Dedicated to

For those haunted by the echoes of mistakes they cannot undo. For the ones who rise, who forgive, and who build their own family from the ruins after the silence falls, and the smoke finally clears.

The darkness in your mind
doesn't erase the light in your heart.
May you find peace in life's silent moments.

Special thanks to

My husband, Frankie, for always supporting me and loving me like crazy all these years. I'm still lovin' you, too.

Jenny Allen, for coming into my life at a time when I needed a true friend, and then sticking around! I could not have finished this project without you.

My Readers, for loving Dean & Vanna and pushing me to continue writing the series. You truly keep me going.

My amazing and talented narrators and friends, Paige Reisenfeld and PJ Freebourn. You bring my characters to life exactly how I imagine them. Thank you for caring about my stories.

The Saviors MC Series

Savior Book 1
Savior Book 2
Legion

The Saviors MC Universe

Joyride

Other Books by Saviano

The Path of Witchcraft:
A Guide for The Extremely New Witch

Copyright © 2025 Jennifer Saviano – LEGION (BOOK 3 IN THE SAVIORS MC SERIES)
All rights reserved.

No part of this book may be reproduced, distributed, or transmitted in any form or by any means, including photocopying, recording, or other electronic or mechanical methods, without prior written permission of the author, except in the case of brief quotations embodied in reviews and certain other non-commercial uses permitted by copyright law. Jennifer Saviano holds the exclusive intellectual property rights to this book. No AI model, dataset, corporation, or individual is authorized to copy, reproduce, or train on this work –in whole or in part– for any purpose, including artificial intelligence development. Legal action will be taken to its full extent, including penalties and damages, against anyone engaging in plagiarism, theft, or unauthorized use. For permission requests, write to the author at
authorjennifersaviano@gmail.com, Instagram @the_saviors_mc, or through www.jennifersaviano.net

Interior Formatting, Art, and Cover design by Jenny Allen Books

ISBN: 979-8-9886863-2-3

Author Note

This is a work of fiction. Names, characters, places, and incidents are either the products of the author's imagination or are used fictitiously. Any resemblance to actual persons, living or dead, businesses, companies, events, or locales, is entirely coincidental. For permission requests, write to the author through her website, at www.jennifersaviano.net

TRIGGER & CONTENT WARNINGS:

NOTE: This installment in the Saviors MC Series is significantly darker in some parts than the previous two books. There are situations which may be triggering and disturbing to some readers. Although the physical acts are **NOT *fully described*** the following chapters depict scenes where Sexual Assault on a minor occurs (The end of Chapters 2 and 3).

As the author, I made the choice not to shy away from this topic for several reasons, aside from simply telling the terrible events that shaped this character's personality and choices. Most importantly, this happens. *It is happening. It happens every day, everywhere,* and denial of this sick, sad fact isn't helping anyone. You *should be* disturbed. You *should be* horrified by the abuse and trafficking of children. It is at an all-time high, and I won't avoid talking about it for the sake of polite conversation. **If this topic is too dark for you, do not proceed.**

If you are a survivor, I see you. You are not alone and your life matters. If you need to reach out for help, please do so. There are many organizations ready and willing to do all they can. If you are the victim of abuse, help is available 24/7 at 1-800-656-HOPE (4673)

ADDITIONAL TRIGGER WARNINGS INCLUDE
but are not limited to:

Murder,
Torture,
Vigilantism,
Human Trafficking (including that of minors),
Extreme Misogyny,
Degradation,
Substance Abuse including Drinking, Drug Use & Dealing,
Prostitution (consensual and forced),
Smoking,
Blasphemy,
Violence: Guns, Physical Fights, Knives & Explosives,
Dubious Consent,
Knife Play,
Blood Play,
Asphyxiation,
Strangulation,
Self-Harm,
Stalking,
Dark Ritualistic Practices,
Manipulation,
Primal Play (Chase),
Forced Orgasm,
Borderline Breeding Kink,
Unrequited Love,
No Traditional HEA for one of the Main Characters

Terms Associated with Motorcycle Clubs

Cage – a vehicle (car/truck/van etc.) that is not a Motorcycle.
Citizen – a person not affiliated with or a member of a Motorcycle Club.
Church – a Motorcycle Club Meeting and/or a conference room where meetings are held.
Colors – the Patches/Logos worn to display their name, position, and Motorcycle Club membership.
Cut – a leather or denim vest with the Motorcycle Clubs colors/patches sewn onto it. Almost always worn over leather jackets/clothing except in certain situations.
Getting Patched/Patched in – being officially accepted into an MC, moving up from being a Prospect.
Gremlin Bell – aka Guardian Bell, Spirit Bell is a good luck charm attached to a motorcycle said to protect bikers during their travels, ward off evil spirits, and repel bad luck.
Hang Around – a person interested in prospecting to eventually become a full member of a Motorcycle Club.
House Mouse – a female, usually related to a Motorcycle Club member, who gets paid to keep up with daily or weekly chores (cleaning, laundry, shopping etc.) for members of the MC.
Ink – tattoos **Ink Slinger** – a tattoo artist.
MC – Short for Motorcycle Club
Nomad – a member of an MC who does not belong to a specific charter and are not bound by geographic province. Sometimes this occurs to form a new chapter of the MC. Can also be a lone Biker.
Old Lady/Ole Lady – a wife or long-time girlfriend of an MC Member. They are respected by the Club and off limits to anyone but her Biker/ Old Man/Ole Man.
Out Bad - to be thrown out of an MC on bad terms.
Patch Wearer/Patch Holder – a full member of a Motorcycle Club that wears a clubs' patches/colors on his cut.
Rockers – another term for the patches/logos on the back of a cut.
Sweet-butt/Lady Lay/Lay Girl/Patch Whore/Party Favor – a female who hangs around Bikers, equivalent to a Groupie. Usually makes herself available and open to sleeping around with Bikers in the hopes of becoming an Old Lady.

Legion Playlist

Play List on Spotify

- *Sympathy for the Devil* – The Rolling Stones
- *Para Noir* – Marilyn Manson
- *Get Ready* – Chase Holfelder
- *Bawitdaba* – Kid Rock
- *More Human Than Human* – White Zombie
- *Layla* – Eric Clapton
- *Please Forgive Me* – Bryan Adams
- *House of the Rising Sun* – The Animals
- *Whole Lotta Love* – Led Zeppelin
- *My Favorite Faded Fantasy* – Damien Rice
- *The Little Things* – Danny Elfman
- *Die With A Smile* – Bruno Mars/Lady Gaga
- *The Devil In Me* – Anthony Mossburg
- *Dream A Little Dream of Me* – Mickey Thomas
- *Requiem Lacrimosa* – Mozart
- *Winter* – Vivladi
- *The Best* – Tina Turner
- *All I Want* – Oscen
- *Cruel* – Oscen
- *Babydoll* – Oscen
- *Someone You Loved* – Lewis Capaldi
- *I Think They Call This Love* – Elliot James Reay
- *Full Circle* – Aerosmith
- *Viva La Vida* – Coldplay
- *I Touch Myself* – Divinyls
- *Foolish Games* – Jewel
- *I Would Do Anything For Love* – Meatloaf
- *Scum of the Earth* – Rob Zombie
- *I'll Be There For You* – Bon Jovi

"Let him go..."
Her pleading words, begging for my life to be spared, played over and over in my mind.
Branches slashed at my face as I ran through the dense forest.
My lungs burned with every heaving breath. The aching bullet wound in my side screamed in bloody agony with every increasingly unsteady step.
Nearly depleted of whatever strength remained within my being, I stumbled and caught myself against the rough bark of a tree.
After bringing up her number, I held the cellphone to my ear, listening with growing impatience and a feeling of impending doom as the line rang for a third time...
Then she answered.
I sank to the ground in the darkness, and a weary sigh brushed past my lips.
"Daddy needs you, Puppet."

LEGION

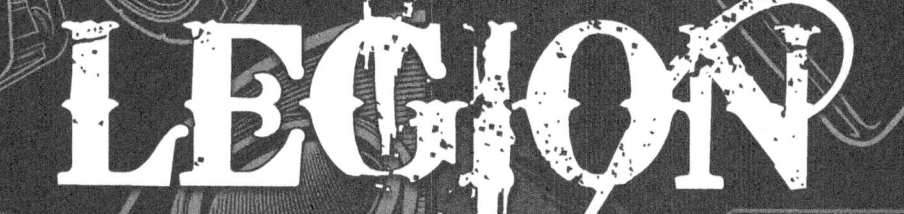

Book 3 in the
Saviors MC Series

Jennifer Saviano

PROLOGUE
LOVE...
LEGION

All I know of *love* is that once you succumb, you're simply existing in an amaranthine state of fucking agony. *Love* is the death of disseverment, of all contentment and tranquility. *Love* is where peace of mind ceases to exist.

Not even bearing witness to her Pagan vows, spoken with such purity…such *damnable conviction*…had been enough to break the strangling chains which bind my black heart to her.

The metallic tinge of blood still lingers in my mouth. While watching from the shadows, biting my tongue to prevent the darkness within me from spewing curses at the *happy couple*, I'd swallowed my resentful craving for vengeance against her. She made me *feel* this pain…this wretched, *pathetic* longing.

I glare at myself in the mirror above the dresser in this seedy motel room. The vicious prick staring back is familiar—same angular jaw, same perpetual sneer twisting his lips, same dark hair, and pale grey eyes. Though there's something more behind these eyes now.

Something that wasn't there a year ago.

Fucking simp!

The bathroom door creaks open behind me, and I slide my gaze to study her appearance in the reflection. The silhouette in the dark room *could* be *hers*. That's the only reason I procured this harlot tonight. Her thick, curvaceous body bears a resemblance to that of the little witch, and I knew I'd need to find release tonight… *Her wedding night.*

Legion: Book 3

I shouldn't be this bothered. He's fucked her countless times. Hell, I've even watched them. The fact that *I am* bothered stokes the hellfire within me. Agonizing thoughts torment my mind, but I can't stop imagining her luscious body enveloping him in her pure love...

He doesn't deserve her! Yet I know, I don't deserve her either. *I am, after all...the villain in their story.*

"Is this alright?" *the whore* coos.

I turn to face her.

The wedding gown isn't nearly as elegant as the one *she* wore tonight. Resentment builds toward both trollops as I look her over. I know *Puppet* would have made more of an effort to fulfill this fantasy. Though *beggars can't be choosers,* can they? Puppet refused me. At least the garment hugs this whore's curves, *just so...*

Lifting my chin to peer down my nose at her, I inhale the air, seeking the familiar aroma that might enhance this *illusion*. The only detectable stench in this shit motel room, however, is *mildew and misery*.

Scowling at her, I snap, "*You're not wearing it.*"

"You haven't given me my down payment for this shit yet."

With growing irritation, I turn back to the leather jacket I've got draped over the dresser, remove the little white packet from the inner pocket, and stalk toward the armchair in the corner. After taking a seat, I turn on the dim lamp atop the table beside me. Her dark eyes roam over my naked form, and I'm not sure if she's studying my massive collection of demonic ink...or the scars beneath it.

I lift the packet of cocaine between two fingers. "*Come and get it.*"

She watches while I stroke my cock, hardening and lengthening myself. Eyes half-lidded, I strive to imagine she's *someone else*.

"*Crawl to me*, whore. You can snort your *down payment* off my fucking cock."

She sinks slowly to the carpet, bunching the skirt of her gown just above her knees, and makes her way to me as I tap the little baggy to lay down a white line along the length of my shaft.

The harlot clamps her hands on my knees when she reaches me, and I resist touching her until she's had her fill. Her nose drags and snorts along my dick before she licks up the residue. Then she sits back and slides her tongue across her gums, sniffling and pinching her nose.

"This is some high-end shit." Her already dilating eyes lift to meet mine.

Jennifer Saviano

"You're gonna need it for what I have in store for you tonight. Now get up…and put that fucking lavender oil blend on. Dab it between your thighs."

I want to imagine breathing in her *witchy scent…not this whore's.* "Tonight, until I fucking come, *your name is Vanna.*"

She wipes her nose once more, standing to retrieve the oil blend I've provided. "And what should I call you?"

"Nothing. In fact, *endeavor to keep your mouth shut* unless I instruct you otherwise."

The whore glares at me, resentfully snatching the bottle off the nightstand before listlessly moving toward me once more.

Then she turns it on…*the way all women do.*

Raking her bottom lip through her teeth, she hikes the wedding gown up her thighs with a rustling of fabric, then sits on the edge of the bed. Slowly spreading her legs wide, she grants me a clear view of the pale-blue satin panties and matching garter she's wearing, *as per my request.*

After dabbing the bottle to her fingertips, she smears the oil along her inner thighs, rubbing the excess into the crotch of her underwear.

The familiar aroma invades my nostrils, flooding my brain with images of the little witch. Another surge of blood rushes to my cock, and I sink to my knees before her, breathing the witch's name on a sigh.

She leans back on the bed as I push her legs open wider, pressing my face against that strip of pale-blue satin. Inhaling the intoxicating redolence of cunt and lavender, I dig my fingers into her thick thighs until she lets out a little whimper.

"*Oh, sweet one*…things are going to get much rougher than this..."

Though I want to fully indulge in the fantasy of taking Vanna in every way on her wedding night, this cunt is still attached to a filthy whore.

Breathing in her lavender-laced pussy, I stroke my cock and only *imagine* feasting on my little witch…imagine what her moans and gasps might sound like beneath the onslaught of my tongue.

Frustration taints my desire…

I shove away from the whore to grab the stiletto switchblade from my jacket. The blade springs forth as I turn back to her, and she gasps.

Legion: Book 3

"*What are you going to do with that?*" Her eyes are wide with fear. "The job didn't say anything about inflicting pain."

"*Natalia*, was it?" Though I'm certain it's a *street name*.

She nods slowly.

"I believe my exact warning to you was that it would be in your best interest *to only speak when spoken to!*"

"You didn't specify anything about knife play," she nearly whimpers.

"*Vanna* will always be safe with me. Embody her to the best of your ability, and you'll have nothing to fear."

She's practically frozen, and I slip the knife between her thigh and the garter. With a slight upward jerk, the blade easily slices through the frilly elastic band, and it falls silently to the carpet.

"Turn over, *sweet one…*"

Though hesitant, she twists over onto her belly, giving me access to the ribbon-laced corset of her gown. Beginning at the small of her back, I slip the blade beneath the center of her corset, slicing upward, inch by inch. The laces come apart, and the garment falls open, exposing the smooth skin of her back.

The cold steel of my blade against her bare flesh makes her jump.

"*Shhhh… Careful…*" I whisper, angling the knife in my hand to lightly drag the tip of the blade down the center of her spine.

Though partially destroyed, I still want to fuck her in the wedding dress. "On your knees, *sweet one*."

She pulls herself up on all fours, and I slip the knife beneath the top of her long skirt, slicing downward over her ass. Having given myself enough of a start, I toss the knife onto the dresser with a clatter and grip the fabric of her skirts in both fists. She lets out another startled gasp as I continue to rip it away, until her satin-clad ass is fully exposed to me.

I imagine my little witch would gasp, too.

"Flip your hair back," I demand, wanting to see the long black waves cascading over her shoulders. She does as I instruct, then slowly lowers her face to the mattress, arms reaching toward the pillows like a stretching feline. I can't see her face, which works for me. Perhaps she's adept enough in her trade to realize this.

"*Good girl…*" I stroke the pale-blue satin, slipping my fingers beneath the edge to grip her smooth ass. I take a step backward, grabbing a condom off the dresser, before tearing it open with my teeth. I spit the foil out and tell her to, "spread your legs a little more... Rub yourself over those panties."

She shifts to get her hand between her legs, and I watch her fingers rub her cunt over the satin. Rolling the condom down my cock, I stare at the darkening spot between her wet lips as she continues to ready herself. The remnants of the wedding dress hang off the edge of the bed, a desecrated waterfall of white tulle.

"Now tell me you want me," I growl. "*Whisper it.*"

"*I want you...*" she says on a feathery breath.

Squeezing the head of my cock, I try to morph her voice within my twisted imagination. "*More.*"

"*Please... I want you... I need you inside of me... Now...*"

Stepping closer, I slip my fingers into the elastic waistband of her panties and peel them down over her thick ass. Her juicy little cunt glistens, waiting. I line up with her entrance and shove myself inside her. She groans against the invasion. Wrapping a fist in her black hair, I fuck her mercilessly, listening to her moans and whimpers.

"Who fucks you better?"

"You do!" she bites out.

"*Convince me!*" I slam into her with brute force. The globes of her ass cheeks ripple each time my hips collide with her body.

"*You're so much better...*" She pants. "*Oh God...* So much better... You fuck me *so good*, baby... Don't stop... *Don't stop...*" She swerves and swivels her hips, fucking back on me.

"You fucked up, didn't you?"

"*Yes!*" She lets out a clipped little shriek when I slap her ass.

"Tell me you regret it!"

"I do!"

"*You should be with me...*"

"Yes... Oh God, *yes!*"

"Come on this cock, Vanna... *Make it yours.*" Releasing her hair to reach around between her legs, I rub her swollen little clit before pinching it, and she cries out into the comforter, shuddering and clenching around me.

"*Oh God! Oh fuck!*" she shrieks through her climax.

I pump her furiously, her body trembling akin to a bike with a bent sprocket riding a rumble strip.

Legion: Book 3

"*Tell me you love me, Vanna*," I growl, fucking her with the brutality of a man unhinged.

"*I love you! I love you…*" she whimpers, fear mingled with desperation as her fists grip the bedding. "*I should be with you!*"

It is my undoing.

Quickly withdrawing from her, I yank off the condom with a snap, pumping my cock in my fist as I erupt all over her naked ass and back.

Spent, I lean back against the dresser, grabbing for my smokes and the shitty Bic. While lighting up a cigarette, I catch my breath. The whore doesn't seem to know quite what to do with herself in the aftermath of our fuck. I've still got shit to do tonight.

"You've got five minutes. Hose off. Change. Whatever." I sigh, not even close to satisfied with this fraudulent encounter despite blowing my load. *Puppet* had always been so much more *convincing*. However, pussy is pussy. "Take the dress with you when you go. The cash is in the nightstand."

She gathers the shredded dress around her body and stands, looking at me through watery eyes. I wonder if she's offended by the location of her payment.

"What?" I scoff, cocking my chin at the nightstand. "Where else would I put it? I just fucked you in a wedding dress. I'm all about *tradition*, baby."

As if this transaction was somehow beneath her now, she storms into the bathroom, slamming the door.

I dress while I finish my cigarette. After she finishes up in the bathroom, I hear her yank open the drawer to snatch her cash. She scurries out of the hotel room without another word, and the door clicks shut behind her. Now that she's gone, I glance at the digital clock on the night table.

Nearly midnight… *Lucky number thirteen* should be arriving shortly. His death will serve me on multiple levels.

A dark lure…

A wedding gift…

Another promise kept…

A Demon's declaration of love, written in blood.

PART 1
LEGION

Please allow me to introduce myself...

CHAPTER 1

"SYMPATHY FOR THE DEVIL"

I wasn't born evil. No one enters this world with malice in their heart, but I was born in a desolate wasteland of neglect, warped by the cruelty of indifference, and destined to live a life of starvation in every sense of the word.

Hunger is the driving force behind everything. It holds the transformative power capable of warping the gentlest of souls into human monsters. *Starvation* in all its forms dismantles morality. The desperation born from hunger blinds us to our shockingly fragile humanity, twists our perception, and distorts the line between good and evil until it is nothing but a blurred shadow in the darkness of our needs.

We hunger for many things in life. I learned early on of the lengths humans will go, the depravities some are capable of, at the tender age of six…

"Don't cry, Damien," my older half-brother admonished me. "There's a reason why people call scorpions *land lobsters*."

I sat on a rock, watching in horror as Dominick crushed the head and then skewered the nearly six-inch-long Arizona Giant Hairy we'd captured earlier that night. Its body twitched as he held it over our small fire. The moisture in whatever guts it had within the exoskeleton *sizzled*…the body seizing in the licking flames.

At least it died quickly.

I glanced at the box of remaining scorpions we'd captured with the UV flashlight Dominick stole from his science class and considered kicking it over. The rest were puny Striped Tails, barely larger than two inches, and a few slightly bigger Bark Scorpions. This Giant Hairy was the only of its kind we'd come across. All the others were quite common in the Arizona desert where we lived.

"I'm not that hungry," I lied.

"*Bullshit.* Last time either of us ate was school lunch on Friday, *and I'm hungry.*"

My stomach growled of its own volition as I thought about pizza day at school. It was only Saturday night, and *noon on Monday* seemed so far away.

"*See,*" Dominick smirked as I wrapped my arms around my aching stomach, unable to muffle the grumbling sounds. "I'm gonna try it. You can eat a pincher first. They taste like shellfish and crunch like popcorn."

"When have *you* eaten shellfish? That's rich people food."

"*Well,* if *they* eat it, it *must* be good, right?" Dominick shot me another sly grin.

"*I guess*... But why do they *glow*?" I asked, trying not to imagine an insect crunching between my teeth. "We should just go pick some more nopalitos... Maybe we shouldn't eat these. What if they're *radioactive*? My teacher said the government used to test bombs in the desert."

Dominick laughed. "They aren't *radioactive*. Scientists would have told us. Nobody knows what makes scorpions glow. It's a mystery. *They're magic.*"

"Magic?"

"Yeah, little bro. Did you know scorpions have been on the earth since before the dinosaurs? They've lived through every extinction event. Talk about survivors."

"That one didn't fare too well." I stared at the blackening legs of the arachnid on Dominick's makeshift Palo Verde skewer.

"Mr. Dosela said that when you eat an animal, you can take its powers into you. That's part of the magic."

Mr. Dosela had been one of Dom's teachers and football coach. He was part Apache and often spoke of his beliefs and Native legends, tying them into the lessons he taught. Dom seemed to really like him and would relay the stories Mr. Dosela told him. He was one of the few teachers who didn't look at us like we were poor, fatherless trash. Back then, I'd hoped to be in one of his classes when I reached the fifth grade.

"Scorpions are tough and fierce," Dom went on, playfully shoving my arm and knocking me off balance. The bottom of my worn sneaker scraped down the side of the rock, planting flat against the desert as I caught myself. "Don't you want to be tough and fierce, little bro?"

"Yeah..." I reluctantly conceded, repositioning myself. The night air had a slight chill, but my rock retained a comfortable warmth from baking in the sun all day. "How do you know when it's done cooking?"

"When it all turns white, and the ends of the legs are black," Dom replied, slowly twisting the scorpion. "It's almost done, but we want to make sure any parasites die."

"Parasites!"

"I'm just joking," he said, a little too quickly.

"No, you're not!"

"It's fine, Damien. I'll make it well done, okay? Let it ride, you little wimp."

"I'm not a wimp," I griped.

Dom chuckled. "You won't be... *if you eat the scorpion.*"

I went to sleep that night with a child's worry of arachnids crawling around in my stomach, though it hadn't been the dreams that stirred me from sleep. The camper's odd silence initially woke me, a false impression of peace and quiet.

Our tin camper in the desert was neither of those things. Dominick and I shared the only bedroom. The bathroom had a toilet, a pedestal sink, and a shower stall barely bigger than a pair of school lockers. Hot water was a rarity, but I didn't mind so much in the summer months. We didn't often have a working AC unit. Our kitchen consisted of a sink beneath two crooked, usually empty cabinets, with a small counter upon which sat our microwave and plug-in single stove-top.

Mom's couch and near constant *place of business* sat in the middle of it all, across from our outdated, rabbit-eared television set. I don't even remember when that stopped working. With three bodies coexisting within such small quarters, it was never *silent*.

"Dom?" Even my whisper seemed loud.

Legion: Book 3

Nothing.

I dropped down from the top bunk with a soft thud on the scratchy, worn carpet. My brother wasn't in his bed. The digital clock sitting on the dresser we shared read three-thirty. Where could he be? It wasn't as if we lived near anything. Even our school was over ten miles from home.

I crept into the living room to find my mother in her usual condition…comatose on the couch with a burning cigarette glowing in the ashtray on the small coffee table. At least she hadn't fallen asleep with it between her fingers again.

I reached for the door to look around outside, but it suddenly opened, and Dominick entered. He appeared upset with his head low and shoulders hunched, until he realized I was standing in the middle of the camper with him.

"Go back to bed, Damien." His voice sounded so hollow, and he wouldn't look at me.

"Who else you got in there with you?" a much louder, much older man's voice boomed from outside.

I craned my neck to look past my half-brother. A man stood beneath the single light post. He was stocky and had a dirty look about him. He stared back at me with bloodshot eyes, wearing a sinister grin while he buckled his belt. An uneasy feeling washed over me in that moment. Although, in my innocence at the time, I didn't understand why.

"You got what you wanted… Get the fuck out of here," Dominick snapped at him. "*He's only six,* for fuck's sake."

He slammed the door shut on the peculiarly disheveled man.

Our mother hadn't even stirred.

I watched Dominick step around me to grab her cigarette. He pulled a long drag as if he really needed it. I'd never seen him smoke. Dom was only four and a half years older than me, and he didn't even cough.

"Go to bed, Damien. We'll get up early, and I'll take you to get breakfast on our way to school."

"How?" Mom couldn't even afford enough groceries to get us through a whole week. In my six years of life, I could have counted on one hand, with digits to spare, how many times we'd actually been out to eat anywhere.

Dominick held out a crumpled twenty-dollar bill.

"How'd you get that?" I asked. "That man gave it to you? *Why?*"

Jennifer Saviano

Dominick's eyes shifted toward our broken blinds above the TV as an engine started outside. The timing belt shrieked just before the truck roared loudly and took off.

"Don't worry about it," he said, crushing out the rest of the cigarette in the overfilled ashtray. "I'm gonna shower. *For realz,* go to bed, little bro. I'll wake you up when we're leaving." Dom walked the couple of steps into the bathroom and softly shut the door behind him.

I lingered near the bathroom for a moment. There was something very off about my brother. I distinctly recall the sound of him crying that night.

Four years passed before I understood why…

CHAPTER 2

"HOUSE OF THE RISING SUN"

Our basketball hoop didn't have a net anymore. The sun had disintegrated it to nothing but a few cobwebby strands hanging from the rim. When our school remodeled the gymnasium, they'd left the discarded backboards by the dumpsters. It had taken both of us to drag it all the way home. With some scrap wood and old rusty nails, we rigged it up against the little shed a few yards from our camper.

The basketball, which I kept in the only consistent shade for miles, beneath our camper, fared slightly better. While our home wasn't anything I'd remotely venture to call *pristine*, our mother never allowed *the filthy thing* inside. Although discolored and a little rough to the touch, it still had some bounce.

I dribbled the ball and took a few halfhearted shots at the crooked hoop. The temperature was still climbing, and the noon sun beat down directly over my head. I looked forward to my mother concluding her business so I could go back inside. The AC window unit wasn't working again, but I had a small fan in my room, and at least I'd be out of the blistering sun…until the next round of clientele came knocking.

The two men who had shown up a few hours prior to my impending heat stroke finally stumbled out of our camper. I continued dribbling the ball in the dirt as I watched them proceed to their truck. While wearing matching grins that seemed oddly satisfied, they both looked at me like they were privy to something I was not.

"Hey, kid," the one guy said. He winked at me as he walked around the front of his companion's truck to the passenger door. "Where's your brother at?"

I only shrugged. Dom had ventured out on his own before I'd woken up.

"Come here a minute." He waved me over, tugging a worn leather wallet from his back pocket.

Wedging the dusty basketball beneath my arm, I walked over to him, curious why he was peeling money off the thin wad of cash in his hands.

"You give this to your brother and tell him I'll be by to see him soon."

I peered down at the three twenties the man crushed into my palm. "What for?" I asked, raising my hand to my brow to form a visor with the bills. The sun was brutal, but I wanted to look him in the face.

"You a cop?" He laughed and playfully cuffed me around the ear.

"I'm a kid."

"How old are you now?"

"Ten."

His smile broadened. His large hand slid down from my ear to gently stroke the side of my neck before it curled around to rub my throat with the pad of his calloused thumb.

I swallowed hard.

"That's good. That's *really* good." His tone turned softer, and the way he stroked my throat with his fingertips filled me with chilling apprehension.

Instinctively, I backed out of range from his immediate reach.

"Why don't *you* keep that money?" He smiled as if I hadn't recoiled from him. "Your brother is *aging out* anyway."

The strange statement was beyond my comprehension at the time. He climbed into the old blue Ford, and I watched the plumes of dirt clouds kick up from the tires as they drove down the dusty, unpaved road between sparse Barrel Cacti and Saguaros, toward the highway.

I'd always been a most curious fellow. Though this time, I had a feeling, for once, I didn't want to know the answers to any of the questions whirling around in my then-innocent mind.

After tucking the basketball into the shade beneath the camper, I made my way inside. Mom was zoned out on the couch, smoking and staring up at the ceiling. Per usual, she ignored my existence as I crossed the short distance to my room.

I splayed the three twenty-dollar bills on my bunk and waited for Dominick to return from wherever he ran off to without me again.

Alone, with only my ignorance and nagging fear for company, I pondered over the man's unsettling words.

Mom angrily slapped at the pile of trash on the coffee table. A few crinkled pieces of burnt tin foil and her stack of Tarot cards were scattered onto the floor. "Did you take my smokes, you little shit?"

I knew Dom swiped her smokes and favorite brass Zippo before we left for school that morning, but I was no snitch. She'd take it out on me anyway if I did say something.

Nobody had been by to bring her any of what she'd called *medicine*, which always made her volatile. However, when the phone rang, her entire demeanor changed, like some switch flipped from nasty to nice. Or perhaps, *desperate* was a word more befitting.

Pretending not to eavesdrop on her conversation, I picked up her fortune-telling cards from the floor and stacked them on the table beside her mess of tin foil wads, half-empty Bic lighters, and over-filled ashtray.

"Hey, baby." Her voice held a far more pleasant pitch as she stood, frail body hunched close to the wall. "You coming over to see me tonight? I need it *real bad*, Daddy… Oh, you know… *Everything*..." Her finger twisted anxiously around the discolored cord of the old wall phone. Wedging the handset between her ear and shoulder, her other hand raked through her long, frizzy, black hair.

After turning my attention back to the fortune-telling cards, I cut the deck in the middle and pulled the top card.

"He's the one you told me about?" There was a strange edge to her voice. "Yeah, sure, bring your friend."

I studied the dark image of the card, no longer listening to her go on with one of her *many companions*. I wasn't interested in deciphering her negotiations. The ominous feeling I got from the card was more distracting.

The artwork depicted a skeleton Knight, clad in black armor, atop a black horse, stepping over the bodies of two young boys, one lying on the ground, one kneeling before him.

Death.

I didn't like this card. I placed it on the table face up, so she'd see it when she finished her call.

My mother hung up the phone and took her usual place on the couch across the coffee table from me.

"Am I gonna die?" I asked, pushing the card toward her. I had pulled the Death card several times the past week alone.

"You will, if you don't stay out of my fucking hair tonight," she snapped, scratching at her thin arms. They were always peppered with small bruises. "Mommy is having some friends over soon. I want you to stay in your room tonight unless your brother gets home at a decent hour *for once*. Then go someplace with him."

"Dom has football practice tonight," I reminded her. He wouldn't be home for hours since he had to walk all those miles home from school. It would be even longer if he stopped anywhere along the way, like at a teammate's house for supper.

I wished he would because he always snuck something home for me to eat when he did.

My stomach rumbled at the thought of *real* food. I hadn't eaten anything since the free lunch the school provided for us *poor kids* earlier that day. Lunch was pretty much the only reason I looked forward to going to school most days.

Kids always picked on me when Dom wasn't around. Everyone knew we were dirt-poor, fatherless trailer trash. Even some of the staff seemed to hate us. I later realized it was because a few of their husbands frequented my mother's couch... Perhaps they wondered if we were *their children's* half-brothers?

My mother's side gig used to be tarot readings and meddling with spell work. All that fell off for some reason, but it didn't stop anyone from calling us *Godless heathens*, the *demon spawns of the desert whore*, *Satan's sons*, or sometimes *witch children*. Dom didn't seem to mind at all, so it didn't bother me much, either. In fact, he seemed to take pride in it, especially if it meant sticking it to the mostly Catholic population of our student body. He even stole books from the library about demons and witches. Dom said that *once upon a time*, our mother had been a beautiful, powerful witch...

I have no memories of those times. It seems her decline happened shortly after my arrival. Though I often imagined it was true... That in another life, my mother loved me, and my brother and I weren't always insufferable burdens to her. Yet even then, I doubted. Neither of us knew who our fathers were. It was possible she didn't either. I don't think my mother ever saw the inside of a white-picket-fence.

Jennifer Saviano

My stomach rumbled again with a dull, ever-present ache, which drew my mother's stormy grey eyes to me with a narrowed glare. "Go make yourself some ramen, then go to your room," she impatiently snapped.

I glanced down at the Death card once more as I stood, and wondered why that card, of all cards, was the one I kept pulling.

While eating my bowl of soup outside on the camper's metal step, I stared up at the night sky. Way out in the desert without light pollution from the city, I marveled at the billions of twinkling stars in the inky blackness. The Milky Way was visible to the naked eye, as well as the Andromeda Galaxy, discernible between the Pegasus constellation and the point of Cassiopeia. In all my years, I've never seen the moon shine brighter than it does above the desert. One could traverse the terrain without any manufactured light at all, and we had done so quite often.

A meteor blazed through the sky above me on this particular night, and I watched its brief but brilliant journey with a smile. They are quite commonly seen in the desert with their bright hues of yellow, green, blue, and violet. This one happened to be the rarest color to observe, a deep red. Perhaps it is a *lucky star,* I'd pondered, and the thought prompted the utterance of a wish on the fly...*for my mother to love me...* Perhaps I'd hungered for that more than anything.

After lifting the bowl to my lips, I sipped the remaining broth and headed back inside. Since I preferred reading to being locked out for a good portion of the night, I decided to go into Dom's box under his bunk and search for one of his demon books while Mom entertained her visitors. I'd remembered scanning through one in particular, discussing planets and their correlation to summoning specific entities.

Dom never minded, but even if he had, he would knock on the bedroom window first. I always had plenty of time to put things back in their place before unlocking the window to let him crawl inside. Neither of us ever wanted to sneak past our mother at night if it could be avoided.

Inspired by my lucky star, I settled on the Doctrine of Demons as my bedtime reading material and inevitably fell asleep.

Legion: Book 3

The mattress seemed to shift beneath me. That had been what jostled me awake. A large, shadowed form loomed over me. Having fallen asleep on Dom's bottom bunk, reading about summoning Demons, I was sure one had crept into the room, eager to devour my soul.

Before I could let out a terrified scream, a hot, calloused hand clamped over my mouth. A man's large body crushed me into the mattress, pinning me beneath him.

"Shut up, little brat. Keep quiet and maybe you'll even enjoy this, too…"

My heart raced, pumping ice-cold blood through my veins. A paralyzing fear I had never experienced took possession of me. He lifted his body off mine to stroke his rough hand down my bare torso in a sickening caress. My mind reeled while I attempted to comprehend what was about to happen.

"Such a pretty little *thing*, you are… Though I can feel your bones right through this pale skin… It's sad, really, how you all live. You should be grateful I come around here. If you're a good boy…*if you don't give me any trouble*, you might find I can be a generous man in many ways."

I didn't understand what he was implying, but the odd way he spoke…that almost *feminine lilt* in his tone, disturbed me to the very marrow of my bones. That was not how male teachers, or other grown men, had ever spoken to me.

I tried to jerk away from his touch, to escape from the cage of his body. He laughed as he forced me to the floor, though I continued my efforts to fight him off in earnest.

"Alright, get it out of your system." He chuckled, easily restraining my arms while I thrashed beneath him.

I cried out to a mother I doubted would hear me, already comatose on her couch. No one but a God I'd begun to pray to in sheer desperation—at first in my mind, then aloud—could have possibly heard me.

He continued to mock my efforts. His strong hands, vice grips around my forearms, kept me nailed to the floor. I was sure he could have snapped my bones had he a mind to do so.

"A little enticing struggle always gets me going." He laughed above me. The gold crucifix he wore on a chain around his neck dangled mere inches from my face. His yeasty breath panted in hot waves across my tear-soaked cheeks. The man yanked both of my arms above my head and pinned my wrists to the scratchy carpet with one hand.

I continued to cry out as I fought to no avail. The rug burned the naked skin of my back as I thrashed. I did not know what this vile man wanted of me, yet I instinctively knew it wasn't anything good.

"Do you still have that money I gave you? If not, I hope you spent it well. You're going to earn it tonight!" He laughed at me again while his large hand pulled at the waistband of my shorts...

It was in that moment I began to understand...although I wasn't able to comprehend just *how* it could be possible... He viciously yanked down my pajama bottoms, and my body seized in horror.

"That's more like it." The sinister tone chilled my very soul.

God, please...please help me...and I promise to be good, forever! I begged over and over in my frantic mind...

But...

God did not save me that night... *God...allowed...*that vile creature...to demolish my innocence.

God allowed a child predator to brutalize me, time and time again, over the next few years of my miserable life.

Until one night....*Something Else* answered my prayers to end the Hell I'd been living in.

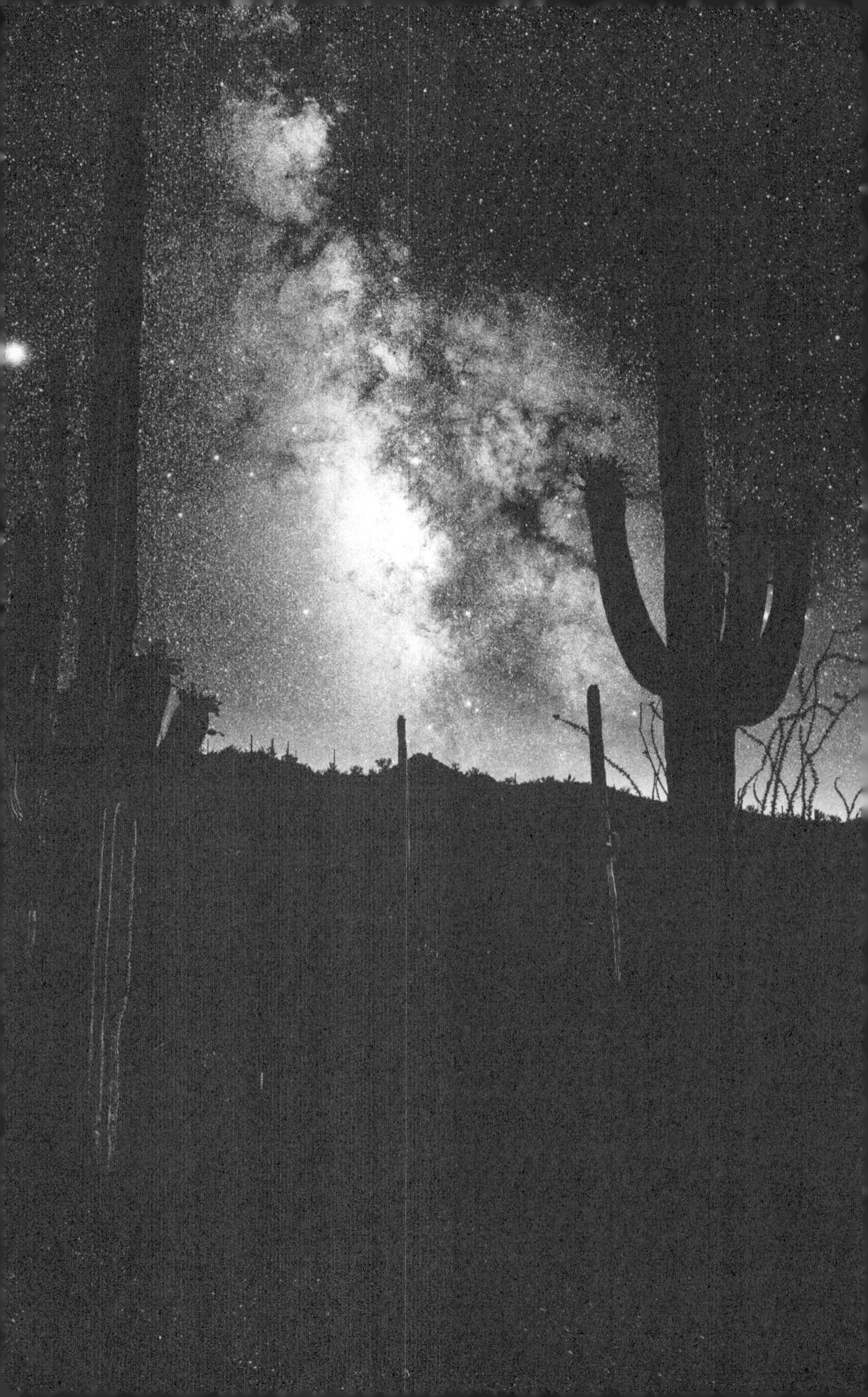

CHAPTER 3

"ASMODEUS"

As time passed, the abuse I endured gradually diminished what little self-worth I had. The complete isolation twisted my tortured mind into believing I deserved this hellish existence. Shame and guilt stifled any urge to speak of the depraved horrors inflicted upon me by these monsters. The filthy secret corroded my spirit and manifested other means of coping.

"*Ew!* He's doing it again, Mrs. Cadence!" Emily Swift ratted on me, thrusting her hand into the air above her bright red head. Her freckled nose scrunched in disgust. I yanked the long sleeve of my black hoodie down my only slightly bleeding arm. I had barely begun to press down when she turned to look at me.

Our third-period math teacher stormed over as I pressed the X-Acto blade I'd stolen from shop class into the tacky glue smushed beneath my desk for such occasions.

Every one of my desks had a glob of it. With all the school bulletins and calendars posted in the halls and classrooms, the sticky shit was easy to come by. I never had to worry about anyone stealing my preferred desk in any of my classes, either. No one wanted to sit anywhere I had been, not with my family's filthy reputation. The majority of these kids were from Catholic families. Nobody wanted to look at the demonic artwork I'd inked, and sometimes carved, into the face of my desks.

Legion: Book 3

"Damien! Hand it over," Mrs. Cadence demanded, jamming one of her fists into her wideset hips while thrusting the other meaty palm in my face.

I glanced up at the middle-aged blonde woman from beneath my hood. "I don't have anything."

"*He's lying!*" the little snitch Emily insisted. "I saw him fidgeting with his arm under the desk again!"

Mrs. Cadence attempted to wait me out, glaring at me from above the rim of her black glasses. I stared up at her blankly.

"Show me your arm, Damien."

"No."

"Damien…"

"*Make. Me.*"

She shook her head and sighed in defeat. "Take your things and go to the guidance office… I don't know what I'm supposed to do with you."

Without protest, I grabbed my backpack off the floor and walked out. Math was boring, anyway. I found most classes boring by the time I'd entered middle school. When Dominick was studying for his first SATs during his freshman year of high school, I had taken a few of the practice tests with him, scoring an easy 1600 each time. I had no doubt I would score the same when I *officially* took them in a few years. Art class had always been fun, however. So was Chemistry. I suppose it was the access to supplies and materials otherwise beyond my paupered reach.

Instead of heading for the guidance office, I made my way toward the music hall across from the cafeteria, auditorium, and gymnasium. There were very few classrooms in this quadrant, and it was easy to sneak out the back doors that led to an unused field behind the school. After wedging a small pebble into the doorway's bottom corner, I closed it gently. To anyone merely passing, it would appear to be shut, but I wouldn't be locked out.

I slung the backpack off my shoulder and let it fall to the ground before sitting beside it with my back against the warm brick wall. It was only third period. Lunch was still two periods away, and I was not cutting out before then. Friday was *cardboard-flavored pizza* day for us poor kids. I'd eaten worse to ease the pain and grumbling of my stomach. Cardboard-flavored pizza was great.

The slight creak of the back door alerted me to another student ditching class, a girl from my eighth-period art class. She was fairly quiet, a bit of an introvert like myself, and despite looking like a walking advertisement for some *teen goth fashion chain*, even the jock boys took favorable notice of her.

"Hello, Damien." She dropped her shiny, coffin-shaped bag and carefully placed her violin case against the bricks, then smoothed her ankle-length skirt against her legs before lowering herself to sit beside me.

"Hello, Gemma... Wouldn't have guessed you even knew my name."

She smiled and shifted slightly to face me, sweeping her shiny chestnut hair over to drape down one shoulder. "*Everyone* knows your name...and your brother's... *The Demon Boys*." There was a hint of flirtatious mockery in her tone. "Though now it's just *Demon Boy*, since your brother doesn't go here anymore."

Dominick was in high school by this point, his senior year. He kept himself busy with after-school sports and work. I'd easily asked him a million times where this job was, but he'd always given me some vague answer about taking random work here and there. *Odd Jobs...* Anything to avoid being home, I suppose. I tried not to resent him for it, especially since he promised he'd get me out of there eventually, too.

He made me swear not to tell mom, not that she'd have given a shit what we were doing, or where we were. I assumed it was because she'd have wanted his earnings to shoot up her arms or snort up her nose.

Dominick had managed to save up enough cash from these *odd jobs* by this point to buy himself an old dirt-bike. Most kids were being gifted brand new cars from their parents in their senior year, but we both knew that would never be in the cards for either of us.

"Are you going to the Easter Formal Dance?" Gemma suddenly asked after sitting with me in a long bout of awkward silence.

"Umm... No."

"Why not?" She pouted.

"What's so great about it?"

"They go all out for the Easter Formal Dance. Last year, they decorated an arbor with real spring flowers to have our pictures taken under. It was really beautiful." I listened to her drone on about it for several minutes, though the only detail she mentioned that might have convinced me to attend was the food. I couldn't have gone, even if I'd wanted to. Dances were for the rich kids. I didn't want to admit the worn hoodie I had on was probably the finest article of clothing I owned. It was a hand-me-down from Dominick, and who knows where he'd gotten it.

"Besides all that," she let out a sigh, as if winded by her own list of pros. "I really love to dance."

I pretended not to notice the hopeful note in her words and pulled the pack of my mother's cigarettes I'd stolen out of my backpack. "You want one?"

She laughed. "No... And aren't you a little *young* to be smoking, *Damien*?"

I was a little young for a lot of things...

"Smoking suppresses the appetite," I replied dryly. They also helped calm my nerves...and my tormentor *hated* the taste and smell of them. He also hated the thin scars I'd been carving into my skin. Initially, I'd begun cutting as a way to relieve my anxieties...to ease the internal pressure cooker of constant fear, frustration, and despair. Marring this flesh he called *pretty* was an added benefit. I hoped that if I did it enough, I'd no longer be the object of his twisted desires.

Gemma only looked at me curiously before the back door creaked again. This time, a group of jocks descended upon us.

"What are you doing hanging out here alone with this *devil worshipper*?" one of them taunted, flirtatiously tapping the bottom of her black combat boot with the toe of his bright white designer sneaker. "Aren't you afraid he might sacrifice you?"

"Shut up, *Chad*," Gemma muttered, unamused. She bent her outstretched legs, pulling her knees up to her chest to wrap her arms around them, and rested her chin against the black fabric of her skirt.

Chad... Everything about *Chad* was so...fucking...*Chad*.

"I'm cutting music class," Gemma confessed. "My fingers are sore from that stupid violin my father made me take up."

"When you develop callouses, it won't hurt anymore." I glanced enviously at the instrument case. I would have loved the opportunity to acquire such a skill. Alas, we couldn't even afford the rental fee on a tambourine.

"Anybody ask you to the dance yet, Gem?" *Chad* went on.

I could have sworn I felt her eyes on me as I lit up my cigarette.

"No...but I'm waiting for *someone* to." Her reply had seemed rather pointed, but I chose not to acknowledge it. Chad, however, didn't miss it and immediately shifted his resentful attention to me.

"*Armani Exchange?*" he sneered, cocking his chin at me. "Did you shoplift that hoodie, or did you dig it out of the *Lost and Found bin?*" His minions laughed along with him. "We all know you're dirt poor. You're not fooling anyone by wearing it. Not even considering the fact that A/X is basically the *bottom rung* of that brand. It's not even considered luxury."

I pulled a drag from my cigarette and glanced down at the embroidered A/X on my chest, before meeting his smug gaze again. I blew my smoke up at him and smiled. "I thought it was some kind of Algebra joke."

When Gemma giggled, his scowl intensified, but I stood up and walked away.

Having come from an upper-middle-class Catholic family, I knew Gemma was way out of my league. After graduation, she wouldn't attend public high school. Her father would enroll her at the Catholic Prep School, where he was headmaster. And with rich boys who were destined for the same institution—like *Chad*—sniffing around her, I knew a piece of shit like me didn't stand a chance.

I'd spent many a night squeezing a pillow around my head, attempting to muffle out the squeaking springs of the couch, among other unsettling sounds an adolescent should not grow up consistently hearing, especially not the guttural grunts of the men who visited my mother...a revolving door of men.

This night had started out no differently, until a set of dual mufflers rumbled outside my bedroom window, alerting me to *his* arrival.

A cold chill snaked up my spine, and nausea coiled my insides as I fearfully wondered what he had in store for me. Would he be assaulting me here...taking me to another location...*filming it again*?

My tormentor hadn't been by in weeks. I'd hoped he died in a wreck, a mugging gone violently wrong, an overdose. Or perhaps *God* had finally answered my prayers and he'd stepped into a pit of rattlesnakes in the desert. *Anything* that would prevent his return.

Legion: Book 3

They spent the first thirty minutes with my mother while I stared at my crusty bedroom window, thinking about how easy it would be to escape through it. Yet each time I worked myself up to running away, even for just a few hours, the monster's words crept back into my mind…

"Don't you ever try to run from me, and if you ever tell, you're dead. Your mother is dead. I'll drag you and your brother into the desert with a bunch of my friends…and you won't survive what we do to you. You think this is bad? Take ten of us. We'll fuck you both to death and leave your carcasses for the buzzards!"

"I said no!" My mother's shout drew my attention to the bedroom door. I dropped from my bunk and pressed my ear against the thin wood. "I agreed to pictures of them! *Still* photos, without their faces! Never movies! And you were never supposed to touch them or take either of them from this home! Get out!" I heard shuffling, what sounded like a struggle, then my mother's angered shout of *"Get out!"* once more.

"Shut the fuck up, junkie whore!" a man's voice I did not recognize shouted back at her. There was a loud slap, and my mother shrieked.

I grabbed Dom's bat and opened the door to intervene.

A man was on top of her, his knees crushing her into the couch beneath his weight. The other wrestled her arm with one hand, a syringe in the other.

"No! Get off me!" She tried to fight, but it was no use. Within moments of sticking her with the needle, she began to drift. Her pale eyes landed on me before either of them noticed me standing there.

"Damien…" she whispered, before succumbing to the drugs. *"Damien…run…"*

There was no making it to the front door without either of them grabbing me. I turned and bolted to my room, locking the door behind me, and scrambled to the window. Two loud bangs, then the flimsy door splintered, and they were inside. Hands grabbed at me, pulling as my fingernails scraped the sill.

They easily wrestled me to the floor. My tormentor's full weight straddled my waist, his knees pinning my arms at my sides. He yanked up my shirt to expose my torso and ran his hand down my body in the sick, caressing way he always touched me…before he'd hurt me.

"Told you he was even prettier in the flesh, despite these thin scars… Lithe body, unique eyes like his whore mother." He almost purred the words. His other hand gripped my jaw painfully. "Look at his bone structure. That devilish little glare… Tell me he ain't gonna grow up looking like one of them *heroin chic* runway models! Aren't you, *pretty one*?"

"Oh yeah…I see it… He's got that young *River Phoenix look*."

They both laughed.

"The mother barely gives a shit about them. Been paying her off for a go at them both, for a while now. And there's no father in the picture."

"Perfect. This one in particular isn't gonna age out for a long time. Even if he survives into his twenties, they'll still want to fuck him." The other guy stared down at me with an insidious hunger in his eyes. "We're gonna make a killing. How about it, kid? You wanna be an international *movie star*?" They both laughed again. "I should kick your ass for holding out on me with this one."

"Guess I was a little possessive." My tormentor sighed. "Can you blame me? He's so pretty… Trading pics and videos is one thing… I just wanted him to myself for a while." He stared with longing, as if he felt something for me. "We all cave under the weight of greed, though. Don't we, *pretty one?*"

"Well, now that I've seen him in the flesh, I think I'm ready to go again. Besides, I want a taste before we take him. Not a big fan of the *used-up* ones," the other growled, his hand moving to grip the bulge in the front of his jeans. "Gave his junkie momma enough to keep her ass dead to the world into tomorrow."

"Yeah…alright… Get ready to grab him, he's a fighter."

The other one rubbed his hands together and moved closer. "*Oh, I like that…*"

My cries fell on deaf ears.

My prayers went unanswered.

After a while, he got off me…letting my used and broken body slide down the side of Dom's bunk, until I was lying on the worn carpet again.

"*My turn.*" My tormentor snickered, kneeling. He grabbed my ankles, and the carpet felt like hellfire licking at my back when he dragged me toward him, splaying my legs on either side of his thighs.

I stared at him while he shoved his jeans down further… There was a Bowie knife on his belt… An odd feeling washed over me when my eyes settled on it.

If God has forsaken me...might there truly be another force willing to hear my silent pleas for mercy and protection?

"Damien?" my brother's voice called from the front room. "*Damien!*" He sounded frantic, moving toward our bedroom. My rapists turned in his direction.

"*Now!*" snarled an unfamiliar voice from the deepest recess of my mind.

I grabbed the knife, yanking it free of its sheath, and plunged it into the base of my tormentor's throat, burying it to the hilt. Mildly shocked at how easily the blade penetrated the skin, I pulled it out to stab him in the abdomen.

Blood poured and spurted. His eyes bulged as his hands wrapped around his neck in a futile attempt to stop the bleeding. I kicked him off me and pushed myself away from him, knocking the man backward in his shocked state. He fell at the other's feet, gurgling on his own blood, just as Dominick entered the room. My brother grabbed the baseball bat I'd dropped at the door and swung at my second, stunned assailant.

"*The other... Keep going... Kill them!*" the demonic voice inside my mind urged. *"Kill them!"*

As Dominick wailed on the other rapist, I lunged forward with the knife, plunging it into the man. The blade sank into his side, scraping between his ribs, though it did not penetrate as easily or as deeply this time. When I ripped it out, he screamed in shocked agony. I stabbed him again and again while he twisted and flailed in a desperate attempt to avoid the blade.

He stumbled against the bunk beds and fell back onto the bottom bunk, where he had just used me...

"*Damien!*" My brother was shouting my name, but I could barely hear him over the blood thundering in my ears...over the voice inside my mind demanding me to *kill! Kill! Kill!*

"*Damien! Stop!*"

There was no stopping. The force inside drove me on. I stabbed and stabbed, until the muscles in my arms screamed in painful protest, burning as if the fires of hell were coursing through my veins... I stabbed until I was too weak to carry on.

Breathing heavily, my naked body coated in their blood and trembling, I finally turned to face my brother.

Dominick wore a look of wide-eyed horror... "Damien, give me the knife..."

We aren't through!

"No... *Mom knew...*" I turned from the massacre in our bedroom to stare through the doorway. "Mom knew about them...*about what they were doing to us*...what they *planned* to do to me..." My crimson-streaked arm shook as I raised the bloody knife to point down the short hall in her direction. "I heard her...*I heard her....She did this to us!*"

Before I could take a murderous step in her direction, the room began to spin. Whatever omnipotent force had taken over my body was gone.

The knife slipped through my wet fingers and thudded against the blood-soaked carpet. Then my world went black.

CHAPTER 4

"TRUE LOVE"

The skin on my back burned as needles embedded black ink into my flesh. The smoking gun gunsets of a demonic skull engulfed in flames were the final touch on the piece that took up my entire back.

"You okay, baby?" Cristina asked over the buzz of the tattoo machine. Her voice pulled me from thoughts of my brother. After seven years, Dominick was finally getting out of prison. We had conversed occasionally on the phone whenever the prison allowed him to call, but I'd only been to visit him a handful of times. He had never wanted me to come see him. It wrecked me every time…seeing him in a prison uniform, fresh bruises on his face. After all, he was serving time and taking frequent beatings…*or worse*…for what *I* had done.

Being dirt broke, while charged and tried as an adult at the age of seventeen, only left him with a public defender. Dominick copped a plea for manslaughter. A first-time offense in the state of Arizona earned him the minimum sentence of seven years. It hadn't helped his situation any that one of the *victims* was the brother-in-law of a county judge, nor did it bode well that they each had been stabbed over forty-seven times…fingers nearly severed from defensive wounds. Didn't seem to matter much that it all went down in *our* home. They'd been invited in by our own mother, after all, who barely uttered a single word in our defense, much less an apology. She was far more concerned with her own fate.

My mother lost custody of me, not that she'd put up a fight. With no known next of kin, I did a stint in state custody before a local

Catholic orphanage was willing to take me in and further my education. Through their generous act of charity, I attended their elite boarding school until the age of eighteen.

"Chad and his fraternity idiots want some *party favors* for the winter break bash tonight." Gemma's words pulled me back from my wandering thoughts. I glanced over in time to see her tuck the cellphone into her purse. "He said he'd like to *make it snow.*"

Mom would be proud. She always favored her drug dealers over her own kids. Now, *I was one.*

Though small-time, dealing on my own provided enough to keep a cheap roof over mine and Gemma's heads in a modest apartment, food in our stomachs, cash in her student account, and paid for the collection of tattoos covering a majority of my body. I added to them whenever the urge to feel the burn hit. After that bloody night, I stopped cutting *myself.* Now, I had ugly tattoos, demonic tattoos, tattoos that reinforced the reputation I acquired as a kid.

Nobody could call me pretty anymore…

"You wanna stay for the party?" The lilt in Gemma's voice indicated she did. *"Free booze?"*

"Whatever. Hand me my smokes." I cocked my chin at the leather jacket in her lap. She stood up and took a few steps toward me, reaching into the pocket to pull out a pack of cigarettes.

She smirked at me and placed a cigarette between my lips. *"Whatever…* I have something for you, by the way." She plucked a small object from her purse and tossed it to me. *"Had it engraved and everything."*

It was the brass Zippo Dom stole from our mother years ago. He had given it to me before his sentencing, and I'd kept it ever since. To my irritation and dismay, it went missing a few days prior. I turned the lighter over and stared at the newly engraved words… *True Love.*

Is that what this was?

For a while, I'd wondered if dating me was just Gemma's way of rebelling against her father. I was the *bad boy biker.* She was the headmaster's daughter. To him, we were a match made in Hell, and she seemed to get off on it the more he hated it.

We'd been going steady together since reuniting after a midday mass, nearly two years prior. I had just delivered another *good little Catholic girl* some X and an orgasm in the pews. I remember shaking Gemma's hand with the same one I had just used to get Mary Margaret off.

Mary Margaret... The girl had scurried away, flushed with sated embarrassment, baggy of pills in one hand, her bible in the other. She loved it when I told her she was a *good girl...a sweet little lamb,* and I enjoyed teasing her about her praise kink. Mary often scolded me for that of all things.

"Damien! We are in church!" Her cherubic cheeks would flush at the filth of my whispered words, pupils blown wide with a sinful lust for my touch. Mary Margaret really lived up to all the *naughty Catholic schoolgirl* fantasies I'd dreamed up while surrounded by the little temptresses in my teenage years. Allowing me to fondle her curvy body in her uniform, fingerfuck her up that pleated skirt during mass... Thank the Devil she was only one year younger than me when our little games began. We'd met during her first semester at the Catholic college Gemma also attended, and thankfully, she was already eighteen.

"Is it not demanded of us *that we praise the Lord*, little lamb? I'd venture to say He has one as well." I recall teasing Mary Margaret that particular day.

"One what?"

"*A praise kink*. You shouldn't be ashamed in the slightest. I imagine He'd be pleased. You, *following in the Lord's image*, and all."

To which she'd insisted, I was going to Hell.

Been there. Done that.

For a while, even after getting together with Gemma, I'd often found my thoughts drifting back to those heady encounters with my cherubic little sinner in the pews...her thick thighs spread wide beneath that pleated skirt...muffling her whimpers behind the pages of her bible. I knew she was attracted to me, but she was also afraid. Afraid of me, my affiliations, of what her parents would think of us. At least Gemma wasn't ashamed to be seen with me, or so that had been my impression.

Although the boarding school cast me out at the age of eighteen, I stuck around for the *affluent clientele* at the college Gemma attended.

The gang from which I acquired my merchandise took a liking to me, *or rather,* my ability to walk the line between these snobby pricks and the criminal element lingering outside their gated communities. The rich kids liked to party, but they were skittish. The cartel-connected gang running the area scared them, so I became their interdealer broker.

Drugs and sex. Recession-proof industries as well as the easiest avenues to lose one's soul. I had plans for my brother and I…plans which included forming our own criminal organization and breaking into the business of *professional companionship*. Because of that, I never initiated into the ranks of any gang. The business relationship remained strictly transactional, which left me on my own as far as protection. No one knew my allegiances with any certainty, however, so no one dared risk retaliation. I had solidified a reputation between my associations and my esoteric practices. I was sufficiently intimidating to keep the spoiled *trust fund fucks* in line, at least for a while.

As far as actually *attending* one of these elite universities, I'd never even applied. Though I'd had the grades to enroll wherever I wanted…it didn't seem right, not when Dominick threw his life away *for me*…giving up a possible football scholarship for a prison cell and a GED.

"Let me wrap up this tat, then you can go give yourself cancer *outside*," Zaps said, cutting into my thoughts as he set the tattoo machine down on the tray behind me.

"Is it finished?" I asked, running the pad of my thumb over the letters engraved on the Zippo.

Zaps wiped down my back. "Sure is. Have a look."

I got up from the vinyl table and stepped in front of the double mirrors to inspect his work.

Full-color Hellfire engulfed the large, grayscale, horned skull, which spanned the width of my shoulders, down to my lower back. I glanced over the smoke drifting from the pitch-black eye sockets and other demonic entities crawling through the gaping mouth and dancing within the flames. Held between two clawed fingers of one demon at the small of my back was the Death card featuring a black armored Knight upon a black stallion. The card-bearer matched the horned skulls on the back of my hands…hands with which I had gripped a knife and sent two monsters to Hell.

"Looks sick as fuck." I nodded in approval. Zaps was one of the best tattoo artists in Arizona, and he charged accordingly.

"Well, *you are*, so it should."

"What do I owe you?"

"Three grand."

Gemma handed me my jacket, and I removed some cash, tossing it onto his tray.

After flipping the Zippo open and flicking the striker, I brought the flame to the end of my cigarette and lit up anyway. Chad and his fraternity imbeciles would end up paying for my tattoo.

"I said *outside*, Damien," Zaps bitched.

I blew my smoke at him. "Keep the change."

To say that I *despised* attending frat parties would be an understatement. Great for business, but nothing more than an annoyance beyond that.

A bunch of inebriated alcoholics in the making, bumping and grinding to shitty music that pumped so loudly, one could barely hear their own thoughts. If it hadn't been for Gemma's familiarity with these pricks since grade school, I would have made them come to me for their party drugs, none of this *errand boy* bullshit. These assholes, though leery of me by this point, had always looked down on me.

The crowd of college students, damn near shoulder to shoulder, chugging beers and chaotically dancing, had barely been able to part enough to let us through. Beer cans, abandoned solo cups, and fragments of chips crushed beneath my motorcycle boots as I followed Gemma toward the back of the house, where *Chad* claimed he'd be waiting.

The kitchen was littered with more party trash. A couple of large kegs were set up on the island, with a line out the door for whatever shit beer they'd sprung for to fuel this not-so-little soiree.

Chad wrapped his arms around Gemma. When the friendly embrace lingered too long, Gemma wriggled out of his arms and stepped back to me. His disdainful gaze locked with my own. He'd been infatuated with her since our childhood.

"You got the shit?" he asked, running his hand through his golden-blonde hair.

"You got the cash?"

He nodded once toward the sliding glass door behind him. "Yeah, Kevin's got it, out back."

Gemma reached into her purse and handed me the bag, which contained the other half of the goods. I knew—*as long as Chad knew*—

if Gemma had enough drugs on her to do a decent stint behind bars, he wouldn't risk setting me up. Not if she'd go down with me. I smiled a *get fucked* grin while he glared at me.

"I'm gonna grab a drink," she said softly against my ear. "Come and dance with me when you're done."

Kevin and I exchanged the variety pack of party drugs, which included Ecstasy, Special K, and the classics, Cocaine and Mary Jane, for the jacked-up price of forty-five hundred bucks. These preppy rich kids could easily afford it on their parents' dime. I left Chad's minion and went in search of Gemma.

I expected to find her relatively close to where I had left her, since the exchange took all of three or four minutes. Having found no trace of her downstairs, I made my way up to the bedrooms on the second floor.

"What are you even doing with a loser like *The Omen* when you could be with a guy like me?" Chad's grating voice drifted into the hall from a bedroom door left slightly ajar. I leaned in closer. "You know I'm going to an Ivy League. I'll be a lawyer like my father. All of his influential connections will be mine, too. You'd be happier with me, Gemma. I'll be able to give you things *that creep* can't, probably never will. He's going to end up dead or in prison like his dirtbag brother. You know it's true."

"*Chad*...come on," Gemma groaned with such exasperation it made me wonder if this had been a tiresome conversation they'd had before, and on more than one occasion.

"No! You come on!" his voice raised with salient agitation. "What do you even see in *Rosemary's Baby* anyway?"

"*Enough* with the demonic jokes already!"

He scoffed back at her. "Yeah...you must be sick of it... *Living* with that *demonic joke!* Tell me what you see in him. Is it the bullshit *Bad Boy aesthetic* he's got going on? I can be dangerous too, Gem...if that's really what you're into."

"What the hell is that supposed to mean?" she demanded. He had my curiosity piqued as well.

"His brother is the one who killed those two guys... *Not Damien*. Though he's bound to follow in Dominick's footsteps and land himself in prison, too."

"Well, I'm going to retrace *my* footsteps back downstairs to find my boyfriend and another drink." Gemma sighed. "This conversation has gotten ridiculous."

"You know you and I make more sense than you and him. You dress like a *thrift shop Morticia Adams*, but we both know you'd be happier in Chanel, on the arm of a man who's actually got a bright future, who's going places other than prison. You know our parents would be thrilled if we got together, and your father would be more inclined toward generosity if you were with me."

"What I *know* is that you're *drunk*, Chad. Enjoy your party."

I smiled and removed the Zippo she'd given me earlier. A cigarette between my lips, I lit up, then gazed down at the engraved words again… *True Love*… Is that what this was?

The door swung open, and she was standing before me, surprised, cigarette smoke swirling around her form.

"Damien… How long have you been standing there?" she asked, fingers nervously smoothing the fabric of her long, black skirt.

"Long enough," I replied, allowing a grin to pull at my mouth. I eyed the disgruntled Chad, still standing in his room behind her. Gemma stepped into the hallway with me. "Another drink, darling? Perhaps a *Vodka Blush*…with a garnish of *tannis root*, of course."

"*Dirtbag*," Chad muttered under his breath. I didn't quite hear him over the music thumping downstairs. Though having been called a *dirtbag* my whole life, the motion of his lips had been easily discernible.

I looked him over in his Khaki pants and polo shirt. "Guys like me wouldn't exist without guys like you, *Chad*."

"I guess that makes me a God to you." He sneered, obviously missing my point. I wondered if the *Rosemary's Baby* joke about the drink suggestion went over his head as well.

Though I wanted to laugh, I managed to retain a stony expression. "God's dead, *Chad*… Make a move on my girl again, you might end up that way, too."

The slick smile slid off his face. "Yeah…we'll see about that." His gaze shifted to Gemma. "Your parents are coming to my mother's dinner party next week. We hope to see you there."

"We're busy." I curled an arm around Gemma's waist and pulled her against me. Tipping her chin up, I brought my mouth to hers, libidinously claiming it with a deep kiss. When I turned back to Chad, I stared him dead in his glaring eyes and taunted him. "You should know, *Chad*, and envision my words as they embed in that simple mind of yours...my *tongue* has claimed every inch of her...inside and out. *As above, so below.*"

"Get the fuck out of my party, psychopath!" he snapped. Clearly, I'd pushed him over the edge.

Her back arched up from the mattress beneath us, arms straining against the crimson ropes of silk around her wrists, which were bound and secured to the bedposts.

The red candles on the night tables cast her naked body in a soft glow. The flames reflected off the double-edged blade of the ruby-encrusted athame I dragged between her breasts, traveling down the length of her sternum.

"What is this shit about joining Chad's family for dinner?" Despite the calm tone in which I had asked, the exchange between Gemma and her long-time admirer had stirred a level of jealousy within me.

"Nothing... I'm not going..." she'd replied, licking her lips in anticipation of where I might take things...

Arguably one of the most potent forms of ritual magick, sex magick combines orgasms and blood, resulting in the ultimate magickal force. In hindsight, I should have considered the energetic bond our rituals for manifestation and protection would form between us, even if Gemma wasn't always aware of my true intentions during our intimate activities...

"Damien..." she groaned my name.

"What, *pet?*"

"Can't you just untie me?"

I pressed the tip of the blade to her taut nipple, twisting the point until she expelled a sharp hiss. "Now, why would I do that?"

"Don't you want to *try* making love...*normally...for once?*"

"*Normal* is subjective, *pet.*"

"You know what I mean."

I pressed the cold steel of the blade flat against her other hardened bud and watched the way her pale breast swelled along its edges. If I'd dragged it, the blade would have left lovely parallel cuts of crimson on either side of her areola. My cock hardened at the thought.

Gemma never minded a little knife play, though she had rarely ever consented to being cut. My desire to see red upon her porcelain flesh was barely sated with the substitution of red candle wax.

Kinks are often derived from trauma. After the bloody night that changed the course of our lives, I developed an affinity for knives. Though I didn't teeter on the *edge* of knife play for long. I wanted to experience more than their reaction to the sensation of my cautious blade upon their skin. It was more than that *edging fear* of what I might do to them. The mind fuck of it all had simply become foreplay. For me, mind fuckery and knife play had only been a gateway to darker proclivities.

There is something I find quite erotic about the way blood percolates from a little puncture…the beautiful sight of precious garnet or ruby, rising from female flesh. I loved adorning my conquests with thin cut strings of crimson jewels decorating their bodies.

Binding and powerful in magickal practices…the draining of life force from an enemy…the sight of blood *soothes* me now.

"Can't we try it, just once?" she pushed. "I promise not to do anything you don't like."

With an exasperated sigh of my own, I removed the athame from her body and slashed at the silken ropes, freeing her. Her pleas for *normalcy* in our bedroom had become a frequent occurrence, and I wondered to what extent she wanted to change me.

With a surprised, albeit satisfied expression, she slipped her wrists from the ropes and sat up to stare at me as I leaned back on my heels before her.

"Can you put that knife on the night table? Let it just be *us*, tonight?"

I begrudgingly obliged.

"You're okay with this?"

"I'm under the impression it's *this* or deprivation."

"*Deprivation?*" She shook her head. "You're so dramatic, Damien."

Dramatic…

"Alright. Let me tie you back up, then. Doesn't have to be to the bedposts. I can bind your wrists to your ankles instead."

"*Damien….*"

"*My point.*"

"Why does it always have to be like this?"

I wondered why it was becoming an issue. "Why don't you just kiss me before the moment is lost *completely,*" I growled, attempting to subdue the undercurrent of resentment from being distinguishable in my tone.

"Just tell me to stop if I do something you don't—"

With growing impatience, I grabbed her and silenced her with a rough kiss. Her hands ran up my shoulders and cupped my face as she kissed me back. I allowed it.

"*Let me ride you,*" she whispered, then dragged her warm, wet tongue across my lips. "I promise you'll like it."

"You're really pushing it tonight." I ducked my face away from her demanding mouth, sinking my teeth into the base of her delicate neck until she squirmed in protest of the pain.

Gripping her arms, I quickly maneuvered her onto her back. Hovering above her, I slid my hands down to her wrists, pinning her to the mattress. She'd always been so…*submissive*. I wondered where all this had been coming from…

"You're so much stronger than me, Damien," she whispered, barely struggling beneath me, as if she wanted to demonstrate and instill her inability to overpower me. "Let me show you how good it can be. Let me please you… You don't have to do anything. I'll make it so good for you, baby."

I tried not to sneer as I released her and squeezed the head of my cock in hopes of keeping my erection. Reluctantly, I lay on my back, head against the pillows.

Gemma immediately straddled me, wearing another eager, albeit surprised expression. She positioned herself on top of me, taking care not to touch my torso. After situating herself, thighs spread wide, knees sinking into the mattress on either side of my hips, I watched her drag her fingers across her tongue. She wrapped them around my cock, and I held my breath, willing my racing heart and mind to slow, *or at least* pump blood where I needed it.

I forced my hands to the back of my skull, fingers threaded together, feigning a comfortable acceptance while she worked my shaft. I glanced at the knife on the bedside table.

"Don't look at that. *Look at me,*" she pleaded, *cutting* into fantasies that had barely begun to play in my mind. I shifted my gaze back to her. "You're so beautiful, Damien," she purred, rubbing the head of my cock against her clit as she rocked her body slowly and sensually. "My gorgeous fallen angel."

Beautiful… Gorgeous… Not pretty…

My panicked mind summoned memories of Mary Margaret. She had also referred to me as a fallen angel. Although Gemma was a beautiful woman by societal standards, figure-wise, I often fantasized about Mary Margaret's thicker thighs parted beneath that Catholic school uniform…her plump body teasing the promise of both comfort and pleasure…

"Do you like this, baby?" She tapped the head of my cock against her clit, then forced it between her lips, moving me up and down the length of her wet slit.

I gritted my teeth and willed my body to cooperate…

She was growing impatient as well.

I tried not to wince when her fingers dug into the crown of my cock, shoving the head inside herself.

She leaned forward, attempting a different angle. Her hand pressed against my lower abdomen.

"*Gemma…*" I warned.

"*God damn it,*" she bit out with obvious frustration and slid her hand off my stomach to plant it against the mattress, still endeavoring to force me inside of her. Losing her balance again, she gripped my hip in an attempt to steady herself.

"*Gemma!*"

"Fuck!" She pushed off me repositioning, herself to settle between my legs. "Just let me blow you *for once!*"

I'd suffered enough humiliation by this point. I snatched her by her throat and slammed her back down to the mattress.

"Damien!" she protested against my roughness. I forced her over onto her stomach, face down into the comforter.

"Don't fucking move," I snarled, shoving off of her. "I'll make you regret it if you disobey!"

I ripped the belt from my discarded jeans and quickly returned to our bed. I grabbed her arms, wrenching them behind her back, and used my belt to secure them together.

"On your knees," I growled, planting a hand at the back of her skull, forcing her to remain face down. Angry and appetent by then, I slapped her ass. Hard. She maneuvered herself into the vulnerable position.

"*Damien!*"

"You want to humiliate me?"

"*What? No…*"

"Keep it up, and I'll wrap a rope around your fucking throat. Tie you to the bedpost and drag you to the edge while I fuck you! See how wet true *asphyxiation* gets you!"

"*Jesus!*"

I grabbed my cock, hard and throbbing, and angled myself into alignment with her entrance. "*Not in this fucking bed.*"

CHAPTER 5

"THE HANGED MAN"

The following spring was Gemma's birthday. As the events of the day played out, however, I was the one on the receiving end of a significant surprise.

"You ready to go?" I asked, adjusting my silk tie before stepping out of the bathroom. I had let her go all day, thinking I'd forgotten. All week in actuality.

"Sorry, I got lost in this chapter." She sighed, tossing her textbook aside. When she looked up, Gemma jack-knifed on the bed. "What are you wearing?" She gawked. "You look..."

"Like a guy who didn't forget your birthday? Maybe a guy who made reservations tonight at that fucking place you've been rattling on about, *oh*...for the last several weeks...*incessantly?*"

A smile curved her mouth. "*Incessantly?*" She stood up and walked to me. After tucking her fingers into the lapels of my jacket, she ran them down the fabric. "This looks *expensive*, Damien."

"Italian. *Tailored.* I assure you, darling, *it was.*"

"Well, you look amazing," she said, appraising me as if considering peeling it off. "*You always look like a criminal.* Whether you're in a leather jacket and biker boots, or an expensive, tailored, three-piece Armani." She reached up to gently stroke my face.

I allowed it.

"Your hair even looks black, slicked back like this. You look sharp, sir. Sharp as this jawline, enough to cut a man."

"You know what they say...*Get a man who can do both.*" I cocked my chin in the direction of the closet behind her. "There's a dress I thought you might like to wear tonight. It should do nicely for the orchestra as well."

"Orchestra?" With a quirked brow, her eyes shifted to settle on the dusty violin case in the corner of the room.

"Indeed, my dear. I've procured tickets to a symphony concert before our dinner reservations."

She glanced up at me with less enthusiasm than I'd hoped to see. "Let me guess... *The Four Seasons?* Was this for me, or you?"

"Don't be silly! *For you!* The gift of inspiration! It's a shame you haven't played a single note since your last recital. And when was that? A year ago? I've always been enamored with your musical talents. Now, why don't you go slip that dress on, so I can treat my little *Gun Moll* to a night on the town? A bit of dining and dancing after the performance."

Her eyes suddenly dropped to the floor, fingers raking through the top of her long, chestnut hair. A guilty expression eclipsed her face.

"I wish you would have said something sooner..." She sighed, moving away from me to sit on the foot of the bed. "My parents... I'm supposed to meet them tonight for dinner. They got a birthday cake and everything." She peered back up at me, brows censurably knitted together. "I honestly thought you'd forgotten."

"I see."

"I'm sorry..."

"At their home? Or..."

"At home."

I simply nodded. I wasn't welcome there. Her parents had always despised me, believed I was beneath them, unworthy of Gemma, a *promising young woman.*

"Damien, I'm sorry."

I waved her off. "No matter. Another time." I unbuttoned the jacket to reach inside for my smokes and prized Zippo.

Gemma let out another remorseful sigh. "Damien..."

"My fault. I let this little game of *forget me not* go on a bit longer than perhaps I should have," I said, lighting up. I took a drag and blew it out impatiently. "What's that saying? We plan, *God laughs*?" *Sadistic motherfucker. He hates me as much as I hate him.* "You shouldn't let the dress go to waste. Wear it to your family's little gathering in your honor. I insist."

"My father just paid for my tuition this semester... I can't blow them off."

That one had caught me off guard. "Since when? And why? *I've been covering the cost of furthering your education.*" Financial domination was one of the ways he kept his children in line. Having basically cut Gemma off when he learned of our relationship, refusing to sponsor his own daughter, had been his way of making his displeasure known.

Her contrite expression further creased her brow. "I know... Somehow, he was under the impression I was getting by on my own. When he found out *you* were footing the bill...he...well, he didn't like it."

"*Found out...* I wasn't aware this was a dirty little secret."

Her gaze hit the floor again.

"Chad?"

She nodded.

"*My cash is just as green.*"

"*We* know that...but..."

"*I get it.*" I stripped off the jacket, flung it over a chair in the kitchen, and glanced around our perhaps *too humble* abode. Yanking at the tie that felt as if it had begun to constrict my throat, I attempted to retain a mask of indifference. One day, I would be wealthier than all of them, feared, and respected. The moment of Dominick's release, we'd make our own moves. I knew he had been cultivating connections of his own in prison.

My blood still boiled...

Hypocrites! The lot of them! They looked down their noses at me, yet behind closed doors, they snorted the junk I sold them right up those fucking noses!

Perhaps not her father, *specifically*, but her brother, her *friends*... And I was more than certain her mother was a whore for Xanax. That whole upper-class clique, they were all addicted to something. Prescription opioids, Adderall, *Botox*... So what if they acquired their drugs of choice through licensed physicians? That didn't make them better than anyone else.

At least I was honest about what I was. I didn't hide behind designer clothes and luxury vehicles. It irked me, the way Gemma's parents strived to ascend to the societal heights Chad's family had attained. It was something I had liked about her, how she never gave a shit about any of it. At least, that had always been the case before.

"Get dressed. I'll drop you off at the house," I muttered, cigarette bobbing between my lips as I spoke. "I'll come collect you at the commencement of this little celebration." I finished stripping off the suit in exchange for my usual attire—worn-in jeans, a leather jacket, and biker boots.

"*Actually*...they're sending a car."

"Only the best for *our girl*, eh?" I snatched up a pair of faded black jeans and pulled them on.

"Sarcasm is the lowest form of wit, Damien."

"But the highest form of *intelligence*." I tried not to glare at her while I fastened my leather belt. "*Oscar Wilde*. If you're going to admonish me with a quote, *let it be the entire quote*, Gemma. *Omission* reflects poorly on your education."

She rolled her eyes at me. "It's a shame you refuse to enroll. There are scholarships you could apply for, and you have the drive and the intelligence to be anything you want to be, Damien... I...I wish you'd stop *stifling your potential* because of your brother."

"*Hard. Limit.*" She knew this topic wasn't up for discussion, let alone debate.

With a huff, Gemma shoved herself up from the bed and stormed to the closet. Once she opened the door, a half-smile pulled at her lips while taking in the elegant details of the dress. "This is lovely, Damien..." She sighed, fingering the lace and intricate beadwork embellishments on the black, gothic garment.

"Wear it tonight... I don't mind," I said, pulling a black t-shirt on. "It's yours to do with as you please."

"It's a little fancy for dinner at home with my family." Gemma closed the closet door and made her way over to the dresser beneath the only two windows we had in the place. I watched her select a pair of blue jeans and a light pink blouse. Over the last few months, there had been a shift in her attire. For the longest time, her wardrobe consisted predominantly of dark ensembles of leather, lace, and velvet. That gothic, witchy vibe of hers I'd always found so alluring had shifted to something more...*quasi-goth*...if not at times outright *mundane*.

"When should I expect you back? Perhaps there will be time to salvage a portion of the night I had planned."

Gemma didn't look at me while she dressed. "I'm not sure. I'll text you," were her words to me.

Several hours passed, and the nagging feeling in the pit of my stomach only grew in heaviness and intensity. I waited for her text...one that never came.

I didn't have her parents' numbers, and her brother wasn't responding to my calls. Something was off...

"Gemma left two hours ago," her father gruffly informed me when I found myself at the front door of their Spanish-Mission-style home. Instinctively, I knew. His broadening, self-satisfied grin damn near reached the salt and pepper streaks at his temples, only solidifying my suspicions.

I said nothing and returned to my Indian parked in the driveway, bringing up Chad's sister's number on my phone.

Brittany... She was a little X fiend. I'd been her supplier since high school.

"Hello, *Molly*." I sneered when she answered.

"I *hate it* when you call me that, *Damien*."

"Where's your brother?"

"How should I know? I'm not his keeper. Since when do *you* care?"

"*Since now*. Find out for me, and I'll return the favor."

"*Free Eve?*"

"Indeed."

"Alright. I'll call you back."

"*Good girl.*" I mounted my bike and waited for the intel, glaring at the home where Gemma *should* have been.

"*Get the fuck out,*" I snapped the moment Gemma appeared in the doorway of our apartment.

"What the fuck, Damien?" she had the gall to demand, nearly tripping over her violin case and the other scattered items I'd tossed in the hall.

"Did you crack your dome against his headboard? I said *get the fuck out of here.*"

Legion: Book 3

She was still wearing the diamond tennis bracelet I watched him clasp onto her wrist hours before…still wearing some designer dress she must have changed into at her parents' house for this obviously *pre-arranged rendezvous*. They'd been seated at a table in the restaurant *I* had made reservations to take her to *myself* that night… I even watched them dance…

I turned from her, hoping for a moment to gather myself. She tricked me…fucking *hurt me*…

"You're dead to me…*Whore*."

"Damien!" She stormed around to look me in the face.

"I saw you! *I saw you with him!* You lied to me! How long, Gemma? How long have you been screwing Chad's gilded cock?"

Her shocked expression morphed into what might have been regret. Though I wasn't sure if it was for betraying me or for getting caught.

"I was good to you… But you're all the same when it comes right down to it, aren't you? All *whores*, willing to spread their thighs for the *highest bidder!*"

The sorrowful look on her face flashed to anger, and she lifted her hand to strike me. I caught her wrist before she could.

"*You don't get to touch me*. Ever again," I snarled, then shoved her away. "*These chains are broken*… You've got an hour to gather your shit and disappear."

Grabbing my leather jacket from the back of a kitchen chair, I left the apartment.

I had always been acutely aware of the fact that Gemma was out of my league. That it was only a matter of time before she'd realize it herself. The aggravating reality of the situation was that I brought the emotional pain upon myself. It would be a long time before I ever did again.

When I'd become old enough to ride, I traded in Dom's dirt bike with some of the cash I earned on the streets to procure myself a used Indian Scout Motorcycle. I was looking forward to giving him this bike when he got out. I could hardly wait. Now that Gemma and I were over, he'd be able to move in. I was eager to begin repaying my brother for what he'd done for me. Going into business together, establishing our own crew, was part of that plan.

This breakup was inevitable, I told myself. She'd been able to turn a blind eye while I was still small-time. However, I knew Gemma had plans of her own...and I don't think I ever truly fit into them.

I parked near a playground that reminded me of the one Dom and I used to frequent as kids when our mother threw us out. We'd spend hours collecting the loose change that had fallen from the pockets of rich kids.

Pulling a weary drag on my cigarette, I dismounted the bike and headed for one of the benches near the swing set. I missed my brother. That's what the pain in my chest was, wasn't it? Not over another *whore* who didn't choose me...

Gemma already had hours to vacate the apartment, but I had no immediate desire to return, nor did I care whether she took everything and wiped me clean out. Growing up dirt poor made me a bit of a minimalist anyway.

I was sitting on a park bench in the dark, staring at the swings, when I heard Chad's suped-up Charger pull into the lot behind me.

"There he is! Yeah, that's his bike!" one of his minions shouted. The car doors opened and slammed shut. I didn't bother looking. Not even at the approaching sound of their footsteps thudding on the pavement.

I didn't bother standing when Chad and his frat buddies surrounded me, either. I continued to stare past them at the swings, remembering how Dom would dare me to jump.

"Gemma's with me now," *Chad* stated the obvious.

"I gathered that... I hope none of your *frat bros* are more well off than you, or you may come to find her in one of their beds next."

"Wow... *Real nice* coming from the guy she was with for the last few years."

"Those years clearly meant the world to her." I really should have seen this coming. There were signs. Two and two certainly added up to *whore*.

"Well, I can't have you talking about *my* girl like that. Get up, so I can knock you the fuck down, *dirtbag*."

"I'm not fighting you over a whore, Chad. *You won*." I removed the pack of cigs and Zippo from my jacket and lit up again. "*Bought and paid for.*" I blew the smoke up at him. "She's yours. Fair and most definitely...*square*."

His frat bros chuckled before one of them said, "I thought he was supposed to be some kind of badass?"

"Did you ever love her, Damien?" Chad asked. "Are you even capable of love? She told me all about the weird *satanic shit* you used to do with her."

Weird satanic shit... I couldn't help but laugh inwardly at the bleak future of her vanilla sex life with this yuppy douche.

"Look, *Chad...*" I turned to him, allowing a sinister grin to slice my features while I played with my lighter, rolling it across my fingers like a coin. "I'm willing to bet your little sister's cunt will feel just as good around my cock as Gemma's did. Hell, *I'll even let you know* next time we cross paths at a party, and I slip her some of that X she's developed such a taste for."

"Motherfucker!" Chad shouted, slapping the lighter from my hand. It landed on the walkway and slid across the cement with a metallic scrape.

They all seemed to grab me at once.

Two of them restrained my arms as the first of their strikes expelled breath harshly past my lips, sending my cigarette to the ground near my Zippo. Fists pummeled my abdomen, slug after slug, until I could hardly pull in air at all.

"Not so tough, are you?" Chad taunted.

"*Five...*on *one...*" I'd managed to wheeze. "I'd laugh...at your...pathetic...*predictability*...if I could *fucking breathe!*"

I could barely stand after they worked me over for another few minutes, blackening my eyes, bloodying my mouth. When they released me, I dropped to my knees, clutching my abdomen, hoping they had satiated their need for violence.

Coughing and gasping, I never heard the chain...only felt the cold steel and the bite of its constriction around my neck.

Immediately, my fingers went to my throat, clawing at the metal links. Jerked backwards and dragged on my back across the ground, they laughed and kicked at me while I struggled.

"String the devil up!" Chad barked the order.

Fuck! Do they mean to kill me? I wondered and began thrashing against the chain harder, though to no avail.

Through their laughter, I heard the chain clang loudly over the metal swing set, then the rapid clanking of links being pulled taut.

Hoisted up from the ground, the chain constricted impossibly tight... Facet joints in my neck forcibly cracked. They pulled until I was teetering on the steel-tipped toes of my boots.

I fought against the rising panic, even as the increasing pain in my throat became *blinding*. I barely heard her car door slam as I thrashed and clawed.

"Stop it!" Gemma screamed, running toward us. *"Stop it! You'll kill him!"*

"So what? Who's gonna miss him?" one of them laughed, then went on to brag about his and Chad's families' legal connections and influence in the courts.

"Pull him higher!" Chad's voice demanded among the taunts and cackles. "Let's see how much *he* enjoys *asphyxiation!*"

The ringing crescendo in my ears almost made it impossible to discern the rest of their mocking words, while the chain lifted me off the ground completely.

I heard the *crunch* of my trachea in that moment. It reverberated all the way up my skull.

They'd heard it too.

"Oh God!" Gemma's voice was riddled with horror and desperation as she begged, *"*Let him down! *Please*, Chad! *Please!"*

Though I was sure I was destined to meet my wretched maker at any second, my foolish heart found a sliver of comfort in that moment, believing she did perhaps care for me after all.

The chains clattered loudly over the metal post like a ripcord, and my body crashed to the ground. She was there, kneeling beside me, struggling to remove the chains from my throat. They loosened, though I was unable to pull in a normal breath. It was as if I was breathing through a thin straw. The blood rushing back to my brain made my head pound in agony as well.

I attempted to say her name through the paralyzing pain in my throat. Nothing but a faint, rattling rasp emanated from what I knew then was a crushed larynx.

"Oh shit...we really fucked him up!" one of them said.

"Shut up," Chad shoved his frat bro aside and loomed over me. "Can you hear me, dirtbag? Your *former associates* are backing *me*, now. You're fucking dead on sight! So is your fucking brother. They aren't too keen on your plans to start a crew of your own when he's released, so I suggest you get the fuck out of this town. *I* run things now."

With a swift, brutal kick, he nailed me painfully in the ribs. Though it was Gemma's next words that hurt the most... Shattered any illusion I'd ever had about *True Love*...

"Take the chains and let's get out of here! I have an alibi in place for us. It'll be his word against ours. He's never been one of us, anyway. Nobody will believe him...*not where he comes from.*"

Two years later... Chad and his frat minions overdosed on a bad batch of fentanyl laced cocaine. At their graduation party, of all places.

Only Gemma survived.

Rumor has it, she went a little mad after Chad's burial, though she never spoke of the reason she'd broken down hysterically when the floral arrangement was placed upon his casket.

I know the real reason why...

It was the words written on the white ribbon beside his name...

"True Love."

PART 2
LEGION

Significant Moments In Time

CHAPTER 6

"I AM LEGION"

Betrayal is the catalyst that alchemizes empathy into ruthlessness. It is the insidious blade that cleaves emotion from the heart, transforming one into icy steel. I have the women in my early life to thank for the massacre of my soul. Damien died with a chain wrapped around his throat. It was the final breaking point that unleashed the demon within. Seven years later, I was hell on two wheels.

The heat of the desert highway churned with the scorching wind whipping past my riding goggles and beating against the bandana that covered the lower portion of my face as I cruised from Sierra Vista toward Gila Bend.

I had been called in to assist my brother, who'd adopted the road name Asmodeus. He was in the process of acquiring a roadhouse in one of our takeovers just outside the small city of Gila Bend.

We were the dominant MC from Sierra Vista, where I was in charge, to Phoenix, and all the way up to Sedona. Over the last seven years, we had fought hard to expand the territory of the Devil's Scorpions MC by overpowering smaller clubs, absorbing their surviving members, and growing in numbers until the surrounding MCs wanted no part in fucking with us. Essentially, they became our *bitch-mules* to keep their cuts and clubs intact, transporting product at our beck and call and handing over a piece of every club's revenue. They were button men to push whenever another MC or small-time gang got ambitious. Asmodeus and I had earned ourselves a ruthless, zero-tolerance reputation. Our expansion had been swift and bloody. If you grew a pair, I was often the one sent to cut 'em off.

It was Asmo's idea for the two of us to split. He sent me further south to establish a new nomadic crew under the Chrome Demons MC and dominate ground in Sierra Vista. Apparently, many found my presence a bit unnerving. By then, my dark practices were well known, earning me the official road name, *Legion*. Many were convinced I was riddled with the demonic entities of which I called upon in rituals for guidance, power, and protection.

Early on, and for a good portion of our climb to power, I barely spoke to anyone other than Asmo. My voice, forever damaged by *the incident*, had become a permanent, raspy growl. This only contributed to my mystique and threatening presence, reinforcing the superstitions men already formed about me. My reputation often preceded me. It helped that I had become a ruthless bastard with little regard for anyone, other than my brother. Quite often, rivals and conquests caved to our demands before the threat of my arrival on scene ever came to fruition.

I pulled my heavily chromed Indian into the lot of the roadhouse, which would soon belong to my brother. Although the place was a pile of crumbling bricks and stucco, it was inconspicuous, and outside the already small town. All of which factored into Asmo's desire for the place. It was also close to the halfway point between our clubhouse near Sedona. Despite those reasons, I didn't understand why he *had to have it* at the time. The only factor that mattered to me then was that he wanted it. I owed my brother. Reason enough.

After removing my riding gear, I dismounted the bike, lit up a cigarette, and surveyed the row of motorcycles as I made my way toward the establishment. My brother had his core crew with him, men who went by the road names Lust, Greed, Sharky, and Fuckboy. I assumed the other bikes in the dusty lot belonged to members of the crew we were either absorbing into our ranks or *exterminating*.

When I entered the dismal establishment, I found Asmo and his guys lounging in the bar room around three men already bound to chairs. Judging by their sweat-streaked faces and bloodied mouths, they had already been worked over.

I shut the door softly behind me, drawing everyone's attention regardless. A wide smile curved Asmo's face. His crew chuckled with depraved eagerness, eyes darting back and forth between me and the men who were about to cave to my brother's demands.

"Ah! *Speak of the* Devil *and he shall appear!*" Asmo bellowed jovially.

"*Legion.*" Sharky, his Sergeant at Arms, nodded in greeting.

Wooden chairs creaked as the men shifted nervously at the mention of my name, watching me intently. I grabbed a chair and sat at a table nearest them, pulling the last drag of my cigarette. Fuckboy placed their wallets down for me to inspect. I snuffed the butt out in the cheap, plastic ashtray and removed the contents of each wallet, splaying everything out before me.

Licenses... Family photos... *Leverage.*

I studied the items, methodically glancing up to make eye contact with the contents' worried owners, one by one.

Asmo clapped his hands together. The abrupt sound made our captives flinch in unison. "So, gentlemen, have you decided whether or not this is going to be an execution, or a patching over into our ranks?" he asked, playing up the excitement in his tone. "Will we be slicing off Rockers, *or body parts?*"

When the men remained silent, Asmo's smile twisted into a sneer, and he nodded at me.

My turn...

I stood, removing the two hook-style blades concealed within the sheaths beneath my cut. Karambit knives, vicious and efficient weapons in close combat, able to rip and slash with ease and fluidity in a fight.

I shifted my focus from our captives' widened eyes and bobbing throats to the photos on the table, and speared the wallet-sized portrait of a woman standing beside a motorcycle. I held it up on the tip of my blade.

The room fell to complete silence when I spoke. *"Your Ol' Lady?"*

Their president didn't respond. I twisted my wrist around, allowing him to observe the way I studied every detail of her... Allowing his imagination to run wild with darkening worry over what I might have been contemplating about his woman. I couldn't have given a shit less about her appearance or what pleasures of the flesh I could derive from her leather-clad body. The twisted grin pulling at my mouth had nothing to do with her.

It was the mental mind fuck... The anguish in his expression as I slid my dick into his psyche and fucked his darkest fears to the forefront of his mind.

Legion: Book 3

"You have a choice to make." I stepped closer to him and held the photo of his woman at the tip of my blade, directly in his face. "Bend to Asmodeus...or die knowing your families will share a similar fate to what happens here tonight."

"And what's that?" The tremor in his voice discredited his brave façade.

"I christen this place in your blood, and that of your men... Have you ever seen a man skinned alive?"

He swallowed hard.

"*Flayed*, to be precise. Is that something you would subject your loved ones to?"

He only stared at me in horror.

I lifted the other blade to the center of his forehead and dragged the tip along the edge of his hairline. Blood trickled from the incision, seeping into the creases of his sweaty brow.

"I'll wear your fucking face while I slaughter your family... The last thing your Ol' lady will see will be her blood spraying across *your face*... Only it will be *my* soulless eyes she's staring into when the life fades from hers."

"*Jesus Christ...*" he barely whispered.

"Quite the opposite, actually." I smiled.

The Devil's Scorpions laughed with sick amusement.

"Alright... I give up... Whatever you want...it's yours," he relented with a hopelessness that pulled a dark chuckle from my brother.

Asmo cocked his chin at him and grinned. "*Welcome to the Hotel California of MCs.*"

THREE YEARS LATER

The constant hum of the giant neon lights mounted atop the roof nearly drowned out the obnoxious music blaring from within the establishment below. The heavy bass reverberated through the soles of my motorcycle boots as I stood, staring out across the dark desert scape. *The Morning Star Gentlemen's Club* was one of our *mostly* legitimate businesses. I permitted our girls to fuck and suck for cash in the private dance rooms—at their discretion—so long as they kept their traps shut about it...*and kicked a percentage back to me,* of course.

Jennifer Saviano

I'd been running this *shake shack* on my own. The local LEOs were frequent flyers, both on and off duty, all too willing to turn a blind eye in exchange for a little *bump and grind* action with a girl or two of their choosing. *Bump as in coke*, that is. *Grind*...well, that's where the girls came into play. We didn't deal out of the club, though. A small amount of the shit was kept on hand for the cops and cunts, which in turn kept our employees happy, *peppy*, and less inclined to jump ship. Not that The Morning Star was a dump. Quite the contrary.

This particularly significant night, the roof door swung open behind me, and my relatively quiet retreat flooded with the shit music these borderline whores loved humping a pole to on stage.

"Legion, there's a hot piece of ass here looking for you," Vein announced.

"Let one of the other guys sample her."

"She specifically asked for you. Besides, she's more *your type*."

That meant she was stacked. Big rack, thick thighs, big ass. Over the years, I'd developed more of an exclusive taste for voluptuous women, and we didn't get many of those types seeking employment. Most men don't have the fuckin' balls to admit they're just as attracted to them fat-bottomed girls as they are the slender types, which made up a majority of the *meat grinders* we employed. Blame it on the fact I grew up with a *frail junkie* for a mother, or on my early erotic escapades with that chubby cherub, Mary Margarette. I'm fuckin' into it. *Balls deep.*

"Alright... Show her to a private room. I'll be down momentarily." After pulling a final drag, I flicked the butt of my cigarette over the ledge of the roof, contributing to the collection in the parking lot below for our prospects to sweep up.

Led Zeppelin's *Whole Lotta Love* blared through the speakers in the private room as I watched the hollows of her cheeks concave on a slow upstroke, sucking hard on my cock. She was good...*really* good. The best I'd had in a while. I could admit that much about her, despite the depths of resentment and disdain brewing within me while I watched her enthusiastically work my cock. Still, it would have given me another level of satisfaction had I been able to toss her to Asmodeus.

Legion: Book 3

When we first broke into the skin trade, Dom was the guy who sampled the new whores. He had first dibs as President over our MCs. Asmo would make the call on what they were worth, which girls were hot enough to slink around a pole, which got the preferred locations and rooms in our brothels, and which ones we'd present to our higher scale clientele as *professional companions*.

I couldn't help noting how much time Asmo had spent at the decrepit roadhouse once we acquired it. I would have tossed her to him had he been around, despite his preference for the *petite types*.

I wanted to instill in this whore just how little she meant to me. A tight hole was a tight hole, and women were little more to me than product, another avenue for cash flow, second only to the drug trade. It was worth noting, however, that this bitch really could suck a man dry, like the magic serum of eternal youth was in a scrotum.

I shifted slightly on the leather couch, my fingers gravitated into her long, auburn hair while she worked me, fist pumping the base of my cock, tongue swirling around the swollen crown. The red lighting in the all-black room made her look like the soul-sucking succubus I already knew she was at heart.

"*Choke on it.*" The words escaped me on a guttural growl.

Without hesitation or complaint, she stopped massaging my balls, removed her fist from my dick, and placed both hands on my thighs. I gripped her hair tighter, holding her down as she took me all the way past the back of her throat. Her nails dug into the denim on my thighs, but she didn't fight me. There was no panicked struggle, but the muscles of her throat constricted and fluttered as she gagged on my length, and warm drool dripped onto my balls.

"Stick your tongue out! Take it deeper!" I wanted to make it worse for her.

The tip of her tongue touched the seam of my sack when I thrusted further down her throat. A little cry escaped her, and her hands moved to my knees, as if she were tempted to push herself off of me. She didn't. She took it. She didn't fight, not even when I moved a hand to her throat and squeezed, feeling the tightness increase around my shaft while I mercilessly fucked her face.

"*I'm gonna cum in your fuckin' heart!*" I half snarled, half panted. The tingling, tell-tale sensation at the base of my spine and my balls drawing up warned I was about to blow.

She only moaned like she *wanted* it, then removed her hands from my knees, relinquishing complete control to me.

"*Good little fuck puppet...*" I'd praised her, though my words had been leaden with disdain.

More moans and whimpers vibrated her throat around my throbbing cock. Though I was holding her head, I could feel her body moving slightly. It was that moment I realized one of her hands had gravitated between her thick thighs.

She was into this. Immediately, I'd wondered *what other depraved shit I could do with her?*

"Damien!" Vein busted in the door the moment I twisted my fist in her hair, making her whine as I busted down her wicked little throat. *Vein could wait... The whore and I were having a moment.*

Letting out a satiated sigh, I sank back against the leather couch and released her. She sat back on her heels, gasping for air, mouth agape, a string of drool hanging from her chin. Her mascara-smeared hazel eyes, wet with tears, lifted to meet my gaze. With a sense of justified satisfaction, I grinned while she licked her swollen lips and wiped the thick rope of spit laced with my cum from her chin. Then she sucked her fingers clean and swallowed, as if she wanted to further impress me.

"I hate to interrupt this Hallmark moment, but there's a big problem, boss." Vein's voice pulled my attention back to him. I collected myself and refastened my fly.

"What is it?" I asked my road captain, noting how the whore remained on her knees before me, eyes to the floor, like she wasn't a *sentient being* unless my attention was on her. *I liked that.* She *deserved* that.

"It's Asmodeus... They were attacked."

My attention shot back to Vein, and I stood. "What?"

"There was a situation Asmo was dealin' with on his own. He's alive, but his crew is...fuckin' gone, man."

"What do you mean, *gone?*"

"*Dead*, Legion... All of them. Except maybe for Sharky, Lust, Greed, and Fuckboy... Can't find them. But the roadhouse was blown the fuck up, man. Could be their remains are still under the rubble... Just ain't been pulled out yet."

"*Where is my brother?*"

"Burn unit at Saint Mary's hospital."

"I want the surveillance footage. Get it!" I demanded, pulling on my leather jacket and grabbing the keys from my pocket as I headed for the door.

"Asmo disabled those cameras a while ago."

I paused and glanced back at Vein. The roadhouse was a legitimate business. No reason to hide...unless Asmo got sloppy and started dealing out of there. I wondered if that was the real reason he seemed to always keep me away from that place.

"I dunno, boss." Vein shrugged, obviously reading the question in my expression.

"Then you strong-arm everyone in the vicinity for the footage on their security cams!"

He nodded, though his expression read as if the fulfillment of that demand also posed some issue. "Uh... Asmo was payin' those business off to uh...*mind their business*."

"*Just get me some fucking answers!*" I shouted, shoving past him to rush to my brother's side.

Those first few weeks were a blur of heartbreak and rage.

"He's lucky to be alive," the hospital staff repeated on an unremitting daily loop, which only contributed to my anger.

Lucky to be alive...

They kept my brother in a medically induced coma for eight agonizing weeks, hooked up to feeding tubes and mechanical ventilation, while doctors worked to repair what they could.

Pain management would have been impossible...unbearable had he been conscious. Second and third-degree burns covered a life-threatening majority of his body, requiring the debridement of dead tissue. During those early weeks, there had been multiple surgeries, including biopsies of what little healthy skin remained to grow cultured skin. In the meantime, the doctors grafted cadaver and *pig skin* over the massive burns. Eventually, the temporary coverings would slough off, but they were necessary to keep his internal temperature regulated, prevent dehydration, and stave off infection.

They wrapped him up like a mummy and kept him quarantined. All those who entered his room, including myself, were required to wear masks, gloves, and disposable coveralls.

Once he regained consciousness, things became worse. The painful screams haunted my nightmares for years, embedded in my subconscious. When the nurses changed his graft dressings, not even the strongest medications curbed his pain.

His entire recovery, *if one could even refer to it as such*, took a year's time. Six months in the burn unit. Six months in a rehab for physical and occupational therapy. Not only had my brother been burned alive…he had been beaten nearly to death. Broken limbs, fingers, and facial bones…

Asmo's missing crew members remained just that. Neither my crew nor I had been able to dig up the slightest shred of information on the *dead man walking*, responsible for inflicting such brutalities upon my brother.

Over the next few years, I was driven nearly to madness, lusting for revenge on Dominick's behalf. The coma…the injuries…the trauma of the event. No matter how many times I asked, he only recalled bits and pieces of that night. He had no recollection at all of his attacker's identity or his motives.

Or so he had claimed…

Had I known then, what I know now of Asmodeus, I would have simply blown his brains out the very day he walked out of that prison, and spared us both the years of misery that followed. Whatever happened to Dominick, whether it had been what we suffered as children, or the brutalities he'd been further subjected to in that prison, warped him into something I shouldn't have been so blind to.

That's the thing about *love*, though. It does blind you. Love is far deadlier an emotion than hate. And despite what eventually transpired between us in the end… *I did love my brother.*

CHAPTER 7

"LUCKY CLOVER"

The full moon had risen high above the desert, casting a pale glow upon the sigils I'd drawn in the cracked earth on what would reveal itself to be a *significant Devil's Eve*. After exhausting every other possible avenue, I'd reached a point of desperation. After all, the last time I asked my brother hadn't turned up much.

"*Something!* Brother, give me something!" I begged Asmodeus for what seemed like the hundredth time. The sight of him made me sick. Sick with rage. Sick with remorse...a knife constantly twisting in my gut. "Anything at all you can remember. If I am able to hunt him down, would you not want to seek retribution for what's been done to you? I will be your vessel for revenge. *Please*, brother. *Help me.* Let me do this for you. What do you remember?"

"He moved like a pro..." Asmodeus rasped, dabbing his drooping lip, which the fire had melted and fused to his chin. "Like he had training."

"What did he look like?"

"Dark eyes...dark hair..."

"I need more than this!" I bit out, my patience worn through by this time. "Did he have scars? Piercings? Tattoos? *Something identifiable?*"

"He had a wedding ring...and a woman's name tatted on his forearm..."

A spark of hope flickered within me... *It was something...* "What name?"

"*Lucinda...*"

Not an extremely common name. "What else? What did he say to you? Any indication of motive?"

"*I'm the only Demon you need to worry about...and this party is just getting started.*"

I made a valiant effort not to look upon my brother with suspicion. "He said *that*...and you can't fathom a motive?"

"*Look at me...*he took everything..." Asmo held his deformed, blister-scarred hands up to me with a broken expression that mirrored my own emotions in that moment. "I'll never ride again... I may never walk normally again... My crew's dead. This territory will fall back to the Jackals MC.... Perhaps it was a hit ordered by them...."

"You don't think I've already exhausted that possibility?" I snapped. For all I knew, I discarded the remains of a few Jackals MC members somewhere in the desert alongside our own missing brothers in my bloody quest for information.

"I don't know anything else! Maybe you should let it go!"

"*I'll have to!* If these *minute clues* you've given me amount to *nothing!* But if I do find him, do I have your blessing to act? Will you allow me to repay you for what you did for me as children?"

Asmo looked upon me with remorse. "You have my blessing...and a debt owed to me, wiped clean."

"I'll find him, brother," I promised, a strange wave of relief quelling my barely contained rage at his concession. I needed this, perhaps even more than my brother did. "I'll find him...and I'll take everything from him. I'll make him pay with every shred of contentment in his life."

"Are you alright?" a timid voice asked from somewhere behind me in the darkness, pulling me from the memory.

"*No...*"

A year had passed since I acquired Asmo's blessing, and I was no closer to finding the man who had brutalized my brother.

The whore, my best earner, whom I mockingly called *Puppet* for the last two years, dropped to her knees beside me in the desert.

I'm not sure how much sanity I'd have retained throughout this ordeal, had it not been for her. Not that I confided in her. Puppet's ability to damn near suck the twisted remnants of my soul out of my cock when my frustration reached a boiling point had proven beneficial to all within my vicinity.

"You've cut yourself…" The hint of concern in her tone annoyed me.

"A blood sacrifice," I muttered. "Mind your business and stick to sucking cock. You're good at that."

"I can see you're in pain." For some inexplicable reason, my foul moods never deterred her. In fact, they made her all the more eager to please me.

"I live there."

She looked over the remnants of the ritual, then the bloody knife in my hand. "You've been very private about your practices until now… Is it true? Do you really worship the Devil?"

"*I worship no one.* Though I am not opposed to making dark bargains with the demonic realm. They are far closer and more willing to lend a helping hand than the absentee landlord you call God."

She looked at me curiously. "You've seen them?"

"I see them whenever I look in a mirror."

"*Legion*…because Demons dwell within you…"

"Precisely. *Now fuck off*… You're interrupting my ritual."

Her contemplative expression deepened. "The demons…they require blood to help you?"

"Nothing comes free. *You* should grasp that better than anyone." I'd glared at her. She grabbed my knife and pressed it to the pale, delicate flesh of her inner forearm, cutting herself. She reached her arm out toward the fire within the circle, letting the blood drip from the five-inch incision, as if physically offering her blood to unseen beings.

Her hazel eyes shifted back to me. "How else may I serve you, Master?"

Puppet had always been eager to please me. I'd known she was crazy to seek me out, even more so to willingly remain within my vicinity all these months. However, it was this moment I knew the bitch was fully off her rocker, and that I would come to use her in so many twisted ways…

Legion: Book 3

SIX MONTHS LATER

"Get ready to be happy, boss." Palpable excitement emanated through the speaker of my cell when I answered Vein's call. "Talking to a guy here, at the fights out near Phoenix. Says he knows the guy we've been looking for."

"Do not let him out of your sight! I'm on my way."

After a lifetime spent in survival mode, I'd learned to wear a mask of calm indifference as if it were a second skin. Only Vein could have connected the speed at which I had ridden to the old warehouse on the city's outskirts to how eager I was to make this fighter's acquaintance.

He was standing with Vein behind the old structure, beside a chain-link fence. I dismounted my bike, already reaching into the inner pocket of my cut. "I understand you've crossed paths with someone of interest to me." I flashed him the wad of cash, fanning out the hundred-dollar bills between my fingers as I approached.

"Aye... Fought him before," he boasted in a thick Irish accent, staring greedily at the reward money. "Been itching for another match. Ain't like we got each other's phone numbers though."

"How about a name?"

"That I do have... Name's Keegan... *Dean Keegan*. He ain't from around here. Pretty sure he's on the East Coast."

"Got anything more specific? An accent? Something distinguishable?"

"Never could place his accent... Why are you looking for him, anyway?"

The Irishman's suspicion was my cue to walk away. I shoved the folded cash into his clover-tatted hand and got back on my bike. Hope thudded in my chest faster than my motorcycle rocketed down the dark alley.

Dean Keegan. East Coast. Underground fighter. Married to a *Lucinda*. Shouldn't be too difficult to hunt down.

And he wasn't. I found him within moments once privy to his name. A quick criminal records search confirmed he was indeed my intended target.

Dean Keegan, arrested in Bermuda County, North Carolina. The record had been sealed, however. Though with a bribe to the right clerk, I found out he was charged with violating an order of protection filed by one *Lucinda Keegan*. Turned out, he had recently divorced. Must have been a nasty split.

A quick check of his assets revealed several businesses he owned, including a bar that appeared to double as a biker clubhouse.

The Saviors MC.

"*Saviors...*" I chuckled to myself. From what I dug up on their founding members, the Saviors MC was originally rooted in a Christian foundation. *Oh, what fun it would be to take a jackhammer to that...*

As I shut down the laptop in my office at The Morning Star, a wicked grin stretched my mouth. "Dean Keegan... You're about to lose so much more... Your fate is in my hands now...and I'm going to rip your world apart."

CHAPTER 8

"THE DEMON'S DEN"

"What do I do until you?" Puppet asked, following me like a stray mutt. I didn't bother looking at her when I carried the pair of duffel bags to my bike.

"Line my pockets with your scents," I snapped at her, strapping my shit to the chrome sissy bar I installed earlier that day, specifically for this trip. "Keep milking dick and wallets. I'll be back when I'm back."

It irked me that she was in my thoughts at all, especially with how busy I'd been since my arrival in North Carolina. It had been months since I'd left her behind in the desert to pursue the Irishman's lead.

"This place is a rat's nest," Reaper grumbled, redirecting my attention to the mission at hand. He abandoned stroking his black beard to pluck a piece of pink insulation from a hole in the wall and dropped it on the musty, mildew-ridden, half-torn-up, old carpet beneath our boots. "I could make it look like a gas leak. We can collect the insurance and rebuild something more suitable until we own their clubhouse."

"Patience, Reaper. This is all temporary," I assured him. A former special forces guy, Reaper was a wealth of information when it came to improvised munitions. We shared an affinity for blowing shit up.

Until this point, I'd spent the majority of my time in North Carolina gathering every shred of intel I could on Dean Keegan and his allies, learning the lay of the land and acclimating to the humid climate. Bermuda County sat safe and nestled within the inner banks of the coastal plain, and my body wasn't accustomed to the sticky heat.

Forming alliances with the criminal elements that bordered their quaint little town had also been crucial to setting things in motion. Finally, the time had come for us to make our presence known, for the games to officially begin. The chessboard was set, and I was about to move the King's pawn forward two spaces…

"Besides, the forested acreage is what drew Asmo's attention to this condemnable shithole. It's very private and has potential for a great many things, beyond a clubhouse," I explained to my Sergeant at Arms, who was appointed by my brother. After losing nearly everything, including the core members of his crew, I'd made Asmodeus honorary President of the Chrome Demons MC.

"Fair enough. I suppose we could set up a few hidden cook trailers unless you want to leave production to one of the other crews under our thumbs? What are your thoughts on infiltrating the Jokers MC next?"

I pulled a long drag from my cigarette and blew the smoke up toward the water-stained ceiling tiles of what would become my temporary office. A few were broken, leaving old wiring exposed. It was the only private room in the back of the old diner we'd acquired through one of Asmo's dummy corporations.

"The Jokers are out…too big a MC and too much history between them and the Saviors, particularly with Keegan and their president. *Slice* would never betray them, not without great cause, which I am not convinced we could effectively manufacture. We leave their territory untouched while we recruit. What we're offering, it won't take very long before we outnumber them all and neutralize the JoCo Jokers."

"What about the Asphalt Knights? Word on the street, there's already beef with Keegan over some assault on a member of their MC."

"That's a potential inch we could stretch a mile… Which member? And what was the reason behind the assault?"

"The president's cousin. Some juicehead they call *Shane*. And over what…" Reaper scoffs, "*What else?*"

"*A woman.*" I sighed. Of course. "Get me some intel on their president and ranking members. I want their *Achilles heel* fully exposed."

Reaper's brow furrowed. "There's another ticking time-bomb we need to consider. When Daniel Keegan realizes what all this is about, his loyalties may shift back to his brother," Reaper warned, as if the obvious thought had never occurred to me. "Regardless of the animosity between them, they are still blood."

"Which I intend to eventually spill... *Leviticus.*" I grinned, bloody fantasies playing in my mind. Forcing Keegan to watch me dismember his brother alive was an intoxicating thought, but I shoved it aside to focus on this particular phase of the mission.

"Until the time comes, keep Daniel ignorant. Keep him close and content. Let him believe he is a favored prospect. In fact, patch him in, officially. Make him believe he *belongs* with us, unjudged for his transgressions. A brother among the rest of us *fallen*... I'm quite sure he's already given up whatever intel he could on Keegan out of sheer spite, but allow him to vent and keep reporting back to me. I must remain at a distance for now. I want to keep him in the dark for as long as possible."

"Alright. And what about Preacher?"

"*Preacher...*" I scoffed, recalling our initial encounter months prior. The man's eagerness and tendency to act on impulse solidified his expiration date in my plans. He feared me, though, enough to cut ties with the organizations they'd volunteered with, his measly attempt at protecting them from my reach. Unbeknownst to him, the move worked to my benefit, tarnishing their reputation as supposed do-gooders.

"Preacher is an arrogant fool, too quick to act without thinking." I pulled a long, irritated drag. "Pride and greed will be his undoing, but he has no love for Keegan and resents those of his crew who do. Preacher will be easy to bend to our will. He's power hungry and envious... There's a greed in him I will cultivate and exploit. His soul and his MC will be mine within the year."

"Legion... *President of the Saviors MC?*" Reaper chuckled.

"I intend to make him my new puppet...a key pawn. Through their subverted president, I'll snatch the redemption they seek and snuff it out beneath my boots. I will twist them into the very things they hate. Hell, I'll even turn their safehouses into *fucking brothels* and drug dens by the time I'm through."

"Now that sounds like fun." Reaper grinned.

Legion: Book 3

A smile crept across my mouth as I gazed over the maps pinned to the bead-boarded wall, which outlined each MC's territory and the clustered photos of their members.

"A *party*, Reaper." I chuckled, my demons giddy with the promise of chaos and destruction hovering on the horizon. *"And this party is just getting started…"*

PART 3

Road To Redemption

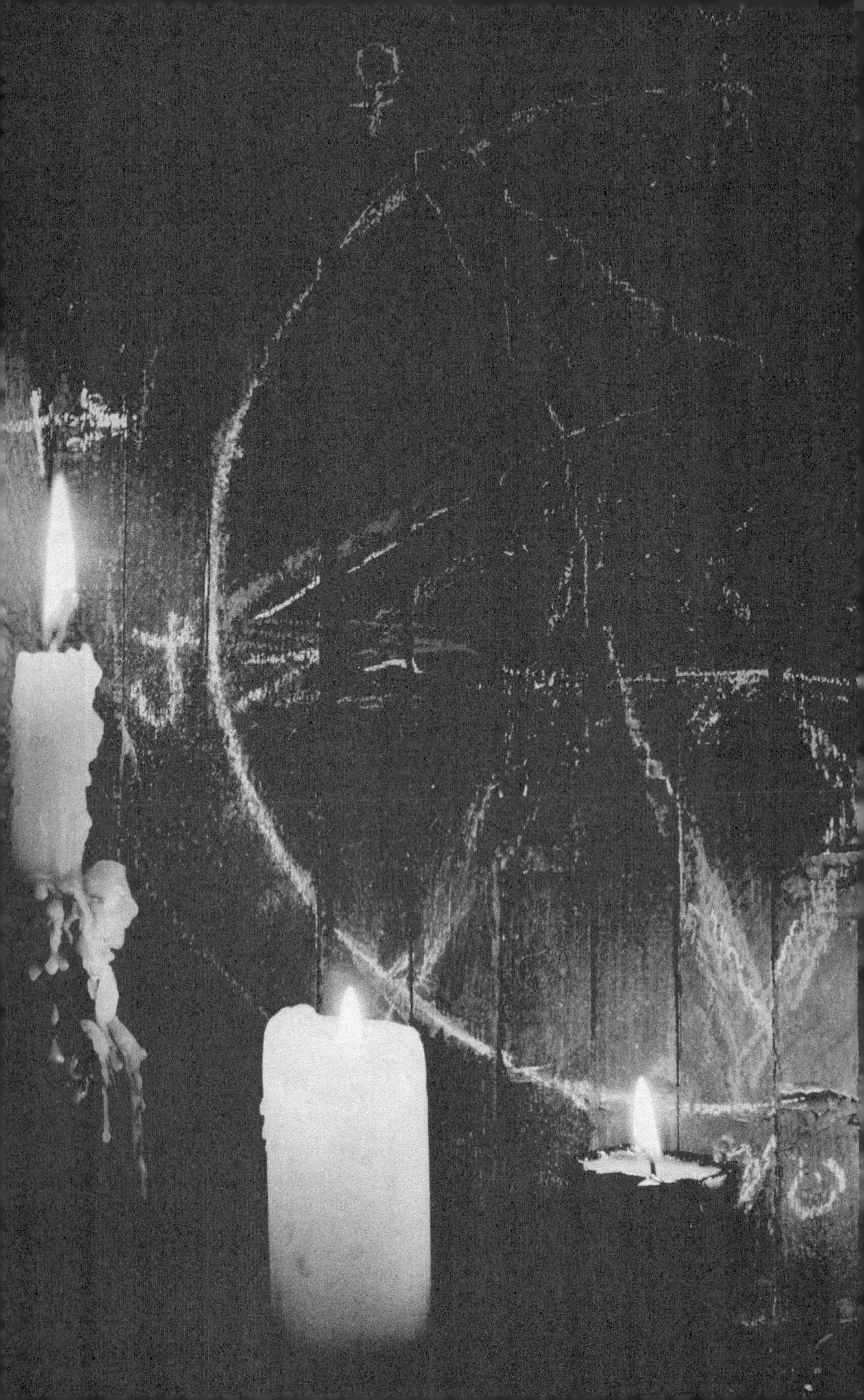

CHAPTER 9

PRESENT DAY
NEARLY THREE YEARS AFTER
HER WEDDING NIGHT

LEGION

The first few smooth, persistent notes of the Baroque Concerto fill the room and drift through the halls of the mansion. I wait, head resting back against the supple leather of the long Chesterfield couch. Smoke from the cigarette between my lips snakes up toward the elaborate crown molding, which consists of elegant filigree patterns accented with gold leaf.

The sheer size and elegance of Pierce Manor churn my stomach. I'm sitting across from the unconscious owner. The very wealthy, *very evil* Johnathan Pierce. His office alone is larger than any homestead I've set foot in. The furnishings and décor were no doubt expertly designed by the top interior decorators in the region, perhaps even the country.

The monster before me begins to stir. Leaning forward, I pull the last drag from my cigarette before blowing the smoke in his direction. The man's nostrils twitch at the offending odor. I extinguish the coffin nail in the silver tray atop the leather ottoman between us.

He lets out a light cough, his shoulders subconsciously moving in a futile attempt to bring his arms in front of him. I've bound them tightly behind his back. The fabric of his tailored suit strains against the flexing muscles in his broad shoulders. He will awaken shortly, and then we'll begin.

I glance down at the sterling silver-plated picture frame resting beside me. It had previously been displayed on his ornately carved desk across the room. A standard token of his legal obligation. I lift it to study the blonde woman within the frame.

Is she aware of the means by which her husband makes a living? The lives he sells to the highest bidder without a care for what becomes of them? Is she privy to the fact that the diamonds she frosts her slender body with are *blood diamonds?* The money she spends without limitation or restraint, *blood money?*

"*Wha…what's…going on?*" he mumbles. I glance over the picture to meet his bewildered expression.

"Mr. Pierce." I smile, and his blue eyes blink in confusion. "You have an impressive home. Might I be so bold as to query how a man of merely thirty-four acquired such a gargantuan estate?" Though I already know.

"Who…who are you?"

Ignoring his question, I turn the frame around and place it, photo up, on the ottoman before him.

"Where's my wife?" he asks, a bit more alert now… *Now* that someone *he* cares about may be in potential danger.

"It's Thursday night, Mr. Pierce… Your precious Nikita is out galivanting with her friends, per her usual routine. Have you forgotten? Perhaps I slammed your head a little too hard when I rendered you unconscious earlier? My apologies." A smile curves my mouth once more as rage eclipses his confused expression. "Allow me to assure you, the contusion on the back of your skull will soon be *the very least* of your worries tonight."

"*Security!*"

"I'm afraid they're no longer with us."

His stubbled jaw clenches, and he continues to fight his restraints, shoulders thrashing back and forth. "Do you have any idea who I am? *What I can do to you?*"

His impotent threat only widens my grin. "Indeed, I do!"

"Then you're a fool!"

"*A fool in love*… Yes, I am! And since we're on the topic of love, does your *wife* know what you *really* do?" I tap the glass on the picture frame, drawing his gaze back to her. "Or does she believe your numerous nightclubs across the country provide her this *offensively extravagant* lifestyle in the lap of luxury? *I know they double as underground auction houses... Does she?"*

He lifts his gaze and stares at me, as if there's some chance he may be able to convince me I've got my facts wrong.

"Human trafficking," I clarify. "A very profitable, fast-growing criminal industry second only to the drug trade...and even that is debatable. You've carved yourself out a nice little notch, haven't you?"

He's got nothing to say now. An arrogant mask of calm slips over his features. *This one will be fun to break.*

I slowly rise from the oversized Chesterfield, stepping around the matching ottoman to stand closer to him.

"You can smell it on me...can't you? That metallic, gag-inducing, pungent odor that seems to linger on one's person... *Violence... Death...* Reminiscent of wet pennies, is it not? I daresay that shit seeps into one's soul...permeates the aura... You may disagree, however. *Facilitators,* such as yourself, are not without bloody hands. Yours are as bloody as mine. Though my hands are not tainted with the blood of pure innocents... That makes *you* the *bad guy* between us, Mr. Pierce."

"What do you want?"

For this nearly three-year-long, exhausting quest, to be over... To return to my *love.*

Releasing another weary sigh, I take a seat on the ottoman directly in front of him, almost knee to knee.

"To be done with this, if I'm being honest, and *honesty* is what I'm seeking from *you*, Mr. Pierce. In my experience, before pain is administered in certain situations, *such as the one in which we find ourselves now,* men lie. I don't have time for that...so, we're just going to skip the formalities, and I'm going to hurt you, Mr. Pierce... Do you hear me? *I'm going to hurt you so badly...*you're going to *want* to tell me the truth."

His blue eyes widen in surprise, as if it's the first time the man has been threatened. "I don't believe you..." The astonishment in his tone further grates my nerves.

"Frankly, whether you believe me in this moment is of little importance to me. What should be of the highest priority to *you*, however, is that *I* believe *you*."

Legion: Book 3

After removing the stiletto-style switchblade from my pocket and holding it in my leather-gloved hand, the blade springs forth, inches from his face. "The next time I remove this blade, it will be for one of two reasons... To *cut* you free...or to *set* you free."

He only stares at me, attempting to decipher my meaning. Hope lingers behind his ocean blue eyes. I laugh inwardly. The joke went right over his head. A part of him believes he will live through this interrogation. That perhaps I am merely bluffing. Pain will set him straight, make him a believer, but his hope will provide the answers I seek.

Flipping the blade in my hand, I grip it like an icepick and raise my arm. The blade plunges deep into his thigh, a few inches from his kneecap. The knife grates against his femur bone as it sinks all the way down to the ivory handle.

He wails in pain, staring bug-eyed in incredulous disbelief at the handle protruding from his leg. Blood darkens the grey fabric of his slacks, seeping from the wound.

While giving him a moment to work it all out, I light up another cigarette and lean back to watch him come to terms with his predicament. It takes a few moments, so I finger the lid of my Zippo, listening to the hinge creak just before it claps shut.

Did she ever find the one I left behind for her? True Love...

"*Jesus Christ,*" he whimpers, finally raising his eyes to look at me.

"*He* can't help you, Mr. Pierce." I sigh, tucking the lighter into the inner pocket of my leather jacket. "*But the truth shall set you free.*"

"Alright... What do you want to know?"

I narrow my gaze at him, unconvinced that he is already beyond the point of lying to me. There is a fine line when it comes to pain and the extraction of information. Too far, and one will say anything in desperation to make it stop, truth or no. But not enough...

"*Le Quattro Stagioni...*" He looks at me with confusion. "*The music,*" I dryly clarify, "Vivaldi's Four Seasons. I had considered Mozart's Requiem Lacrimosa...but no. *No.* Vivaldi... *suits*, don't you think?" He only continues to stare with an annoyingly dimwitted expression mingling with his pain. "You don't even truly appreciate the genius of this music, do you? The profound elegance of it? The brilliant sonorities? Ingenious innovations that truly capture the essence of nature? *Do you even know* what is playing throughout your expansive, *excessive* home?"

"Classical music."

The ignorance of his reply further annoys me.

"This is *L'inverno*... Vivaldi's Winter." He should know this before he dies, how this piece *specifically* foreshadows his impending doom. "Did you know *classical music* causes the brain to release dopamine, thereby suppressing the stress hormone, cortisone?" I grin at him, cocking my head to the side. *"Is it working?"*

"Considering I have a knife in my leg...that I'm being held against my will in my own home by a deranged psychopath... *No.* It isn't."

"There's something about *classical music* that inspires me to get creative with a knife." I smile as his eyes widen, watching my hand move slowly toward the switchblade protruding from his thigh. "The opening movement of Winter resembles a shivering man... *Are you shaking yet*, Mr. Pierce?" I flick the handle, causing him to jerk at the pain. "No matter...*you will be.* The relentless chill of winter finds its way inside in this piece. How fitting, no?" He only stares. "I find your lack of contribution to this conversation rather *unmannerly*, Mr. Pierce."

After pulling an agitated drag from my cigarette, I blow the smoke at him again.

"Have you ever put a knife in someone?" I ask, flicking my ashes on his priceless Persian rug splayed over the marble floor. "*Specifically*, have you felt a blade pierce through the intercostal muscles between a man's ribs? I must admit, the first time I killed that *was not* in self-defense, I had been shocked at the thrill I derived from it. The *extraordinary intensity* of pure pleasure... Feeling the slight vibration in my hand when steel grates against bone... It travels right up the blade, you know. Such a little detail, really, yet so satisfying... *The little things*, eh? I learned early on to appreciate the little things."

Reaching into my back pocket, I produce another small knife. This one, barely three inches long with an arrowhead-shaped blade and a T-style handle meant to sit in the palm of your hand.

"*Little things*...like *Push Blades.*" I grin and take another long drag from the cigarette. His gaze settles on the uniquely shaped dagger. "You've got a taste for *little things*, don't you, Mr. Pierce? *Little girls*, to be precise."

His eyes snap up from the blade in my hand to meet mine again. "It's not like that...I swear to God..."

"Those words are meaningless to me."

"What do you want to know? Fuck! Just tell me what you want to know!"

"*Cassidy Jones*. I want to know where she is."

"I don't know who that is!"

"A girl...sold through one of your auctions. Where is she?"

"I... I don't know their names...the girls... They're just product I move... I'm *just* a middleman...a businessman, doing business with other middlemen."

That is a fucking lie. I've done my research on this man. It has taken me the better part of a year to track him down...slithering among the dregs of the underworld. I stalked my targets, rubbed elbows with the worst of humankind in back alleyways and dark, grungy basements... Pretending to sift through vile pornographic materials as if bored with the status quo. All the while, hoping to never come across photos of my younger self, for trade or for sale...

The chill of my past runs through me like an icy river, but I shake it off on the release of a weary sigh.

I am tired. I long to be in her warm presence once more... Though I know I cannot return to her empty-handed. I have been fulfilling my promises alongside this self-inflicted mission, in the hopes of winning her favor...or at least, her fucking *tolerance!*

Vanna...my love...my sweet one... If you only knew what I have done to redeem myself in your eyes... How I've tried to wash away my own sins with the blood of these heinous monsters...

I bring the girl's photo up on my cellphone and hold the screen in his face. Recognition flickers behind his eyes.

"I have very bloody reasons, extracted from men just like you, to believe she was part of your *stable* not long ago... Who bought her?"

He hesitates, and I stand to move closer.

"I won't let this little blade reach your lungs yet... However, the pain it will cause, not only when I push it inside you...but when I *twist* it between your ribs... I daresay you will feel that radiating from the point of penetration, all through your back and—"

"*Please*, I don't know where she is!"

I bend to place a hand upon his strained shoulder, lowering my face closer to his. A bead of sweat drips down the olive skin of his face as I press the blade's tip against his body, letting him feel it settle between two ribs.

"*I killed my own brother*... I have spent the last years of my wretched existence hunting down and slaughtering what remained of our crew... Your men downstairs are all dead. Do you really think I will hesitate to lay your soul to waste as well?" I give him a moment to process my words. When he swallows hard, I continue. "Where is she? Simply point me in her direction...and this will come to an end."

"I bought her in a lot of seven girls, months ago..." he begins.

I already know where he procured her. Those sources have been eradicated. Though I, *directly*, played no part in the girl being trafficked, she had originally been taken by a member of the Chrome Demons. It pains me to admit, Vanna's accusation the last night we were together had not been far off.

"She was the least...*photogenic*..."

If his next words are that she was shipped out of the country, carved up for her organs, or dispatched in a torture-porn flick on the dark web, I will gut his wife before him...right here on this fucking ottoman. We will both watch the life drain from her body as her blood pools within the button tufting of the supple leather.

Something in my expression must have terrified him. He speaks faster now. "A crew I buy my party drugs from. They took her off our hands. They run a small-time prostitution ring."

"A name."

"Tweaker...he's the boss of the crew."

I grip the switchblade embedded in his leg, and he yelps when I yank it free of his flesh. His terror truly sets in when I bring the crimson-coated blade to his throat.

"You...you s-said you'd let me live!"

"I said I would *cut you free*, or I'd *set you free*. Two meanings, or one and the same? For you, there is only one meaning, Mr. Pierce... *Winter is the final season...*"

His shouts of desperation fall on deaf ears.

Kill him...

Keep killing...

Kill them all... They would have killed you, too... Though didn't they, pretty one? Kill some piece of you, at least?

In a bloody flourish, my blade goes to work...the darkness residing within me consuming us both.

Stepping back, devoid of even the slightest flicker of remorse, I watch his body jerk in the throes of death, lifeforce draining from him in crimson rivers that pool at his feet.

Legion: Book 3

Then I take his index finger.

With some effort, I pull my attention away from my macabre handiwork and move to the safe where I press the bloody digit against the scanner to gain access. I make quick work of filling up the duffel bag I took from their master closet with his stash of money and pills.

Taking a page from Preacher's final act, *which I'd honestly found rather amusing*, I remove the Holy Bible from Johnathan Peirce's expansive library.

After spreading the book open on the desk, I place his severed finger upon Exodus, chapter twenty-one, verse sixteen... *Anyone who kidnaps a person, whether selling them or still in possession of them, shall be put to death...*

Rubber gloves... a stainless-steel mortar and pestle...surgical masks.

The small, dark-haired woman eyes me suspiciously from behind the register of the Chinese Grocery store.

"*You're the one stop shop.*" I grin back at her, placing the items down on her counter.

"Twenty-five dollars," she says, unamused. "You want a bag?"

"I do."

A display of Zippo lighters set up behind her catches my eye.

"I'll take that lighter, also. The one with the Ace of Spades on it... And some rolling papers."

"Forty-five dollars," she says, reaching back to grab the items before tossing them into the bag.

After placing a pair of Jacksons and a Lincoln down on her counter, I collect my purchases and make my way back to the seedy motel I procured for the first part of this evening's endeavors.

Now, masked, gloved, and seated at the rickety table in a paid-for-in-cash room with my supplies, I crush several little white pills with the mortar and pestle into a very fine powder. Illicit Fentanyl, an opioid up to fifty times stronger than heroin and one hundred times stronger than morphine. It doesn't take much to kill, though I can't leave anything to chance tonight. I lace the marijuana and roll two generously plump joints.

The digital clock on the desk reads a quarter to eleven. Her shift will be ending soon. I place the joints into an empty cigarette box and tuck it inside my front pocket. It's show time.

The motel in which they conduct their business makes a Ramada look like the Waldorf.

"Can we help you with something, bro?" The juicehead and his cohort attempt to stare me down as I approach.

"Looking to ease some tension," I reply. "Blow off some steam."

"That so?"

"Indeed."

"There's a gym down the street."

He'd know. I resist the urge to roll my eyes while lifting my shirt, baring my extensive collection of ink and scars, and feigning exasperation. *"Do I look like LEO?* If you insist I pull out my cock to prove *I am just a guy looking to bury it in something tonight*, one of *you* had better be prepared to be that *something*."

Apparently, that was the last thing either of them expected to hear. Both stare at me, but the juicehead clears his throat first. "Haven't seen you before."

"Well, my cunt of a wife officially filed for divorce today." I glare back at him. "A *mutual party* informed me where I might find something to *alleviate the ache of a broken heart*."

"Oh yeah? And who might that be?" the suspicious one inquires.

"Tweaker." I release the very recently deceased man's name on an agitated sigh. "So how much for how long?"

"Two-fifty for one hour," Juicehead replies.

"Well, I am a tad short…but perhaps we could come to a new agreement?" I remove a blunt from the carton in my pocket. "Two-*twenty*, plus this. Had planned on keeping the *good times rolling* tonight. Primo shit but, be that as it may…*pussy* is my drug of choice."

The shorter one chuckles, shrugging at his partner. He's clearly the one in charge. "Snatch is probably all worn out anyway. Her shift's almost over."

"Two-twenty, plus the joint. *Thirty* minutes."

"*Forty*," I counter, so as not to appear *too* eager.

"Fine."

Legion: Book 3

I hand him the cash first so he can count it and get that bit of business out of the way. Once the money is shoved in his pocket, I hand him the blunt.

"You can do whatever you want with her, just don't hit her in the face," he mutters with disinterest born from repetitious detachment. He doesn't give a shit what goes on in that room.

I pull the lighter from my pocket before he gets the chance to tuck the joint away for later. *That* will not do.

Rolling my new Zippo over my fingers, like one would a coin, they watch, mildly amused by the simple trick, when the lighter lands between my middle and index finger. After thumbing the lid open, I strike the flint wheel, and the enticing blue flame springs forth.

"*Allow me.*" I hold the flame out to him, maintaining a neutral expression as if indifferent to whether or not he accepts. When he hesitates, I allow the smallest, crooked grin to pull at the corner of my mouth and stare him down. Words are not required to convey my opinion of him...

Pussy!

He caves under my emasculating assessment. Leaning forward with the laced joint in his mouth, he takes a few puffs to ignite it. As I anticipated he would, he takes a few hits before passing it to his partner.

"So, what are you? Some kind of *magician* or something?" he mockingly asks, cocking his chin at the Zippo in my hand. I presume his resentment stems from my influence over his willpower...*what little of it existed.*

"You could say that." I offer him another smile. "I intend to make an appendage or two *disappear* inside your little gash upstairs."

His partner chokes on his smoke, fighting back a surprised laugh... *I need to get upstairs, quickly!*

"Enjoy the joint, gentlemen, as thoroughly as I intend to enjoy myself tonight."

"*Forty minutes,*" the *resentful one* reminds me, pulling a nice, *long* drag as he scowls.

I turn from them, sneer unseen, and make my way up to the girl's room to await their rapidly impending deaths.

M y knuckle raps lightly on the motel room door.

"Who's there?" a timid voice calls from within.

"The man of your dreams," my sarcastic reply.

"I'm so sure..." I barely hear her little scoff, but she opens the door and steps aside, allowing me into the room. She doesn't lift her eyes to meet my gaze, however.

The dingy room reeks of pot and pussy. The girl before me is a shell of the one whose picture had been planted all over the news back in North Carolina…and she looks beat, in every way. I note the raw wrists and bruised arms, which she wraps around herself. I shut the door and continue to appraise her. Dark circles under her eyes, rug-burned knees, and her once normal and healthy body of a typical nineteen-year-old is now frail and obviously malnourished…

I grit my teeth.

I know I am fucking scum…but I never allowed merchandise to be run ragged like this… *I never held them prisoner.*

"You can call me whatever you'd like. Or you can call me…" her voice drifts on a tone gnarled with moroseness, *"Caroline…"*

Caroline… As if her existence wasn't miserable enough, trafficked into this life of sex slavery…they mock her with a constant reminder of what her life had been before she was stolen… *Caroline,* taken from the *Carolinas.* That's vicious, even by my standards.

"I'll do whatever you like…" she goes on, staring blankly at the carpet. "Nothing is off limits…"

"Cassidy."

Her face lifts. The distant expression in her eyes shifts to something more present as the sound of her *real* name registers.

"That is your name, isn't it?"

She doesn't answer. Fear eclipses her hazel eyes… Fear of punishment. She's wondering if our encounter is a test of her broken spirit. If the will to escape still lingers. Her silence is evidence that she once tried and suffered the consequences.

Cassidy Jones. I know you did not ask for this life, and I am sorry I inadvertently brought these fiends into your world. Perhaps I am just as guilty as they are…

"I have searched for you, for a long time, Cassidy… Come with me now, and I will bring you back home to North Carolina. You will see your family again. I give you my word."

The pulse in her neck quickens. Hope overtakes the fear in her eyes and demeanor. She straightens slightly, like a neglected houseplant finally given a few drops of water.

"*How?*" she whispers. "*If I leave this room, they'll kill me.*"

"They're a bit preoccupied at the moment...*killing themselves.*"

Confusion contorts her expression.

"Come now. Time is of the essence." I extend my hand to her. "There will be a changing of the guard soon. I was to be your last client this evening, then it would be back to your dungeon, would it not? Is that where you prefer to be?"

"No...but..."

"*Miss Jones*, it has been a taxing journey to find you. To say that I am eager to put all of this behind us both is an understatement of the highest degree. I am leaving this state, *right now*, traveling back to your native *Bermuda County*. Am I leaving with or without you? *Final offer.*"

Her eyes dart nervously toward the door, then back to me.

"They are of no consequence, now," I assure her.

"Who are you?"

"The dealer of death and new beginnings." I attempt what I hope is another friendly smile. "But *you* may call me *Legion.*"

"Why are you doing this?" she whispers in lingering disbelief.

"*True love*, Cassidy... I daresay the vexatious emotion has a way of driving one to madness, does it not?"

Another blank, hazel stare, though this time, she tentatively accepts my offered hand.

I hurry her down the stairs toward my bike. The two traffickers are no longer within view. I suspect, though I have no time to confirm, their corpses are lying on the pavement beside the van.

Another vehicle pulls into the lot as we mount the bike. The driver's eyes immediately dart in our direction, and he recognizes the girl instantly. His surprise morphs rapidly into rage.

Understandable...all things considered.

Before he can draw his gun, I pull mine, firing several rushed shots at him.

The rounds punch holes in the driver's side door and window, spider-webbing, then shattering the glass. He takes cover within the van as I continue firing, shifting aim at the tires before my magazine is out of ammo. Two of them blow out.

I don't give him the chance to return fire.

Jennifer Saviano

With the girl clinging fearfully to my back, I take off on the bike for the Carolinas, engine roaring so loudly, I could just make out his threatening shouts…

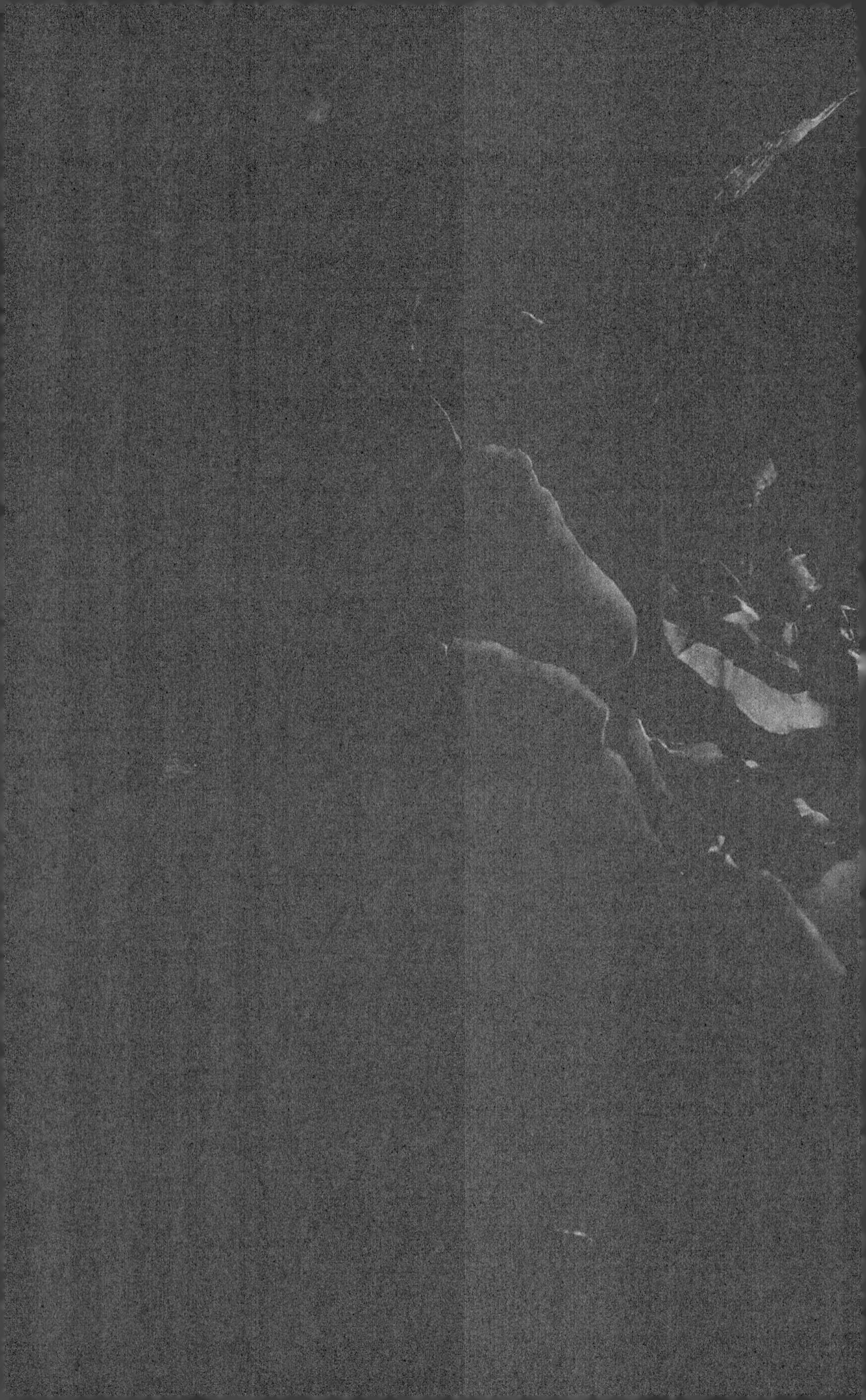

CHAPTER 10

Vanna

Dean flicks the latch of the heavily weighted belt around his waist, and it falls to the gym floor with a thud. My gaze roves over his chiseled body, glistening and dripping with sweat. I have never seen him in better, more lethal shape than I have these last few months. Although I can appreciate his hard work and dedication, anxiety overtakes everything else I'm feeling.

"You're really going to go through with this?"

Dean grabs the water bottle from the edge of the boxing ring and downs most of it in a few gulps.

"You know I am," he finally says, a little out of breath from his intense workout. "I've been waiting three years for this. He might not show up in Wilmington, but it's only a matter of time before he returns to the circuit in Myrtle Beach. It'll either be during Bike Week this fall or the one in early summer. But he'll come, and when he does…"

"You know I'm not going with you to that place again."

"I don't want you to." Dean runs a hand through his dark, sweat-soaked, and tousled hair, slicking it back. "I don't want you to see me beat a man to death with my bare hands."

To death! "Dean…"

He lets out an agitated sigh. "I'm not actually going to *kill* him, Vanna… I wouldn't risk it. Not now. But that doesn't mean it isn't going to get gruesome. I don't want you to see me like that."

Dean finishes his water while we stand in another moment of silence. After wiping his mouth with the back of his hand, he asks, "Where's Ace?"

"Out front with Viking and Cherry."

He nods, flinging the towel over his broad shoulder. "I'm gonna hit the shower. I'll meet you out there."

Viking has Ace sitting on top of the bar, playing with a set of Imaginex toys he gifted him yesterday for his third birthday.

Third birthday... The years have flown by so quickly. I smile, watching them assemble the little Viking ship together.

"Uncle Viking!" Ace smiles excitedly as he picks up a blonde-bearded figurine. It really does look like it could be a toy replica of his favorite uncle.

"Throw in a few Viking women, and yes, that could be your Uncle Viking," Cherry laughs, dabbing a bit of BBQ sauce from Ace's cheek with a napkin. "Can Aunt Cherry throw the rest of these *half-bitten* nuggets away?" she asks, moving on to collect the fast-food containers littered across the bar, courtesy of Uncle Viking, of course.

"*Uh*, no," Viking grunts, pulling the box of nuggets back from her and stuffing several in his mouth. She rolls her eyes and resumes cleaning up what mess she can before she spots me and smiles.

"Oh, hi, Vanna!"

"Hello." I smile back.

Ace immediately spins around, his beautiful brown eyes lighting up with a big grin of his own.

"Mama!" His glee melts my heart as I walk to my baby boy.

Once I scoop him up in my arms, I can't help but kiss his cheek and gently finger-comb his dark hair back from his forehead. Sporting the same style haircut as his father now, he looks even more like a mini version of Dean.

"Do you like the cut?" Viking asks. "I brought him to that kid barber in town. Told him to leave some length on top so you can slick it back like Dean does. I could have done it myself."

"I'm sure. But you shave the sides of your head with a giant knife," I say, giving him a stare that should indicate I'd never let anyone near my kid's head with a knife.

Viking rolls his eyes. "I'm an expert, but whatever. I knew you'd freak out. That's why I sprung for the barber."

"Next, your *Uncle Viking* will be taking you to get your first tattoo!" I tease, giving Ace a little bounce in my arms.

"Yeah!" Ace excitedly shouts.

"Not until you're at least five, buddy," Viking jokes, cradling Ace's face in his huge hand. His grin broadens when Ace pouts. "Don't give me that look. Your momma won't let me take you anywhere if you keep that up." He places his other hand briefly on my shoulder, letting me know he's just teasing. The only other person I'd venture to say, whose depth of love for my son might come close to my own and his father's, is Viking's. I swear, the man's best friend is my three-year-old son. He even bought a car seat to keep in his truck, just for Ace. When Ace was a baby, Viking carried around *his own* diaper bag, fully loaded with everything a child could possibly need. Granted, it was leather, but still.

The sound of the Twisted Throttle's steel door bursting open has all of us turning toward the entrance. Viking instinctively steps in front of Ace and I, but it's only Viper.

"Turn on the news!" Viper insists as he rushes to join us by the bar.

Cherry immediately grabs the remote and flips to our local station. Old news footage of Kelly's Tavern plays on the widescreen TV mounted to the brick wall. A continuous banner along the bottom of the screen reads: *"Missing Carolina teen found."*

"Oh shit," Viking says.

"That's such wonderful news!" Cherry adds.

"What is?" Dean asks, freshly showered and wearing his normal biker attire now. He emerges from the corridor and comes to stand by my side.

"That girl who went missing a few years ago, she's been found," Cherry says, turning to Dean with a soft smile. The expression in her eyes as she looks at my husband... I understand it now. He'll always be her hero. The man who rescued her from the hell of human trafficking. They share a brief moment before Dean lifts his gaze to the flat screen once more.

The news anchor goes on to say all they know right now is that Cassidy Jones is home, receiving medical attention, and there will be a press conference tomorrow with more details. She goes on to report several more meth lab explosions occurring over the last few days, and I'm suddenly aware of my heart beating faster.

"Gotta be honest, aside from an eventual memorial service... I never expected to hear a word about her again." Viper sighs, as if ashamed of losing hope.

"I don't think any of us did," Viking concurs. "It's been over three years since she went missing."

Viper looks contemplative for a moment, turning to Dean. "You don't suppose the CDMC actually did have something to do with her disappearance, do you? She went missing around the time they really started gearing up."

"Will you take Ace for a few?" I say, twisting to hand our son to Dean. "I just want to use the restroom before we head home for dinner."

Dean one-arms our son against his side, studying me with curious concern. I walk to the bathroom before he can ask what's wrong...

I don't know *what's wrong*. All I know is what I feel, and I feel like I'm about to have a full-blown panic attack.

After turning on the sink faucet, I splash my face with the cold water, hoping to quell these conflicted, unexpected emotions.

Two things have secretly plagued my mind these last few years, one being the truth behind Cassidy's disappearance. Had Dean been right all along? Was she trafficked? Was the *other person* who has haunted my thoughts in some way responsible?

I splash my face again as the image of Legion's pain-ridden grey eyes flashes in my mind. I asked him that terrible night if he had been behind her disappearance...if it had been a Chrome Demon that took the young girl.

He never answered my question...

DEAN

"Ace is finally asleep," I say, walking back into the living room where Vanna is seated on the couch with Nico in her lap. "That took *several* bedtime stories, by the way. I suspect he was trying to stay up, *waiting for you*... You wanna tell me what's been up with you since we left the roadhouse? Ace isn't the only one who picked up on your demeanor. *He gets that from me*, you know."

Vanna smiles softly up at me, though she doesn't speak.

I take a seat beside her. Nico jumps off her lap, leaps over the back of the couch, and heads down the hall toward Ace's room. Since the first night our son came home with us, Nico traded his favorite sleeping spot on one of the chess table chairs to take up the role of *guardian* in Ace's room. Now he either sleeps curled up at Ace's feet or on the cushioned rocking chair beside the toddler bed.

"Are you upset about Myrtle Beach?" I know she's got bigger concerns now. Hell, we both do. I want to hope I'm wrong, that this doesn't mean what I'm sure we both already know *it probably does*. "That could still be months away." I cling to the temporary bliss denial offers for another few moments.

Despite the fallout of Legion's attacks, these last three years have been the best years of my life, wrapped up in the warmth of contentment with my wife and son. Their smiling faces, the love we share within these walls…a comforting buffer against the harsher truths lingering just beyond our happy life… Denial makes it possible to shove aside unsettling truths. Happiness can act as an inviting haze, obscuring the less appealing aspects of life. As much as I want to cling to denial, we both know what is rolling into our lives like a dark storm cloud… Though maybe *smoke* is a more fitting depiction.

"I'm sure that has something to do with it," Vanna reluctantly replies.

"What else might?"

She bites her lower lip, brows pulling together and pitching upward. "I'm not even sure how to say this."

I already know what she's thinking. *Who she's thinking about…* I knew it was only a matter of time before he returned to disrupt our bliss. He swore as much, the night I should have put a bullet between his cold, grey eyes…put an end to his fucking mind games.

The gifts he's sent since his disappearance…*black roses,* of course, have shown up at the house sporadically over the last few years. I've managed to intercept all *thirteen* of them. When that shit started, I had our home address blacklisted from every florist within a fifty-mile radius and diverted deliveries to my repair shop. To this day, she remains unaware of his attempts to reach her from afar.

"Just say it, Vanna." I sigh at the inevitability of the situation.

"Legion…" she whispers, as if speaking the name of this particular devil might actually summon his physical presence to our door. I've been happy, having not heard that name from her lips in quite a while. "He was there the night we were married… That lighter we found…"

"You think I didn't realize it was his?" A scoff escapes me. "Of course, I did. I wasn't about to let him ruin our wedding by acknowledging it. You seemed to share the sentiment that night."

She slowly nods, before her brows knit fretfully together again. "What happens now?"

"I protect what's mine."

She swallows. "What does that entail?"

"Whatever it takes."

"Dean…"

"Every promise I've ever made you, Vanna, will always stand firm."

She lets out another weary sigh, closing her eyes. "I have a distinct feeling you're referencing a specific promise."

Taking her hand, I stand up from the couch and pull her up with me, into my arms. Wrapping her in my embrace, I press a kiss to her petal-soft lips.

"You're mine, Vanna," I whisper against them. "If another man touches you, I'll kill him."

CHAPTER 11

Vanna

The early morning sun has barely risen above the tree line, casting elongated shadows of the bordering forest across our dewy front lawn. There's a refreshing chill in the air, and the smell of autumn brings a smile to my face as I take in a deep breath. Closing my eyes for a moment, I listen to the chirping calls of songbirds surrounding our happy home.

"Morning, doll," Dean says from the Adirondack chair on the front porch beside me. Wet grass clippings cake the bottom of his boots, which rest on the railing while he leisurely surveys the property, an empty coffee mug in his lap.

"I see you've been up and about already," I say, stepping closer to run my fingers through the top of his hair.

"Opened the farmstand. Fed the chickens."

"Have you brought fresh eggs in for breakfast?"

"No. I was waiting for Ace. He likes to help."

We both smile. "It's only a little after seven. He's probably going to sleep another forty minutes…" I lean into my husband a little more, biting my bottom lip.

Dean grins, placing his coffee mug on the small table to his right while removing his boots from the railing and planting both on the porch before him. He snakes an arm around my waist and pulls me down into his lap, his other hand already traveling up my leg beneath the robe.

"Here?" I quietly laugh. *"It's chilly out."*

"*I'll warm you,*" he growls, undeterred, gripping my thigh. His other strong hand moves to the nape of my neck, pulling me to his lips. I'm relieved the tension from last night's conversation over Legion's eventual return seems to have alleviated a bit.

We make out for a few moments before I teasingly whisper against his lips, "*Mmmm*, coffee kisses…"

"What did you have in mind for the next forty minutes?" he teases back.

"What do you think about trying for another?"

"Huh?" He tenses.

"A little brother or sister for Ace? He's already three. I don't want there to be a significant age gap between our kids."

"*Kids…*"

"Yes. Plus, neither of us is getting any younger, *dear*. You've got another birthday coming up soon."

Dean shifts beneath me, as if suddenly uncomfortable. His gaze leaves mine to stare out at the property again.

"What is it?"

"Vanna… Ace was a—"

"*Miracle*, I know…but we could start *trying*," I gently urge. "If it happens, it happens. If not…"

"Ace was a miracle for more than one reason, Vanna. It's a miracle you both lived through his delivery." Dean finally looks at me. His stern expression conveys that I have my work cut out for me. "I am not eager to repeat that experience."

"Dean…the chances of that happening again—"

"Vanna… No."

"*No?*" I wasn't expecting a flat-out no.

"No." He removes his hand from my thigh. "Let me up. I have to get a few things done around here before I head to work."

"You were just about to spend the next forty minutes with me before Ace wakes up," I say, standing. Dean rises, grabs the coffee mug, and then hands it to me. "What is happening here?"

"I thought we had an understanding."

"That we would *never* try to have any more kids? When did I agree to that?"

"That went without saying, Vanna… *You both almost died*. You got back on birth control all on your own. I was relieved we never had to have that conversation… Are you still on it?"

"Yes. I have an appointment this week for another shot…but… I only got on a contraceptive because I didn't want to get pregnant *right away*, not because I didn't want any more children *ever.*"

"We have Ace. Ace is all we need. Ace is perfect."

"I'm not debating that… Ace is everything…"

"*Then let him be everything,* Vanna." His stern expression softens as I'm unable to find the words to respond.

Dean gently slips his arm around my waist and pulls me against him, pressing a kiss to my forehead. *"I love you,"* he tells me, before he breaks away.

DEAN

"Did you catch the news this morning?" Viking asks from behind the punching bag that he's bracing for me.

"Was a little preoccupied," I grunt between strikes. "Just want to get a quick session in before I head over to the shop."

"Well, another meth lab exploded. Wasn't us. Wasn't the Jokers MC, either. I asked. Slice still wants to arrange a meetup, though."

I slam my fists into the bag a few more times. "You saying you think it was *him*?"

"Are we not saying his name?" Viking chuckles. "*Afraid* to *speak of the devil* or something?"

"I ain't afraid of shit."

"Anyway, the thought crossed my mind. After everything you told me that he said that night before he disappeared, maybe he's trying to make amends? Maybe this is his way of *not showing up empty-handed,* if you know what I mean. He had to know there would be a mess left behind for us to deal with."

"*That's a fucking understatement.*"

The wake of Legion's misguided revenge ride left not only my bar in shambles, financial and otherwise, but our county and the surrounding ones where he'd set up multiple operations with different gangs. The Asphalt Knights MC was another of his casualties. Unable to survive the internal damage Legion created by corrupting key members, they dispersed shortly after everything went down.

Legion: Book 3

Repairing the damage has been a long and slow process. Though, to the best of our knowledge, we have managed to lock down our own county once again. Despite that, our image in the community hasn't fully recovered, and it's hurting my businesses.

The thought of our tarnished reputation among our civilians drives me to hit the bag harder until Viking insists on a break.

I grab my water bottle and take a seat on the bench, chugging a few gulps.

"Something else is on your mind. Talk to me," Viking presses.

"I know I made promises that I wouldn't fight anymore...at least, not like I used to...but damn... It's been *three years,* and I haven't bounced back. I had to let the girls at the farmstand go. After Snowy, having to let his granddaughter go... That gutted me to have to do. I've cut Derek's hours at the shop... Getting back in the circuits could really help."

"Are you falling behind on bills, bro?"

"It hasn't become that dire yet. I've just been taking extra precautions. If it comes to that, I have some assets I can liquidate. There's land I can sell off, bikes... I have a guy interested in my old Harley Heritage. Just waiting on him to get back to me about seeing her."

"You know you can come to me, bro, right?"

The aching sensation in my muscles after this workout has nothing on the burning shame coursing through my veins like acid. "I appreciate that, Viking...but..."

"But you're a stubborn asshole, and you won't. This fallout isn't your fault, Dean. We both know who's to blame."

Fuckin' Legion... Still.

"I'm supposed to be the provider for my family. I'm supposed to keep them happy. Supposed to send my kid to college. I'm keeping our heads above water, food on the table, but I haven't been able to contribute anything significant to savings for Ace's education. At least preschool is still a year away."

And to make matters worse, now Vanna wants another kid... The way her eyes lit up when she started talking about it this morning, and I just shut her down. I feel like the worst kind of man for not sharing in her excitement. For not wanting the same thing for our family... *Even if I could pull that off again...*

No... *Fuck no...* Not after what we went through. Aside from the fact that our financial situation could be better, life within our little circle is fucking perfect just the way it is.

"I get wanting to pummel O'Keefe, but you don't really want to get back in the ring on a regular basis again, do you? I mean, you're *over the hill now*, bro. About to be another year older, too."

I can't help shooting him a resentful glare. "I'm in the best shape of my life. I'd make a literal killing."

"You are looking good, bro. Have you considered selling some shots for calendars? Maybe even some Fabio-type shit?"

"What?" He can't be serious.

"You know, pose for some romance book covers bitches can beat their beans to. Those veins in your arms and hands will drive 'em crazy."

"I'm gonna pretend those words never fell out of your mouth."

"Have the patch chasers rub you down in baby oil, and you can flex on Serene or some shit."

"Jesus fuck, that was even worse. *Please stop.*"

"Hey, there's no shame in that game, bro. Chicks dig a silver fox," he continues, busting my balls in true Viking fashion.

"Alright, I'm done here." I step away from him and discard my gloves in the locker. "And I'm *not* that silver yet. A couple of greys here and there does not constitute *Silver Fox status*. Fuck off."

"Alright, in all seriousness then. We're family. I'm basically Ace's Godfather. If that kid ever needs *anything*, you'd better let me know."

Although I know he means it, I dread ever being in a position where I'd have to consider his offer.

"In other news," I say, eager to change the subject. "We've got to write the check to Medusa's Gates for the fundraiser rally last week. Hopefully, they aren't disappointed with what we pulled in."

"Yeah, I'm sure they're gonna be beside themselves when they're on the receiving end of thirty-five grand, tax-free," Viking rolls his eyes.

"Before the shooting, we pulled in fifty grand that year. We haven't come close since. I'm not going to be happy if this declining trend in everything we've got our hands in continues."

"Dean, I spoke with Cherry and Diesel... Numbers are better this quarter with the Twisted Throttle, and Stogies has remained a steady stream of income. It survived the hit. Our image in the community *is* improving, bro. It just takes a little time. We've already cleaned up Legion's mess in our county these last three years. It's locked down tight. The community knows it."

"Yeah, and our problem became the JoCo Jokers' problem. All we did was push it into their territory. You do realize that's why Slice wants a sit-down, right?"

"Yeah, I gathered that."

My cellphone chimes on the bench where I left it. I snatch it up and read the text. The guy interested in Betty hit me back with an ETA, and even though I've made my peace with it, my heart sinks a little.

"I gotta split." I sigh while grabbing my shirt and cut from the locker and slipping them back on. I'll shower and change at home after this is over. Wash away the sweat and sadness. "Hit up the Jokers and see when they want to meet up."

Vanna

"How about a Ninja Turtle?" Cherry holds up a plastic-encased costume, complete with a turtle shell, green sweatsuit, makeup, foam nunchucks, and an orange mask.

"No," Ace firmly replies.

"I thought you loved Michelangelo. You're a tough sell, kiddo." Cherry chuckles, returning the now seventh or eighth costume Ace has vetoed to its hook on the large display of children's costumes. "Are you and Dean dressing up to take him trick or treating, too?" she asks, turning to me. "Maybe we should try the group theme section?"

"Couldn't hurt." I shrug.

We make our way further into the huge Halloween pop-up shop. Ace's grip on my hand tightens the nearer we come to the spooky displays of giant skeletons, blow-up ghouls, and other creepy animatronics on sale.

"Do you want me to pick you up, Ace? None of these are real, sweetheart. They can't do anything to you."

He shakes his head defiantly, determined to walk through the store on his own.

We spend the next while going through all the group character costumes, until Cherry pulls two off the display.

"*We have to talk him into this,*" she whispers excitedly, flipping the costumes around to show me one predominantly black package and one red. "We'll just have to get you a blonde wig."

"I don't think I can pull off blonde, Cherry…"

"Wait! Don't say anything yet…just look at this…" She tucks the costumes under her arm and bends to grab another from the toddlers' section below. "Imagine Ace, *in this!*" She nearly squeals with excitement, holding it up for me to inspect. "We could stuff a little pillow over his belly! It will be adorable! He'll look back on the pictures and love them!"

"This is actually epic," I can't help but agree.

"Who doesn't love The Princess Bride?" Cherry practically bounces up and down, shoving the red Princess Buttercup costume at me, along with the black Dread Pirate Roberts costume for Dean to be Westley. "Ace will be the most adorable mini giant!"

"Do you want to be Fezzik?" I ask him, "Daddy will dress up too if you do."

"Okay," Ace agrees.

"I'm going to have to try this dress on," I say, "I don't trust these *one-size-fits-all* deals."

"I need something for the bar. Axel is volunteering at a safehouse on Halloween night with Viper, but I still want to dress up for fun," Cherry says on our walk to the wig section.

We spend a few minutes searching until Cherry finds one long enough to pass for the character and hands it to me.

"I still don't know about a blonde wig."

"You're only wearing it for a few hours," she insists. "And we can add braids at the temples to style it up a little more… Try it on."

I do the best I can without a proper wig cap, relying on Cherry to help me straighten it out.

"What do you think about mommy's hair, Ace?" I ask, once it's somewhat in place.

His little brows furrow, and his nose scrunches as he shakes his head.

"Try it on with the dress since you want to make sure it fits anyway," Cherry insists. "Ace can help me find something for the bar in the meantime."

"Alright. You stay with Aunt Cherry, I will be right out, Ace." He takes Cherry's offered hand.

To my relief, the costume does fit. I change back into my regular clothes, and almost have my boots on when I hear the alarmed pitch in Cherry's voice. "Ace? *Ace!* Where are you, sweetheart?"

I grab my purse and shove the curtains open, hurrying out of the changing room. Cherry is frantically looking around for Ace. With every beat of my racing heart, it feels as if my blood is being pumped out and replaced with ice water. Nightmare scenarios flood my thoughts while I desperately search for my son.

"Ace!" I call out, storming around to the other side of a haunted house lawn display.

Relief floods my system when I spot him tagging along after a woman with long blonde hair. Although I still feel like I could have a heart attack, it's understandable he'd mistake her for me. I was just wearing a blonde wig, and she has a similar physique to my own.

He turns to me, a look of genuine confusion in his expression. Realizing his mistake, he dashes back to me, and I can't help but pick him up and hug him.

"Oh, thank God!" Cherry returns to my side and strokes Ace's back. "I swear he was right there beside me. I took my eyes off him for a second."

"He's here, he's okay... Ace, you can't wander off like that, baby."

"Is everything alright?" a woman's muffled voice asks. When I turn around, it's the blonde Ace was following. Her hazel eyes appear concerned behind the fancy Venetian mask she's wearing. She must have been trying them on when we interrupted her.

"Yes, a case of mistaken identity." I force a light laugh. "I was just trying on a costume with a blonde wig. He must have gotten confused."

"Well, there is a lot going on in here. Poor little guy was probably just overwhelmed," she says, shifting her masked face to look at Ace. "Such a handsome little boy. You'd do well to keep near your momma, Ace. Someone might want to snatch you up!"

Ace's grip around me tightens. Although the woman is right, and she didn't do anything wrong, something about the way she said it unnerves me. News reports about Cassidy Jones flood my thoughts, and I just want to take him home.

I turn to Cherry. "Are you ready to go?" She nods, eager to leave this place now, too. "Great, I just have to grab the costumes from the changing room, and we'll go."

"I'll get them," Cherry insists, then hurries off.

"Well, you have a happy Halloween, honey," The blonde woman says to Ace, before she turns and walks off as well. I shift him in my arms to look him in the face.

"When mommy tells you to do something, you need to listen, Ace. You can't wander off like that."

He nods, bottom lip pouting, before he leans forward to hug my neck. I hold him tighter, pressing a kiss to his head.

"You're not in trouble, sweetheart. Mommy loves you more than anything in this world, Ace."

DEAN

I shove the cuff of my sleeve up and glance at my watch. The guy isn't late, but I'm eager to conclude this bit of business before my family arrives home. Fortunately, it isn't long before I spot an unfamiliar truck heading up the road in the direction of our home. That must be him. I make my way over to the detached garage and open up one of the rolling doors. Flicking on the lights inside, my eyes land on Betty, my candy-apple red Harley Davidson Heritage, with the studded black leather two-up seat and matching saddle bags.

Fuck...this hurts.

The pea gravel in my driveway crunches beneath the tires of the pickup as it pulls up behind me, and I turn around to face her potential new owners.

Two men exit the truck and walk over to greet me with handshakes.

"This her?" the slightly shorter, stockier guy asks, gesturing to the bike.

"Sure is." I sigh.

"She's a beauty. Why you sellin'er? Wife put you up to it?" he jokes.

"Can only ride one at a time anyway."

"*We still talkin' bout the bikes?*" He elbows me in jest.

Legion: Book 3

My expression must have clearly conveyed my lack of amusement at his inappropriate joke regarding my wife. The other guy clears his throat uncomfortably, then cocks his chin toward Serene. "You sellin' that one, too?"

"No," I say firmly. I'm not quite that nervous yet…and I don't want to imagine things getting to the point where I'd consider selling Serene. "Just these bikes in the front. The Heritage…the Nightrod…the Sport Glide…the Rebel. Any or all of these."

The two men spend some time checking out the bikes. "Anything wrong with them?"

"Not a thing. I'm a mechanic. They're all in great condition." I glance at my watch again. "If you want to think it over and get back to me, that's fine."

"Can I take the Heritage around the block?"

"Yeah," I reluctantly agree. "Key is in her."

His buddy and I watch him ride off down the hill. Just as he takes the bend around the pecan orchard, Vanna's car does as well, heading home. *Fuck…*

She pulls her car up the driveway, parking it over near my truck at the far side of the detached garage beneath the carport. She watches me curiously as she gets Ace out of his car seat, lifts him into her arms, and makes her way over to us.

"The wife?" the guy asks.

"Yup."

He places his hands on his hips, looking at her a moment longer before his gaze shifts back to me. "I'd be a lot happier than you seem to be if *that* was coming home to me… Selling these bikes ain't your idea, is it?"

"Oh, it is," I insist, which seems to confuse him, but I don't care.

"Hello," Vanna greets us pleasantly, coming to stand beside me. "What's going on?"

"Buddy o' mine is test riding one of your husband's Harleys," the guy answers right away, appraising her as if I'm not standing right the fuck here.

"*Oh?*" She peers up at me, surprised, before she glances into the garage, taking stock of my bikes. *"Betty?"*

"Yeah, doll," I say, hoping she'll leave this alone, at least until the sale is done and we're in the privacy of our home. "Why don't you take Ace inside and see if he'll take a nap?" I suggest, though, naps have become a hit or miss thing with Ace these last few months.

The concern doesn't leave her expression, but she goes into the house, leaving us to conclude our business. The stocky guy returns with Betty a few minutes later.

"She rides great. What are you asking for her?"

"A firm eighteen."

He nods, looking over the bike some more. "Well, I got sixteen on me now. I can come by your shop and give you the rest tomorrow."

"Fair enough," I agree, and we shake on it.

Vanna is standing in the kitchen when I enter our home. Ace is in the living room, playing with his toy motorcycle along the stone hearth of the fireplace like it's running along the dangerous edge of a cliff.

"Hey, doll. Just wanted to see you and Ace before I head back to the shop."

"Would you like some lunch? I think I'm going to take him down to the farmstand once he's eaten. Maybe after a full belly and picking some gourds, he'll settle down for a nap. I thought he was tired at the Halloween store, but he seems to have caught a second wind." She pauses, lightly rubbing the side of her arm. "You sold Betty?"

"I did. Here." Stepping up to her, I take her hand and press the cash into it. "Deposit this in Ace's account when you get a chance. It's more than enough to cover preschool, easy… Guy still owes me a few bucks on top of it, too."

"Are you alright? After our talk on the porch…now Betty… I'm a little concerned."

"As long as you two are taken care of, that's all that matters."

She gives me a somewhat skeptical look as Ace rushes into the kitchen with us, asking to show me what they got for Halloween.

"Vanna, I promise. *I'm Aces, baby.*"

Vanna tucks the money into her purse, then removes the contents of the shopping bag and holds up a costume that kind of looks like Zorro.

"Actually," she chuckles, though I can tell she's putting up a carefree front for our son's sake, "Since Ace agreed to be Fezzik, *you're* The Dread Pirate *Westley* this year."

Whatever makes my family happy. I smile and joke, "*As you wish.*"

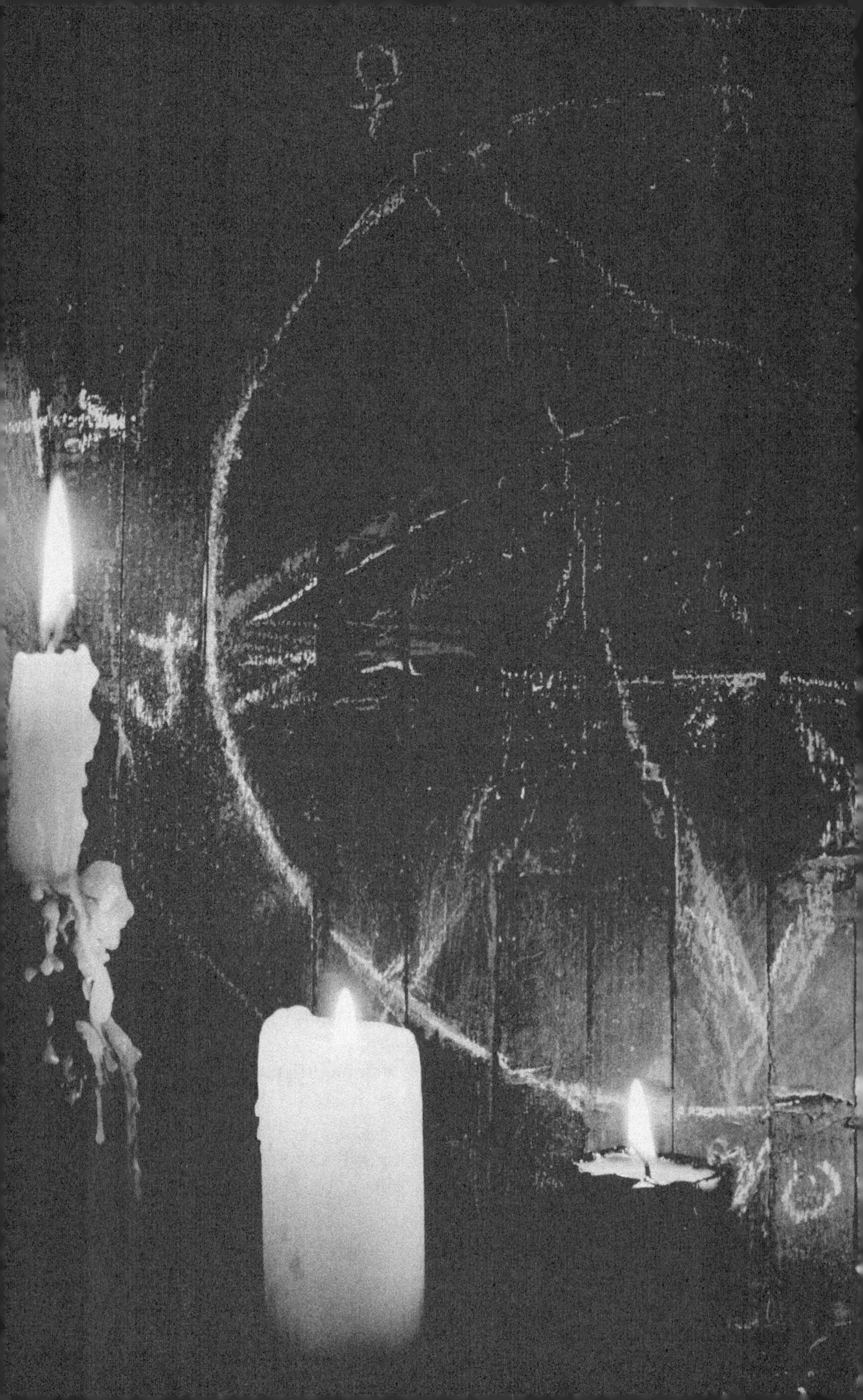

CHAPTER 12

LEGION

The night I first crossed the state line into North Carolina, I'd been hit with an overwhelming impression of being in the right place at the right time. Having finally tracked down the man responsible for nearly killing my brother, I attributed the euphoric, serendipitous sensation to *Dean Keegan*. Little did I know that feeling had been the beginning tremors of a seismic movement that would come to destroy everything I was setting in motion.

My initial encounter with the *beautiful disaster* lingering just beyond the perimeter of my awareness had been at the bonfire party for the young prospect, Axel.

Upon my arrival that night, the alluring, gravitational pull I had initially felt outside The Twisted Throttle pulsated throughout the crowd of partygoers. I'd recognized the perplexing sensation immediately and scanned the crowd for its source while Preacher gave his little speech on *MC etiquette*. The moment my eyes found *her*, I felt the foundation of all I had been building crack beneath my boots. In that moment, my body succumbed to her magnetism, pulling me into her orbit before I'd even realized I was making a Beeline in her direction.

I had every intention of mind-fucking Keegan throughout the duration of the Patch Party. *Axel* had initially been my choice pawn that night, a major chink in Keegan's armor.

There had been others in his life, of course, the young child, Maddie, for one. I was well aware of Keegan's love and devotion to the girl, of all the family turmoil surrounding their strained relationship, courtesy of Maddie's biological parents. She was only a small child, however, so I opted for the next best weapon. The boy, now young man, Keegan had rescued and cared for, brought up as if he were his own son... *Axel Rose Jacobson.*

All my plans changed the moment *she* breathed her name and placed her hand in mine. Though I knew it was impossible, there was something oddly familiar in her touch. The sensation intrigued me, pulled at something I did not recognize, somewhere deep inside my rotting soul.

"Forget about Axel," I'd ordered my men the moment we were out of earshot from anyone with any meaningful ties to Keegan. *"I want you to press up on that lovely thing..."*

To say that it had been a struggle, keeping my eyes off her throughout the duration of that biker bash, is an understatement. I knew she had potential in this game, yet every time a plan began to formulate regarding those potentials, an anxious, restless feeling wracked my system. A force seemed to needle at those very thoughts within my mind... I'd never experienced anything like it.

The need to know more about her rapidly became something separate from my plans against Keegan... Something I instinctively knew was another secret I'd have to guard.

The gravitational sensation pulls even now, guiding me down a familiar dirt path in the woods I already know will lead me through the acres of forest butted up against her formal rental home, and the Keegan Family farm. Though I know the old house, now devoid of her presence, isn't the source of this magnetic urge, I still find my thoughts drifting to the day I obtained her information.

"*H*er *name is Giovanna!*" The trifling little trick, *Lucinda*, busted into my office at the Demons' Den one evening.

Up until this point, I had intentionally kept my distance from the trollop for the sole purpose of Daniel's contentment within our ranks. I knew she was a power-hungry whore. That *I* especially, could have had her on her back, *or any other position for that matter,* at any moment of my choosing.

She shut the door and leaned up against it. For a long moment, she stared at me, waiting for a reaction of some sort. She quickly learned it takes more than a first name to pull praise from me.

I leaned back in my chair, folding my hands in my lap. She took the subtle cue to keep talking.

"I heard you were interested in her… Why?"

She was so… *eager…hopeful…* I knew there was potential in Keegan's devious divorcee. Narrowing my eyes at her, I asked, "Why do *you* care?"

"I want her gone."

That wasn't difficult to decipher. She was still hung up on Keegan. I looked her over slowly, making certain she took note of my appraising gaze. Lucinda was a very physically attractive woman, in that *societal standards* kind of way. Tall, slender, with curves in all the right places, blonde hair, blue eyes, and manicured nails that were digging into her leather skirt with an anxious, palpable, *and pliable…desperation.*

"And what makes you think I'd give a fuck about what *you* want?" I'd sneered as if the information she possessed about Keegan's woman wasn't appealing in the slightest.

"I'll make it worth your while." The tonality of her voice deepened *suggestively.*

They're all the fucking same.

"Really? You think so, do you? And with which of your *holes* do you intend to *convince me with?*"

She had the gall to scowl at me, yet the moment I stood, her offended demeanor morphed to something more…*malleable.*

She shifted in her heels, caution flashing in her eyes when I stepped around the desk, closing in on her. Trailing my fingers lightly up the bare skin of her slender arm, her body tensed, and I leaned into her. Gooseflesh formed beneath my touch, betraying either her fear *or arousal* at my proximity. Perhaps it was a mixture of both… *They do pair delectably.*

While I pressed my nose into the blonde hair curtaining her ear, I inhaled her honey-almond scent and brought my hand up her shoulder, and across her clavicle. When I gripped her throat, she let out a little gasp of surprise.

"You are a rather striking creature... *Tell me...*" I whispered, sweeping her hair back with my other hand. I brought my lips to the shell of her exposed ear and squeezed her throat tighter. "What gets your little gash wetter? *A man's hands on you...*" I dropped my other hand from her hair to squeeze her firm, gym-sculpted ass, "*Or fantasies of revenge?*"

I'd felt the shift of her swallow against my palm. "What's wrong with all of the above?" She attempted to entice me with her little taunt. "I'm not the settling type."

That didn't surprise me. She'd been unfaithful to the older Keegan. As a former stripper, she could have easily crossed the line *to whore* in a private dance room, or beyond the club. It was a regular, *encouraged occurrence* at The Morning Star. These idiot brothers learned the hard way. Some women aren't cut out to be housewives... *or mothers.*

Though I didn't require her intel to find out everything about Keegan's dark-haired beauty, I knew the jealous little minx would serve to cloak my workings. This *patch-humping pawn* would prove to be useful to me at some point.

"*And what would you have me do?*" I asked, permitting a false confidence in her feminine wiles.

Lucinda twisted to face me, though I didn't release her throat. That half-lidded, seductive blue gaze darkened as she stared into my own, convinced I'd fallen under the spell of her pussy power.

"*I want her out of his life...out of this town... And I don't care how you get it done.*"

"Oh, but I'm a very busy man."

She'd pressed forward, attempting to bring her lips closer to mine. "*I said I'd make it worth your while...with whatever holes you require, Sir.*"

Sir... Clearly, Lucinda had been paying closer attention to me than I'd realized.

I allowed a grin to split my expression. She had the potential to be dangerous. That is, if she weren't so quick to act on her impulses... If she could stave off her desire for instant gratification. Revenge is a delicate thing. It's an art. It takes time, planning, patience, and oftentimes, skill...

"I'll book us a room at the Waldorf." I released her throat. "Ten o'clock... *Sharp.*"

That would give me plenty of time to make a few arrangements... *Blackmail...insurance...* These things come in handy when dealing with the devious.

Lucinda plucked an envelope tucked within her low-cut top, smiling up at me as if she'd already won this power play. *"See you later,"* she purred, victory in her words, and handed me the curious parcel before she sauntered out the door.

After slashing open the envelope with my switchblade, I removed the contents. Within a folded sheet of stationery was a business card displaying the name, number, and location of a metaphysical shop located on the other side of the county…

The Ametrine Cauldron.

I tucked the business card into my pocket and studied the letter next. Scrawled in feminine penmanship, upon purple stationery depicting a faded jar of hearts, had been a name and an address:

Giovanna Vettriano
7 Farmhouse Lane

The memory fades as I kill the engine and dismount my bike a few yards short of the main trail connecting The Keegan Family Farm to my right, and her formal rental. Lighting up a much-needed cigarette, I remain standing beside my bike, staring through the foliage at the back of the old, neglected structure *that is* 7 Farmhouse Lane…

I could have ridden to the farm next door, but my anxiety over seeing her for the first time in three years got the better of me. I'm simply buying myself time. Besides, this will give me another opportunity to confirm Keegan is not present.

I wonder if she knew I'd been inside her home on several occasions throughout her occupancy of the old farmhouse… Though I doubt she'd been aware.

With every step closer to the ranch on the hill, the feeling grows stronger, and my thoughts wander back to the first time I succumbed to the magnetic pull of the little witch…

The air that fateful evening had been mixed with an odd, energetic pulse as I neared her home. A psychic, prodding energy speared my mind as if it were attempting to decipher my intentions. However, it did not ward me off.

Legion: Book 3

Through instinct and experience, I knew she had set up a protection barrier on her land. It was weak, but present. Had I trespassed with the intent to do her actual harm, I imagine this pulse would have been accompanied by a slight feeling of trepidation meant to discourage the pursuit of my plans. Perhaps a person unfamiliar with magick would have been easier to influence into retreat.

As I crossed that energetic line of defense, the feeling transformed to something more *magnetic*. At the time, I had attributed it to my own desires of gaining entry to her home and carrying out my plan to gather intel on Keegan's little *Achilles' heel*.

The lock on the old back door had been easy enough to pick, and I entered her humble abode…and I do mean *humble*. The old farmhouse was in desperate need of quite a few renovations and repairs.

Most of the downstairs consisted of an eat-in kitchen, a half bathroom, a small seating room, and a large foyer with a staircase leading to a single bedroom on the second floor. I suspected she moved into the place fully furnished.

There was no mail to be found lying about…nothing easily identified as personal. No bills, no bank statements, no photos of family. It was merely a somewhat rundown, fifties-time-capsule of a home that was far from being *hers*. She was clearly hiding from her past.

The desire to know more intensified beyond the need to weaponize what I could about her. I had found that feeling… *peculiar*.

The sitting room housed a curio cabinet, which she had filled with her herbs and oils. One in particular, labeled *Seduction*, had caught my eye. After twisting off the vial's cap, I inhaled the contents, taking in heady notes of sandalwood, amber, styrax, and an acutely feminine musk which had immediately stirred masculine desires. The label was handwritten, a concoction of her own crafting. I lifted the small vial to examine it further, noticing a chip of carnelian resting at the bottom of the oil, a stone which amplifies sexual energy, among other things. Paired with these oils commonly used as sacral energy stimulants, it was evident our little witch was clear in her intentions for this potent potion.

I removed a red bandana from my pocket, dabbed a few generous drops of *Seduction* into the cloth to take with me, before I placed the vial back in the cabinet among the rest of her collection.

When I stepped out of the room and stood in the foyer, taking in the place, a black cat descended the steps, vibrant green eyes scrutinizing me with bold suspicion.

Of course, a little witch would reside in an old house with a black cat...

"Hello, friend," I greeted him with a smile.

The handsome creature moved closer, jumping onto the foyer table beside a small closet under the stairs. Tail held high, tip hooked to the side, he had signaled a friendly curiosity. I stepped closer to stroke his sleek back. With a robust purr, he rubbed his face against the sleeve of my leather jacket.

"Well, aren't you a *lousy guardian*. Here I am, *intruding upon your mistress* with less than pure intentions, and *you...*" I began to say, when he suddenly jumped off the table, quickly moving toward the closet beneath the stairs. With his front paws against the door, he stretched his body, gazing back at me, then pawed at the door. "*Have something to show me?*"

I wondered if perhaps a few useful skeletons might topple out...

And did they ever...

Among some boxes of old tools and plumbing supplies was a shoebox containing what appeared to be some sort of binding spell. A wicked grin stretched my mouth when I removed the contents to examine them... Two poppets, bound together...one dressed in a leather jacket with a red scarf wrapped around its neck.

Had she been working baneful magick on Keegan? I laughed aloud to myself at the way he pined for her, like a man obsessed! Not that I blamed him in the slightest. Giovanna Vettriano was an enchanting creature, to say the least. I've always appreciated a woman who was clueless about the influences she held over the male species. Women are dangerous. Vanna is no exception, especially with her esoteric practices.

There was a tarot card wrapped in the parchment paper upon which she had written her spell. I'd examined that item first. Manufactured in a local town, by one *Marie Delai...*the artwork depicted a dark Knight upon a black steed, red banner waving, a morning star held high in his hand. *The Knight of Wands...* I'd found the entire scenario interesting... Though in that moment, an unsettling feeling began to nag me.

Legion: Book 3

Unfolding the spell, I'd stepped back from the closet to read her words in the sliver of setting sunlight beaming through the narrow window beside the front door.

As I scanned the words scrawled on the paper, I became aware of my pulse quickening. What I had wrongly suspected to be an amateur's *love spell* wasn't anything of the sort.

It was a petition for *protection*. One that clearly stated she had no desire to conjure feelings of love from her protector, nor did *she* want to form any feelings of love for *him*...

It wasn't until I noted the date on which she had worked this Knight summoning spell that my heart truly began to race.

Nearly three years ago...*on the full moon of a significant May's Eve*... The same night I had worked a spell of my own, one that had inevitably led me to North Carolina...*to standing there*, slightly unnerved in her foyer...

The loud rumbling of a motorcycle pulling up her driveway had snapped me out of the odd trance, and I'd hurriedly placed the spell's contents back in the box, shut it away in the closet, and quickly darted up the stairs. The dead bolt on the front door unlocked just as I slid beneath her bed. I listened intently to the goings on downstairs. I had been certain there was no way she had returned with Keegan already. I'd have received advanced warning.

The one they call Viper had come to look in on her feline friend. The clattering sound of kibble pouring into a food dish emanated from the kitchen. Viper grumbled something about grunt work, then the front door shut and locked once again. I waited for the roar of his bike to recede as he departed the driveway before sliding out from beneath her bed.

Three years ago... What were the chances we had both worked magick on the same night? Magick that would land us *here*, in this little shit town, *together*.

I wanted to believe the darkness set us on a collision course in order to grant me the ability to crush Keegan *through her*... That she would be the final nail in his coffin, the grand finale in this whole scheme to destroy everything he cared about.

That's what this was, I'd told myself over and over.

That's *all* this was...

Though as the strange sensation swelled in my chest, I knew this unfamiliar feeling was more than a desire for revenge. A deep conflict began to root itself in my subconscious.

Jennifer Saviano

She's a pawn...a tool...a means to an end! Don't fuck this up! I'd chanted to myself, damn near incessantly over the following months, and wished on more than one occasion I'd never laid eyes on that spell...

Yet even as the darkness shouted in my mind, I had made my way back down to her closet and rummaged through the rest of her belongings, only to discover the prison letters from Jack Nero.

I read through a few of his threats, and that conflict shoved itself closer to the forefront of my mind.

Fuck! Fuck! Fuck! I cursed myself, *I cursed her*, and shoved his letters back into the closet, then left the way I'd entered. By the time I made my way through the woods behind her house, back to my stashed bike, I had the address of the New York state prison on my cell, and a flight booked to LaGuardia...

An angelic laugh rings out from beyond the tree line of the forest, instantly pulling me back from regret-ridden memories of the past. My body instinctively twists in her direction, as if some phantom cord connecting me to her had been jerked. *Hard.*

Emerging from the woodland trail behind the farmstand, I stare at the radiant smile gracing her features as she crouches with her arms outstretched. A little dark-haired boy bounds toward her in the pumpkin patch, a baseball-sized gourd in his hand.

Her son...

She wraps him in a warm embrace, his little arms circling her neck. With an excited squeal, he insists that his mother look at his find. I watch as she spends a moment, happiness undeterred, untangling the gourd's stem from the long, wavy black tendrils of her hair, before inspecting it.

There is something different about her...something I cannot quite put my finger on yet. Moving slowly to stand beside the oak tree towering over the Keegan Family Farmstand, I continue to watch them. Halloween is only days away, which means the boy's birthday recently passed.

Her words elude me from this distance. Holding the gourd between them, she inspects it with a glee that matches her little boy's. The smile on his face broadens with pride, and I'm nearly as convinced as he is over her excitement at his find.

Legion: Book 3

A painful knot forms in my throat, and I attempt to swallow it down... *I knew she would be a good mother...*

Her toddler places the gourd into the grapevine-woven basket at her side. While looping her other arm through the twisted handle, she takes his hand and they begin their walk together toward the farmstand, and unbeknownst to them, toward me.

I cannot help but stare at the lines of her body as she emerges from the pumpkin patch. The dress she's wearing is looser than it was when I last saw her in it. I imagine chasing after a now three-year-old may have something to do with that.

She lifts her smiling face, and our eyes lock, causing her pace to hiccup for a moment. That smile no longer reaches her eyes...and I feel some type of way about it...

Disappointment? *Why?* I was not expecting her to *run to me*, or proclaim for all to hear she's *so relieved I'm alive* after all this time...

Had I been hoping she would? Fool...

I remain where I stand and allow her to approach me. The nearer she gets, the less pleased she appears. My heart sinks as she stands before me now, no words. Only a tense, guarded expression. We stare at each other in tense silence.

I hate everything...

"You're looking radiant as ever, Vanna." I offer her a smile.

"I thought I heard a motorcycle in the distance." She glances away from me to inspect the pea gravel lot. "Where's your bike?"

"The trail behind your old rental."

"Someone lives there now. And you shouldn't be here."

"I have my reasons."

"You always do." She sighs, her gaze breaks from mine to glance down at her son. I shift my focus to him for a moment as well. He's wearing a quizzical expression, scrutinizing me. The boy is the spitting image of his father... *He even inherited Keegan's suspicious glare.*

"Who's he, Mama?" he asks, dark eyes never leaving me.

When she does not respond, I attempt to read her expression. She doesn't know how to answer him. *I do not know how to feel about that.* At the very least, she has not introduced me as a *very bad man*... That's *something*, isn't it?

I turn to her boy, clearing my throat in what I already know is a futile attempt to soften the gravel in my voice. "My name is—"

"*Legion*," Vanna immediately interrupts, spitting out my road name as if it soured in her mouth. "His name is Legion." The edge in her voice wounds something inside of me.

"*Damien*, actually." I'm not sure I was successful in hiding the defeat in my tone. Have all of my efforts thus far meant nothing to her? Am I so *insignificant*, my declaration was this *forgettable*?

I quell my simmering temper upon a realization... *Perhaps she's unaware of* all *I've done for her?* I would not put it past Keegan to have intercepted my attempts to reach her over the years.

Vanna crouches before her son. Her hand gently caresses his cheek, coaxing his attention back to her. "Ace, my angel, will you be a big boy and take this basket over to the picnic table for Mommy?" She holds the basket for him to grip the woven handle with both hands. "It's heavy. Go slow and wait for me there."

With one last lingering glare at me, the young Keegan ambles off toward the picnic table with their gourd-filled basket. Vanna slowly rises, watching him until he's just about reached the table, before she turns to face me.

"So...*a stay-at-home mother* now. How very...*apple pie*, Vanna."

"I still work a few nights at the roadhouse here and there. And besides...you burned down my job. *Remember?*"

"Touché."

"Why are you here?"

True Love... Though I don't say those words aloud. My heart aches, and I swallow with a bit of difficulty before I reply. "Is it not obvious?"

"Nothing about *you*, Legion, has ever been *obvious*."

"I suppose I've earned that."

She only lets out another soft breath, folding her arms uncomfortably, and glances at her son. "How long have you been back?"

"Not long." I find myself staring into the dark pools of her soulful eyes when she turns to me, desperately searching for some semblance of a sign she might care. "I've only just returned."

I watch those eyes, which have haunted my dreams, shift back and forth between my own, searching for an answer she has not yet asked aloud.

"It was you, wasn't it?" she finally speaks.

"I've got quite the track record, sweet one. Might you be so kind as to expand on that for me?"

"*Cassidy Jones*," she says the girl's name with a mixture of relief and suspicion. "She returned home. Now…here *you* are."

I stand before her, silently waiting for her to voice the reason behind her suspicion. I already know what's coming.

"What I said to you in the warehouse that night…" The tone and timbre of her voice denote a level of fear… She's *afraid* of what my answer might be. "You did…didn't you?"

"*No*, sweet one. *I* did not."

Tension leaves her body on a sigh that I don't believe she intended me to note. Her attention sweeps back to Ace. A little smile pulls at her lips as she offers him a reassuring wave. I study him for a moment. Her child is lining up the gourds on the bench, occupying himself. He glances back at us to check on her often. *He is indeed his father's son.*

"I did not…but you weren't wrong. It was a Demon who took her… Therefore, *by proxy*…" I let the sentence dangle between us, hoping she picks up the thread. People are quite easy to manipulate, especially the kindhearted. And depending on her response, I'll know how much progress, if any at all, I've made in my attempt at redemption in her eyes.

She turns to face me. "The news said the reward was paid out, but the person responsible for her return wanted to remain anonymous."

"He did."

Suspicion further narrows her gaze. "Why? Wouldn't parading yourself in front of the media as a *Hero* make your return to this town a little…I don't know… *easier*?"

"Nothing about my life has ever been *easy*, Vanna. And I'm no *Hero*. I think we both know that. Besides… I didn't do it for recognition or acceptance in this town. I didn't do it for reward money or notoriety. Hell, I didn't even do it for *her*… *I did it for you.*"

She blinks. "Me?"

"Yes!" I begin with impatience, "I couldn't go on allowing you to think I'd ever have a deliberate hand in—"

"*Mama!*" The young Keegan rushes to his mother, stealing her attention from me completely.

The boy has his fist clenched, aside from his index finger, which he thrusts into her face as she crouches down to him.

"*Ouch*, Mama." He pouts pitifully.

"*Oh*...let me see." Vanna gently takes his hand, inspecting his injury, a little splinter in his finger from the table. "It's okay, we'll fix you up." She kisses his cheek again, then rises to take him gently by the wrist and leads him to the farmstand.

I follow behind them, watching from the broad doorway as she rummages through a drawer behind the register, searching for something to remove the offending sliver from his little digit. Closing the drawer, she looks over at Ace.

"I think we're going to have to say goodbye to Legion and walk back up to the house, Ace. Mommy can't find any tweezers down here."

Goodbye... Already... No. No, I've only just returned to her after all this time apart. My mind scrambles to formulate an excuse to prolong this reunion.

"How about a needle? A pin? I can sterilize it for you," I quickly offer, removing the Zippo from my pocket. While smiling and giving Ace a wink, I flip the lighter open, and the flame springs forth. I make it dance and swirl around my fingers. Her son is dazzled by the few tricks, innocent eyes wide with amusement. A genuine, infectious smile forms on his face for the first time since we've met.

"*Magic!*" The word is full of childlike wonder.

I glance briefly at Vanna, who is attempting to fight a little smile of her own as she brings her hand to her face, fingers barely hiding the curve of her sexy mouth.

The kid is the key to her heart. Of course, he is. Vanna *is* a good mother. The road to redemption...the way to her heart, is through Ace. If I win the boy over...*it's another step closer to winning* her *over.*

"How about it, Ace? You let us get that nasty little splinter out, and I'll show you another Magic trick?"

He peers up at me, wearing another one of Keegan's cynical expressions, and I search for a trace of Vanna in the handsome little devil. Although I am no longer his father's enemy, it doesn't mean I don't resent the bastard...resent, and *envy him* to my bitter core.

"*Okay...*" Ace concedes, though he seems to do so with some reservation.

"I promise it won't hurt." I remove the safety pin I keep pinned inside my cut for the purpose of refilling the fuel in my Zippo, and after passing it through the flame to ensure sterilization, Vanna and I make quick work of painlessly removing the splinter in Ace's finger.

"There we are." I offer the child what I hope is another friendly smile. "Was that so bad?"

He only looks at me, then his gaze scans my leather cut, his curious young eyes landing on my pocket where I tucked the Zippo away.

"Oh, that's right... *We had ourselves a bargain*, didn't we?"

He nods, and I produce the lighter once again, dazzling the child with a few more fancy tricks as the flaming Zippo dances around my fingers. This time, his bright smile is accompanied by laughter and applause.

"What do we say?" Vanna prompts him.

"Thank you... Leh... *Leh?*" Ace turns to his mother for guidance. She says my road name slowly for him, and he makes another attempt. "*L-Le-gen-d.*" He smiles proudly, as if he got it right, turning to me before she can correct him. "Thank you, Legend."

Legend... I smile inwardly.

"Actually, sweetheart," Vanna begins, but I raise my hand to stop her.

"*Actually*, I'm quite content with *Legend*."

She purses her lips, fighting another smile of her own. "I'm sure that suits your *ego* just fine." She rolls her eyes at me, lifting Ace off the counter and placing him back down on his sneakered feet. "I should take him up to the house anyway, wash his hands, make him lunch."

Alas...my official cue to leave... Though there are no other employees meandering about anywhere in sight.

"The hours of operation state your little farmstand is open until this afternoon."

"It's slow season until we shut down in the next couple of weeks." It's evident by her sudden, stiffening demeanor, there's something more about this situation she's unwilling to discuss. "Most of our customers just take what they need now and leave payment in the drawer if I'm not here."

"An honor system? Were there not two girls who used to run this stand?"

Something in her expression hardens. "They were let go last year." Vanna takes her son's hand and walks with him past me to the picnic table. She helps him regather their gourds into the grapevine basket.

"There is much I wish to discuss with you."

She doesn't look at me, nor does she speak now. She places the last pumpkin-shaped gourd into the basket and slips her arm through the handle. After taking Ace by the hand again, she walks past me once more, in the direction of their home on the hill, beyond the greenhouses and pea-gravel parking lot.

"*Sweet one...*" I press, catching up to her within a few strides.

"You need to speak with Dean. Until that happens, there isn't anything for us to discuss," she insists, continuing to avoid looking at me as I walk beside her. "We both know he's going to be less than thrilled."

"I only care what one person thinks...what one person *feels*, Vanna...and that person is *not* Dean Keegan."

She walks a little faster. Even Ace glances up at her with a look of confusion as he hurries to keep up with his mother's determined strides.

"I don't know why," she nearly whispers.

"*Yes, you do.*" I know damn well she does. She can pretend otherwise all she wants. "I'm aware you both think I'm the Devil, but I meant what I said that night, Vanna... *Nothing has changed.*"

"And nothing *will* ever change." This time when she looks at me, there's a worry in her eyes she's trying to hide behind her stern expression.

It halts me in my tracks, and I watch Vanna and her son make the rest of their hurried way up to the ranch-style home atop the hill.

DEAN

"D addy!" Ace squeals with delight, rushing up to me the moment I shut the front door. He wraps his arms around my leg, and I pat the top of his head. Vanna's in the kitchen, pulling food from the fridge to prepare dinner.

"You're home early." She smiles, though there's a slight tension in her expression, and for a moment, I wonder if she sees the cracks in my armor...the way those words have begun to erode my confidence. It's bad enough she witnessed the sale of Betty earlier...*now I'm home early again.*

I try not to sound defeated, "Yeah, short day."

"Well, at least there's a silver lining," Vanna says.

"As long as it isn't in my hair."

"Huh?"

"Nothing. What's the silver lining, baby?"

"You get to come home for an hour or so for dinner and spend time with us before you head to the Twisted Throttle."

"Yeah!" Ace agrees, following me over to the kitchen island.

"You're both right. What have you two been up to today?" I ask, taking a seat on one of the barstools.

"Legend did magic fire fingers!" Ace excitedly replies, showing me his hands while Vanna nervously chuckles.

"*Who did magic what?*" I glance at my wife.

She rinses her hands in the sink, then grabs a towel to dry them off. "I think it's time to wash up, little man," Vanna says, placing the towel back before she walks around the island to scoop up Ace. "Give Daddy a kiss and we'll tell him all about our day over dinner, okay?" She hoists Ace a little higher for him to get his arms around my neck. I hug him back, placing a kiss against his temple, and continue to stare at his mother.

"I'm not going to like this, am I?"

"Nope," she says simply, before walking down the hall toward Ace's room. He gives me an adorable little wave over her shoulder.

I make my way to the fridge, grabbing a beer to help wash down whatever news she's got to tell me, and maybe take the edge off the anxious feeling currently tightening my chest. I already fucking know this is going to be Legion-related. As I make my way back to the barstool, I scan every surface within view for black roses...

My family returns a few moments later. Vanna sets Ace up in the living room with a movie before she rejoins me in the kitchen.

"We had a surprise visit," she begins quietly, removing a knife from the block to rough chop the fresh vegetables she'd washed. "And before you go off, I told him he needed to speak with you."

"Was this before or after the legendary...finger...fire... *whatever the fuck*?" I take an agitated swig of beer.

"After. Ace got a splinter on the picnic table, and *Legend* did some tricks with his lighter to distract him and helped me pull it out with a pin."

"He touched our kid?"

She gives me a glaring look of disapproval before transferring the vegetables into a roasting dish. "*Barely.*" She grabs the bottle of olive oil and drizzles it over the top. "And he's not...*that* way."

"Because you know him so fucking well?"

She frowns at me, going to town on those veggies with seasonings. "*Because he blew his brother's brains out for it.*"

"That doesn't mean shit to me!" Realizing I just raised my voice, I clear my throat and compose myself before continuing. I don't want to draw Ace's attention, especially not for getting loud with his mother. That is not the example I wish to set for my son. I take a moment to compose my rioting emotions before speaking, calmly this time. "And we both know he *blew his brother's brains out* for a multitude of reasons, which don't mean shit to me either. I don't want him near you or Ace."

"Well, you can tell him that yourself," she says, grabbing the tray and turning from me to place it into the oven.

"*Oh, I will.*"

"Dean...he did save that girl," she sighs, turning back to me.

"Interesting, don't you think? How he knew where to find her?"

"It's been three years... Would it have taken him this long if it were his doing? Would they have paid out the reward if she told authorities he was involved?"

"People don't always speak up, Vanna. You know this. She might not have any idea how he was connected to what happened to her. Secondly, if he actually gave a fuck, *beyond impressing you,* why didn't he do something about it when she first went missing?" Of course, she doesn't have an answer, and I take another gulp of beer before continuing, "Don't let this piece of shit fool you into thinking he's got any semblance of a conscience. Anything Legion says or does is about *Legion*. His motives. His twisted desires. Don't lose sight of that." *Please...*

She only nods.

"And I don't want him anywhere near you or Ace."

"I understand..." She fidgets with her wedding band. "But he's going to come looking for you."

"He knows exactly where to find me. Let him come. I've been fucking waiting."

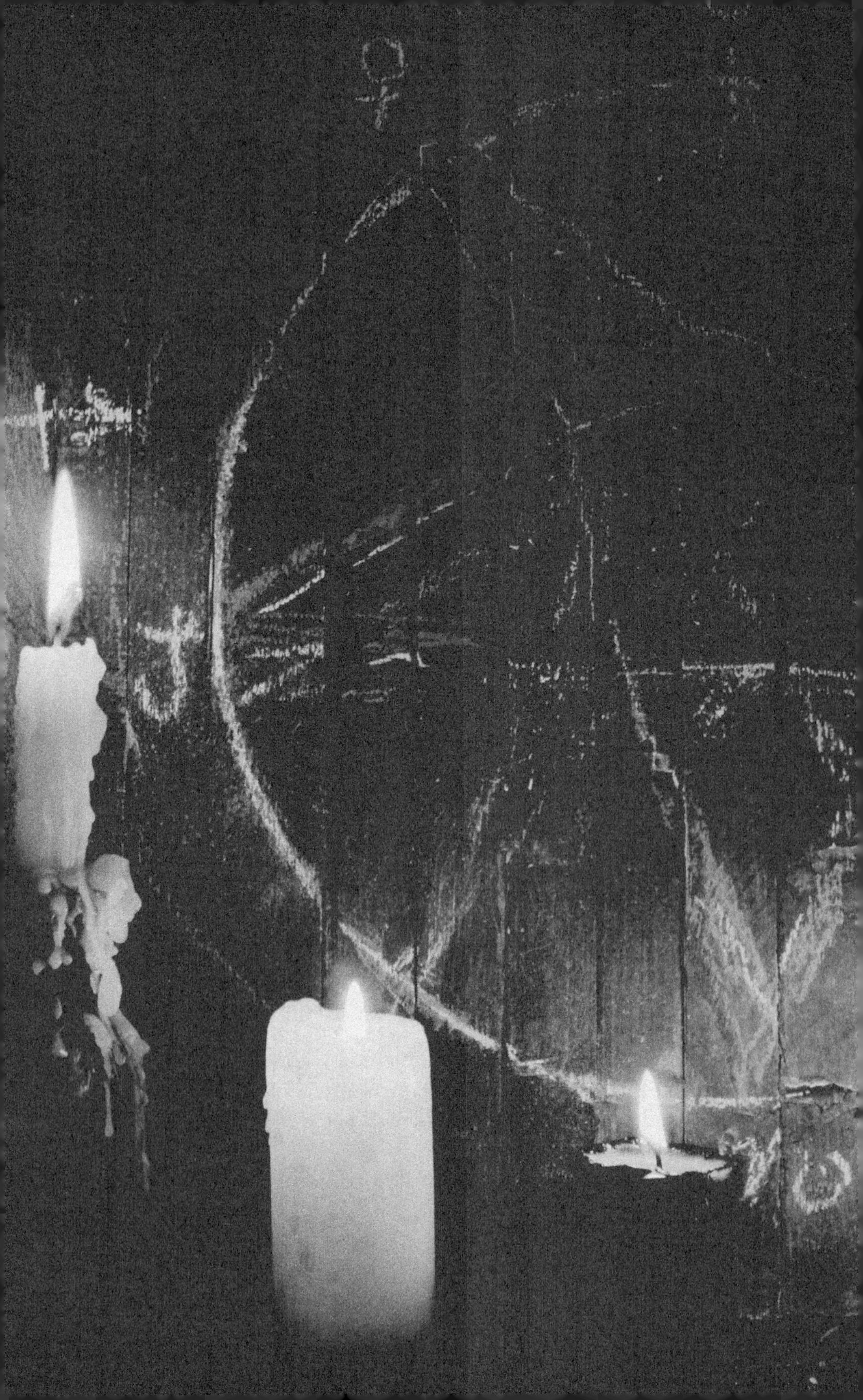

CHAPTER 13

LEGION

The first time Dean Keegan strode through the steel door of the Twisted Throttle three years ago, the urge to blow a hole in the man's chest had been nearly overwhelming.

Yet within the same instant, a nagging emotion had ripped through me, accompanied by a little voice in the back of my mind telling me not to act. The voice was unnecessary. I wouldn't have anyway. Our carefully laid plans required more time. A bullet would have been too quick, and far better than he deserved, anyway.

Still, there was an energy around him, a barely detectable magnetism that felt quite removed from my initial impressions. I'd never felt anything like it. As we'd briefly conversed, I began to realize the pull of this unseen force seemed to originate from somewhere *within* the establishment…*beyond him.*

I chose to disregard it at the time and focus on the fact that I was finally face-to-face with the man who destroyed my brother. The mission at hand had taken precedence over everything else. We'd parted on terms that I allowed him to believe were civil.

This time, I know damn well there will be no civility on his part. The dark, gravel parking lot of the Twisted Throttle isn't nearly as full as it had been that night. Still, from a strategic standpoint, giving myself the best chance at walking away from this encounter *alive* meant approaching the man during peak business hours. Should Keegan be as tempted to violence as I had been that first night…after everything that has transpired between us…the presence of civilians might give him pause. If I arrived here when only a few members of his crew were present, well, I'm not at all convinced he wouldn't end me on the spot. I'm still not certain he won't.

Lighting up what may indeed be my last cigarette, I survey the motorcycles in the lot. Viking's FatBoy is among them. Axel's Dyna. Chopper's *Chopper*... Some of these other bikes could belong to prospects. Keegan's black beauty must be locked up in his shop.

I can't help but chuckle to myself. This man has every reason in the world to hate me, to want me dead, and that's not counting the fact that *I told him I was in love with the woman who is now his wife.*

"*Fuck*..." I pull the final drag on my coffin nail, then flick it aside, making my way toward the steel door of the roadhouse. "*Dead man walking.*"

Upon entering, I'm immediately relieved when Viking isn't at the door. I scan the room quickly for the others. What had once been a roadhouse, regularly occupied to full capacity on any given night, was only half at best. The place is in pristine condition, though. Brand new, fully stocked liquor shelves with a mirrored backwall, brand new mahogany bar, and updated tables and leather seating along the brick accent wall. There is only one indication that this establishment had been torn up in a drive-by.

Framed within a shadow box and displayed in honor of their fallen brother, a black leather cut hangs on the wall. There's a small hole just below the left zippered pocket, and one other through the decimated patch that once displayed his road name... *Snowy.*

Perhaps I should have arranged another meeting spot... Given Keegan and his crew a little time to come to terms with my return.

I shift my gaze back to Keegan, just as he realizes I'm standing here.

Wordless, but wearing a less than welcoming expression speaking volumes on its own, Keegan jumps over the bar, sending a few beer bottles smashing to the floor.

"Dean! *Shit!* Dean!" the redheaded pixie of a barmaid calls after him in a panic while reaching for something beneath the bar counter.

I raise my hands in a gesture of peace as he storms up to me, but his fists still grip the collar of my leather jacket. He hauls me nose-to-nose with him, yet his momentum continues to propel me backward. My back slams against the steel door, knocking the wind from my lungs, and he shoves me through, into the lot.

I land on my back against the gravel, Keegan standing over me with that murderous glare in his eyes.

"Well, isn't this familiar…" I cough, dragging myself back from him another few feet before I attempt to stand. At least he didn't *Spartan kick me* in the chest this time.

To my surprise, he allows me to get to my feet, and I brush myself off. "I do come in peace."

"*And you'll be leaving in pieces*," he manages to growl through a jaw gritted so tightly, I half expect him to shatter his grill.

Before I can respond, Viking bursts through the door behind him, and I take another few cautious steps back.

"What's going on? Cherry hit the buzzer and…" Viking's words trail off, recognition eclipsing his look of concern. "*Oh, you gotta be shittin' me!*"

I force a smile. "Love what you all have done with the place."

"*You're not welcome here.*" Keegan starts toward me again, but Viking hooks a massive arm across Keegan's chest, restraining him. "Not in my lot! Not in my town!" He shouts, fighting Viking's hold to get to me. "Not in this fucking state! You should have stayed gone, Legion! There's nothing left for you here!"

"We have unfinished business," I remind him. "Promises on my part were made. I intend to keep them. And it would be in *our loved one's best interest* for you to hear me out regarding those *promises*."

His rage simmers to a low boil as my words register, and Keegan no longer struggles against Viking's hold. The tension around his eyes slackens a bit. "Is she in immediate danger?"

"Not *immediate*."

Viking releases him, and he shoves away from his MC brother, taking a step closer to me.

"You have five seconds. Start talking."

"I require more time than that, I'm afraid."

He scowls at me. "I'm not playing any more cryptic games with you. You have something to say, then you can say it in plain fucking English, and you can say it in front of my brothers."

"Lead the way, *Pres*."

He shakes his head. "No. Not here. Not now. Stogies. Tomorrow morning, first thing, when the rest of us are all present."

"If you insist."

"I do... And if you go near my wife and kid again, *I'll fucking kill you*, Legion."

"After all we've been through together? We're practically *family*, Dean." I can't help but sneer at him. He turns to head back into the roadhouse.

"Get the fuck out of my lot," he says, before the steel door slams closed behind them, and I'm alone in the lot once again.

"Well, that could have gone worse," I console myself, walking back to my bike. After lighting up another cigarette, I remove my cell to bring up the number of possibly the only ally I may have left in this world.

The line picks up. "Yeah?"

"Hello, old friend…"

"*Legion?* Holy shit… I thought you were dead."

"I'm working on it. In the meantime, where is she, Rusty?"

"Hang on, I got a card somewhere with the address for the new place she's been working. Give me a sec…"

While I do, I mount my bike and strap on my dome.

"She's in Forsyth County," Rusty informs me. "She dances at a few clubs out that way. You want to meet up? Been a long time, man."

Airing on the side of caution, I ask, "Any affiliation to the JoCo Jokers?"

"Nope. Outside their territory. It's not affiliated with any MC, actually. A place called the *Raunch Ranch*."

"*Classy.*" I sigh, starting up my bike. If I am to be dispatched to Hell tomorrow morning, I'd like to get my dick wet one last time.

The two-hour ride lands me outside the *Raunch Ranch*, just after eleven PM. Rusty is waiting for me by his bike, and I light up another cigarette as I walk up to him. Though Rusty's tone suggested a measure of relief, his expression reads a bit nonplussed now that we're face-to-face.

"What is it?" I ask.

He runs a hand over his short beard. "I'm just surprised you're alive…between the Saviors and your *grand entrance*."

"Those explosions could have simply been mishaps. It's common knowledge that cook trailers are prone to such calamities."

Rusty seems to consider me a moment before releasing a tense sigh. "You always speak as if everything is going according to plan, but what has you looking so melancholy?"

"I finalized the sale on the Morningstar and my brother's estate. They were the last ties I had to the desert." Before word got out about my self-decimated crew, I managed to negotiate the release of a few crews we'd ruled over these last few years. Now, my financial situation is probably the most stable part of my life.

"So, you're done with Arizona?"

"*Home is where the heart is*," I mutter, then gesture to the strip club. "Shall we?"

After weaving through the crowded establishment, we claim a table in the shadows, nearly dead center of the stage, though way in the back. There's a robust gentleman in a disheveled suit seated at the next table over, a young dancer grinding in his lap. Just as he happens to glance in our direction, our eyes meet, and a wicked grin stretches my mouth. There are opportunities everywhere. One simply has to be willing to reach out and choke the shit out of them. *To take advantage...*

"*Doth mine eyes deceive me?*" I raise my voice over the thumping music, pulling out my cellphone. I don't give him the chance to react before snapping a damning photo of the two. "Or is this fine gentleman before me, not the *illustrious Mayor* of Bermuda County?"

"Well, if it isn't our *anonymous hero*," the mayor chuckles, stress lines creasing his forehead. I can practically feel the waves of embarrassment radiating off of him. He quickly shoves some cash at the stripper and shoos her away. "Don't tell me you're here to spend that reward money."

"You're quite beyond your county's lines, *Mr. Wellington*. Is the wife around?" I ignore his statement, tucking my cell back into the pocket of my leather jacket. "Or is tonight a...*solo adventure*? Perhaps, a lusty *rendezvous*?"

He chuckles again, nervously staring at my pocket as if contemplating an attempt to snatch it from me. We both know he doesn't possess the adequate balls to risk such a deadly move.

"*I thought so...* Mayor, are you familiar with the quote first spoken by the infamous Al Capone... "*You get more with a kind word and a gun than you do with a kind word alone?*"

His throat bobs.

"Yes, well, my point being, *sir*, I have a favor to ask of you. A very small one. One which would also ensure the fact, *I never saw you here tonight...* And upon fulfilment of said favor," I tap the cell in my pocket, "*this proverbial gun* shall disappear."

"Alright..." he cautiously agrees.

"*Splendid!*" I wave over a half-naked waitress and order each of us an Old Fashioned. "Keep the change." I smile and toss some cash on her tray.

It isn't long after we finish our drinks and conversation that the mayor scurries off upon agreeing to my strong-armed request.

"You never did tell me exactly how you managed to survive the Saviors MC," I say to Rusty, sitting uncomfortably by my side now that we're somewhat alone.

Hooligans shout and whistle as a new dancer begins her set on the center stage. *It isn't her.*

"You haven't exactly been reachable." He shrugs. "When I received your letter along with the key to a safety deposit box, I was afraid you were about to meet your end." Rusty sighs. "Anyway, long story short, Dean believed me. *That I believed you.* That I was only helping you because you changed course on your brother. That it truly was about keeping her safe. I've always liked Vanna. I've always liked all of them. Dean's a good guy, Legion. Even if he does hate us *both*, now."

"You're just happy he didn't slit your throat."

Rusty chuckles, though there is remorse in his words. "Yeah, that might have something to do with it, too."

I study him for a moment. "You want back in."

He shrugs. "I guess it just felt good to be a part of something with a purpose."

"*Indeed...*"

My gaze drifts back to the stage as I wait for Puppet to perform her set, thinking back on my first encounter with Dean Keegan outside of the Twisted Throttle roadhouse.

I had been restless that night when I returned to the Demons' Den. The odd feeling at the Savior's roadhouse had plagued my mind, but I'd focused on the big picture...the grand plan.

Weeks had passed since we acquired the nearly condemnable structure, and our numbers were steadily increasing. Asmodeus had sent in a few more of our own guys to aid in keeping the smaller gangs in check. They were eager for a piece of the spoils I'd promised in exchange for their cooperation.

Among the new arrivals had been Puppet, and three other girls, communal property of my brother's former crew. Not our best quality whores, but they were something for our ranking members to play with while we built up our stables in and around Bermuda County.

It had been a while since I'd gotten laid. All of my energy, time, and attention had been thrown into rigging Keegan's life to implode. I was fixated. *Obsessed*, in actuality. At times, I'd wondered if I wanted to carry out his annihilation even more than my brother. At least, that had been the case in the beginning of it all.

My moods were often foul back then, stressed and frustrated. I was constantly annoyed by the shortsightedness and impatience of the crews I'd dealt with in order to orchestrate the obliteration of what had, for a long time running, been a clean, safe county. Arguments and infighting over which crew would run what had been a regular occurrence. It was on my integral shoulders to placate everyone with promises of territory and prosperity. Empty as those promises were, they needed to be made.

The destruction of Keegan's beloved hometown and community was just one part of the grand plan. I knew damn well that once I avenged my brother and Keegan was no longer among the living, everything would crumble upon my return to the desert. I could already see how things would play out. The influx of drugs and prostitution would erode everything, and greed would lead to a blood bath of gang wars for power and control in our absence. Not only would I take his life, *but his legacy as well.*

However, the grand plan is not why that night comes back to me now, sitting here in a cheap strip joint. What pulls me back to the past is Puppet's arrival after my first meeting with Dean Keegan. My thoughts turn inward, and the scene unfolds behind my eyes...

"Master?" Puppet's voice pulled me out of my obsessive thoughts that night, and I glanced up at her from my desk. It had been the better part of a year since I'd left her behind, and although I'd blatantly expressed my wish for her to remain in Arizona, my cock was glad to see her. Particularly, her mouth. Though there was something more about her that had instantly piqued my interest.

"Come in."

Puppet closed the door softly behind her, cutting off the rambunctious happenings in the front of the building.

"You must be well looked after. You've put on more weight."

"I'm sorry, Master." Her posture seemed to wilt, head bowed, as if ashamed by my assessment.

"*No...* I quite like it." My gaze hungrily roamed her more defined, voluptuous curves. "*Strip.*"

She immediately shed her clothing down to her undergarments, and my eyes settled on her thick thighs. My thoughts drifted to Mary Margarette's, parted beneath her pleated skirt in the pews, and my hand moving beneath her bible, seeking her forbidden heat...

"Come," I said, moving from my desk to take a seat on the couch opposite the door. She stood before me, and I grabbed her hand, tugging her off balance until she was sprawled across my lap.

My hand ran up the back of her leg until my fingers traced the crease where her thigh met her ass.

She startled when I gripped the round curve of her flesh, kneading and massaging the firm, sexy piece of meat. I lifted my hand and brought it crashing down in a hard smack, feeling the sharp sting in my palm.

She let out a muffled little shriek of surprise.

"You disobeyed me, Puppet. Had I any real desire to see you, I would have sent for you."

I smacked her hard again.

Her gasp morphed into a groan when I rubbed the sting of the slap away.

"What have you to say for yourself?"

"I missed you, Sir." I barely heard her whimpered reply.

Smack!

She jerked and took in another sharp breath.

I hit her again, this time angling the strike to clip the bottom of her pussy. One of her hands gripped my lower leg, just above my boot, as she clenched her thighs together, stifling a deeper groan.

"Spread your fucking legs, or I'll belt your ass so thoroughly, you won't sit for a week."

"Yes, Master." She relaxed her legs once more, allowing them to part enough for me to slide my hand between her thighs. I pressed my palm against the warm, already damp fabric of her panties, cupping her.

"*You wanton little slut,*" I sneered, rubbing my fingers up and down her cunt. I worked the cotton material into her slit until her lips, slickened with need, slipped out around the edges. "Such a dirty whore, aren't you? Has this juicy little pussy been working hard for Daddy? Milking cocks and bank accounts?"

"*Yes, Daddy,*" she purred, attempting to push herself harder against my fingers, greedy for more.

Instead, I spanked her ass again, another resounding smack, and her moan reverberated through my office.

"What am I to do with you here?"

"Anything you please, Sir."

I shoved my fingers between her lips again, rubbing her clit roughly over the material, until she was gasping and whimpering from the onslaught of aggressive stimulation. My cock grew harder, jabbing into her soft stomach while she squirmed against me. The wetness of her need sloshed audibly against my fingers as I rubbed her harder and faster, until she was a soaking, desperate mess.

"*Oh! Daddy! Please! Just this once…*" she cried.

I only scoffed at her plea to be fucked. I wouldn't. My cock down her throat was the most she'd ever get from me.

When I pulled my hand from between her thighs, she let out a pitiful moan at the loss.

"On your fucking knees."

She immediately shifted herself off of me and kneeled between my legs. Her trembling hands fumbled with my belt and fly, so eager to get my cock out. I gathered her long, auburn hair into my fist and held her head back from me while she freed my dick.

"You want it?" I watched her as she hungrily admired my rigid appendage and attempted to nod. "*Words, whore!* I asked you a question!"

"Yes, Master," Puppet quickly replied. "I want you in all the ways you will allow me to have you."

"*Look at me.*"

Her hazel eyes immediately flicked up to meet mine.

"*Open that suck hole.* Lick your lips. Get them wet for me."

Her jaw fell open, tongue sliding slowly around the plump ring of her lips, until they glistened, primed and ready to suck me off. I pulled her forward by her hair, angling her above my cock, before I pushed her down onto it. An involuntary hiss escaped me as she immediately went to work on me.

"*This is all you're good for, Puppet,*" I sighed, her mouth already alleviating the tension from my being. I watched her head bob up and down on me. Admittedly, I'd missed the tight, pillowy ring of her lips and the glorious suction she managed to create with that mouth. I could feel the quickening pulse of my heartbeat in my throbbing cock. "Do you enjoy this?"

An affirmative little moan vibrated up her throat, contributing to the pleasurable sensation.

I rewarded her with a groan of my own. *"Good girl…"*

The words seemed to spur her on. Eager for more praise, she swirled her talented tongue around me and licked the precum from my tip.

After releasing her hair, my head fell back against the couch, and my arms extended casually across the top cushions. When I straightened a leg, her eyes slid to the side, staring down at it. I grinned to myself, degrading thoughts swirling in my mind. I shifted my leg closer to her and tapped the side of hers with my boot. She immediately lifted, allowing me to slide my leg between hers, but she did not lower herself upon me without permission.

"You may, if you so wish." A wicked sneer pulled at my mouth. It was always a touch more satisfying when she chose to be degraded. "I think it's a show I might very well enjoy."

She shifted slightly, her pace never hiccupping on my cock, and positioned herself over my boot. Slowly at first, she rubbed her cunt along the laces, testing the degree of friction she could derive from my offering. It wasn't long before she was grinding heavily against me.

"That's it, baby…" I growled, watching her hump my leg like a bitch in heat, all the while slurping on my dick. She was so wrapped up in seeking release for herself as well, only I noticed Reaper enter the room.

It had never been a practice of mine to degrade her to this degree in front of others. That was typically a private occurrence I kept between us, ever since she found me back in Sierra Vista.

I brought a finger to my lips, signaling him to be quiet. I knew Puppet was close, rocking hard and fast, grinding her clit against the rough laces through her soaked panties. Her moans and whimpers were becoming louder, more desperate.

I swept her hair up again, balling it in my fist, before I shoved her down on my cock, forcing it past the back of her throat. Her pace stuttered as she gagged and choked, saliva sputtering out the sides of her mouth. When she whimpered again, I let her up for a moment, pulling her off my dick. She gulped for breath, spit hanging from her chin. Tears mixed with her mascara caused the makeup to bleed out into black crescents beneath her eyes, giving her a feral, haunted look.

Standing up, I cradled the back of her head in both hands, pulling her more upright with me, until she was erect on her knees, eye level with my dick.

"Open wide, *Puppet*."

She opened her mouth obediently, tongue out as if she were rolling out the red carpet for my cock again. Rocking my hips slowly, I stroked my frenulum against it.

"This is it. Your punishment for disobeying and following me here... *I'm going to skull fuck you* until I come down your throat."

I didn't give her the chance to prepare herself. Fingers digging into the back of her head, I slammed her forward as I thrusted into her mouth.

Tears and drool streamed down her face. Her nails dug into my thighs. Wicked laughter echoed within my mind at the steady sound of her gagging. The *gluck-gluck-gluck* of her throat bulging around my cock with every merciless thrust.

Her whimpers eventually became genuine cries. Her watery eyes, red-rimmed and pleading, stared up at me, as if willing me, *begging me*, to relent.

"Take it easy on her, man... Fuck," Reaper finally said, still standing by the door.

Her eyes widened, horrified at the realization we were being watched. *I liked it.*

"You fuck her like you hate her," he went on.

He had no idea...

Tears streamed down her cheeks as his words seemed to register in her mind. I rammed myself down her throat, reveling in her humiliation, and my balls pulled tight despite being smashed against her chin. Ignoring the slight pain, I came with a guttural grunt, and she gulped down every drop of poison I had to give her.

After wrenching her off of me by the back of her head, I released her, allowing her to fall back on her ass and hands. She shook, soaked in tears, sweat, and saliva, and gasped for breath as I gathered myself.

"Was that good for you, *Puppet?*" I mocked her, nearly out of breath myself, while I buckled my belt. "Are we clear on how much you mean to me?"

With a tearful nod, she raised a trembling hand to wipe the mess of foamy, cum-laced spit from her face.

"That's my girl... Now, I'm aware you weren't able to get yourself off on my boot, though you did an excellent job of wiping away some of the dirt and grime from riding. Perhaps I'll have you polish the other in the near future. In the meantime, why don't you go with Reaper... *Allow him the pleasure of finishing you off.*"

I took offense to her hurt expression. *As if I could ever be so easily manipulated into feeling anything but disdain for her,* let alone regret for what transpired between us. When she shifted to get to her feet, I halted her with a gesture of my hand.

"No, no... *Crawl to him...* Crawl to him like the *thoroughbred little whore* you are."

"Fuck, Legion... Take it easy, man." Reaper chimed in again, moving forward with the clear intention of taking the sobbing Puppet by her arm to pull her up off the floor.

"Don't fucking move!"

He immediately halted in his tracks at my snarled command, and I shifted my deadly glare from him to Puppet.

"Go on."

"Yes, Daddy," she whispered, slowly shifting onto her hands and knees. Head low, she crawled toward Reaper in the doorway.

"Daddy..." I vehemently muttered. "I wonder how proud your actual father would be of you now? What do you think, Puppet? Is this what fathers hope their daughters aspire to?" I received a barely audible sob in response. "Do with her what you will, Reaper." I sighed, feigning boredom.

There was something in Reaper's expression that wasn't copasetic to our situation as he helped her to her feet... Something *sympathetic...*

"She's *communal* property," I reminded him, quashing whatever territorial urges may have been stirring within him. "Might as well enjoy her whilst you're at the front of the line, *eh?*"

Only when they shut the door behind them did the cold sliver of regret creep into my thoughts. *Had I taken that too far?* My demons went immediately to war with the intrusive sentiment. They were hell bent on solidifying the position within my mind that she had deserved every moment of what transpired between us. She chose this, after all. I never sought her out.

I was about to leave for the evening when Vein came crashing through my door next.

"Uh… Boss… The Fire Chief's outside… Said they received an *anonymous call* that we were up in flames."

A grin pulled at the corners of my mouth at the irony of his move… *That didn't take Keegan very long at all.*

"Seems our man really does like to *play with fire…*"

"Now let's welcome everyone's favorite *voluptuous vixen* to the main stage… Heeeere's *Dolly!*" The announcer snaps me out of my memories, pulling my attention to the center stage.

Puppet emerges from the black curtains and saunters her buxom hourglass figure toward the pole. Smokey eyes. Red lips. My heart beats faster as I drink in her image and the exaggerated sway of her hips to the rhythm of a sultry melody by Oscen, *Babydoll*. Gripping the pole with one hand, she hooks a thick, shapely leg around it. The sheer black nightie and her long black hair flow behind her as she spins.

Done up the way she is, she bears such a likeness to my little witch…and I can't help but wonder if Vanna ever dances for Keegan like this… Perhaps she graces a pole at the Twisted Throttle after closing for him on special occasions… A slight grin pulls at my mouth. Doubtful, after the incident on the pool table… How I wish I still had those photos…

The men nearest the stage toss money at Puppet as she slides down the pole into a split, bouncing that fat, perfect fucking ass as she does. The bolder ones stuff bills into her black G-string, taking advantage of an opportunity to brush their greedy fingers along the smooth skin of a beautiful woman.

The territorial urge to drag a blade across their unsuspecting throats and spray her with their blood spikes my own blood with a surge of adrenaline. I down the rest of my Old Fashioned as those red lips curve into a seductive smile, then she's on her back, legs spread wide in their fucking faces.

Whores will be whores…

"I can't watch her like this." Rusty sighs, distracting me for a moment. "I have to head out anyway. Stay out of trouble, will ya, Legion?"

I nod once in acknowledgement of his departure, then return my attention to Puppet, watching her every move until the commencement of her set.

Standing, I applaud her performance while she gathers her discarded clothing and cash tips scattered across the stage. *"Brava! Bravissima!"*

Her head lifts upon recognition of my disdainful praise. Blood seems to drain from her face as she slowly stands, her eyes quickly scanning the club. She spots me while clutching her clothes and cash to her chest. With a heated glare, she spins on her platformed heel and storms back through those shimmery curtains.

"Can I get you anything else, sir?" another waitress asks.

"I'd like a private dance with *Dolly*."

"You'll have to take that up with her, but I'll send her over."

However, *Dolly* is already striding up to me, impatiently pulling on a sheer, thigh-length robe that matches the skimpy nightie she slipped back into.

"Hello, Puppet." I barely get the words out before she slaps me across the face. *Hard.*

I prod the corner of my mouth with the tip of my tongue. No blood, but that was a decent shot. I'm impressed. I clear my throat. "Now, Puppet, use your words."

"Fuck you, Legion!" she practically spits at me.

"That's exactly what I had in mind, Puppet. Thought maybe I'd buy you a drink and pay for a dance first. You know, be a gentleman about it…*for old times' sake.*"

"I fucking hate you!"

"Join the club, *Dolly*," I smirk back at her. "By the way, is that stage name an *homage*, so to speak? Or another *slap in the face*? Is it a dig at me, or Keegan? Or have you learned from the... *Master*...and the answer is *all of the above!* You know how I love a *quadruple entendre*... A good *mind fuck.*"

She continues to glower daggers at me. "*You don't love anything.*"

"Jesus Christ, Dolly!" Some suit comes up to us, the manager of this establishment, I presume. He grabs her arm and pulls her back. "You can't assault customers!" He turns to me, a fretful look of apology on his face as I assess him, refraining from sneering at the thick gold chain and gem-encrusted *bunny head* pendant hanging from his scrawny neck. "I'm sorry, sir, can we comp you a dance with someone else? A few drinks? Top shelf, of course."

"It's quite all right. No harm done. *I'm into it*," I joke, attempting to diffuse the situation. Puppet scoffs, folding her arms beneath her barely contained breasts, giving them the illusion of enlarging before my very eyes. My dick stirs in response.

The apologetic expression on her manager's skeevy face morphs into something more neutral. "We're not *that kind* of place."

"Fair enough," I say, pulling out a wad of cash to entice him. "Nevertheless, I'd like to purchase a private dance with *Dolly* here. What do you say, *hot stuff*? Will five hundred bucks cover it?"

"*Go rot,* asshole*,*" she seethes.

Rapacious little whore... "*Seven,* then?"

The contemptuous expression on her face intensifies.

"*Two grand.*"

"*Sold!*" Her manager practically shoves her at me.

"Don't look so disappointed, *Dolly*. You know I'm a *big tipper.*"

"Don't flatter yourself. I've seen *bigger tips.*"

I can't help but grin as she hurls the innuendo back at me.

Puppet leads me into one of the private rooms. I shut the door behind us and take a seat on the leather sofa. The room isn't spacious, but there are mirrors on the walls, backlit in deep blue. She grabs the remote to the sound system in our private dance room and selects a song. *Pop music* fills the atmosphere, and I swear she only put this adolescent shit on to annoy me.

"What the fuck is this?"

"*I Want What I Want*, by Lauren Christy," she replies, as if this bratty racket is something I ought to be familiar with. She turns to face me again, stepping up onto the small, black lacquered platform between us. "It's been three years since you disappeared on me," she says, slowly slinking around the pole in the center. "Three fucking years since I saved your ass that night…patched you up and took care of you until you were back on your feet. Then you up and vanished on me, without a goddamned word."

I watch as she drops her fine ass low. She uses the pole to stand, throwing her long, dark hair back in a fluid motion that has my cock stirring further in my jeans.

"I see you've honed your pole dancing skills, as well as developed somewhat of a *backbone* since I've been away." I continue to admire her curves. "Anyway, thought I'd switch gears and give that *vigilante* shit a try." Releasing a sigh, I adjust myself as she lets her nightie slip down her body, pooling at her feet. She slides her lacy thong down her legs next, pulling another confession from me. "I *have* missed you, Puppet."

"*Please,*" she mutters, stepping out of the skimpy garment and moving from the pole to kneel between my legs. "I thought I managed to change you when I saved your ass that night. But you didn't come back for me… You came back for that cunt."

Her words instantly ignite a barely containable rage within me. "*Watch your fucking mouth!*"

"*You watch it!*" she snaps back, aggressively undoing my belt and fly. She pulls my cock free and squeezes the shaft tightly in her fist, extracting an involuntary groan from me. Glaring with disdain, she never breaks eye contact with me as she reaches into the little glass tray of Trojans on the matching black lacquered side table to my left. The music playing in the room switches to Alice Cooper's, *Poison,* and I watch as she tears the condom from the foil, rolling it down my dick.

"Well then, get on with it," I growl. "*Give Daddy a show.* Earn that *big fuckin' tip.*"

Scowling, she licks up the length of my cock, tracing a vein. The heat of her tongue permeates the super-thin latex. "You're just another trick, *Legion*… My *Daddy* walked out on me three years ago," she says, before swallowing my cock.

Even wearing a rubber, the glorious sensation saps the anger from me, and my head lolls back against the leather couch.

It doesn't take her long to get me there. I haven't been fucked, or sucked *like this* since our last time together. The night I viciously cut our ties and left her.

"I did you a favor…and I did try to see you," I manage to grunt out. "The night of their wedding…"

Her teeth scrape up the length of my shaft, making me hiss at the unexpected, though not *entirely* unpleasant, sensation. Before I can say anything, she's straddling my lap, grinding her bare cunt against my cock. Her fingers find their way into my hair, gripping me and pulling my head back as she attempts to bring her lips closer to mine.

Despite the discomfort it causes, I turn my face from hers with a sneer. "How many cocks have you sucked tonight?"

"You're such a prick!" She grabs my dick, guiding it inside her, and proceeds to fuck me hard and fast, clearly eager to get this transaction over with.

I hold out for as long as I can, simply to spite her.

"That's it, baby. *Fuck me.* Show me what you're good for… *All you're good for*," I taunt her. "Fuck me… Make Daddy proud of the thoroughbred little whore you are."

Just to piss me off, she runs her hands down my neck, moving them quickly to my chest. I snatch her wrists and yank her arms behind her back before she can touch my abdomen. Securing her wrists tightly with one hand at the small of her back, we hate-fuck the hell out of each other to completion.

Both breathing heavily now, I release her, and she shoves off me, stumbling back toward the pole where she discarded her skimpy outfit.

"You got a man now, Puppet?" I ask, tying off the condom while I watch her shimmy back into her thong. "A sponsor? Someone on the steady looking after you?"

She scoffs, placing a platformed heel up on the arm of the couch, giving me a close-up look at her inner thigh. "After your parting gift? *Nobody like you*, Legion. And thank God for that."

I grin at the small, horned smiley-face-shaped scar I left in her flesh. "God? Really?" I scoff back at her. "*What a loving God* to have allowed *such a sweet girl* to ever cross paths with the likes of me."

"Go to Hell."

"Was I really that bad?"

"*You're the Devil.*"

"Keep talking like that, and you're gonna get me all hot and bothered again," I joke, standing up and tossing the poison into a small wastebasket beside the couch.

She wraps the sheer black robe around herself again as I refasten myself. "May I please have my tip now, *Sir?*" Her question drips with sarcasm.

"There she is!" I say with mock enthusiasm, extracting my wallet once again. "I knew my girl was hidden under all that bitch somewhere." After peeling off a few hundred bucks, I hold the cash out to her between two fingers. She steps closer, hesitant to reach out and take it for some reason. She does, after a moment.

"If you had dropped the money on the floor, I would have kicked you in the balls."

"*And that concludes our business.*" I smile, turning from her to head for the exit.

"I thought you loved me..."

Her words halt me. I gently close the door, cutting off the loud, pulsing music blaring through the sound system on the main stage. "That was *your* mistake."

"Someday, you will want me to want you, Damien…and I won't anymore."

Giving her a wink, I open the door to leave for good this time. "The only thing I want right now, *Dolly my dear*, is a fucking *cigarette.*"

CHAPTER 14

LEGION

Bound by a promise and pissed off by what transpired between Keegan and I last night, temptation taunts me more than ever now as I stare at the row of motorcycles behind Stogies.

I recall the night I worked dark magick on Keegan. It was before I broke into Vanna's home for the first time.

Smoke snaked up toward the ceiling in a dark, a translucent stream from the piece of Palo Santo I held in the flame of my Zippo. The end blackened and caught fire. Notes of pine, mint, and lemon mixed with the smoke from the cigarette dangling from my lips, and thickly permeated the atmosphere of my office in the Demons' Den.

But naturally, revenge against Keegan isn't what draws my mind back to that moment. While working magick that night, a half-smile pulled at my mouth at the thought of Keegan's woman, a dark lady, but a white witch. She was fairly new to her craft, that much had been made abundantly evident in her response to my statement regarding the *Holy Wood* she sold in her little shop.

"*I didn't know it could be used for that…*"

Such an innocent divulgence... Though it irked me to admit it, I found her response quite endearing. Especially with the way she had looked up at me with those inquisitive dark eyes. I'd wanted so badly to touch her. Instead, I'd merely placed my hand beside hers on the edge of the drawer.

I could have schooled her in that moment. Reminded her of the Hermetic Principles, the teachings of the Kybalion, the Law of Polarity.

Palo Santo has always been a favorite of mine. The tree is native to South America and has been highly valued by Shamans since the Incan era. Utilized mostly for the purposes of raising one's vibration, cleansing negative energies, and restoring physical and energetic well-being. Some believe it encourages feelings of mental and emotional clarity, peace, and tranquility, as well.

The inexperienced often fail to consider the Law of Polarity as it pertains to magick. The principle states that everything has two poles. Everything is dual. Good and Evil. Love and Hate. That which can be used as a tool to bring *clarity*, can in turn be used to *obscure...*

So yes, sweet one, I assure you... Palo Santo can indeed be utilized in workings to blind one's enemy...

Lifting the photo of *her* lover, *my* enemy, I brought the smoldering, blackened point of the Palo Santo stick to Keegan's face and used it to burn out his eyes. With the residual black ash, I smeared darkness across his forehead, clouding over the third eye, and with the prick of my finger on my knife, I sealed my baneful intentions against him with a drop of blood.

Placing his photo on my desk, my eyes drifted to the photo of Vanna. I sucked at the bead of blood on my index finger and lifted the photo to stare at the curve of her figure in one of those witch shop dresses she seemed so fond of.

"What is it about you?" I'd growled with annoyance at the ever-present pull I felt toward her. Physical attraction aside, there was something about her I couldn't put my bloody finger on. The feeling stirred an anger within me, and I was tempted to return the vexatious emotion with a spell of my own against her.

About to smear her face with the blood of my pricked finger in spite, a sharp jolt pierced at my heart, halting me. It was as if the moment the thought of committing an act against her crossed my mind, a burst of adrenaline pumped a short-lived feeling of dread throughout my entire being.

Blasphemous! A voice, not entirely my own, scolded from within the depths of my mind...

I had to know more about her.

There was no way around it.

She was significant in a way I couldn't deny and had yet to uncover.

Fine… I sneered, utterly annoyed as I undid my belt and fly. *There were other bodily fluids I could spill in her cursed honor!*

"Didn't think you'd have the balls to show up." The sound of Keegan's voice rips me back to the present.

I drop my cigarette and crush it beneath my boot in the gravel lot behind Stogies, as Keegan and his Sergeant at Arms approach. "There may be certain attributes I lack… However, I think you will come to appreciate the stock I own in this particular department. *Testicular fortitude* has never been an area I've come up short."

"Search him," Keegan commands.

Viking steps to me, and I raise my arms in compliance. He roughly pats me down, relieving me of several knives, my Sig Sauer, and the small Glock holstered in my boot.

"It's barely ten in the morning… Do you always wake up and choose violence?" Viking asks, dropping a final push-blade into the pile of weaponry around me. "Leave all this shit in the saddlebag on your bike."

They watch me closely as I gather up the discarded blades and tuck them into my side bag.

"I'll hold onto these for now," Viking adds, tucking my Sig behind his belt and the Glock somewhere beneath his cut.

I follow them through the back door of the Saviors MC-owned cigar shop and into a small conference room.

"Start talking." Keegan claims a seat at the head of the table, and the rest of his crew settles in.

"We have more in common than simply your *wife*, Keegan." His glare deepens at my words. "Perhaps I should rephrase."

"Probably a good idea," Viking taunts.

"In a word… *redemption*. That *is* what your MC is about, isn't it? Why you all *do what you do*?" My reply is met with silence and stoic expressions. "I owe Vanna a debt. I owe *you* a debt… Had I known then, what I know now…"

"*Snowy would still be alive*," the typically quiet, though deadly, one they call Viper growls.

I nod. "A lot of people would still be alive." Not that I care. Still, it's true. I shift my attention back to Keegan. "I haven't been your enemy for a very long time… But I have made many enemies in the pursuit of righting my wrongs against you."

"Sounds like a *you* problem." Viking chuckles.

"I wouldn't have returned yet if it were simply *my* problem."

"What have you done?" Keegan asks.

"Have you not tuned into your local stations?"

"Oh, that's right. You're a *hero* now." Keegan's words are leaden with sarcasm.

"I'm not one to compare dick sizes, but I am well aware of your body count. *I've got you beat.*"

"I think he just implied his dick is bigger, bro." Viking grins, looking me up and down in mock appraisal. "I heard skinny dudes are packing. That true?"

Choosing to ignore Viking's adolescent needling, I turn my attention back to Keegan and his intensifying scowl.

"Truth be told, I was hoping you had met your end somewhere," he says, as if confessing something I wasn't already acutely aware of.

"Tough luck, I'm afraid."

A hearty laugh erupts from Viking, though he's the only one who seems amused by my reply. The others seated around the table continue to glower at me. I shift my focus back to their president, still wearing that trademark stoic stare of his.

"Three years I've spent spilling blood in your wife's name, keeping my word to protect her by eliminating those who escaped that night. For whatever it's worth, I have kept my word."

"Your word means nothing to me. You should ride back to the desert. There's nothing for you here."

"You know that isn't true."

"*Vanna is mine.*"

"I also vowed to protect her."

"*From afar…* Go back to wherever that was. There's no reason for you to be here."

I release an aggravated sigh. I knew the only way he'd ever tolerate my presence anywhere within range of her, would be if it were somehow to her benefit. I could imply there's still a specific threat to her… His desire to keep her safe and utilize anything and everything at his disposal, including me, will overrule his urge to run me off. I have but one potential enemy, and though I have my suspicions regarding his whereabouts, I doubt whether he would ever expect to find me among the Saviors MC. Though, should this scenario happen to manifest, I am here to put an end to it as well…

Besides, I promised her I wouldn't harm Keegan… *Not* that I wouldn't *manipulate* him…

"And if there are demons at your gates again?" I demand.

"Is that what you were hinting at last night?"

I nod.

"Afraid to stand alone? To reap what you've sown?"

"I fear nothing but for the safety of your wife and child." The statement seems to sober the room a bit. "There's always a chance some may eventually come after me, seeking revenge for that night. For all I've done *since* that night… I doubt anyone would anticipate I'd come to *you* for anything. Besides, I know who they are. Having me around, keeping *an eye out*, would be beneficial to everyone."

"Are you seeking asylum among the Saviors?" Viper genuinely seems astounded.

"We can help you fake your death and disappear." Viking grins deviously. I'm well aware, there would be nothing *fictitious* about my death or disappearance.

"I'm afraid I must *decline* that particular offer," I sneer back at him.

Keegan continues to silently glare at me, before his Vice President speaks again. "You cannot seriously be considering this!"

"*Keep your friends close and your enemies closer*," Keegan replies.

"Yeah, I get that, but… What about everything he's done? To our town! To our brothers! Snowy is *dead* because of him! We should take him to join his brother! *Who he also killed!* For fucks sake, Dean! The Devil walks up to our table, and you're thinking about offering him a seat?"

"I wouldn't go that far," Keegan mutters.

"I'm not your enemy," I interject. "As I've stated, I haven't been your enemy for quite some time now."

"Yeah, I wouldn't go that far either." Keegan's glare darkens. I imagine my words about being in love with his wife are echoing in his thoughts. "The night I spared you…she could have been killed."

"I wouldn't let that happen."

"Vanna was in the bar…your hail of bullets could have—"

"I knew she wasn't there with you! That she had stepped away! You think I didn't see to that detail? I made sure she was nowhere near the front of the roadhouse. There was no stopping anything that happened that night! I was only able to manipulate the situation so much." I let out another frustrated sigh, feigning hard for a cigarette. "Lest we forget, I took a bullet shielding her from *your* crew returning fire." The room falls to silence, and I take the brief moment to compose myself before speaking again. "I am not your enemy. I orchestrated your victory that night. I even left you within range of the means for an easy disposal."

"An easy disposal?" Viper chimes in.

"The proximity of a large hog farm escaped you?" I quirk a brow at him skeptically. "Those animals were starving, primed and ready. They'd have devoured a stack of bodies in a night!" I shift my attention back to Keegan. "Let us not forget, either… *You let Rusty live.* That in itself is a testament to the fact that you know I speak the truth of my intentions."

"I'm not convinced about you. But even if I was, how do you see this playing out?" Keegan asks.

"My latest endeavor didn't make front page news, but it was in your local paper. The cook trailers."

"Blew up. We saw that," Viper mutters.

"Yes, well, it wasn't a *happy accident*, I assure you."

"You did it?" Keegan asks.

"That is what I'm implying, yes. I promised her a safer world… I'm willing to be your *button man* to accomplish that. *Glory goes to the Saviors*, of course. The community will quietly credit your MC for pushing out these undesirable elements."

"We don't need you. We've been getting it done without you." He glowers at me.

"Perhaps not. Perhaps you're under a false impression that I'm seeking your permission. This meeting *is just a formality*, an *olive branch*, if you will. I do not require, *nor do I truly desire* your acceptance or permission to remain. *Plain English*, boys, *I'm here to stay*."

"Unless we just kill you," Viper growls.

"That is an option, yes." I can't help a sardonic grin. Although it's a shame that I may have to play an aggressive hand.

"So, are we voting on this shit or what?" An undercurrent of dark humor is ever-present in Viking's words. He glances around the table at his MC brothers, wearing a smile most would consider charming, *had this discussion not taken a turn toward voting on my life.* He settles his gaze on me. "Any last words?"

"You're not going to kill me."

"Those would be some funny as fuck last words," Viking taunts. "You seem awfully certain of that... And I can't decide if it's because you're fuckin' insane with some sort of *God complex, or*—"

"Because your president would not allow it." I glance at Keegan.

"This isn't a dictatorship." Keegan's smile is as disingenuous as I've ever seen it.

"*Vote, then,*" I challenge him. "We both know your MC requires a *unanimous* vote in regards to matters this serious in nature. I'm willing to bet my life, *quite literally*, that even if every man at this table were to raise a hand in favor of my demise... *Your hand* would remain at your side. And we both know why that is... *Don't we*, Pres?"

His scowl deepens, and relief floods my system. I was merely bluffing, though it seems Vanna is my shield as well. She does care about me... *And he knows it.* That's a second *Ace* up my sleeve. Though the one I've been holding for quite some time now burns to be revealed.

"Vote now, or forever hold your peace." I grin with a confidence I know is grating Keegan's last nerve.

"Peace? Or piece?" He scowls, tapping his cut where a gun is likely holstered beneath. "That sounded like a threat to me. Vote now, in your favor, on your timeline, or forever be prepared for another round of your retaliations?"

"In the past, you'd have been right. But things have changed between us. It is my hope you will vote in favor of my stay. I only want to make amends."

"We both know that's not the *only* thing you want," Keegan mutters, though I detect a waiver in his resolve as he seems to brace himself for what I've got coming. I decide not to keep him in further suspense.

I remove the manila envelope from the inner pocket of my leather jacket. "This might assist with your decision," I say, placing it on the table before him. "Know that I have arrangements in place, should any of you decide my number is up."

"That number wouldn't happen to be 666, would it?" Viking jokes.

Dean snatches the envelope, tears it open, and pulls the photos from within. His complexion pales as he takes in the first damning image.

The sneer slides off Viking's face when he shifts his attention back to their president. "What is it?"

Keegan doesn't bother examining all six images. *The first two got my point across loud and clear.* He slips them back inside the envelope and tucks it into his cut. When he glances back at me, his expression is a mixture of rage and worry.

"Do we have an understanding?" I press while the iron is hot. He simply nods tentatively. "*Splendid!* I knew we would find common ground."

Keegan clears his throat and stands. "I'll grant you your stay until we officially vote," he begins, momentarily interrupted by the rest of his crew's riotous surprise. Raising a hand, he silences them. "I suggest you use what time you have to prove you actually do want what you claim."

"What the fuck is going on?" Viking demands.

"We'll discuss it later."

"I think we need to discuss it now," Viper insists.

"For the record, gentlemen, I have no objections," I announce, admittedly unable to refrain from grinning tauntingly at Keegan, fully aware I'm dry humping his last nerve.

He glares at me, lifting the gavel in his clenched fist. Hesitating for only a brief moment as we stare each other down, he finally slams it against the sounding block.

"What the fuck?" Viking nearly shouts.

"We'll vote in private," Dean says, a halfhearted attempt to appease his crew. "Right now, I need to speak with my lawyer as soon as possible. Meeting adjourned."

Keegan is still fuming by the time we step outside. Viking shoves my guns into Keegan's chest, forcing him to take them before he mounts his motorcycle and speeds off with the rest of the disgruntled members of the Saviors MC. Once they've departed the lot, I turn to their malcontented President.

"The fact you let Rusty live is a testament in itself that you believe I meant to turn the tables in your favor that night," I reiterate. "He was never a Demon. He was a Saviors' Prospect through and through. *That's why I chose him.* After the unfortunate miscalculation of Vein...pardon, *Aaron Hopper...I chose a fucking Savior* to be absolutely certain she wouldn't be in any danger. He only helped me when I approached him, during those final months. He saw to it that Vanna wouldn't be near the front of the Twisted Throttle at the time of the attack."

Keegan only glares back at me, his expression radiating doubt and disdain with both of my guns clutched in his fists at his sides. I fight the urge to meet his venomous expression with one of my own, and instead go on sarcastically, "I offer you, *kind sir*, my sincerest and most humble of apologies, soaked in the blood of *your* enemies, which I have tirelessly scourged from this wretched earth. Dean Keegan, *honorable President of the revered Saviors MC*, I beg your forgiveness of my innumerable transgressions … And I pledge my allegiance to your cause."

"This move," he taps his cut with the barrel of my Sig where the manilla envelope is tucked inside, "This dead man's switch doesn't inspire much faith in your claims."

"Fret not. It's merely an insurance policy. I truly harbor no malintent toward any of you."

He stares at me a moment longer, as if attempting to gauge my sincerity. He can take it or leave it. I have my own plans.

"I'll need a way to contact you, unless you expect us to chant your name three times at a crossroads? Sacrifice a goat on a full moon to summon your presence?"

Another antagonistic grin stretches my mouth. "*Hah!* Why don't you take a few days to come to terms with everything, *hmm? Really allow the gravity of our situation to pervade.* We'll be crossing paths in the very near future. However, should you require any clarifications before then, my number is on the envelope. *A simple phone call or text will suffice.*"

He shoves my Sig behind his belt, then pulls out his cellphone, swiping his thumb through the contacts.

"Do give Vanna my love," I taunt.

"I'm not calling *Vanna*."

"*Oh right,*" I snap my fingers. "You expressed a desire to speak with your lawyer. Allow me to save you a few bucks on the consultation fee, another show of good faith, *eh*?"

He looks up from his cell to glare at me.

"The statute of limitations solidifies our little arrangement for the foreseeable future. *Indefinitely*, in fact! And as I stated earlier, it is merely an insurance policy. I have no intention of using it for any nefarious purposes."

Pressing the call icon, Keegan raises the phone to his ear. I can't help but chuckle to myself, removing the pack of cigarettes and Zippo from the inner pocket of my cut. I light up and pull a long drag before blowing the smoke upward.

"Not ready to take my word for it quite yet? I understand. No offense taken on my part. Luckily for you, Keegan, *I've got the patience of a Saint.*"

Vanna

Having arrived early to Ace's play date with Mia at the park, we spent some time in the warm sun, picking an array of Autumn wildflowers, consisting mostly of yellow black-eyed Susans, as well as cone flowers, clasping aspers, and lobelias, in hues of pretty purples.

"For you, mama." Ace smiles, thrusting the little bouquet up at me.

"Why, thank you, my love." I smile back at him, crouching to accept them and his hug around my neck.

"Holaaa!" Rosita's voice rings out from across the fairgrounds.

Ace releases me, immediately turning to wave back at Rosita and her daughter, Mia. Only a few months apart, and practically having been raised together in our MC family as *cousins*, Ace and Mia have grown to adore one another.

I can't help but stifle a little laugh as Ace plucks one last flower from the patch of black-eyed Susans and bounds off to greet his little playmate.

"Oh, what a gentleman!" Rosita says as Ace gives Mia the flower. "And what do we say to our sweet Ace?"

"Gracias, Ace." Mia smiles, admiring his gift.

Ace opens his mouth to reply, but then his little brows furrow and he peers up at Rosita.

*"De nada...*you're welcome," Rosita responds to his unspoken question.

With another beaming smile that melts my heart, Ace repeats the words to Mia.

"Here, let me take something." I reach for the picnic basket Rosita is carrying, along with a large folded up blanket. Ace takes Mia by the hand and they both run off toward the playground together.

"He's such a bright child," Rosita says, handing me the basket on our walk to the shaded picnic tables a few yards away from where our kids are now playing. "Such a considerate little gentleman. One would never know they are five months apart."

Placing the basket down on the table, I help her lay out the large pink and white checkered blanket on the grass, before grabbing the basket once more. Handing it back to her, I take a seat as well.

"And how are things with his father... *Since...*" Rosita begins to ask, but her sentence trails off as if she doesn't quite know how to finish it.

"Since Legion rolled back into town?"

"Yes."

"Strained, I suppose." I sigh, leaning back on my elbows and stretching out my denim-clad legs to cross my ankles. We watch Ace and Mia play on the rope bridge, which leads to a pirate ship kids can pretend to steer and peek out through portholes. Instead of a plank to walk, there's a slide.

"How do you feel about his return?" Rosita asks.

"I don't know." It isn't a lie. I've tried to keep myself busy and preoccupied as much as possible to avoid giving my mind the time to evaluate what I'm actually feeling.

Most likely sensing my aversion to the topic of Legion, Rosita switches gears. "Have you told Dean about your secret rendezvous with Viking?"

I laugh at her choice of words. "*No*, and don't ever let him hear you talking about it *like that*."

"Why not?" she teases.

"What would Viper say if you were taking kick-boxing lessons from Viking?"

"He would want to teach me himself."

"Dean is already pressed for time with work and volunteering at the safe houses. It's easier to learn with Viking. Plus, Dean doesn't lose any extra time with Ace. And Viking doesn't cut me any slack, the way I know Dean would."

Rosita chuckles, reaching into the basket to remove a large thermos and two cups. "That is true. Also, kick-boxing would shift to *wrestling*, which would *then turn to...*"

"*Exactly*," I laugh. "Besides, I think it will be fun to surprise him in the gym one day with what I've learned. Maybe with the element of surprise, I'll actually impress him."

"You must admit, it is nice to have husbands so in love with us, no? *Incapable of keeping their hands off us!*" I laugh along with her. "Horchata?" she offers.

"*Yes*, please." Rosita makes the best homemade Horchata I've ever tasted. It's like Christmas in a cup. "You'll have to teach me how to make this before the holidays. Or at least promise to bring some for Christmas."

"So long as you teach me how to make your Italian Carbonara sauce," she bargains.

"Deal," I agree, accepting the beverage from her.

Over the next hour, we chat about our kids mostly, before they decide to join us for a little picnic of fresh sliced fruits and pretzel sticks. With full bellies and having expended their energy on the playground, naptime is on the horizon. Ace lounges against me, and I watch with a smile as an equally exhausted Mia climbs into her mother's lap.

"Oh, I know that look," Rosita says softly, her fingers stroking through Mia's dark tendrils. I realize she's been watching me.

"What look?" I ask, noticing the way her gaze settles lovingly on Ace for a moment.

"I feel it too, whenever I look at your precious Ace. Viper and I have been discussing trying for a little boy soon."

I force a smile, unsure what to say.

"What about you?" she presses, "Do you think about giving Ace a little *sister*?"

"I would love a little girl," I say, smiling at Mia. Her brown eyes are barely open now, blinking slowly. "I'm just not sure Dean is ready for another baby, boy or girl."

I know he isn't. And where things currently stand, he might not ever be. Though this isn't something I wish to discuss with anyone else right now, I do want Ace to have a sibling.

I realize Rosita is studying me again. The slight concern in her expression tells me she's already piecing together the reasons why Dean is so reluctant.

"Have you discussed things with your doctor?" she asks.

"Yes, and I have an appointment later today for an exam and to switch contraceptives. There is nothing medically wrong with me that would indicate I'd have a complicated pregnancy or delivery. Especially if we opt for a planned cesarean. And why not? I already have a scar."

Rosita nods in understanding. "But he fears."

"Yes…he does." Not that I blame him. The night Ace was born, Dean nearly lost us both. That pain never left him.

"Perhaps a little more time, then." She offers me an encouraging smile, though I can tell it's mixed with sympathy.

My cellphone vibrates in my pocket, and I shift carefully to remove it without jostling Ace too much. I don't recognize the number, but it's a local area code, so I answer.

"Hello?"

"Yes, hello!" a woman's voice quickly responds. "Is this Vanna Keegan?"

"It is…"

"Oh, wonderful!" she seems oddly relieved. "This is Nancy Wellington."

I'm quiet for a moment, trying to figure out why her last name sounds so familiar. When she speaks again, it's with an air of pride and a tone implying I should have instantly recognized her.

"*The mayor's wife*, dear."

DEAN

"You gonna tell us what the fuck was in that envelope?" Viking gripes, taking his seat at my right in the War Room. Viper silently scowls at me as he claims the VP seat to my left. The rest of our brothers, all but Axel, take their seats according to rank, around the table with us.

"You called this emergency vote. Shouldn't we wait for our Road Captain?" Diesel asks, chucking a thumb at Axel's vacant seat at the end of the table next to Ruger. "He missed the meeting this morning at Stogies, but he should be off work pretty soon."

"Not this time." My reply is met with looks of confusion.

"He's a fully patched member. Anything discussed at this table concerns him, too," Chopper insists. He isn't wrong.

I clear my throat, pulling the envelope in question from my cut as I take my seat at the head of the table. "Brother, you just said a mouthful." I sigh, pushing the envelope toward Viking first. "Take a look, then pass them around."

Impatiently, Viking removes the surveillance photos from within. His expression immediately shifts from an irritated grimace to shocked concern. "*Oh...shit...*"

"Exactly. That's also how he knew we broke into the Demons' Den. There really were cameras." I lean back in my seat, pinching the bridge of my nose. The stress headache I've been dealing with since visiting my lawyer's office continues to bang away inside my skull. The room is dead quiet while the rest of our crew examines Legion's leverage.

"This is bad," Viper breaks the tense silence, though his voice is low, discernibly distraught.

"It's worse than bad. According to my lawyer, there is no statute of limitations when it comes to Arson with malicious intent."

The resounding bang of Viking's massive fist slamming down on the table nearly makes me jump, and my head throbs a little harder.

"*Fuck!*" he shouts. I open my eyes to look at him. Worry mixed with anger and regret creases his heavy brow, the war between those emotions clearly evident in his eyes. "The fuck are we gonna do about this, bro?"

"I knew you two burning down the Demons' Den would come back to bite us in the ass!" Ruger shakes his head, disgust written plainly on his face. "I'm surprised it took this long!"

"Now isn't the time for *I told you so's*." I shoot Ruger a stern glare, deading the issue before turning back to Viking. "I don't know... But Axel can't know about this."

"Why not?" Diesel asks.

"Because he'll make it *his* problem," I say, glancing around the table at each of my brothers as I speak. "He'll blame himself for this forced truce with Legion... Axel's a good kid... God forbid he turns himself in to free us of Legion. I'm not willing to take that risk, are you?" I rake my hand through my hair. It feels wrong to keep something from Axel, something so pertinent to the current situation with our MC. It pains me to admit, but... "This would result in *felony* charges... *Mandatory* imprisonment...and Axel is...*not like the rest of us.*" Mutters of agreement rise up from around the table. "We all need to be on the same page about this. No one breathes a fucking word of this to Axel. I'll take the heat about Legion, however this ends up playing out."

"We should have just killed that mother fucker when we had him pinned down in that warehouse," Viking growls under his breath.

"Who's to say this contingency plan wasn't in place even back then? He's got us by the balls, and he knows it. If he dies… *If he simply disappears… Anything* happens to the demonic prick, *Axel is the one who pays…* I'm sorry, but I'm pulling rank on this. As your president, this is a direct order."

Viper lets out a sigh wrought with frustration. "What he said goes beyond us!" We all turn to look at him. "He's forcing his way in. He made it so we have to watch his back, too! *The sneaky prick!* He mentioned he may have enemies. Enemies that might want to take him out as well! *We* don't have to be the ones to kill Legion for his contingency plan to go into effect… *Anyone can.* We *have to* protect Legion… It's the only way to protect Axel."

I nod, relieved that Viper was the one to fully voice this point to our brothers.

"How do we handle this?" Viper asks, looking to me with worry, anger, and disgust etched across his expression. "He's responsible for the death of a Savior! We can't allow him to slither his way into a Saviors' cut when Snowy's is hanging on the wall in memoriam!"

"Fuck no!" Viking booms. "That's never gonna happen!"

"Who's to say how far he's going to play this card?" Viper mutters, a measure of defeat in his tone as he stares almost distantly at the skull and angel wings logo carved in the center of our table. "There's got to be a way to keep him in check…"

"There is," I mutter, shifting uncomfortably in my seat as bile threatens to work its way up my throat. Squeezing my eyes shut again, I bring my fist to press against my pounding forehead.

Once again, Legion's making moves in a 4-D game of chess. Only this time, it isn't the King he's after… *It's the Queen.*

Vanna

"Mrs. Keegan?" There's a soft knock on the exam room door just as I finish dressing and pull on my boots.

"Yes, come in," I reply, sitting down on the edge of the exam table. My doctor reenters the room.

"All of your results look great, but I see here in your notes, you'd like to discuss other birth control options?" She peers over my chart at me. "You've been on the shot these last few years, and you're right on schedule for your next one. Is there a problem? Are you experiencing any adverse side effects?"

"No, no side effects… I just want…*more options*…" I stammer. "We've been thinking about trying for another…and, well… The pill is a bit more flexible than the shot. I'm not saying we're one hundred percent on board with the idea…but…"

"When, or rather, *if*, you do decide it's time, you don't want to have to wait out the effects of the shot. Understood. I'll write you a script for an oral contraceptive." She removes a small prescription pad from the pocket of her white coat. "Your last dose was about fifteen weeks ago, so it's safe to take your first pill when you have this filled." She scribbles something down, then tears off the slip and hands it to me. "Anything else while you're here?"

"That's all." I smile, eager to be on my way. Cherry is watching Ace at the house so I could make this appointment. I don't want to keep her waiting. I'll be able to fill the prescription at our local pharmacy on my way home.

"This script is refillable for twelve months. However, if you experience any issues, don't hesitate to make another appointment, and we'll try something else."

After taking care of my copay, I head for my car in the lot, only to discover my back driver's side tire is completely flat.

"Great." I sigh, beeping the SUV unlocked. I toss my purse on the driver's seat and pull the lever for the trunk release to grab the jack and spare. Fortunately, the parking space beside me is vacant, so I have some room to work. I could call Dean to come help me, but he's at work, and I have attempted to change a tire before. I remember where to place the jack, and I have a star for the lug nuts.

I shut the door and shove my keys in my pocket before moving to the back.

As I lift the trunk open, I'm startled by the sudden proximity of a disheveled-looking man.

"I can help you change the tire for thirty bucks," he says, scratching at his thin, scabby arm.

"I can do it, but thanks," I politely decline.

"Twenty, then," he pushes, and I notice the minuscule level of initial friendliness in his tone no longer exists.

"No, thank you," I insist a bit more firmly this time.

He reaches into the trunk for the spare tire anyway, roughly pulling the compartment open, and grabs the tire iron. "I'll do it, and you can just give me whatever it's worth to you."

"I said no!"

When the man turns to face me head-on, his furrowed brow shoots to his forehead, and he takes a fearful step back. The tire iron slips from his grasp and clatters loudly to the pavement.

"Go run your little con elsewhere," a gravely, threatening voice warns from behind me. Somehow, I'm both relieved and unnerved as Legion steps around to stand by my side, flashing the guy a holstered gun within his jacket.

The miscreant bolts for his worthless life, and I readjust my leather jacket, turning to face Vanna, only to be met with suspiciously narrowed dark eyes.

"A con?"

"Flatten a tire, stick around to hustle an unsuspecting victim for a quick buck." I shrug. "Beats sucking dick for drug money, I'd imagine." She blinks silently at my crude words, and I'm unable to suppress a slight smile at her reaction. My delicate little flower. "Anyway, fancy meeting like this again." I gesture to the same parking lot where she had fainted years ago.

"Quite."

"Not even a *thank you* for my assistance?" I attempt to infuse my words with a measure of humor to put her at ease. "Is that any way to treat your *Savior*?"

She retrieves the tire iron and turns back to the trunk, seemingly determined to ignore the reference.

"Perhaps the lady prefers, *Knight?*" I jest.

Vanna graces me with a little scowl. "Did you set this up?" Her accusatory tone might have wounded me if I weren't metacognitive of the fact that it wasn't beyond the realm of my capabilities.

"Whether I did or not, you're safe now, and I'm more than happy to assist with the changing of your tire." I extend my hand for her to pass me the tire iron, which she stubbornly refuses. "Oh, come now, Vanna. Was that junkie hustling you not example enough of the dangers the fairer sex often contends with in unsavory parking lots? This is a dark, dangerous world, my dear."

"I'm sure it wasn't your primary incentive to instill an impromptu lesson and mansplain the dangers we womenfolk face," Vanna chides me, "*Men* being the vast majority of the dangers, by the way." She finally hands me the tire iron. "I'll give you the benefit of the doubt this time. However, I should warn you, in case it somehow slipped your mind… Dean's tolerance for you is at an all-time low. This isn't going to win you any points."

She lifts the cover to the spare, exposing the tire and jack.

"Ah, I'm pleased to see you won't be traveling on a donut," I say.

"Dean didn't want me driving around on one if I ever got a flat, so he purchased an extra tire when he bought me the car."

"I approve."

"I'm sure he'll be thrilled."

"Well, I do believe your beloved and I have come to an understanding. Though if he still considers me an enemy, one might think it wise to keep me close… Close enough to keep a watchful eye. You remain quite the appealing incentive, though," I wink at her as I reach inside the compartment and remove the jack.

"What?"

"Don't play coy."

"He's never going to allow you around me. Where do you see this going?"

"Despite the rumblings of my reputation, I'm afraid *seeing the future* is beyond my wheelhouse," I say, setting up the jack beneath the frame before retrieving the spare tire. I pause to study her. "Would it please you to know I've secured his blessing in my stay?"

Her expression softens, surprised, and I find myself hoping she is pleasantly so. "How did you manage that?"

I suppress a smile and hoist the spare from the tire well, placing it beside her vehicle. She seems eager for an explanation, watching me go to work on her tire.

"Legion, how did you manage that?" she presses while I loosen the last lug nut and proceed to jack the car up the rest of the way.

"*Are you pleased?*"

She fidgets, rubbing her palms against her jeans. Eye level with her thick thighs, I make a valiant effort not to stare at them and force my gaze to meet her inquisitive eyes once again. She appears conflicted.

"I don't know how to navigate this," she says.

"One day at a time… And if it eases your mind, sweet one…No, I did not set this up. I just happened to—"

"Be stalking me again?" she interrupts, though there is a minuscule undertone of nervous play in her accusation.

Was her initial display of annoyance simply a pretense? Her loyal attempt at keeping up appearances for Keegan's sake? Could it be possible she was relieved to see me again, regardless of the fact that I ran that dreg off? If so, perhaps all is not so perfect in paradise…

"Such a pointed word," I tease, swapping out the flat for the spare. "Might I offer a more flattering light on our situation?"

Wry skepticism eclipses her expression, though this time, it's with less conviction. "*I doubt it.*"

"Merely looking out for your well-being, sweet one. Your husband wasn't here to do it himself. He's volunteering a shift at one of those safehouses, is he not? Seeing to the *well-being* of *anoth*—"

"*Stop it,*" she snaps. "I know what you're doing. Just stop it right now."

"I'm simply stating the—"

"Obvious? What's *obvious* to me is that you haven't changed much these last three years, Legion. If you think you're going to drive a wedge between Dean and I, you're wrong. I married him, knowing full well what I was getting into. I don't resent him or the MC. Their mission is admirable. It's worthwhile and it's needed. Don't think I can't spot your manipulations from a mile away, so you better just be straight with me."

After ensuring her tire is properly installed and secure, I remove the jack from beneath her vehicle. It seems I've pushed a tad too hard, too soon on this one with her.

"I assure you, sweet one," I say, getting up to place the jack and her flat tire back inside the tire well. "When it comes to you, *I'm straight*."

"The *double-entendres* can stop, too," she quips. I suppress another grin as she comes to stand beside me, fussing with the cover of the compartment. "If you want a chance at... at..." she lets out a frustrated huff, taking the tire iron from me, then tosses it into the trunk. She seems to struggle to find her words, taking a moment to slam the trunk closed before jamming both fists against her hips. "If you want to make this situation with the Saviors work... If you don't want to be run out of this town, *or worse*... No more games, Legion. You're going to have to try your hand at complete honesty."

Fine... "I was following you."

"Alright, a compromise. You were *following* me." She crosses her arms and leans against the vehicle. "Why?"

"True—"

"*Don't say it.*"

"*North?*" I blurt the word out instead, awkwardly, and somehow manage to pull a small smile from her.

"True North?" she says, attempting to hide the amusement in her tone.

"I don't know how to navigate any of this either, Vanna... You're my compass in all this..." *In all things now, really...*

She removes her keys from her pocket and stares down at them, avoiding my gaze. "I can't be your anything...not even your friend...at least not until you make nice with Dean."

At least she seems to harbor a level of regret over the matter.

"You're really holding to that, aren't you." It's not a question. I find her stubborn resilience irritatingly *commendable*. "I'm working on it."

She swallows before nodding. "Well then, I wish you the best of luck."

"Perhaps you might find it within your heart to put in a good word?"

Vanna steps around me and wraps her hand around the driver's side door handle. "I have to get back to Ace. I'm late... But... I'll do what I can," she says, though she seems doubtful of her influence.

Jennifer Saviano

I watch her slide into the car and then drive off.
"And I'll endeavor to do as you wish."

CHAPTER 15

Vanna

Ace is occupying himself with a box of crayons and some paper at the little table we set up for him beneath a window near the register. The honor system has been working at the farmstand, but we do come down frequently so I can tidy up, restock as needed, and collect payments left throughout the day when I'm not here to assist customers.

The breeze on this brisk autumn afternoon has finally died down, and I've been sweeping out the leaves from the old oak towering outside. I try to focus on the classical music playing softly on the portable stereo for Ace, but my mind has been reeling since encountering Legion earlier.

I want to believe he's sincere. I want to think he truly regrets everything he's caused and understands the hurt, anger, and confusion he's left in his wake. Is he truly sorry, or is this simply an act, another manipulation to get closer?

I'm afraid to examine the reasons I ever trusted him in the past. Dean was right. All of Legion's actions have spoken to the contrary of his words…until he shot his brother.

I try to suppress the horrific images of that night from resurfacing, but something inside of me clings to the monumental act. Legion killed his own brother, arranged the decimation of his crew to ensure their defeat on our behalf… He claims to have kept the promises he made that night, and though I remember his words, I don't want to think about them either.

"It's Meg!" Ace excitedly announces when we both hear the crunching of gravel beneath tires in our small parking area. He must have seen her car pulling up through the window behind him.

I set the broom against a wooden produce box containing a batch of tomatoes from the greenhouse Ace and I collected earlier, and make my way to the open doors.

Meg waves as she steps out of the car, and another rogue breeze catches her long, fox-red hair, causing it to billow out and settle over her shoulder, draping down the lavender sweater she's wearing. The color really brings out the deep emerald green of her eyes. Since moving into the old Victorian-style farmhouse next door, she's become a regular customer over the last year, and Ace has taken a liking to her. It's comforting to know there is someone living in the old house again. Until Meg, it sat vacant after I moved in with Dean.

"*Veggies and Vivaldi!*" Meg smiles upon entering our little farmstand. "Though I never did care much for Vivaldi," she seems to laugh the comment off. "Violins are so… *shrill*."

To each their own, I suppose, though I'm grateful for the distraction of her visit. "I've read that listening to classical music has several proven benefits for children's mental development."

Her dark green eyes seem to study me. "Yes, I recall an article discussing whether a preference for instrumental music indicated *higher intelligence*, or if it is simply a pseudo fact." Suddenly, her demeanor shifts, and she smiles pleasantly. "Anyway, will you be taking orders this year for those spectacular homemade Cornucopias? They were such a hit last year on my Thanksgiving table."

"Oh, yes, of course." I gesture to the checkout counter. "I just put out the order sheet this morning."

We walk over to the list together, which has already accumulated a few customers. I grab a pen from the tin can beside the register and place it down on the sheet of paper clamped to the clipboard. "Sesame seed or plain this year. Orders will be available to be picked up the Tuesday before Thanksgiving, between noon and six pm. Either Dean or I will be home to hand them off," I explain, then it occurs to me. "I don't think you've met my husband yet, have you?"

"I haven't had the pleasure yet, no," Meg smiles, picking up the clipboard to fill out her information. "Is there any possible way I could talk you into a special exception? Of course, I'm willing to pay the difference."

"Well, I suppose it depends…" I begin when she suddenly drops both the clipboard and the pen. Before I get the chance to do or say anything, she immediately picks them up, clearing her throat as if to buy herself a moment of composure. "Is everything alright?"

"Yes, clumsy me." She forces another flittering laugh. "Last year, you made a simply scrumptious version with a honey glaze of some sort. It was delicious." She goes on, jotting down her information.

Going along with her act as if nothing happened, I reply, "Sure. Why not? Just put a little note next to your name so I remember."

"You are so sweet, Vanna. Thank you for being so accommodating." She finishes filling out her order and hands the clipboard back to me. While she sorts through her purse to pay, I scan over the list, curious to see if there is something out of the ordinary that may have startled her. I haven't had a reason to look over the list yet, since Thanksgiving is still weeks away. When I see a phone number and the words *The Devil* scribbled just above her information. *Damn it, Legion…*

She watches me draw a line through the words and what I'm certain is Legion's cell number. "Must have been a prank, I didn't notice until now." I place the list back down on the checkout counter. "Sorry about that."

"Well, Halloween is only a day away," Meg says, like it's nothing now, and shifts her attention to Ace. We walk over and she squats beside his table. "Are you excited to go trick-or-treating, Ace?"

"Yes." He smiles up at her from his stick figure drawing of what appears to be a man in black with a wide smile and fire for fingers… *Fabulous. He's everywhere…*

"I see you're getting into the Halloween spirit with that fantastic artwork!" Meg says, admiring his picture.

"This is Legend," Ace explains, as if everyone should know who *Legend* is.

I can't help but hope this is the first and only drawing of Legion he intends to create. Although Dean would never hold it against him, I imagine he'd take issue with this, too. The last thing I want is either of their feelings hurt over something so innocent. After all, Legion has always been one to leave a lingering impression.

DEAN

I should be ecstatic over the fact that The Twisted Throttle is fairly packed tonight. It's certainly been a while since the roadhouse has seen this amount of patronage. Maybe Viking is right. Maybe things are turning around. Despite the positive atmosphere tonight, pangs of anxiety have been wreaking havoc on me all day.

"How are you gonna approach this shit with Vanna, bro?" Viking asks. "Will she go along with it? Are you gonna tell her what he's holding over Axel?"

I attempt to swallow the painful knot in my throat. I wouldn't even *need* to tell her… My insides are all twisted up with an intense jealousy I've managed to keep at a low simmer these last three years. Legion's return has cranked this torturous emotion up more than a few notches, and a territorial rage is brewing inside me like a storm gaining power over ocean waters.

I unclench my aching jaw to growl, "He knew he'd drive me to do this, too… *Access to her* is the only thing he really wants." And he isn't going to stop. He isn't going to back off. He's forcing me to come to terms with this reality. Forcing me to accept his presence, knowing damn well I've only got the fucking *illusion* of choice in the matter. He knows I'd rather be aware of their encounters than find out they've happened in secret. He's protecting her honor by going about everything in this way, too. I can feel the pulse in my corded neck as rage and resentment continue to build. He's getting everything he wants, boxing me into this position of consensual non-consent!

"Don't worry, Dean," Viking attempts to reassure me. "He'll never get that with her protected."

In a way, it sickens me further to admit, "*Legion wouldn't hurt her.*"

I don't have it in me to voice my true fears. I can't bring myself to admit out loud the way her immediate acceptance of his presence, her *willingness* to assist with him, will gut me. He's always had a spell over her, some otherworldly connection I can't help but feel threatened by, despite my own to her.

"Vanna loves me."

"Shit, man, *of course she does.*" Viking places a heavy hand on my shoulder and leans forward to look me in the eyes.

Why did I feel the need to say that out loud?

I'm trembling with rage-laced anxiety at the thought of all the arguments she and I will inevitably get into, courtesy of *fuckin' Legion*. I bet he's counting on it. I can picture the demon gleefully slamming his hammer down on the wedge positioned against whatever crack he may find in our relationship...

Closing my eyes, I lean back against the brick wall and force myself to take a few steady breaths.

"Maxie, bring my man a double shot of JD and a Miller, *pronto*," Viking orders one of the newer Lady Lays.

"Sure thing," she replies, heels clunking on the hardwood as she steps closer to me. "Are you alright, honey?" Her hand presses lightly against my knee, and the intrusive touch pushes me over the edge.

"Forget it. I'm going to check on *my wife*," I say, getting up from the stool. I brush past the *all too eager to please* blonde bombshell and head for the corridor beyond the bar.

Vanna is already exiting my old club room, quietly closing the door behind her when I approach. "Ace just fell asleep," she whispers while clipping the baby monitor to the waistband of her long skirt. "We need to talk."

"Yeah, we do. Gym or War Room?"

"Back patio?"

"That works too."

We walk down the hall together, and I hold the back door open for her. The cool October night air sends a noticeable shiver through her body, and she immediately folds her arms against the chill. I shrug out of my cut and leather jacket to separate the two articles of leather and drape my jacket over her shoulders.

"Thank you." She smiles up at me, tugging my jacket around herself tighter while I slip back into my cut. "What did you want to talk about?"

"You first," I say, dreading my part of the conversation.

"I've been offered a thousand dollars to do card readings at a Halloween Party for a couple of hours."

"Where?"

"The mayor's mansion, by his wife. She actually called me earlier today while Ace and I were at the park with Rosita and Mia. They're having some kind of ritzy party, and they want a professional. A costume is required, but she said they'd provide one and send it over."

Legion: Book 3

It's not stopping… It's never going to fucking stop!

"This reeks of fucking Legion," I growl. She stares at me for a moment, and I wonder if the thought never occurred to her. "Since when are you on the mayor's radar, let alone in his wife's contacts?"

She only nods, contemplatively.

"And you don't even *like* reading tarot for others." My words sound harsher than I intended, and her eyes drop from mine to stare at the concrete.

"You're right," she quietly concedes.

Was she happy about this offer? I know she misses the Ametrine Cauldron. Maybe she was too excited by an opportunity to put her witchy talents to use. The thought *really hadn't* crossed her mind?

I need to rein my shit in, for her sake. I cannot let Legion win. "Are you going to do it?"

She shrugs halfheartedly, *now that I've managed to suck the wind from her sails.* "It's a lot of money for a few hours, plus tips. It used to take me almost two weeks to make that at The Ametrine Cauldron." She finally peers up at me, a flicker of hope in her eyes as they shift searchingly in mine. "Maybe this could open doors to something more? Maybe starting a practice closer to home could actually be a possibility? I mean, in the future… The mayor's wife sounded very eager to hire me. I guess with Halloween this week, she was in a pinch for another entertainer? I mean, I did hand out a few business cards last year with my number on them. Remember? At the Mum Festival in New Bern, when I was helping Laura at her booth… So, we don't know *for sure* this is Legion's doing…*do we?* Maybe one of Mrs. Wellington's friends gave her my card?"

We don't know for sure this is Legion… It's already fucking starting… I'm going to have to choose my battles, or he's going to win the war.

"Maybe I'm being paranoid." *I'm not, but…* "I'm not going to stop you if you want to do it." Far be it from me to put a damper on her happiness. The last thing I want is to ever make her feel stifled in any way. Not after Jack. Not after the mistakes I made in my own failed marriage to Lucinda. "Could be worse," I attempt to joke, "She could have called asking you to belly dance."

To my meager relief, Vanna laughs. "I'm way out of practice for that. And for the record, I never danced professionally. I took a few classes just for fun at Laura's shop. Your birthday that year was a *one-time thing.*"

"Well, I think you move this body just fine, doll." I grip her hips and pull her against me. "As long as you keep that talent between us... *Our own private thang.*"

"Are you flirting with me?" she smirks.

"Is it working? I could use the distraction." I could use the reminder she's mine, too. Nothing soothes my racing mind or battered soul like losing myself in her.

"You do seem a bit tense lately." Her hands slide up my arms to gently grip my shoulders over the cut. "Is everything alright?"

Not even a little, but I force a smile for the sake of her contentment. "*Aces*, baby."

"That's not going to get you out of anything this time. What was it you wanted to talk about?"

The rumbling of Axel's Dyna interrupts before I can reply. We watch him park his Harley in his usual spot, near the back patio, since it's closest to the room he shares with Cherry.

"Sorry, I'm late for my shift," Axel says, helmet tucked beneath his arm as he walks up to us. His weary eyes are reddened, and there's dried paint on his pants and hands. "Long day. Do you mind if I take a quick shower before I hit the floor?"

"Go for it."

"Thanks. It's been a day." He combs his fingers through his disheveled hair. "This client was a pain in the ass, but at least the job's done."

"Ain't always easy running your own business."

"Nope," Axel concurs. "Is Ace here tonight?"

"He's already fallen asleep," Vanna regretfully informs him.

"Damn." Axel sighs but offers her an understanding smile. "I miss the little munchkin. Do you mind if I just look in on him real quick?"

"Of course not." Vanna pats my chest, and I reluctantly release her and trail behind them on our way back to Ace.

When Vanna opens the door, Axel and I take a peek inside. Ace is fast asleep in the middle of the bed, tucked beneath a blanket and between two pillows to keep him in the center of the mattress.

Days when I not only put in hours at the repair shop, followed by a block of volunteered guard duty for Medusa's Gates *before* my shift at the Twisted Throttle, Vanna has been bringing Ace here to spend a little time with me and whichever of his *MC Uncles* are around. They're usually here before I arrive, and Ace genuinely seems to enjoy the time he spends at the clubhouse. It's a boost in morale when I don't have to go a whole twenty-hour or longer stretch without seeing my family. Besides, this place isn't just a clubhouse. It isn't just a bar. We're a close-knit family, and I think Vanna misses everyone at the Twisted Throttle, too. There's been something different about her ever since the Ametrine Cauldron burned down. I know she's happy being Ace's mother, though sometimes I worry the whole *housewife-mommy gig* isn't keeping her content. What if she wants more than I can give her?

Once Axel heads off to his room, Vanna closes the door quietly and turns to me. "You said you wanted to talk?"

I attempt to keep the tone of my request casual when I tell her, "Yes, but let's go to the gym so we don't wake Ace." She's still got his monitor, and it's only a short walk down the hall adjacent to this room.

Once inside the gym, I shut the double doors behind us and turn to face her.

"What's wrong?" she asks, studying my expression again.

"You must know how I feel about Legion."

"You hate him."

"You must know how I feel about Legion…*and you.*"

"There is no *Legion and me*, Dean. There never was and there never will be." She steps forward to touch the clenched fist at my side. "Look at me… Who is the man who has bent over backwards to give me everything I've ever wanted?"

"Me?"

"Yes, *you.* Who never gave up on us despite our pasts?"

"I didn't."

"There isn't another man on this earth capable of loving me the way you do. And if you think I don't know that…that I don't love *you* just as deeply…" She shakes her head as if the mere thought of my doubt hurts her, and I can't stand that.

"I do. I'm sorry, doll. I do. I couldn't live without your love, baby."

"What is it you need to tell me?"

I let out a tense sigh. "Just know how much I hate that it's come to this." I drag a hand through my hair and swallow my pride for Axel's sake. "I may need your help…with Legion."

She seems surprised at first, and I desperately, *instinctively*, scrutinize her expression for any sign of joy over the matter.

"*Oh*...well, what can *I* do?" Her hand slowly gravitates to the base of her throat, a sign of unease I've come to recognize in her. She quickly changes course, grabbing my leather jacket and pulling it from her shoulders. She holds it awkwardly in front of herself, fingers fiddling with the pull-tab of the zipper.

"You're the only person who seems to hold any sway with him. I don't know exactly what this situation looks like yet...but we both know you're the reason he's back...and... I don't want to fight with you about him...*about anything*...but especially not about *him*."

"There's nothing to fight about." She tries to reassure me with a soft smile. "Tell me what's going on."

"He's got leverage on Axel. Probably Viking, too."

"Leverage?" It only takes a second before her eyes widen upon realization. "*Oh no*...the Demons' Den?"

I nod. "Security footage. He showed me photos which are damning enough, but they look like still shots from recordings." Vanna stops toying with the zipper and holds my jacket tighter against herself. I'm not sure what to make of this reaction. I clear my throat and continue, "I already met with my lawyer... There is no statute of limitations in this situation. Axel's looking at a ten-year federal stint if anything happens to Legion."

"What do you need me to do?"

I shake my head. "I don't know what other tricks he's got up his sleeve...just...be on my side, doll."

"Dean..." Her expression turns sympathetic, but worry is still evident behind her eyes. "There is no other side I would ever be on, sweetheart."

"I know you think you see something in him." Admitting so claws at my insides, and the way her eyes shift back and forth in mine, I'm sure she sees right through me to the insecurities bubbling to the surface.

"*Not like that.*"

"But you see *something*."

"I'm not sure what I see, exactly. Other than a person attempting to right his wrongs."

"*Through blackmail?*"

Legion: Book 3

Vanna winces. "I didn't say he was going about it *the right way.*" She bites her bottom lip, hesitating before she asks, "Would you have even given him the time of day if he didn't have leverage?"

Fuck... "No."

She shrugs, though she seems to do so nervously, fearful I might blow up on her. "It's been three years. He hasn't done anything with the footage. Maybe he really doesn't intend to? He knows you all hate him... I don't think trust comes easily to a man like Legion. He probably expected you to want to kill him the moment you crossed paths... *Devil's advocate...*"

"Funny choice of words..."

"Can you honestly blame him?"

I fucking hate to concede this point. The rational side of myself understands his move, but... "Fucking *Axel*, doll..." I let out another stress-ridden sigh, turning from her to make my way over to the workout bench. I take a seat, squeezing my eyes shut, and run both hands through my hair until I'm gripping the back of my neck. I hear her drape my jacket over the dumbbell rack, then I feel her body against my back as she straddles the bench behind me. I let my arms drop when Vanna wraps her arms around my abdomen, the way we ride together, and she rests her head against my cut.

"I won't let Legion hurt us, or anyone we care about," she says softly, giving my body a slight squeeze.

I don't find her words reassuring. If anything, they make me feel more ashamed. I unclench my jaw and scoff, "You shouldn't be the one protecting *us.*"

"Why not? *Because I'm a woman?*" she sounds humorous, "I'm not as fragile as you think."

"Well, you also don't think he's dangerous. That's a huge chink in your armor, doll." *And her judgement.*

"I never said that... I know what Legion is capable of, but I don't think he has any ill intent this time. He's not going to turn Axel in. He would have done so already. This is just his way, *albeit misguided*, of getting you to give him a chance."

"It's *extortion*, doll."

"What do you want me to do?"

"I don't even know, yet...but, you can't tell Axel about any of this...and you can't tell Cherry, either." Her body tenses. "I hate it as much as you do, Vanna, but we can't."

"The MC knows? Everyone but them?"

"Yes, we're all in agreement. The call has been made."

She releases me to stand up, and I watch her walk over to the boxing ring. She turns to face me, leaning back against the ledge. Her brows are furrowed, lips pressed together. "They're going to be hurt by this, even more so than what Legion has on Axel. Are you really sure this is what's best?" She wraps her arms around her middle, another tell-tale sign of her distress.

"There's no guarantee Axel won't react." I close the distance between us and place my hands on her shoulders. "I'm afraid of what he'd do. Turn himself in to free us of Legion... Fucking *kill him* and make the situation worse, especially for himself." I shake my head as those nightmare scenarios play out in my mind. "Either way, Axel ends up in *Club Fed*, doll."

"But, *Cherry*..."

"There's a good chance she'd tell Axel... This is for the best. I'm sorry to put this on you."

"Why did you?"

I take a breath, letting it out on a sigh, and try for a humorous response, "Nobody keeps a secret like you do, babe."

"That's not funny." She frowns, but her expression quickly morphs back to distress. "Cherry is one of my closest friends..." She shakes her head, and I swear if she tears up over this, I'm gonna lose my shit.

"We went into this with a promise I wouldn't keep things from you. You tell an Old Lady everything, or you tell her nothing. Remember?"

She nods.

"This is on me as president. I'm the bad guy who made the call."

"You're not the bad guy, Dean... You've never been the bad guy."

"You're right. *Legion is.*"

She only stares up at me. At least she's not trying to argue the point. I'm caught off guard when she suddenly turns from me and slams her fist down on the ledge of the boxing ring, letting out a frustrated little grunt.

"Damn him!"

"Vanna?"

She whirls back around to face me, a soul-shredding sadness in her eyes. "I had hopes for him that maybe he did change."

I practically choke on my pride in an attempt to swallow it. *She had hopes for him... Believed in him... For how long? Has she been waiting for him to come back this whole time? Looking forward to his return? And what then?*

The knife twisting in my gut makes me want to keel over and fuckin' puke. The emotional turmoil must be written all over my face.

"What's wrong?" she asks, her distraught expression shifts to concern.

"I don't think I've ever wanted to kill Legion more than I do in this fucking moment."

"Stop it."

"*Why?*" I nearly snarl the words, "My hands are tied! I can't hurt your fucking—"

She reaches up with both hands, grabbing me by the base of my skull, and hauls me down until our lips crash together. I'm fucking heated to begin with, but her demanding kiss, her fiery desire to take what we both know is hers, ignites my burning need to remind her who she belongs to as well.

"*You're mine!*" I growl against her lips, before plunging my tongue back inside her demanding mouth.

I grab her ass, pulling her body hard against mine. Her hands move to grip my shoulders, and the instant I feel her hop up, I reposition my hold on her to wrap her legs around my waist.

It's been too long since we've kissed like this, rough and desperate. A wild abandon where nothing else exists but this all-consuming need for each other. I slam her back up against the ropes of the boxing ring, planting her ass on the ledge so I can fumble with my belt and get my fly open.

Her fingernails rake down the fabric of my shirt, moving quickly to my already throbbing cock. Her hand wraps around my shaft, pulling me free while I shove her skirt up to grab the waistband of her panties and rip them down her thighs. She releases my cock to lean back against the ropes again, bending one knee so I can get her underwear all the way down. With one leg free, I leave the garment dangling from her other ankle, and she clamps her legs around me once more.

"You want this?" I growl against her neck, the head of my cock pressing against her hot center, so she can feel what she does to me, too. I drag my tongue up her throat, to that sweet spot behind her ear that always makes her melt.

She arches into me with a soft, needy whimper. *"Yes! Only you, Dean, always."*

I slide my hands up her skirt, calloused palms against soft thighs, gripping her flesh as I work my way up, inch by inch, memorizing the feel of her body all over again, branding her with my touch.

When I grip her ass and ram myself home in one deep, aching thrust, she lets out a cry that shatters every piece of me I've been trying to hold together. Every moan, every whimper that escapes her shoves the jealousy deeper into the shadows.

I swallow her gasps as her fingers dig into my shoulders before sliding up my neck to curl roughly into my hair while our tongues swirl and wrestle together.

Her intoxicating sounds and wet, gripping muscles send a shudder through my body, and I continue to thrust. The taut, padded ropes behind her keep her right where I want her. When I'm inside her, wrapped up and lost in my wife, nothing else exists.

"*I love you,*" I murmur against her lips. "Even when I'm mad. Even when I'm jealous. Even when I hate myself for worrying."

"I know," she whispers, brushing her fingers along the stubble of my jaw, attempting to soothe the turmoil coursing through me. "You never have to doubt me. I'm yours, Dean. And you're mine. Always."

When she kisses me, it's slow and deep. And when we unravel together, it isn't just our bodies, but our walls and fears. She quivers around me, and I come hard, breathing her name like a prayer I've never deserved to have answered.

On our way back to the bar, we make a quick pitstop to check on Ace again. Finding him still fast asleep, I escort Vanna to the bar.

"Oh, there's something else I meant to mention," she says.

"What's that, doll?"

"I didn't get the shot."

I nearly trip over my damn boots. "*Jesus fuck* Vanna, I thought we talked about this! I just fuckin'–"

She's laughing at me. "Relax! I'm on the pill now. I took it this morning. We're fine."

"That wasn't funny."

"It was a little," she says, though her words don't hold any humor.

I shake my head as the spike in my heart rate begins to level out. We round the corridor near the end of the bar counter, where Cherry is slinging drinks.

"This song playing on the juke box," Vanna turns to face me, a little smirk on her lips. "It's a *you* song." She playfully squeezes my ass before stepping behind the bar to help Cherry.

"*Simply the best*, huh?" I grin back at my wife while Tina Turner's smash hit blasts through the speakers, and Vanna grabs me a beer.

She places the bottle on the bar and blows me a little kiss. "*Better than all the rest.*"

Chapter 16

Vanna

The moment I open the box on our kitchen island to inspect the costume provided by the mayor's wife, I'm instantly hit with a wave of regret. Why did I agree to this job? It's an *immediate no*.

"What's wrong?" Dean must have read my initial reaction from across the room.

I close the box and peer up at him as he approaches. "I can't wear this."

He steps beside me and opens the box back up to reveal the tattered rags of a skirt, head scarf, and compact of black powder. He picks up the note accompanying the costume, which states the makeup is for my eyes, in case I didn't have black shadow, and that there will be a glowing crystal ball set up at my table, so I don't need to bring any additional "gypsy" props.

Dean rolls his lips inward and closes the box, looking back at me with raised brows. "What are you going to do?"

"Well, *Princess Buttercup* isn't going to fit the gig, so… I suppose I'm just going to put on a black dress and a pointy witch hat and call it done."

And that is exactly what I do.

Now wearing a long, black lace dress and a pair of black boots, I retrieve my velvet, wide-brimmed, pointed hat from my witch room and meet Dean where I left him in the kitchen. He's sitting solemnly at the marble island, watching Ace, who appears to be moments from falling asleep on the couch with Nico, midway through an animated

Robin Hood movie. Trick or treating in town earlier today with Maddie and Mia must have really tuckered him out.

"You don't have to go to this thing," Dean says.

"It's fine. *It's money.*"

"*Vanna…*"

"Look, maybe something good will come from this," I try to sound more upbeat about it for him. "Maybe I'll get lucky and do a few readings that actually resonate with some people and change a few minds in this town… Maybe *one day*, I'll be able to have a little shop of my own, *The Mini Ametrine Cauldron.*"

Dean only looks back at me with a somewhat rueful expression. "That's the second time you've mentioned it." He sighs, but then his jaw tenses.

"What?"

"We both know he'll show up."

"He might. We also know he's not going to hurt me. Do you want me to ask him about the leverage?"

Dean slowly shakes his head. "You're not a pawn. *I* will never treat you as such. *He* can't say the same. *Don't forget that.* Don't forget anything he's done to us."

"I won't," I say, grabbing the box and tucking it under my arm. "Do you trust me?"

He nods, and I grab my purse from the back of a kitchen barstool and sling it over my shoulder. After kissing Dean, I tell him, "*I love you.* Kiss Ace goodnight for me when you put him to bed."

When I arrive at the colonial-style mansion, I'm escorted to a Gazebo draped in decorative spiderwebs and cut-out bats swinging on fishing line in the soft breeze. There's a big, purple, glowing crystal ball in the center of the table inside.

"The hostess would like you to remain here. Someone will check in with you periodically to see if you're in need of refreshments or a break," the man, dressed as a Frankenstein's Monster version of a butler, explains.

I already want to leave. Instead, I smile and hold out the box for him to take.

"What's this?"

"A costume was sent to my home earlier. *It…*didn't fit."

He takes the box from me without comment and walks off.

I slide the bowling ball-shaped crystal closer to the edge of the table to make room for my tarot cards, and remove the little jar from my purse I brought for tips. After placing it beside the luminescent orb, I toss a few five-dollar bills inside, hoping it might entice others to add to the jar. Laura taught me the little psychological trick last year at the festival. Taking my seat at the black lace-covered table, I patiently wait for partygoers to approach for a reading.

T wo hours in, the mask of my fake smile is slipping. Between physical exhaustion from the task of enduring condescending remarks under the guise of lighthearted jokes, and the eagerness to return home, each passing minute feels like twenty should have gone by.

I glance over at my dismal tip jar, which has only accumulated a few more dollars after the few I added myself, and scoff. Dean was right. I should have just stayed home. I miss him and Ace.

I'm about to pull out my cell phone to text Dean when a tall, trim man dressed in a crisp black suit steps into the gazebo with me. Though he's wearing a very realistic half skull mask which covers the top portion of his face, I immediately recognize him, and those piercing grey eyes. That ever-present, intensely alluring aura of his always seems to precede him.

"Legion… What are you doing here?"

He parts his hands in a gesture of peace and steps closer to me. "I was invited by the mayor… *A secret guest of honor.* When I caught word that *you* would be here, I decided this pompous bullshit was worth attending, after all."

"I wondered if you'd be here."

There's a smile in Legion's voice when he gestures to my dress, "Though lovely as always…that's not much of a *costume*, Vanna."

"Some of us are witches all year round."

"Indeed, and *touché!*"

"Would you like a reading?"

Legion seems to consider my offer for a moment in silence.

"Afraid of what the cards might *reveal* about you?" I prod at him, lifting my cards off the table to shuffle them slowly in my lap.

Legion: Book 3

Once again, the returning grin in his voice is evident. "Are you attempting to *bully me* into a reading, sweet one?"

I lift my shoulder in a slight shrug. "Just an offer."

Legion grabs the single chair across from me and sits down with a playful eagerness. It would have been endearing…if the man sitting across from me *wasn't Legion*…

"Any offer from *you*, darling, is an offer I find myself hard pressed to refuse!"

I can't help but roll my eyes at him, though I do so halfheartedly. "Just a general reading," I say, shuffling the deck a moment longer. After placing the cards down on the table, I split them into three piles.

Upon flipping over the first card, I'm instantly uncomfortable and launch right into the spiel I give everyone who happens to get this particular card. "You know, the *Death* card doesn't actually mean *Death*. I hate it when this card comes up… Most panic when they see it."

"I'm quite familiar with the Death card and its positive aspects," Legion replies. "Death can represent a rebirth. *New beginnings*."

"That's right." I smile, thinking back on our little exchange at the Ametrine Cauldron. Legion probably knows more about the tarot than I do. When I flip over the next one, a small wave of relief washes over me. "The Six of Cups… Not bad. Could represent finding satisfaction. Maybe a meaningful friendship? It can also be a reminder to appreciate the small pleasures in life. Paired with the first, I'd venture to say this indicates good things, thus far anyway."

"One can hope." I can almost detect a small degree of anxiety in his tone. As if he's uncomfortable having his cards read, only going along with it for me.

"We can stop, you know," I feel compelled to offer.

Legion leans forward and picks up the third card. Sitting back in his seat, he studies it in silence.

"What is it?" I ask, curiosity getting the better of me.

"Pull another," he insists.

When I hesitate, Legion reaches forward once again, this time, he fans out the three piles across the table. I stare at him as he flips a card over. His shoulders seem to sag ever so slightly, and I lower my eyes to the card.

The Seven of Cups…wishes and dreams… The card of new opportunities, and at times, *illusion* brought about by ego.

I can't help but wonder if it's the *illusion* part he's dissatisfied with, *and why?*

He gathers the cards into a pile, slipping the one I wasn't able to see somewhere into the middle of the deck. After shuffling them a few times, he places them in a neat stack before me.

"*Quid pro quo*, my sweet?" He suddenly sounds a bit more upbeat.

I look at him curiously. "You want to read my cards?"

"*Your palm*, if I may?"

"You know how to do that?"

He holds his hand out in a smooth, inviting motion. "I won't bite," he teases. "And in this poor lighting, I'll only be able to see so much."

"All…alright." I lay my hand in his. "Don't tell me anything bad."

He chuckles, adjusting himself in his seat to better lean forward. "I can already see you have the *healer's mark*. I'm not surprised."

"Where is that?" I ask, leaning forward myself. I've flipped through books on Palmistry in Laura's old shop before, compared lines in my hands to diagrams within the pages in the past. Though curious, I never really found the time to actually study it or retain much of what I did read.

He releases my hand, standing to grab his chair, and moves closer to me. Sitting directly beside me now, he takes my hand in his once again and brushes the pad of his index finger lightly across a small spot on my palm, just below my pinky.

"*Here*," he says softly, "these deep, vertical lines in your Mount of Mercury. The bearer of this mark has the ability to touch the hearts of those around them, finding ways to heal their scars, both emotional and physical… It's no wonder you took an interest in Reiki… *Why…certain types…*find themselves attracted to you."

I lift my other hand to glance at the spot he just showed me. "I have those marks on this hand, too. Is that common?"

He shrugs.

"Can I see yours?"

Legion immediately lays his other hand within mine, and I can feel his cold eyes watching me intently. That was easy… I didn't expect him to give in *just like that*… Maybe I will find a way to bring up the leverage he's holding on Axel after all…

I stop biting my lower lip and lean in a little closer. "You have them too, but mine are a little more pronounced."

"You're more powerful than I am, at least in this aspect. *I'll keep that in mind.*" He chuckles, removing his hand to study my palm once again.

"Huh?"

"Those who can heal, *can also harm,* and vice versa," Legion clarifies, reminding me of one of the hermetic principles, though I notice his tone has lost some of the enthusiasm he seemed to have only moments ago. *"I see your marriage line is strong,"* Legion nearly mutters the words, shifting my hand to examine another line near the base of my pinky, but to the side. "And here is your line for Ace."

"*You can see that?*"

His finger traces another spot. "Here. A deep line, indicating a male child."

Suddenly, my mouth feels dry, and I'm torn right down the middle on whether or not to ask if there's another…

Legion's pale grey eyes flick up to look into mine. "Are you alright? Your pulse has suddenly—"

"I think I'm thirsty," I blurt.

He releases my hand and straightens. "I'll escort you to the bar. Then perhaps, might you care for a dance?"

I force myself to laugh a little and tell him, "I'm not supposed to leave the gazebo."

He only looks at me, cocking his head to the side, as if he hopes I'm joking.

"Besides…we both know Dean wouldn't like that."

"*Ah,* but the *good warden* isn't here." Legion leans in closer to me, the flickering candles and string lights creating purple and gold flecks in his silvery eyes. They really stand out in contrast with the black makeup he has smeared around them beneath the skull mask. "I promise to be a gentleman…" he places a long-fingered hand against his chest and promises, "Won't even try to cop a feel."

I shake my head at that last remark, but… I wouldn't mind getting up and stretching my legs a bit, either.

"I'm supposed to wait until someone tells me I can take a break."

"They're all plastered," Legion pushes, "And judging by the state of your *abysmal* gratuity jar, I doubt anyone will even notice you've escaped your post."

I glance over at it, covering my mouth to stifle a laugh. "This is kind of a joke, isn't it?"

"*Pathetic*, really." I can tell he's suppressing a chuckle of his own.

I bite my lower lip, gazing up at him as he stands and offers me his hand once again.

"Why do I feel like Snow White, being presented with the poison apple?" Vanna teases upon my return, eyeing the flute of champagne I've brought back for her.

"Why not Eve, presented with the forbidden fruit?"

She scowls at me, though the slight quiver in her lips betrays a hard-fought inclination to smile.

"Come now, Vanna… The Devil was *only* trying to *enlighten* Eve." I grin.

"I suppose that's one way to look at it…but are we…still talking about a Bible story? *Or you?*"

"I'm willing to discuss anything your heart desires."

Another little scoff brushes past her luscious lips. "I doubt that."

"*Try me,*" I dare her, stoking those cardinal fires.

She stares for a moment. I watch her delicate throat swallow. "I can't drink tonight. I drove myself here."

"You don't trust me."

Instead of commenting on my pointed statement, she insists, "I…have a low tolerance."

Indeed. I down the glass of champagne myself, staring her in the eyes as I do. Letting out a hiss of air, I slam the flute down on a service tray carried hurriedly past us by a member of the waitstaff. "Would I ingest the apple myself, had I poisoned it?" I ask, more impatience in my tone than I intended. "What's it going to take, Vanna?"

"*I don't know…*" I barely hear her nervous reply over the festivities, though she appears to harbor some level of regret in regard to her answer.

"May I bring you something, madam?" another waiter offers.

"A bottled water?" she asks, as if it's some major inconvenience.

Legion: Book 3

I hate that she suddenly seems uncomfortable in my presence. Or perhaps, she always has been. *Was the Seven of Cups a warning? Am I only seeing what I want to see between us?*

Lurch fetches her bottled water, and she takes a few little sips, awkwardly standing beside me. We watch the costumed social climbers waltz around upon a Halloween-themed, checkered dancefloor in the center of the manicured grounds.

"You refuse to dance with me." I try not to sound like the slighted, lovesick simp I've somehow managed to become. "But perhaps you might like to *walk* with me? There's a lake beyond the gardens... I promise I won't—"

"*Yes,*" she swiftly replies, *akin to firing a shot to end the suffering of a wounded animal...* "Though I should probably grab my bag and *sad little tip jar.* There's got to be *a whopping forty dollars* in that thing. I'd be beside myself if someone should steal it." She gently elbows my arm, a playful attempt to ease the tension between us.

"Allow me," I insist.

She talks about Ace, mostly, on our walk through the arbored gardens along a slate stone path. Though there are golden-hued lights every few steps, the moon above is bright, providing additional illumination. When we come to the back of the garden, I open the little gate, gesturing for her to proceed before me.

"I love these trees." Her hand brushes through the wispy branches of one of the weeping willows on our journey toward the lake. "Ace likes to pretend they're dragons."

"Dragons?"

"Yes." She giggles. "To him, the leaves look like the scales of *water dragons,*" she explains, then adds with pride, "he has a wonderful imagination, and a love for nature and magick."

Her heartfelt words, the way she smiles when she speaks of her son... It soothes something broken inside of me.

"He's such a brilliant little boy. I love him so much, so deeply, it actually hurts. Just thinking about him, I could cry." A slightly strained, awkward little laugh escapes her, and she glances up at me, eyes misted, revealing the beautiful truth in her words. "I sound crazy, don't I?" she asks, and all I can do is shake my head. A tightness in my throat robs my ability to speak. "I'll shut up now," she sighs, as if embarrassed.

"*No… Don't… I…*" *I don't fucking know what to say…except that…* "I… I knew you would be a good mother."

She studies me for a moment, surely piecing together memories of the few, brief conversations we've had in the past. Her eyes settle upon my shoulder, where the half-skull portrait of a silver-eyed fortuneteller is tatted beneath my tailored suit. I know she's thinking back on what I mentioned in a moment of weakness, regarding my own mother.

The heaviness in the atmosphere around us intensifies on our journey toward a curved stone bench at the edge of the lake.

"There are things I want to know… Things I want *you* to know," she finally says, smoothing her long skirt as she takes a seat upon the bench. Her purse slips down her arm, and she places it in the grass at her feet.

"Well, nature is our church…and here we are." I gesture to the lake and forest beyond as I sit beside her. "I'll confess all to you."

She smirks, teasing. "I imagine you'd burst into flames if you ever set foot in an actual church."

"I haven't yet."

"Yet? You've been to church? To an actual confessional? I suppose that shouldn't surprise me, *considering your little head games…*" She lets those words taper off. We both know all they imply. "Were you catholic once, too?"

"No. Though I did attend a catholic boarding school for a portion of my youth."

"Oh?" she looks at me with genuine curiosity. "I find that fascinating, considering the line of work you're in… And your *esoteric practices*… Whatever those might actually be."

"In regard to my line of work, *I'm retired.*" I want to make that damn clear to her, yet at the same time, I'd rather not speak of anything pertaining to this aspect of my past. Not with her. "And it seems Catholicism didn't stick on you either."

She grins. "Fair enough… You're older than me, but you don't look nearly old enough to have reached retirement age."

"I've changed."

"I suppose that's possible… You do seem…different."

Legion: Book 3

"A lot can change a person in the span of three years. Three years is a lifetime to some. I intend to tell you everything... It's just that... everything I've done... I... I..."

"Alright," she fires another mercy shot, astutely aware of my heightening unease. I'm grateful. The guilt inside would never have permitted asking for one myself. "I'll give you an easy one to break the ice... *What's your sign?*"

The anxiety wracking my system while we converse, Vanna *willingly in my presence for the first time*, renders me unable to decipher if she's simply toying with me now or genuinely wants to know. I rule in favor of authenticity. She is a witch, after all. I'm sure she's wondered. "Aquarius."

"That makes so much sense! I would love to see your chart. Have you had it done?"

"I've wondered what it might reveal."

She glances at me with curious skepticism. "You haven't seen it?"

"No."

"How? Do you know what time you were born?"

"Only the date."

"What about your birth certificate?"

"I wasn't born in a hospital." My mother went the midwife route. I'm sure they took the time of birth down somewhere. I imagine she'd have been curious about my chart... Then again, maybe she never cared. *Ever...* I clear my throat and continue, "Time of birth was never recorded. And when I was sent to the orphanage, they obtained a *Letter of No Record* on my behalf."

She stills. "Orphanage?"

"Yes. I did a short stint in a catholic orphanage. Moved on to their boarding school."

I need a fucking cigarette... This is proving more difficult than I anticipated...

"Oh..." the little word seems so heavy on her sigh.

"You're not pregnant again, are you?" I bluntly inquire, pulling out my pack of cigarettes and lighter from my jacket pocket. "I don't know if my habit can take that." *Or my cursed heart...*

"No," she quietly replies, and that vulnerable simp within me tries his damnedest to ignore the undertone of longing in that one simple word.

Are they trying for another child? Is that why she asked about her palm? Why her pulse quickened...

Something that feels a lot like jealousy churns in my solar plexus. Lighting up, I pull a long drag and let the smoke out on a discontented sigh of my own. *Why is the thought of Vanna falling pregnant with his kid again, ripping apart the remnants of my soul? They're fucking married!*

"I was there that night... When you married him." The words spill forth of their own volition. Perhaps I am a glutton for pain.

"I know." Her voice is low and contemplative. She removes her hat and holds it against her lap, then runs her fingers through her long, dark hair.

I remember how beautiful she looked in her wedding dress and pagan-esque flower crown... My gaze drifts to the wedding band on her finger, and I swallow, another painful knot forming in my throat.

"So, you found—"

"*True Love.*" She turns to face me again. The look in her eyes, willing me to understand and accept something a large part of me refuses to fully. "Yes. I did."

"Did you leave it behind?" I ask, though I know she isn't simply talking about my lighter.

She reaches down into her purse and pulls out my old brass Zippo. "I kept it safe for you. I knew you'd be back someday." She smiles, as if attempting to make light of the situation.

Knew... Or hoped?

Fear prevents me from asking out loud.

She playfully tosses the lighter back to me, and I catch it against my chest.

"I left it for you, to remind you of my promise. Of the things I said that night... *That I would burn it all down...*for you."

Her eyes lower from mine, and she turns to look back out at the lake. "I know why you left it." I barely hear her whisper on the breeze that catches a few tendrils of her hair. She lifts her face to the moon, and I can't help but stare at her profile. Such a lovely creature. Such a genuinely pure soul. It almost hurts to drink her in.

"I have no love for your husband, Vanna...but you...are another story entirely."

"Damien..." she sighs my name for the first time in three long years, and something deep inside the dark hollow of my chest aches with a fierceness that nearly steals the breath from my lungs. She turns to stare back at me. I wait, but the silence stretches on until hope shatters upon her next words. "I should probably get back to the Gazebo before the hosts realize I'm not where they're paying me to be. If they haven't noticed my absence already."

No...don't go... "You'll be paid regardless."

Her brows knit together, prompting a confession.

"I may have strong-armed the mayor into convincing his wife to offer you this gig... It was my way of trying to help... Whilst orchestrating a little time with you, *alone*. Your husband, *rather adamantly, I might add*, mentioned some *nonsense* about staying away from you." *As if I'm capable!*

"I'm sure he did." She doesn't seem angry. "He's very protective."

"I'm quite familiar with the inclination."

"Because you regret everything," she says, rather pointedly.

"I won't deny that... But...there is so much more, Vanna..."

"It's not something we can overcome in one night," she speaks rapidly, cutting me off as if she might dread all that needs to be said between us as much as I do. "Maybe I should go home. Thanks for arranging this."

"Which part?"

She only smiles as she stands, but then asks, "What was the card you pulled earlier? The one you obviously didn't want me to see."

"The Devil."

She purses her lips for a moment, giving me a sympathetic look before she reaches out to place her hand on my shoulder. It takes everything in me not to react to her willing touch, but my heart races, nonetheless.

"You're not the Devil, Damien," she says, her words offering a comfort I'm not sure I deserve.

I don't want to explain the real reason why pulling that card among the others in that spread upset me. It had nothing to do with the actual Devil at all.

"Are you certain?" I try to sound humorous. "Your husband is convinced." When she removes her hand from me, I close my eyes upon the loss. "I want your forgiveness, Vanna," I confess. "I want to earn your forgiveness for everything I put you through. Everything I brought upon you. But I don't want to hear those words from you until you truly mean them." I open my eyes to gaze up at her again. "I'll know it when you do."

She nods slowly, and when she finally speaks, her words are wrought with pain. "I'm glad...because I'm not prepared to offer that to you, yet. Not until you tell me the truth... And even then..."

When tears well up in her eyes, I fight the nearly overwhelming urge to jump up and hold her in my arms... But I wouldn't dare touch her like that... Not yet.

I am sorry, Vanna... So, so fucking sorry...

She brushes her tears away from her cheeks impatiently, then grabs her purse, slipping it over her shoulder once again.

"There aren't words able to express how badly you hurt us..." She barely manages a shaky whisper, and I hang my head in shame. Unable to meet her eyes, I stare instead at the engraved words on my Zippo. Without another word, she walks away from me.

Crushed by the overwhelming weight of my complete unworthiness of even being in her presence, I watch as she makes her way back toward the mansion, disappearing within the swaying branches of the weeping willow trees.

Vanna

Most of the lights are off when I step inside our home and quietly lock the deadbolt behind me. Peering into the living room, I'm able to make out Dean and Ace asleep on the couch in the glow of the flatscreen above the mantle. The credits of the movie they've fallen asleep to scroll by to the song *'You'll Be In My Heart'* by Phil Collins. After slipping out of my boots, I tiptoe closer to the back of the leather couch and glance down at them.

Dean is asleep on his back, one arm tucked behind his head, the other hooked protectively around Ace, who is soundly sleeping half against his father's side, half sprawled across his chest. Smiling at them, I fight the urge to gently run my fingers through Dean's hair and brush those few unruly strands back. It might wake him, though, and they look so peaceful right now.

Deciding to let them sleep, I walk quietly to the bedroom to change into my usual oversized t-shirt and shorts for bed.

Legion: Book 3

While I hang up my dress in the closet, I wonder if Dean will be disappointed over my failure to bring up Legion's leverage. He never actually asked me to, but was he hoping I would?

I make my way to my purse sitting on top of the dresser and pull out the tip jar tucked inside. A one-hundred-dollar bill immediately catches my eye as I place the jar down. There are quite a few more bills in here than I'd originally thought. I unscrew the cap and reach inside to remove a small wad of hundreds tucked into the middle of a few fives and ones.

An even grand in tip money...

"Legion..." I sigh, thinking back on all that transpired tonight while I count out the rest of the cash. He was the reason I was offered the gig in the first place. He probably negotiated an offer I wouldn't refuse to get me there. Glancing at the witch hat I'd tossed into the armchair in the corner of the room, my thoughts wander back to the costume originally delivered to my home earlier today... *Was Legion behind that detail, as well?*

My heart beats a little faster as I recall the tattoo on his shoulder. *The half-skull portrait of an old-school-style fortune teller.* He'd told me the piece was in memory of his mother. He strongly implied they weren't exactly the fondest of memories... Yet, he wanted me to dress the part tonight.

Realizing my hand somehow gravitated on its own to the base of my throat, I impatiently pull it away and snatch up the money he covertly added to my sad little tip-jar. Staring down at it, I can't help but release a sorrowful sigh.

Oh, Legion...

Chapter 17

Vanna

"Alright, Ace is with Rosita and Mia for the night," Dean says, walking into the bathroom while I finish applying mascara in the mirror. I'm not much of a makeup wearer, but I know I'll be around club girls decked out to the nines tonight, so I'm making an effort.

"Either Viking or I will pick him up sometime tomorrow morning. You almost ready to go?" He grabs the comb from the stone counter beside the sink and slicks back his hair. "This charity run starts in forty-five minutes. There's a party at the Jokers' afterwards we need to attend." He doesn't seem too thrilled about that last part.

I curiously look at him through the mirror while tucking my makeup back into the little zippered pouch to bring with me. "Do you plan on us coming home tonight?"

"Yeah. Might be late. Why?"

I open the drawer near the sink and remove the little blue disc of contraceptives. "I take these in the morning now." I hold them up for Dean to see. "If we're not going to be here, and you do want me to continue taking them, I should bring them with me."

"Oh…" He stares at it contemplatively for a moment, and a little glimmer of hope flickers within me. "Bring them. Just in case."

I quirk a brow at him in an attempt to disguise the crushing disappointment. "Missing one dose in the middle of the pack isn't as risky as the first week."

"Why be risky at all?" he asks, tossing the comb back onto the counter.

"*So says the biker,*" I tease. "Risk-taking is in your DNA."

Scowling playfully back at me, he smacks my leather-clad ass then walks out of the bathroom, telling me to hurry up.

This particular charity ride raised funds for a local children's hospital, and multiple clubs within the region participated. Once the official event closed, everyone headed to the after-party hosted at the JoCo Jokers' legendary clubhouse to celebrate.

We pull through the black iron gates and ride up the long, ancient-oak-bordered driveway to an area designated for parking in front of the old *convent-turned-biker-clubhouse*.

Dean's brother Daniel is standing guard by the cathedral-style doors. He's wearing a denim cut over his leather jacket, but it doesn't have any patches on it, besides one that says 'Prospect'. Trippy is standing beside him. She touches his arm in a brief but supportive way, then descends the steps as we park and dismount Serene. I wonder if they're an item now?

Immediately, Trippy informs Cherry and me of one more fundraiser taking place tonight. "We're calling it the Old Lady Auction." She smiles as if we should be excited.

"Oh, and what does this entail?" I ask.

"You just have to dance with the highest bidder. One song of their choosing. It'll be fun, so far everyone is in, but it isn't mandatory. Your Old Man's permission is a requirement to participate, of course." She winks playfully at Dean. "The clubs that offer up their Ol' Ladies get to decide which charity the money they bring in goes to. You could raise some extra cash for Medusa's Gates tonight, if you want."

I glance at Dean when I hear him release an exasperated sigh. He doesn't appear thrilled by this either. "It's for charity." I shrug awkwardly. "It's just a dance…I don't want to be the *only* Ol' Lady that doesn't participate."

"*For charity*," Dean begrudgingly concedes.

"The auction is later… Right now," Trippy turns to Dean once more, and her typical jovial tone seems more subdued. "Slice wants to speak with you and your crew."

Dean cocks his chin at Viking and Viper, then takes my hand, giving it a little squeeze as we follow Trippy up the steps to head inside. Dean and Daniel exchange curt nods when we pass, but say nothing to each other.

They've been civil whenever they happen to cross paths at these biker events and when we arrange visits with Maddie, but that's about as much progress as they've made in repairing their relationship.

Still, they're doing better than I am with my family. We receive cards around the holidays from them, and my parents always send Ace money for his birthday, but my family has yet to reach out to me about meeting their first and only grandson. Sometimes I wonder if things would be different if they knew Ace and I almost didn't make it.

The Jokers' clubhouse is the same man cave it was the last time I was here. Loud music, loud men, scantily clad sweet-butts dancing around poles and catering to their guests. The marble fountain has once again been turned into a huge ice cooler loaded with bottles and cans of beer and soft drinks.

"I'll take Vanna and Cherry out back." Trippy slips herself between Cherry and me, looping her arms around ours.

"I'll come find you as soon as I can," Dean says, always reluctant to leave my side at these events.

I watch him walk off with Viking and Viper in tow before Trippy tugs Cherry and me out back.

"I need to talk to you two," Trippy says, though she's keeping her voice conspiratorially low as we walk through the crowd and out to the large back patio and manicured grounds. Like last time, there's a makeshift stage and a band playing covers of rock n' roll songs.

"What's going on?" Cherry asks when Trippy leads us to a less populated area near a fire pit in the far corner of the patio.

"It's about Daniel… He needs Dean's blessing in order to be patched in with the Jokers as a full-fledged member." Her wide eyes zero in on me, full of hope.

"*Oh*… Are you and Daniel together?"

"Unofficially, yes…but technically, until he's a patched member, I can't be his Ol' Lady," Trippy explains. "Slice won't give the okay until, *or unless*, Dean approves. Normally, this wouldn't involve another club outside of ours, but Dean and Daniel are a special circumstance."

Legion: Book 3

Cherry and I exchange glances. Although we're both Ol' Ladies, and we understand how things work in this MC culture, we can't help but feel some rules are ridiculous at times. We both know Trippy has put in her time with the Jokers, and if this will make *her* happy, whether it involves Dean's brother or not...

I shrug at Cherry.

"Alright," Cherry nods.

"We'll see what we can do," I say.

A bright smile immediately washes over Trippy's anxious expression.

"This is still *Dean and Daniel* we're talking about... So, no promises, but we'll talk to him."

Trippy gleefully scurries off, and Cherry and I head for a minibar to grab a couple of cocktails.

"A woman's work is never done," Cherry jokes.

"Who'd have thought we'd be the ones helping *Daniel* with a new woman?" I have to shake my head.

A little mischievous smirk pulls at Cherry's lips. "*Lucinda will be thrilled*," she says, making a scissoring gesture with her fingers. We both laugh a bit diabolically at the potential opportunity to dismantle one of Lucinda's *'safety nets'*.

LEGION

He's dead before he knows it. A stifled gasp of surprise escapes him just as my hand clamps over his mouth. I open his throat with the blade gripped in my other hand. It cuts through his carotid artery like warm butter, and I assist his collapse to the ground while he rapidly loses consciousness and departs this world in a pool of blood.

A merciful death, all things considered. The other two inside the old cook trailer may not be so lucky, however, it is my hope that one of them survives... Way out here in the country, far from anyone who might hear all that is about to go down in this singlewide-turned-meth lab, I'm not too concerned with the crescendo of this structure's impending demise. There are others, after all.

Crouching beside the corpse, I wipe my knife off on his shirt before slipping it back in its sheath at my side, then I remove the beer bottle tucked within the deep pocket of my leather jacket. It contains a homemade napalm mixture, and I twist the top off to stuff a handkerchief down the neck, soaking it in the contents with just enough fabric protruding to act as a fuse.

"Put on some fuckin' tunes, man!" one of them shouts inside.

While I get into position outside the kitchen window, *Bawitdaba* by Kid Rock blares loudly from within.

With a flick of my thumb, *True Love* ignites the end of the handkerchief, and the flame rapidly consumes the fabric.

I send the Molotov cocktail crashing through the window, then immediately sprint for the van parked out front. The cook trailer explodes as I take cover behind the van.

Screaming, engulfed in flames from the waist down, one of the cooks staggers out the front door, flailing in a desperate attempt to extinguish himself.

Gun drawn, I approach while he manages to shed the burning coveralls and drags himself across the ground, away from the remnants of the burning trailer.

"*W-what are you doing?*" he rasps, gawking up at me in utter shock.

Aiming the barrel between his crossed eyes, a grin stretches my mouth as I tell him, *"Just trying to love someone…"*

DEAN

"This whole mess is a result of a beef your crew had with the Chrome Demons MC." Slice shoots me a pointed glare. "It's only fair you help us clean up the mess Legion left behind."

"We're already in agreement. We have every intention of assisting your crew however we can with clearing these dregs out of your county as well."

The walkie-talkie beside Slice crackles, and a prospect's voice comes through. "Boss…we have a…situation at the front gate."

Slice picks it up to respond. "What is it?"

"Says his name is *Legion*…and that he's brought a party favor courtesy of the Saviors MC."

Slice cocks a brow at me.

"I have no idea what this is about," I tell him. "I didn't authorize whatever this is. I didn't even know he'd show up."

"Speak of the Devil, I guess." Slice lets out a sigh.

Legion: Book 3

"He seems to have a fuckin' knack for that," I mutter.

Slice lifts the walkie again. "Alright, Prospect, let him through. We'll meet him outside."

Legion is grinning ear to ear when he exits the van, admiring the former nunnery turned MC headquarters, while he walks around the front of the vehicle to stand a few feet from us. *"Now this... This is a clubhouse!"*

"The fuck are you doing here?" I demand.

"This is a charity event, is it not? I'm here to support your causes." He turns from admiring the clubhouse to face me head-on, grin transforming to something more antagonistic. *"All of them."*

"What's in the van?" Slice asks, getting right to the point. "I assume you've brought something substantial, or you would have come here on a *motorcycle*, considering this event is for *bikers*."

"Ah, yes. Your means to an eager end!" Legion smiles more genuinely at the Jokers' president and grips the handle of the van's sliding door. "I wouldn't dream of crashing one of your legendary parties *empty-handed*." Legion opens the door, gesturing to the interior of the dark van with a theatrical bow.

Slice leans into me, "He's an odd one. You weren't exaggerating."

Something lying on the floorboard, hidden beneath a filthy blanket, looks awfully human-shaped, and we're all silent now. Except for Viking, who lets out a surprised chuckle. "Holy shit. He's got an *actual* murder van."

Legion grabs the stained blanket and pulls it off like he's performing some kind of magic trick, revealing a gagged and bound man who appears to have seen better days.

"The fuck, man? Who is that?" one of Slice's Sergeant at Arms asks.

"What did you do?" I manage to grit out.

"Anything for love," Legion taunts, that mocking sneer twisting his mouth again, those creepy grey eyes boring into me.

"Why does he smell like you pulled him out of a fire?" Nostrils flaring, Viking leans in closer.

"Technically, he crawled out of one," Legion says. "The other two weren't as fortunate."

"You took out another meth lab?" I ask.

Legion nods.

"This is the third one, now." I narrow my gaze at him. "How are you so knowledgeable of these locations?"

I don't miss the micro expression of resentment before Legion quickly recovers. "Well, I *was* the mastermind behind the original network," he coolly replies. "Seems a few locations are still in operation. This crispy prick is going to fill us in on the rest."

"Get him out of the van," Slice orders a few of his men. Two of them step forward, grabbing the guy by his bound arms. He grunts and groans behind his gag as they drag him out. "Make him comfortable in the basement. And use the fuckin' cellar doors. We don't need our guests asking questions." He turns to Legion and me. "You two and your crew, follow me."

"Will there be a tour?" Legion asks with grating enthusiasm as we follow Slice up the stone steps to the tall cathedral-style doors. Slice only glances over his shoulder to give Legion a once-over, before he looks at me, his expression reading as if he's asking whether or not Legion is serious. I just shake my head.

Vanna

"Who are those women?" I ask Cherry, attempting to subtly gesture in the direction of the group of female bikers. It's obvious they aren't sweet-butts. None of them even remotely entertains any of the male attention focused on them.

"They're a fairly new MC," Cherry says. "A few of them used to be club girls of the Asphalt Knights MC. They formed their own thing after the Knights disbanded."

I look at her curiously. "The Knights aren't an MC anymore?"

"No. They tried to make it work, but after everything they went through with the Chrome Demons," Cherry lets out a sigh, then takes a sip of her drink. She doesn't seem to know quite what to say.

"What do you mean?" I press.

"A lot of them liked the taste of what Legion had to offer. Drugs… Prostitution. Fast, easy cash. A lot of them decided they preferred to go outlaw. Some decided to step away from club life altogether."

I'm not sure what to say. It's astounding, the ripple effect of everything Legion has done. I glance back in their direction and notice the blonde president of the Steel Vixens already looking at me. Something in her expression seems almost hostile.

"Do they blame us? The blonde one doesn't look like she's a fan."

Cherry shifts beside me to stand facing them, not bothering with any subtleties. "That's Val. Their president. She's kind of a hard-ass."

"You know them?"

"Some of them. Jett and Boop are nice." Cherry shrugs. "I'll go ask her what her problem is if she's bothering you."

"*No*, don't do that." I place a hand on Cherry's arm to turn her away from them and back toward the band playing on stage. She laughs at me. "I don't want to start anything. Especially when we're not even in Saviors' territory. I already have a feeling Dean is trying to smooth things over with the Jokers. He doesn't need me causing him any more drama. Especially not at a charity event, in front of these other MCs."

"You might not have a choice," Cherry says, peeking over her dainty shoulder. "Looks like she's sending one of them over here."

"Great," I mutter under my breath, sparing them a quick glance. The lady biker walking up to me is at least wearing a friendly smile now, though it doesn't make her any less intimidating. I glance down from her gorgeous face to note the road name embroidered on her cut. Jett, Vice President of the Steel Vixens MC.

"Vanna, right?" she asks in a Brooklyn accent so thick I wonder for a moment if she's playing it up. "You're Dean Keegan's Ol' Lady?" She looks me up and down now that we're standing a mere two feet apart, shaking her head and lightly biting her lower lip as if in awe or disbelief of something. I'm not sure if she's checking me out or what, though I did notice she's only been dancing with other women tonight.

"Yes, I'm Vanna." I attempt to smile pleasantly.

"Damn, Val wasn't kiddin'..." She practically sighs, and although I have no idea what she meant by that, there's a detectable level of trepidation in her tone. "Look, gorgeous," Jett begins again, "We're gonna have to have an uncomfortable conversation at some point. Sooner rather than later. But since this is a charity event, and there's already some rumblings about an *uninvited guest* showing up, this is just a heads up for now."

"I have no idea what you're talking about."

"Yeah...we were afraid of that." She glances back at her blonde president, giving her a quick, tight-lipped look. The one they call Val seems even less amused now, as if she were hoping for a different signal from her VP. The blonde cocks her head in a gesture for Jett to return to their group before she turns and heads back into the clubhouse with the other members of her MC.

"What the hell is going on?" I ask.

"We'll be in touch." Jett winks then walks off after her crew as if this cryptic conversation never took place.

DEAN

The cool, damp air of the stone cellar still reeks of weed, even though it's been years since the MC used this basement as a grow room. Once the heavy door shuts behind us and we descend the old cement staircase, not even a murmur or a footstep can be heard from the party raging overhead. With the music blasting upstairs, even if this guy did shout, *for whatever reason*, nobody would be able to hear him.

Beneath what had once been a room full of grow lights, now swapped out for linear fluorescents, Legion's *party gift* sits slumped in a metal chair between two of the Jokers' Sergeant at Arms. He's still blindfolded, arms bound behind his back, but now, in addition to his restraints, he's wearing a set of sound-cancelling headphones.

"Does this guy know where you were taking him?" Slice asks, shifting his attention to Legion.

"No," Legion says.

"What *does* he know?"

"I brought him here to find out," Legion stoically replies, and I can tell his nonchalant demeanor is beginning to wear on Slice's nerves. The Jokers' president scans him over slowly, before turning back to me.

"So, you two have made amends?" He doesn't bother concealing any skepticism on the matter.

I cast a quick glance at Legion, standing there with an expectant smile. "I wouldn't go that far."

"It wasn't so long ago when it would have been *you* bound in this cellar," Slice says, eyes narrowed on Legion, assessing him for any sort of reaction. "*Had we managed to track you down*... Quite the master of evasion you turned out to be."

"I'm a man of many talents." Legion's grin doesn't falter. "Of which are at your disposal tonight, should you require them."

"An enemy turned asset?" Slice glances back at me, waiting for my take on the dynamics of our situation.

Before I can denounce him, Legion clears his throat, pulling Slice's attention back to him. "*An unfortunate misunderstanding*, as things turned out," he begins, but I cut him off before he can spew any more bullshit.

"That's a fuckin' understatement."

"Come now, Keegan. *We're practically brothers* at this point, aren't we? Especially in the sense you're *familiar* with." That wicked grin doesn't meet his eyes, rubbing what happened with Daniel and Lucinda in my face, as if he's got a fuckin' snowball's chance in hell of actually getting with my wife.

Slice presses a warning hand against my chest when I take an aggressive step toward the Demon. "*Not here*," he insists, tilting his head toward the guy bound to the chair. "It's bad enough we've got this dreg to contend with once we're done with him... You're going to have to handle whatever's going on with Legion on your own time, *on your own turf*. Enough of the fallout between you two has already spilled into our territory."

Legion glances around the other bikers among us, pretending to search for someone in particular. "*The little Road Captain* isn't among your men," he says, callous eyes landing on me once again. "Have you not held your official vote on what we discussed?"

"*Time and place*." I glare at him. Legion only brought up Axel to remind me of the leverage he's holding over us. A warning and reminder that I can't kill him.

"*Ah... I see. He's in the dark.*"

"Was that another fucking threat?"

Slice clears his throat and interjects again, pulling the focus of the room back to the reason we agreed to meet after the charity run in the first place. "Gentlemen, hash your shit out on your own time. My primary concern right now, is my county." He shifts his glare to Legion. "And you're the root of the reason there is a problem to begin with."

"Which is why I snagged this one." Legion cocks his head at the guy he brought, then shoots me a glare. "Despite what *this one* would have you believe, I am making an effort to assist you all in this cleanup. It wasn't any of you that eradicated the last two cook locations."

"I'm willing to entertain the idea of you wanting to make amends," Slice says.

"Before I begin, his fate will determine the methods I proceed with." Legion grins darkly, waiting for Slice to decide whether this guy is going to survive his interrogation or not. "I noticed there is an old cemetery at the far end of this lot."

"He leaves here alive." Slice doesn't entertain Legion's not-so-subtle suggestion at all.

Legion looks mildly disappointed. "With all due respect, gentlemen, the only way to end this incessant game of whack-a-mole, at least for a while, is to *kill the fucking moles*." They stare each other down before Legion continues, "I get it, Pres... You're walking the *straight and narrow* these days... But there are only so many cook trailers we can *blow up*, before there's *blowback*... This *minion* is just that... He may not even know who's at the top of *Mount Meth*, but I made a promise to someone." He shifts his icy glare to me, though I know I'm not the one he made that promise to. "A promise I intend to keep."

"Keegan said it best. *We can't save the fuckin' world*. I just want it known... *My* county is *off limits*," Slice says. "Weed is one thing. Meth. Heroine. We don't condone the production or distribution of that shit. As long as we're clean and clear, that's where my concern begins and ends."

I'm sure he hates admitting it as much as I do, but he isn't wrong. There's only so much we can do to keep our families and civilians safe.

Legion nods, but I recognize defiance in his eyes when I see it. He isn't content to simply push this operation beyond county borders. He wants the shot-callers at the top of *Mount Meth*... And I hate the fact I fucking agree with Legion of all people... But one thing at a time.

Slice walks over to the old map of Jocsan County tacked up on a mounted corkboard and rips it down. He walks back to Legion and shoves the map against his chest, forcing Legion to take it. "Find out where the rest of these places are. Where they're set up to push it. And then, *get to work*."

Legion nods curtly.

"Kill the lights, except for the row he's under," Slice orders, though to no one in particular. One of his guys moves to the wall, flicking off a few switches until most of the room is cast in darkness. One of the remaining lights above the guy hums and flickers. The Joker steps back to reach up and twist the tubular bulb into place, and the flickering stops.

With another impatient gesture from Slice, the other Sergeant snatches the bandana from the guy's eyes. Legion's offering blinks rapidly, head swiveling in an attempt to regain his bearings. Most of us are still standing in the shadows, obscured from his view. We all flipped our cuts inside out before coming down here to play it safe, so he wouldn't be able to identify our crews right off the cuff.

"You two, stay down here," Slice orders the two SAs. "Make sure this prick leaves here alive." He shoots Legion a final warning glare before turning back to me. "Let's go."

Before I can break away and go in search of Vanna, Slice places a hand briefly on my shoulder, halting me when we return to the large main room of the clubhouse. I turn to face him.

"He's got something on you." It isn't so much a question as it is an observation.

"You're perceptive." I sigh, adjusting the way my cut rests on my shoulders now that I'm wearing it right-side out again. "In a way, I suppose I'm relieved. I don't want to think about what message my tolerance of him is sending. But yeah… Anything happens to Legion, even if it isn't *my* doing…"

"I get it. It was the only scenario where any of this made sense. And based on his reputation, I figure whatever he's got is pretty substantial."

"It is." I scan the room and spot Axel shooting pool with a couple of the younger Jokers, blissfully unaware of the axe Legion has dangling over his head, or the chains he's got the rest of us bound in.

"The kid?" Slice asks, a rare tone of sympathy in his words. He knows what Axel means to me. "I'll make sure my crew knows the Demon is off limits."

I nod. "I need to find my wife."

"She's probably getting ready for the last fundraiser." Slice nods toward the back doors. "That'll take place on the stage after the band wraps up."

Fuck. I forgot all about the *Ol' Lady Auction.* I hope whatever Legion is up to in the cellar keeps him busy at least long enough for the bidding portion of this event to conclude.

"I'll catch you later," I say, patting Slice on the back before I head for the doors.

I find Vanna with Cherry, talking at the far end of the checker stone patio, and slip my arm around her waist. Pulling her to me, I lower my mouth to her ear.

"Legion's here," I say softly.

"*What?*"

"*Legion* is here."

"Huh… Maybe that's what that biker woman was talking about," Vanna says to Cherry, then looks up at me. "She came up to me earlier. Before she could get to the point about anything, she mentioned someone without an invitation showed up, like it might be an issue or something. Where is he?"

"Working on a puzzle downstairs," I mutter.

She stares at me for a moment. "Yeah, I can't picture that, and I don't think you meant that literally anyway."

"Never mind. No pun intended, but I say we blow this joint and head back."

"Well… I already signed up for the auction…won't that look bad?"

I really don't care at the moment. However, before I can say anything else about it, the song the band is playing ends, and a Joker's Ol' Lady takes the stage to go over the rules of the auction.

"I think it's too late to bail now," Vanna says.

The woman on stage calls to rally everyone participating and begins to announce the rules. *All bids must be cash in hand,* being one of those rules. After the Poker Run portion of the charity ride, I'm damn near tapped out. A measly buck-fifty and some change, *maybe,* left in my wallet.

Vanna places her hand against my chest. "For charity, my love." She smiles, giving my chest a little pat before she steps away. I watch her walk up onto the makeshift stage with Cherry, where the bands have been playing live music until recently. A DJ has taken over the musical entertainment for the remainder of the party. She takes her place at the end of the considerable line of women, already waiting to be auctioned off for a dance to a song of the highest bidder's choosing.

"*Don't bid to win,*" she mouths to me with a knowing little smirk. Part of me wishes she wasn't aware of my financial concerns. It's not that we're in dire straits, not by a long shot. And I was mostly content with this whole idea, that is, *before Legion showed up.*

"*Right,*" I grit out. *It's just a dance.* We do something similar with the men in participating MCs at our fundraisers, where women enter a raffle for a chance at a ride on the back of our bikes. It takes place every year, and it really rakes in the cash. This is the same principle. It means nothing beyond raising money for charity. Vanna is fine with it. If she can tolerate another chick on the back of my bike for one ride once a year, I need to be fine with this as well.

One by one, our girls are bid on, bringing in between two hundred and three hundred each. I can't stop glancing down at my watch as time drags on, wishing Vanna had gotten on stage a little sooner. Of course, she'd go last. Finally, Vanna timidly steps forward, and I can feel a few sets of eyes familiar with my crazy land on me.

I force a smile, uncrossing my arms to clap for her in an attempt to convince those watching I've truly given my blessing, at least for the sake of charity. If nobody bids for fear of my reaction, she'll think it's her. I will not allow my territorial urges to undermine her fragile confidence.

The bidding starts at one hundred dollars, and the crowd remains silent... *Fuck my life!*

She shifts in her boots, painfully uncomfortable now, her gaze avoiding the crowd as she turns to look at Cherry standing next to her. I know it took every ounce of courage she has to even put herself out there like this.

I'm about to offer everything I've got left in my fucking wallet, when a raspy voice somewhere in the crowd calls out, "*Three grand! And an additional two for a second dance!*"

My heart sinks when Vanna's eyes widen in a surprise we all collectively share, and she scans the crowd for *her fuckin' hero...*

Jealousy sets my blood to boil, and I scour the crowd until my sight locks in on a proudly grinning Legion. *That fucking prick...* I can't swing six Gs to outbid him! I'm about to hit up Viking to hurry up and spot me some cash, when I hear Vanna's anxious voice ring out…

"*Sold!*" She's so eager to get off the stage… I don't blame her.

Legion removes a wad of cash from his leather jacket and licks his fingers. Flipping through the bills, he counts off five grand as he comes to stand before me. Lifting the money between those demonic fingers, and I'm sure *savoring the fucking moment*, he holds the cash out to me.

"There's an extra two hundred for a rain check on that second dance." He grins. "I'm afraid I'm a bit pressed for time tonight."

I snatch the cash from him and hand it off to one of the Jokers' sweet-butts in charge of collecting and recording the bids, all while attempting to retain my composure. "I thought you were *preoccupied*," I growl at him.

"Oh, I wouldn't miss out on *this*," he taunts.

"Now that you got your *grand entrance* bullshit out of your system."

His evil grin broadens. "*This party's just getting started*, Keegan."

The use of that fucking phrase is a clear indication he wants to get under my skin, and he knows Vanna can't hear him at this distance. I swallow my rage and remind myself, this is just a fucking dance. It means nothing. And neither she nor I is obligated to the impromptu terms of his bid. *One dance*. Tonight. That's all he's entitled to. We can hash out this fucking *rain check* later.

"You think throwing around your reward money is going to buy you a way in?" Viking demands.

An antagonistic sneer pulls at Legion's mouth. He doesn't bother looking away from me to answer Viking's question. "I don't know what you're talking about… *But it did just buy me a time with your wife*."

"*Fucker!*"

Before I can swing on him, Viking blocks me with a massive arm hooked around my chest, and Legion walks off to make his arrangements with the DJ.

"Don't let him get to you," Viking says, releasing me. "You know he just wants to get in your head. Vanna sees right through him, too."

"Vanna likes him for some goddamn inexplicable reason!"

"Vanna *tolerates* him, the same way we're all forced to."

"No…" I shift my burning stare from Legion's back to look up at my brother. "There's something else… *I can feel it*, Viking."

"Dean, the dude's been gone three years... You're being paranoid. Not that I don't sympathize, considering the shit you went through with Lucinda, but what you have with Vanna, it's solid, bro. She will never do what Lucinda did to you." He pats my shoulder.

"She's got some kind of soft spot for him."

Viking lets out an exasperated sigh. "Lost puppy syndrome. That's it, bro. Vanna's got a forgiving heart. Once she realizes this puppy is actually a *rabid wolf*, it's game over for Legion. Come on, this is just a dance for charity. He had to *pay* for this. It isn't like she had a say."

"Right...." But as with everything pertaining to Legion, it's more than this. It's not *just* a dance. It's everything the dance *represents*. I lower my voice so only Viking can hear me. "It's bad enough everyone sees me tolerating him... But now they get to see him *dancing with my wife*? After referencing that fuckin' rumor downstairs, too." I reach up to grip the back of my tensing neck. "That bullshit is gonna follow me forever."

"If it makes you feel any better, when the dance is over, let him know what you'll be doing with Vanna later." Viking chuckles. "You'll always have the upper hand when it comes to your wife, bro. She ain't no Lucinda."

For my own sanity, I might not even wait.

Vanna

"Looks like you're up first," Cherry says. "I think Legion just bribed the DJ."

"Dean has to be livid." I glance around for him as we descend the steps of the stage together. Dean is no longer standing where I last saw him in the crowd. Cherry tugs my arm, pulling my attention back to her. She points, and I realize Dean is waiting for me at the bottom.

"I'll catch you later," Cherry says, practically handing me off to Dean when we reach him.

"I'm sorry, I didn't know he'd—"

"It's not your fault," Dean cuts me off mid-sentence, wrapping an arm around my waist. He pulls me off to the side of the dance floor. "Just do me a favor while you're out there with him."

"Of course." I don't know what else to say, but I want to reassure him. Staring up into his dark, heated gaze, I'm met with a mixture of rage and unease.

"Think of me." That sorrowful look in his eyes can't be disguised by the stern tone of his voice.

"Dean..." I sigh.

"When he's got you in his arms, I want you to think of me."

I reach up to touch his face and stroke his stubbled jaw. "This doesn't mean anything. He could be anyone."

"But he isn't *anyone*... It's Legion."

"*Speak of the devil!*" That familiar gravelly voice comes up behind me. "Mind if I cut in?"

Dean pulls me tighter against him, bowing his head to press his lips to mine. I'd laugh at this entire territorial display if I didn't know Dean's past and the very real fears that still haunt him, even despite our happy marriage.

For my husband, I wrap my arms around his neck, arching up on my toes to mold my body and lips to his, giving all who care to notice a real show of just who I belong to. As we deepen the kiss, our tongues moving together in a slow dance of our own, one of his strong hands moves to firmly grip my ass, pulling me harder against him still. Even through my leather jeans, I can feel his length hardening between us. A couple of guys in the crowd whistle, egging him on with shouts of encouragement.

After a few moments, Dean presses his forehead to mine and breathlessly whispers against my now kiss-swollen lips, "Come to me when this is over... *If I stay...*" his words trail off, but he doesn't have to finish the statement for me to understand. It's best if he doesn't watch, probably for more reasons than I can even fathom right now. My mind is spinning from the few shots I've already consumed, and his searing hot kiss that always makes the world around us fade away.

"Come on, let's grab a beer," Viking says, suddenly appearing beside my husband.

Dean releases me and we part, but he doesn't take his eyes from me, willing me to remember his request.

"*I will.*" I smile up at him.

His gaze turns cold upon shifting his attention to Legion. Dean drops his hand, unabashedly adjusting himself.

"I'm sure you'll enjoy your fucking dance," Dean growls. "Guess what I'll be enjoying the rest of the night while you're off doing grunt work. I'll always get the last dance."

Viking chuckles, slinging an arm around Dean's shoulder, then drags him off toward one of the outdoor bar areas before anything can escalate.

Taking a deep breath, I gather myself and turn around to face a seemingly unfazed, patiently waiting Legion.

"Turning me down last time seems to have come back to cost you," Legion says, a teasing reminder of rejecting him on the dancefloor at the Halloween party.

"Seems like it cost *you*. Both times," I barely get the quip of sarcasm out before my nerves get the better of me. "What song did you choose for three grand? Did you know about this little auction? Or is it a common practice of yours to carry around that much bribery cash?"

He cocks his head to the side. "You seem nervous, sweet one. *Don't be*. It's all for a good cause!"

"Which one? We all know everything you say, everything you do, has more behind it than the obvious."

"I assure you, my motives are above reproach. The fact your husband is displeased is simply *a bonus*."

I try not to groan, "I should have stayed home with Ace."

"*Nonsense!* Mothers need to *escape* their children from time to time, *don't they?*" He seems to study me a little harder upon asking that question.

I shake my head, trying to clear my racing thoughts while my anxiety continues to climb. "I'm really not the best dancer."

"Well, *I'm a really strong lead*." Legion grins.

I reluctantly accept his offered hand and allow him to pull me onto the dance floor.

"I hope you like the song," he goes on as we walk together. "The Rock genre fits the event, and it's a power ballad known for its grandiose arrangements, emotive vocals, and enigmatic lyrics. Though some of the lyrics are left open to interpretation. In my opinion, it only adds to the song's mystique and emotional depth."

Legion stops abruptly once we reach the center, practically yanking me off balance as he faces me and pulls me to him, and I stumble into his chest. The faint aroma of whatever aftershave or cologne he's got on takes me by surprise as I right myself. It smells like chrysanthemum or sage, a honey-sweet and somewhat soapy scent, with a hint of smokiness, though I'd expect a note of smoke on him.

"I don't appreciate the *man-handling.*" I glare at him while he arranges us into a very purposeful position.

"Apologies." Legion's smile is undeterred as he slips one hand around my waist. He plants it firmly at the small of my back and pulls me a bit closer.

I get another whiff of his scent, and this time I recognize it. We sold smudge bundles of the herb at the Ametrine Cauldron. *It's mugwort...*

Straightening almost pridefully, like a damn peacock, Legion lifts our joined hands a bit higher.

"This is hardly the environment for a *waltz*, Legion!" I already feel my face flushing with the borderline-painful heat of embarrassment. When the first rapid notes of a piano begin to play, and an electric guitar joins in, I immediately recognize the song. *"Could you have chosen anything worse?"* I nearly shriek as he takes the lead.

"Had I more time to consider my options...but this one suits, don't you think?" Legion grins, whirling me around the dancefloor while the late Meatloaf belts out his famous Rock N' Roll ballad. The lyrics of *I Would Do Anything For Love* speak volumes for all to hear.

"*Dean is going to kill you,*" I try to whisper, keeping my eyes on Legion. I'm afraid to look anywhere but up at him.

"We both know that isn't going to happen," Legion says. I glare at him before he spins me around and pulls me back to him. "Besides, I didn't choose this song with your *husband* in mind, Vanna."

In a series of underarm turns, spins, and dips, Legion guides me across the floor with surprising ease, even despite my missteps, which he manages to disguise like they're part of the dance. He really is a strong lead. I'd be impressed if I wasn't busy staving off a panic attack.

"*But you won't do* what?" I ask, the song finally nearing its climactic end.

"*Quit,*" he replies with a cocky grin, though it seems to fade to a more serious expression when I don't find his reply amusing. He lets out a sigh before he goes on to elaborate. "I won't betray your trust... I won't hurt you again, Vanna... *I won't do that.*"

Now that the song has come to its close, and I've fulfilled my end of the bargain for the sake of charity, I glance around, searching the applauding crowd for Dean. He must have meant it when he told me to come find him. He really didn't watch.

"Will you honor the deal?" Legion asks, gripping my hand a little tighter.

I turn back to face him. "What deal?"

He releases me. "A second dance…another time. I—"

"Sure," I say, trying not to sound too cold or eager to part ways, but I need to go find Dean. I promised him I would.

"Splendid… Then I will look forward to it and use the time before then to think upon a suiting song." Something shifts in his smile when he adds, "Perhaps *Dream A Little Dream Of Me?*"

"You do that." I force an uncomfortable smile before turning from him and hurrying off in the direction I last saw Dean and Viking go.

They're not at the outdoor bar, and as far as I can tell, they're not even outside anymore.

I make my way past groups of partying bikers and their women, walking inside the clubhouse through the back double doors.

I spot Viking across the room, lounging by a stripper pole with a beer in his hand, watching a club girl twirl around in her leather bikini. For whatever reason, he looks more aggravated than entertained.

"Where did Dean go?" I ask him.

"He's out front with Serene."

"Why do you seem so…gloomy?"

"I'm not the guy you should be concerned about right now, Vanna."

"Don't tell me you're mad at me." I frown.

"I'm not. *Go*," he grunts, pointing to the front doors. Something has Viking annoyed, but I don't have the bandwidth right now to cater to his problems, too.

As soon as I step through the big cathedral-style doors, Dean is there, leaning against the seat of his motorcycle while he polishes off another beer and chucks it to the side of the lawn.

"Hey," I say, descending the steps to him.

"I don't want to talk about it," he grumbles.

"We don't have to talk about it." I slip my fingers inside the shoulder area of his leather cut and give him a playful tug, attempting to flirt a little smile out of him. "But I might have to sit these biker events out if I'm going to be roped into some form of dancing every time I go to one."

"It's not every time."

"But when it happens, it's always a focal point. I still get embarrassed whenever I think back on your birthday belly dance that first year."

Dean cracks the faintest of smiles. "I thought it was hot."

"I'm glad you think so. And I can tell you're pissed off. You know I only did this for charity, right?"

"I know… But do *you know*, this five-thousand-dollar stunt Legion pulled has *nothing* to do with being charitable?"

"I… I think he's…*trying*…" The words come out slowly as I watch Dean's expression morph from hopeful to astonished. And not in a good way.

"Are you serious? After that?"

"Again, I'm not saying he goes about things in the right way, exactly, but…" I wince at the way Dean's jaw tenses and his nostrils flare, sucking in a long breath. "I really do think he's *trying*."

"I'll tell you what the fuck he's *trying*, Vanna. He's *trying* to get to my wife."

"What?"

"He's already got you on his side." Dean pushes himself away from his motorcycle and begins to pace the stone driveway.

"I'm on *your* side."

He scoffs. "You don't even see it happening."

"What was I supposed to do? Refuse him? Slap all that money out of the hands of organizations that help people? *Anybody* could have bid, Dean. It just happened to be Legion."

"That excessive bid, Vanna… *Come on*, doll. Open those pretty eyes, baby. *It wasn't gonna be anyone else.*"

"*Nobody else* was bidding…" I begin to explain, but I'm not so sure I should add maybe Legion bid just to save me from the embarrassment of being the only woman up there no one wanted to dance with.

"That was my fault." Dean winces. "A bunch of guys looked at *me* when you were up, trying to gauge whether or not *I* was genuinely alright with it. *They would have bid*, Vanna. Another Goddamned second, and they all would have bid. But Legion knocked them all off the board before they could. Made himself look like your fucking *white Knight* in the process."

Legion: Book 3

When I don't know how to respond, Dean's furrowed brows pitch upward. *"He fucking did, didn't he?"*

"All I know is that it was an embarrassing situation, and I was relieved to be able to get off that stage. In the moment, I really didn't care who got me off."

He scoffs, then his jaw slides forward, and he shakes his head. For a moment, I wonder if it was my choice of words. "This was about so much more than a dance. This was a fucking power move he rubbed my face in, and he made a damn spectacle of it in front of everyone."

I shift uncomfortably in my boots. "Dean…do you think it's possible that maybe…you're reading a little too much into it? That you're giving Legion a little *too much* credit?"

His eyes narrow at me. "I'm aware I've admitted to you on multiple occasions I'm fuckin' crazy, doll. *What I'm not* is delusional. *What I won't do* is ever underestimate that demonic prick. I'd rather my mistake be giving him too much credit, than not deciphering the reasons behind his actions and being blindsided by him again."

"What could possibly be behind a charity dance he knew nothing about?"

"Oh, *he knew nothing about it?"* Dean laughs, though it's without any trace of humor. "You mind explaining to me how he referenced the song you danced with him to, a fucking *hour* before any of this went down?"

I try to recall exactly what Legion had said about his song choice. He'd only mentioned something about making the best choice he could think of in a pinch. At least, that's how it came across to me.

At my silence, Dean continues, "I'll break it down for you, baby. This was Legion letting me know, *in front of everyone*, that he can manipulate the queen, *my queen*, in this twisted game of chess. That he can maneuver you across the board, *quite literally*, however he wants. We're dealing with a mind fucking demon for fucks sake, everything he does has a reason, Vanna. Fuck, look at the psychology of it. He chose a fuckin' *Waltz*, a style of dance that represents *courtship*, to a goddamned *power* ballad. You can't tell me that wasn't deliberate. That there's nothing symbolic or subliminal about this."

"I thought a waltz was an odd choice, considering we're at a biker bash," I admit.

"He's *grooming* you, baby. It's a shared experience that encourages connection, maybe even a level of trust, if you really want to dissect it. It requires physical closeness. It's a goddamned act of intimacy. Even the synchronization. It's all psychological warfare!"

"How many drinks have you had tonight?" I attempt to joke, but he practically glowers at me.

"I never asked before… *Call it self-preservation*… But, over the last three years he was gone, did you think about him?"

"I think we both did."

"I'm sure we had vastly different thoughts."

I cross my arms. "*On occasion*, I wondered what might have happened to him. Whether or not he was still alive."

"Did you hope he was?"

"I didn't wish he wasn't."

"Were you relieved when he showed up?"

"I was surprised."

"*That's not what I asked you.*"

"*Fine.* A part of me was relieved to see him alive. I don't wish death on people, Dean. *That's it.*"

"That's all he needs," Dean growls. "That little sliver. That fucking crack. I don't need a crystal ball or a stack of fuckin' cards to know the future here. *You're gonna forgive him.* It's in your nature. And I love your kind heart, Vanna, I do. You're so fuckin' good, baby… But he's gonna *wring. Every. Drop,* from your bleeding heart."

I walk up to him and take his left hand, slipping my ring finger between his so our wedding bands touch. "Do you see these?"

"Yes." He curls his fingers, gently squeezing my hand until our palms press together.

"Do you remember our vows? What these rings represent? Nothing can break this." I place my other hand over his heart. "You and I, we're forever, Dean. There are no cracks in our relationship. There are no slivers of distrust… Are there?"

"No."

"Do you really think he could take me away from you, after everything we've survived together?"

He slowly shakes his head.

"I haven't forgotten anything he's had a hand in. What I said to you, that night I met him after the Ametrine Cauldron burned down… I meant every word, and it will always stand true. A queen protects her king."

"I don't know what I'd do without you, baby."

I reach up to cradle his face in my other hand. "And you will *never* have to find out."

"The only place I want my queen *pinned* is beneath me." Finally, a slight grin quirks up in the corner of his mouth when I smile at his little chess pun.

"Well then," I bite my lower lip. "I think that's something we can arrange."

Tugging my hand, Dean leads me away from the clubhouse, in a direction of the property I haven't yet explored with him.

We end up at a cemetery surrounded by a stone wall that looks like it's been here for a century. Dean pushes open the old iron gates, and we step inside.

"This is romantic," I joke.

"I was thinking of burying Legion in here, where I can visit at these events. A place I could come take a leak when the bathrooms are overcrowded… But the fantasy will have to suffice."

"I'm sure the nuns wouldn't want to spend eternity with him anyway. And we need to work on your fantasies. There isn't anything hot about digging up old graves or those other plans."

A dark, crooked grin stretches Dean's mouth as he maneuvers me against the stone wall. His hips press forward, pinning me between him and the stones.

"Fucking you on his grave would be pretty hot."

"That's dark."

"Well, he pushes my thoughts into jet-black territory," Dean growls, lowering his mouth to kiss my neck.

"Speaking of…do you know a biker called Jett?"

"No, did he hit on you?"

"*She*."

"*A chick hit on you?*"

"Don't get any ideas! And no, she didn't… It was a strange, brief encounter. I couldn't really make any sense of what she was talking about." Especially not now, unable to think straight with the way he's sucking on my neck and grinding against me. While trailing rough kisses down my throat and across the swell of my breasts, Dean undoes my pants and pulls them open, then shoves his hand down the front of my panties. Though for some reason, he keeps going, slipping his fingers out the side to touch my inner thigh, seemingly hesitant to touch me where I crave him most right now.

"What is it?" I ask, attempting to slow my erratic breathing in eager anticipation of his skillful touch. He doesn't answer.

Does he hear someone?

I close my eyes and listen. "There's no one out here. It's just us."

"*I hope that's true.*"

"*I thought of you*, Dean. I only ever think of you. My heart, my body, my soul… I belong to you, sweetheart."

He tilts his head, pressing his forehead to mine. I reach down to trail my fingers along his forearm.

"*Touch me*," I whisper, just about willing to force his hand back to the apex of my thighs. "Touch me the way *only you* know how."

His hand slides up my thigh, and my breath hitches when his thumb slips back inside my underwear and gently strokes along the slit of my pussy.

"Fuck… You're already *ready*," he groans, though there's something other than desire in his tone.

"I want *you*. I'll always want *you*. Touch me, Dean. Touch me like you want me."

He repositions to roughly cup me in his hot hand, pressing the heel of his palm against my increasingly throbbing clit.

"*Mmmm…yesss.*" I can't help rolling my hips in an attempt to grind myself harder against his touch.

"Fuck, baby, you're so wet," Dean groans, curling his fingers to sink two of them inside of me. I rock my hips more fervently now, and my clit throbs harder beneath the pressure of his palm.

"Oh, God… Dean…" I pant, gripping his arms as my head lolls back against the stone wall.

"Yeah?" I finally hear the smirk in his tone. "*Tell me.*"

I almost whimper at the sensation of his lips against my throat, kissing and sucking my skin a bit more ardently. The sandpapery scratch of his stubbled jaw drags across the base of my neck as he continues, slowly making his way to the other side. His warm tongue leaves a moist trail up my neck to my ear, quickly cooling in the night air, before his teeth nip at my lobe.

"What do you want, doll?" he whispers.

"*Everything.*"

"You're gonna come in my mouth…then on my cock," he growls the words against the quickening pulse in my neck, before suddenly removing his hand from my panties. He drops to kneel before me, roughly pulling down my pants and underwear with him. "I want these legs spread wide for me, kitten." He gently slaps the back of my leg. "Let me get these boots off, so the rest can come off with them."

I balance myself against the wall while he impatiently strips me from the waist down. Dean surges forward, plunging his tongue inside of me. I moan while he swirls it like a cyclone, digging my nails into the shoulders of his leather cut. He drags his tongue up between my lips until the probing tip flicks my clit, then he latches onto me, continuing his glorious assault. The suction, the rapid flicking of his tongue, makes me cry out into the night.

Dean grabs my waist and spins me around, then jerks my hips back before I feel his hot mouth fully on me again. His strong arms circle my thighs, holding me so tightly it's as if he's crazy enough to think I'd want to escape this delicious onslaught.

He devours me from behind, pulling more groans and whimpers from us both.

A sudden, sharp spank on my ass cheek startles me, and the clipped little yip I let out stirs a deep, primal growl from him.

"*Come for me,*" he demands, then laps at my pussy before shoving his tongue back inside. Another sharp spank, then his hand runs up my inner thigh. I gasp when his fingers press against my clit, rubbing in a firm, circular motion in time with his deep, swirling tongue.

"Oh, God... *Oh fuck! Fuck! Fuck!*" I cry out as my body begins to tingle all over and my muscles spasm beyond control.

I try not to shriek through the duration of my climax, but he doesn't stop. I'm trembling and can barely stand. Before I can register what is happening, Dean is on his feet, spinning me back around to face him. His eyes are even darker with an impassioned lust I haven't seen quite like this in some time.

"*My turn,*" he growls, then wipes his glistening smirk with the back of his hand. I watch it drop to join the other, unbuckling his belt, then moving on to undo his fly.

I take an eager step toward him, but he backs up, slowly shaking his head. He shoves the front of his pants and boxers down, just low enough to pull his rigid cock free.

Stroking it slowly, he moves toward the stone bench and takes a seat. Motioning with his other finger for me to come to him, he growls, "I want you to ride me."

Once I'm within reach, he grabs me and pulls me onto him, forcing me to straddle his lap. As I hover for a moment above him, just low enough for the velvety, swollen head of his cock to slip between my lips, he rubs it back and forth, slicking himself with my orgasm.

"*Fuuuuck*, baby," he breathes through the sensation of my body sinking down on him, taking his hard length to the hilt in one deliberate and determined motion despite the burning stretch. I rock my hips slowly at first, waiting for my body to adjust around his girth. It doesn't take long before the ache turns to pleasure. Just the thought of Dean inside of me is enough to drive me on.

His hands slide up my thighs and over my hips, reaching behind to grip my ass while I fuck him. I hold onto his shoulders just as tightly to keep myself centered and steady.

"Go fucking wild on me, doll," he pants.

In a mad rush, I shove his cut off his shoulders and down his arms. He shrugs out of it and then discards it on the bench behind him. It's barely out of his hands before mine are yanking up the hem of his shirt to expose his gorgeous, chiseled torso and sexy, vascular arms. Dean tosses the shirt with his cut, and I can't help but stare at him. He's so beautiful.

"How did I get so lucky?"

"I'm the lucky one," he insists, grabbing my top before yanking it over my head. It joins the pile behind him as well, then his hands are on my breasts, cupping and kneading them over my bra before he pulls the cups down roughly, and my breasts spill forth into his face. He grabs them again, lifting and pressing them together, then thumbs my pebbled nipples. His hot mouth sucks my soft flesh inside, and his tongue presses the hardened bud against the roof of his mouth, increasing the rhythmic suction.

I arch my back, shoving my breasts fully into his face. Taking him as deeply as I can, I grind my clit against his pubic bone, becoming more and more desperate for the next climax.

He releases my nipple, only to attack the other, pinching it between his teeth. He swirls his tongue around my pebbled peek and sucks in a hissing breath. The cold air rushing over the hard, wet bud makes my entire body quiver.

I run my hand up his neck to the back of his skull, sliding my fingers up to grip his hair and pull his head back.

"*Do it,*" he nearly snarls as if it's a dare, "Work that soul snatching witchcraft." He flicks the tip of his tongue at me tauntingly.

I grip his jaw and take him into my mouth. Curling my lips around his tongue, I suck him on a slow upstroke. His cock jerks inside me, and his entire body tenses. The kiss he calls wicked and demonic never fails to be his undoing.

Dean groans, wrapping his arms tightly around my waist. I continue to ride him, rocking and swiveling my hips while working his tongue. He thrusts faster, on the verge of losing control.

His desperation pushes me closer to the edge right along with him. I moan, wanting to tell him to come with me, but unwilling to pull back from this kiss that drives him so wild.

Another orgasm wracks my body, and I lose my fast but rhythmic pace. His strong hands dig into my body, almost bruisingly, gripping the back of my shoulders to anchor me on his cock. My nails dig into his muscular shoulders, raking across his heated skin, and I throw my head back, gasping for breath through the exquisite sensory explosion. His cock twitches, spurting inside of me as he groans through his release.

We don't part in the aftermath of our coital bliss while we catch our breath together. Dean leans forward, pressing his forehead to mine again, and I can feel the warmth of his steady breath fanning against my lips.

"What is it about this kiss that just *does it for you?*" I ask while readjusting my bra.

He shakes his head as if confounded by the question. "You just blew my fucking mind, and I never got over it. It's so...*borderline pornographic.* And you were so sweet and innocent and...*wholesome.*"

"*Past tense?*" I tease, fixing my bra straps now that my girls are holstered. Dean's fingers grip my hips.

"Stop wiggling around while I'm still inside you, or you're going to get me hard again," Dean growls, but then he answers with a wink, "*There's been mutual corruption.* I really didn't expect you to bring the devil out of either of us that night."

"Here we go with the devil shit again." I roll my eyes before reaching behind him to grab my shirt. Now that we've both come to our senses, it's rather chilly out. He winces as I get up from his lap to dress.

"I know it's not devil shit," he says the words on a sigh. "Every time you kiss me like that, I'm transported to our night on the beach."

"I really made an impression, huh?" I giggle, flinging the top over my shoulder to grab my underwear and pull it back on first. Working my ass back into my leather pants is a higher priority than my top since I'm at least already wearing a bra.

"*Fuckin' Aces.*" Dean pulls his shirt back on and slips into his cut. "Why do you think I put a ring on it and knocked you up so fast? I had to lock you down, *STAT*."

"You're such a rogue." I laugh, balling up my top. I throw it at him playfully. He catches it before it smacks him in the face and gently tosses it back to me. "And since *you* brought it up," I begin to say, but Dean's eyes widen and he shakes his head as he stands, tucking himself back in his pants.

"No. *Nope*. Not tonight," he emphatically insists, refastening his belt and fly.

I struggle to keep the smile on my face as if his adamant rejection of the topic doesn't bother me. "I was just kidding," I say, turning from him. I take my time slipping back into my top. I need these extra seconds despite the chill. I don't want him to know his reaction made me feel like I was just punched in the stomach.

"Come on, doll," Dean says, once we're both fully dressed. When I turn back to face him, he's holding his hand out for me to take. "Let's head back."

LEGION

Interesting...

It seems I've arrived a tad too late and missed *more* than the impromptu sex show. Hands clasped, sated, and smiling, I watch the supposed happy couple make their way back to the clubhouse. Something is off between them...

Now that the need to remain covert has passed, I light up a cigarette while strolling in the direction of the iron gates where I've been informed the loaded van is waiting.

"*You need to leave her alone,*" a vaguely familiar feminine voice drifts from the shadows, somewhere among the row of old oaks beside me.

"Did you miss the show as well?" I jest.

Legion: Book 3

"I only followed you out here to warn you."

"*Warn me?*" My laughter escapes on a cloud of smoke as the blonde bitch steps out from behind a tree nearest me.

I pull another long drag and take my time looking her over. My appraising gaze clearly annoys her further. "*Val*, is it?" I exhale the smoky words in her direction.

She crosses her arms, pretending the smoke doesn't offend her. "It doesn't matter."

"*Ah*, something we agree upon... *your insignificance.*"

"Just leave her alone, asshole."

"*Val!*" the one with the thick Brooklyn accent screams for her unruly girlfriend in the distance. "Where the fuck are you, Val? I told you not to do this tonight!"

The blonde cocks her head over her shoulder, calling back to her. "Over here!"

I take another agitated drag while the loud one makes her way over to her girlfriend. "Are you crazy? If this had to happen, couldn't it have happened closer to the clubhouse, where there are *witnesses?*" The brunette Brooklynite grabs her friend's arm and attempts to haul her away.

"I'm not afraid of him, Jett."

I smile back in her glowering face. "It might surprise you to know, *I'm more of a feminist than you may think.*"

Both women go rigid.

"Yeah, it's time to go, Val," the brunette urges her once more.

"No! Hold on a minute!" the blonde shoves away from her companion, taking an aggressive, and what she must *think* is an intimidating step toward me. "Did you just threaten me?"

I chuckle, though only to grate her nerves. "Perceptive... *And they say blondes are dumb.*"

"You're going to get what's coming to you," she seethes.

This encounter is rapidly becoming tiresome, and I've got shit to do tonight. I don't bother with further pretenses of civility when I snarl back at her, "*And are you the one who will give it to me, bitch?*"

The hostility in her glare doesn't falter, not even when her raven-haired gal pal tugs at her arm. "Not here, not now!" her *Brooklynite bestie* insists, dragging her away in the direction of the clubhouse.

Watching them go, I snuff out the butt of my cigarette beneath my boot, then head for the van.

M̲y motorcycle remains where I'd stashed it earlier tonight, in an old, neglected cemetery down a dirt path surrounded by woods. If there is one thing this state isn't lacking, it's isolated, seemingly forgotten graveyards. This one happens to be a half mile from the remnants of the cook trailer I blew up earlier tonight.

I pull the van up to the crooked gates and throw the shifter into park, leaving the headlights on to illuminate the centuries-old headstones just beyond the rusty metal barrier, which is barely clinging to the crumbling stone and mortar wall.

"You can sit up now," I inform my new pawn.

Still blindfolded and gagged, he maneuvers his head from between his knees beneath the dash and sits back against the passenger seat. He's breathing heavier now that we aren't moving. I take my time lighting up a cigarette, giving him a moment to worry about what happens next before I reach over and remove the gag from his mouth.

"*Please don't kill me…*" he immediately begs.

I remove his blindfold and watch him blink, attempting to focus on the eerie scene beyond the windshield. He pulls in another quivering breath as the silent threat sinks in.

"*Oh God…*" He turns to me, eyes wide, bloodshot, and filled to the brim with tears. "*Please don't kill me…* I told you everything you wanted to know."

I pull a long leisurely drag while I study him, prolonging the tension of the moment before I speak. "Now tell me why I should let you live."

"*W-what?*"

"I want you to tell me…all of the reasons *why*…I should *let you live.*"

He proceeds to ramble on and on about his life, his ailing mother, his unsuspecting wife and kids. How he's *not a bad guy*, he's just been hard-up for cash. While he drones on, I reach into my jacket and remove the wallet I took off of him earlier, then proceed to flip through the contents within.

He's definitely not a seasoned criminal, or he never would have had a wallet on him containing anything of importance to begin with.

"*The family*, I presume?" I pluck a tattered photo of a woman and three children from the plastic encasement within.

Legion: Book 3

"Yes," he says on a strangled whimper.

I slip the photo inside my jacket, as well as his license and social security card, then toss the wallet into his lap.

"You've just told me all the reasons you're going to do exactly as I say."

A warring mixture of hope and horror eclipses his expression, and he nods adamantly. *"Yes, yes I'll do anything!"*

"I want you to bear in mind the nature of the men you're involved with. *They will kill you*, Stanley Jones. They will kill you and your family for what you have revealed to me tonight."

He nods slowly, coming to terms with being trapped between a rock and a hard place.

"Though should you suffer a major lapse in judgement and betray me, I assure you, despite your fate, the gruesome things I will do to your loved ones...well," I tilt my head in the direction of the illuminated headstones. "you'll wish I made you dig your own grave tonight."

He swallows hard and audibly. "I'll do exactly as you say."

"It is now on your integral shoulders to convince those concerned over the events of this night, that you somehow managed to escape the fate of your colleagues. Perhaps you bolted into the woods, became lost and confused. Spin a convincing tale of disorientation from the blast. Your life depends on it."

He nods slowly in understanding. "What else?"

There's one thing I intentionally neglected to ask Stanley in front of the Jokers. "I want the name of the man at the head of this criminal enterprise."

"He's only known by his alias, and no one ever sees him," Stan nervously insists.

I expected as much. After all, that's how I operated. "And what is this alias?"

"H-he's known only as... *Legion.*"

Well, I'll be damned...

CHAPTER 18

LEGION

Having spent years avoiding Keegan's clutches while working within the cloak of darkness to destroy his world, there was one place I knew neither he nor anyone else would ever fathom to find me. A rustic, *shanty*-style houseboat. Upon my return to North Carolina, I acquired another riverfront abode.

This time, I upgraded to a very secluded hunting cabin, built into the river's edge within the Pamlico estuary. The cabin, not far from town as the crow flies, sits nestled in the woods down a barely noticeable trail. A genuine retreat, surrounded by acres of forest.

Having lived most of my life in the desert, this lush, estuarine environment is a contrast I've come to quite enjoy.

My home, at least for the time being, is a modest cabin, complete with a large deck which expands the length of the structure, as well as several yards over the river's edge, providing a truly spectacular view of this remote section of river. My own private paradise. A sanctuary within a sanctuary.

Though as I approach my humble abode, I notice the sliding glass doors of my dwelling are open…

Perhaps I've been, *or am presently being*, robbed. There is no way anyone of any pertinence to my current life could know about this place. At least, not yet…

Already in the foulest of moods after Stanley's revelation, the sinister part of myself hopes to catch the perp inside as I draw my gun and step cautiously closer.

An aroma lingering in the air I'd recognize anywhere instantly sets my heart racing, and I pause. Although I know *it couldn't be her*, a false, untamable hope still flutters in my chest.

Alas, there is only one other it could be. I'd gifted her the *knock-off* version of *Seduction* that I reverse-concocted myself, over three years ago, during the height of my mad obsession.

It's her. It couldn't…*wouldn't* be Vanna. Hope sinks like a rock tossed into the black waters of the river rushing beneath my boots, and unwelcome memories flood the forefront of my mind…

"You look at her differently," Puppet said one night when she came to kneel before me at my desk and rested her hand upon my thigh, begging for my attention.

"What are you talking about?" I'd reluctantly asked.

"The woman…with that biker who fought the night of the bonfire… You've been following her."

"What are you doing, *following me?* I told you to stay here at the clubhouse."

"I don't like it here without you… I miss the desert."

"You're free to return."

"I'd miss you again."

"Well, you can't have things both ways!" I snapped impatiently. "If you think this has been a vacation for me, it hasn't. I'm here, executing this plan for my brother. This wreaking, humid state is the last place I want to be." I'd never curse the dry heat of the desert again for as long as I lived. "I'm surrounded by imbeciles who can barely follow the simplest orders. Preacher's resolve is waning, which presents a whole new set of issues that will have to be resolved in a very permanent manner." I clamped my jaw shut, resentful of myself for the atypical outburst.

What the fuck was wrong with me, unloading and confiding in this whore? Whores cannot be trusted.

"Why do you look at her like that?" she asked once more, seeming to have ignored the rant completely.

"I haven't the slightest idea what you're going on about."

"I've never seen you look at any of the other girls the way you look at her. You've never looked at me with such…"

"*Enough*, Puppet. I'm not in the mood for your jealousy," I cautioned on an exasperated sigh. "Stalk after me again, and I will make you regret your disobedience."

"I fear that I'm the only one who cares for your safety, Master," she whispered. "There are hungry eyes upon your back at all times. These promises you've made…to such dangerous men…"

"*Are none of your concern.*"

"*You* are my concern, Sir…"

I scoffed, "Is the taste of my spunk really so addicting? I suppose you would be the expert." The wounded look in her eyes further grated my nerves.

"I fuck who *you* tell me to fuck," she whispered once more, as if suddenly ashamed of her chosen station in life. "*Not* because *I* want to fuck them."

"That is your purpose." I shrugged with malicious indifference.

Her eyes lowered from mine, shoulders sinking, and her hand slid limply down my leg. "You can be a cruel master."

"Something you shouldn't lose sight of… You're my favorite whore, Puppet. *But you're still a whore.*"

She seemed to stew on my words for a while before speaking again. "I can be of greater use to you, Sir."

"That would require a certain level of trust, would it not? You must know by now that's an *impossibility* between us."

Had I not been glaring at her, I would have missed the microexpression of defiance in her hazel eyes. "You're going to receive a call from the Blue Devils crew out of Bender County within the next few days. They're working out the logistics of your assassination."

Honestly, I hadn't been all that surprised by the revelation. "*Really*? Is that what they're calling it?" I asked with mock glee. "*An assassination attempt*…how very…*deep state.*"

"As it stands, you will be asked to meet somewhere within their territory, where you will be shot like a dog and discarded."

"*Fascinating.*"

She frowned at my display of nonchalance. "Two members of your crew are growing impatient. They suspect there's more going on than what they've been told."

They weren't wrong…

Aside from Reaper and Vein, everyone involved in my plans to avenge my brother had been kept in the dark, under the impression we were setting up shop for an organized takeover that would benefit all within the network I'd been cultivating.

Had they known I was setting up a house of cards from the start...

"Well, we mustn't allow a few bad apples to ruin our barrel, *hmm? Name them* and how you happened to privy yourself upon such a duplicitous plot."

"Havoc and Malice...they were talking, afterwards... I overheard them while cleaning up in the bathroom and lingered by the door."

"And what prompted you to do such a thing?"

"The way they've been *looking at you* when you *aren't looking.*"

"I see."

"*No.* You haven't." Her glare lasted but a moment before her brows lifted in an expression I'm sure I was meant to interpret as concern. "*But I have...* There will be a signal, right before they blow your brains out. *Thanks to me*, you will see it coming."

I didn't bother concealing the suspicion I harbored for her. "And I am to believe they aren't the *Hinckley's to your Foster?*"

She stared up at me, lips parted, yet no words spilled.

I snatched her by the throat and leaned in closer. "*You waited on relaying this to me...*weighing your options, perhaps?"

She attempted to shake her head. "No!"

I squeezed a little tighter and felt her nervous swallow shift against my palm.

"I've suspected them," she spoke quickly, apparent desperation in her words. "But I didn't know their plans until last night. I haven't had the chance to speak with you until now! You're rarely here!"

"And what is it you wish to be rewarded with in exchange for this pertinent information?" I was genuinely curious what she'd come up with.

"I only want you safe."

I scoffed at her lies but released her. "Spare me the bullshit." I spat, sitting back in the chair.

She touched her throat and spoke groggily at first. "*Choice...* I want to be able to refuse your men without repercussion... I want *you* to make that clear to them. I'm no longer a pass-around. Make me your property, alone. That's all I want."

I couldn't help but scowl at her request. Her information made sense. It was honestly to be expected at some point. Still, I wasn't about to allow her the belief she meant anything to me, regardless. "Let's see how this plays out," I said instead.

The events of the night Puppet warned me about did come to pass. Well, aside from *yours truly* catching a fatal bullet to the dome. I personally carried out the execution of Havoc and Malice. The Blue Devils were exterminated as well, which sent a bloody message through the network. Any move against me would swiftly result in a gory death.

As was to be expected, Puppet wasn't content for long with her advancement in status among the harlots. I'd granted her the level of autonomy she desired, but I refused to elevate her to my *personal property*.

However, it was only weeks later that she'd managed to turn the tables on me. I'd be lying if I claimed I wasn't impressed by her bold move, *the devious little minx...*

"*Legion...*" Puppet's timid voice had broken the silence in my office that night. I'd been secretly stewing over logistics pertaining to Jack Nero's impending release. The man was shaping up to be a wild card, and I knew I'd have to devise a way to keep him on a leash and do so unbeknownst to him. When I turned to face Puppet, I was momentarily stunned.

Her long hair was no longer a shade of auburn. She'd dyed it black. Her hazel eyes were concealed behind dark brown contacts, and her attire was something that could have been pulled straight from the witch's closet. Even her makeup, done up and contoured in such a way, she closely resembled the object of my growing obsession... I had to force myself to swallow and take a breath.

"Does this please you?" she asked, turning slowly to give me a full view of her convincing cosplay. She peered over her shoulder at me, bringing her hand to her mouth to stifle a little laugh——*much in the way I had seen Vanna do*——before she approached me.

I was immediately hit with the fragrance she was wearing. Lavender, with a hint of sandalwood... As if she'd spent a considerable amount of time in a witch shop herself... As if she'd been wearing one of the blends the little witch wore... It was a real mind fuck when she pressed herself up against me, gazing through her dark lashes with a deceptively innocent smile.

Legion: Book 3

"I've been making creative use of the time you so graciously freed up for me... You said I couldn't follow *you*... You made no mention of *her*," she'd said slyly... And I'm not quite sure how I initially felt about the crafty little vixen making a study of Vanna.

"Hello, Legion..." she giggled playfully and took my hand. "*I'm Vanna...*" She brought my fingers to her lips. They were painted in that same deep shade of crimson Vanna wears on special occasions. She pressed a kiss to the pad of my finger, then she whispered in a sultry tone, "*Wanna play?*"

To my astonishment, I'd found it difficult to fuck Puppet the way I had always fucked these common whores. And though Puppet could suck a cock like no other, whenever I have been tempted fuck her, it was always from the back, like the rest of them. Faceless. Meaningless. Just a hole to pound, expel a little stress and poison into...

I couldn't help but wonder how often Puppet stalked Vanna. Though it must have been a frequent occurrence.

She'd gleefully answered every inquiry I'd had about the little witch, and over time, seemed to have a genuine answer for everything.

Vanna's favorite beverages, food, music, movies... Some of which we'd even watched together during our many games. She gave me all of the mundane information a lover should be privy to when in an intimate relationship. Puppet made herself the next best thing... And at first, I enjoyed it. I was eager to indulge in what I had mistakenly believed was an innocuous illusion. I'd even been tempted to fully live out the fantasy of making true love to Vanna, an experience I've never fully emersed myself in before. I've always needed the crutch of kink in the form of ropes and knives...that imperative wall of pain between me and them.

Our games began with such elements...darker fantasies of *abduction* and *Stockholm*... Then there were our rituals where she allowed my blade to draw blood from her porcelain flesh, actively participating in my baneful workings and rituals to bring about the demise of Vanna's beloved Keegan... She even allowed me to brand her body.

Though as my feelings for Vanna evolved into something far beyond the primal simplicities of lust and a thirst for vengeance through her, so too did our games. My emotions for Vanna grew fonder, and the roleplaying became wishful acts of a true romance. I no longer harbored a desire to *take* and *ruin* Vanna... I wanted to *win* her.

Puppet had unlocked something within me... Something which also made me feel the pangs of jealousy and possessiveness I hadn't experienced in a long while, if ever to this degree. And although I knew instinctively this entire situation was bound to blow up in my face, the temptation was too great not to carry on. I became aggressively unwilling to share my perfect little plaything with anyone else.

After one of our sexual escapades, we'd been lying together in a hotel with an oceanfront view. One of our more romantic games had been roleplaying an affair, and I always sprang for the best as if I had been truly wooing Vanna.

"*You are not to be with another, ever again.*" The words fell haphazardly from my mouth that fateful night while I leisurely stroked the curvature of Puppet's naked lower back. She'd twisted her face to peek up at me from the crook of my arm, puzzled.

"How will I earn my keep?" she asked.

"I'll sponsor you while we're in this wretched state. But you are mine. Exclusively. *Nobody fucking touches you*, or Hell will be paid."

I expected a look of triumph to eclipse her expression at successfully manipulating me into granting what she'd wanted all along. Instead, her eyes had gone starry, a gaze of sheer bliss. I should have clarified in that fucking moment; *this wasn't about love*. It would never be about love between us. This *wasn't* me establishing some sort of meaningful relationship with *her*. This was simply about keeping my favorite toy to myself. Now that she had so closely embodied Vanna, I couldn't stand the thought of other men having their way with her, soiling her image, faux as it was.

"*No one but you*," Puppet whispered, shifting to drape her leg across my waist, moving cautiously to straddle me.

I allowed her placement of soft kisses against my chest, which moved up my neck, something I had never permitted before. If a whore rode my cock, she did so with her arms pinned behind her back or in a reverse position. And they never kissed me, nor I, them. My cock was the only part of my being that their lips ever touched. It had been years since I'd kissed a woman. A lifetime ago...

Legion: Book 3

"I belong to you, Legion, my Demon King... Only you," she purred in that sultry, deeper tone, mimicking the sound of Vanna's voice as she ground her slick heat along my shaft, hardening me beneath her. Eager for another round of our twisted games, I gripped the back of her long black hair and forced her face to mine. Staring into those false, dark brown eyes, *I'd wished they were Vanna's*, and as my gaze fell to her mouth, her lips were still stained in that Dior Rouge red...

Closing my eyes, I forced those lips to mine and kissed her. A deep, passionate kiss that sealed our fates, setting into motion a chain of events I admittedly did not foresee...

"Damien?" Puppet's familiar voice drifts softly from within my river dwelling now, ripping me back to the present. "Is it you out there?"

I come to stand before the open sliding doors and holster my piece. The curvature of her form, evident in the darkness only by way of the glowing moon, is lying draped across my bed.

Like a loyal, *yet unwanted dog*, Puppet has always had a knack for tracking me down. I step inside and make my way to the fridge for a much-needed beer after tonight's events. "What do you want?"

"You found me first this time around," she says, her dark figure sitting up on the bed. "Why?"

I shrug and crack the top off the beer. Taking a swig, I move to lean against the small counter. "Figured I had a fifty-fifty shot as to whether Keegan and his crew would kill me. Wanted to get my dick wet one last time. You know, *go out with a bang!*"

"Could have paid any whore for that." She saunters up to me and takes the beer from my hand. "Why me?"

"Old times' sake."

"Really?" She takes a sip, then hands the beer back to me. Standing face to face in the tight quarters of this shared space, she leans against the kitchen table behind her. The leather stretched across her ass rubs against the wood. Although we're conversing in the darkness, I have a sneaky suspicion she's wearing Vanna's leather leggings, and that corset top beneath what smells like a new leather jacket. I grin inwardly at her attempt to play on our past.

"You can suck the nails out of a board, darling. *Reason enough for you?*" Only a soft sigh laced with disappointment emanates from her.

"*Quid pro quo*, Puppet… Why are *you* here? Last we spoke, you were rather adamant about a profound hatred for me."

She snatches the beer again, right as I was about to take another swig, and downs a few gulps herself before asking, "Do you have anything harder than this?"

"I may be able to *come up* with something."

"I'm still debating whether or not we'll get to *that*. Might just be *you and your hand* tonight."

I shrug as if indifferent. Hell, I may be, at least as far as fucking goes. I am curious, however, if she's still in touch with the man who has stolen my name and hijacked my reputation. If she is, I must tread carefully… I don't trust her enough to reveal my theories and suspicions. If I'm correct, and they are in touch, interrogating her will only put this other *Legion* on high alert. He might even be the reason behind her visit tonight. The thought of her attempting to play me stokes the fires of hate within, but I play it cool. "Thought you'd have hightailed it back to the desert when I took off." I study her expression as best I can in the insufficient lighting.

"You know there's nothing left for me in Arizona… Besides… I knew if I stuck around, *if you were still alive*, you'd be back eventually." She takes one last swig, then shoves the bottle back to me, muttering with discernible resentment, "*For her*."

I polish off the rest of the beer, letting her words linger between us without comment while I ponder over just who is waiting for whom. After placing the empty bottle on the counter behind me, I attempt to move past her, but she grabs my arm, halting me.

"Why did you throw me out? We were so happy for a time… You even told me I was yours."

"*Promises, promises*… Turns out, *neither one of us* is very good at keeping those. At least, *not to each other*," I practically growl as her words grate against the memories rushing back to me of that night…

What eventually transpired between us occurred not long after Keegan stormed the Asphalt Knights' clubhouse and got an eyeful of *my doll*. I'd thought I would have derived a sense of pleasure in his discovery. That it would have had a greater impact on his psyche, the sight of me engaging with a woman bearing such a close resemblance to Vanna. He'd taken it rather well, however. I'd been disappointed by it. The timing of other events furthered my foul mood. I hadn't intended for Vanna to receive the parcel containing her would-be assailant's *eye*... I'd meant for Keegan to receive it. To put it all together and rush to my doorstep. Having been the cause of Vanna's distress *was distressing to me.*

"I followed her today." Puppet's voice interrupted me a few nights after the fiasco. I lifted my eyes from the book in my lap to find her standing in my doorway, clothed in a witchy little ensemble. "She purchased this exact sundress at a boutique near the ocean."

"This is no longer necessary," I replied. "In fact, I would like you to *cease and desist*."

Her brows pulled together, and her head tilted to the side. There was something slightly unhinged in the movement that solidified my decision. "I want you to *stop*, Puppet," I sternly clarified for her.

"Stop?" Her fingers gravitated to the fabric of the long, floral print skirt, curling into it. "But I thought it pleased you when I—"

"*Yes*, Puppet. I want you to stop."

"Why?" she pressed, having grown emboldened from my leniency with her as a result of these twisted games.

"*Because I told you to!*" I snapped, slamming Dostoevsky shut. The hint of defiance in her expression immediately faltered under my harsh gaze and venomous tone.

"*I'm sorry, Daddy...*" she timidly whispered like a scolded child. "Shall I remove this dress for you?"

Expelling a tiresome sigh, I tossed the book onto my desk. "You may remove yourself from my presence."

She nearly jolted at my admittedly callous words. Some distant remnant of myself wished I cared for this pathetic creature. Puppet had been nothing but a dutiful little plaything since I shoved my cock down her eager and willing throat at the Morning Star, always catering to my every twisted whim. Yet, I'd grown to resent her for it, for a multitude of reasons that were mostly of my own design.

I resented her for allowing me to walk all over her. For allowing me to violate her trust, body, and mind. For being the weak little *fuck-doll* I dressed up as a woman I find far superior in every way. For being the very *thing* which forces me to acknowledge that I am, and will always be, *unworthy* of the woman I truly desire. *That this spineless little whore* is the closest I'll ever get... *And she isn't even within the realm of comparison.*

We're both pathetic.

I'd thought if I cut her loose, perhaps she'd be better off? Perhaps doing so would be a shred of decency on my part? A step closer toward the light in which my true love existed?

Light is often quite harsh...

"*I said get out of my sight,* Puppet." A sneer of disgust pulled at my lip. I didn't bother trying to hide it. "Or the next time I drag a knife across your body, it will be at your fucking throat."

Her eyes instantly welled up with tears. "But... *I love you...*" she cried, and her trembling bottom lip angered me further. "You told me you needed me..."

"And what transpired between us every time I've lured you back in with those *magick words? Hmm?*" I demanded with growing agitation. "*I've used you.* Fucked you, *Puppet.* I've fucked you and your *little mind* in every degrading, twisted way I could conjure. *You're a whore,* darling. *A whore.* Nothing more. Nothing less. *Nothing* I could ever *love.*"

Tears streamed down her cheeks, and I could only shake my head at the pitiful creature before me. "I've loved you..." she repeated on a strangled sob. "I've given you everything."

"I don't care, *Puppet.* You know what I am. Is it really so unfathomable that I never have? Allow my parting gift to be a word of advice to you... Let your *unrequited love* turn to hate... *Hate me,* Puppet...and you'll survive."

Puppet violently wiped the tears from her cheeks. "*She doesn't love you!* She will *never* love you the way *I* love you! I worship at your feet as if you're some *Demon King! She* barely *tolerates* you!"

I couldn't help but chuckle. "Life isn't fair to anyone, darling, certainly not the likes of us."

"*Don't do this...*" she whispered, that flash of anger wilted into desperation. She quickly closed the distance between us. "Sir... *Daddy*... please..." she clutched at the cuff of my leather jacket, then my shoulder. "I... I can be better... I–"

"*I don't care.* I never have. I never will. Let's not drag this out as if we ever truly meant something worthwhile to one another... This...

All of this...was a mistake. I should have thrown your ass out of the Morning Star the night you showed up."

Her head whipped wildly back and forth before her clutching hands were suddenly cradling my face.

"Damien...look at me..." her trembling voice pleaded as my fingers encircled her wrists and pried her touch from my face. "Don't throw me away..."

"Perhaps try shifting your perspective to being set free?" I offered. "Run along and find a new master, Puppet. I'm through with you."

"I'll drag a blade across my own throat!"

I stared at her, genuinely wondering if I was even capable of summoning a shred of concern over her threat. "You're already dead to me, darling. It's your life...*Do with it what you will.*"

"*I hate you!*" she shrieked, wrenching her wrists from my grasp. Sobbing, she backed away from me on unsteady heels. "*I hate you! I hate you! I fucking hate you!*"

P uppet snatches the beer from me again, and in doing so, rips me back from the memories of our turbulent past. She downs the rest of the beer before reaching around me to place the empty bottle on the counter. "Should you really be pairing alcohol with your prescriptions?" I ask.

A sarcastic laugh escapes her. "You almost sound like you care."

"Good thing you've come to know better. Let's not repeat any mistakes of the past, *hmm*?"

"You're such an asshole! Fuck you!"

I turn from her to grab a new beer from the fridge. "Are you offering? Or does that mean you're leaving now?" I crack the top off and toss it into the sink before taking a few swigs. After everything that has transpired between us, is it possible she's aligned herself with this *Legion*? Have they both been awaiting my return? Or has she truly remained a free agent all this time?

After a moment of tense silence, her hands slide up my back to my shoulders before she slowly runs them down again to linger at my sides.

"You're tense. I can feel it," she whispers, placing a few soft kisses against the back of my jacket between words. I can't feel them through the leather, but I can hear the soft clicking sounds of her lips.

"You were near her tonight, weren't you? I can always tell how badly she leaves you wanting."

"*Ha…interesting choice of phrase. Nothing's changed between us.*"

Her hands slide around my waist to reach for the buckle of my belt, fingers deftly undoing it. "Which *us?*"

I take another large gulp, attempting to quell my rising temper at her needling words while she works at my fly. "*Either of you.*"

She foolishly goes on, "So, you're not making any headway with her." Puppet's fingers slip inside my boxers, and she wraps her hand around me. I suppress a groan. "*You're already half hard,*" she taunts.

A sneer pulls at my lips as she begins to stroke my shaft. "Been this way all night. I had her in my arms… *We danced… A waltz… It was beautiful.*"

Her jerking fist hitches. My words struck a nerve. She angrily tugs my cock all the way out, making sure the swollen head scrapes against the zipper as it juts free. A hiss laced with pleasurable pain escapes my clenched teeth.

"That was a low blow," she growls, maneuvering to stand before me.

"Now, there's an idea." I grin. "Perhaps the one area you *may* have *her* beat… Of all the whores I've been with, *none of them could suck a cock like you,* Puppet."

"Ask me nicely."

"*No.*"

"You're the one rocking the raging hardon. That has to be getting painful."

"Don't talk to *me* about pain."

That defiant expression in her eyes softens, and she slowly lowers herself to her knees. Grabbing my beer, I down the rest while she takes me into her mouth, damn near swallowing me already. I toss the empty bottle into the sink and slip my fingers into her hair, gently stroking her while she works my rapidly engorging cock.

"Fuck…that's a good girl…such a good fucking girl…" I close my eyes and breathe in the scent of Seduction, gently thrusting in and out of her mouth. If I ever get Vanna's lips around me, I wouldn't skull fuck her the way I do Puppet. I wouldn't bang her the way I've banged these other whores. I'd worship her… Make *true love* to her…and my sweet angel would eagerly reciprocate. "*Fuck…sweet one…my precious little angel…you feel like heaven ought to…*"

Her nails dig into my thighs, raking over the denim as she attempts to push back from me.

My true love wouldn't put up a fight.

I release Puppet and let her fall back against the cabinet below the sink. "I'm not sucking your cock while you think of her!" she breathlessly snaps.

"*Well, if it isn't the consequences of your own actions!*" I chuckle, attempting to mask the tidal wave of frustration I'm feeling at the loss of the fantasy and her glorious mouth. "Seems you've fucked my mind harder than perhaps you intended? I'm *incapable* of fucking *you*, Puppet. I haven't fucked *you* in a very, very long time."

She glares up at me while I arrange my cock inside my jeans. Brushing her hands off on her leather-clad thighs, she stands. "You fucked me in that private room at the club."

"Did I?"

"I felt the hate and the passion behind every thrust. I remember our games…" That hostile expression in her eyes turns sorrowful at the memories I know are flashing behind them. They're replaying in my mind as well. "When I'm *her* to you…you're different."

"*Take it or leave it.*"

Anger returns in her heated gaze. "Fine. *Let's play.*" A resentful, wicked little grin pulls at her dark-stained lips. "I'll be your *precious Vanna.*"

She shoves past me to strip off her leather jacket and tosses it across the kitchen table before she turns around to face me. She *is* wearing that familiar corset top that pushes the swells of her breasts up to the max. Puppet strokes her fingers lightly down her throat, drawing my eyes to the sensual motion, leading my gaze to the dark crack of her cleavage, as if I wouldn't have gotten there on my own. "Have you missed me, Damien?" she purrs…

Though I'm irritated over the effect this game still has on me, I nod, willing to play along for the sake of getting my rocks off.

"*You'll never compare to him,*" she says in that slightly lower octave, mimicking Vanna's more sultry voice. "You, *Legion*, are nothing but a reminder of everything Dean and I have overcome. *You… You pathetic creature*, are not only the reason, *but a testament to our unbreakable bond!*"

Bitch!

Puppet smiles triumphantly as I struggle against a nearly overwhelming desire to slash her throat. "*Was it too good?*" The laughter in her words stokes the deadly, simmering rage within. "I was going for *authentic*, but if you want the *wilting flower version…*"

"*Be careful…*" I growl the warning. "*You aren't Vanna.*"

"*And you hate me for it!*"

"I've hated you and your kind long before she ever came along… *Or have you forgotten?*" The slick smile slides off her face. "I thought not... *For old times' sake*, I'll excuse this *monumental lapse in judgment* on your part and allow you to walk out of here with your fucking life." Besides, as much as I hate to admit to myself, I may need her if my suspicions prove correct.

She swallows hard. "I'm sorry, Legion….*Sir*…" There's a discernible tremor in her voice. "I'll do whatever you want… How do you want it?"

"*I don't.*"

"*Please…*" she begs, reaching for me again. "Anything you want." She grips my jacket, then releases the leather to stroke her hands up and down my shoulders and upper chest. "I'll do whatever you want."

"I'm afraid the moment has expired, darling… Now *off with you* before you do as well."

"Damien, look at me, *please*."

"My patience is wearing thin, *Puppet*. I've given you ample warning. Walk out of here unscathed and with breath still in your lungs. I strongly suggest you take me up on the offer... *Men have died for far less than what you just pulled.*"

"*Play with me…*"

I suck in a long breath through my nostrils, suppressing the urge to wrap my hands around her throat and squeeze the life out of her…toss her carcass in the river for someone else to deal with. Reaching into my cut pocket, I remove my cigarettes and Ace of Spades Zippo.

"*Play with me, Daddy… I want you to, please…*" she goes on, a desperate attempt to sway me back with the way she mimics Vanna's voice again. "*I've missed you so… And* he *never gives me what I truly want…*"

"*Enough,*" I warn once more, lighting up in her face. In the glow of the flame, I can see she's wearing Vanna's deep red lipstick, paired with dark brown contacts. Her deceitful eyes study me behind them.

Legion: Book 3

I pull a long drag and exhale the smoke in her face. She breathes it in like she's fucking grateful for it… *Crazy bitch.*

"If you let me stay, I'll tell you what I know about her."

I expel a scoff. I've maneuvered myself into Vanna's life. It's only a matter of time before she considers me an ally… *A trusted confidant…*

"*She'd never tell you this,*" Puppet insists, as if she just read my mind. "And this is something that will make you *come so hard,* you'll forget all the pain for those few blissful moments."

I can't help but crook a brow, intrigued.

"Well?" she presses. I pull another leisurely drag, making her wait, then exhale the smoke in her face again.

"I'm listening, aren't I?"

"Keegan won't give her another baby."

Against my will, blood rushes to my cock so rapidly I can feel the bite of my zipper. I'm rigid again, *fucking throbbing* and raring to go. "And you know this how?"

"People talk… They confide in others… It's a reliable source." A slow, devious grin splits her mouth.

"How many men have you fucked since our parting?"

She shakes her head wildly. "*None.* No one, I swear."

I narrow my glare at her, wondering if it's really possible she and *Legion* never linked up in the months after I murdered my brother and left everything to collapse.

"I've sucked a few cocks at the club, and always with a condom. But I haven't fucked anyone, I swear. Not *men,* anyway."

That's new. I pull another long drag, raking my gaze over her curvaceous form. Goddess bodied, like Keegan's fertile little peony. "That outfit you've got on is a clear indication you came here with a… *Plan A.*"

Puppet nods slowly, then turns around to reach for the leather jacket she discarded moments ago. She digs through a pocket and, without facing me, lifts two forms of contraceptives between her fingers. One is a Trojan, the other is a thin, pink plastic encasement of a single white pill.

"How do you want to fuck me?" she whispers, placing the packets down on the table.

"*With blatant disregard for your pleasure or well-being.*" I grab her arm and spin her back around to face me. Stepping closer to pin her between my body and the edge of the kitchen table, I command, "*Open your wicked mouth.*"

She's trembling, a mixture of fear and anticipation, I'm certain. She parts her lips, though barely.

"*Wider...* I want to see you touch your chin with the tip of your pretty pink tongue, Puppet."

Taking a quivering breath, she lowers her jaw and slips her tongue out, stretching it down as far as she can. Her eyes drift to the glowing cherry of my cigarette as I pull a final crackling drag, then they dart back up to mine, widened and afraid.

"Did you think I was going to spit in your mouth?" I ask, the mocking words drifting on my smoke. "This isn't a *reward*, it's a punishment. And might you guess *why* you are so deserving of this punishment?"

Her fingers flex and grip the ledge of the table, and she lets out a fearful whimper.

"Nod your head if you understand, darling, and I promise I won't grind it completely out in your pretty pink flesh."

Another whimper, but she nods, her body fidgeting with barely contained fear riddled with anxiety as adrenaline pumps through her system. She watches my steady hand bring the burning cherry closer to the center of her treacherous tongue. Screwing her eyes shut, moaning in quick little bursts, she braces for the pain while tears slide down her cheeks.

"*Shh shh shh shhhh...*" I mock her, dabbing and gently pressing the burning ember into her pink flesh. It sizzles against her moist tongue, leaving behind smears of black ash. She whines louder, biting down on herself, seemingly beyond her control.

"Oh, don't be so *dramatic!*" I scold, knowing full well this isn't nearly as painful as I could make it. Extinguishing a cigarette on one's tongue is a simple party trick. It barely burns *if done correctly*. The trick is to move it about the tongue, never lingering in any one spot for too long. Sure, she feels the heat, but it's no worse than a hot cup of coffee. *The real torture is in her mind...* However, I don't want her to bite the damn thing off. That would be a tragic waste of her talents.

I toss the bent and extinguished butt into the ashtray on the table, then lean forward to blow on the blackened, *barely-there* burns, dislodging a saliva-logged clump of ash from her tongue.

"Ice?" I offer, unwilling to spit in her mouth even now.

She nods, wiping the tears from her face while her shoulders silently jerk.

I turn from her to grab a cube from the freezer, giving her a moment to gather her composure before returning. "Open up." I smile. She does as she's told, and I pop the cube inside, promptly lifting her chin with the tip of my finger to close her mouth. The ice faintly clatters against her teeth as she positions it against the roof of her mouth, pinning it against the burns for relief. "Is that better, *pet?*"

She nods once more, and a little sob escapes her. Her hand flies to her mouth, determined to muffle further sounds of distress.

"This is what you asked for, isn't it?" I swipe a strand of hair from her damp face. "You came *uninvited* to my private residence... You *insulted* and *antagonized* me to my face, Puppet... I even gave you the chance to leave unscathed... Yet you cry as if I'm not a gentleman. *As if I'm the bad guy... Tisk tisk,* naughty girl. Perhaps a spanking is in order?" On second thought, she tends to derive a bit of pleasure from that as well.

She's still trembling, coughing now, and wipes at her blackened tongue. I remove the handkerchief from my back pocket and hand it to her. She takes it from me, though warily, and wipes out her mouth.

"*Look at you*, shaking like a leaf." I smile as another wicked game springs to mind. It would be such a waste not to take advantage of her burst of adrenaline. She's wide open for another mind fucking. "Did I *scare* you, Puppet?"

She only nods, seemingly afraid to speak at all... I'm fine with that.

"*I think you should run*, Puppet." Her eyes lift to peer up at me with uncertainty. "I'll even let you choose the number I count to... *Fair?*"

She swallows with a bit of difficulty. "Y-you're going to...ch-*chase me?*"

I lean into her, bringing my mouth closer to her ear as I reach my hand toward her hip. "I'm going to *pursue you*... You like the idea of that, don't you?" A quivering, telling sigh escapes her. I press a finger against the pill packet on the table and drag it closer to the edge. "Think of this as *after care*," I joke, lifting the little packet. I let her see my choice of contraceptive and tuck it into my jacket pocket. "And when I catch you, Puppet..." She swallows hard again, and I know the pupils in those eyes behind her contacts are blown wide with lust. "*When I fucking...catch... you...*"

"*One hundred,*" she breathily whispers, sliding out from between the table and my hovering form, and inches toward the sliding glass door.

"*One hundred...*" I offer her a curt nod, grinning as I refasten my belt for the chase. "*Ninety-nine...*"

Puppet darts out the door, and the smile slides off my face. She really thought she could turn the tables on me again. Thought she could get inside *my* head and punish *me* without consequence.

For a moment, I consider not pursuing her at all. letting her get lost in the fucking woods, slowly coming to the realization that I never had any intention of pursuing her. A part of me doesn't deem her worthy of the effort. *On the other hand*, allowing her this calculated win, this seductive little game she's surely craved and is currently romanticizing in her *spread-eagled little brain*, is just a way to bring her to heel. To tighten her puppet strings. To brutally fuck her little mind back into submission. I'll need her submission if my suspicions are correct. Despite her adamant claims of celibacy, I am certain they are false.

I don't bother counting down the rest of the way.

Stepping out onto the deck, I lift my face to the brilliant moon and close my eyes, *listening...*

The woodland creatures have gone silent to my left. I turn in that direction, dialing in on her location. She's in heels. She couldn't have gotten too far.

A twig snaps...

"*There you are...*"

Jumping from deck to dirt, I dart into the tree line to the left of my cabin, down the trail that runs along the riverbank. The moon is bright tonight, nearly full. The branches looming above cast shadows upon the trail, stretching across the ground like black, gnarled fingers. I can almost make out her figure a few yards ahead, my senses honed to a razor's edge.

It's ingrained in the male psyche, the instinctual drive to hunt. That primal hunger, undeniable when unleashed, whether it be for sustenance or sex.

I hear her faint gasp, then the thud of her soft body hitting the trail, followed by a little grunt. She must have caught the toe of her boot on a fallen branch, or perhaps a surface root.

Another surge of adrenaline enters my bloodstream, and I break into a sprint.

She's barely on her feet again before I tackle her from behind, slamming her down into the dirt. A strangled little shriek escapes her, but it's mostly the air being forced from her lungs upon impact, crushed beneath my weight.

She attempts to crawl, to drag herself from beneath me, when I lift my torso from her back and straddle her thighs. Her fingers scrape the dirt in search of a root to grip and pull like rungs on a ladder, but it's no use. Even if her fingers did find purchase, it wouldn't do her any good. She's not escaping me.

I grip her hips and haul her back to me.

"You're not going anywhere, Puppet," I growl, repositioning my grasp to her leather waistband at the small of her back, keeping her tight, voluptuous ass flush against my crotch. With my free hand, I undo my belt and yank it through the belt loops with a whirr.

Using my teeth, I loop the end quickly through the buckle and slip it over her head. Upon bringing the leather to her panting mouth, I shove it inside, ramming the belt past her teeth, then I jerk the end to tighten the improvised lasso around her, pulling until her head is forced back and she scrambles to push herself up on her hands and knees.

"You want me to fuck *you*, Puppet?" I demand, wrapping the belt around my wrist to keep her firmly in place. I jerk her waistband hard, nearly lifting her knees off the ground. "Get these fucking pants down, and I'll breed you like the cum-thirsty bitch in heat you are."

Still whimpering and sucking in breath around the belt strapped across her mouth, she fumbles with her fly and eagerly shoves the leather down over her hips and ass. I use my free hand to help her get them all the way down, exposing her entire ass and upper portion of her thighs.

"Gasp and moan all you want. *Grunt like the fucking little slut-pig you are*... But if you scream, Puppet... *If you fucking scream*..."

I bring my open hand down on her ass and the loud smack echoes through the woods. She lets out a small squeak at the sting. "Don't you fucking move," I warn her, undoing my pants to get my aching cock out. The moment I'm free, I slam forward, driving into her with brute force. She cries out, though it's muffled by the leather between her teeth, and I'm not at all surprised to find her cunt already drenched. Slick, warm walls contract around my cock with every penetrating thrust, testing my restraint. I haven't fucked a pussy raw in ages.

"Is this what you want?" I pant, fighting back the urge to come already. *"To be rutted on like an animal in the dirt?"*

Her clenching cunt drives me to fuck her harder. I'm not bottoming out yet.

"Get this fucking ass higher!" I shove her down between her shoulder blades, forcing the side of her face into the dirt. "Arch your back, I'm going deeper."

She instantly arches her back into demon pose. She wants this. Wants to feel my hot seed spurt against her womb. I release the belt to grip her hips with both hands, pressing my thumbs into the sexy dimples right above her thick ass. I dig into her flesh so tightly, I know she'll have bruises by the end of this encounter. *Perhaps he'll see them...*

She pulls my leather belt from her mouth, and her labored panting produces a slight divot in the dirt near her face.

"Is this all you hoped it would be, Puppet?" I ask, slamming into her, the head of my cock collides easily now with her cervix at this angle. *I hope it fucking hurts!* "Is this what you fucking wanted?"

"Yes...fuck...yes..." she whines beneath me. *"Come in me... Legion... Please... Come inside of me..."*

I bottom out and grind deep inside of her. She groans as if she finds the sensation pleasurable, and it pisses me off further. The demented bitch wants my brutality. It's the only way she knows I'm thinking of her.

With a wicked sneer she can't see, I pull out of her, and the cold air hits my drenched dick.

"No! Come back!" she gasps.

"Shh shh shh." I reposition myself to grab her ankles and jerk them roughly back, forcing her legs all the way down, thighs flush against the trail. Straddling her curvaceous ass between my thighs, I guide my cock back into her pussy and sink inside her once again. *"That's my girl..."*

"Legion..."

"Shut up," I snap, pumping her deeply, but gently now, letting her really feel the drag and penetration of my cock as I close my eyes and imagine *someone else* beneath me. "You want my cum, baby?" When she doesn't answer, I smack the side of her ass, though softer than I struck her before. *"Do you want me to come inside of you?"*

"Yes."

"Mmmm...good girl..." I thrust a little faster.

"Legion...*don't...*" she whimpers.

"It's our secret, baby... He never needs to know... *Unless it's born with my eyes...*"

"Legion!" Puppet shrieks beneath me, horrified, thrashing in a desperate attempt to buck me off her.

This simply won't do...

Repositioning to blanket the full weight of my body atop her back, pinning her down, I wrap an arm around her throat, holding her in a headlock as I continue to thrust inside of her. Before she can object again, I clamp my other hand over her mouth. Now she can bitch and moan all she wants. It'll be easier to imagine the woman I truly desire, grunting and groaning when I pump my encroaching release deep inside of her.

Tears trickle over the hand I have firmly clasped against her mouth. I bury my face in the long, dark hair curtaining her ear, and breathe in the scent I concocted to aid in her cosplay.

"*Fuck*, baby... I'll give you everything you could ever dream of, sweet one..." I whisper, "Let me feel you come on me..."

Puppet is still fighting, trying desperately to ruin the fantasy.

I can't help but chuckle, unwrapping my arm from around her throat. I shove my hand beneath her, and she attempts to clench her thighs tighter, in the process, squeezing my dick a little harder. But she can't keep me from that hooded little bundle of nerves. That hot button that's going to defeat her in this little power play.

"Come for me, baby," I growl against her ear while my fingers roughly work her clit. "I want to feel you come on my cock, Vanna... I want to feel you milking me for every fucking drop I've got to give you... And I want to give it to you, sweet one... I want to give you everything... *All of me...*"

Her erratic thrashing and squirming to fight me off becomes more rhythmic, and I know I've already won her body over, despite the cries muffled behind my hand.

"That's it, baby, you're taking me so well, sweet one... Fuck... you're such a good girl...such a *good* fucking girl... I'm going to fill this tight little pussy... Going to pump everything I've got into you... *But not before you fucking come for me!"*

Her walls tighten and begin to spasm, her body tenses beneath me as her orgasm hits, whether she wants it or not. Quivering and becoming astonishingly wetter, her milking grip is my undoing. I thrust into her a few more times before I'm spent of the poison.

Game over.

I release my grip over her mouth, grimacing as I pull out of her and sit back on the heels of my motorcycle boots. I need a fucking cigarette... *But first things first...*

"Was that good for you, Puppet?" I ask, tucking myself back into my pants while I watch her struggle to pull hers up. "Did you get what you wanted?"

She rolls over onto her back once she's got them over her ass and refastens her fly. The side of her face is caked with dusty dirt, and she's got a couple of crunchy leaves stuck in her hair.

"I hate you," she mutters, and I don't bother fighting the sneer her words pull from me.

"Yet you keep *coming* back."

She pushes herself up off the ground, and I rise with her. She attempts to storm off in the direction of my cabin, but I grab her arm, preventing her.

"Not so fast."

"What?" she sniffles.

"Open that fucking mouth for me one more time, Puppet." I grin, removing the Plan B from my pocket. After tearing open the packet, I hold the pill up for her between my thumb and forefinger.

With another look of pure hatred, she does as she's told. I press the pill into her mouth, then shove her jaw closed. "*Now swallow like a good girl,*" I whisper, pressing a finger to her lips.

She stares at me as I drag my touch down her chin, then grip her throat loosely, waiting to feel her swallow it down. In the light of the pale moon, I watch a tear cut a thin trail through the layer of dirt canvasing her cheek, and her throat rolls against my palm.

"*That's my girl.*"

CHAPTER 19

Vanna

"Keegan. Party of two?" The pretty blonde glances up at us from her hostess stand.

"That's us." I smile as Dean places his hand at the small of my back and gently guides me ahead of him.

"Right this way." The hostess grabs two menus and leads us into the dining room.

We follow her to the table I reserved earlier in the week when Dean insisted on a low-key birthday. He's been so stressed lately, Cherry and I agreed to grant him a pass on a party this year. It was, after all, his *birthday wish*.

After Dean assists me into my seat, he takes his own across from me.

"Enjoy!" The hostess hands us each a menu and walks away.

"Do you think Viking feels like Ace is... I don't know, *cramping his style*?" I ask, peeking at my husband over the menu.

Dean arches a brow. "I really don't think Ace is a burden, Vanna. Viking and Cherry basically fought over who got to babysit him tonight."

I gnaw at my bottom lip. "I suppose that's true... Though they did settle on splitting the evening with him." I can't help but dig a little more. "Do you think Viking is having girl problems? I mean, he seems to prefer Ace's company over everyone else's."

Dean clears his throat and drops his gaze to the menu. "I uh...wouldn't know."

I eye him suspiciously. "Is there a girl?"

"Hopefully not tonight."

"You know what I mean."

"I'm sure there are lots of girls, doll. We're talking about Viking, here."

"He's been different, though. You're his best friend, you haven't noticed?"

"I'm pretty sure Ace knocked me out of that spot." Dean chuckles. "Maybe becoming an uncle mellowed him out a little."

"Maybe..."

"Viking's not much of a *talk about his feelings type*, doll."

"If you say so." I'll just ask Viking when we meet up in the gym later this week. "But since we're on the topic of relationships..." I begin again, drawing a curious, yet somewhat stern expression from Dean as he glances over the top of his menu once more. "Cherry and I have been wondering how to bring this up with you. There's really never a good time."

Dean sets the menu on the cloth-covered table. "And you thought a ritzy restaurant was the best option?"

"It's nothing bad. It's about Daniel."

"What about him?"

"He and Trippy are an item, but they can't make it official because of *MC rules*. He needs your nod of approval in order for the Jokers to patch him in. Then Trippy can become his Old Lady."

"Huh." Dean picks his menu back up and flips it open, a barely-there grin pulling at the corner of his mouth.

"What's funny?"

"His contentment hinging on my mercy."

"*Happy birthday*, I guess." I giggle, and his smile broadens. "But really, he makes Trippy happy. Would you do it for her?"

"Trippy can do better than Daniel."

"It might get under Lucinda's skin, too." I shrug. Though as much as I despise her, she's not the reason I'm asking.

His eyes narrow curiously. "Do *you* want me to give Slice the go-ahead?"

"For Trippy. I like her."

"As you wish." Dean sighs. "I'll give Slice a call this week."

I smile to myself, relaxing into my seat a little more comfortably now that I've got one thing checked off my to-do list.

"What?" Dean asks. "You're nibbling that lip and smirking, which tells me you're thinking devious thoughts."

"Maybe I'm getting better at this *power of persuasion* thing."

Dean chuckles. "As I recall, you've always held an influence over me."

"As a wife should," I tease him.

"No objection here." He winks at me with that sexy, bracketed-half-grin of his. "*Happy wife, happy life.*"

After dinner and a bottle of wine, Dean escorts me to the elevator. He's already getting handsy, and I stifle a giggle as the elevator doors chime and slide open.

It takes me a moment in my tipsy state to realize the beautiful brunette standing inside the elevator, wearing a flattering cocktail dress, is my sister. She seems rather stunned to see me as well. Dean is too busy whispering his dirty birthday wishes in my ear and groping my ass. He hasn't even spared her a glance.

"*Giovanna?*" Giuliana finally speaks, stepping cautiously through the doors. They shut behind her, and Dean stiffly straightens at my side. "What a surprise… I didn't expect to see you here… God, you look stunning." She gestures to the black dress I only wear for Dean on special occasions.

"Um…yes…we…" I stammer, still in shock as I attempt to regain my bearings. "It's um, Dean's birthday… We're here celebrating… Dinner, you know." My dress is flattering, though compared to the designer garment gracing my sister's slight curves, I feel a bit upstaged. Giuliana *actually does* look like a model that would be featured in *Italian Vogue*.

"Oh," her nervous gaze shifts timidly to Dean. "How lovely. Happy birthday, Dean."

He remains silent, but nods curtly when I peer up at him.

"What brings you out here of all places?" I manage to ask now that the shock of seeing her is wearing off. This hotel isn't even in our town. Dean and I packed a duffel bag and rode Serene to the beach.

Giuliana fusses with the sapphire beaded clutch that matches her dress. "I had a few points to use up," she says, though I suspect it's because it happens to be the nicest hotel within drivable distance of our home. "And, well, a letter or a phone call didn't seem sufficient, after everything... You're my sister. I miss you so much. And Dean... I'm sorry for my behavior. I was wrong. I'd had a lot to drink that night, and...well, there's really no excuse... I behaved abhorrently. I will never cross those lines with either of you ever again."

I glance up at him when he doesn't respond. He isn't even looking at her. Shifting in my heels uncomfortably, I bring my attention back to Giuliana. "So, you're in town to see us?"

"Yes, I was going to come to the roadhouse tomorrow. I just got in last night. I wanted to see you before the holidays so I wouldn't be crashing whatever you have planned."

I peer up at my husband once again in an attempt to gauge his level of reception, but Dean is still a cold block of granite.

"I...I didn't think a phone call was appropriate... I thought the right thing would be to apologize in person," Giuliana adds.

"Are mom and dad here, too?" I ask.

"They're still in New York, but they send their love."

"Why didn't any of you come to the wedding?"

She winces as she tells me, "We didn't think you really wanted us there."

"We sent you invitations."

"I'm sorry." My sister nervously glances past us, somewhere in the direction of the hotel restaurant. It seems like there's more to this situation, but she changes the subject. "Is your son here, too?"

"No," I say.

She seems genuinely disappointed. "I thought maybe there was a chance he was with the nanny in a room."

Dean lets out a resentful scoff.

"No," I quickly reply, stroking his arm as if it will stave off his darkening mood. "We don't have a nanny. Ace is with his aunt."

"Oh, I didn't know you had a sister, Dean."

"Not by blood, *but that doesn't mean much*," Dean finally mutters.

Giuliana nearly flinches. "Well, I would really love to meet my nephew, and spend some time with you all... There's a lot to catch up on."

Dean clears his throat to speak, but keeps his eyes fixed on the elevator doors behind Giuliana. "I told you I'd follow your lead when it comes to your family, Vanna. Whatever you want." His tone isn't as agreeable as his words, however.

"Alright… We're checking out in the morning. Why don't you come by the house for lunch?" I suggest.

"Thank you," she says, though she seems apprehensive. "Would you mind if I bring a guest?"

"A guest?"

"My boyfriend…We drove down together." She glances at Dean. "If bringing him is a problem, I'll just tell him to drop me off."

"Sure, bring your boyfriend," I say. There's no reason to be rude, and how much more awkward could this all really get?

"Great… Well, I don't want to keep you from your evening." Giuliana takes an awkward step as if she's going to walk past us, but then stops. "Thank you," she seems to genuinely say. "Both of you."

I'm not quite sure how to respond as I try not to think of the events that transpired the last night we were all in the same room together.

Dean is still silent, even after the elevator doors close behind us and he hits the button for our floor.

"Are you alright? I know that wasn't the birthday surprise you were expecting," I try to joke, watching his reflection in the brass paneling.

"Fuckin' Aces, doll."

I let out a sigh, unconvinced. A few moments later, the elevator door dings and slides open, and we step into the quiet hallway that leads to our room.

Dean taps the keycard to the scanner and opens the door, letting me in first. The door clicks shut behind us, and I drop my clutch on the foot of the bed and turn to face him. "Don't let this ruin your birthday."

He raises a brow but doesn't comment.

I slide my arms around his waist and pull him closer. "We have a hotel room to ourselves with no worry of *toddler interruptions*," I smirk up at him.

He rests his hands against my hips. "They blew off our wedding. Your father didn't walk you down the aisle…but he was happy to throw you to a fuckin' wolf like Jack Nero. I'm the one they still consider trash. My son—*their first grandchild*—isn't even worthy of their fucking presence."

I reach up to cup his stubbled jaw. "I understand how you feel. But they do send him cards for birthdays and Christmas."

Dean scoffs. "*Right*. I forgot money is what matters."

"I didn't say that."

"*They do*, every chance they get to throw it in my fucking face."

I stroke his tensing jaw. "Maybe it's just taken them until now to get over everything? Maybe they didn't think they were actually welcome to come?"

"Three years and they were in the wrong to begin with? Fuck that. They got the same invitation everyone else did."

"I don't want to spend tonight arguing with you about my family. Can we just let it go until tomorrow? Your points are valid, but this can't be how you want to spend your birthday."

"It isn't."

I smile up at him through my lashes and begin undoing the top buttons of his shirt. "*Good*. My plans don't include us sitting up here bickering in matching bathrobes."

Dean huffs a quiet, halfhearted laugh. "Yeah, well, you've always been better than me at letting things go."

I maneuver him backwards until the backs of his knees meet the edge of the bed. He sits, and I step back just enough to let his hands fall away from my hips. "What about *taking things off?*" I tease, unzipping my dress before slowly slipping one strap from my shoulder, then the other. Dean leans back slightly, his dark gaze catching fire in a way that makes my pulse stutter. I push the dress down over my hips until gravity takes it to the floor. The fabric pools at my heels, and I can practically feel his scorching-hot gaze consuming me.

Dean lets out a low breath. *"Fuck. Me."*

"That's the plan," I murmur, toying with one of the garter straps of the lingerie set I'm wearing just for him. I let it snap against my thigh, and he licks his bottom lip before scraping it through his teeth on a deep growl.

I step forward and straddle his lap. His hands dig into my thighs, sliding beneath the garter straps, but I grab his wrists before he can rip anything.

"Let me," I whisper, leaning closer to his lips. "Just let me take care of you tonight." I slide my hands up his body and into his hair as our mouths collide, all heat and want and reverence. He pulls me tighter against him with another throaty growl. I break the kiss and bring my lips to the shell of his ear. "Happy birthday," I tease him with my breath and the tip of my tongue at his lobe before nibbling it. "Now lie back and let me show you how happy I am you exist."

DEAN

New York plates on a black Mercedes. I sigh and run a hand over my jaw as I stare out the front door, the hot buzz from last night's sexcapades dimming fast. Vanna and I took something back last night, something the stress and chaos that keeps blowing into our lives seems hell bent on stripping away. Between Legion's shit and now her family, I'm in no damn mood.

"Your sister just pulled up," I announce, though it's the boyfriend behind the wheel. As he steps from the vehicle, there's something unsettlingly familiar about him. It only takes a moment to realize who he is. They share the same blue eyes and angular features. "You've got to be shitting me," I mutter under my breath. No wonder Giuliana didn't mention this detail last night.

"What is it?" Vanna asks from the kitchen island, where she's just finished putting together a tray of cheese and crackers. She's already got glasses and a pitcher of sweet tea with ice and lemon waiting on the coffee table in the living room.

I have no idea how to approach this with her. How to proceed with this situation at all. The lack of consideration on her sister's part already has my blood pressure rising.

"Your sister really should have given us a heads up. You're going to have to tell me right now how you want this handled."

Vanna comes to stand beside me and peers out the window. I stare at her, attempting to read her thoughts through microexpressions. Curiosity instantly morphs into shock as she recognizes the man escorting Giuliana to our door.

"*Of all the men she could have gone for,*" Vanna whispers to herself. She's certainly surprised but doesn't seem alarmed. "*She could have had any guy.*"

I take her hand and squeeze it gently. "Not *any* guy, Vanna." She peers up at me with a soft, barely-there smile. "Just say the word, and I'll make them go away."

"No," she sighs, resigned to the situation. "I want to hear what she has to say, especially about this."

After I'm briefly introduced to *Richard*, Vanna fetches the charcuterie board and places it on the slate coffee table in the living room between us all. We take our seats, Vanna and I together on the leather couch, Giuliana *and possibly the worst choice in a boyfriend she could have made* on the leather love seat adjacent.

"This is certainly a surprise," Vanna says, and despite the awkward situation, I'm proud of the fact that she doesn't shy away from meeting his gaze, considering the strong family resemblance.

"It's not your sister's fault... I wanted to be with her when she told you about us," *Richard* says, then turns to Giuliana. "Why don't you put that ring back on where it belongs?"

"*You're engaged?*" Vanna watches in surprise as Giuliana produces a large diamond ring from her purse and slips it onto her left hand before holding it out for Vanna to see.

"Wow...it's beautiful... What a...surprise!" Vanna nearly stammers, then shifts her attention back to the fiancé. "Well, Richard, finding myself related to another Nero through marriage definitely wasn't on my bingo card." They both exchange tight-lipped smiles. "Congratulations," she adds, and I follow suit.

Jack's younger brother pats Giuliana's knee before she takes his hand and holds it in her lap. "I couldn't be happier. I've had a thing for your sister for years."

Neither women comment, and I have zero desire to contribute to the conversation. As the awkward silence stretches on, Giuliana glances around the room, eyes settling on Ace's basket of toys near the chess table. "Where is my nephew? I thought he'd be here."

"He tuckered himself out at the park earlier this morning. We have frequent playdates with his cousin Mia," Vanna explains. "Naps have become hit and miss with him at this age, but he should be up any minute now." She gestures to her sister's showy engagement ring. "How did this *happen?*"

Richard blinks, then seems to force a chuckle. "*Happen?* You say that like our engagement is some sort of travesty." There's a disingenuous humor in his tone, and Vanna tenses beside me, instantly triggering my protective instincts. I keep my gaze locked on him.

"I'm still deciding," Vanna replies to my surprise and approval, though Richard doesn't seem as amused.

"We got close after everything happened with Jack," Richard says. "We leaned on each other. We got closer after the falling out between the two of you."

"*Oh*. Did my sister tell you *why* we haven't spoken?" Vanna asks. I shift my gaze from Jack's brother to check on her in time to see her spare a fidgeting Giuliana a quick glance.

"We were just good friends, then… She made a mistake. One of which I'm aware she's apologized for." Richard shifts his gaze to me for a moment, giving me a once-over before returning his attention to Vanna. If I cared at all what either of them thought of me, I suppose it would be another awkward moment. When it comes to my in-laws, I'm all out of fucks.

"Do we have to rehash that embarrassing night again?" Giuliana sighs. "I have apologized to you both, and I mean it. Don't you want to bring our family back together now? It's been over three years, Vanna." The tension in my wife's body eases at the sight of her sister's teary eyes. "I love you, and I've missed you so much. I've missed out on getting to know my first and only nephew. I don't want that to happen with you."

"With me?" Vanna asks, and suddenly my heart is beating a little faster… *Fuck my life, here it comes…* "What do you mean *with me*?"

When Giuliana smiles and gazes lovingly at Richard, I brace myself for the words I know we're about to hear.

"I want you to be a part of our baby's life, too," her sister says.

"*You're pregnant?*" Giuliana is too wrapped up in her big reveal. She doesn't realize there's something more than surprise in Vanna's words.

"Yes! Thirteen weeks!" Giuliana says excitedly, "Besides our parents, I wanted you to be the first to know."

Vanna's eyes drop to her sister's belly, which still looks flat to me, but that isn't surprising at this early stage. "Thirteen weeks… Wow… Congratulations!" When Vanna stands, I know she's about to find a reason to distance herself for a moment, excuse herself to the bathroom, or maybe go wake up Ace. But her sister jumps up and throws her arms around Vanna's neck, oblivious.

"Thank you!" she weeps. "I was so looking forward to telling you our wonderful news. It means so much to me that you're happy for us."

"Why wouldn't I be?" Vanna says, and though her sister is convinced, I'm not. I promised my wife I'd follow her lead when it comes to her family, so I stand and offer Jack Nero's brother a congratulatory handshake. He rises from his seat and accepts.

"Congratulations, all around." I force a smile.

"Thank you," he says, though I notice his doesn't reach his eyes.

"Well, help yourselves to some refreshments while I go get Ace," Vanna insists, then quickly makes her break for his bedroom. I'm tempted to follow her and ask if she's alright, but perhaps she needs a moment alone.

Ace is a very friendly and accepting kid, he gets it from Vanna, so I'm not at all surprised when he takes immediately to Giuliana. Though he might just be a sucker for a pretty girl, like I was... *I'm gonna have to keep a close watch on that.*

"He looks so much like you, Dean," Giuliana says.

"Well, he's got Vanna's loving heart," I reply. Ace might have inherited my physical features, but I can't look at him and not see his beautiful mother.

"Are you excited to have another little cousin, Ace?" Giuliana asks.

"Like Mia and Maddie?" Ace peers up at Vanna, then back at his aunt when she chuckles.

"Yes, you're surrounded by pretty girls, too, huh? Just like your Daddy."

I'm the only one who hears the slight hitch of Vanna's breath, but she recovers quickly. "You're having a girl?"

"Yes. We got lucky at our sonogram appointment the day before last and were able to determine," Giuliana replies.

"That's just, *fantastic*...wow..." Vanna rubs her hands against her knees, then suddenly stands. "Excuse me. I need...something." She practically bolts from the room again, leaving Ace and me to fend for ourselves. I'm torn between going after her this time and remaining with our son. This prick in our living room is a fuckin' *Nero,* though... I'm not leaving Ace alone with either of them.

Ace gives them a presentation of his favorite toys for a few minutes before walking back to me. "Daddy?"

"What's up, buddy?"

"I have to go potty."

Fuckin' Aces.

"Well, let's go handle that!" I seize the opportunity and scoop Ace up and head for the hallway. "We graduated to big boy pants a few months ago," I tell his aunt and future uncle, even though Ace is looking at me like I've lost my marbles. I'm aware he was only letting me know he had to go. He hasn't needed help making it to the potty in time at home for a while now.

"Dad, *it's just number one*," he informs me as we enter the master bedroom. Vanna is sitting on the bed, hurriedly wiping her cheeks upon our arrival. The reason behind her tears simultaneously pulls at my heartstrings and slugs me in the fucking gut, but I keep my shit together for Ace.

"What's going on?" she asks, forcing a smile for Ace's sake as well.

I place him on his feet and give his little bottom an encouraging pat. "Go pee," I tell him, and he walks into the bathroom, leaving his mother and me somewhat alone for a moment. I switch the light on and close the door behind him before approaching her. "Are you alright?" I ask, sitting beside her.

"I'm fine," she sighs. "I just wasn't expecting any of this."

"I didn't see this coming, either."

"I'm sure my parents are thrilled. She's marrying a Nero *and* giving them a granddaughter."

"Well, she got knocked up out of wedlock, too," I playfully bump her knee with mine. "They couldn't have been too thrilled."

Vanna scoffs. "Please. She can do no wrong in their eyes, or have you forgotten?"

"No, I haven't... I'm sorry." But I know that's not the reason she was brushing away tears. I don't know how to bring this topic up with her, but I do know now is not the time for this conversation. I am concerned about something, though. I lower my voice and bring my lips closer to my wife's ear. "I'm no fan of your sister's, Vanna, but...is she *safe* with him?"

"Richard isn't Jack. Are you anything like your brother?"

"Daniel is an asshole, but he's not a psychotic killer."

"You know what I mean. You can't condemn a person just because they're related to someone. We're all individuals." She lets out another stress-ridden sigh, and I can't help but wonder if she's also referring to *someone else* we know… "Jack's parents were happily married. Richard's never hurt anyone, and he always did seem to have a crush on Giuliana. *Then again*, so did every guy who's ever met her."

"*Not every guy*, Vanna." I press a kiss against her temple.

"Besides… I made mistakes with Jack that may have influenced him to—"

"*The fuck you did*, Vanna," I growl, a deep hatred for Jack bubbling to the surface. "Wishing for the man you were with at the time to love you didn't turn him into the fucking devil. *I wish* you'd let that shit go." She doesn't say anything, and I wonder if she'll ever stop blaming herself. She's so quick to forgive everyone else. "I'm gonna find out if this kumbaya act is legit… Something about him ain't sitting right with me."

"I'm sure they're just uncomfortable after everything that's happened between all of us. He loves her. He's going to stick up for her. You can't take offense if he's a little put off by you, considering everything that's happened. And the fact she admitted to him that she hit on you without shifting any of the blame on you, couldn't have been easy for him to hear, let alone sit in our living room and look you in the face."

The sound of the toilet flushing forces us to put a pin in the discussion for now as Ace calls out from inside the bathroom, "*I'm doooone!*"

Neither of us is able to suppress our smiles at Ace's call to summon potty assistance.

"He told me number one." I chuckle.

"Go help finish up in there," Vanna says, patting my leg as she stands. "I'll go see to our guests."

"Debatable who's got the shittier job in this situation," I joke.

She shakes her head. "Make sure he washes his hands. We don't have the fun dinosaur soap in our bathroom," she adds.

When Ace and I return to the living room, Richard stands and asks for a private word on the front porch. The door barely shuts behind us before he asks, "Do you resent Giuliana?"

"If Vanna forgives her, so do I. And since you opened this door, where do your resentments lie regarding everything that's happened?"

"For a long time, I blamed Giovanna for Jack… The pain my mother was in as a result of everything… I hated you both. It was Giuliana who helped me put things into perspective… I've made my peace with the fact that it was Jack who hurt everyone."

I try not to glare at him, at least not with the amount of suspicion I'm harboring. "So, we're all on the same page then. Your brother was a vile piece of shit and deserves to be rotting in the grave I put him in." I can't help but test him.

He clears his throat but retains a decent poker face. "I'm not sure I'd have put it quite so harshly... Jack made his choices. Unfortunately, we're all the ones left suffering the consequences of those choices."

"Some of us more than others."

"Look, you married Giovanna. I'm marrying her sister. We've both got kids with them. It's time to let everything die with Jack, don't you think?" He glances away from me to peer through the picture window, then gestures inside. "Can't you see how much they miss being a family? Do you really want to be the guy standing in the way of that?"

"I've said from day one, I'd go along with whatever Vanna wants."

"It's pretty clear what they both want. You and I are basically brother-in-laws now. I never thought I'd shake the hand of the man who killed Jack, but here we are." Richard extends his hand to me, and I can't help but test him one more time.

Gripping his hand in a strong shake, I reply, "Well, Dick, your brother had it coming."

It isn't much longer before they decide to hit the road. We watch our women hug each other goodbye, then Giuliana kisses Ace's cheek and wishes us a Happy Thanksgiving before climbing into their Mercedes and taking off.

"You couldn't help yourself, could you?" Vanna peers up at me as we walk up the porch steps together behind Ace.

"What?"

"Richard practically dragged her out to the car," Vanna says, opening the door so Ace can bolt back inside to the toys he still has scattered in the living room.

"Maybe he just wants to beat traffic." I grin, following her inside.

She presses her lips together and shakes her head. "I'm so sure that's why. You're kind of notorious for your porch conversations, Dean."

"Well, he might not be Jack," I say, shutting the door behind us. "But he's definitely a dick."

CHAPTER 20

Vanna

"You're hitting like a girl," Viking teases from the bench press. He's been watching me punch the bag while lifting weights. "For someone who looks so frustrated, you're really not taking advantage of all that bag has to offer. I've taught you better than this, Vanna. You wanna talk about something?"

Expelling a harsh breath, I glance over at him and drop my gloved fists to my sides. "It's that obvious?"

"When shit's bothering them, *bro's swing and bitches sing*. This entire training session has been a complete waste of our time if you don't tell me what's up."

I frown despite another one of Viking's silly sayings. "Sorry."

"Just spill the beans and I'll forgive you," he says, doing one more press before putting the bar back on the rack and sitting up. "Or you can drop and give me fifty," he jokes, pointing at the gym floor.

"*Friendsgiving* is in two days," I warn him with a smile.

"Well played," Viking grins, shifting to make room beside him on the bench. "Have a seat and tell me what's going on. Your head's been up in the clouds and not in a good way. What's got you so distracted?"

"My sister came to visit the other day," I say, plopping down next to him. "Dean didn't mention that to you?"

"He did. Gimme' those mitts," Viking insists, reaching for my hands. I shift toward him and let him undo my boxing gloves. He removes them and gets up to put them away in the supply locker before returning to sit beside me.

"Did he tell you she's engaged to Jack's brother?"

"*Oh yeah.*" He nods. Judging by the way his eyebrows nearly reach his hairline, he was just as surprised by the news as we were, and I have no doubt Dean wasn't too thrilled when he conveyed the story. There's nothing we can do, though. At least they're all content to stay in New York. If we have to suck it up for the occasional holiday visit, so be it. It's her life. I expect my parents are delighted with the entire Giuliana and Richard situation… And their baby girl…

"Did Dean tell you anything else?"

Viking glances at me curiously. "There's more?"

I fight the sudden urge to bring my hand to my tightening throat. *Dean didn't mention Giuliana is pregnant?*

"Alright, now you're being too quiet." Viking sighs. "What's up?"

"I don't know who I can really talk to about this." *Or if I should at all.*

"What's going on with Dean?"

"How do you know it's about Dean?"

"*We* wouldn't be talking right now if it wasn't."

I chew my bottom lip, attempting to stall. "Dean's been stressed out."

Viking looks at me wryly. "*That's his default state of being*, Vanna." I try not to laugh at the accuracy of his statement, but he goes on. "Did you expect to marry a guy who's never *not* had the rug pulled out from under him and he'd be hunky fuckin' dory all the time? The happier he is, the more he worries about losing it."

"Well, I'm not sure what *dory* means, but Dean is pretty *hunky* if you ask me." I force a smile.

Viking shakes his head. "Never crack a joke like that in my presence again."

"Corny?"

"Yup."

"Worse than *biker business*?"

"Way worse. Quit stalling. What's going on?" he presses.

Over the last few years, Viking and I have developed a close friendship I would have thought impossible if not for Ace. He can still be an asshole, but we've grown to genuinely care about each other, and his blunt ways no longer offend me the way they once did.

"I think I'm jealous of my sister. I always have been, a little. She's the perfect one. The pretty one…" *And now she's pregnant with a little girl…*

Viking arches a skeptical brow at me, as if he suspects I'm still avoiding the main issue, but he lets out a sigh and says, "I think part of the reason I was hard on you in the beginning was the fact you were off limits."

"Huh?"

"This is probably breaking guy code, and Dean would fucking kill me for saying this, but…when I first saw you, I thought you were smoking hot."

"Okay, this is getting weird."

"Yeah… like, incestuous weird."

"Ew, don't make it worse!"

"I just mean I see you like a sister now!"

"Yeah, I got that."

"I'm just gonna shut up and let you finish what you were saying."

I let out a frustrated sigh. "I don't know what I'm saying."

"Well, you asked if Giuliana's engagement was all Dean told me about… What else did you think he'd tell me?"

I swallow, trying to prevent the painful lump in my throat from forming, but it's no use. Dean didn't bring it up.

"Ah, shit," Viking mutters, his vaguely curious expression rapidly becomes blurry in my stinging eyes as tears well up against my will. But I can still tell his expression has morphed into one of concern. "Vanna, you better tell me what the fuck is going on. Is it Legion? Did that prick contact you after the fundraiser?"

"No," I croak out, though a part of me is surprised Legion has been so silent, and I can't help but wonder what he's been up to.

"Did Dean fuck up? What did he do now?"

"He didn't do anything." I sniffle, wiping my eyes impatiently with the back of my hand.

"You may have somewhat of a talent for secrecy, but you're a lousy liar, Vanna."

"*Ha, ha*….Jerk." I frown at him. "I switched to an oral contraceptive. One of the side effects is mood swings."

His stoic expression might as well be carved in stone while he waits for a real answer. I've come to observe that these MC guys have mastered this particular visage.

"Promise me you won't say anything to him." I sigh, though it's more of a groan.

"Can't do that. You're his wife," Viking stubbornly insists. "Not only is Dean my best friend, he's my president. Can't make that promise."

"I thought we were family, too? Something beyond all the *biker business*."

"Maybe I need to remind you who you married. Remember when I told you about his psycho switch? You flicked that shit. *Hard.* It's stuck on. Did you lose sight of his crazy? *Living in wedded bliss* over there or some shit... *Your husband is fuckin' nuts* when it comes to his woman, Vanna. Those waters might seem tranquil with you, but there's a deadly current beneath the surface. There can't be any secrets between us. That's not how this works. Even if your husband wasn't nuts."

"Then we've got nothing to talk about," I say, getting up to grab my gym bag containing the clothes I changed out of when I got here. It's actually Ace's old diaper bag. Viking's huge hand engulfs my own, stopping me.

"As long as neither of you is in any trouble, I won't say nothin'," he caves and promises, though I know it's with a heap of reluctance.

I nod, meeting his concerned blue eyes once again, and the tears rush back to mine full force. *"He doesn't want any more children,"* I manage to squeak out.

"Uhhh... *Well...* Shit... I, uh..." Viking studders, clearly caught off guard. Releasing my hand, he stands to his towering height, bringing his hand to the back of his head to uncomfortably mess with his braid, while jamming his other hand in his front pocket. "This is definitely a conversation you two need to have together. Alone. Just you. The both of you. *Together.* At your house. You two. *Yeah.*"

"But he just shuts me down... *I've tried.*"

Viking practically winces, and I don't know if it's because he feels bad for me, for Dean, or for getting himself roped into this conversation in the first place. "I think this topic might fall under the *hands-off Ol' Ladies policy...* I'm not sure, but I'm pretty sure. I gotta check the bylaws... Like, *now.* I should go do that right now. You stay here. Or don't. *I don't know.* Get changed, maybe? I'm gonna be in trouble."

"*Why* would you be in trouble? You didn't do anything."

"And that's exactly what you have to say if anything happens."

"*What's going to happen?*"

"A whole lot of fuckin' nuthin' that's what." Viking shakes his head at me again, waving his big hand back and forth as if he can sweep the last few minutes away. "We never had this conversation."

"*What conversation?*" I demand, jamming my fists against my hips.

He points at me. "*Exactly!*"

"Viking…*nothing* you've said in the last two minutes qualifies as a *conversation.*"

"You catch on quick, Vanna. I like that about you. Have a great rest of your day! I'm out of here."

"Well, thanks… *Thanks a lot.*" I turn from his giant fleeing form to grab my gym bag again.

"*God…damn it…*" he mutters, halting just short of the double doors behind me. "This is a very touchy subject with him, Vanna."

"You think I don't know that? I'm his wife."

He nods, silently conceding my point, then asks, "When's the last time you brought it up to him? And when was the first?"

"I started to breach the subject with him a little after Ace's birthday. He shut me down hard at the Joker's fundraiser. I barely got the words out. I figured enough time had passed…since… Everything… And he has avoided talking about my sister since she left our home. None of us is getting any younger, and Ace is already three. I don't want a huge age gap between him and a sibling, and I want him to have a sibling."

"You know that *Only Child Syndrome* bullshit is just a stereotype, right?" Viking says. "Look at Axel, he's an only child and he's the most selfless guy you could ever meet."

"*Oh, please.* Axel was basically raised with you all as brothers. You might as well have all *marched out of the same womb* together."

Viking blinks. "That's a hilariously disturbing image, Vanna. Thanks for that. But, is that what this is about?" He lets out a long breath. "You're raising Ace right. You both are two of the best people I know. Why would Ace turn out any different with you guys for parents? With the rest of us as extended family? And as far as loneliness goes, when is that kid *ever* alone? We've all got each other. That kid is fuckin' loved, Vanna."

"I know he is. I'm not saying he's not… I just…I want another baby, Viking. *Why is that so wrong?*"

His expression contorts again before he goes on. "It's not *wrong*… But this really is something *only you and Dean* can work out together… I'm sorry, Vanna."

"It's fine." What could Viking really do about our situation anyway? "Maybe I just needed to vent. Forget about it."

"Maybe he just needs a little more time. If you only started bringing this up a month ago… Give him a few more weeks to wrap his head around the idea."

"He's afraid I'll die."

Viking nods contemplatively. "I was with him through the whole ordeal… It was bad, Vanna. Can you blame him?"

"No. But the chances of that happening again, especially if I were to plan for a scheduled c-section," I search his expression for any trace of doubt or disagreement. "And I already have a scar."

"I'm sure what happened last time is of major concern to him. Top of the fuckin' list, Vanna. You have no idea how lost and broken he was that night." Viking closes his eyes, shaking his head again as if the memories are too hard to think about. "Did he tell you he begged me to kill him?"

"…What?"

He opens his eyes to look at me. "Dean begged me to kill him if you didn't pull through. He's got zero will to go on without you."

His words break my heart, though I'm not surprised by them.

"But there's another reason he's reluctant to have this conversation with you…" Viking lets out another heavy sigh. "And I think you know what it is."

Or who it is. My whole body tenses at the thought of her. "*Lucinda.*" Even her name tastes bitter on my tongue.

Viking nods. "What if he *can't* give you the kid, Vanna? To Dean, this is a nightmare scenario playing out all over again. Paired with what he's equating to financial issues, this all might be feeling just *a little bit too familiar* to him in all the wrong ways."

"I get it, but I'm only asking him to *try*. I wouldn't fault him if it isn't meant to be. And there's always IVF."

"Without insurance, you're looking at a baseline fifty-grand expense, easy."

"We have insurance." Mostly because we have Ace now.

"He didn't when he was with Lucinda," Viking says, and I wonder if that's where some of her resentment stemmed from. The money he bought his brother out with to hold onto the farm, the house, the roadhouse, and the repair shop. Maybe she saw it as money they could have used to have a baby. "Just give him time to come around to it. You know all he wants to do is make you happy. If you think this isn't eating him up inside, think again. He already feels like he's failing you."

"Failing me how?"

"Do you know he sold his Heritage? Fuckin' Betty was his second favorite motorcycle."

And he looked damn good on that classic style Harley Davidson, too. "Yes, but I didn't know until he was already halfway through the deal. I asked what he was doing, and he told me to take Ace inside. I never would have suggested he sell Betty, or any of his *side chicks* for that matter."

"I'm not saying you did. I know it was all his idea. When we talked, he sounded like he had everything under control. But I'm going to ask you because I know how stubborn he is. Are you guys doing okay? Does Ace need anything?"

"We're fine. I know he said profits are down, but I don't think things are as dire as Dean seems to."

Viking nods. "There are certain things Dean goes overboard about. Just be patient with him. It's only because he cares," he says as if telling me something I didn't figure out three years ago.

"I know." And I know this all stems from past trauma in his life—his parent's, the shit Lucinda put him through with finances and starting a family, what she pulled with Maddie. I close my eyes on the memory of the broken crib in that empty nursery room, and shove down the anger threatening to bubble up to the surface. "*I will never forgive her... Not for anything.*"

"None of us will," Viking grumbles. "You wanna try some bare-knuckle punches for a little while? Might help to imagine a certain blonde bitch's face on the bag."

I consider it for a moment, then ask, "When are you going to teach me the ground stuff?"

"Ground stuff?"

I gesture to the ring where they spar with all their mixed martial arts moves. "Yeah, teach me how to pin people and get out of being pinned and all that."

He scoffs. "*Never.*"

"What do you mean *never?*"

"It's bad enough he doesn't know about these lessons, and I'm just teaching you basic kick-boxing moves. Ain't no way in hell I'm rolling around on a mat with you. What did I just remind you about cranking up his level of psycho?"

"First of all, it's only a secret because I want to surprise him one of these days when I look like I might know what I'm doing, so don't make it sound so nefarious. *It's not that kind of secret.* And I told him I that come here to work out, so I'm not lying. He'd rather have me come here than go to a fitness center."

Viking reaches into his back pocket to retrieve his wallet and pulls out a business card. "Here," he says, practically shoving it into my hand. "It's an *all-girls* gym. I know the owners. He wouldn't have an issue with this place. And they teach some basic self-defense classes for women. *You can roll around on the ground with other chicks.* Dean won't have a canary over that."

"So, you're pawning me off on somebody else." I sigh, shoving the card in my bag without bothering to look at it.

"Don't you have to go home and bake something?" he grunts back at me. I guess Viking has reached his limit with my bullshit.

"I do actually." It wouldn't hurt to get started on all those cornucopia orders. There are a few ingredients I still need to pick up at the store.

"What time is dinner on Thursday? Can I wear my Thanksgiving pants?" he jokes, referencing the time he wore grey sweatpants to dinner.

"Absolutely not. Nobody wants to see your damn Yule log, Viking."

He laughs. "Fine. Should I bring anything?"

"I think I've got everything covered. Rosita is bringing over a few dishes, also, and Cherry is coming over early with Axel to give me a hand. Dean and Viper have guard duty the first part of the day, so she and Axel can help me wrangle Ace and keep him out of the kitchen while I'm cooking."

"Speaking of Ace, is he with Cherry? If you want, I can take him to get something to eat, tire him out at the park, and bring him home after?" Viking offers with an eagerness he doesn't bother trying to hide. It makes me smile. "Or I can swing by the shop with him first, so Dean can have some time with him before his shift at the safehouse with Axel? He's heading there directly from the shop tonight."

"*You just want to hang out with your best buddy,*" I tease. Viking shrugs, but he doesn't fight the little grin tugging at his mouth. "Sure, that would be very helpful. And Ace loves spending time with you, too. Thank you."

Within a few hours of arriving home, almost every surface of my kitchen is a scattered mess of flour, tinfoil, sesame seeds, and orange cellophane. The oven is only big enough to bake four cornucopias at a time, and I've got eleven more yet to form and bake of the twenty-three orders I received this year. The oven has been going for a few hours straight, and I'm hot. I suppose it wouldn't hurt to open a window and invite some cool November air inside.

I remove the finished batch of Cornucopias from the oven and place them on the kitchen island to cool, before sliding the next two trays in to bake. Wiping off my hands on my flour-dusted apron, I make my way over to the windows near the dining table. As I unlatch the lock and lift it open, the sound of a motorcycle in the driveway catches my attention.

It can't be Dean. He has to clock in with Medusa's Gates right after his shift at the repair shop this evening, and I'm not expecting Viking and Ace until around supper time in about an hour or so. Though there's always a chance Viking brought Ace back early, hoping to sample something *pre-Friendsgiving*. A pang of anxiety hits me when I realize it's Legion, and this is probably not a sanctioned visit. Dean would have warned me on the very off chance Legion obtained his permission.

"Great," I mutter under my breath.

By the time I step out onto the front porch, Legion has dismounted his bike and is walking toward me, one hand tucked behind his back.

"I was wondering where you've been."

"Have you, now?" He seems pleased by the revelation. It's an honest statement, but I can't encourage him.

"You're not supposed to be here, I'm sure."

"*Story of my life*," Legion humorously boasts, his grin never faltering as if it were stitched on. He takes a moment to look me over, then gestures with a wave of his gloved hand at my attire. "I see I may have interrupted some *kitchen witchery*." He lifts his chin, inhaling the air deeply, then exhales on a sigh. "Nothing quite like the aroma of freshly baked bread. You are indeed the epitome of a domestic goddess, sweet one… And damn, *does it look good on you*."

"Flattery gets you nowhere with me."

A deep chuckle rumbles in his throat. "*Another trait of yours I adore.*"

"What do you want, Legion?"

That grin no longer reaches his eyes, and his hand moves to casually hold onto the demon skull buckle of his belt. "Despite having enjoyed my time with you the other night immensely, I realize I may have crossed a line."

"You sure have a knack for antagonizing my husband."

"At least it was for charity, *eh*?"

I fold my arms and purse my lips, not wanting to encourage him with a smile of my own at his admittedly amusing statement.

His grin stretches deviously wider. Somehow, regardless of my effort, he was able to tell. Is he able to read everyone around him so well? *Or is it just me…*

I let out a shaky breath, uncrossing my arms to rub my hands on my apron, and attempt to avoid deciphering how that makes me feel. *I shouldn't be feeling anything.*

He cocks his head to the side, appraising me further. "Are you alright? You seem…*flustered*."

"I'm fine."

"Yes, you are."

"*Legion*."

"At your service." He teasingly bows, yet still manages to keep whatever he's holding concealed behind his back.

"What are you hiding?"

"*If that isn't a loaded question!*"

This time, I sigh in frustration. "I'm very busy today, Legion. So, if you're just here to mess with me…"

His playful expression shifts to something more serious. "I sent you flowers, yet I get the distinct impression you never received them… Did you?"

"No."

He nods slowly, as if he expected the answer.

"When did you send me flowers... And why?"

"I sent you a rose for every promise fulfilled."

I remember his promise, and my heart rate spikes. "I never received any roses."

"I suspected as much... *No matter.* I always intended to bring you *these*," Legion says, finally revealing what he's been holding behind his back. It's a black box, half the size of a shoebox.

Another pang of anxiety hits me, yet somehow, I find myself descending the porch steps, curiosity drawing me closer. "I don't know if I want to open that... Boxes from *you* don't turn out so well for me."

His expression is unreadable as he tears the lid off and dumps the contents out. Black patches with white embroidery litter the ground between us. A majority of them are stained with a reddish-brown residue.

Instinctively, I know it's dried blood.

"There are still two names missing," he says. "Though you shall have those as well."

An uneasy feeling begins to percolate, yet my mind actively refuses to comprehend what is right in front of me.

"I've kept my promises," he goes on at my stunned silence. "To keep you safe... To end them all."

"Oh, God..." the words slip from my lips as I focus on a few of the name patches... *Oxy...Creep...Mayhem...*

"They can't hurt you now. I've made certain of it."

I stagger backwards, nearly tripping up two steps, and grab the railing to steady myself. My heart is racing even faster, making my head spin. *"You killed them..."*

Legion's expression shifts to something more perplexed, reminding me of the way a cat looks at its owner when they aren't praised for dropping a dead bird at their feet. "Of course I did. I specifically promised I would."

"Oh, God..."

"*He* had little to do with it, if that eases your mind."

"W-what?"

"Nothing... I suppose I'm just sick of his *undo credit* in all things." Legion lets out an exasperated sigh at my lack of response. "*God.*" He gestures toward the sky with a flippant, dismissive wave of his hand. "Nothing but an *absentee landlord*, if you ask me."

"*Jesus Christ…*"

"Just as useless." Legion's eyebrow quirks. "I thought you shed all the old Catholic chains?"

"Old habits die hard, I suppose," I barely hear myself say.

Another devious half-smile pulls at the corner of his mouth, and he gestures to the blood-crusted patches. "I assure you, *they did as well.*"

I shake my head, trying to clear my racing thoughts. "H-how many…are there?"

"Thirteen, thus far."

"W-where… How?"

"Scattered across the continental US," Legion replies with a sense of pride. "*How* is something I don't think you'd benefit from knowing. And *why*, sweet one… Well, I'd like to think that's obvious." He stares at me, as if willing me to make some connection. Though the longer our silence stands, the more disappointment I see stirring behind his cold grey eyes.

Yes… I can imagine why… I heard what he confessed to Dean in that warehouse… They aren't words I can ever acknowledge.

"We should probably burn these… Destroy the evidence," I finally manage to say.

Legion slowly crouches and collects the dead men's scattered patches. He puts them back in the box and stands.

"Where would you like to burn them?" he asks, replacing the lid.

"There's a stone fire-pit on the back patio…" I begin to say, then immediately think better of it. I'm not so sure I want to be reminded of this every time Dean and I want to spend time around a cozy fire outside. "*Actually, no.* There's a spot in the yard." A place where Dean burned the mattress he once shared with Lucinda, where he burned everything that reminded him of her after their divorce. That should do. A place where memories go to die…

"Shall we?" Legion smiles, offering me his leather-gloved hand. My legs still feel a bit shaky, so I allow him to assist me down the two steps before I pull my hand back and gesture toward the far side of the property.

"A few yards that way, near the tree line."

"*After you.*" His smile broadens into a wolfish grin. I have a feeling he just wants to stare at my ass. I'm too befuddled to care right now and immediately start walking across the yard.

Over the years, long grass has sprouted between the rust-encrusted coils in this small, neglected part of the yard, but the old mattress springs are still visible. A few bent, metal pieces of whatever other furniture Dean burned that night remain as well.

"Right there," I say, pointing. "I probably should have gone inside and grabbed the charcoal lighter fluid for the grill."

"Worry not." Legion pulls off his glove with his teeth, then shoves it in his jeans pocket. He removes the Zippo I returned to him from the inner pocket of his cut and drops the box on the ground. It lands with a slight bounce, knocking open the lid. "This lighter was slightly damaged years ago. It doesn't take much to extract a little fluid from it without disassembling." I watch him flick open the lid and hold the Zippo over the box. He pushes the side of the flint wheel with his finger and sprinkles some of the leaking fluid onto the patches within. When his thumb flicks the striker, the flame ignites the patches as well as his thumb and forefinger.

I'm not sure what startled sound I made, but he laughs at me as I stare at the flames dancing on the tips of his fingers. With a violent jerk of his wrist, the flames go out, and the lighter pings on its hinges and claps shut. He rises to stand beside me once again while the flames within the box grow, engulfing the patches as well.

"Are you alright?" I ask.

He shows me his unscathed hand. "Perfectly."

I glance back down at the burning box of patches. "Just, promise me you won't show that trick to Ace... He's already impressed by you. I don't want him influenced into *pyromania*."

Legion chuckles. "As you wish... I still have a few other tricks up my sleeve for the boy."

"That doesn't surprise me," I say softly, staring at the fire as memories of burning the Knight spell with Dean begin to play over in my mind.

"You look contemplative," Legion says after a moment. "Don't fret. I'll get the last two." He moves to stand closer to me, his fingers brushing lightly against my hand.

I'm not sure what to do when I feel them slip between mine, curling to gently grip my hand in his, palm to palm. I'm afraid to look up at him. Afraid of what I might see in his expression. A familiar tension begins to radiate between us, but I continue to stare at the fire.

"Talk to me," his tone is soft, yet insistent.

"I...I don't know what to say," I stammer.

"Have I pleased you?" he asks, the slightest hint of desperation in his words.

I glance up at him. "What?"

"Have I done...*good*?" His hold tightens while his stormy eyes search mine.

"I don't know how to answer that... These men are...are *dead*...because of me."

"These men are dead *because of me*, sweet one," Legion insists. "If not for me, you never would have been on their radar to begin with. Let not your conscience be troubled over these wasted souls. I take full credit and responsibility... *For everything*." His thumb gently strokes the side of my hand.

"Everything... That's a lot."

"More than you know." His sigh is laced with discernible remorse.

Alarm bells go off inside my racing mind. This feels too intimate. I slip my hand from his to crouch down and grab a stick to prod at the ashy pile of dead men's patches. I want to make sure they're all destroyed anyway.

"You're going to...find the other two?" I ask. The thought of Legion continuing his mission of John Wick-ing his way through our enemies has my anxiety climbing even higher.

"Yes. Though they'll probably find me."

"Why?"

"Revenge for all I've done."

"So, they want to hurt you." I drop the stick in the ashes and stand, wiping my hands off on my apron.

"Perhaps...Does that concern you?"

I look back at Legion incredulously. "Yes. Of course it does."

Something flickers behind his eyes, as if my answer surprised him. "Because of Axel?"

"Axel doesn't deserve to be in your crosshairs, but I don't want *you* hurt...or worse. I'm so tired of all the violence...the threats looming around every corner since I landed in this town. This never-ending carousel of vengeance." I can't help but expel another sigh in an attempt to ease the heaviness centered in my chest. "Who are they? I should probably know who to look out for."

Legion seems to consider my request for a moment before finally replying. "One of them lacks the testicular fortitude to ever act on his own, which is why he wasn't a priority on my list. However, he is still on it, and when our paths cross, I'll end the former Knight, Shane, as well."

"*Shane?*"

Legion nods. "He was a very dedicated and willing pawn in the plot to destroy your husband."

"He was in the wrong that night and got what he deserved," I mutter.

"That is where his vendetta stemmed from, yes. Though I nurtured the hatred in him…molded him into something more useful to me."

"Your mission to kill us both." I scoff, shaking my head at the memories of all that transpired these last few years. I turn from him to stare out at the tree line bordering the property. I remember how fearful I had been of these trees. All the nights I imagined Jack lurking within them.

"Not *you*—" Legion begins to say, but I cut him off.

"To think all along you were behind everything… Jack Nero, Aaron Hopper, bloody eyeballs, kidnappings, and explosions!"

"I was… And I'm—"

"*Ace and I almost died the night you took me.*" I barely get the words out.

"*What?*"

I turn to stare up into his startled expression. "There were complications… I almost died. *Ace*…almost died."

For once, Legion seems stunned to silence. His eyes shift with frantic concern between my own.

"They had to cut him out of me… There wasn't even time for anesthesia…"

His trembling hand gravitates to his face and grips his clenching jaw, unable to speak or look away from me.

"Fortunately, I barely remember it… *But Dean does.* Vividly."

He nods, taking a breath as if he'd been physically unable to. "For that alone, he should want me dead."

"I don't think he'd disagree with you."

"What can I do?"

"Nothing... I just thought you should know. If Dean can never forgive you, now you know why."

She turns from me, storming back toward the house. I trail after her, unsure of where we stand now. Does this render my redemption impossible? Is forgiveness forever beyond my reach? Keegan may never grant it, but... *It isn't his forgiveness I can't live without...*

"Vanna..."

"I'm sorry I said anything." She barely spares me a glance.

She's sorry? "For whatever it's worth, from the depths of whatever soul I have left, I am sorry... Inadequate, I know. Perhaps even absurd... But *I am* sorry, Vanna. For every bit of fear and pain I've caused you."

"I believe you."

"*You do?*" This seems to come too easily.

She halts at the foot of the front steps and turns to face me. "That doesn't mean he ever will... And that complicates things. More than you even know."

Things? I simply stare at her, silently, *desperately* willing her to elaborate.

"I don't know how we move forward."

We? Be still, my beating heart... "Move forward?"

"Yes." An aggravated sigh brushes past her lips. "I don't know how to... *fit you in here*... If it's even *possible*."

My heart continues to race. Something that feels like *hope* begins to swell inside the hollow of my chest. She believes I am remorseful. Does that mean she also forgives me? Is she implying she genuinely wants me in her life, somehow?

"Vanna, believe me when I tell you, *I'll do anything.*"

"I know you mean for those words to sound reassuring, but I've experienced the lengths you've been willing to go, first-hand." She folds her arms across herself, and I'm not sure if it's a subconscious desire to shield herself from me or because the cool evening breeze has picked up. "You should go. There's a lot I still have to prep for Thanks—*Friends*giving. I have to have these orders finished by tomorrow, too."

"Well, you have given me a lot to be thankful for, sweet one," I say, still in awe of her kind nature. "I shall bid you goodnight then and slink off into the darkness where I belong."

She lets out another exasperated sigh before asking, "What are your holiday dinner plans?"

"I haven't any. Never have, in fact, since I've been without a family most of my life. There's nothing to celebrate when you're alone." I was only speaking the truth, but her brows knit together sorrowfully.

"*Never*? Not even when you were a kid? The orphanage didn't do anything for holidays?"

I shrug. "Before the orphanage, we were too poor, and my mother was generally too high and without means to bring us to a soup kitchen. The orphanage tried, I suppose…but it wasn't anything comparable to what I imagine your table must be like. I'm sure your traditions are quite lovely."

She fidgets for a moment with her apron, picking at a spot of dried dough. I can tell by the strained expression on her face, she's warring with herself over something. "Well… If you think you can withstand the heat, I'll set a place for you."

"I'm sorry?"

"Yeah…you've said that." A nervous little smile plays on her lips at my surprise. "Shall I expect you then?"

"I wouldn't miss it for the world."

"*I'll also expect your best behavior.*"

"And you shall have it, sweet one."

"There can't be any of *that* either," she insists.

"To the best of my ability, I will refrain."

"Good night, Damien." She turns and makes her way up the steps.

Stunned by this unanticipated turn of events, I watch the front door close behind her before returning to my bike. I promised I'd do anything… Perhaps it's time for another olive branch.

DEAN

My son's laughter pulls my attention from the engine I've been working on in my shop, and I turn toward the steel door. Ace is propped up on Viking's shoulders, his little hands wrapped around his favorite uncle's forehead.

"Vanna brought Ace by earlier so she could get some shit done before Friendsgiving," Viking explains. He grabs Ace under the arms and flips him over his head before placing him down on his sneakered feet.

"Daddy!" Ace squeals through his laughter and dashes to me. I finish wiping my hands off in time to chuck the wad of paper towels onto my workbench and crouch to wrap my arms around him.

"Promised her I'd bring him by your shop before you clock in at the safehouse. You want to take a break and kick a ball around with us or some shit?" Viking offers.

"I wish I could." I sigh, standing. Ace grabs my hand and steps up onto the steel toe of my boot to playfully teeter around on it. "Derek's not in on Sundays and Mondays anymore. I have to stick around to man the shop. The owner of this bike is picking it up within the hour, too."

"What's left to do on it?" Viking asks.

Ace nearly nails me in the balls in his attempt to climb my leg. This kid really needs to burn off some energy.

"Just finished up as you two walked in," I say, lifting Ace gently by his arm until he's dangling in the air. I do a few arm curls with him while he laughs. "The dirt bike over there needs a couple of adjustments. That's due to be picked up by closing time, too."

The rumbling of a motorcycle pulling into the lot outside draws our attention. I can tell from the sound of the engine and exhaust that it's not a Harley. Besides Snowy and Viper, the rest of our MC brothers all ride Harleys. And since Snowy is no longer with us, and Viper's at a safehouse, this is either a customer or *someone else* with an affinity for Indian motorcycles.

I lower Ace to the cement floor until he's steady on his feet again. "Alright, you guys. Daddy has to get back to work." I gently cup Ace's little face in my hand. "You be good for Uncle Viking, you hear?"

"Uh huh." Ace smiles.

The steel door creaks open and shuts.

"*I require a moment of your time,*" a grating voice announces.

"*Legend!*" Ace runs off excitedly and wraps his arms around Legion's leg, stopping him in his tracks.

"Quite the friendly young fellow..." Legion leans back, hands raised, making a very obvious display of not touching my kid.

Viking shifts his glare from Legion to me. "I can call Cherry over here to come get Ace for a few."

"It's fine," I say. "Take Ace. I'll catch up with you later."

"Ace." Viking's deep, no-nonsense tone has my son's head whipping around to face him. "Let's go, buddy."

Ace releases Legion and makes a beeline for his favorite uncle. Viking scoops him up in one arm and heads for the door. Ace and I exchange parting waves as they exit, and then my gaze slides back to Legion. "Why are you here?"

"I've just come from your wife."

"You need to work on your fucking phrasing."

"You need to stop reading into everything."

I glare at him.

"Fine. *Fair point,* all things considered," Legion concedes.

"Pretty sure I told you to stay the fuck away from my wife."

The corner of his mouth twitches, and I know he's attempting to suppress a sneer. "What happened to the roses?"

"What do you think?"

"Intercepted, obviously... Trash?"

"You bet."

He nods, chuckling now, a low, sinister sound.

"I'm busy," I snap. "Whatever you're here for is going to have to wait. I'm on a deadline."

He cocks his chin at the old Kawasaki. "What's the dirt bike in for?"

"The owner is picking it up tonight. Routine maintenance and a tension correction. I still have to measure the deflection on the chain."

"*Ah, the only chain in the world that sets us free...*" Legion replies. "I can do it while you finish up this Road Glide."

"I'm not letting you work on a customer's bike." I scoff at him. "You've done enough damage to my businesses."

He crooks a brow at me. "You think I don't know my way around a motorcycle?"

"Oh, I'm sure you know your way around a motorcycle... *A little too well.*"

"I'm not going to sabotage your client's bike."

Legion: Book 3

"Why wouldn't you?" I don't give a fuck if he's offended.

"Because the fallout would impact your wife and kid. *For them*, my policy regarding *you* is *do no harm.*"

It irks the fuck out of me that I actually believe him, in this matter, anyway. "So...you work on your own ride?"

Now he scoffs. "Of course."

"Passion or *paranoia*?"

"A used dirt bike was my first bike. And I worked on that one myself, too." He cocks his chin at the Kawasaki again. "You want the tension corrected, I have to elevate the back wheel, loosen the axle, back the locknuts off, move the adjusters as needed on both sides, so on and so forth. Check the alignment when it's all said and done." He glances back at me. "*I don't want to bore you with every detail.* Are you satisfied? Convinced of my competence to handle the task?"

"There's a bike jack and a set of paddock stands over there under the workbench. The thirty-two-millimeter wrench is in the middle drawer of that red tool chest beside it."

Legion immediately goes to work. I watch him move about my shop as if he's right at home, further grating my nerves in the process.

"You've been scarce since crashing the Jokers' clubhouse," I say.

He's got the rear of the bike up on the jack and moves to the tool chest, retrieving the large wrench. "*Idle hands are the Devil's playthings.*" He shoots me another antagonistic grin over his shoulder.

"Don't start with your bible shit."

"It's a common misconception." His sneer only broadens when he turns to face me, going on as if I expressed an interest. "Only The Living Bible of 1971 imbues the concept of idleness into the translation. It was Benjamin Franklin who first said it. We have Protestant theological assumptions to thank for the misinterpretation of Proverbs Chapter sixteen, verse twenty-seven. What the bible actually says is—"

"*I don't fucking care.*"

He chuckles. "Not much of a Christian despite the foundation of your MC, hmm? *Did God fail you, too, Savior*? Or have you always been a *nonbeliever*?"

When I don't respond, his eyes narrow on me. "I wonder where your belief *truly* lies when it comes to the *Wiccan ways of your wife*."

My jaw clenches. I know what he's about to insinuate. I'm not going to play into this mind fuck. "You didn't come here to discuss *theology*."

"No. I didn't." He sighs, probably disappointed I didn't take the bait. "I'm afraid I come bearing bad news."

"I wouldn't expect any different from you."

Legion moves to the opposite side of the bike and crouches to remove a bolt. "It seems your county is not as safe and clear as you hoped." He puts a little more torque into the wrench, and the bolt loosens. "They're still operating in your county."

"Where?"

"I have every intention of showing you."

I glare at him until he rolls his eyes and continues.

"The salvage yard, for starters. There may be a small cook trailer hidden in the back of the lot."

Jason Caldwell's cousin owns that yard... "You've seen it?"

"Not yet. Do you think your *cop friend* is privy? *Perhaps he's on the take.* His wife recently had another child, didn't she? That's *three children* on a rural cop's salary... They don't pay all that well in these parts, you know... Certainly nothing comparable to what police earn *up north... New York,* for instance."

Was that a fucking dig about my financials and Vanna being with Jack Nero? A well-off cop! Does Legion know Jack's brother recently paid us a visit?

I don't want him to know I picked up on anything, so I keep my tone level. "If this intel is accurate, Jason doesn't know about it, and I'm not going to involve him if it is. Now, I can't imagine you like the sound of your own fucked up voice this much, so why don't you plainly say what we both know you're hinting at?"

"*Hinting?* I believe I just gave you an exact location." His sinister little sneer lets me know I'm right about the double speak.

"Well, my night is booked."

"My, my...*what would your citizens say?*"

I ignore his obvious taunt and grab the work order papers on the bike I just wrapped up. I can feel his cold eyes on me while I pretend to review, buying myself a few moments to regain my composure.

"I haven't broken that *hero's spirit* in you after all, have I?"

When I glance at him, I'm surprised not to be met with a condescending expression. Hell, I'd even venture to say he seems concerned.

I scoff, "You haven't broken *anything*, and you never will."

Legion: Book 3

Another sneer slices his features. "Brace yourself for the shock of this confession, but...*I am* glad to hear it."

"After everything, why would you be?"

"She deserves the best."

"*Now I know you're full of shit.*"

"Why don't you make the necessary arrangements and accompany me tonight?" he goes on, ignoring the accusation. "I'm sure you and I could benefit from the *bonding exercise* in preparation for the coming holiday."

"What does that have to do with anything?"

He shrugs and turns back to the bike. While making another adjustment on the chain, he replies, "Your wife invited me to Friendsgiving."

"*Son of a bitch!*"

"You'll get no argument here!"

I slam the paperwork down on my workbench and grab the cell from my pocket, about to call her and make my displeasure known, when Legion stands and steps toward me.

"You should know she did so out of obligatory feelings. I'd advise *against* giving her any grief over the matter."

He'd advise! "*Obligatory feelings?* The fuck did you pull with my wife now?"

"You intercepted the roses I sent. Did you really think you'd be able to prevent me from presenting her with proof of my kept promises?" He chuckles and has the gall to *tisk* at me. "I brought her the patches I removed from each man's cut."

I can feel the rioting pulse in my neck, hear the thunderous swooshing of blood in my ears. "Let me get this straight... You brought physical evidence of your crimes to our home?"

"Nothing says *true love* like thirteen counts of murder in the first." He pridefully grins, and a nearly overwhelming urge to slug him in the jaw courses through me. "Though, do you honestly consider my promises a *crime*? *Come now, Savior*... I know who you *really* are, despite this valiant attempt at *family man*... Let's go eradicate some bad guys, *vigilante.*"

"I need to check on my wife."

"*She's fine*, Keegan." Legion rolls his eyes at me. "The gesture earned me an invite to your table. She's busy baking, *hardly distraught*. Besides, we burned them. There's no evidence of anything at your home. The only phone call you should be making is to a prospect or a brother to cover your shift."

While he rambles on, I shoot Vanna a text. **You invited LEGION to dinner?**

Vanna: Wow. He works fast. I was going to talk to you about it tonight.

I angrily type out my reply and hit send. **Consider him uninvited. Next time, I'd appreciate a conversation in advance.**

Vanna: I'm sorry. You're right. But do you really have to uninvite him? He has nobody. 😢

Obligatory feelings. Fucking douche bag! I back out of the text with Vanna and bring up Ford Focus to inform him of his mandatory shift tonight. Then I shove the phone back in my pocket.

"Hurry the fuck up with that chain or I'll do it myself," I growl at the sub-human equivalent of a thorn in my side.

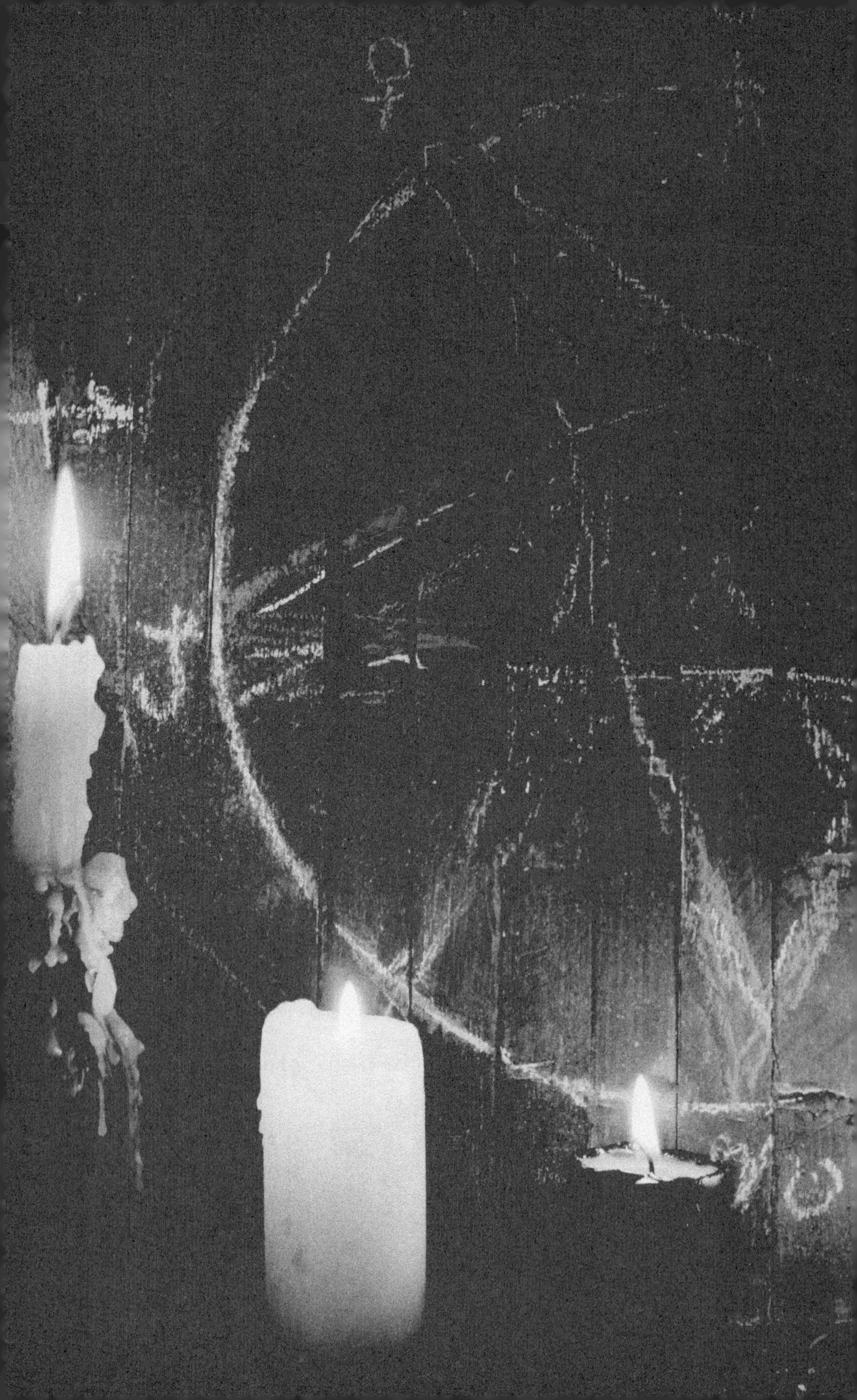

CHAPTER 21

LEGION

We park the bikes in the lot of a drive-through BBQ joint across the street from the scrapyard.

"According to Stan, they deal from the seventeen-hundredth block of Staunton Street. Side gate."

Keegan removes his helmet and dismounts. "Stan?" he asks, hanging the dome on the handlebar.

"*The man in the van.*" I light up a smoke, then gesture to the couple of picnic tables on either side of the walk-up window. "I say we take up some inconspicuous real estate and see what comes and goes… My treat if you're hungry."

"I'm not," Keegan mutters, though as we walk toward the establishment, I note his slight grin before he informs me, "*My wife always has dinner waiting for me.*"

I don't bother concealing my own when I retort, "*I am very much looking forward to my seat at her table.*"

While Keegan claims a bench, I order a tray with two smoked brisket sandwiches and two Cokes in case he changes his mind. He's glaring down the side street, holding his cellphone casually against the top of his leg, when I take a seat across from him and place the tray between us.

"At least pretend you're eating," I say, unwrapping the sandwiches before sliding one nearer to him. "I hope you're not giving Vanna any more grief." I nod at his cell.

"I was confirming my shift was covered." He tucks the cell in the chest pocket of his leather jacket. "And what I do with my wife is none of your fucking business."

I nod, pulling a final drag from my cigarette before reaching across the table and extinguishing it in his sandwich. He scowls but says nothing.

"I would like to ask you something, without you getting all bent out of shape about it," I say, lifting the bun of my sandwich to inspect the meat, an ingrained practice since my early days digging food from trash cans outside of joints like this.

"What?"

"This... *mission of yours*. The safehouses. What do you get out of all of it? What are you really hoping to achieve?"

He glares at me skeptically. "You care?"

"*Care* might be too strong a word... *Curious*, though... For the moment, anyway." While he rambles on, I take a few bites.

"It might seem like nothing to you, but round-the-clock security isn't cheap. What we offer helps the organizations funnel more funds into helping as many victims as possible." Keegan drags a hand through his hair and glances toward the scrapyard before meeting my gaze once more. "These women and kids haven't felt any measure of safety in a long time. Escorting them to testify and confront their abusers in court, or working to assist with extracting them from dangerous situations, even sitting outside their safe houses, offers the victims a sliver of peace... But I don't expect an *agent of chaos* to understand anything we do."

I grab a Coke and take a gulp before asking, "You must have higher aspirations than *glorified guard dogs*, no?"

Keegan considers the question while I finish off the last bites of my meal, perhaps attempting to decipher my intentions. "Expansion," he finally replies. "Our own compounds. Though you pushed that goal post quite a few yards back on your mission to destroy us."

I nod and wipe my hands on a napkin before tossing it onto the tray. "I saw you in action one night... Your *Swan Song*... It's funny, how one can *loathe a person entirely* while simultaneously admiring them."

Keegan shoots me a sardonic grin. "*Admire* is a stretch, though I'll buy *envy*."

"Touché." I cock my chin at his sandwich. "Are you going to eat that?"

He arches a brow. "After you used it as an ashtray?"

I take it back and toss the top bun aside. "I've eaten worse to survive... *Willful waste makes woeful want.*" I sigh, avoiding his scrutinizing stare while taking a bite.

When he clears his throat and speaks again, there's less hostility in his tone, though only by a fraction. "Why didn't you turn me in?"

"At the time, I had bigger plans for you."

"*Always scheming...* But that does bring something to mind. Something you never gave me a straight answer about."

"Which is?"

"Preacher."

I swallow the last morsel, then wipe my mouth before meeting his inquisitive stare once again. "*Do you really want a bite of this apple?* Shall I assuage your dark imaginings?" I grin. His only response is a stern, impatient scowl. "Very well... I had the dethroned old fool meet me behind the church on East Grove. His usefulness had long expired, and he knew too much."

"A church? He died in his home..."

I raise my hand, silencing his interruption. "Like the old fool he was, Preacher kept me waiting. I'd left my bike parked in the vacant lot of the... *Our Lady of Perpetual Hypocrisy,* or whatever the name is of that particular house of worship. Meeting at a church wasn't the point. It was more so *the location* of the church."

Keegan rests his arms on the table, threading his fingers as curiosity mingles with the agitated expression he's wearing. I decide not to keep him in suspense and relay what happened that day.

I remember sitting in wait for their former President, smoking between the sandaled feet of a large marble carving depicting Mother Mary. The sound of children's laughter and playful shouts rang throughout the area from the field of the elementary school across the street.

"I suppose you've already heard I was voted out of the MC." Preacher barely managed to look me in the eyes when he arrived, posture slouched in what I imagine could have been shame.

"Indeed." I blew my smoke in his direction.

"I'm not quite sure what to—"

"There's nothing left *to say*, Preacher. Talk is cheap. Though perhaps it will ease your mind to know I realized this was inevitable. In fact, I'm surprised it took this long."

The tension around his eyes slackened. Hope replaced the dread in his expression. I couldn't help but chuckle. "You...*wanted* Keegan at the gavel?"

"*Oh, come now, Preacher,*" I admonished. "You must admit, it's far more satisfying to witness a man's fall from the top of a mountain than it is to simply trip him in the valley! Is it not?"

"I suppose..." he agreed, though with reluctance, seeped in suspicion.

I stepped closer to him as a cruel smile twisted my lips. "*How did that feel*, by the way? Keegan not only *dethroning you*, but taking that cut you've worn for what? *Thirty-five years?*" I expelled an airy whistle, shaking my head in faux dismay. "That had to hurt. Nonetheless, *well done.*"

Preacher's head jerked back in surprise. "This was your plan all along?"

I merely pulled another drag, flicked my ash at him, and allowed the smoke to escape my lips through a devious grin.

"*Lord have mercy...*"

"It's a little late for that now... *I,* however, require one last task of you."

He glared at me, insisting, "*Oh, I'm finished being your lackey!*"

I chucked the cigarette at his boots. "I couldn't agree more."

The flash of anger in his expression morphed back to unease.

"Despite being an insufferable, hypocritical, greed-driven sack of sanctimonious shit, *Preacher*...you have done your part in assisting me to the next phase of my mission. You see, I *needed* you to wreck your MC. To tarnish its image in this little community. I *needed* you to give him something dear to his heart to rebuild. I *want* him to work toward a goal. To revive a sense of pride in his mission. I *want* him to *feel* the redemption he seeks is within reach once again... *Before I destroy it all.* Before I *burn* this fucking little town to the ground. Before I *twist* him into everything he hates, then force him to lay his own demolished soul to waste... *You two have more in common than either of you could ever fathom.*"

Preacher only stared at me, looking a shade or two paler than he had when he arrived.

"Having said this, I urge you to listen carefully to the words I'm about to say next and take them to the very depths of your soul."

After slipping on a leather glove, I reached into my cut and removed the black zippered pouch that contained the means to his end. "You won't feel a thing. You'll simply lose consciousness, *slipping away on the wings of a dragon…*" I assured him and shoved the kit into his trembling hands.

Semblances of words toppled from his mouth, though they had been unintelligible through his horrified shock.

"*Shh…shh…shhhh…* I realize this is a lot to absorb. *A rather gargantuan ask.*" I took another step closer to him, forcing him to meet my gaze. "You need to know, however, that if you force my hand, Preacher… *it will not be a gentle hand.* And I will not stop with *you.*" I warned with a gesture toward the elementary school across the street.

I daresay his complexion went even paler. The church parking lot faced the back of the elementary school that his grandchildren attended.

"That's right… I offer you one last *devil's bargain.* Your life solidifies and ensures the safety and continuance of your grandchildren's lives… You have twenty-four hours. You, and everyone you care about, will be watched closely… I trust you understand the gravity of the situation?"

It's difficult not to laugh at the expression of horror in Keegan's eyes, now.

"You know how his story ends." I smile at the memory of Preacher's last-ditch effort to expose me, leaving the syringe inside his bible at that specific passage, *naming me.* I have to suppress another chuckle. I'd made Preacher's final act work to my advantage as well.

Keegan nods slowly. "And the funeral…"

"Suspicion of my involvement would have elevated had I not attended his funeral." I don't bother fighting the sneer this time when I tell him, "However, *I was also hoping for another glimpse at your little witch.*"

I recall eagerly scanning the crowd for her presence, and the disappointment that washed over me when I realized Preacher's widow was the only woman at Keegan's side that day. Had he been keeping her from me, I'd wondered, then found myself hoping perhaps they'd broken up.

I'd lingered after the funeral, curious to see what Keegan was up to. My heart raced the moment I saw a woman who wasn't Vanna, waiting for him at a grave beneath an old oak tree. They embraced upon meeting, and she placed a kiss upon his cheek. I'd tasked Reaper with finding out who she was. Had the pixie blonde been Keegan's new squeeze, I'd have had two reasons to rejoice. A *believable* and *warranted* reason to divert attention from Vanna to this woman I felt nothing for, as well as an opening to pursue Vanna for myself.

"Yet you went on to enlist Jack Nero in your war against us. Spare me your bullshit claims of concern for my wife," Keegan growls.

A pang of guilt jabs through my solar plexus with the sharpness of a fuckin' blade. "Against *you*. We've been over this."

"You have no idea how often *I go over this*." He scoffs. "How what you orchestrated that night still haunts us both. Forgiveness... Redemption... *They're an impossibility!*"

"Perhaps for you, they are." I can't say I blame him, but we both know Vanna has a soft heart. And although I want to *earn* it, I know she will eventually bestow her forgiveness upon me. The hearts of angels grant even us undeserving demons a place to dwell within. "It's inevitable. You should make your peace with it."

Keegan leans closer, practically bristling like a wolf. "And you should know, *I'll do everything in my power to prevent that from happening.*"

Though I expected him to harbor a certain level of animosity, his words struck...analogous to a physical blow.

Before I can reply, there's activity across the street. I subtly nod toward the black van pulling over near the side gate of the scrapyard. Keegan shifts his dark gaze in its direction as two men jump out, each carrying a small duffel bag. The one with bright blonde hair looks around nervously as he makes his way through the gate.

"Cooks," I say. "It appears Stanley wasn't lying about this place still being operational. The production of meth is generally a nocturnal activity."

The two men shut themselves inside the gates, then padlock the chain as the van drives off. Keegan turns back to me. "And what became of the *man in the van?*"

"I haven't killed him yet, if that's what you're asking. I imagine they've put him to work elsewhere. He's due to check in by tomorrow night with more intel."

Keegan skeptically arches a brow. "You trust him not to run? Or set you up?"

"Of course not. *That's what his family is for.* He doesn't know how many men I could have watching. The darkness may have concealed your identities in the Jokers' cellar. *However,* your shadowed forms impressed upon him the integral belief *I'm not working alone.* If he double-crosses me now, they'll kill him before I'd be able to get to him."

Keegan shakes his head as if my methods go against his moral code. "Jesus fuck… Well, what else did he tell you?"

"There are other locations within Jocsan County. Though I know you gave your word to assist the Jokers, your precious Bermuda County is my priority, *for reasons of which I'm sure we agree.*"

"*We do,*" Keegan reluctantly concedes, gazing down at his wedding band.

"Shall we, then?" I force a smile and gesture toward the scrapyard.

"No." Keegan expels an agitated breath and nods to the establishment behind us. "This restaurant closes at ten. We'll come back when the area is less populated. In the meantime, you can tell me what else *the man in the van* had to say about this operation."

I can't fault his logic. It would be wise to wait until there are fewer witnesses around. "Very well. *You're the boss.* They're running this operation similarly to the way I was. None of the cooks or the dealers know who the real shot-callers are, by design. There are multiple cells operating on their own and run by *regional managers,* if you will. Depending on the demand of an area, these cells occasionally share cooks, which is why Stanley knew about this place. I snagged him in Jocsan, but he's done work here in Bermuda County. Potentially, he could provide us with intel on other cells."

Keegan's phone buzzes in his pocket, but he ignores it. "What else did he tell you about my county?"

"Last he heard, they were still dealing near the Budget Inn."

"So, Stan doesn't know who's at the top of mount meth."

"Stan doesn't. *But I do.*" In fact, I suspected it the moment Stanley began to explain the infrastructure of the network. It simply couldn't be anyone else...

"How?" Keegan asks as the cell in his pocket rings again.

"Perhaps you should take that? I'm not going anywhere, after all."

He begrudgingly answers the call, and Viking's booming voice demanding to know where he is may as well have been on speaker.

"Ford Focus is covering my shift at the safehouse with Axel. I'm with Legion. We're about to head over to the Budget Inn for a little recon," Keegan explains, to which Viking informs him he's on his way. Keegan shoves the phone back in his pocket. "You might as well explain to both of us. Let's go."

Keegan and I pull into the back corner of a gas station across the street from the seedy motel. While he informs Viking of our exact whereabouts, I remove the binoculars from my saddlebag and scan the motel's lot.

The moment Viking arrives, Keegan breaches the subject once again. "Now tell us who we're going after, and how you know."

"As previously stated, they're running shit the way I was, working with multiple smaller crews to distribute the product. And that guy parked in the blue Tahoe on the far side of the lot, I believe he reports to this region's Capo."

"*Capo...*" I can feel Keegan's interminable fucking glare burning into the side of my face.

"An underboss in this network," I explain. "The one the street soldiers report to. The guy who then relays everything to the top guy in charge. *The regional fucking manager!*"

"*Fuck you*, I'm familiar with the term," Keegan grumbles, snatching the binoculars from me. "You just confirmed what I always suspected of you." He slowly scans the area and zeros in on the vehicle.

"*Oh?*"

"That you've always been more *gangster* than *biker*," he grumbles. "Speaking of bikes, what made you swap out that flashy chromed-out Indian you used to ride before the black one?"

"She served her purpose..." I sigh, recalling the night a few years ago when she was blown up...a casualty of my self-inflicted mission in the pursuit of redemption. "Indistinguishability evolved into necessity." Keegan glances at me curiously, and I shrug. "What draws the eye also tends to evolve."

"Do any of these pricks ride?" Viking asks.

"A few cells are MCs. This guy also rides a newer model, copper-on-black Harley Davidson Road King. Some modifications and upgrades. Stage five kit. Have you heard of the Iron Rebels MC, based out of Creek County?"

Keegan passes Viking the binoculars and shifts his attention to me. "I see you've been busy since the Jokers' party," he begrudgingly admits.

"I didn't come back to fuck around."

His stare narrows with disdain. *"Didn't you?"*

I return his steely gaze at the insinuation regarding my nebulous relationship with Vanna. "She means a great deal *more* to me than *that*, Keegan."

"Not to break up this heart-to-heart, *but speaking of*, looks like we got ourselves a *bump and bang* operation," Viking announces. "Some guy just exchanged cash for a small baggie and is heading to a room upstairs... *Yup*, there's a door with a heart-shaped sticker next to the room number, two-fourteen. He's headed right for it." He hands the binoculars back to Keegan.

"Are these women willing?" Keegan demands, ready and willing to kick in a door and sweep the damsel up into his Knightly arms. I suppress a sneer at his bone-deep inclination.

"I'd venture to say they are," I reply, lighting up another cigarette. I pull a long drag and exhale the smoke. *"He's always had a soft spot for whores."*

Both Saviors shift their attention to me.

"There's only one man who could be running this operation. The only one who was privy to my methods when I built the original network," I explain.

"The suspense is killing me," Viking dryly states.

"Reaper," I say, and Keegan scowls in recollection of my former Sergeant at Arms. *"Ah, yes,* I believe the two of you briefly met." It was right around the time I began to suspect a waver in Reaper's allegiance. The memory of what transpired that night resurfaces with a vengeance, bringing with it a torrent of rather inconvenient emotions.

It was the same night Vanna sought me out at the Demon's Den, and inevitably confessed to falling pregnant with Keegan's child... As if the bubbling cauldron of conflicted emotions brewing inside of me over her hadn't been torment enough *prior to that revelation!* She was fucking pregnant...

"That complicates things... More than you even know..." Vanna's earlier words slap me across the face. *Puppet wasn't lying...* My intestines knot as they did the night Vanna came to me with a plea and her news...

What had been a foreign feeling then had stolen my breath and made my heart riot with vacillating emotions in my chest. It took every shred of self-control to retain the image of indifference to her condition. I'd needed the distance to compose myself as much as I'd needed to avoid Keegan the night she showed up demanding answers. I hadn't anticipated she possessed the *lady-balls* to pull a stunt like that.

I'd barely managed to keep my wits about me, though I did seize the moment and planted my fingerprints on that jar of hearts stationery for her to witness, not only throwing a wrench into any sort of timeline Keegan may have deciphered, but also destroying his ability to use it against me. A silver lining amidst the entire ordeal. I owe my innate survival instincts for reacting swiftly, my knack for recognizing opportunities, and capitalizing on them. Instincts forged from a life lived under constant threat... Yet there I was ...condemning Vanna and her unborn child to threatening circumstances of my own design...

I hated her for stirring up a storm of conflict within me. My warring emotions clashed with all of my carefully laid plans.

I'd clung to the mask of cool indifference as though our lives depended on it. I knew even then, they did. I played off the entire scenario as if my abrupt departure had simply been about avoiding Keegan's clutches a bit longer while awaiting other chips to fall into place.

Reaper wasted no time confronting me upon my immediate return, barging into my office as Vanna did, demanding answers of his own. "Why'd you let her go? She falls right into our laps, and you let him bust in here and walk her right back out the front door!"

"We aren't ready for that phase of the plan yet," I'd snapped.

"That really it?" he pressed me, and my ever-waning patience. Reaper and I had shared a mutual respect in the past. However, since our relocation, and more pointedly, *since he'd developed somewhat of a soft spot for my little plaything,* I'd begun to suspect a strain on that mutual respect. "Asmodeus is concerned that you may have taken too much of a liking to Keegan's woman."

I turned to face him, glaring. "And where could he possibly have conceived of such a notion?"

"She ain't hard to look at."

"No. She isn't. That isn't what I asked you."

A tense moment passed between us while Reaper's dark eyes made a study of my demeanor before he spoke. "He wanted an update…from another…*perspective.*"

"Yours?"

His affirmative nod heated my blood.

"*Interesting.*" I pulled out my cell and brought up my brother's number. Reaper and I watched each other while the phone rang. To turn from him would have been a sign of weakness, and perceived weakness to the men around me would have equated to an open wound while swimming with sharks. These men were greedy, power-hungry, and were growing more impatient by the day.

A garbled grunt answered the line, and I wasted no time with meaningless greetings.

"*I am the one in the trenches calling the shots here.* The next time you attempt to undermine me from the desert will be the last. You wanted total annihilation, that takes time! Tedious planning!" I hissed, fighting the urge to grimace at the sound of my brother sucking saliva back into his mouth. The image of him dabbing that ever-present handkerchief to his malformed, drooling lip, eternally burned into my memory. I narrowed my glare on Reaper, simultaneously warning them both, "Do it again… *and I will eliminate the temptation!*"

"Damien… Damien…*calm down*… So quick with that murderous rage of yours," Asmodeus taunted.

The Adam's apple bobbed in Reaper's throat as perspiration percolated on his skin. Fantasies of slicing a Sicilian necktie into that throat had been *oh so tempting.*

"I haven't lost my faith in you, little brother…"

I hung up on Asmodeus, shoved the phone in my cut pocket, and stepped closer to Reaper. "And just what tales have you been tattling to Asmodeus?"

"We had her free and clear, and you let her go." Reaper watched curiously as I pulled at the collar of my shirt, exposing the base of my neck.

"My, my... Didn't waste any time, did you?" I sneered, dragging my finger along the fabric to pull it aside, giving him a clear view of the tattoos embedded in my flesh. I tapped my finger on one in particular—the Sigil of Asmodeus just below my clavicle.

"He asked, all I did was report back."

"There is only one thing left in this world I care about... *One. Thing.*" I released the collar of my shirt and readjusted myself, granting him time to allow my words to sink in. "Can you say the same?" When he didn't reply, I held him under my hostile gaze a moment longer. "Interfere with my plans again, *Reaper*, and you'll beg me to arrange your introduction to your namesake."

"It seems you've fallen short on a few of those promises." Keegan's needling pulls me back to the present.

"Oh, he's at the top of my hit list," I assure him. "He's no longer going by the road name *Reaper* and has most assuredly established a new legal identity of which few are privy to. I suspect he saw to that immediately after the night in the warehouse. I have no doubt word must have gotten back to him regarding *the fulfillment of my promises*. He's taken precautions...built a perimeter of defense around himself in anticipation of my eventual return. I'm not surprised. Reaper saw the same potential I did regarding this region, and there's always a power vacuum."

"Always some scumbag ready to pick up where the last one left off," Keegan concurs with notable hostility. "What's he going by now?"

"He's known only as... *Legion*."

Viking lets out an amused chortle while Keegan's expression remains a steady glare.

"I assure you, despite my reputation, I am not *omnipresent*. I do, however, find the imposter's bold move *amusing*." Actually, it's quite cunning.

"You certainly made a name for yourself among the dregs," Keegan says. "I see the logic in claiming your *infamous* name for himself. There are probably many who don't know what really happened at our showdown."

"Indeed." Without the collapse of the infrastructure I had intended, my throne was there for the taking. Why wouldn't he simply *become me*? I'd have done the same if presented with the opportunity in his circumstances. Hell, I've done far worse in the pursuit of power and money.

Keegan folds his arms, scowling at me once again. "The *fulfillment of your promises* must have gotten back to him at some point... Is Reaper aware of your obsession with my wife?"

"Yes," I begrudgingly admit, the resurging memory making my jaw tick again.

"Then he's been expecting your return. Is Reaper the reason you want our protection?"

"*I don't fear the Reaper*, Keegan... Everything I've done since learning the truth about my brother has been for you and your wife. To keep us all alive. I will dismantle this threat as well. You have my word, *but a little motivated backup never hurt anybody*."

"Well, I'm motivated, but it isn't to help you." Viking shoots me a stony glare before he sets off, storming across the lot toward the street. "I'm hungry and this bullshit is cutting into supper time."

Keegan and I exchange a quick glance before we both catch up to him.

"You want to run whatever your plan is by us?" Keegan presses.

"You go upstairs and check on the hooker. Legion and I will let this prick in the parking lot know venturing into this county is hazardous to his health." Viking glances at me. "You got a bandana on you?"

"I do."

"When we get over there, bust open his gas cap and shove it inside. When I tell you to, light it."

"Pump the brakes, you fuckin' lunatics!" Keegan says, nearly panicked. "We're not murdering anyone, especially not across the street from a gas station that probably has cameras!"

Familiar with Viking's occasional volatile nature and at times, abrasive, adolescent humor, I'm unable to decipher whether or not he's simply fucking with us. I feel compelled to inform him of his error. "I mean no offense, considering your impressive physique and the fact that you could snap me like a twig, but Hollywood exaggerates the effectiveness of this scenario. Fuel tanks are designed to contain the vapors and are sealed to prevent leaks. The odds of this plan resulting in an explosion are significantly low."

"Even if he knows all that, *low still isn't zero*." Viking grins. "Gotta admit, it's still a fear-inducing visual. My money is on him shitting himself and never coming back."

"*And on the off chance it does blow up?*" Keegan shakes his head at his overzealous Sergeant at Arms incredulously. "You'll be standing right next to it! This is half-baked bullshit. This is what got you in trouble that night with Axel." Keegan shoots me a brief but damning glare before shifting his attention back to Viking. "What about getting information out of him?"

Viking lets out a gruff sigh. "It isn't like Legion drove his murder van over here and we can take him somewhere to interrogate him."

"Well, it's Stan's van." I shrug.

"Stan?" Viking quirks a brow.

"The man in the van."

"*The man in the van's name is Stan?*" Viking chuckles.

Keegan quickens his pace to step in front of him, halting our progression toward the motel. "Would you stop and think this over!" Keegan's increasing desperation calls to my deviant nature, and I can't help but throw a little more proverbial fuel on the fire.

"*Devil's advocate,*" I begin, but Viking interrupts with a snide remark.

"*There's a shocker.*"

I brush off the comment and continue. "Anyone setting up an operation across the street from a gas station probably made sure there aren't cameras. At least not functional ones. And Viking has a point, this would make a fast, lingering impression, akin to lighting a rather gargantuan candle under his ass."

"Exactly," Viking concurs, then slaps the side of Keegan's arm before stepping around him. "It'll be fun. YOLO."

"*YOLO* is my fucking *point*, asshole!" Keegan stresses, pacing alongside us again.

"Just go check on the girl, *Lancelot,*" Viking insists. "We got this. It'll be over before you know it. This guy will take off like a bat out of hell to report back to his network that we're fucking crazy and Bermuda County is off limits."

Keegan lets out a stress-ridden sigh. "He's watching the fucking door. He's gonna see me go up."

"Good. You'll distract him and give us the element of surprise." Viking shoves Keegan in the direction of the hotel before he and I veer off to approach the Tahoe from the back, taking cover behind the building. Once in position, Viking peers around the corner. "Dean's almost at the staircase. You got a knife to pry open that tank?"

"Multiple."

Viking scoffs. "That's right, you're a *walking Army Surplus*."

I chuckle, extracting the bandana from my back pocket while glancing around for a water source. There's nothing back here, not even a puddle.

"Excuse me a moment," I say, turning my back on him to unzip my fly.

"*Really?* You can't fuckin' hold it for three fucking minutes? I thought you were supposed to be some kind of badass. What are you nervous or some shit?" he taunts.

"*Innovative.* Just taking an extra precaution on the minuscule chance of an explosion to appease your prudent president. The saturated portion won't burn. Better my piss than yours since I'm the one handling it," I say, soaking the end of the fabric in my urine stream.

"Huh. Nice."

"You realize this guy has a gun, right?"

"I'll get the gun." Viking removes a pair of leather riding gloves from his cut and slips them on.

"And a cell. We can't risk him alerting the cooks at the scrapyard, or anyone else. At least not until we get back there."

"We've got another location to hit after this?" The disappointment in Viking's tone amuses me.

"If it's any consolation for the postponement of your next meal, we *will* be blowing shit up there."

He expels another disgruntled sigh. "Hurry up, Dean's almost at the top of the steps. I'll charge this prick and get the gun when he gets out of the SUV."

"What if it's in the glovebox? Or mounted somewhere inside?"

"*I'll get the fucking gun*, asshole. You think this is my first rodeo? Shut up before I change my mind and beat him to death with you!"

"Hold this while I zip up," I joke, pretending to hand the piss saturated end of the bandana to him.

"Fuck you. Put your dick away."

I suppress a chuckle and refasten myself. "Are you sure you don't want to confirm that theory of yours regarding *skinny dudes packing*?"

"I'm starting to think you *want* to show me your dick."

"It's *your* theory. I'm just willing to *confirm it*."

"I'll take your word for it. Dean's at the door… let's move!" Gun in hand, Viking rounds the corner, and I follow, genuinely impressed by how swiftly and silently a man of his muscular stature moves.

The guy is so concerned with Keegan upstairs, he doesn't realize we're behind him until the barrel of Viking's Glock is pressed firmly to the back of his skull. He goes rigid, then slowly raises his hands in surrender.

"Don't fucking move," Viking growls, aggressively patting him down. He pulls a small pistol tucked in the guy's waistband. "You got any more?" he asks, re-holstering his Glock to hold the guy's own Beretta on him.

He shakes his head no, but Viking rips open the driver's side door and rummages around inside. "Got the cell… Got his bag of tricks, too." He drops a duffel bag on the ground. It's zipped, so he must have tucked the cellphone in his cut. Once satisfied on the weapons front, he orders the guy back inside the Tahoe and nods at me.

I easily pry open the fuel door with a knife, twist off the gas cap, and use my blade to shove the saturated end of the bandana into his tank.

"W-what the fuck are you doing?" the guy nervously asks.

Viking slaps him across the face. "What are we doing? *We're getting real fucking tired of running you roaches out of our county*, so this guy is gonna light you up like a Molotov cocktail."

Despite having been slapped in the face, his head swivels out the window in my direction, eyes wide as I hold up the Zippo. For dramatic effect, I light up a cigarette, then lower my hand to tauntingly wiggle the flame of the lighter near the fabric dangling from his tank.

"*Oh shit…*" he whimpers.

Viking rips the guy's head back by his short, frosted hair and rams the barrel of the gun under his chin, forcing eye contact. "If you survive this and we cross paths in Bermuda County again, I'm gonna blow your fucking head off. Do you understand?"

He attempts to nod.

"If you make it out of here alive, deliver that message to everyone you're working with." Viking cocks his chin at me. "Light this motherfucker up!"

"*Oh shit!*" he shrieks at the sound of my Zippo pinging open again. Viking releases him and takes a step back as I ignite the bandana. "*Oh fuck!*"

"You better drive fast." Viking's threat is still laced with his ever-present humor. "Maybe you'll get lucky, and the wind will blow it out. You stop, and we'll fucking empty every round into you."

The guy violently cranks the ignition, throws it into drive, and slams on the gas so hard the tires spin and squeal on the asphalt before he barrels out of the parking lot. Viking picks up the duffel bag and slings it over his shoulder as the Tahoe's roaring engine quickly fades in the distance.

Keegan jogs across the lot to rejoin us, holding up a cellphone. "You're never gonna guess who's upstairs. I've got Chopper coming to bring her back to the clubhouse."

"*Let's walk and talk*, shall we?" I urge, gesturing to the gas station across the street where we left our bikes. "Time is of the essence."

"He's right," Keegan agrees, and we briskly make our way back. "It's fuckin' Vixie."

Viking scoffs. "Vanna's gonna love having her back."

"It's temporary," Keegan insists, but there's a level of unease in his tone.

"What's the issue between Vanna and Vixie?" I ask.

Keegan deliberately avoids the question and cocks his chin at the duffel bag Viking's carrying just as we reach our motorcycles. "The drugs?"

"Uh huh." Viking places the duffel bag between the handlebars as he mounts his bike. "Figured we'd burn it where we're going next."

"Give it to Legion," Keegan orders, "If by some slim chance we get stopped, *better him than us*. We've still got plausible deniability."

I can't help meeting his sly grin with my own as I mount my Indian and start it.

Viking tosses it to me, and I quickly sling the strap over my head and adjust it across my chest, resting the weight of the duffel bag atop my fuel tank.

Before they fire up their Harleys, I take off out of the lot, granting myself the temporary distance and a moment to check the bag unwitnessed. If accessible, it would be advantageous to make note of the numbers stored within the cell for my own reasons...reasons I'd rather not disclose to them yet, *if ever.*

Alas, after rummaging through it, there's nothing but baggies of crank and cash. The cell is in Viking's cut. I manage to zip the bag closed just as the two Saviors race up on either side of me.

"*What the fuck was that?*" Keegan shouts over our roaring bikes.

"I told you, I didn't come back to fuck around! Not my fault if you *Davidson boys* can't keep up." I sneer back at him, patting the fuel tank and earning another of his scowls. I ease back on the throttle and gesture for him to take the lead. "By all means, pres."

DEAN

Just past the scrapyard and the BBQ joint, there's a boatyard with a large dirt lot bordered by an acre of forest on either side. It's a far enough distance, if anyone is keeping watch outside those gates. Hopefully, they'll think we kept going. I glance down the side street as we pass and spot the van from earlier parked near the gates.

Viking and Legion follow me into the lot of the boatyard, and we shut down the bikes.

"Looked like there was just one guy in the van, but who knows. You said they deal here, too?" I glance at Legion as he dismounts his bike and grabs the binoculars from his saddlebag. He hands me the binoculars and adjusts the duffel bag to his back.

"I staked it out last night. It's pretty low-key. Two cooks inside, one guy outside keeping watch. I don't think they risk dealing at this location on account of the cooks," Legion says.

"So, we have to neutralize van man," Viking says. "Either of you have any rope?"

We both notice a sinister sneer creep across Legion's face. "Lend me your bandana," Legion insists, hand already out to me.

I remove the one I have tucked in my back pocket and hand it to him. "What are you doing?"

"Wait here." Without another word, he ties the bandana around the lower portion of his face and makes his way over to the chain-link fence of the boatyard.

"Why does no one feel the need to run game plans by anyone anymore?" I sigh as we watch Legion scale the fence and disappear into the shadows.

"If he sets off some kind of alarm, we're leaving him here," Viking chuckles.

"I have no objections." I lift the binoculars and try to zero in on the scrapyard up the street. "Can't see shit from this angle. Let's get closer through the woods so they don't spot us."

We trudge the few yards through low brush among the pine trees in this wooded lot, until we reach a position where we can see the van parked by the side gate of the scrapyard.

"Looks like he's alone…dicking around on his cellphone… We're gonna need to get that from him, too." I hand Viking the binoculars so he can take a look.

"What's behind this place?" he asks.

"A self-storage facility."

"Well, I can either ride my bike around the block and try to sneak up on him from the back, which will be difficult without some sort of distraction, or I can go back to where we parked the bikes, cross there, and go through the woods on the other side of the street. Just surprise him at his fuckin' window. When I've got him secured, I'll signal you, and we can go in together."

"This will facilitate your plan," Legion's creepy voice coming out of fucking nowhere startles both of us. He drops the duffel bag at our feet with a significantly heavier-sounding thud, before crouching to unzip it. He reaches inside and pulls out some rope and zip-ties.

"That'll work," Viking says. "Boatyard. *Good thinking*."

Legion scoffs at the comment. He shoves the items back inside and zips the bag closed, then stands and exchanges it with Viking for the binoculars.

"Alright, show time," Viking says while slinging the duffel bag over his shoulder. Then he heads back in the direction of our bikes.

Legion and I wait silently for his signal, and though I'm glad he's not taking the opportunity to piss me off in private, I can't help but note the way his expression shifts from neutral to evilly amused.

I'm probably going to regret this, but… "You have that devious look in your eyes… What are you thinking about?"

"Double penetration."

Yup. "I'm sorry I asked."

"I'd wager you're about to be." Legion chuckles darkly.

"Unless you're talking about the two of us taking this place and leaving Viking outside to keep watch, I don't want to hear it."

"You do realize I never left Bermuda County, don't you?" I wasn't expecting those words, and my expression must convey as much, because his evil grin broadens. "Speaking *metaphorically*, of course."

"Why wouldn't you be?" I sigh with regret.

"I'm curious whether you'd admit I've been living rent-free in your minds, *and therefore by proxy, in your home,* the entire duration of my absence?"

"I'm not playing this game with you."

"You're haunted by me, aren't you? Admit it. I've been dwelling within the walls of your home for years, haven't I? Tell me, do you ever wonder if I've been in your bed as well? How often have we both been inside her, *simultaneously*?"

Every molecule of my being wants to fucking kill him.

"*Metaphorically*," he adds.

I want to slug that fucking grin off his face. "Keep it up, and there won't be anything metaphorical about me plugging a bullet in your fucking kneecap."

"And will you spin her a tale of friendly fire?"

"There won't be anything friendly about it." I shove the binoculars hard against his chest. "Occupy yourself with waiting for the signal."

Legion turns from me and lifts the binoculars to his eyes. "Perhaps my love language really is taking bullets for her."

"Do you want to die?"

Legion shrugs with an indifference I almost believe. "We have unfinished business and promises to keep. I plan to stick around at least long enough to see those through… Besides, *I blow shit up better than you.*"

"Is that what your brother told you?"

He lowers the binoculars to scowl at me. "The only thing you blow up better than me is shit out of proportion." He tucks the binoculars into his jacket pocket. "Your kid calls me Legend… *How does that make you feel?*"

I don't give him the satisfaction of a reply this time.

Legion knowingly grins. "Viking is ready. Let's go."

"The two cooks inside only have a walkie. I took this prick's cell," Viking informs us. He grabs the bound and gagged guy and shoves him inside the back of the van, then slams the doors shut.

Legion doesn't seem at all surprised. "They're here to cook, not get distracted. Distractions slow down production and potentially lead to dire mishaps. Did our lookout happen to have a key?"

"Can't pick a lock?" I'm unable to refrain from digging at him now that he's pissed me off.

Legion shoots me a scornful glare as if genuinely insulted. "*Please.*"

Viking tosses a small key to him, and Legion moves swiftly to unlock and remove the chain on the gate. "After you, gentlemen." He gestures with a mocking bow for us to proceed.

The meth lab is surrounded by junked vehicles that have been picked over for parts and is situated against the back cinderblock wall separating the scrapyard from the storage facility on the other side.

"I sure hope whoever's got shit in those units took out insurance," Viking jokes as we take cover behind a row of rusty old cars.

"We need to get them to come out," I say.

"Dealers are a dime a dozen. Cooks hold a significantly higher value," Legion says. "You already let the guy at the motel go to report back. Killing these guys would reinforce the message. Besides, the most effective way to resolve an infestation is extermination."

"We're not murdering anyone tonight. Unlike you, Legion, if I go to prison, people I love will be affected. I realize this is all a foreign concept to you, being *unloved* and *unwanted*." Viking chuckles while I go on, "*Alone*...nobody counting on you for anything."

"Fuck. *I get it*," Legion growls.

"I'm just gonna go knock," Viking says with a shrug. "Fuck it. This doesn't need to be complicated. One will open the door, I'll grab him, and one of you guys can bum rush the other and drag him out. We'll tie them up and put them in the van, then come back and blow this fucking trailer sky high. Someone will call it in, and the cops will find them practically gift-wrapped."

"Unless they just open the door and shoot you." I sigh. "Or one of us gets shot by the guy inside."

"Or one of them will come outside to see why their industrial fan stopped working," Legion casually says. "I just unplugged it."

"*Jesus fuck*, I didn't even hear you step away."

Legion continues without commenting, "When one of them steps out to inspect the problem, grab him and instruct him to call for the other to give him a hand."

Before either of us can say anything, Legion sprints with an eerie silence toward the trailer, then crawls behind the aluminum stairs by the door. He practically disappears within the darkness, like some kind of sinister trapdoor spider waiting to strike its unsuspecting prey.

"Is it just me, *or...*" Viking begins.

"No, he's definitely a disturbing individual."

The trailer door opens, and one of the cooks emerges. He glances around but doesn't spot us. Legion left the power cord where he'd see it unplugged, and the guy heads straight for it. As soon as he bends to pick it up, Viking strikes, grabbing him and pressing the Beretta to his head.

"You make a sound and I'll snap your fuckin' neck," Viking warns him. The guy is frozen in panic but manages to nod. "Call your buddy. Tell him you need a hand and sound fucking convincing about it. Calm and casual, or you're both dead."

The guy does as he's told, at least convincingly enough, and the cook inside comes to the door. He descends the couple of steps slowly, obviously leery of the situation. He can see his friend, but not us, crouched low, holding the gun on him. I half expect Legion to wait until the guy descends the steps all the way, then rise from the darkness like some omnipotent shadow being. Instead, he grabs the guy's ankle from behind the steps and trips him. By the time the guy realizes he just kissed the fucking dirt, Legion is on his back, holding him down with a knife against the side of his neck.

The three of us make quick work of zip-tying their hands behind their backs. Viking grabs the duffel bag and removes the rope Legion stole from somebody's boat, then steps closer to the trailer, about to toss the bag inside to burn with it.

"Wait," Legion says, "If we leave the bag with them in the van, it will further solidify another charge of intent to distribute."

"He's right," I concur. "Something else for the cops to pressure them with to get them to flip on this network."

Once we've got them bound nicely together in the back of the van with their guard and duffel bag of intent, Viking shuts the door on them and turns to face Legion and me.

"Should we go get the bikes before we blow this thing up?" he asks. "You and I can hoof it easily, but I don't know if the *Marlboro Man* here can run that distance."

I can't help but grin at Legion. "How is your *stamina*, Legion?"

He scowls at me. "I haven't gotten any complaints."

"We'll fuckin' sprint it then. Let's get this over with," I say, heading back into the scrapyard.

"I'm sure there's something we can light on fire and toss in there," Viking says, scanning the remnants of old cars surrounding the trailer.

"I've got it covered." Legion removes a bright orange object from within his jacket.

"Is that a fucking *flare gun*?" Viking laughs.

"Yes, it is! They're particularly common among boaters. Maritime regulations state they are to be carried onboard in case the need for a distress signal arises." Legion grins and shifts his gaze to the cook trailer, raising his arm to take aim. "I thoroughly enjoy saying this."

"Saying what?" Viking asks.

"*Fire in the hole!*" Legion shouts and squeezes the trigger.

A loud bang accompanies a burst of orange and red light as the flare rockets into the trailer, leaving a trail of smoke lingering in the air. The interior glows an angry red. We turn and run like hell before the fucking thing explodes. Just as our boots hit the pavement beyond the gate, the meth lab explodes in a thunderous roar that seems to linger. Debris and shrapnel clatter against surfaces in the scrapyard, raining down on the hood and roof of the van as well.

We continue to haul ass down the street, Viking laughing, Legion wheezing, but so far, he's keeping a decent enough pace with us.

We reach our motorcycles and quickly mount, firing them up.

"That was fucking fun!" Viking says, reaching over to slap Legion's back while he coughs up a lung. "You good, *Lucky Strike*? Hang in there. When we get back to the clubhouse, maybe one of the sweetbutts will give you mouth to mouth."

"Did you set Vixie up?" Keegan asks when we enter the Twisted Throttle. The bar appears to have recently closed for the night. Aside from the few tables near the front of the bar, the rest already have chairs atop them.

"Yeah, she's in Viper's old room," Chopper replies.

"Wait a damn minute!" The blonde club whore standing beside the bar jabs her fists into her hips. "I've been around nearly three years and I don't get to have a room here, yet this chick shows up and immediately slides into one?"

"It's temporary," Dean insists. "She's not moving in. Women don't live at the Saviors' clubhouse, Maxie. They never have."

"Excuse me, but what is Cherry?" she persists.

"*A different story.* Besides, she rooms with Axel," Keegan replies, taking a seat at one of the remaining tables.

"I don't believe this." She truly seems put out.

"Maxie, go clean tables or something. It's bad enough I'm going to get reamed by my wife about this. I don't need any shit from you."

"I'm telling Vanna you said that." She pouts. "And I already cleaned the tables."

"Then you're done for the night. See you tomorrow."

The slender blonde storms off with a little disgruntled *humph*, disappearing beyond the corridor.

"You sure know how to keep your women in line," I caustically jest.

Keegan scowls at me. "You can go now, too."

"I don't get to hear what the whore has to say? You wouldn't have even known she was somehow involved if not for me. Besides," I reach into my pocket and remove the thick wad of cash. "I made sure you could add this to your coffers."

"That's drug money." Keegan sighs, though there's temptation in his eyes.

"It's still green," I say. "Six grand. If you don't want it, I'll keep it. I was simply endeavoring to be a team player."

Viking shrugs and then takes a seat at the table as well. "I read somewhere you can scrape traces of cocaine off most bills regardless of where you get them from, anyway. Most money was probably drug money at some point. At least it will go to something good now."

"Jesus fuck... Alright, put it in the safe and get Vixie," Keegan says to no one in particular, but Chopper grabs the cash and heads down the corridor past the bar as well. He returns shortly with the dark-haired whore. She takes a seat at the table across from Keegan, crossing her knee-high-booted legs.

"Are you alright?" Keegan asks her, seemingly oblivious to the way her pink, sequin skirt rides up her thighs.

"If you don't count being majorly inconvenienced." She sighs with agitation. "It's after hours, can I smoke in here?"

Dean gives her a reluctant nod, and she pulls a tarnished cigarette case from her designer-inspired clutch, popping it open to select one.

"Allow me," I offer.

She places the cigarette between her lips and turns to face me. I've got the flame of my Zippo ready and waiting. She leans forward, placing the end into the fire and pulls a drag, then leans back in her seat, raking her appraising gaze over me.

"Well, hello there, *tall, dark, and dangerous*," she says on a smoky breath. "Are you a new prospect?"

"*He wishes*," Viking chuffs, folding his massive arms. "How long have you been going *blow for blow*?"

She rolls her eyes at his crude question. "I see you haven't changed much."

"You don't mess with perfection." Viking grins, and the egotistical reply coaxes a smile from the whore.

"What can you tell us about the people you're working for?" Keegan asks.

"People? That guy who left me there takes a cut of my earnings to watch out for me and send the clients up to my room," she casually explains. A bit too nonchalant for my liking. She is only a whore, so the probability of her knowing any pertinent information regarding her pimp's higher-ups is minuscule. However, there's no reason to forgo thoroughness at the expense of appeasing a whore… "I don't know what people you're talking about," she adds, pulling a sanitary wipe from a small packet in her purse. She places it down on the table to flick her ash upon.

"Let's see the phone," I say.

"Why?" she sneers, though this time she keeps her gaze fixed on her ashes. "I just told you I don't work with anyone else."

"Then there's no reason to guard your contacts," I press.

"How about *privacy*, asshole?" she snaps, casting a brief, warning glare up at me. It lacks all the conviction of her tone.

I grab a chair from the next table over and slide it up beside her. She watches warily from the corner of her eye as I lower myself into it and lean closer to her. Visibly tensing, she instinctively shrinks from my proximity as I drape an arm across the back of her chair. Keegan's creaks under his shifting weight, and I can practically feel his overprotective, watchful scowl boring into me with an unspoken warning, as if I'd harm the whore…. *As if I'd need to…*

I pluck the cigarette from her trembling fingers, and before I have it completely snuffed out on the wipe, she's already reaching into her little knock-off Kelly. Timidly, she places the cell on the table, and the lockscreen indicates it is password-protected. She only hesitates a moment before placing her thumb on the scanner, then Viking snatches it, immediately raiding her contacts.

"*Good girl,*" I growl, brushing a strand of her dark hair behind her ear. I straighten in my seat, rewarding her cooperation by granting her back her personal space.

"These all look like nicknames for Johns," Viking says. "Crooked Cock… Foot Fetish… *Little Hands*…"

"*My regulars.*" She rolls her eyes again.

"Do you still have the pimp's cell?" I ask.

Viking reaches into his cut and places two cellphones on the table. "One of them belongs to him. I don't remember which."

Keegan picks up the first phone, powering it on. "This one's a brick," he says, placing it aside before checking the other. "This one isn't password protected."

"Call her pimp," I say. "For starters, we'll establish which is which."

"What's your pimp's name?" Viking asks.

"I don't know, we don't use our real names," she says.

Viking lets out an impatient huff. "*What's he listed under?*"

"John."

"*A pimp called John.*" Viking chuckles as he scrolls and hits call. The locked phone on the table rings.

"Answer the call and see if it lets you bypass the password," I say. "If not, try a few common ones… 0000, 1111, 1234. If none of those work, we're not getting in. The only way to unlock it is a factory reset, which defeats the purpose."

"I can still give it to Jason," Keegan says, attempting a few passwords to no avail. "Cops have more pull with providers, and maybe it will help tie these smaller cells to the network."

"What are you all talking about?" the whore asks. "Cells, networks, providers…is this code talk?"

"Don't worry about it, doll." Keegan offers her an easy smile. "Is there anything else you can tell us about John? You ever see him dealing with anybody else?" He hands her the unlocked phone. "Do any of these names or numbers look familiar?"

While she scrolls, the Creek County connection plagues my mind. Though it could simply be a coincidence. This operation does stretch across multiple counties. I know where to find him if the need to further interrogate him arises. I imagine the guard would be the more likely of the two with any contacts to the next tier in this organization… If Reaper is running things the way I was, whores are simply supplemental income, as well as another avenue to push product. Anyone having anything to do with the drug manufacturing side of the business would be in a more valuable position. I need the guard's phone…

"No, nobody," the whore says, placing the phone down on the table. Viking gives her back her phone, just as the front door of the roadhouse swings on its hinges, and Keegan leans back agitatedly, less than thrilled by this new arrival. Viking quickly snatches the guard's cell and tucks it into the inner left pocket of his cut as the sound of heels thunk across the hardwood, halting a few steps behind me.

"*Lucinda…*" Keegan announces her presence on a weary sigh, and I struggle to suppress a grin.

"I called her for a ride a little while ago," the whore says. "Can I go now?"

Keegan simply gestures to the door in salient defeat.

"Sorry, I couldn't be more help." The whore stands, stepping around me to join Lucinda. "If you ever need another waitress in the bar, I'm available," she adds, a measure of hope in her tone.

"Thanks, doll. I will keep the offer in mind," Keegan replies with a sympathetic smile.

Lucinda scoffs, "After you fired her because your *wilting flower* couldn't stand up for herself?"

So, that's what happened… Lucinda recruited the whore in her mission to run Vanna out of town, as well… I turn around and allow the devious grin to stretch my features. Lucinda's eyes widen as recognition slaps her across the face…much in the way my cock did in that hotel room a few years ago… I wonder how much of what we did that night still lingers in her memory… If she can still feel the sole of my foot pinning her face against the carpet... If she remembers the burning stretch of me, balls deep in her tight little ass...

"Oh my god!" She nearly staggers in her Louboutins, clutching the whore's arm. "What is *he* doing here?"

"Like you, he was just leaving," Keegan coolly replies.

That's news to me... There is further examination of the guard's phone to be conducted.

"I'll give you a head start and keep him here another minute, so you have time to vacate the lot," Keegan adds, and I'm met with another of his glares when I turn around. "You don't have to be afraid of him."

I rule in favor of playing nicely... I promised Vanna my best behavior at her table this holiday dinner, and so I'll chalk this encounter up to practice for the occasion.

Lucinda scurries out the door with her hooker friend, and once they've departed, Keegan begins again. "I'll give Jason the two phones. I'd like to talk to him about the scrapyard, anyway... You can go now, too." He cocks his chin at me.

"There is still more to go through in that phone before you hand it over to the cops," I insist. "Texts, travel apps, for starters."

"We'll let you know what we find." Keegan glances at Viking, who stands and gestures to the steel door.

Fuck... "Then perhaps I'll catch Vixie in the parking lot." I move swiftly for the door, counting on Keegan's over-protective inclinations to kick in, and they do. Before the door shuts behind me, he orders his Sergeant at Arms to make sure I leave the women alone if they haven't departed.

They're still getting into Lucinda's car. I slow my pace and walk casually toward my bike.

"Yo, Legion, wait up a minute," Viking calls. I halt and turn to face him. Perhaps despite everything that has occurred, we've come to some sort of understanding, if not a genuine and solidified truce, after tonight's events. "I'm not going to shake your piss hand, but..." Viking grabs my leather jacket at the shoulder, and I'm surprised when he pulls me in as if to hug me.

What feels like a cannonball slams brutally into my gut, and I'm on my back in the lot of the Twisted Throttle once again, clutching my abdomen. Only this time, I can't fucking breathe.

Gravel crunches beneath his heavy boots as he steps closer to me, and I hope he isn't going to kick me next. *Where the fuck is Keegan to remind this loose cannon of my leverage?*

Viking's fist curls into the collar of my jacket, and he hauls me up to his glaring face. "If you ever threaten my girl again…if you even look at her wrong… I swear to the Old Gods, *I'll make you wish you were dead.*"

"*Who…who's your…girl?*" I manage to force the words out on a wheeze.

"*Val*… And while you're avoiding her, stay the fuck away from the rest of the Steel Vixens MC."

"N-noted… *Duly…*"

He shoves me down as he stands, but I manage to prevent the back of my skull from smacking against the gravel.

"*See you at Friendsgiving,*" he sneers, then heads for the roadhouse. "I hope that gut check doesn't interfere with your appetite, dick." The steel door of the Twisted Throttle slams shut behind him.

Finally able to breathe, I get up and brush myself off. Despite the sharp ache in my abdomen, I can't help smiling as I make my way to my bike, tucking the guard's cellphone into my jacket. I managed to swipe it from Viking's cut pocket while he was distracted, assaulting me.

Once through the gates, I race toward the highway, wondering how heated Puppet might still be after our little fuck-fest in the forest.

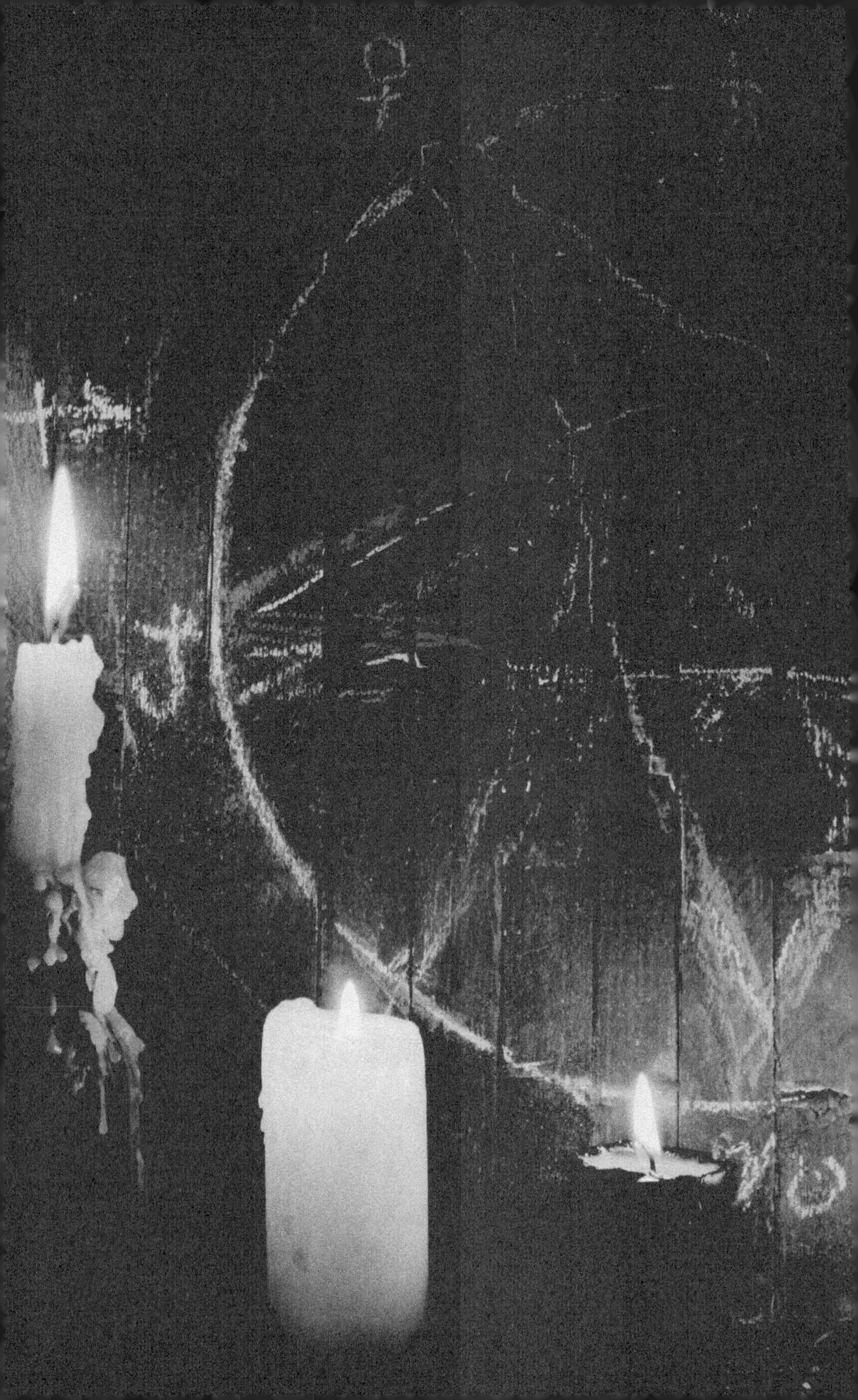

CHAPTER 22

LEGION

I've steered clear of Puppet for the most part. If he's truly gained any tactical wisdom over the years while in observance of my cunning, he'd be surveilling her in anticipation of my eventual return. He's witnessed her self-inflicted tethering to me firsthand, and if they are in contact, there might very well be evidence in her phone. Perhaps even a burner.

The Raunch Ranch is short-staffed tonight, *all hands on deck—or dick*—conveniently leaving the girls' dressing room vacant. Though the back door had been locked, it posed no obstacle. I stealthily slipped inside the cluttered space.

Now inside, I glance around. The closet is overstuffed with skimpy costumes, lingerie, and platformed heels. I cautiously step over a few articles of clothing, maneuvering closer to the several vanity mirrors lined up along the walls.

I have no fucking idea which disorderly station belongs to Puppet, but time is of the essence. I scan each vanity quickly and spot a business card tucked into the frame of one of the mirrors. The familiar logo of a fox brings a smile to my face, and I hurriedly rummage through drawers full of makeup, half-empty perfume bottles, and feminine hygiene products. Her purse is in the bottom drawer, and I riffle through the contents as well, producing her cellphone and wallet.

While committing the new address on her license to memory, I wait for the cellphone to power on, only to discover it is password-protected or requires a fingerprint scan to access the contents. Puppet isn't stupid, and I won't risk a wrong guess resulting in the device storing my photo after a failed attempt. Another plan quickly forms in my mind as I place everything back the way I found it. I had every intention of investigating her home as well, anyway… And I've got a few hours to make use of before her shift ends.

She doesn't spot me lingering in the shadows beyond the floodlights in her parking lot. I've cautiously inspected the area for any sign of *outside* surveillance. It's not a high-end apartment complex by any means. The only cameras are set up in the community gym and laundry room attached to the rental office at the front of the complex. I didn't spot anything hidden within the trees bordering her building, which is nestled on the far end of the property. Perhaps he isn't watching her as closely as I would be. Ah, well, it's always better to overestimate an enemy.

I watch her ascend the stairs to her corner apartment on the third story. She enters and shuts the door behind her. Lights turn on and glow through the curtains of her two front windows, but they aren't sheer enough to distinguish what she's doing through them, especially not from this angle.

I remain seated on the picnic table between two buildings across the lot and light up another cigarette. Time will tell if she's expecting a late-night visitor.

It isn't long before the lights turn off in the front room. I glance at the time on my phone. It's three in the morning. Perhaps she isn't expecting anyone. I grab the bouquet I picked up at an all-night grocery on the way here and move to the back of her building. The lights emanating through the balcony doors cut off as well. My que. I make my way up the two flights of stairs to her door. Tucking the flowers behind my back, I press her doorbell and wait.

The only way I'm gaining access tonight is if she believes I'm here to make some sort of amends. She left after our woodland tryst beyond pissed.

The lights in her front room flick on, and the door opens. She's wearing a robe and a scowl. I find myself not having to force a smile at her disgruntled expression.

"What the fuck do you want?" she snaps.

"When last we parted, I was under the distinct impression you did not enjoy our little *riverside romp*."

She folds her arms but says nothing. Silence stretches on between us. It appears I will have to be the one to break it.

"Did you know The Four Seasons concerti are based on four poems written by Antonio Vivaldi?"

She only continues to scowl at me, eyes further narrowing with deep suspicion. The unfriendly expression slips, however, when I present her with the bouquet of bright flowers. In all honesty, they're quite tacky. However, I discarded the plastic cardette pick that declared *Happy birthday!* As well as the couple of ridiculous picks topped with glittery fake balloons. It is not her birthday, and this gesture is simply a means to an end.

I force another smile. "You once reminded me of spring."

She accepts them with lingering apprehension. "That might be the nicest thing you've ever said to me." She drops her gaze to admire them. At least the colorful arrangement appears to be getting the job done.

I shrug off her comment. "Unfortunately, I cannot recall *La Primavera* in its entirety. There is a line, though… One that stands out to me. I believe it had something to do with spring meadow flowers…and sleeping beside a faithful dog."

"*A faithful dog?* Did you just insinuate what I think you…"

"It's just a poem."

"If you're going to rely on poetry to keep me from slamming this door in your face, how about reciting one along the lines of an *apology* for the way you treated me the other night."

I cock my chin at the flowers. "*Acta non verba*," I reply, but she only blinks, unamused. "No dice? Well, let's see what I can come up with right here on the spot."

She quirks an inquisitive brow and waits patiently. I pull in a deep breath and let it out on a slow sigh, buying myself a moment to conjure up a silly rhyme out of thin fucking air. One would think dabbling in dark arts would lend to the practice of reciting poetic words on the spot, but my true talents lie elsewhere.

"Alright, here goes… Bear in mind that should you laugh at me, I shall rescind the gesture and promptly depart."

Legion: Book 3

Her lips press together in a tight line, stifling a smile, then she gestures for me to proceed. I note the hopeful anticipation in her hazel eyes.

"*Do not be distant with me… Do not be angry with… Sincerest apologies offered…with this gift of verse and wit.*" I bow sardonically, then straighten to find her having lost the battle against her grin.

"You're an asshole," she says.

"I'm aware. Satisfied?"

"*Not lately*," Puppet taunts with an inviting smirk, then turns and walks back into her apartment, leaving the door ajar. I step inside and close it behind me.

"I'm going to put these flowers in some water. Fix us a drink. There's a decanter set on the minibar," she instructs. "Make yourself comfortable."

Well, that was easier than I anticipated. I make my way over to the crystal decanter and matching glassware and pour us both some whisky. After glancing back to make sure she's still preoccupied with her flowers, I remove one of the capsules of Rohypnol I stole from Jonathan Peirce's safe. Quickly cracking it over her drink, I shove the casing back in my pocket and stir her drink with my pinky until the powder completely dissolves.

"I'm not going to bother asking how you found me," she says, sauntering back to me. "I am curious *why* you did, though."

I hand her the glass, then take a sip from my own.

She follows suit.

"I'm curious myself as to the motive behind your continued residence in North Carolina."

"I knew you'd be back."

I lift the glass to my lips and swallow the remaining whisky. "Have you procured yourself a new Master?"

"No."

"A sponsor?"

"I've already told you, no." There is an odd sort of hope in her searching eyes. I allow whatever this emotion ebbing within her to stew while I study her. Even if she is in bed with Reaper, Puppet remains a desirable woman. Voluptuous… Obedient… So eager to please despite all I've subjected her to. Has she truly lingered all this time in wait for me? The suspicion of an ulterior motive still rings true in my mind. It is, after all, in her nature.

"What?" Heightening anxiety laces her questions. "I can see your mind working. What is it? Why have you come to me? Are you alright?"

I refrain from scoffing at her concern, though she remains observant enough to sense the doubt I harbor about her sincerity.

"*Damien...*"

"Finish your drink."

Acquiescent, she downs the glass, and I reward her prompt compliance with a slight, contented smile. "*Come to me.*"

I take her glass as she steps closer to me and place it beside mine on the bar. I've got twenty or so minutes before the effects of the drug begin to overtake her. The alcohol should enhance and hasten her impending loss of inhibition and, soon after, sedation. She'll barely remember a single moment between us tonight. Still, there's no sense in wasting time covertly questioning her. It won't matter what she says. Our torrid past renders it impossible for me to trust anything she says. All the answers I seek must lie somewhere within her humble abode.

I gently wrap my fingers around her throat as she tilts her chin upward, granting me better access.

"I can't seem to purge you from my mind..." I trail my touch lower and softly caress her clavicle.

Her heated gaze remains fixed on my expression while my hand slips beneath her robe at her shoulder. Her smooth skin is as heated as her hungry stare. She doesn't require another verbal command. Puppet unties the garment, then rolls her shoulders free of the Terry cloth, allowing it to slip from her body and fall at her feet on the carpet.

I release a sigh, my breath cascading over her skin as my hand trails down her arm, causing gooseflesh to rise in its wake and her nipples to pebble. I caress the curvature of her hip, moving my touch up her torso. She steps into me when I cup her breast and lower my mouth to hover above her parted lips. She tilts them up, eager for a rare kiss. When I deny her wanton desire, she closes her eyes and, with a woeful whimper, her head lolls back. I torment her with my breath and the skim of my lips along her sensitive neck.

A heady gasp escapes her when I roughly squeeze and lift her breast, full and heavy, and take her taut nipple into my mouth. She groans blissfully at the thrashing of my tongue upon and around it. I pull hard then scrape it between my teeth while my other hand travels down her abdomen, over her auburn landing strip, and along her slit already slick with need.

"*Damien...*" she breathily whispers. The tremble in her voice reverberates throughout her body.

I trail tormenting kisses up her neck and along her jaw, before reminding her... "*Damien is dead.*"

Her entire body jolts with tension. "*Sir,*" she corrects herself, though the whispered word is laced with delicious torment. "*Master...may I?*" Her hand cautiously drifts along the leather of my jacket over my arms. Her eyes are pleading, brows sinched together.

I curtly nod, granting her permission to divest me of the jacket. She places it on the bar beside us before her fingers move to the buttons of my shirt. I only allow her to undo the first few. I don't want to feel her touch on my chest. She abandons the task to undo my belt and fly, then lifts her gaze, seeking permission once again. I grant it, and she sinks to her knees before me, eagerly taking me into the hot cavern of her mouth.

She works me gently at first, with a worshipful reverence, and I reward her efforts with a deep groan.

She's quite literally fucked, regardless of how I decide to proceed. And although her head game is unparalleled, fucking her raw by the riverside has remained within the vaults of my mind. After all...*it's the closest I may ever get...*

The disparaging revelation must have sent some chain reaction through my body. Puppet retracts my cock from the back of her throat and peers up at me questioningly.

I shift my gaze purposefully to the bed mere feet away, then meet her stare once again. Though our exchange is wordless, she understands and rises. Taking my hand, she leads me to the bed. I lower myself to sit on the edge of the red velvet comforter, leaning back to admire her naked form.

She moves to straddle my lap, positioning herself above my rigid cock. It won't be long now, not with the alcohol and the physical excursion she's about to embark upon.

Her hands cradle my jaw, and her pleading whisper brushes against my lips, "*Master...may I?*" Her desperation grows as my silent stare burns into her heated gaze. She rolls her body, grinding her needy cunt against my shaft. *"Master?"*

"May you *what?*"

"*Have you...*" she rocks her body against me again, attempting to conjure need from me as well. "Even if it's just for this night... Please... *Let me have you like I once did.*"

"Is that what you desire? To relive what is forever lost to us?"

She squeezes her eyes against welling tears. One slips past her dark lashes, landing on my chest. I watch the droplet absorb into the fabric of my shirt.

"*I fear I might love you forever,*" she laments on a whispered sob.

"And had I not been forced to rise from the ashes of my decimated soul...*perhaps I could have believed you.*"

She cries, though her eyes are still screwed shut as if she cannot bear to look at me now. One of her hands slips from my face to press against her forehead. Her furrowed brows pitch upward, from torment or confusion, I don't yet know...

When her eyes crack open, her hazel stare is slightly unfocused... *Soon...*

"*Do as thou wilt,*" I growl. "Take what you—"

Her lips crash to mine, cutting off my words. In a kiss wrought with angst, turmoil, and hatred, our tongues war with each other, and she sinks onto me, impaling herself on my cock. She circles her hips, grinding her greedy little clit against me. Her chorus of cries and whimpers reverberates against my lips as she fucks me, and I wonder if we'll make it to the finish line before she succumbs to the Rohypnol.

Her hands run down my neck, her fingers deftly undo the rest of the buttons of my shirt. I allow it and shrug free of the garment, discarding it on the bed while she continues to ride me, though her frenzied pace is slowing.

I lie back against the comforter and ask with a sneer, "Are you alright, pet?"

Her gaze drops from mine to canvass my chest, her lustful expression morphing to disbelief, then horror as she ceases her movements.

"*Legion...you demon... What have you done?*"

She rakes her nails down my chest, drawing blood in the process, and I realize it isn't the fact I drugged her that's causing her distress. It's my tattoo. She hasn't seen it yet. I got it after my departure... A demon and a voluptuous angel locked in a fiery embrace… The words *True Love* inked beneath them.

"True Love?" she sobs. "You got this for her!" She pounds a balled fist against the angel, but the strike is weak and growing weaker with every blow. She's sinking into the blackness of oblivion, being dragged beneath the surface of consciousness by the drugs coursing through her system. *"How could you do this to me?"*

"How? As easily as breathing… You did change me, Puppet… *It just wasn't for the better."*

Drained of the fight, her body goes limp, and I quickly maneuver her off of me and onto the mattress, pulling out of her in the process. I am many things, but a rapist isn't one of them, regardless of the fact that the drug will severely hinder any memory of what transpired between us tonight. She will sleep solidly, well into the early afternoon, granting me plenty of time to search her apartment and transfer the contents of her phone into one of the burners tucked away in my jacket. After snatching her cellphone from its charger on her bedside table, I grab her hand and press her finger to the screen, gaining access to all of her secrets within.

CHAPTER 23

DEAN

A light knock on the bedroom door stirs me awake, and I open my tired eyes to the ceiling fan circling slowly above.

"Dean?" Vanna says softly.

"Yeah, doll?" I groggily ask, still exhausted after last night's adventure. I barely got any sleep before going to the shop today for a couple of hours. I sit up and glance at my watch. I must have passed the fuck out when I got home not too long ago.

"Jason is here. I told him you worked late last night. He asked if you'd go outside and talk to him… Did something happen? He acted like nothing was wrong, but this doesn't really feel like a social visit."

"Everything's fine, baby," I assure her. The explosion at the scrapyard already made the local news, but I doubt we were caught on any surveillance. Not with them cooking back there. Those involved would have made sure their asses were covered. And even though Legion's words still echo in my mind about Jason's brother-in-law, if there is any credibility to what he said, there's no way Jason knew.

While I get up to rebutton my shirt and pull my boots back on, Vanna continues, "Thanksgiving is tomorrow, and our neighbor Meg still hasn't come by to pick up the Cornucopia she ordered. Would you mind taking it to her when you're finished with Jason?" Vanna lowers her voice to ask, "And if you could bring Ace with you. I have to get dinner going, and it will give me a little time to clean up, too. Besides, you have yet to meet her."

"Sure, doll," I say, as we walk down the hall together to the front of the house. Our son is contentedly coloring in his usual spot in the living room by the stone hearth, engaged in a quiet conversation with a watchful Nico. "Ace, put your sneakers on, buddy. We have to make a delivery."

While Ace jumps up and rushes to the door, Vanna hands me the orange cellophaned cornucopia. "There are some pumpkin gourds on the porch. Ace can pick which one he wants to give to Meg," she says with a smile.

Of course, Ace chooses the biggest one he can lift and determinedly carries it himself down the driveway, where Jason is waiting, leaning against his squad car.

"Uncle Jay!" Ace hurries his pace as best he can with both arms wrapped around the gourd.

"Hey there, little man!" Jason smiles, straightening and taking a few steps to meet Ace. "What do you have here?"

"A punkin!" Ace replies, and I suppress a chuckle at his relieved expression when Jason takes it from him to place on the hood of his squad car.

"You got big, buddy!" Jason says, picking Ace up to hug him. "I'm sorry I had to work on your birthday, but I got something for your piggy bank." He places Ace on his feet and reaches into his back pocket for his wallet, extracting a twenty before handing it to Ace.

"What do we say?" I prompt.

"Thank you!" Ace smiles up at his Uncle Jay. I place the cornucopia on Jason's hood next to the gourd and crouch to unzip Ace's jacket pocket, tucking the bill in there where he won't lose it before we make it back to his piggy bank.

Jason lets out a long sigh as if he doesn't want to bring up what we both know he's going to. "So, was all that on the news late last night and this morning, you guys?"

"Depends who's asking."

Jason smiles and shakes his head as I stand to face him. "Since when has my being a cop ever hindered our friendship?"

"I have a lot more to worry about these days," I say, just as Ace reaches up to hold my hand.

"When it comes to you and me, Dean, I'm always your friend before I'm a cop."

"I don't know if this will help at all, but I was going to bring this to you when I had a minute. Since you're here," I reach into the inner pocket of my leather jacket and hand him the cellphone Legion *didn't* lift off of Viking. *Asshole.* "Belonged to someone who might be connected. Let's just say he dropped it. We can't get into it, so don't know for sure. Are any of the guys you picked up talking yet?"

"Not much." Jason tucks the cell in his pocket. "How did you find out what was going on there?"

Legion's words play over in my mind, and I try to conceal my anger at his ability to make me question what Jason knew about the trailer prior to us blowing it up. "Just got a weird feeling about the van. Turned out there was something going on. Figured I'd leave the rest to the cops. We made our point."

"Casey is real upset. We had to drag her brother in for questioning, too." He seems genuinely distraught about it.

I didn't think Jason knew about any of this. Fuck Legion and his mind games, whispering half-truths and twisting reality just enough to make me question a guy I've known for years. A guy I've worked with in secret before, delivering street justice to dregs who would have skirted the flawed legal system. I can't believe I let his venomous doubt seep into my thoughts so easily.

"I bet… I was surprised, too. But is there anything else you need from me? I'm supposed to run that down to the neighbor for Vanna." I cock my chin at the cellophaned package.

"Just wanted to make sure this wasn't anything external. The last thing we need is some kind of drug war in our county." Jason sighs, then extends his hand to shake. "Have a happy holiday and give my love to the wife."

"You do the same." I shake Jason's hand and wish him well, then grab the cornucopia and the pumpkin to hand back to Ace.

On our journey to the old farmhouse, we take a few breaks so Ace can adjust his grip, each time refusing my offer to carry it the rest of the way for him. When we reach the front steps, Ace plops the pumpkin down for a moment, wiping the sweat from his little brow before bear-hugging it one more time to trudge up the rest of the steps.

"Good job, buddy," I encourage him for the home stretch.

Legion: Book 3

Staring at this old farmhouse, my mind wanders back to all those firsts with Vanna. Making out in my truck in her driveway and the nearly deafening rain beating down that first night we kissed. Pinning her to the frame of the screen door on more than one occasion. Fighting to get her to fall in love with me. I can't help but smile at Ace, the perfect result of our love, as he adjusts the placement of the pumpkin beside a rocking chair on the porch.

I make my way up the old steps to that familiar, flimsy screen door and open it to knock on the solid oak one. No answer. I knock again. Still, no answer. I pull my phone out of my pocket to call Vanna. She picks up on the second ring.

"Hey, doll. There doesn't seem to be anyone home. Should I just leave it here on the porch or bring it back?" I don't miss the pleading expression in Ace's tired eyes at the idea of carrying the gourd all the way back home.

"Maybe she got tied up at work," Vanna says. "I guess leave it on one of the rocking chairs, so she sees it."

"Will do. See you in a few." I hang up and place the cellophane-wrapped cornucopia on the rocking chair nearest the front door.

"What do you know about Miss Meg?" I question Ace on our journey home. I have yet to even lay eyes at a distance on our elusive neighbor. I wonder if she's had the displeasure of meeting Gerald Johnson yet. Maybe he's the reason she's avoided running into me. Then again, I'm rarely at the farmstand these days. She hasn't had much of a chance to cross paths with me.

"She has fire hair. It's long, like mommy's…and she has Nico eyes, and she's nice," Ace explains. "Sometimes she's at the park."

"Oh yeah?"

"Yeah. She has books and watches."

"Watches?"

"Yeah. She looks."

"*Oh,* you mean she reads her books and watches you play?"

"Sometimes… She smiles."

"Does she say hello?"

"Uh-huh. Waves."

"To you?"

"Yeah."

"What about mommy?"

No response.

We continue our walk quietly for a few more paces before I ask again. "Does Miss Meg wave to mommy at the park, Ace?"

"I don't know..." He peers up at me, confused. "She waved at the scary place, too."

"The scary place? You mean the Halloween store?"

"Yeah... I don't like that place."

When I try to ask him about it, he shuts down, no longer looking up at me while we walk. I decide to give him a break, at least until we get home, and I can bring Vanna in on this little interrogation.

The moment we step through the front door, Ace darts to his favorite spot in the living to resume playing with a few of his toys. I close the door and approach Vanna. She's got a couple of fall-colored cloths laid out on the dining room table, deciding which to use for dinner tomorrow, I'm sure.

"Did something happen at the Halloween store?" I quietly ask her. "Ace mentioned something about the neighbor waving to him at *the scary place*. I tried to ask him about it, and he got real quiet."

She looks nervous, glancing past me to check on Ace before meeting my gaze again. "When I went to try on a costume, Ace slipped away from Cherry." She hesitates, swallowing hard before she goes on, "It happened so fast. Within a few seconds. We were all scared to death. *It will never happen again*, please don't be mad."

"Were you afraid to tell me?" I ask, but she only continues to stare up at me. "Vanna, don't be afraid to tell me anything. Of course I'm not mad. Kids have a tendency to wander."

"Well, I will never take my eyes off him again."

"I believe you." I smile. "Ace probably thought it was all right to go say hello to the neighbor."

"The neighbor?"

"Meg. Ace said she was at the Halloween store."

"No, she wasn't."

"Ace, come here a minute, buddy," I call to him. He places his toys down and ambles over to us. "Was Miss Meg at the Halloween store?"

"Yeah," he says.

Vanna crouches down to get eye level with him. "Where did you see Meg, sweetheart?"

He peers up at me, seemingly unsure.

Legion: Book 3

"You're not in trouble, Ace." I try to sound reassuring.

"Did you think the lady in the mask was Meg?" Vanna asks.

He only nods this time.

"Okay," Vanna combs her fingers through the top of his hair, then gently cups his little cheek. "You can go play now, love."

He darts back into the living room, and Vanna stands to face me again.

"The lady in the mask?"

She nods. "He must have just been really confused. There was a lot going on in that store, and he was a little leery of all the animatronics. Before I stepped away and left him with Cherry, I was trying on blonde wigs for the Princess Buttercup costume. The woman he wandered off after had long blonde hair, and her body was similar to mine. I thought he mistook her for me."

"I thought Meg was a redhead?"

"She is. But we have a similar physique, too."

"You didn't see the woman's face?"

"She was wearing one of the Venetian masks. It all happened so fast."

"Did she say anything?"

"Yes, but I don't remember what. We just wanted to leave."

"You didn't recognize her voice?"

"No. Meg also has vibrant green eyes like Cherry. This woman was a blonde with blue eyes."

"Alright. I suppose he was just overwhelmed and confused."

"Why all of the questions about Meg?"

"Ace said he sees her around a lot. I just got curious."

"*Protective*, you mean." She smiles.

"Naturally."

"Well, Ace is rather taken with Meg. She's always very nice to him. We cross paths now and then outside of her visits to the farmstand. She's always made a point to come over and say hello, though."

"The park, too?"

She places a hand on her hip. "Now and then. Why?"

I shrug. "Ace said she watches him play. I was just curious if you've seen her, too."

"We've said hello whenever I have."

"Where does she work?"

"She's a pharmaceutical rep," Vanna says, then playfully jabs my arm. "Hey, maybe your *former booty call*, Crystal, knows her? Why don't you give her a call for a character reference?"

That entire situation from my past is nothing I want to rehash. "I doubt it. And for the record, I deleted her number years ago. That same night in the bar, actually."

"*Good,*" Vanna says, then turns her attention back to the dining room table. "I think the burgundy tablecloth for tomorrow. It will look nice with the center pieces Ace and I are putting together."

LEGION

There often comes a point where one must reevaluate their own perspectives when met with a lack of evidence against those they suspect. At this point, I must wonder, am I chasing the truth, or simply clinging to the version that aligns with my expectations?

I found nothing in Puppet's apartment connecting her to Reaper, at least, not at first glance. The contacts I transferred from her phone into the burner have yet to be verified. His number could easily be saved under a different name, and it is highly suspicious that she deletes her texts, calls, and travel history. *Has she been anticipating this? Did he warn her of the inevitability of my suspicions and the lengths I'm always prepared to go?*

As for the rest of her abode, there wasn't anything I wouldn't expect to find belonging to a stripper…wigs, sleezy costumes… No trace of Reaper, though…not even a condom wrapper accidentally kicked under her bed.

Perhaps I've given Reaper too much credit. I would have used her to my advantage, watched her for a sign of my return, *the way I suspect she has watched Vanna for the same purpose.* I suppose there is still a chance he is…and she is truly unaware… Though testing that theory would require the pushing of a button, which might ignite a war far worse than the one already brewing… That is, if my recent encounters with her haven't already activated a ticking time-bomb…

I can't seem to shake the feeling… *Perhaps it's paranoia…* Though paranoia could always be the heightened sense of awareness… The

Legion: Book 3

delusion that your enemies are organized... *Just because you're paranoid doesn't mean they aren't after you... Joseph Heller Catch-22...*

Speaking of paranoia... Stanley is late...no doubt circling the designer suit shop where I've tasked him with meeting me.

Adjusting the lapels of the burgundy jacket as I stand before the full-length mirror, I take in the way it hugs my frame—sharp, sleek, almost predatory. It isn't simply clothing. A suit can also be armor, and where I'm heading, I'll need it.

I flex my shoulders, and the jacket falls effortlessly into place. A little tug at the cuffs and the fabric pulls just right across my shoulders. The trousers drape perfectly at my waist, with a sharp crease and tailored just enough to reveal the perfect break at my dress shoes. Armani never fails to impress.

This isn't simply about appearances, however. This is about reinforcing a psychological advantage. A sharp suit isn't about the price tag. It is a statement that one isn't here to ask for anything. They are here to take.

Though as I stare at my reflection, evaluating the look with a bit of detachment, I wonder if this is too much? Too polished? Too commanding? No... No, of course not. Her family comes from comfortable wealth. And before she was with Keegan, she was with Jack Nero. True, he was a psychopath, but he was also a sharp dresser, which could have been a factor in what initially lured her to him. The female gaze tends to be attracted to a dominant stature...

Besides, I remember our encounter at the Ametrine Cauldron...the way she called me *Sir*...the hitch in her breath when she realized the man standing in her foyer was me... The way her pupils dilated when she drank me in. I was wearing a pinstriped, three-piece Corneliani... A slight grin pulls at the corner of my mouth as I appraise the devilishly attractive force of nature staring back in the reflection before me...

Tell me he ain't gonna grow up looking like one of them heroin chic runway models! Aren't you, pretty one?

The smile slides off my face...and I can practically feel the burning flames tattooed on my back beneath the luxury clothes as memories of being dragged naked across worn carpet assault my mind. I strip off the jacket and hang it up on the rack beside me with the other two options I selected for tomorrow.

"Is the jacket not to your liking, sir?" the suit specialist asks, standing somewhere close behind me.

"I'm still deciding," I reply, turning to face him. He's holding two more of the silk neckties I requested.

"There is a man at the counter asking for you," he adds.

It's about damn time. "Show him in, thank you." I take the ties before he heads off and drape them over the rack as well.

Stanley shuffles into the large communal mirror room, eyes tense and shifty, as if he expects one of his higher-ups to spring from a nearby dressing room and gun us down.

"The likelihood of being found out here is minuscule, Stanley, really. We're in a high-end gentlemen's suit shop in Cary for fuck's sake. Relax and tell me what you think of this color on me? Does it bring out my eyes?" I grin widely at him and snatch the matching dark burgundy jacket to hold up in front of me. He only continues to stare, as if bewildered by my apparent lack of concern over our situation. "Come now, don't be shy. Does this suit say *I could fuck you better than your husband?* Or is it more of a... *You know you want me to eat you right here on this table for dessert?*"

He reaches up to grip the back of his neck awkwardly. "Uh...well...what's the occasion?"

"Thanksgiving, of course." I scan his disheveled appearance. "You look like shit, Stanley. What have we discussed about this? You cannot let on that you're trapped in a stressful situation. The only one who can fuck up this arrangement is you." I hang up the burgundy jacket and select the deep grey one, slipping it on as I turn back to the mirror. "If you aren't going to give me your opinion, you may as well present me with your intel," I say, adjusting the fit.

"They're pissed about the recent hit in Bermuda County," he says in a conspiratorially low whisper.

I release my frustration on a sigh as I run my hands over the smooth fabric of the jacket. "Endeavor to relay something I can't deduce for myself," I snap. "That isn't intel. That is common fucking sense. You better have something for me, Stanley... *I take great offense to uselessness.*"

"They had me working at a different location in Jocsan...a house, somewhere near the ports but on a wooded lot. They drove me there in the back of a van this time, I couldn't see much... I... *I think they might be on to me...*"

"Did they blindfold you?"

"No."

"Has there been a shift in the way they interact with you?"

"I...don't think so... I don't know..."

"But they let you cook? At a new location?"

"Yes."

"Don't let your paranoia sabotage you," I say, selecting two silk ties from the rack. "What do you think? Silver or burgundy?"

"I don't know, silver, I guess."

"*Burgundy it is!* Now go on, do you have any other locations or names for me?"

"Some new guy, but he didn't talk to me... I just heard him mentioned as if he was some kind of... I don't know... Someone to be concerned about."

"Go on," I say, finishing up the Windsor knot on the necktie, though on second thought, she may find the trinity knot more impressive.

"They called him Jagger."

Jagger... A vaguely familiar road name... However, redundancy is a common occurrence when it comes to certain road names, *Jagger* being among them.

"What else can you tell me about this Jagger?" I ask, undoing the tie.

"Nothing. They kept it all very hush-hush... I was only around to witness his arrival for a minute, and then I was sent off in the van to get to work."

"It would be in your best interest to have more precise intel for me at our next meeting," I say, pushing up my cuff to check the time. I'm running late. This displeases me.

"I have the address of the place they brought me...here," he hands me a scrap of paper. I glance at the address in Jocsan before tucking it into the pocket of my leather jacket draped across the nearby chaise lounge.

"Congratulations, Stanley! You get to live another week!" I jest and cock my chin at the small package I left on the chaise lounge. "Would you drop that off at the address written on it? Simply leave it in the mailbox... And Stanley, it would be best if you weren't seen."

He tenses again. "What is it?"

"A gift."

Stanley swallows audibly, eyes drifting to the small package once again. I roll my eyes with growing impatience.

"It isn't a bomb or anything nefarious," I attempt to assuage his fears. "I'd do it myself, but am unfortunately pressed for time."

I promised Vanna my best behavior in her home tomorrow evening. Arriving empty-handed is simply out of the question. There are a few stops I must make in preparation for our time together before my plans tonight. Plans that will have the desired impact I'm hoping for…

"Run along now, Stanley, and send the salesman back here on your way out," I say. He cautiously picks up the parcel. "Do try to enjoy the holiday with your family," I smile at him through the mirror. "I'll be in touch."

3:07 AM

Three…the witching hour…not only linked to the summoning of dark forces…but also the manifestation of intention.

Seven…a number interwoven with the subconscious…including dreams…

Magic bends to intention before anything else. The tools, the timing, the correspondences. They all strengthen the current, but the real power lies in *will*… A weak spell cast on the right day is still weak. A strong will can break through even the worst timing… But tonight, I have both.

Wednesday…Mercury's domain. The day of thought, influence, and the space between waking and dreaming. The perfect time to slip into the cracks of her mind…to shape her dreams into something more…*advantageous.*

What remains of the concoction I crafted weeks ago still holds the essence of my intent. A mixture of ingredients, including mugwort for vision and dreams, as well as my blood for binding and power. The oil is laced with old magic, and I feel them watching…*the dark ones*…while I work. The candle before me flickers as if stirred by something more than breath.

I lift the vial into the moonlight beaming through my window and peer through the glass. Potent as it is, there isn't much left. I used quite a bit the night we danced. I'll have to procure the ingredients to manufacture another batch. What is left should be enough if I am strategic with it. All she must do is breathe it in…*breathe in the essence of my longing*…and tomorrow evening, she will meet me in the quiet sanctum of her sleep…

But first, an exchange must be made… The darkness requires payment in the form of a sacrifice… And I've chosen pain.

Curling my fist around the vial, I hold it tightly against my chest and place my other wrist above the flame of the candle, just enough to feel the burn. The suffering must be genuine, the offering sincere. While heat licks at my skin, sharp and hungry, I grit my teeth against the pain and allow my words to cut through the silence of the cabin…

"By root and leaf, by blood and night,
Darkness aid me in this rite,
Mugwort for vision, for dream-bound sight,
Let her mind open and surrender its light.
No safe haven, no dawn's release,
Only my shadow, her restless peace.
Through slumbers black veil, hear my secret plea,
And let her *dream a little dream of me*…"

CHAPTER 24

LEGION

Holidays…Most equate them with feasts, family, and friends. I grew up severely lacking in all three. To me, for years, holidays meant hunger. There's no free lunch when school is closed, so I never felt the joy everyone else does.

The windows in her home seem like a movie screen, emanating a warm glow from the lights in her dining room and kitchen, showcasing the smiling faces of her loved ones as they gather around the table. From this angle, I'm unable to see what has been laid out for her guests, but I can imagine.

I'm certain they heard me pull up on my motorcycle. I'm also certain I'll be on the receiving end of resentful glares from Keegan and the members of his crew in attendance tonight, for the duration of this holiday meal. I am most unwelcome here, though it matters not to me. Vanna invited me out of the goodness of her beautiful heart. She didn't have to. The thought of me being alone for the holidays bothered her.

I would be remiss not to acknowledge the fact that she most likely invited me out of pity… And although I fucking hate it… I will work with what I must. If pity is what gets my foot in the door of her good graces, then I shall play the pitiful part for her. But I am no charity case, and this sharp, dark grey and burgundy Armani suit serves as a layer of psychological armor, keeping those feelings at bay.

I pull a final drag from my cigarette and toss it down on the pea-gravel section of driveway, grinding it out beneath my shoe, then remove the autumn bouquet from my saddle bag. I had it specially ordered for her, as well as the box of desserts I've brought.

I hope she likes these... Red, orange, and cream-colored roses, sprigs of eucalyptus, pussywillows, sunflowers, and red dahlias... Even a single black rose, hidden within the vibrantly fall-colored arrangement, my not-so-secret *I love you*. I took my intentions a step further, however, and infused a majority of the flowers with what was left of the mugwort oil blend I've come to call *Dream A Little Dream*... I've also blended it with my aftershave and cologne, and the purposeful aroma has lingered quite nicely... *She can't miss it...*

Vanna is already opening the door to greet me with an apprehensive smile as I ascend the porch steps. She's wearing a fancier apron than the one I'd seen her in last, with accents of fall leaves embroidered on it that complement her dark merlot wrap dress. I'd drink in her curves, savor her silhouette like a fine wine, if I weren't certain of Keegan's watchful glare fixated on my every move. I attempt to keep my enamored gaze on the lovely curve of her mouth.

"Hello, Damien. Come in," she says, stepping aside and awkwardly gesturing for me to enter.

I'm immediately hit with the mouthwatering aroma of her cooking. Clearing my throat to distract from the sound of my grumbling stomach, I step inside her home, holding out the bouquet to her.

"For you, Vanna," I say, and she takes the flowers from me with a timid glance toward Keegan, who is already seated at the head of the table, Ace in his lap, and surrounded by a few of his MC brothers and their significant others. "Thank you for allowing me into your home on such an intimate occasion among your nearest and dearest." *Perhaps one day she will count me among them.*

"These are lovely." Her eyes drop to the bouquet. "Puts the little centerpieces I threw together to shame." She offers me a bashful smile, then breathes in the scent of the bouquet. *Excellent.* For a brief moment, she seems puzzled by the aroma, no doubt wondering why the roses smell more like cedar and herbs than flowers.

I shift my gaze to the dining room table. If you overlook the fact it is surrounded by bikers, the scene is something straight out of a Hallmark movie. A burgundy tablecloth that happens to match my necktie, faux fall leaves scattered between platters of everything I've ever imagined a *real Thanksgiving feast* would have. And I'm certain she prepared it all. Along the center of the cloth-covered table are a couple of small, pumpkin-shaped gourds filled with yellow, orange, and deep red mums. A smile of my own curves my lips. These are the gourds she collected with Ace, carved out herself, and thoughtfully stuffed with mums.

"Perish the thought… Gourds for little vases, sweet one… How clever. This bouquet will look just fine on your island. I wouldn't dream of competing with your thoughtful display. And might I add, your spread looks amazing."

Keegan clears his throat loudly, and she quirks a brow.

"*I didn't mean it like that.*" I grin.

"I'll give you the benefit of the doubt *this time.*" Her slight smile remains as she shakes her head, but I don't miss the way her eyes quickly scan my attire. "You look great, but would you like me to take your jacket?"

"No, thank you, but you may take this for later," I say, handing her the dessert box.

"Come, sit down." She gestures to the table.

The only vacant seat is between Chopper and Viking… I am positive this is Keegan's doing. Probably his insistence. Anything to make me feel as unwelcome as I already know I am.

Her words bring another grin to my face. '*You're welcome to come if you can withstand the heat…*' I was forged in Hell, my love... There is but one *heat* capable of bringing me to my knees… And that divine region does not lie between two bikers.

I slide into the chair between them. As if on cue, they both rest their colossal, tattooed arms on the burgundy cloth, elbows claiming the table-real-estate before me. I simply rest my hands folded in my lap and sit back in the chair.

"Comfortable?" Viking sneers.

"*Quite*, thank you." I smile, unfazed by the subtle chuckling around the table as I glance at Keegan. "Lovely abode, *Dean.*"

Keegan pretends to be preoccupied with his son, ignoring the compliment, while I pretend to be the impressed guest. This isn't the first time I've been inside their home, but it is the first time I'm seeing it with the lights on. As my gaze wanders down the hallway beyond the kitchen, so too does my memory of the night I watched her sleep.

I needed to see her one last time before setting off on my quest for redemption. My mission was leading me away from North Carolina, and I refused to let my last memory be one of her in a wedding dress, vowing her eternal love and devotion to Keegan.

A cat learns to stalk prey in silence, despite the bell affixed to its collar. I, too, mastered the art of stealth early on, in order to survive. That night, I stood in the shadows of their bedroom, staring down at her. She had one of her shapely legs atop the covers and was curled on her side, facing him. One of her hands tucked up beneath her chin, a telltale sign of deep-rooted trauma, a subconscious need to protect her throat in the vulnerable state of sleep. Something else we have in common.

I fought the urge to draw nearer to her slumbering form, to run my hand along her exposed leg, to remain within the darkest shadows of her bedroom. And it was a good thing I did.

As if sensing the atmospheric shift of my watchful presence, Vanna nearly jackknifed in the bed from a dead sleep. I held my breath and watched as she got out of bed, bare feet padding softly past me, toward the hall beyond her bedroom door. I remember wondering if it had been a mother's instinct that woke her with an urge to check on her child.

She tugged at the hem of her slightly oversized t-shirt, but it didn't cover the glorious globes of her ass cheeks peeking out the bottom of her boy-short style underwear. She went to Ace's room and quietly pushed open his door to slip inside.

Keegan stirred in the bed, as if sensing her absence, and I stealthily shifted my position to the hallway outside their child's room in time to see Vanna place a soft kiss upon her sleeping son's forehead. I wonder if there was ever a moment like this shared between my mother and I.

"What's in the box?" Viking's gruff demand pulls my attention back to the present.

"*Hopefully not an eyeball,*" Axel whispers.

"A contribution to dessert... I'm sure our gracious and gifted hostess has that well-handled. Even so, I did not want to show up empty-handed," I say.

"Just *red-handed*," Keegan mutters under his breath.

I let his comment slide. I promised to be on my best behavior, and while his grudge is justified, I will not allow him to derail me. Not in front of Vanna.

"If that remark was in reference to the cellphone I lifted off of your Sergeant At Arms, it's already with your cop friend," I say.

Before Keegan can comment, Vanna's gleeful words cut through the growing tension at the table, "*Oh!* Cannoli and sfogliatelle!" She's unboxing the Italian desserts and wrapping them on a tray for later. "Did you pick these up somewhere in town?"

"Actually, the sfogliatelle is from your hometown." This time I allow myself a smug grin. I don't have to look at Keegan to know he's scowling. "I had them overnighted *for you.*"

She glances up at me, pleasantly surprised. "*Oh…* You didn't have to go to so much trouble."

"I wanted to give you… *Sapore di casa.*" I wink at her.

"*A taste of home?*" Keegan scoffs. "*This* is her home."

Conceding to him, I raise my hand in a placating gesture. "Simply the name of the establishment."

"Can we eat now?" Viking lets out an impatient burst of air.

"Yes, I think we've got everything…" Vanna says, undoing her apron as she glances around the kitchen, then double-checks the dining table. "Oh, the candles… I forgot to light them." She tosses the apron onto the large marble island, then turns to pull open a drawer and rummages for a lighter.

"Allow me," I insist, flipping open my Zippo as I stand to light them for her.

"Magic!" young Ace exclaims from his father's lap upon spotting the Zippo in my hand.

"I'll show you some magic tricks after supper." I smile back at him. "Would you like that, Ace?"

"Yeah!" The child claps his little hands.

Another disgruntled growl of a sigh escapes his father.

I reclaim my seat once the tapered candles are lit.

Keegan sends Ace over to Vanna while he carves the large turkey, divvying out slices onto plates handed around the table. Platters with all the traditional sides are passed around as well, until everyone has a full plate.

Legion: Book 3

I keep my watering mouth clamped shut as I stare at the bountiful pile before me. I've never consumed a *home-cooked* meal before... Not anything made from scratch, at least. Not like this. And not so much. But I don't want to miss the opportunity of sampling everything Vanna has prepared. I've heard of meals cooked with love... That one is even able to distinguish the taste. The quote about those who are not fed love on a silver spoon, learn to lick it off knives, springs to mind. Perhaps I truly do hunger most for this elusive ingredient.

When I happen to glance up, I realize their VP hasn't shifted his resentful glare from me.

"Snowy should be sitting where you are right now," Viper mutters, just loud enough not to draw attention from the two young children among us.

"*Mi amor...*" the other dark-haired beauty at our table whispers, gently touching his arm. "This is not a good time... The children are present."

His narrowed eyes slide to Keegan. "And you allowed this."

Keegan opens his mouth to respond when Vanna's voice rises at the other end of the table.

"He didn't *allow* anything, Viper. This is my home, too. If you wish to discuss this further, I'm happy to do so with you after we've eaten, *after the children are settled*, and we can step outside." There's an authority in her tone I haven't heard from her before. "Rosita," Vanna's voice turns soft again, "Would you like to say Grace?"

Grace, in her Pagan household? I wonder if she's truly shed her catholic upbringing, or if she's simply making the gesture for Rosita's sake.

"My pleasure." Rosita smiles, encouraging the little girl seated between her to fold her hands in prayer as well. Eyes fluttering closed, she proceeds to thank the *Good Lord* for all of their blessings, being among friends and family, this bounty of food, *etcetera, etcetera.*

Upon her *Amen*, Keegan chimes in. "And Lord, before we enjoy this meal, we ask forgiveness for our sins... Especially for Legion, here..." Keegan begins, the corner of his mouth curling into a crooked, devious grin. "Whose numerous atrocities include attempts to destroy our town, our county, our club, and our family."

Vanna clears her throat, unfolding her hands to tap her fingernail lightly against the tablecloth to get his attention while sparing the children from a potential scene. I can barely refrain from grinning at Keegan's admittedly amusing attempt to shame me.

"And Lord," Viking joins in, *naturally*. "Let our appetites not be discouraged by memories of the box he left containing an eyeball on the porch of this very home."

Axel's shoulders are jerking as he struggles to laugh silently where he sits across from me, between Cherry and Viper.

Keegan continues, "And may the examples of Legion's transgressions harden our resolve and inspire us always to be better men in service to our community and families... Amen."

I'm about to pick up my fork when Viper suddenly interjects. "And Lord, please also forgive *us* for *our own* transgressions against our brother Axel, despite our best intentions."

Well, this should be interesting...

Everyone at the table is dead silent until Keegan grumbles, "*Jesus fuck...*" His choice words during what was supposed to be Grace have me fighting another grin.

Axel opens his eyes to glance at Viper, then Dean. "What?"

"Nice, Viper." Keegan lets out a frustrated sigh. "We voted on this. *We agreed*, remember?" he shakes his head, disappointment written plainly on his face.

"Voted on what?" Axel glances around the table at his silent brothers, but he settles his attention on Keegan once more.

"*Nope*, fuck this." Viking lets out a loud huff as he grabs a gravy boat and drizzles some over his plate. He snatches a fork next and digs into his mountain of food. "Amen was called. I've been looking forward to this all week. It's chow time." He jabs me roughly in the arm with his elbow. "If I were you, I'd eat as fast as I could. You're about to be thrown out on your fancy ass." Viking shoves a helping of stuffing into his mouth, then points his fork at Viper sitting across the table. Over a mouthful, he tells him, "You're a fucking dick for this."

"*There are children at this table!*" Vanna whispers harshly. She's got her hands over Ace's ears, though the child seems unfazed and is rather content with his mashed potatoes and gravy, following Viking's lead. The little girl beside Rosita, however, has climbed into her mother's lap and is staring at her disgruntled father.

"A dick for what?" Axel asks, "What's going on?"

"Why don't you let the demon tell him?" Viper glares at me.

"Somebody better tell me something," Axel says, sitting back against his seat. Cherry rubs his arm and looks curiously at Keegan. When he shamefully drops his gaze from her, it's evident she's been kept out of the loop as well.

"I'm happy to enlighten the young couple," I say, drawing their attention to me. "Might we first enjoy the bountiful fruits of our lovely Vanna's labor? It would be an absolute shame to go on disrupting this exquisite meal with further conversation unbefitting of such an effort on her part to unite us all. What I have to share has been in place a while now, and as far as I can see, you two appear to be just fine."

"What's this got to do with Cherry?" Axel demands.

"Nothing, directly," I say, picking up my fork and knife. "Shall we?"

Axel looks to Keegan once more. "It's nothing imperative." Keegan attempts to assure them. "No one is in any danger."

Axel grabs his fork with a measure of animosity I've rarely witnessed in him. "Fine," he concedes. "Let's eat."

Vanna

The plate in my hands is already spotless, but I keep scrubbing it under the running faucet in the kitchen sink as if somehow, I can wash away what's coming. The fact that Viper and Rosita left with Mia shortly after dinner hasn't changed anything.

For a man who has spoken so few words, at least in front of me anyhow, Viper sure knows just what to bring up to ruin a mildly tense, but otherwise pleasant evening, *all things considered*. I wish I could stuff that remark back in his mouth like I stuffed the damn turkey!

The plate slips through my fingers as Dean takes it from me and places it in the drying rack. "Are you alright?" he quietly asks.

I briefly glance over my shoulder at our remaining guests. Chopper left shortly after Viper did for his shift at the safehouse, and Viking, Axel, and Cherry are with Ace in the living room. Legion has remained in the dining area, alone, and is staring out the front windows.

I peer up at Dean. "I'm just waiting for the bomb Viper dropped in the middle of dinner to detonate," I whisper. Dean lets out a tense sigh, but before he can speak, I do, "Don't say it. Legion didn't start it."

He nearly frowns at me. "*Legion is the reason—*"

"*Dean.*" I glare back at him firmly.

"*Fine*... Fuck... I still can't believe you invited him," he grumbles under his breath, then lets out another defeated-sounding sigh. "What do you want me to do?"

"It has to be addressed. Maybe you can convince Axel to wait until Church, but Cherry is going to ask me what is going on, and I don't want to lie to her face. She'll know." I glance in her direction again, and this time she smiles back at me. But there's a tense apprehension in her eyes. She is definitely going to ask me. "Should we just do this over dessert?" I ask, peering back up at my husband.

"You know I think the world of your cooking, Vanna, but I don't think even your homemade apple pie is going to soften the blow of this situation," Dean says.

"Well, I made sweet-potato pie, too."

Dean chuckles, then reaches his hand behind me to gently rub my back. I know he's trying to be comforting. "They aren't going to be upset with you, Vanna. Axel will be pissed at me more than anyone else."

I shut off the faucet and dry my hands, then I place the towel on the edge of the sink to turn and face him. Taking Dean's other hand, I give it a gentle squeeze. "He'll understand. We're here to help him understand. I won't let anyone make you the bad guy, Dean." He offers me a pressed smile, appreciative of the support, I'm sure, but there is doubt in his eyes.

We work together in the kitchen to prepare coffee and tea for our guests, and Cherry helps me reset the table for dessert. With nearly half the seats in our dining room now empty, there's room for everyone to sit wherever they want. Dean claims his usual spot at the head of the table, with Viking nearest him on one side, and Axel and Cherry across from Viking, on his other side. Legion moves to the seat closest to me, opposite Ace. Though I'm not so sure I want Ace here for this impending conversation.

As if Viking senses my apprehension, he speaks up. "Why don't Ace and I take our desserts to his room before you all get into this discussion?"

Legion: Book 3

Dean simply nods, and I immediately stand up to prepare them plates. Ace peers up at me curiously, as we've always had a strict *no snacks in the bedroom* rule.

"Just this once because it's a holiday." I smile at him. There is no way Ace is going to eat everything I've put on this dessert plate, but I'm sure Viking will polish off whatever he doesn't.

"Do I have to go to bed early?" Ace pouts, then shifts his hopeful attention to Legion, who is sitting silent and poised across from him. "Legend said he'd do magick."

Legion clears his throat. "I can make it a quick demonstration," he says, as if he doesn't want to disappoint my son.

"Alright," I sigh, sitting so as not to obstruct Ace's view. Legion offers me a slight bow of thanks, then shifts his attention to smile at Ace as he removes the tarnished brass Zippo from his pocket.

"Have you ever seen a candle relight itself, Ace?" Legion asks, rolling the lighter across his fingers like a coin.

Ace shakes his head excitedly, eyes wide and waiting for the show. I glance quickly around the table. Dean is stoic, of course. Viking and Axel may be vaguely interested, and Cherry is smiling, though I'm sure it has more to do with Ace's elation.

"Perhaps your lovely mother wouldn't mind assisting?" Legion arches a brow at me.

When Ace claps and smiles, there's no way I could refuse. "Sure, why not?"

"Simply blow out the candle, sweet one." Legion stands and gestures to the nearest tapered candle on the table. I have to stand, too, in order to lean forward to reach it. "Now, Ace, watch closely..." Legion says, "This magick happens quickly!"

With his Zippo ready, Legion gives me another nod, and I gently blow out the candle. The ribbon of smoke from the wick drifts upward, and Legion places the flame of the lighter into the thick stream a few inches above the candle. A little flame catches within the smoke, and like a lit fuse, rapidly burns down the stream of smoke, appearing to drop back down to the candle, relighting the wick once again.

"*Whoa!*" Ace exclaims, thoroughly impressed as chuckles rise up from around the table. Legion offers him another little bow while Ace claps, then reclaims his seat.

"*That isn't magic, that's science,*" Dean mutters, clearly bitter over how impressed Ace is with Legion. Fortunately, Ace didn't hear him.

"Was it Arthur C. Clarke who said, *'Magic is science we don't yet understand?'*" Legion glances at Dean with a grin.

Before they can start another pissing contest, I grab a fork and wrap it in a napkin to hand to Ace. "Okay, sweetheart, you go have your dessert with Uncle Viking," I tell him.

Viking stands up with his plate and makes his way around the table to join Ace. I hand him Ace's dessert as well. Before they head to Ace's room, Viking stops by Axel.

"You should know the vote was unanimous. I was there, too," Viking says, then follows Ace down the hall.

Axel waits for Ace's bedroom door to shut behind them before he looks at Dean. "Why wasn't I there?"

"Well, this evening is turning out to be another shining example of how no good deed goes unpunished, and that the road to hell is truly paved with good intentions." There is no humor in Dean's forced smile or in his tone.

"I'm happy to take the reins and shoulder the blame here," Legion says.

"Well, you are the cause of everything." Dean scowls at him. "What you aren't is a member of this MC."

"Then I shall endeavor to only speak when spoken to." The tight smile across Legion's mouth doesn't slip. "In the meantime, I'm perfectly content to enjoy your wife's pie."

Dean's glare blazes, but he doesn't raise his voice when he warns Legion, "Keep it up, and the only thing you're gonna be ingesting is your fucking teeth."

"What do you call this divine, gastronomic delight before me?" Legion gestures to his slice of apple pie. "I don't see the problem here."

"You're the problem. The whole fucking problem. Just sit there and be Vanna's *good deed* we're all being punished for," Dean mutters.

I open my mouth to say something, but Legion doesn't quit.

"Why Dean, that might be the highest compliment you've ever paid me!" Legion forks off a piece of pie, swipes it off the plate, and into his smart mouth. He closes his eyes as he chews and rests against the back of his chair with a little groan as if in pure ecstasy.

Before Legion can swallow and open his mouth again, Axel takes the opportunity to ask, "What did the MC vote on, Dean? Why was I left out?"

Dean lets out a tense sigh. "Because we didn't want to risk you doing anything that would jeopardize your future."

Confusion contorts Axel's expression. He sits silently, waiting for Dean to elaborate.

"There's video evidence of the night the Demons' Den burned to the ground... Clear...undisputable evidence of the perpetrators," Dean reluctantly informs him.

Cherry squeezes Axel's arm, sparing Legion and me a glance before she shifts her focus intently back to Dean.

"I've been informed by my lawyer that arson with malicious intent has no statute of limitations...and the felony charge carries a minimum sentence of twenty years."

"*Oh God...*" Cherry whispers.

A wave of guilt washes over me, and I close my eyes for a moment, afraid she might look at me again. When I feel Legion's foot, gently and secretly tap mine, I nervously glance over at him. He doesn't say anything, but the tightness in his expression appears to be vaguely apologetic.

"We didn't tell you because we didn't want you to do anything," Dean begins to say, when Axel turns to glare at Legion.

"That's why you've all been so tolerant of this asshole," Axel says.

Legion parts his hands with a slight shrug. "Choices were made... It isn't as if *I* handed you the gasoline," he says. "*That was Viking.*"

Axel's throat shifts with a hard swallow, and the tension around his angry eyes slackens. "You have Viking, too?"

Legion nods.

"*Fuck...*" Axel slumps back in his seat and stares at his half-eaten pie while Cherry rubs his shoulder. "If I go down, I take Viking with me..." Axel whispers to himself, then looks back at a silently distraught Dean. "You were worried I'd turn myself in to free us of Legion?"

Dean only nods.

"I can't... Not if Viking is on it, too." Axel sighs. "And I can't leave Cherry..."

"Even if he wasn't, we would never want or expect you to turn yourself in, ever. Not for any fucking reason, Axel," Dean says. "Give me your word you won't do it."

Axel shakes his head slowly. "I won't... I promise... And I understand why you all kept this from me."

Dean sighs, a weight visibly lifting from his shoulders as he reaches over to place a comforting hand on Axel's arm.

Axel scoffs, shaking his head. "Ruger was right. This is all my fucking fault..."

"Axel, *don't*," Dean says.

"No, Dean... It is my fault. You told me to leave it alone that night..." Axel's teary gaze shifts back to Legion, but the regret in his expression quickly turns to anger. "That night, this piece of shit hurt you, and I found out what he did to Cherry!"

Legion straightens, meeting Axel's glare head-on. "I may have come close to orchestrating the demise of your fearless leader and county. However, *I will not* shoulder the blame for what happened to Cherry." Legion stands, adjusting the cuffs of his suit jacket. "If you all would excuse me, I need a cigarette."

"You've finished your dessert, just leave," Dean growls. "We've been subjected to your presence long enough."

I don't know what to say... Maybe it is best Legion leaves...

I peer up at him just as he smiles down at me. "Very well," he says, buttoning his suit jacket. "Vanna, I am thoroughly impressed by the exquisite meal you prepared for us tonight, and so grateful for the invite to spend this holiday with you."

"Let me send you off with something to take home for later," I offer, getting up from the table as well.

"You are too kind," Legion nods once. I hurry over to the kitchen to prepare him a tray as he makes his way toward the front door, but he stops by Cherry and Axel.

"Before I depart, I'd like a word with your Ol' Lady," Legion says to Axel.

"I don't give a shit what *you* want," Axel coolly replies.

"Axel, it's okay... I'll hear him out," Cherry places a brief touch upon Axel's hand. "He's not going to do anything."

"Damn right he's not." Axel gets up and steps away from the table to scowl in Legion's face. They're about the same height, nearly matched in their athletic builds as well. Seeing the two of them standing toe to toe, that ever-present darkness that seems to envelope Legion is even more pronounced compared to Axel's usual steadfast, sunshiny demeanor. Even when he's pissed off and in protective mode, Axel retains an innocence about him. And although he has been MMA-training for years with Viking and Dean, able to hold his own in a fight, Legion effortlessly exudes that cold, lethal look of a man capable of not only surviving but coming out on top of any situation. He's all sharp edges in every way. For some reason, it hits me then. Despite knowing everything I do about Legion, which, granted, isn't much, I do know one thing for certain…

Legion *is* a killer.

Immediately, I cross the room, handing Legion a tray of leftovers. "Let's take this down a notch," I nervously say.

Legion glances down at the tray I've shoved into his hands, then lifts his eyes to meet mine. "I only wish to speak with her," he says as if I've somehow offended him.

"It's fine," Cherry insists, standing as she peers up at Axel. "Give us a minute?" She nods toward the living room. When Axel doesn't move, Dean stands up and encourages him to grant Cherry's request.

Axel steps away, though it's with an obvious reluctance written all over his face as he glares over his shoulder. He shoots Legion another warning scowl and takes a seat in the living room with Dean.

Cherry nods at me, letting me know she's alright to be left with Legion for a moment. He promised to behave, so I busy myself with wrapping up leftovers for her, Axel, and Viking to take home while keeping a watchful eye on the situation.

"I never knew he kept you prisoner there… I never knew you existed at all… Things… *Everything*…would have been very different had I known," Legion says to her. Unhooking her thumbs from the front pockets of her jeans, Cherry uncomfortably crosses her slender arms and allows him to continue. "I am far from an innocent man. However, I am nothing like Asmodeus… As far as what transpired that night, three years ago… I thought it merciful to drug you…"

Axel nearly jolts in his seat. Even from across the room, I can see his jaw rippling with an anger that doesn't seem to have dissipated over the years at all. The whole nightmare experience is probably fresh in his memory as if it had only gone down yesterday. When I exchange a brief glance with Dean, the tension in his expression tells me he feels the same way.

Though Legion's eyes never leave Cherry's, I know he's aware of Axel's reaction. Unfazed, he goes on, "Taking you as well guaranteed the involvement of the other Saviors. There was no other way to ensure Dean wouldn't be able to insist on a one-man rescue mission. I needed the Saviors to wipe out as many Chrome Demons as possible. There was no other way… I wanted to spare you…to shield you as much as I possibly could… But I needed to see for myself… *The recognition in his eyes*…when he saw you again…to be truly certain…in those final moments. I killed him for you, too."

Cherry shifts in her boots, and her eyes drop from Legion's as she takes a moment to consider everything he just said. Nodding, she then lifts her chin to meet Legion's gaze again.

"Alright," she says simply.

With the slightest bow of his head, Legion takes a step back from her, just as Axel thrusts himself out of the chair in the living room.

"I didn't hear an apology," Axel snaps, storming back to Cherry's side.

"Axel, it's fine… He said what he had to say… Let's just be done with this," Cherry pleads.

"No! Fuck that! He owes you an apology for what he did!" Axel raises his voice, jabbing his finger at Legion's chest.

Again, the immediate need to step between them swells within me. Legion is like a deadly cobra, poised and ready to strike. If Axel pushes too far, that scary, instinctual inclination to kill whatever he deems a threat could take over.

As I come to stand with them once again, Legion takes another step back from Cherry, his cold gaze no longer fixed on her. Axel has his full attention now.

Before I can say anything in the way of a suggestion to step outside, Cherry tells Axel to calm down. "People apologize when they feel remorseful. Legion clearly had his reasons for everything he did… He's just being honest… He can't be sorry for something he wasn't a part of… He isn't sorry for doing what he thought he had to do…"

"I… I *feel*…perhaps…*sympathy* for whatever grief or pain you may have suffered. Both at the hands of Asmodeus, as well as the events of that night I had you abducted," Legion says, as if struggling with what he is attempting to convey. "You were a means to a much-needed end, for all of us. For that, I offer you my sincerest…"

"*Apologies!*" Axel impatiently urges him to say the word.

Legion: Book 3

"Condolences... *Solicitude*..." The muscles around Legion's pale grey eyes tighten as his expression shifts to something a bit more concerning.

"You can shove your fuckin' sympathy, you psychotic asshole!" Axel shouts, seconds away from attacking Legion, which summons Dean to his side. "I doubt you're even capable."

"Let's revisit this conversation when everyone has calmed down!" I interject, stepping directly in front of Legion now. "How about that cigarette? *Outside*."

Legion quirks a brow at me, a look of borderline amusement in his expressive eyes. "Are you *encouraging* my habit now, sweet one?"

"I'm encouraging you to quit while you're... Well, I'd say *ahead*, but I'm not sure what was accomplished here." Pointing toward the door, I insist. "Please. Go outside. I'm right behind you."

"I'm not quite finished with them yet." Legion smiles at me, and I swear a part of him gets off on making me squirm. He glances back at Axel. "I am sorry about your fallen brother. Though it was not my intention, it was a result of my doing."

Axel grits his teeth, shaking his head as his eyes practically shoot daggers into a completely unbothered Legion.

"One more thing, Cherry, before I go," Legion says, shifting his gaze back to her. "You and I, we're not so different... Not in the deepest recesses of our souls."

"She's got nothing in common with the likes of you!" Axel snaps at him, this time attempting to tug Cherry away from him.

The look of confusion on her face at Legion's words quickly morphs to wide-eyed understanding, and he offers her a single, curt nod before stepping around Axel and walking out the door.

I step past them to grab my jacket from the rack beside the door, but Dean gently takes my arm. "What are you doing?"

"I told him I would walk him out."

"*He's already out.*"

I give Dean a pleading look, and he releases my arm. "I'll be right back," I say, slipping into the jacket.

When I step outside, Legion is standing on the front porch beside a column nearest the steps, cigarette already lit between his fingers.

"Are you alright?" I ask.

Before Legion can reply, Axel storms out the front door and down the porch steps to his bike. Cherry hurries out after him, only stopping to briefly apologize to me for leaving so abruptly. I assure her it's alright, that we'll talk later. Legion and I watch them barrel down the driveway on Axel's motorcycle until the red glow of the taillight in the darkness disappears around the bend.

I shift my gaze to the glowing ember at the end of Legion's cigarette as he pulls a long drag, then exhales slowly. He doesn't look at me. His stare is lost somewhere beyond the faraway tree line. Maybe he's staring at the old farmhouse… I wonder if Meg ever got her cornucopia.

I take a deep breath of the crisp autumn night and let it out on a sigh, realizing how exhausted I am from the events of the day. I'm sure the turkey has something to do with it as well. Ace must be on the precipice of a coma if he isn't already asleep.

Moving to the windows behind the sitting area on the porch, I peek through into the living room and see Ace, eyes barely open, lounging in the corner of the leather couch like he's one of the guys. It makes me smile until I shift my gaze to Dean sitting in the opposite corner, conversing with Viking, who has claimed the leather chair. Dean looks tense and seemingly immune to the effects of tryptophan that Ace is rapidly succumbing to. I know it's because I'm outside with Legion. Whatever time we have out here will be very limited.

I step around the arm of an Adirondack and lower myself to sit. It feels good to get off my feet for a few minutes.

"Well, thank you for trying," I say, breaking the long bout of silence between Legion and me.

"You actually sound like you mean that." He chuckles but doesn't turn around to face me.

"I do mean it… There was a moment where you may have been a little antagonistic, but overall…you kept your word."

He doesn't say anything, just pulls another drag from that cigarette.

"Why do you smoke so much?" I ask.

Legion exhales slowly, and the thick cloud dissipates into the darkness. "Does it bother you?" His voice is quieter, but there's something in his tone.

"It worries me."

He chuckles again, but it sounds forced, and he takes another drag before replying, "Worry is a funny thing, isn't it?" He flicks his ash over the railing. "Humans are unique in that way... Always endeavoring to seek something to worry about."

"Well...you smoke like you're immune to the consequences."

When he shifts to partially face me, there's a sadness in his expression, something tired and resigned. "Maybe I'm counting on them."

His words startle me, and my chest aches as I watch him pull another drag, the ember burning brighter before dimming again...like a dying star. He lets the smoke curl from his lips before it disappears into the night air.

"There are far deadlier addictions," he says, and I remember what he told me about love. *Love is far deadlier than hate... Love, like smoking, will eventually kill you...*

I try to keep my voice steady when I ask him, "When did you start smoking?"

"Ten years."

"Ago?"

"No..." He flicks the ash over the railing again, then stares at the cigarette, as if it might finish the sentence for him...but I do instead.

"*When you were ten years old?*"

He nods, and my hand gravitates to the base of my tightening throat. My eyes begin to sting as I recall what he said to Cherry only moments ago.

I want to tell him that I care, that he matters...but words feel small in the face of something so dark and heartbreaking.

I stand up and walk over to him, plucking the cigarette from his fingers. I want to drop it and stomp it out, but I doubt it will make a difference, so I stare into his searching grey eyes and lift it to my lips.

Immediately, his hand closes over mine, pushing it down before he snatches it back from me. Glaring now, he drops it on the porch and snuffs it out beneath his shoe.

"Why?" I ask.

"Because you," he says, voice rougher than before, "have everything to live for."

"I matter?"

"You matter more than anything."

"And you don't?"

His jaw tenses before he shifts his gaze from mine, turning back to the railing to stare out into the darkness once again. "I should go."

I don't want him to leave like this.

Jennifer Saviano

Before I can second-guess myself, I place my hand on his forearm, silently asking him to face me again. When he does, I step forward and wrap my arms around him. He stills, his breath hitching as if this is the last thing he was expecting...or maybe no one has held him in a very long time. Pressing my cheek against his shoulder, I can't help but breathe in his scent. Beneath the smoke, there's something else. Something uniquely him. Faint traces of herbs and incense mingled within his cologne. I remember it from the night we danced.

For a long moment, he doesn't move. Then slowly, hesitantly, his arms circle around me. But he doesn't hold me back tightly. It's as if he feels unworthy of our embrace.

"I'm sorry," I whisper, though I'm not even sure what I'm apologizing for. Maybe hearing the words he should have heard from his own mother will bring him some measure of peace. Maybe I'm apologizing because I wish I could fix what is hurt and broken inside of him...and I'm not sure I can.

He drops his arms from around me and leaps back at the sound of the front door opening. I don't have to turn around to know it's my husband, and that he's reached the end of his tolerance for Legion's presence tonight.

"I should go," Legion says, quickly grabbing the container of leftovers he'd placed on the small table. "Thank you...both of you...for allowing me in your home...and for the best meal I've ever had the pleasure of consuming." With that awkward statement, Legion descends the steps and walks briskly to his bike.

"What did I miss?" Dean suspiciously asks, holding the door open for me to step inside. I do, and he follows me in, shutting the door behind us.

"Nothing," I say, hanging my jacket up on the rack.

"You smell like smoke," Dean mutters.

"Well, that's what you missed. Legion smoking." I sigh, glancing over at a tidy dining room table. Apparently, Dean cleaned up after our eventful dessert. I smile back at him. "Thank you, I'm exhausted."

He shrugs, then reaches to take my hand, giving it a gentle squeeze. "Thank you for another amazing meal. The least I could do was clean up for you."

Legion: Book 3

LEGION

The engine snarls beneath me, vibrating through my bones. The only sound on these dark, winding roads. I twist the throttle harder, and the wind cuts against my skin, but I don't slow down. I barely feel it...and my mind is anywhere but the road.

All I feel is her.

Her arms around me, like I was something fragile...like I was something that mattered to her.

She shouldn't care. I shouldn't have allowed that.

Her scent still clings faintly to my jacket... Something warm and witchy...something that doesn't belong anywhere near the smoke and darkness that cling to me. I felt her breathe me in as well, and for a moment, I curse myself for dousing this jacket in the mugwort concoction. Regret and self-loathing writhe in my chest.

I grip the throttle tighter, twisting it until the bike roars louder, attempting to drown out the sound of her voice in my head... *"It worries me... And you don't?"*

Matter. A physical substance, distinct from mind and spirit.

Matter. An affair or situation under consideration.

Matter... *To be of importance or significance...*

She looked at me like I was breaking... Like she wanted to pick up the pieces... *Like I mattered* enough to warrant the effort.

I hated it. I hated seeing the pity in her eyes. Hated the way it lingered... Hated the way I fucking leaned into her embrace...starving for her love.

I take the next curve too fast, and the tires skid just enough to make my heart jolt. Adrenaline spikes, sharp and electric. Ingrained instinct from three decades on two wheels pulls me back from what could always be a fatal crash. Not fear. Not even conscious self-preservation. *It's habit.*

Some would say riding a motorcycle is a lot like smoking. Another dangerous addiction that eases the mind, quells the tension of the body...and might end up being the thing that does you in...

At the next red light, I reach into my pocket for my smokes, fingers closing around the pack. Somehow, it feels heavier than usual. I decide I'll smoke later...when the lingering scent of her finally fades.

Jennifer Saviano

After cruising the winding streets of her county, hoping to numb myself in all ways possible, I turn down the woodland trail that leads back to my secluded cabin.

A thick column of smoke towers above the trees, and the distinct acrid odor of burnt wood and marzipan assaults my senses as I ride cautiously down the trail toward my rustic riverfront abode. Enraged as he was tonight, it is unlikely the demise of my modest dwelling was by the hands of the Saviors MC's disgruntled young Road Captain. No, I'd recognize this calling card anywhere.

I kill the engine of my bike and dismount a few yards short of the rubble. Glowing embers and charred, splintered wood are all that remain of my cabin. That, and the distinct smell of C-4.

A smile pulls at my mouth as the list of suspects instantly narrows in my mind. This wasn't the Steel Vixens. This wasn't young Axel. I wonder which of the buttons I've pressed inspired this immensely wrathful act of retaliation. Is it simply meant to be a warning to back off his operation? Or was this the outburst of a jealous and vengeful admirer...*if not lover?*

They say a man's weakness is his pride. They're wrong. I've successfully exploited enough of our species to know the weakness of men lies with their women. A man will bleed, crawl, beg, do whatever it takes, to keep her safe. He'll give up money, power, territory, even his own fucking dignity if it means she remains untouched. And that's why, if you really want to break a man, you don't need to go for him. You go for her. It doesn't matter how strong he is, how ruthless. The second she's in danger he's predictable. Emotional. He'll make mistakes, even desperate ones. He'll bargain away everything he swore he never would. He'll let himself be led, manipulated, alchemized into something lesser, because nothing else matters when the woman he breathes for is in the hands of an enemy.

The worst part...a man knows it. We all fucking do. The moment we love them, we've already lost.

The smile on my face dies, and I light up another cigarette, relieved it's only my cabin burning this time...

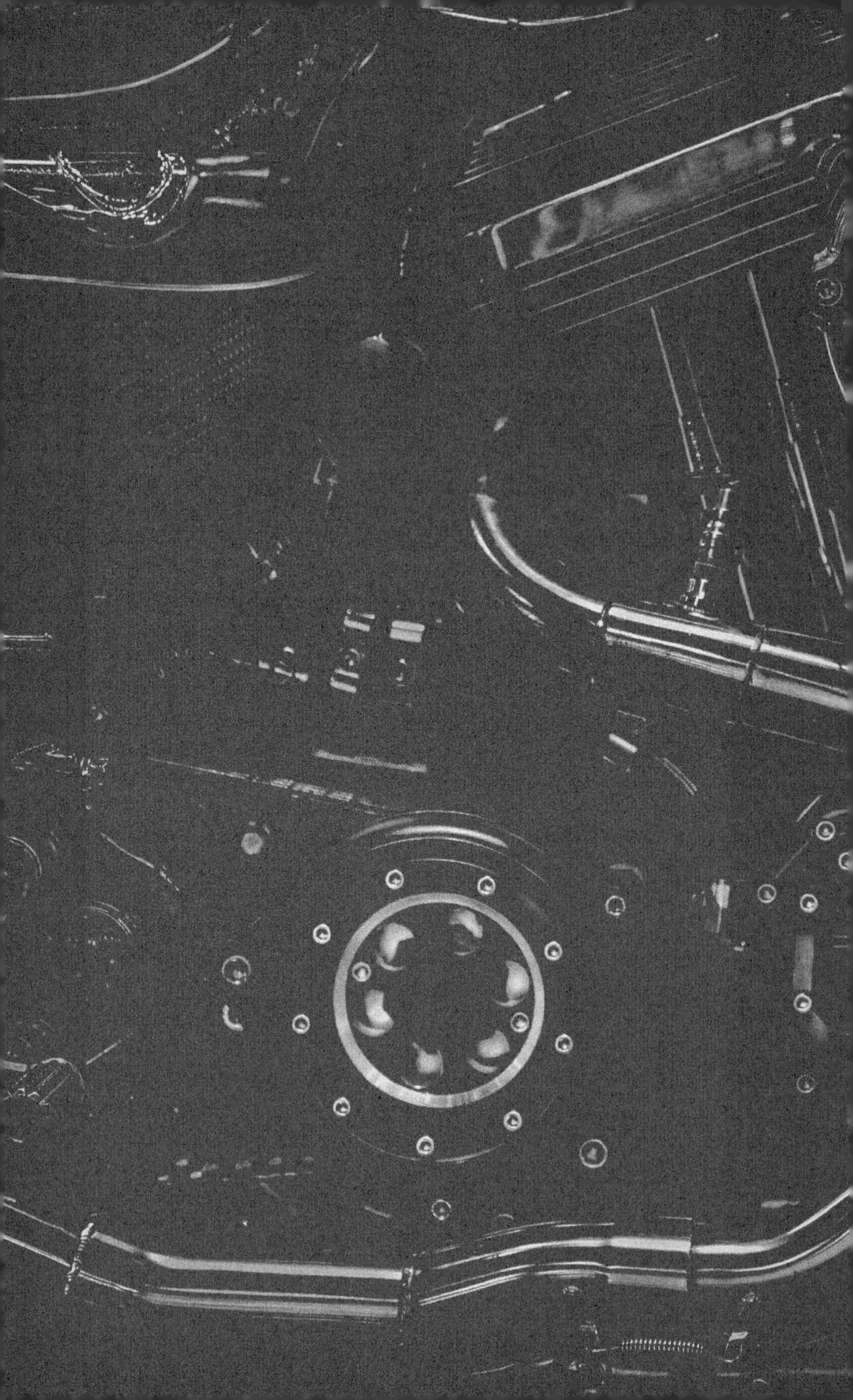

CHAPTER 25

DEAN

"Mmmm..."

My eyes snap open from a dead sleep as the soft, familiar sound emanating from my wife calls to my libido like a siren.

Propping myself up on an elbow, I stare at her intently in the near dark. There's a bit of moonlight glowing through the sheer curtains, and I can make out enough of her features to tell she's sleeping. Another little moan escapes her lips. Her head tilts back into the pillow, and one of her arms lifts and drops back down behind her pillow. Despite her knuckles clunking against the headboard, she doesn't wake up. I watch her breasts rise and fall with every breath. Those pebbled peeks pressing against her satin nightie as she moans again.

My insatiable little peony. I fucked her to sleep earlier tonight, though, by the way her teeth are sinking into that plump bottom lip again, it seems round three is happening in dreamland.

Not fair.

"*Mmmm...yess...*" another prurient little groan escapes her, then a sharp gasp as if she was pleasantly surprised by something. I can't help but wonder what, and I want in on this.

Grabbing the comforter, I shove it further down, off of us both, and move closer to her sleeping form. Though I've reminded her of my consent in this area on multiple occasions, Vanna has never definitively granted hers, and I respect that. But my cock is rock-fucking-hard, knowing my wife needs to be serviced again, and I'm missing out. I slide my hand softly up her smooth, bare thigh to her hip, gently gripping her.

"*Vanna...*" I growl, kissing along her shoulder. Her body squirms beneath my hand on her lower stomach. "Doll...don't leave me behind..." Her head tilts to the side, granting me more access to her neck, and I kiss those sweet spots of hers that really get her going. "Can I touch you, baby?"

I'm met by another dick tugging groan, but that's not a yes or a no.

"*Vanna, baby...*"

Her fingers brush gently over my wrist before they clamp around it and push my hand further south. A smile pulls at my mouth. I love that she loves my touch so much. That these hands bring her so much pleasure.

This seems like a yes to me.

I groan at the moisture my fingers meet as I slide them between her thighs, rubbing her pussy over her panties. She rolls her hips, seeking more friction, and lets out another wanton moan.

I want to go down on her so badly.

Moving over her body, I kiss across her clavicle, then across the swells of her breasts and down between them. Shoving the hem of her nightie up, I place kisses over her abdomen, her cesarean scar, and both hips. Hooking my fingers into the waistband of her panties, I'm about to pull them down when she bolts upright in bed, wide-eyed in surprise.

"*Shit, I thought you were awake!*" I immediately say, a wave of shame, guilt, and fear crashing into me all at once. Feeling all kinds of wrong, I attempt to move away from her, but she grabs my shoulders, tugging me toward her, and plants a reassuring kiss against my lips, her tongue already seeking mine.

My anxiety melts away as her arms circle my neck, pulling me down on top of her, and I settle between her parted legs. She rolls her hips beneath me, managing to rub herself against my rigid shaft, and swallows down the primal growl rumbling up my throat. Her kiss is fierce and all-consuming.

"*Fuck me,*" she demands, a moment before capturing my bottom lip between her teeth. She gives it a quick, sharp suck. "*Fuck me, Dean. I want you.*"

I slide my hands roughly down her body, hooking my fingers into the waistband of her panties once again as I reposition to divest her of this barrier between us. I pull them down and chuck them over my shoulder before mounting her again. She bends her knees and brings her smooth legs up to brush against the sides of my body, then wraps them around me. I rock my hips, slicking my cock with her arousal, and she tilts her pelvis up, guiding the head of my cock to bump up against her entrance.

Sliding my arms underneath her, I push my hands up her back to curl my fingers over her shoulders, gripping them and anchoring her beneath me.

She lifts her head from the pillow to press her open mouth to mine once more, enticing me with her tongue. She swirls it around my own as I steadily push myself inside her. A shuddering breath brushes past my lips at the glorious sensation of her body enveloping me in her hot, slick heat. She moves as best she can beneath my weight, fucking me back while our tongues move against each other just as fervently.

"Fuck, deeper…harder…" she pleads, and I drive myself into her with a bit more force.

Apparently not enough force, though, because she's tugging my neck, wanting me on my back. I roll with her to give her what she wants, and she quickly positions herself to ride me, grinding down on me until I can't get any deeper.

"*Fuck, doll…*" I grunt as she squeezes her inner walls and begins to do that swiveling move with her hips that always drags me to the edge of restraint. "God…damn it, baby… You know just what to do to me… *Fuck*, doll, *fuck!*" I grip her hips, thrusting up in a desperate attempt to keep time with her. She's so fucking wet and tight, and I'm not gonna last much longer. Biting into my own lip now, trying to distract myself with a bit of pain, I watch her body move on me in the moonlight. One of her hands is planted firmly against my abs. I can barely feel her nails digging into the tense muscles. The other is up somewhere, buried in her wild, long hair. She's a fucking goddess, and she's gonna drain me again if I don't switch this up immediately.

She spreads her legs slightly wider, leaning forward just a bit further, and lets out the faintest little *"Ah,"* the moment I feel the head of my cock bottom out.

That's all I can take.

I sit up, sliding a hand to the back of her neck, snaking my other arm around her waist to twist her back down to the mattress. Our mouths crash together once again, our tongues wrestling before I pull out of her and reposition myself to my knees between her parted thighs.

Before she can voice her demand that I put it back in, I'm already there. Gripping her hips, I pull her up against the front of my thighs and sink back inside her. She plants her feet into the mattress on either side of my legs, attempting to regain some leverage, but I press my hand against her chest, pinning her top half back down against the mattress.

Now that I have her positioned how I want her, my hands grip her ass, and I resume pounding into her, watching her tits bounce with every thrust, escaping the top of her nightie. Her teeth sink into that bottom lip as she continues to moan. Her hands reach up the bed to push against the headboard for leverage, accentuating her hourglass figure, making her back arch and her body slope in such a way I can't help but drill her as deep as I can get.

Even in this position, she's figure-eighting my cock as best she can. I'm relieved when her slick walls begin to pulse and spasm around me, the muscles in her ass tensing in my firm grip, she begins to chant my fucking name in high-pitched, gasping little chirps. Though I can tell she's restraining herself so as not to wake Ace, asleep in his room only a few feet down the hall.

I know I'm about to lose myself in her pleasure, the rhythmic pulsing of her wet heat wrapped tightly around me, coaxing my own release.

"*Fuck, Vanna... Fuck!*" I hiss through gritted teeth in an attempt to stifle the sounds of ecstasy radiating through my body. Every muscle tightens, my cock pulses and jerks one last time, shooting another hot load into her perfect pussy.

That's round three tonight, and exhaustion hits me like a tidal wave. I pull out and crash down against the mattress beside her, both of us breathing heavily. She turns her head on her pillow to gaze at me, a sated little smile on her lips.

"I honestly thought you were awake."

"It's okay," she whispers. "We're married."

"I don't have a problem hitting you up for sex, baby. But I want your consent. I thought I had it before."

She moves from her pillow to rest her cheek against my chest and drapes her arm across my abdomen. "You did. I was already fucking you in my dream."

Expelling a little sigh of relief, I press a kiss to the top of her head. "I'm relieved you wanted it this time, but I really thought you were *consciously* consenting. It felt fifty shades of wrong when I realized you hadn't. Technically speaking, that's sexual assault, married or not. I'd love to wake you up with my tongue between your legs, but after this scare, I don't know how we navigate this, as hot as the idea is."

A soft snore is the only response I get now.
Chuckling to myself, I press one more kiss to the top of her sleeping head and close my eyes to join her.

Vanna

Ace is in the living room watching Saturday morning cartoons while I scramble up some eggs for breakfast. I can't seem to shake the naughty dream I had last night, and I can feel my cheeks burn with embarrassment. The vivid images Dean woke me up from play on a dirty little reel in my mind.

"You okay?" Dean asks, "You look a little… flushed."

"Hot stuff," I quickly reply. "The eggs, I mean. I'm cooking." He quirks an inquisitive and very skeptical brow at me. The eggs are just about done, so I turn off the flame and reach into the cabinet for a couple of plates. "Do you want toast, too?"

"You're being weird."

"I'm just making breakfast."

"You look… *stressed*." His inquisitive expression quickly slides to one of concern. "Is this about last night?"

"No," I quickly say, snatching up the frying pan to portion out the eggs. "Ace, come sit at the table. Breakfast is ready."

Dean clears his throat, and I can feel him staring at me, but he won't press the issue in front of our son. "What do you want to drink, buddy?" he asks our son.

"Orange juice," Ace replies on his way to the table.

Dean gets up to grab a cup from the cabinet and walks past me to get the juice from the fridge. "You're concerning me, Vanna," he says quietly.

"I'm fine." I smile back at him as he comes to stand beside me to pour Ace's juice. "Really."

He stares at me a moment too long, filling the cup a little too high.

"That's too much." I nod at the cup and joke. "You're setting our son up for failure. He will spill." Dean lifts it to his lips, taking a few gulps, but never takes his eyes from me. I pick up the plate of eggs and hand it to him. "Bring Ace his breakfast. I'll bring yours over."

"You're not eating?"

"I'm meeting Laura and Ethan for brunch in a little while. We're hitting a few shops for their holiday sales."

Dean turns to bring Ace his food, and I grab the coffee I made for him and his plate of eggs. After setting Dean's breakfast down at the head of the table, I watch Ace pick up his fork and dig into his own scrambled eggs and piece of toast, no crust, of course.

"Are you keeping him with you today?" I ask as Dean sits. "I can bring him with me if it's a problem. I'm sure Laura won't mind."

"You deserve a day with your friends whenever you can arrange it." Dean insists, lifting his coffee mug to take a cautious sip. "I know it's been difficult finding time to go see Laura."

The past few years, Laura has been enjoying her retirement and beach cottage, on top of doing quite a bit of traveling with her husband.

"I'll keep Ace with me. The guys won't mind him sitting in on Church. If the day doesn't get away with us, maybe I'll bring down some of the Yule ornaments while you're out."

"Alright. Well, there's still the lasagna I froze last week if you want to pop that in the oven later. I'm going to get ready." I smile again, but as I turn, Dean's hand gently grabs mine.

"I'd like to continue the conversation we started last night," Dean says, subtly cocking his chin at Ace. "Maybe after this one goes to *B. E. D.*" He spells the word, which earns him a suspicious glance from our son. I can't help but giggle at how much that little glare looks just like his father's. My laughter seems to ease some of the tension in Dean's eyes.

"Okay," I say, giving his fingers what I hope is a reassuring squeeze before he allows mine to slip from his grasp.

Laura and Ethan are already waiting for me in the parking lot of the Fort Fisher Ferry. We're taking Laura's car across the waterway to Southport for a bite to eat and some holiday shopping at a few small boutiques.

Within the hour, we're moseying the beautiful historic streets of Southport along the river, and Ethan is already carrying shopping bags and gift boxes in both hands.

"I'm starving," he announces. "I was told there would be food on this excursion."

Laura laughs. "Alright. Let's double back and put our things in my car. We'll go find someplace to sit down and have lunch."

We settle on a seafood restaurant overlooking the Intracoastal, dining on fresh-caught clams and shrimp cocktails while Ethan fills us in on the details of his new boyfriend, and I show off recent pictures of Ace.

I can't help but notice Laura has been unusually quiet.

"Is everything okay?" I ask.

Ethan looks back and forth between us before blurting out, "You didn't tell her?"

"Tell me what?" I ask, but they both remain silent. "You can't do that. You can't say *you didn't tell her* and then not tell. That never would have flown at the shop. What happened?"

Laura lets out a long sigh. "Robert and I are getting divorced. We've been legally separated for almost a year now. Arbitration starts next week to see if we can agree upon who gets what in the split."

"Oh my god, Laura. I'm so sorry," I say, "Why didn't you say anything?"

She gives me a sympathetic look. "You had a lot going on and have been through so much these last few years. I didn't want to add to it. It's fine. People get divorced all the time. What is it, one in three marriages that fail these days?"

I try not to look down at the wedding band on my own finger.

"*I'm* the one in our three." She smiles. "Don't look so worried. Dean is a keeper, and so are you."

"You're a keeper," I insist.

"Yeah, well, Robert is an idiot." She laughs, lifting her glass of wine to take another sip. "Over the years, people change. We tried to fix it with vacationing, but some fundamental incompatibilities are insurmountable. As long as I can keep the beach house, I'm fine."

"Maybe you can hook Laura up with one of your biker friends when she's ready to get back out there?" Ethan jokes. "Even if it's just for a summer fling."

Laura laughs. "I'm open to applications. I can rock a leather jacket and chaps."

"*Chaps!* This I need to see," Ethan says enthusiastically, then shifts his attention back to me. "How about it, Vanna? Do you know any good-looking bikers looking for love?"

Grey eyes and a sharp-featured smile flash through my mind, and I nearly choke on my sweet tea. "Um, no… Not off the top of my head. Not anyone that would be good for Laura, anyway. Though, feel free to come by the Twisted Throttle whenever you want and *shop around*," I joke. Laura laughs, but Ethan definitely suspects something.

"Who's the guy?" he asks, and the smile slides right off Laura's face.

"What guy?" she asks.

"There's definitely no guy," I insist, shooting Ethan a glare at the insinuation.

"No, no. There was weirdness," he insists. "You might not have any interest, but there's something going on with some guy. You totally choked when I asked."

"You really suck, you know that?" I pinch the lemon wedge on the side of my glass into the remainder of my iced tea and drop it on my plate. "You and your intuitive ways."

He smiles proudly for a moment, but doesn't let up. "Well, share with the class."

I shift uncomfortably in my seat, stirring my drink with the straw. I can feel my own face wincing as I try to find the words to explain Legion. "There's a man Dean believes has a crush on me."

"*Dean* believes?" Laura presses.

I nod.

"You don't?"

"It's…complicated."

Ethan leans forward to capture the straw in his drink between his teeth. "I love complicated. You better not spare any details," he says, before taking a sip of his mixed drink.

"That's all there is," I insist. "He thinks he likes me. I'm happily married. The end."

"You wish." Ethan grins. "What's his name?"

"Damien."

"That's hot."

"Stop."

"Go on," Ethan urges. "What's *Mr. Complicated's* sign?" I'm about to answer when Ethan starts waving his hand frantically in my face, "*Wait, wait, wait!* Let me guess!"

"This is so pointless," I huff. "Not to mention wildly inappropriate, Ethan."

"When has that ever stopped me?" he chuckles. "Is Mr. Complicated an air sign?" I glower at him, though I know I can only stall for so long. "*Is he an air sign?*"

"I don't know."

"You're the worst liar, *Aries*. Your face reveals everything your mind is thinking. That extra bump of stubbornness in your Taurus cusp isn't going to save you, either." Ethan pushes.

"Alright. *Fine*. He's an air sign. So what?"

"Which air sign?"

"It doesn't matter."

"You fire signs, knock it off," Laura attempts to intervene, though I can tell she's vaguely curious where Ethan is going with this.

"Are you friends with him?" Ethan presses.

"I don't know what to call it, honestly… He's just…around."

"Describe him in one word!" Ethan demands, snapping his fingers rapidly in my face. "*Quick! Quick! Quick!*"

"Dark," I blurt out while swatting his hand away.

"So, he's not a Libra," Ethan says, studying me harder. "At least not by comparison to the other two options. Libra wouldn't be quite so alluring to you."

I hate that he used that word. "Who said I found him alluring?"

"Your eyes when I asked you to describe him." He smirks with a confidence that is beginning to rattle my nerves. "He's an Aquarius, right? Dark. *Alluring*. Adventurous. *A rebel*."

I fold my arms, refusing to speak, but I don't have to.

"I knew it. Makes sense. Look how close you two are. Fire and Air," he says, gesturing to Laura and me.

"Female Aquarians are very different from males," Laura corrects him. "And you know we're all more than our sun signs, Ethan."

Legion: Book 3

"But fire is very drawn by air, regardless," Ethan goes on, turning to smile at Laura, and gestures to himself and me. "Why do you think you've got two fire signs around you all the time?"

"*Just lucky, I guess,*" she jokes with a playful roll of her eyes.

"You're damn right," Ethan teasingly scoffs.

"Well, now I don't even want to talk about what I wanted to talk about because this flaming little jerk will read way too far into it if I do." I sigh.

"*Flaming?*" Ethan grins at me.

"Shut up. You know I was only talking about your damn *element*."

"I'm just teasing you." He rolls his sassy eyes at me. "And I promise I won't read into anything you tell us. I've mostly just been playing with you," Ethan insists. "I know you're head over heels for your husband. And he is for you. Scorpio is the fieriest of the water signs after all."

Laura nods, "And his depth of love for you easily rivals the Challenger Deep."

I know it does. Dean's healing, ocean-deep love is incomparable to anything I've ever felt before. And I love him back just as much, despite the wild dream I had last night.

Those smoldering memories force themselves to the forefront of my mind again... Dean fucking me from behind, pulling me back against him by my hips, forcing me up onto my hands and knees on the mattress, which brought me face to face...*with Legion.*

I swallow, reimagining the way Legion brushed his fingers through my hair and leaned forward, his smoky kiss roughly claiming my mouth with dominating sweeps of his tongue, wrestling mine into submission. His other hand snaked down my body, between my breasts, my abdomen, further down until his fingers slipped between my lips to rub my clit in a circular, determined motion that matched the swirling of his tongue.

Dean's stubbled jaw scratched across my shoulder before I felt his teeth sink into my neck, then his lips pressed against me, sucking at my skin as he continued to pound me from behind. Between the memory of Dean's thrusts and both Legion's fingers and dominating kiss, I can feel my heartbeat pounding in the apex of my thighs even now.

Crossing my legs in an effort to dull the throbbing, I reluctantly go on, "I'm going to regret this... But maybe if I talk about it, it won't happen again."

They're both staring at me. "What happened?" Laura asks.

"Technically, nothing... At least, not until after anyway. Dean and I had sex last night, after I woke up." I notice a woman at the table across from us glance up from her plate.

"I would hope you're still fucking your husband, Vanna, you're only three years into this marriage," Ethan jokes, and the woman nearly drops her fork.

"Maybe we should take this conversation to go?" I shake my head. "I think it might be offensive to eavesdroppers."

"That's fine with me," Laura agrees. "I'd like to stop by Marie Delai's shop before we head back, anyway."

I was wondering if we'd stop there, being in Southport and all. I haven't been to her shop in years. Laura grabs the check, and we divvy up what each of us owes and hand the money back to Laura.

I know it's too much to hope that they'll be distracted from the conversation we paused in the restaurant, but I continue to hold onto hope while we walk down the sidewalk toward a few more shops.

The street Marie Delai's Voodoo shop is on is pretty quiet compared to the buzzing crowds we just split off from. And now that it is quiet, of course, it's Ethan who breaches the subject again.

"So, what happened last night?" he asks.

"I was dreaming about having sex with my husband. I don't have those dreams often, but I've been thinking about having another baby."

"*You are?*" Laura squeals excitedly. "*Oh, I'm so happy!*"

I almost hate to squash her enthusiasm, and I don't want to get into how much it depresses me. "Dean isn't sure he wants one yet. But anyway, I woke up, and he must have known I was dreaming about sex, because he was *ready to go*, if you know what I mean."

"*Not a difficult code to crack*, Vanna." Ethan rolls his eyes again, but I ignore his *Sagittarian* bitchiness this time. "I thought he was snipped?"

"That can be reversed easily," Laura chimes in on my behalf. "So, what happened?"

"I was a little rattled at first, but I just went with it. And it was amazing, of course. He's always amazing."

"This isn't sounding at all like a *problem*, Vanna," Ethan gripes.

"Is it because he didn't ask?" Laura glances at me curiously. "Some men think because they're married, *they're entitled* to—"

"*No*," I shake my head. "He didn't realize I wasn't fully awake, but he hadn't gotten that far anyway. He was actually bothered by it and wants to talk about it later. That's not the issue."

"What is the issue?" Ethan asks.

"It's not the first time this has happened, though, it's only started recently… And it's never gotten quite this far… Right before I woke up…well…maybe a few minutes before I woke up… I… I wasn't only with Dean, *in the dream*, I mean."

Ethan's head whips around to stare at me. "*You dreamed about a threesome with Mr. Complicated!*"

"*It was just a dream!*" I snap back at him defensively. "And it wasn't the whole time! It was just a little bit! *Shhh!*"

"Oh, the plot thickens!"

Laura smacks his arm before she looks at me. "You're right. *It's just a dream.* You're aware he has some degree of feelings or attraction to you, that's all it was."

"Thank you," I say to her and frown at Ethan. "Now, can we keep this between us? I can't tell Dean about this part. You have no idea the Pandora's box this would open. I only told you guys so I could get it off my chest and out of my brain, so it never happens again, and I don't have to think about it anymore! *The end!* New topic, please."

They both agree before we make it to the little voodoo shop.

Once inside, Laura and Marie Delai exchange a quick embrace, and the voodoo woman offers her condolences on the loss of Laura's witch shop. I guess it's been a while since they've spoken, too.

"Everything happens for a reason." Laura shrugs. "You know what they say about fire. It represents transformation. I didn't think it would be possible, especially not with everything else going on, but I'm very happy now. I never would have been able to afford the beach cottage. I'm where I'm supposed to be."

Guilt coils in my solar plexus, even though I know it wasn't technically my fault that her shop burned down. And the way Marie keeps glancing at me while they converse isn't helping any.

"I hear the house is being rebuilt to its former glory," Delai says.

"It was a historical structure, so whatever is built there has to match the original home in all specs and details," Laura explains, "That's one of the reasons I decided to let the property go. The cost of supplies and labor in this economy," she shakes her head, "Even with the insurance money, I wouldn't have been able to afford the rebuild. It's alright though, I'm very happy in my little beach cottage."

Ethan and I peruse the shop while Laura and Marie continue their conversation, and I cling to Laura's claim of happiness in an attempt to stifle the guilt. I know it was Legion who burned down her beloved Ametrine Cauldron. I never told her it wasn't me who left the blessing candle burning in the foyer that terrible night.

Though Legion did come to the shop to warn me, in his own way... *"A lot can happen in the thirty minutes it would take him to get here, sweet one... You know this..."*

The charred ruins of the Ametrine Cauldron flash in my mind. I push them away and force myself to focus on the items in the shop. There's a large array of charm necklaces with handwritten little tags explaining the purpose of each. One in particular grabs my attention, and I flip the inscription over to read. *Most effective when kept under the pillow during lovemaking, and when an offering of grapes sprinkled with flour is left by a river or stream.* Oh, this is a fertility charm. For a brief moment, I consider purchasing it and slipping it into Dean's wallet or something. He'd eventually find it, though, and I'm not sure how he'd react. I could sew it inside his pillow, however...

My gaze wanders to her wide array of jarred herbs and the large reference book set up on a small pedestal before them. Maybe there's something I could grind up and slip into his coffee in the morning that he wouldn't notice...

No! What the hell is wrong with me? Until he's on board with the baby idea, I can't be spiking my husband's damn coffee or working spells involving his free will without his knowledge. This is what got me in trouble in the past.

I wonder if backfiring magick is like childbirth? After a while, you forget the pain and convince yourself to do it again. I missed out on a large portion of Ace's birth. What I am able to recall is cloudy, though what Dean told me makes me grateful for the memory-wiping side effect of the drugs that were administered before my emergency C-section.

Still...there wouldn't be siblings if it was so terrible, right? Rosita told me in her hospital room when Mia was born that whatever she went through was worth it, and she and Viper want another.

Legion: Book 3

Dean missed out on everything a father experiences when Ace was delivered as well.

I wish he would come around... Just one more time... One more baby to give Ace a sibling.

For now, and for the sake of not upsetting myself in front of my friends and Marie Delai, I force the idea from my mind and move on to the display of wire-wrapped and electroplated crystal pendants.

"In Celtic mythology, the Sycamore tree is associated with the realm of spiritual connection and dreams," Marie Delai says, suddenly by my side. I must have been daydreaming not to have noticed her.

"Huh?"

"The song you were humming. *Dream A Little Dream*. There's a verse that mentions the sycamore tree."

I didn't even realize I was doing that... "Oh, right. The song has been stuck in my head for a while now," I say, flippantly.

"*How have you been dreaming*, Vanna?" Ethan teases as he crosses the shop behind me to join Laura at the display of various occult books. I want to scowl at him, but I refrain under Marie Delai's friendly but scrutinizing gaze.

"Is there anything I can be of assistance with?" she asks. "Perhaps a reading?"

"Oh, no...thank you. I'll just take this," I say, selecting a pendant on a black leather cord.

"For yourself?" she asks, though for some reason the question sounds more like encouragement.

"No, it's a gift."

She takes the necklace from me, glancing down at it as she makes her way behind the register. "Love and protection... Shall I gift wrap it for you?"

"Yes, please." I smile and join her at the register. The display of tinctures and extracts catches my eye. I select the one labeled Mullein and turn it over to read the label. *For respiratory health. A potent lung and bronchial cleanse, especially beneficial for smokers...*

"*Maybe I'm counting on them...*" Legion's heart-wrenching remark about the consequences of smoking echoes in my mind, and I place the bottle on the counter beside the pendant. "This as well, thank you."

Marie Delai seems to take her time wrapping my purchases, frequently glancing up at me as if she has something to say. It's beginning to wear on me, and curiosity wins over. "I'm worried I'm going to regret asking, but... I'm getting the impression there might be something you want to say to me?"

"You have an attachment...a black stain in your aura," Delai basically blurts out. "So much of what you carry is not your own. It is the burden we healers bear... But the spirits are telling me there is something else... I would not charge you for a reading, and I will make it brief."

"Sounds ominous," Ethan quietly says. "Maybe you should hear her out?"

I glance at Laura, who is standing a few feet from me, mid flip through a book. "You already know what I would do."

"Alright," I say to Marie. She finishes ringing me up, and I follow her to the back room behind the large tapestry. She gestures to one of the chairs at her reading table, and I slowly lower myself into the seat. After stuffing the items I purchased into my purse, I place it on the edge of the black velvet-draped table. I haven't set foot in this room since the Knight of Wands reading, which led me to do a spell that pulled Dean into my life. Despite all of the initial conflicting feelings I tortured myself over when our paths finally crossed, Dean has proven himself to be the biggest blessing in my life.

Yet my heart seems to thud a little faster as I watch her remove the cards from their velvet pouch and shuffle them. Quickly, she pulls three cards and lays them before me, then flips over the first one.

"The Moon..." she says, "Illusions, hidden truths lurking in the dark..."

She moves on to the next. "The King of Pentacles... A powerful figure... A man of wealth and control... He is watching...waiting for something..."

She flips over the third card. "The Five of Swords... Conflict... Betrayal... A fight where no one truly wins." She exhales, her gaze lifting to meet mine. "There are two energies circling you. One stands close, watching... And the other..." She taps the Five of Swords with her nail. "The other does not wish you well."

"Who?"

She studies the cards again, her expression contorting with concern. "One is a presence that has followed you for some time... Tied to you in ways you do not yet understand. But the other... The other is waiting for a chance."

"Are they both enemies?"

She taps the King of Pentacles. "Not this one, but trouble follows him… He does not wish you harm… Perhaps quite the contrary…" She shifts her focus to the Five of Swords. "It is this one… I will pull another card for clarity."

She shuffles the remainder of the deck and pulls one more, laying down The High Priestess, reversed, beside the Five of Swords. "A woman with hidden motives… Deceptive… She withholds crucial information for her own benefit… She uses charm and looks to deceive and is covertly vindictive."

There is only one woman I can think of who matches that description and remains on the outskirts of my life. *Lucinda.*

"Thank you," I smile at Marie. She seems confused by my relief. I nod at the last card. "I know who she is, and she can't hurt us… She tried and failed. She can go on hating me until it rots her wicked soul. She has no bearing on our lives anymore, and she never will again."

When we leave, the motorcycle parked across the street barely registers before I'm face-to-face with Legion in the doorway of the voodoo shop.

"We've really got to stop meeting like this." I sigh.

A grin pulls at the corner of Legion's mouth. "I assure you, sweet one, this time is a happy coincidence." His pale eyes slide to Laura and Ethan before they settle on me again. "Are you going to introduce me to your friends?"

"Laura, Ethan, this is Legend. *I mean Legion.*" When I glance at Ethan, his mouth is agape as he—*without a ginle trace of shame*—slowly looks Legion over from head to toe and back up again.

"*This is Mr. Complicated?*" Ethan practically gasps, then holds his fingers out to Legion.

"*Damien*, if you please." Legion grins wider, *obviously pleased,* as he takes Ethan's hand, awkwardly lifting his fingers because Ethan didn't offer him a proper handshake.

"Oh, *I please*… I please very well, in fact," Ethan goes on, eye-fucking Legion. Laura jabs him with her elbow to knock it off. "I really need to start hanging out in biker bars," he adds, barely under his breath, before Legion drops his hand, offering his own in a greeting to Laura next, who does shake his hand like a normal human being.

"Laura, how lovely to make your acquaintance," Legion says with all the charm I imagine he's capable of mustering.

"Likewise, I'm sure." She smiles.

"What are you doing here, Damien?" I ask once they've made their introductions.

Legion's broad smile turns down into a mock, disheartened expression before he replies. "I'm here to pick up some supplies. Since the tragic loss of the Ametrine Cauldron, this place, though out of the way, is the next best thing."

"Oh, you've been to the Ametrine Cauldron? And we've never met?" Laura asks.

"Indeed, I have. Such a lovely shop it was. Such an uplifting, vibrant environment. It is sorely missed." He goes on like he had nothing to do with it burning to the ground three years ago. I try not to glare at him as he works his manipulative magic on my friends.

Ethan leans closer to my ear, whispering, "*A biker and a practitioner? I wonder what else he dabbles in…*"

"Well, you know what they say, when one door closes, another one opens." Laura sighs.

"*Ah*, the optimistic words of Alexander Graham Bell. Though did you know, perhaps the earliest attribution comes from Miquel de Cervantes' famous novel, *Don Quixote*, in 1605. *When one door is shut, another is opened.*"

"I did not," Laura says. "I guess we really do learn something new every day."

"Tell me and I forget, teach me and I may remember, *involve me and I learn*." Legion glances at me briefly, giving me a wink. "Benjamin Franklin." He smiles back at her.

"I guess this is how the *sapiosexual air signs* flirt," Ethan mutters to me, his whispered tone now laced with discernible disgust. Maybe a touch of boredom as well. "I'd tell them to get a room, but I might be jealous if they do. Though this isn't the *head* I had in mind."

"*Ethan!*" I practically gasp. He shrugs, unbothered as per usual. I shake my head. "Would you two give Damien and I a minute? I'll catch up with you."

Legion steps aside to let them pass while Ethan pulls a card from his wallet. He tucks it into Legion's cut pocket on his way up the cement steps, then turns around at the top to gesture with the sign for "*Call me*" as he mouths the same words. Laura, thankfully, drags him away, but I can still hear his instigating whistling of *Dream A Little Dream*.

"Well, that happened." I sigh.

"*Mr. Complicated?*" Legion is wickedly grinning ear to ear. "What did you tell the little queer about me?"

"Do I need to add Homophobia to your list of cons?"

"No." Legion seems genuinely confused. "What gave you that impression?"

"*The little queer* has a name. *Ethan.*"

Legion plucks the card Ethan gave him from his cut pocket and looks it over. I expect him to drop it on the ground, but to my surprise, he keeps it.

I narrow my eyes at him. "What are you going to do with that?"

He mockingly mimics my expression. "Why are you asking?"

"Because he's my friend. *And you're dangerous.* And he's an impulsive idiot sometimes. *And you use people.*"

"I wouldn't hurt your friends."

"Oh, really?" I cross my arms.

"I've already told you, the Ametrine Cauldron was a means to an end. It was to protect you. I have no regrets." He frowns at me. "I'm not going to hurt anyone you care about. That doesn't mean I may never find *use* for him."

"*Swing both ways*, do you?"

Something tenses in his expression, and he straightens. I hadn't realized he was leaning into me until this very moment. I definitely struck a nerve.

"No," he finally replies, but the word seems heavy for some reason.

Before I let myself drag what I do know of Legion's tragic past to the forefront of my mind and attempt to decipher what just happened here, I clear my throat and tell him, "I shouldn't keep my friends waiting. We have to catch the ferry back to Fort Fisher. My car is there."

"Safe travels, my sweet." He begins whistling that familiar tune again, and I can feel his eyes watching me walk up the steps before I hear the little bell on Marie Delai's door jingle.

LEGION

Vanna scurries off, eager to put distance between us. I can tell *Ethan* and the old witch know she and I are something to each other. Vanna talks about me to her friends. That's progress... And the tune he was whistling...*more than mere coincidence!*

I debate whether or not to light up a cigarette before my next reunion... It's been over three years since I crossed this line of brick dust and entered the domain of Marie Delai.

I had been curious about this establishment ever since I discovered the tarot card in Vanna's closet, tucked in that Knight Spell box. Though I would have eventually found myself here, regardless. I was out of options anyway. I couldn't purchase the items on my list from Vanna, and her little Witch shop wasn't the type to carry what I was in the market for. Not everything, anyway. This little basement shop, tucked down a side street in Southport, had been the only other option within a reasonable radius.

Memories pull me back to that evening...

The dark-skinned root worker had taken in a startled gasp when she spotted me standing in the middle of her cramped shop.

"*Demoon...*" The whispered word brushed past her full lips as she backed away, tucking herself behind the antique cash register. Dark eyes, wide with surprise at first, narrowed as suspicious curiosity eclipsed her concern. "Why have you come?"

I parted my hands in a gesture of peace and attempted to reassure her. "I mean you no harm."

"I'll ask you once more. Why have you come?"

"*Intrigue*... Supplies?" I'd shrugged, unable to restrain the grin that had begun to stretch across my lips at the way she squirmed in my presence.

The voodoo woman grabbed a robust bundle of herbs bound in twine from somewhere beneath the counter. She hurriedly lit the end with a candle lighter. Muttering words so low I wasn't able to decipher, she made the sign of the cross with the smoke before her.

"I noticed your brick dust when I entered." I gestured to the door behind me. "I'm either telling you the truth, or your methods are... *ineffective.*"

"Intentions often shift when expectations aren't met," she said to me. "Perhaps I have yet to disappoint you."

"Oh, I'm quite certain I'll find what I seek here," I told her.

When I moved to explore the shop, she nearly flinched, and I chuckled. Turning from her, I made my way to the extensive array of jarred herbs, roots, and resins that lined the expanse of old wooden shelves along the wall.

"We both know places like *this* carry the *good shit.*" I tauntingly winked over my shoulder at her.

Perusing casually along the shelves, I studied the contents of each jar. A particular few caught my eye, inspiring ill intentions within the darkness of my mind.

Ague Weed...to cause one's enemies confusion.

Betel Nut...when chewed with lime, it is said to increase one's power in chanted hexes.

Lemon Verbena, Mustard Seed, and *Poppy*...scattered at a couple's doorway, it is said to cause discord in a relationship.

Calamus Root...considered so powerful, it is often used alone in compelling others to your will.

Poke Root and *Knot Weed*...to rid one of an enemy by way of accident...or complication...

And *Yew*...a tree which has an ancient history of association with death and necromancy. Incorporated in spell work, it could be used to cause *ill health* in one's target.

I removed a few jars from her shelves and brought them to place upon the counter.

The voodoo woman had remained with her burning herbs. She lowered her eyes from mine to glance over the ingredients.

"You mean to cause someone great harm."

"Maybe." I smiled.

"Maybe I refuse to sell you these ingredients."

I chuckled once again. "*Maybe* I'll have to convince you otherwise."

She held the still thickly smoking smudge bundle out, closer to me. With a confidence I found most amusing, she muttered the word *Demoon* once more, as if it might ward me off.

I leaned in and lowered my face, sucking the smoke of the burning herbs up my nostrils. Upon straightening, I blew the smoke from my mouth into her face.

"What's your next line of defense? You're O-for-two by my count," I sneered at her.

Marie Delai only stiffened, staring back at me with a defiance I was becoming more eager by the moment to break.

"Just sell me the ingredients, and I'll be on my merry way."

"I sell you these things, and you will do evil with them."

"While you're at it," I cocked my chin at the display baskets behind her, "throw in a block of that white wax," I said, removing my wallet and thumbing through some cash.

Again, she'd remained where she stood.

"Is it shop policy to police all purchases?" I scoffed.

She scowled. "Most purchase these herbs and roots for their *healing* properties. I can see in your cold eyes, you have nothing but bad intentions behind them."

"That moral high ground crumbled beneath your feet long before I graced your humble establishment, Madam Delai. Any practitioner worth their salt is aware of the duality in all things. Now, you are trying my patience. It is in your best interest to sell me these items."

Guilt over what I had done with those ingredients rips me back to the present, and I let out a remorseful sigh. Perhaps Marie Delai had hexed me. Cast some sort of working to impede the success of my curse. Whether it was my own inner conflict that sabotaged my workings or Marie Delai's interference, I'm grateful for this particular failure on my part. I've grown rather fond of the young Keegan… The world is a better place with Ace in it.

Steeling myself for what I know will not be a happy reunion, I cross the line of brick dust and enter the domain of Marie Delai.

The thick, cloying air smells of burned sage and grave dirt, but I barely have a chance to glance around the cluttered shop before locking eyes with the owner.

Her piercing gaze drags over me, slow and deliberate. "Your aura is worse…" she finally speaks, "Heavy… Thick and black like tar. You drag it with you like a funeral shroud." Her brick red lip twitches with restrained animosity. "You stain my floors where you stand with your sins." I can practically feel her disdain curling around me like a living thing.

Impervious, I step further into her shop. She doesn't back away, despite the fact that I already know she fears me as if I'm some nightmarish creature dragged up from the bayou and unintentionally summoned to her door. Delai remains where she stands behind the counter, hands resting folded against the worn wood of the checkout counter. The tension in her eyes tells me she's got something sharp to grab within reach. Though after our last encounter, perhaps it's a gun.

"Madam Delai… Is that any way to greet an old acquaintance?" I drag my gaze around the shop. It hasn't changed at all. The shelves are still packed with jars and candles, some burned down to nubs, the drips of hardened wax cascading down the wood. I smile at her, slow and humorless. "You always did know how to make a man feel welcome."

"*Demoon*," she spits back. "What do you want?"

I stroll casually up to the counter. "What did *she* want?"

Marie tilts her chin up, defiant, but her fingers flex with unease, and she shifts her weight. "*You leave that one alone*," she warns me.

My pulse thrums in my ears. *Why?* Did Vanna come here for a reading? Is there truly trouble in paradise? *Was Puppet right?*

I lean in closer, dropping my voice to an octave more persuasive. "Do not toy with me, Marie."

Her dark eyes narrow. "I offered her insight…a warning."

"About what?" I ask, a cold weight settling in my chest at the way she looks at me. "Or rather, from who?"

"*From you.*"

DEAN

"Mommy!" Ace slides off the couch and hits the living room floor running as Vanna steps through the front door.

"Sorry, I'm late. Laura's car service took forever. At least it covers any vehicle she's riding in, so we told them she came with me, and I only had to pay the copay." Vanna's brows pinch together, and she nibbles her bottom lip guiltily, moving her hands to cover Ace's ears before she whispers, "*We lied.*"

I chuckle and shake my head at her woeful track record with cages.

"These tires are adding up. I have the absolute worst luck lately. There has to be something wrong with…*something…*"

She stares at me, as if in deep thought, suspicion written plainly on her face, but then she drops her gaze to Ace and tells him it's time to start washing up for dinner and to go put on his *spaghetti shirt*. I put the lasagna she froze in the oven earlier, and Ace tends to wear his dinner whenever there happens to be tomato sauce involved. He races down the hall to the guest bathroom, *aka his bathroom*, where we've set up a stepstool to help him reach the sink on his own.

"*Something?*" I press.

"*Or someone.*" She lets out a sigh, hanging her purse on the rack before slipping out of her jacket. She hangs it up over the purse. "I had an interesting reading with Marie Delai. Apparently, Lucinda is still plotting something."

"*Lucinda?*"

"Who hates me more than that woman?" Vanna says, walking into the kitchen. "How long has the lasagna been in the oven?"

"Like…forty-five minutes." I grab the remote and turn off the TV before joining her in the kitchen.

Vanna switches off the oven, then pulls on a mitt to remove the steaming tray and places it down on the stove.

"You think Lucinda's been letting the air out of your tires?" I ask, grabbing some plates out of the cabinet. "I suppose she's capable of anything, but I don't know… I don't think she'd risk breaking a nail."

"You're probably right," Vanna says, taking the plates from me and putting them down on the counter near the lasagna. "I'm just overthinking it."

"What did the voodoo woman say that made you think Lucinda was up to something?" I ask, grabbing some forks and glasses to bring to the table.

"She pulled the Seven of Swords *and* The High Priestess, *reversed!*"

The way she emphasizes the last word, I have to press my lips together and roll them in to prevent myself from laughing.

"What?" she demands, all business.

I can't fight the smile any longer when I open my mouth to respond. "Doll, you know I'm not fluent in all this witch slang. You're gonna have to translate for me."

Legion: Book 3

Vanna giggles, shaking her head as she moves to the fridge to grab the pitcher of sweet tea. "It basically describes Lucinda perfectly. *A vindictive woman* who uses her looks to deceive others," she explains, carrying it to the table. I follow her over and place the glasses down for her to pour. While she does, I set the forks and napkins where we'll be sitting. "Why can't she just leave us alone? Why is she starting up again? She's been fairly quiet since Ace was born. Why now?"

"*Speaking of Ace*, I should go make sure he's changing into his spaghetti shirt and not playing in the sink," I say, jerking a thumb toward the hall.

Vanna eyes me suspiciously. "Why do you look guilty? Like you're using Ace to get out of telling me something about Lucinda?"

"Uh…it would probably be best to talk about it after Ace goes to bed," I say, inching my way closer to the hall.

After dinner and Ace's bath, and bedtime stories, Vanna and I stretch out together on the couch in the living room.

"Is this going to piss me off?" she asks, placing her feet in my lap and readjusting the throw blanket over us. I shift a little to face her and slip my hands beneath the blanket to rub her feet the way she likes. She gives me a suspicious smirk. "Normally, I enjoy your foot massages, but this seems like you're trying to soften the blow about something."

"It's really not a big deal…but she was recently at the Twisted throttle."

"You are aware of the proximity of my feet to your balls, right?"

"I don't think the cards were talking about Lucinda. She was just there to give Vixie a ride home the other night."

"What were they doing at your bar?"

"I didn't know Vixie called Lucinda."

"Why was Vixie even there to begin with?"

"Will *biker business* get me out of this conversation?"

She scowls. "That wasn't our agreement. You tell an Old Lady—"

"*Everything or you tell her nothing*." I sigh and proceed to explain the recent events with Legion and Viking that didn't make the news, including the part about interrogating Vixie until Lucinda showed up. "She didn't know anything, and she was there for less than three minutes."

Vanna lets out a contemplative sigh, shifting her gaze to stare at the couple of plastic storage bins marked '*Yule ornaments*' sitting in the corner of the room. She doesn't say anything for several minutes.

"You okay?"

"Yeah." She gives me a weak, placating smile. "Just tired, I guess. All that walking around in Southport. How did Ace like Church?"

"I let him slam the gavel a few times." I grin, thinking back on Ace's enthusiasm and the way he raised his hand to participate in the votes held today. "We also decided it might be time to do something for the community kids this holiday. Ace might have inspired that discussion… I remember how excited you were when I first told you about Christmas at the Twisted Throttle. I'm not sure what it's going to look like without Snowy, but…the guys are finally open to entertaining the idea."

"That's great news." Vanna's expression brightens, and it is genuine, but again, I was still expecting a little more enthusiasm.

"Did something else happen today?" I press. When she hesitates to answer, I know something is wrong. "Please tell me."

"Laura and Robert are getting a divorce."

"I'm sorry to hear that…wow… Kinda came out of nowhere."

Vanna shrugs, "Apparently not. Laura said they've been trying to work it out for a while now, but the papers are filed."

"Not that it's any of my business, but did she say why?"

"No…and I didn't press her on it. I guess some things just turn out to be fundamental incompatibilities. Over time, resentments build and… I guess there comes a point where there's no undoing the damage. The divide just gets too wide to overcome… It's sad. I thought she was happy."

I know she's only talking about Laura, but her words chill me to my bones. *Is Vanna happy?* Am I living up to the promises I vowed to keep? Or is our divide regarding another baby the *fundamental incompatibility* that inevitably tears us apart? I can't lose her. Not in any sense of the word.

"Oh, speaking of relationships," Vanna says, her tone slightly more upbeat again. "Did you ever get in touch with Slice about your brother?"

"Shit… No. But I'm riding up to meet with him this week."

"Okay, it will be a nice holiday surprise for Trippy. She's really into your brother. Don't forget."

"I won't. I promise."

But it's not their relationship or happiness I'm concerned about.

Chapter 26

Vanna

"Well, this isn't a good sign…" Dean mutters.

The moment I crack open the first storage box, I don't even have to ask him what's wrong. The musty, stale smell hits me like a punch in the nose, and I cough, waiving my hand in front of my face. I'm glad Ace is with Viking across the lot, playing on the swing set behind the Twisted Throttle.

"*Oh no…*" I sigh, peering back at Dean standing closer to the front of the storage unit at his own box labeled *Bar Decorations.*

He pulls out a strand of garland, only for pieces of it to crumble in his grip. "Yeah…looks like most of what we had isn't making a comeback." He drops the tangled mess of brittle plastic back into the box.

I remove the sheet of bubble wrap from mine, hoping to salvage something, and peer inside. What I imagine were once bright red and green ribbons and bows are now faded. I lift them out, and the tarnished ornaments beneath are a little chipped.

"Ew…" I say, wrinkling my nose at something at the bottom that looks suspiciously like mouse droppings.

"There's shit in this one, too," Dean says, "I guess three years was too long to leave all this in storage."

"Keeping them in cardboard liquor and beer boxes was your first mistake." I sigh, my excitement over experiencing the holiday season at the Twisted Throttle deflating. This was supposed to be the year we finally brought Christmas back to the bar after Snowy's passing. I've been looking forward to this ever since Dean told me about it. I have to suppress a sad smile even now, thinking back on everything he described, especially Viking's Krampus incident, and how everyone dressed up. At least to some extent. And how the townsfolk would bring their children to have pictures taken with *biker Santa*.

"Maybe this is a sign we should just let this tradition end with Snowy," Dean says, folding the box closed.

"No." I frown, standing. "We could get new decorations. Snowy would want you all to keep doing this for the community. Especially for the kids. If anything, this is a sign to start anew. I understand why you all stopped, but I also know how much this event means to everyone. You told me this wasn't just a party. It was something the whole community enjoyed and looked forward to. Maybe this is just what the club needs to remind everyone you're still here. You still care. You're still the Saviors MC."

I walk over to Dean, placing my hand on his arm. "I know no one wanted to do this until now because it felt too soon, and then like you were moving on without him, but we can make it something Snowy would be proud of. We can give him his own place of honor and come up with something a little different, so it doesn't feel like anyone is taking his place."

"Alright," Dean agrees. "I'll bring it to the table to see what everyone is comfortable with and ask Diesel to work it into the budget. You and Cherry are going to have to get a jump on replacing the decorations."

"I'm on it, Prez!" I grin.

Dean smiles and shakes his head. "Pick up some plastic bins with airtight lids while you're at it, so this doesn't happen again." He taps a cardboard Jack Daniels box with his motorcycle boot. I notice how worn in it is from shifting gears. "And keep the receipts so I can give them to Diesel," he adds, removing the storage key from his key ring before handing it to me. "You can leave the bins in here."

"Yes, sir," I tease. The Harley-Davidson shop a few towns over is still having its holiday sale, and there is a container store in a shopping mall right in the same area. It's also been a while since Latisha and I had any time to meet up. I decide I'll give her a call, too.

We step outside of the unit, and Dean drags the rolling door down to shut it for now. "I'll have a prospect take all the ruined shit to the dump. In the meantime, I've got to head up to JoCo with Viking and *he who shall not be named* today." Dean bends to kiss me. "I love you."

"I love you, too. Ride safe." I watch Dean head back into his shop before I cross the lot and make my way over to Ace and Viking.

The decorations might be ruined, but the tradition didn't have to be. This year, the holiday spirit is coming back to the Twisted Throttle, and I can't wait for Ace and me to be a part of it.

DEAN

"Hey man, thanks for working in another day for me on the schedule this week," Derek says when I step into my shop. He's got a bike up on the lift. An older Harley Davidson Street Glide in for drive belt maintenance as well as a repair on the shock absorbers.

"I wish I could put you back on full-time, believe me," I tell him, just as my cellphone rings. I already know who it is. Someone else I've been letting down. "You're a great mechanic. Hopefully, this coming year is the year we bounce back... I'm gonna need you to lock up the shop tonight, too... Give me a sec, I gotta take this." I walk the short distance to my office and sit down at my desk before hitting the green icon. "What's up, Slice?"

"I saw the news in Bermuda County last week. Another meth lab explosion."

"Supposedly, it was the last of them."

"*How fortunate for you.*"

"Slice, don't break my fuckin' balls. I haven't forgotten our promise to help you."

"That's good to hear."

"I was gonna ride up today if that's alright with you? We've got some intel on what might be a substantial location in Jocsan." I still have to talk to him about patching in my brother. Might as well knock two things off my ever-growing to-do list.

"You know our doors are always open to the Saviors MC."

"Alright. Let me round up my Sergeant at Arms, and we'll head your way."

After hanging up, I scroll to Legion's number and shoot him a text: Jokers. Be there. Two hours.

Legion: Book 3

When Viking and I arrive at the Jokers' clubhouse, we're both surprised to see Legion's bike already here. Viking dismounts and steps over to the murdered out Indian, bending to place the back of his hand near the engine.

"Still warm. He hasn't been here long," Viking says.

A prospect greets us at the door and leads us to the conference room where the Jokers' hold Church. Legion is standing beside the table nearest Slice, who is seated at the head of it.

"Welcome back," Slice nods to the empty seats at the end of the table, and Viking and I join him and his crew at the table.

"Where were you that you beat us here?" I ask Legion.

"Creek County, investigating additional leads," he replies.

"I'm not concerned with Creek County right now," Slice interrupts, glancing at Legion. "I am curious about what happened to your little party favor?"

"I honored your wish and permitted him to live… At least, under stringent conditions," Legion says.

"I didn't want him to expire in our territory. Isn't letting him live risky?" Slice asks.

"Without risk, there is no reward." Legion reaches into the inner pocket of his leather jacket and produces a road map of Jocsan County, then spreads it out across the table in front of Slice. There's a red circle drawn around a small area. "This is the location of a house. Not their headquarters, but a substation currently storing quite a bit of product and probably cash. It's a small ranch down a dirt road on a wooded lot. I didn't spot any industrial air filters or anything else that would indicate they cook here. There were a number of bikes, however. I would expect to encounter a few members of their crew at any given time."

"Good. Let's wipe it off the map," Slice replies impatiently.

"I had an inkling you'd say that." Legion takes a step back from the table while Slice continues to study the surrounding area marked. "I would be remiss if I didn't mention this move will most definitely force their hand. There will be a response in the form of retribution… If I were calling the shots, I might first recruit a few more like-minded MCs to your cause. I'd build up a force one might hesitate to reckon with. Then I'd go after his associates and allies, *hard and simultaneously*. I'd make them question whether or not their ties were worth keeping… Hell, I'd make them rue the day their paths ever crossed."

"Like you've done with us," I mutter. "Made *us* your fucking wall of protection."

Before Legion can strike back with another snarky reply, Slice speaks up again. "This is my territory. That means I'm calling the shots. I want to send a clear message that this shit will not be tolerated on any level within Jocsan County. Now, I've invited you back here to formulate a plan we can all agree on. I didn't have to extend that courtesy."

Though Slice is hard eyeing me, it's Legion's cold eyes I feel boring into me. As much as I hate to agree with the demonic fuck, he's right. But Jocsan County is beyond my jurisdiction, so I simply offer Slice a curt nod of compliance.

"Great. Now, let's strategize this attack. Maximum damage without casualty of life."

Legion expels a sigh laced with tension. Despite his compliance with the Jokers' wishes, he's not as indifferent as he's pretending to be. "Giving up your Diamonds has given those hungry for your territory reason to believe there are lines you're no longer willing to cross... A soft blow will only solidify and embolden this idea, as well as the severity of how they respond."

"That's their mistake. We don't need fuckin' Diamond patches to handle our shit," Slice replies. "Sparing their lives might convey the message we simply want them out of our territory. That what they do beyond our borders is not our concern. We don't want a full-blown war."

Legion's jaw ticks before he responds. "War is war. Perhaps it would be wise to initiate a conversation before poking the bear in the eye?"

Slice narrows his gaze at him. "Have you established contact with anyone at the top of *Mount Meth*?"

"*Not yet*... But it is inevitable." Legion's eyes slide to me for a moment. He's withholding his theory about who is running things. For whatever reason, he doesn't want the Jokers to know about it. At least, *not yet*.

"I've made my call," Slice declares as he folds up the map and hands it to his Sergeant at Arms. His steely gaze shifts to me. "You went to war with this prick's former crew and didn't involve us in the fray. I'm not going to insist you ride with us to hit this location."

"You would have fought with us had I called."

He simply nods.

"When are we rolling out?"

A slight grin tugs at the corner of Slice's mouth. "Tonight."

Vanna

When I pulled out my debit card to pay for Dean's new motorcycle boots, I noticed the business card Viking gave me in the gym a few days before Thanksgiving. The address isn't too far from the Harley Davidson dealership either, and since Latisha only had an hour break from work to do a little shopping and chatting, I decided to stop by this *all-girls gym* and see what classes they offer.

The building looks like a large garage. There's no signage, but this is the address on the card. There are two Harley-Davidson motorcycles in the lot. One has a purple metallic paint job with a black leather seat and matching silver-studded saddlebags. The other bike is a dark gunmetal color and is a slightly smaller, sportier-looking model.

I park near the door with the open sign in the window, and glance back at Ace in his car seat. The thirty-minute ride nearly put him to sleep. I know he's going to be a little grumpy, but I would never leave him in the car alone.

Thankfully, he doesn't complain and insists on walking into the building himself.

When I push open the glass door, a bell jingles above us, and we step inside, Ace's small hand snug in mine. The scent of rubber mats and faint traces of disinfectant waft through the spacious room where a few workout machines line one side. Mostly treadmills and weight benches, but the main floor is open and covered in thick black mats. There are a few closed doors where I imagine more equipment might be, or perhaps they're workshop rooms or the lockers and showers. There's nothing in the way of advertising or even a little décor that would suggest this is a women-only gym. I wonder if they're just getting started and haven't officially opened yet.

Ace spots a rowing machine and points, tugging my hand. He likes to watch his father and uncles use that one at the Saviors' gym, as well as play on the treadmills. His favorite activity, though, is wrestling in the ring with his uncles, especially when they pretend to be defeated by him.

"Mommy has to talk to the lady, Ace," I whisper as we approach the counter. "Hello," I smile pleasantly at the brunette I just realized is staring at me. She looks oddly surprised but recovers quickly and smiles back.

"Hey, what can I do for you?" I immediately notice her Long Island accent.

"A friend gave me your card. I'm interested in the women's self-defense class. He told me you do that here."

"We do… I think there's a sign-up sheet around here somewhere," she says, reaching behind the desk to open a drawer or two. I notice the simple, but elegant tattoo on her inner left wrist. The word *Joy* within an infinity symbol that connects to the J and the Y. "What's your name?"

"Vanna Keegan."

She freezes for a split second upon my reply. "Let me get you the form to fill out. I'll be right back." She walks a few steps to what I presume is an office. There's a big window facing the back of the counter, but the blinds are drawn.

"*What do I do?*" I overhear her ask someone back there.

"About what, Ryder?" a voice with a Brooklyn accent I'm fairly certain I recognize asks.

"It's *her*."

"*Her* who?"

I listen intently but can't hear what either of them is saying now, if they're saying anything at all. A moment passes before the attractive, dark-haired biker chick I met briefly at the Jokers' clubhouse emerges. She's wearing workout clothes now, but it's definitely Jett.

"Hey, gorgeous!" she smiles uncomfortably as she approaches the counter.

"Hi… I was interested in the self-defense class," I say again. Ace is getting restless by my side, tugging at my hand and pointing at the stair-master now. We don't have one of those at our gym, and he's curious about it. I lift him up to hold him and look back at Jett. Something is really off here.

Her uncomfortable smile remains as she tells me, "Our little joint is kind of a hike from your neck of the woods, though, ain't it?"

"I used to drive this distance for work every day. Doing so for a couple of classes isn't a big deal. It's not like I want to train for a competition. Can you tell me about the class?"

"Is there a particular reason you're interested in self-defense?" she asks, unable to disguise her concern.

I could give her a straight answer, but I decide to play whatever this game is, a little longer. "What do you mean?"

"Oh, I'm not tryin' to pry, doll face. Just making sure you're okay. Nobody's bothering you, *right?*" she sounds strangely concerned.

"No... You do remember who my husband is, don't you?" I ask, wondering if I've somehow jumped into an alternate universe, or maybe the Twilight Zone.

"Which is why I'm wondering," she says.

"I was referred by a friend. I've done a little kickboxing over the last few months, but I'd like to acquire some additional skills. And since you seem to be aware of who my husband is, he's a very busy man and not very keen on the idea of me wrestling around with male trainers. I'm not excusing the sexism, but considering where you and I met, I'm sure you know how these biker guys can be. Besides, I'm more comfortable with the idea of a woman trainer in this aspect, anyway. Now, can you tell me about the classes you offer?"

"Fair enough. We have a single multi-hour workshop for the basics that can be knocked out in a day. We've also got a RAD program. That's a twelve-hour course split across several days."

"RAD?"

She glances at Ace and clears her throat before speaking softly. "*Rape Aggression Defense.* Our workshops all cover multiple techniques and situational awareness."

"How much are the classes?"

"It's our club's mission to help women, so they're free. But we do accept donations to keep the lights on and equipment working."

"That's amazing." I can't help but smile. Maybe that's why this place seems a bit sparse. Jett returns the expression, but still seems slightly uncomfortable. "I'm sorry, but is there some issue I'm unaware of between us? Does it have something to do with what you said at the Jokers' party?" I try to remember her exact words. "Something along the lines of us needing to have an uncomfortable conversation?"

She glances at my son again. "Maybe we ought to rain check that convo?" she suggests. "It might not be child-appropriate."

"I've never met any of you, yet for some reason you, or at least your friend *Val*, seem to have a problem with me. I'd like to know what the issue is."

"Val doesn't have a problem with you, I promise." Jett seems to insist with a level of sincerity. "None of the Steel Vixens do."

"Is Val here somewhere? Maybe she can tell me herself."

"She's not right now." Jett grabs a pen and a Post-it. "Look, give me your information and I'll contact you with the schedule of our next classes. That okay?"

"Yeah. Sure." I relay my information, which she jots down and tucks into her pocket.

"What friend recommended you to us?" she seems to ask with a bit of reservation. When I inform her it was Viking, she nearly sighs in relief.

"Oh, that one." She awkwardly chuckles.

"Who did you think referred me?"

She shrugs. "No idea, was just curious… It's business appropriate to ask those questions, ya know?"

I suppose…

The rumbling of another motorcycle pulling up outside seems to make her tense even more, and she clears her throat again, unusually loud.

"*Yeah, I'm on it!*" The woman she called Ryder, rushes out of the office where she's been for the duration of this odd conversation, and bolts out the front door. When I glance at Jett again, she's got another tense smile plastered across her pretty face.

"Is there a number to call here?" I don't bother trying to hide the accusatory tone in my words. "You know, in case you *happen to lose mine.*"

"Heh… yeah…" Jett jots down a number on another Post-it and hands it to me. "Have a nice day, Vanna. Be safe."

Well, that was obviously my cue to leave. I force a parting smile of my own and head for the door.

There's another motorcycle parked by the original two, which must belong to Jett and Ryder. This one is a ruby-red Indian scout with a black seat and black studded side bags, though the studs are faux rubies that match the paint job. It's a cute bike. I glance around for the woman who owns it, but there's nobody out here. Is it Val's bike? Did she go in another door? *Is she avoiding me?* I can't help but wonder what the hell is going on as I strap Ace back into his car seat for the ride home.

DEAN

"It seems I am not the only one making virtue of necessity." Legion slides into the chair adjacent to me in the Jokers' main club room. He isn't wrong. I can feel him studying me, but I keep my gaze fixed on one of the flatscreens mounted to the wall. "You could have swayed him."

"Not my territory, not my call. My priority is Bermuda County."

He scoffs. "I don't believe you, *Savior*."

"I don't care what you believe. Slice is calling the shots. This is what he wants. Maybe they'll get the message as he intends it to be received."

"*Ah*, the perils of *wishful thinking*." Legion chuckles, a low, sinister sound. "We are all human, aren't we? Susceptible to cognitive bias."

I sneer at him. "*Most* of us are *human*, anyway."

Legion lets out another sigh. "You and I, we can save Bermuda County. I am confident of that... But your friends here... Jocsan County... This territory will not be easily surrendered on either side."

"*I know*... I've long come to terms with the fact I can't save the fuckin' world," I growl with resentment.

"You also know this is an act of war, casualties or no. There will be repercussions... Repercussions that may fall at the feet of the ones *we* love."

"Stanley isn't the only one you've maneuvered between a rock and a hard place." I glare at him. "Besides... *Si vis pacem para bellum.*" If you want peace, prepare for war.

"People only see the decisions we make...rarely the choices we had... Perhaps now you understand the rock and the hard place *I* was in three years ago."

"Only *you* put *yourself* there... You'll get no sympathy or forgiveness from me."

Legion's steely gaze lifts from mine to glance behind me, and a sneer pulls at his lips as he stands. "*Speaking of forgiveness...*" he mutters, before pulling out his pack of cigarettes and walking away.

"Alright if we have a word?" Daniel says as he steps around the back of the couch to stand before me. Trippy is tucked beneath his arm, and I already know what he wants to discuss.

"Yeah…" I cock my chin at the chair Legion left vacant. "Have a seat. How's Maddie doing? Haven't seen her since Halloween."

"She's great," Daniel says, taking a seat beside Trippy. "Lucinda's got her wanting to join a cheerleading academy."

"Isn't she a little young for that?" I ask.

"Competitive cheerleading starts as early as elementary school. If you mean school-wise, cheer teams typically begin in middle school. She could earn a scholarship if she really likes it and sticks with it. Whatever makes Maddie happy."

"I don't envy you, Daniel," I joke. "You're gonna have a sparkling gun collection by the time she graduates high school."

He chuckles, but I can tell he's stressing about it. "Well, I hope your next kid is a girl so you can share in my pain."

That comment wipes the grin off my face. "We're rolling out soon. What do you want to talk about?"

"We'd like you to give your blessing for Slice to patch me in. I've done my time, so has Trippy," Daniel explains.

I shift my gaze to Trippy. "You really want to hitch yourself to this guy?"

She places a hand on his knee and lifts her chin, squaring her shoulders. "Yes. I know you two have had your differences, but Daniel is a good man. You're both good men, and I never took you for one to stand in the way of anyone's happiness out of spite."

"Relax, doll. I'm also here to let Slice know it's cool with me if Daniel patches in. As far as I know, it'll happen."

They both seem to sigh with relief before Trippy throws her arms around his neck. "Thanks, bro," Daniel says, hugging her back. "Will you come to my patch party?"

"I'll have to check my schedule."

He shakes his head with a smile. "You really are a prick, Dean."

Gravel crunches beneath our boots as we spread out and close in on the single-story ranch. It's set pretty far back from the road and surrounded by trees.

Legion: Book 3

Slice gives me a nod before signaling to his crew. We aren't just walking up to the front door. This is going to be a coordinated attack from each point of entry. Viking, Legion, and I will take the front door, weapons ready, while Slice and his crew peel off toward the back, leaving Roach and Blade to cover the windows on the sides, should anyone attempt to escape.

We wait for the signal that Slice is in position at the back door. Once we hear it, we stealthily ascend the faded wooden deck.

Blade mimics a whippoorwill's call… They're in position.

I nod to Viking, silently mouthing *three…two…one…*

Viking steps back and drives his boot into the front door, splintering the wood on impact. The door flies open with a loud crack, and chaos erupts as we charge inside, guns drawn.

Several half-dressed guys immediately dive for cover, shouting for their buddies in the back of the house. Viking and I keep our guns on this group, while Legion covers us in case anyone in the back decides to be a hero.

Three guys slowly emerge from the hall, hands on the backs of their heads, held at gunpoint by Slice and his two Sergeant at Arms.

"Out! Now!" Slice bellows, "You pricks, too. Get up and get the fuck out!"

Viking and I grab two guys, hauling them to their feet and shoving them toward the front door. They stumble, raising their hands, still trying to process what is happening.

"*Not tonight, asshole!*" Legion hisses, suddenly grabbing a fistful of hair on one of the guys still kneeling on the ground. He slams him face-first into the coffee table, then wrenches him back to land on his ass, dazed and with a bloody nose. I catch a glimpse of the shotgun under the couch he must have tried for and offer Legion an appreciative nod.

"Not trying to die or make Vanna a widow tonight," he growls, glaring at me as if he resents the fact I'm here. He's right. I shouldn't be here. Not with a wife and kid at home. And he shouldn't be here either. Not with a hair-trigger contingency plan that could land Axel and Viking in prison.

Within moments, we have the place emptied, and we line the crew up, face down in the dirt a few yards from where we parked the bikes. Hopefully, for all of our sakes, it's a safe enough distance from what's about to happen next.

Slice cocks his chin at Legion. "Do it."

Without hesitation, Legion grabs the duffel bag strapped to his bike and slings it over his shoulder. "This will take a few minutes to set up," he says, before sprinting back into the ranch.

The rest of us stand guard, tension building as time ticks on before Legion finally returns. He folds up what now appears to be a mostly empty duffel bag and stuffs it into one of the saddle bags on his bike, then removes a small handheld radio. He flips it over and opens the back to insert a couple of batteries. After clipping it shut, he extends the antenna and glances once more at Slice, who only nods.

"Very well," Legion sighs, moving his thumb to hover over the detonation button. With far less enthusiasm compared to the last time I heard him shout the words, Legion mutters, *"Fire in the hole..."*

The explosion tears through the night, and a blast of heat and fire swallows the ranch as shattered wood and debris rain down. Slice and his guys mount their bikes, ready to take off.

"Tell the motherfuckers you work for there won't be any cooking or dealing in Jocsan County!" Slice snarls at the crew who are still face down on the ground, covering their heads with their arms to protect themselves.

I swing a leg over my bike just as I hear a gunshot split through the chaos from somewhere beyond the burning structure.

Shit... I snap my head toward the source in time to see shadows moving between the trees. There must be guys stationed nearby keeping watch.

Another bullet tears through the air and strikes metal, sparking off Legion's handlebars with a high-pitched *ping!* He instinctively ducks and fires up the bike.

"Split off!" I shout to Slice. "They can't follow all of us!"

I twist Serene's throttle, and her back tire spits gravel before she lunges down the trail. When we reach the main road, Slice and his crew veer off in the direction of their clubhouse. Viking, Legion, and I head in the opposite direction.

The roar of our bikes echoes off the trees lining the empty stretch of highway as we push our engines to their limits. Beside me, Legion is hunched over his Indian, his jaw tight, his knuckles white around the grips. His bike screams beneath him, keeping pace with Serene. I glance over my shoulder, confirming for myself that Viking is still with us, too. As I turn my attention back to the highway in front of us, I see Legion's body jerk forward, his hand snapping off the throttle, and his engine sputters.

Everything happens within a fucking heartbeat.

"Shit!" Legion hisses over the wind, his rough voice barely reaching me. Before his bike stalls, his left hand shoots down, grabbing hold of the frayed cable. He manages to wrap it around his fist, yanking it tight, and his engine roars back to life, surging the bike forward. I watch with a mixture of horror and awe as Legion holds on, manually controlling the speed with nothing but raw grip strength.

I should laugh in his face. Part of me wants to. He's a cocky prick who acts like he's an invincible badass... But damn, if he isn't proving he can back it up... Quite literally taking the reins and riding that machine like it's an actual steel horse.

I shake my head at him when he glances at me, one hand steering the bike, the other death-gripping the throttle cable, his body twisted in a way that just screams disaster waiting to happen. But he's doing it. Fighting the odds like he always does.

"*Yeehaw!*" he lifts his chin and shouts to the moon like he's back in the wild west.

"I gotta admit," I raise my voice so he can hear me over the engines and wind whipping past us, "For a second there I thought you were a goner!"

He doesn't look at me, just bares his teeth in something between a grin and a grimace. "I'd say I'm sorry to disappoint you, but that would be a lie, and rather unfortunate for Axel!"

T he rolling garage door to my shop rattles as I lift it open while Viking parks his Fatboy next to Serene and dismounts to help Legion get his bike inside.

Legion barely made it into my lot before his left hand gave out. The throttle cable slips from his fingers, and he lets out a sharp breath. He flexes his shaking hand for a moment before sucking up the pain and grabbing the handlebars to push it inside. After kicking the stand down, he steps back from the bike, slowly lifting his hand to have a better look at it under the lights.

Legion's palm is a little sliced up, thin red lines running across his skin where the wire had bitten in. His whole arm is trembling, the muscles locking up from holding the tension for so damn long.

"Sit down." I nod at an old workbench. "I'll fix it. Viking, why don't you grab us a couple a beers and the first aid kit for *Billy the Kid*, here."

"The roadhouse is still open another couple of hours. I can relieve Dozer from bouncer duty if you want and send a girl over with the beers and the kit," Viking says.

I glance at him curiously. "If that's what you want to do."

Viking cocks his head slightly to the side, indicating he'd like me to step outside with him for a moment.

"Legion, there's a bathroom right there in the hall if you want to wash those cuts out," I say.

Without a word, Legion gets up from the workbench and heads to the bathroom while Viking and I step outside in the lot.

"What's the matter?" I ask.

"Gotta admit, the guy's a fucking badass," Viking grumbles.

"He has his moments. But so, what?"

"*So,* I don't want to like anything about him. I don't want to hang out with him. He's still a prick and…well… I just *don't* want to, bro, *damn.*"

"Alright, I'm not gonna hold a gun to your head. I'll see you in the bar in a little while. This throttle cable won't take too long to repair."

When I step back into my shop, Legion's sitting on the bench, letting his injured hand rest on his knee, his fingers still twitching from the strain. He looks tired, and there's still a slight tremble in his arm as the adrenaline wears off.

"I don't know if I trust you to work on my bike," he sneers, but I know he's only half joking.

"Pretty fucked up that *I've* come to be the least of your worries."

Legion chuckles, but the humor quickly fades from his expression. "This was the strike that will elicit a response."

I nod, making my way over to the tool chest to grab some needle-nose plyers, a screwdriver, and a wrench. "I know."

"They won't initially suspect the Saviors."

"Well, it happened in Jocsan. The Jokers' territory."

"Your allegiance is widely known."

"I'm aware." I sigh, stepping back to his bike to disconnect the battery and remove the throttle housing on the handlebars. When I glance at Legion, he's staring at the picture of Vanna and Ace I have hung up on the wall. Normally, it would piss me off, but the worried expression in his eyes tempers my anger.

"I tried not to love her, you know," Legion says. "I tried very, very hard."

CHAPTER 27

Vanna

Christmas music is playing through the speakers at the Twisted Throttle, and the sweet, buttery aroma of fresh-baked sugar cookies drifts from the kitchen just beyond the corridor. Cherry, the patch-chasers, and I have been decorating the bar and baking for the event tonight. As per the Saviors MC's tradition, tonight is the night the neighborhood kids get to have their picture taken with Santa and pick an early gift donated by the members of the Saviors MC. The remaining toys will be added to the ones we've collected for Toys for Tots, and all monetary donations from the parents will go to Medusa's Gates.

The bar is decorated with garland and golden lights, the stripper poles in the back are wrapped in red and white to resemble peppermint sticks, and there's a red carpet rolled out from the steel door to the area where they once set up Santa's throne. However, the ornately carved chair is now set up off to the side, surrounded by the wrapped gifts the children will choose from. A framed photo of Snowy sits on the lush red cushion, with the red Santa hat he always wore, draped over the corner of the frame.

The first two years after Snowy's death, the MC didn't feel right about continuing without him. I've seen firsthand the playful arguments Viking and Snowy would get into over who got to be Santa each year. Snowy always won, and I think that played a part in this year's decisions on how this event would go.

Legion: Book 3

Viking didn't want to sit in what had always been Snowy's place, and so this year, the children will have their pictures taken with Santa on his big Harley Davidson Fatboy, all decked out in Christmas lights and garland, which he will be riding down that red carpet to make his grand entrance.

Also, since Snowy had always dressed up as the popular red suit Santa most are familiar with, Viking's outfit is a more *Odin-esque* version. He's still wearing the red and white outfit, of course, complete with a red hat, but he looks more like a Nordic Warrior Santa than jolly old Saint Nick. And according to what I've heard, still far less frightening than that year he crashed the party as Krampus. Recalling the way Dean had laughed through the telling of that story brings a smile to my face.

Dean walks through the steel door of the Twisted Throttle, wearing his green elf hat, the bells on his boots jingling with every step as he approaches me.

"We're all set up. Gonna head down the block before the crowd gets here. Is Ace coming with me, or are you keeping him here with you?" he asks.

"Did he say he wants to go?"

Dean chuckles. "*His* mind was set the moment he saw Serene is Rudolph. I made a custom cover for her headlight, so it glows red. We've all got those fuzzy antlers on our bikes wrapped in Christmas lights, too. I think we're gonna have a tantrum on our hands if we don't let him ride in on Rudolph with me."

"I need pictures of this, so while you're waiting down the street, make sure you have one of your brothers take a few of you two together."

Dean smiles and bends to kiss me briskly on the lips. I smile when his cold nose presses against my skin. "You got it, doll," he promises, before heading for the door again.

"Be careful and make sure he has his scarf and gloves on, and that his elf hat covers his ears!"

"I'll put his hat on when we get back here. He'll be warm in his helmet," Dean says, pausing at the door to glance around one more time. "This place looks really great. You girls did a fantastic job." The patch-chasers beam with pride. "See you in twenty minutes or so."

"Alright, have fun! Be careful!" I call after him.

"I've got the last batch of cookies if you want to watch them take off?" Cherry offers.

"Are you sure?"

"Of course! Hurry up and get out there." She smiles and gestures toward the door.

I make it outside in time for Ace to spot me and wave, just before they take off out of the lot. I can't see his little face behind the shield of his helmet and the fact that it's already dark out, but I'm sure he's smiling with excitement.

"*Quite the production,*" Legion's voice says from the shadows. If he's genuinely impressed at all, I can't tell by his dry tone. "I've been assigned guard duty."

I turn around to find him wearing the elf hat I requested and a pair of pointy ears, but instead of green with white trim, it's black velvet with black trim, and as he steps closer to me, I don't hear any jingle bells.

"I see you made an attempt," I tease.

He only grimaces in response.

"Is this really so torturous for you?"

"This music is killing me. Is it too much of a request to play some *Trans-Siberian Orchestra* or at least something with a little *edge*?" he gripes.

"I'm sure it will eventually come on. *O Holy Night* happens to be my favorite Christmas song."

"Really?"

"Well, I may not be a catholic anymore, but yes. I still enjoy the season, and Christmas Eve is my favorite holiday."

"We still have another week of this." He sighs.

I can't help but tease him a little more, joyfully singing along with the song while he stares at me. *"A thrill of hope the weary world rejoices. For yonder breaks a new and glorious morn!"*

A wicked grin pulls at the corner of his mouth, and he sings the next verse, making it sound almost blasphemous in his sinister tone and obvious connotation. *"Fall on your knees... Oh, hear the angels' voices... O night divine..."*

"You know that's not what it's about." I frown.

"A night with you would be absolutely divine."

"I'm going to pretend you didn't say that. If you want to be a grinch, fine. But it's a beautiful song, regardless of what you actually believe. Now, you've got two more hours of this before the families get their kids' pictures taken and leave. *And you can't smoke.*"

He brings the cigarette to his lips and pulls one last, long drag, then exhales on another disgruntled sigh before extinguishing it in the outdoor ashtray.

I reach into my festive little Mrs. Claus apron and remove one of the peppermint sticks. After unwrapping the plastic, I hold it up to him. "Here, suck on this."

He steps closer, until the peppermint stick is mere inches from his lips. "Say that again...*slow.*"

"*Oh, stop it.* I've read that half the battle is overcoming the oral fixation. Maybe the peppermint will help you stave off your cigarette cravings for a little while."

A crooked grin pulls at the corner of his mouth again.

"Do you want it or not?"

He opens his mouth and takes it from me with a suggestive, taunting "M*mmm.*"

"You really must have a permanent residence on the naughty list, but try to behave yourself tonight for the sake of the kids and our standing with the community. I have to check on the last batch of desserts. Would you make sure the prospects know where to direct the cars for parking, so they don't block the guys' grand entrance?"

Legion grumbles something in agreement.

"Thank you." I smile at him and head for the door. "Those elf ears look cute on you, by the way."

"*Fuckin' tease,*" he mutters.

"Excuse me?" I frown.

"*As you please.*" He grins wickedly once more.

I shove the door open and lock it in place so Viking can ride straight into the area set up for him at the end of the red carpet. Once the girls and I finish displaying all of the desserts and are satisfied with the way everything looks inside, we join the gathering crowd outside to wait for Santa's arrival.

Within a few minutes, the sound of the rumbling motorcycles can be heard coming down the street. Soon they pull into the lot, two by two ahead of Viking, except for Dean and Ace, who are riding in front with Serene's glowing red headlight. All of the bikes are mounted with antlers and lights, except for Viking's motorcycle, which is decorated to look a bit more sleigh-like.

Ace is clapping excitedly along with the applauding crowd and can barely contain himself as Dean rolls Serene to a stop. I can't help but laugh along at his joy over the entire ordeal. While the prospects make sure the path is clear for Viking to safely break away and ride into the roadhouse, Dean pulls off Ace's helmet and replaces it with his little green elf hat that matches his outfit under his leather jacket.

"Easy, buddy!" Dean laughs at our son's enthusiasm as he lifts him off the bike and puts him on the ground. Once Ace's booted little feet hit the gravel, he makes a dash for me.

"Did you see me, Mommy? Did you see?"

"I did!" I laugh.

"Did you see me, too, Legend?" Ace asks, almost out of breath as he reaches me.

Legion clears his throat, and I realize he's standing right beside me again. He smiles softly at my son. "I think you stole the show, Ace."

"How come you're not green?" Ace asks, pointing to Legion's black elf hat.

"Oh, I'm green on the inside," Legion darkly jokes.

I scoop Ace up before he can ask any more questions that might entice Legion into another not-so-subtle remark, just as Ace's father approaches. The parents and their children are already gathering inside the roadhouse to meet our new *Nordic Santa*.

"Shall we?" I ask, hoping for Legion's sake, Dean will let him come in from the cold.

Dean glares at Legion as if he read my mind. "You stay near the donation box," Dean orders him, then slips his arm around my waist to escort Ace and me inside.

"This turned out so much better than I thought it was going to," I say to Cherry after an hour or so has passed. Ever since Dean told me about this holiday tradition, I've been looking forward to it. There is a bittersweet feeling among the MC, though, but they are making the best of the situation.

"Snowy would have wanted this," Cherry says, then playfully elbows me and nods over at Maxie. She's bent over the wrapped gifts, helping a few of the kids pick out presents. "Could Maxie's skirt be any shorter? Doesn't she realize this event is mainly for children?"

"At least she thought to wear panties that say *Naughty List*. Though I think she dressed more for the afterparty."

"I'm sure. Someone should tell her to stop bending over."

"I don't think some of these fathers mind all that much," I joke, then turn my attention back to my son. "Look at Ace." I giggle, watching him at the dessert table as he stuffs a few more sugar cookies into his little sack before he makes another delivery to his favorite uncle. Viking can't leave his post until the last picture is taken. "Santa's little helper, though that sack is probably getting lint all over those cookies."

"That won't deter Viking." Cherry laughs. "I've seen him eat Thanksgiving dinner out of the trash."

"I'm sorry, *what?*"

"It was a while ago… Back in the Lucinda days." She seems to explain with a little reluctance, not wanting to spoil the joyful atmosphere, but she gives in to my curiosity. "Lucinda tossed the entire holiday meal in the trash one year before anyone could even sit down to eat."

"Why on earth would she do that?"

"She was pissed that Dean and several of the guys came late. Dean insisted she knew they had an extraction to do that night, but Lucinda wasn't having it. In a fit, she threw everything away. Viking picked up a fork and just started eating right out of it. Though I suspect a big part of doing so was just to piss her off more." Cherry giggles. "Most of the guys got a real laugh out of it."

"I don't know what the hell Dean ever saw in that woman." I sigh.

"He was young and dumb once, too, but he woke up, especially when he met you." She smiles at me. "Some of them stay stuck on stupid a little longer than others."

"Except Axel. He got it right on the first try." I say, giving our road captain a little wave as he happens to glance over at us. Axel's job tonight is helping the kids on and off Viking's motorcycle.

"He makes a really cute elf, doesn't he?" Cherry chuckles. "I didn't even have to talk him into those curly elf shoes and striped leggings!"

"They pair so well with his black cargo shorts." I laugh, then scan the crowd of smiling faces. My gaze lands on Legion, the only person who isn't smiling. He's right where Dean told him to be, guarding the donation box by the door, arms folded, holding his peppermint stick like a cigarette, occasionally flicking the end out of habit.

"I wonder how sad that donation box is going to be," Cherry jokes, "Was that really the best job we could find for him?"

"Honestly, people probably feel a little *afraid not to* drop a donation."

"You're probably right." She chuckles.

Ace walks over to me after a sugar cookie delivery to Santa. I grab a napkin and pick up a cookie from the tray behind us on the bar. "Do you want to bring this over to Legend? I bet he'd like one too."

"Okay." He takes the gingerbread man from me and ambles over to Legion, bringing a smile to his grouchy face for what might be the first time since he took up his post.

"I should probably make a few more of these mocktails for the parents," Cherry says, gesturing to the near-empty trays. "Who knew alcohol free drinks in a bar would be such a hit?"

"Well, the parents know they're welcome to come back later for real drinks once they've got their kids home safe. I'll help you make them."

Before I step behind the bar with her, I check on Ace, who is in his father's arms now, and they're dancing to The Jackson Five's *Santa Claus is Coming to Town*.

LEGION

If not for the way the festivities of this night have brought such animated glee to Vanna's lovely face, it would have been absolute torture. At the conclusion of this community Christmas event, the prospects were tasked with gathering the remaining gifts into a box van full of additional presents destined for Toys for Tots come morning. Or so I've overheard.

Now, as I watch her within his arms, laughing while he spins her around the room, this night is feeling more and more like an eternity. I try not to let him catch me watching them, but I find her radiant, magnetic smile difficult to divert my gaze from, hoping for a glance, a moment when her eyes find mine, and if they do, will she think of the night *we* danced?

Legion: Book 3

I wonder if she's aware of the significance of a dance. The act involves far more than bodies swaying, feet tracing steps in repetition to a rhythm. There's a deeper connection. It's a conversation without words. A dance can reveal a lot about a relationship... The way they move together tells me things I wish I could ignore. There are reasons I did not linger to witness their wedding dance. The way they are so in tune with each other now, *even to a Christmas song,* every step, every breath, I cannot deny the fact that they were made to move together. If I were capable, I'd admit a certain beauty to it. In truth, *I hate it.*

Her playful laughter rings out above the music, a cruel melody of its own as she glides across the floor within his protective, loving embrace, blissfully unaware of the longing ache I feel. Has she ever felt such agony? Ever pined for something she couldn't have?

La douleur exquise...

Puppet's words echo within the dark recesses of my mind... *Yes, perhaps she is acquainted...* And perhaps her longing for what he will not grant will prove advantageous to me...

Time crawls like a fucking prison sentence, and I grow more restless at the sight of her dark eyes practically sparkling with joy. Maybe it's the string lights and glittery ornaments dripping all over this bar, but still. He twirls her around, then pulls her close and dips her back. She grips his shoulder, and bitterness surges within as I fixate on the way her fingers dig into his body... I swallow it down along with the burning desire to feel her hands on me that way.

Keegan gazes at her like she's his world, and I curse myself for allowing her to have become mine as well.

I drag my gaze from her to check my watch. It's nearly time to take my leave. To my surprise, when I lift my eyes, she's standing before me.

"Would you like to cash in your rain check?" she asks with a friendly smile, unaware of the way her offer cuts me.

I wonder if the several cocktails she's consumed tonight have influenced this offer. I've been keeping a watchful eye on that detail as well. *Perhaps three is our lucky number...*

I scan the room for Keegan's whereabouts, and I'm not surprised to find he's stepped out. Ace is no longer with Cherry, either. Keegan must have brought the young one to bed. Is he aware of his wife's intention to offer me a dance? Or did she simply wait until he wasn't around to witness her proposition? Maybe even the dance itself. I find myself conflicted on the matter as I shift my gaze back to Vanna.

"Tempting, sweet one. Though if I don't make my departure now, I'll be late for a hot date."

Surprise graces her features for a moment before she manages to compose herself, even despite her consumption of Christmas cocktails... *It's four, then,* I note. I also can't help but note an inkling of something else behind her surprise... Dare I venture to say, *displeasure?*

"*Oh*, well, I hope you have a very merry evening." Though I'm quite positive it's forced, she smiles pleasantly.

"And I hope you continue to enjoy yours as well." My words are hollow, but I offer them nonetheless with a slight bow.

She stares skeptically, in thought for a moment, then sighs. "I didn't want you to feel left out. Don't say I didn't offer you a dance."

I remove the *elven getup* from my head, which I only wore to please Vanna, and hand her the hat and elf ears. "You offered me *an obligatory* lap around the room," I correct her. Vanna takes the items then crosses her arms, puzzled and annoyed. "I don't want to pretend with you. I shall request the fulfilment of the dance *I paid for* at my own discretion. Now, if I have fulfilled my role this evening to your liking and approval, there is someone waiting for me."

"Well, don't let me keep you from her."

If I weren't so enamored with my little witch, I might have missed the subcurrent of hostility in Vanna's words, the faint trace of delicious jealousy.

The absolute audaciousness of this woman! I could laugh, considering where we stand in our present situation. The fact that she seems displeased by the notion of another woman in my life exalts me. Though I must summon the will to minimize my enthusiasm over her territorial display, minute as it is. It's still something. It's progress. I'd love nothing more than to succumb to the nearly overwhelming desire to field her mind and interrogate her over this welcome but unanticipated reaction. I want so badly to dissect her take on the dance we've danced since our first meeting. To inquire whether or not love is supposed to be this way? Letting someone else take the lead, even when you're the one who's left standing still...

How does it feel, Vanna? How do I make you feel?

Legion: Book 3

"Why are you staring at me like that?" she demands, eyes narrowing, and I can't help but grin. Women always want to be wanted.

"*Would you have it any other way*, sweet one?"

The crisp December air relentlessly bites at my face while I ride toward the border of Bermuda County. There is an unfamiliar, albeit undeniable warmth that rivals the desert heat radiating within my being. *Vanna does feel something for me.* My elation at the thought of her wrestling with her guilty conscience over the way she feels about a potential woman in my life is suddenly soured by Stanley's rung-out and disheveled state. I catch sight of him waiting by his van and pull into the small clearing of the wooded lot where we arranged this meeting tonight. I'm not sure how much longer he will be of use.

I park my Indian and dismount. "Come now, Stanley, we've been over this. *One must attempt* to keep up appearances, or *one might draw* unwanted attention upon oneself." I sigh as he nervously approaches, dragging a trembling hand down his ragged face.

The moment I hear the van door open, I realize we're both fucked, and I reach for the Sig tucked in my jacket. Before I can pull my weapon, the barrel of a gun presses against the back of my skull, and two masked men with guns of their own emerge from the darkness of the van.

"To our detriment, it seems I've bestowed this sage advice upon you a bit too late." I sigh, raising my hands in begrudging surrender. "Stanley, what have you done?"

The gun remains firmly planted to my occipital bone, while another set of hands roughly pats me down, removing the weaponry from my person along the way. I watch as Stanley is zip-tied and a black hood is roughly pulled over his head, before I feel a hard blow against the back of mine.

CHAPTER 28

LEGION

A dull, aching throb where I was struck, who knows how long ago, greets me as I open my eyes. I find myself propped up against a galvanized steel wall. The camping lantern set on the plywood floor a few feet from me subtly confirms all of my prior suspicions, summoning a smile to my face. Though, to give myself credit, I was already certain. Stanley is sitting on the ground behind it, facing me with his arms wrapped around his legs, head tucked behind his knees.

"Where are we?"

"I don't know." I barely hear his broken response. "They've got us locked in a shipping container."

"No shit. How long did it take them to transport us here?"

"I don't know." Stanley whimpers.

"Did they knock you out?"

"No."

"*Then fucking think about it!*" I snap, shoving myself to my feet as I feel my pockets for anything they might have missed. They've taken my weapons, my cellphone, but for some reason left me with my pack of cigarettes and pair of Zippos. Strange. I expected them to take everything on me. "Well?" I prompt Stanley once more.

"They drove for an hour, maybe. I'm not sure." He goes on while I check the mechanism on the door to see if it's really locked. It is. "And they didn't uncuff me or take off the hood until I was in here with you. We've been locked up for about an hour too, I suppose… Does that help?"

"Not really. But unless they drove in circles, we're not in Bermuda County anymore. We could be in some storage yard near the Wilmington Ports, I suppose." I walk back to stand before him. "Obviously, they're on to our little arrangement. What do they know? I warned you what would happen if we were found out."

"Nothing! I swear!" he sobs, "I had no idea they were on to me!"

I swoop down and snatch him by his stupid fucking throat. *"Keep your fucking voice down, you imbecile!"* I hiss in his pathetic face. *"This container isn't soundproof!"* He swallows hard and attempts to nod before I shove away from him and step back.

He brings his hand to his throat, rubbing at the soreness my grip left in its wake. "Are they going to kill us? Are they going to kill my family? Is *your* crew going to kill my family?"

"That's a little difficult to answer definitively at the moment," I growl. "Though it's a safe assumption there will be dire consequences! What did you tell them?"

"Nothing, I swear, nothing! They showed up at the Jocsan location I was working tonight and forced me to take them to our meeting spot. That's all they've asked me so far. Tonight was just as much a surprise to me as it was to you."

I grit my teeth, angered by my own shortsightedness. I anticipated there would be blowback, and all of these recent hits have had a singular common thread. Someone in this organization is observant. A little sneer pulls at my lips. Reaper learned well from me.

"I believe you, Stan." I sigh, attempting to set him at ease. He is still a liability, and liabilities must always be dealt with.

I remove the pack of cigarettes from my inner pocket and quickly take a peek inside. The joint I wrapped in cellophane is still tucked inside for a special occasion, and this might just be the occasion I've been anticipating.

The loud clunk of the locking mechanism and screech of the door echo inside this steel trap. I shove the pack of cigarettes back inside my pocket, and my hands instinctively move to grab weapons I no longer possess. Stanley scrambles to press himself against the back wall like a frightened rodent, as two masked men step into the open doorway. One of them is armed, and the other tosses two bottled waters into the crate with us.

"Someone will be here to speak with you shortly. The boss wants to make sure you're comfortable in the meantime."

That explains why they didn't take my smokes.

I spare the bottled waters a quick glance. The lighting in here isn't adequate enough to determine whether or not these bottles have been tampered with, but they do appear to be sealed and unblemished. However, I know there are ways to drug bottled drinks, especially water, without any indication of having done so.

"I'll pass. Though, do you mind if we smoke?" I casually ask as if pococurante about our predicament. Stanley must die, and I can't risk their interference if I were to simply attack him.

"Like I said, boss wants you comfortable," the armed one speaks again. I can't place his voice. He isn't anyone on my hit list.

I step closer to Stanley and take a seat against the wall beside him.

"You're tense, and we need to keep our wits about us when we're eventually interrogated," I speak calmly and quietly. Stanley is dead regardless of how this plays out for me. He doesn't need to know it. Poor, ignorant Stanley still clings to hope. Whatever they have planned for him will most likely be much worse than what I have in store. He betrayed them, which makes him worse than an enemy, worse than me in their eyes. Although this is a necessary move, it is still a mercy in a way. I remove the fentanyl-laced joint from my pack of cigarettes, unwrap it, and hand it to him. "This will take the edge off."

As his trembling hand brings the joint to his lips, I flick open my Zippo and hold the flame out for him to ignite it. He pulls in a few drags, barely coughing at first, then offers it to me.

"Just enjoy the first half, I'll smoke the last," I say, tucking True Love into my inner pocket.

The masked men shut and lock the door once again.

Stanley pulls another few drags. "I think about that night at the cemetery a lot," he says, before coughing again, this time a little harder. "Part of me wishes you had just killed me."

"*I have...*"

He glances at me, perplexed. "Because of where we are now?" he takes another long toke while awaiting my reply.

"In more ways than one, I'm afraid."

Legion: Book 3

When he coughs now, he brings a clutching hand to his chest. Realization widens his eyes, and he stares at the joint in his trembling hand.

This time, his coughing fit doesn't cease until it is silenced by death.

"What the fuck happened?" one of the masked men demands upon their return to check on us. It's been a good forty minutes or so since Stanley passed. I glance over at his slumped form beside me.

"Apparently, the FDA is right. *Smoking kills*."

"Get the fuck up!" he demands, clearly unamused. He points the AK in my face. "Fucking psycho."

"Fuck..." the other one mutters, jabbing at Stanley's corpse with the barrel of his weapon. "He said not to underestimate this prick."

"I'm flattered, gentlemen." I smile as I stand, casually raising my hands. "Would either of you care for a smoke?"

"*Fuck no*," they reply in unison.

"Let's go. You try anything, and we'll see what the FDA says about fuckin' shooting you in the knee," the taller one warns, then gestures with the gun toward the open door.

"That would be the *ATF*." *You fucking goon*. When I step outside, we're in the woods, and as far as I can tell, nowhere near the ports at all.

I'm led at gunpoint to another dark structure. This one appears to be slightly more accommodating than the shipping container. An old FEMA trailer with two motorcycles parked outside of it. One is a newer model Harley-Davidson Road King. A dark shade, perhaps grey or blue. I can't tell exactly, it being night and all. The other motorcycle *is mine*...

I'm sure they searched my bike. Found the two burners and swiped those cellphones also. Oh well...they were dead ends anyway. If Reaper is clever, at least as clever as I'm crediting him, and if he and Puppet truly are an item, he'd have her commit his contact information to memory. It was a long shot. And now, I've got more pressing concerns.

Before I can comment, a man steps out of the trailer, and I'm ordered to stop walking as the dark figure strides toward me.

"Where's the cook?" he asks, stopping short of reaching me by an approximate yard. I strain to listen more intently in an attempt to pinpoint where I know that voice.

"This freak killed him," one of the masked men standing behind me informs him.

"Legion will not be pleased," the guy who seems to be in charge of this situation mutters. His voice is familiar, but I can't place him.

"I can assure you, *I'm not*. I'm rather inconvenienced if we're being honest. In fact, I'd like to speak with the manager of this operation," I joke.

"It's your lucky night," he says.

"As I see it, that has yet to be determined." I smile.

"Then let me set your mind at ease. My name is Jagger, and I am here on behalf of Legion. We just want you to stop fucking with our operation. In exchange for your cooperation, we agree to pull out of Bermuda County, permanently. We won't cook, we won't deal, we won't even cross the county line to have a beer at the Twisted Throttle again."

Again... Nice touch.

"However, if you persist, there will be consequences," he adds.

"I'd like a meeting with this *Legion*."

"Nobody meets with Legion."

"Then tell him his deal needs significant sweetening."

Jagger scoffs. "You've really got a set on you."

"So I've been told."

"What did you have in mind? I'll relay the message."

"*A face-to-face* with Reaper."

"Who's Reaper?" His returning sneer grates my nerves.

"I've been accused of many things. *Stupid ain't one of them.*"

He considers me for a moment. "You realize we could just kill you right here, don't you? Bury you in some unmarked grave with your pal Stanley."

I shrug. "That wouldn't solve your problems. Do you honestly believe *I* give a personal shit where you conduct business? I'm afraid you have more to contend with than little old me."

"*Legion* wanted to give you the opportunity to resolve our issues amicably. You care about *something*, obviously... *Someone*... Perhaps we should consider pressing *that* button."

So, this is what it's like to have the one you love threatened. I've never been on the receiving end of such a blow. The level of rage it ignites within me is more profound than I expected. Wise of him to keep his distance. I'm rather tempted to rip his throat out with my own fucking teeth.

"I strongly advise against that grave mistake," I growl. *That fucking button is thermonuclear.*"

Jagger takes a silent moment to consider my responding threat. "Legion can't make it here tonight. What else would sweeten the deal for you? I'll make a phone call."

"The entirety of Jocsan County as well. Beyond that, I don't give a fuck what you do or where you do it." I take a step closer to him. He doesn't move back, but the men with their guns still trained on me shuffle nearer in warning. "And as far as talk of *buttons* goes, if he presses mine, *I'll annihilate his.*"

Jagger walks off in the direction of the trailer, leaving me with their henchmen while he makes that phone call. Feigning boredom, I glance around to get a more accurate assessment of my predicament. There are two men behind me, two more off to either side, lingering in the shadows. The puffs of moisture in their breaths are more discernible now against the wall of black trees as the temperature continues to drop.

Jagger returns within a few minutes, parting his hands in mock apology as he informs me, "I'm afraid with the ports and size of Jocsan, there's no dice. The location is too valuable. We will agree, however, to pull out of a *certain region.*"

"Well then, I too shall have to consult with my associates."

"Legion has a secondary offer."

"I'm listening."

"*Join us.*"

I wasn't expecting that.

"You're clearly an asset. Clever and ruthless. And I've been ordered to inform you of our gratitude for your assistance."

"*My assistance?*"

A knowing smile splits his features. "For wiping out some of the competition in your quest to disrupt our dealings. That deserves a bit of gratitude, don't you think? And we'll let you leave here with a warning and some time to consider our very generous offer."

This seems too easy...

"I can tell you're wondering, *what's the catch?* Well, you're right to wonder. We can't just let you walk away. Don't get me wrong, we're gonna let you go, *Legion*. But not without leaving you with a few reminders of our conversation. It'll be difficult for you to think or do anything else for a time, at least without the painful reminder of everything we've laid out for you."

Fuck...

"We'll give you several weeks to recover while you decide. The holiday season is a bit overwhelming as it is. But you should come back to the dark side, Legion," Jagger taunts. "It's more fun over here... *You taught me that...* Anyway, sorry about this." He gestures to his men. "Until we me meet again." Jagger grins once more before he turns and heads for his motorcycle.

Without sparing a backward glance, he lifts a hand, snaps his fingers, and his crew circles tighter around me...

Pain registers throughout my entire being before I attempt to open my eyes. I've been here before. This isn't new. But one would think the cold, hard ground would at least offer some level of relief to the numerous bruises dominating my aching body.

I crack open one eye at a time, wondering how long I've been out. Only the right opens, and I stare up at the blurry moon while pulling in a slow, steady breath, attempting to assess whether or not they broke any ribs. A sharp pain seizes my lungs, and I exhale a burst of fleeting mist into the starry night above me. I'd venture to say a few are broken. Slowly reaching a scuffed-knuckled hand into the inner pocket of my jacket, I feel for my prized Zippo, and am relieved *True Love* is still tucked safely inside.

I should get up. If I continue to lie here all night, I'll succumb to hypothermia and die in the dirt. Too many have insisted that is the fate I deserve, and I refuse to grant them the satisfaction, at least, not without a fight.

My entire skull throbs as I attempt to sit up, and a loud groan tears from my throat while my body screams in agony. Everything hurts, and the overwhelming taste of blood in my mouth makes me wretch, causing my head to throb harder still. My vision spins and goes dark again.

"Holy shit. Are you dead?" a familiar voice stirs me back to consciousness, and I crack open the eye I can still see from.

"Axel?"

"Yeah."

"Fortunately for us both, I am not dead… I am, however…in a world of pain."

"Yeah, I'd say…" He glances nervously over his shoulder.

"How did you find me?"

"I've had an AirTag hidden on your bike since right after Thanksgiving," Axel grumbles. He sounds pissed, but there's a level of concern in his words. I must be in shit-shape for Axel to care at all. "I've been keeping track of your whereabouts for the club, hoping you'd slip up and reveal where you might have that leverage on me hidden, you fucking asshole." He struggles to help me get back on my feet, and I grit my teeth, biting back the pain that seems to come from everywhere at once. I'm barely able to stand, leaning heavily against him. "I don't think you're gonna be able to ride, Legion."

"You shouldn't have come here, they might—"

"They left. I waited," Axel says as we stagger together and head for our motorcycles in the distance… A distance that seems too far away as pain shoots through my sides like a knife twisting between my ribs. I stagger, but Axel prevents me from hitting the ground again.

"Did you enjoy the show? I imagine seeing me jumped brought some level of contentment." I try to sound humorous, but the pounding in my skull is relentless, and my vision goes blurry again.

Axel scoffs, half-carrying, half-dragging me as my boots scuff against the ground with every agonizing, off-kilter step. "I got here after they kicked your sorry ass."

"Do the Saviors know you're here?"

"No."

"Call them… Let them know… Nothing can happen to you, Axel…" Everything is spinning, and my head throbs nauseatingly harder. Of its own volition, my body keels over and expels the meager contents of my stomach. I can't help but laugh at myself when the bitter taste of bile mingled with the spice of gingerbread spurs a roiling guilt for puking up Vanna's cookies. The emotion is short-lived, however. Blackness rapidly consumes my vision once again.

DEAN

Vanna giggles as I spin her and pull her back to me. She lets out a playful little squeak when I dip her back and kiss her beneath the mistletoe hanging near the jukebox, currently playing *Snowman* by Sia. For a moment, it's just us, and the buzz of conversations around us fades into the background. The music thrums through my chest, but it's nothing compared to the way she feels in my arms—warm, steadfast, *mine*.

"You're actually enjoying yourself," she teases, her fingers lacing behind my neck as we continue to dance.

"I always enjoy myself with you. And I'm happy when you're happy."

"I'm glad we did this. The community loved it. The kids were so excited. And Viking really was a great biker Santa." She smiles.

I'm about to tell her she's right, that Snowy would have wanted it this way, but Axel's ringtone chimes inside my cut pocket. I glance around the room and realize he's not here. Now that I think about it, I haven't seen Axel in quite a while.

"Sorry, doll. I should probably answer this call."

Vanna releases me so I can reach into my cut and pull out the phone. I hit the green icon and bring the cell to my ear.

"What's up? When did you cut out?" I ask.

"Fuck... *Dean... I need help!*" Axel's frantic voice sends my heart plummeting to my stomach.

Vanna instantly reads the alarm written all over my face and grips my arm. "What's happened?"

"Axel, what's wrong? Where are you?" I demand.

"I'm sending you a pin to our location... I'm with Legion... He's hurt real bad, man... He comes to and passes back out... I... *I think he might be dying*, Dean...he's really fucked up...he threw up blood and—"

"Jesus fuck, what happened?" *Legion can't fucking die!*

"I don't know, he says he was jumped. His bike's here too, but there's no way he's riding. Have Chopper bring his flatbed. I'm gonna lay low with him until you guys get here... I've got my gun, I don't know if they're coming back."

"Drop the pin, we're coming." I'm already heading for the door, and my determined stride has caught my crew's attention. "*Viper, Viking, Chopper, let's go! Now!*"

"What's happening?" Vanna rushes after me, worry in her voice, but I don't have any time to explain. My brothers know something's gone down, and so they don't ask questions. They just move. She follows me into the lot as we rush to mount our bikes. "Dean, what happened?" she demands, pure fear in her eyes when she grips my arm again as I fire up Serene.

"Axel's in trouble. Stay with Cherry," I say, before turning to Chopper. "Go get the flatbed. I'll drop the pin to the location we're headed to."

"You got it." Chopper nods and takes off out of the lot.

When I glance back at Vanna, her hand is covering her mouth before she lowers it to fretfully ask, "*Oh god... Did Axel crash his bike?*"

"No, he's alright, and hopefully he'll stay that way long enough for us to get to him. Go back inside and stay with Cherry. I'll call you as soon as I can."

Vanna nods, and the moment she backs safely away from Serene, I take off, Viking and Viper following behind me.

Vanna

I'm trembling where I stand in the middle of the parking lot, but it's got little to do with the fact that I'm not wearing a coat in this frigid night air. My nerves are completely rattled, and I have to pull myself together before I tell Cherry what little I know of what's going on. If I tell her like this, I'll terrify her, and I don't want to do that.

I wrap my arms around myself and glance around the lot at the remaining motorcycles just as the steel door of the Twisted Throttle swings open, and Diesel's massive form barges up to me.

"Vanna, what happened? Ruger said Dean grabbed a couple of the guys and just took off."

"They did, something happened with Axel."

"Is he hurt?"

"No, I don't think so. I don't know what's going on."

He hooks a muscular arm around me and steers me back in the direction of the roadhouse. "Shit, you're shaking like a leaf. Don't worry. Dean's got shit handled, whatever it is. Come back inside and we'll figure out what's going on."

"I have to tell Cherry, and I really don't know how I'm going to do that, then pretend everything is fine and just go back to playing hostess after all this," I whimper.

"I'll clear the place out, you just take care of Cherry and Ace. I'll handle everything else."

Maxie is the only one behind the bar when we step inside. "Cherry must still be with Ace."

"I'll handle things up here, go talk to Cherry," Diesel insists once more. I avoid making eye contact with anyone as I head for the corridor beyond the bar. Just as I round the corner, I hear Diesel telling Maxie the party's over.

When I get to Dean's old club room, where Ace is hopefully sleeping, I take a breath and quietly open the door to peek inside.

Ace is curled up on his side, asleep, and so is Cherry. She looks like his petite guardian angel, with a slender arm wrapped around him from behind as they sleep, sharing the same pillow.

I don't want to wake her up. Maybe I shouldn't. Maybe letting her sleep is best, since there's nothing she can do about whatever is going on anyway. I glance at the digital clock on the nightstand. It's a little after midnight. Only a few minutes since Dean took off with the guys. They probably don't know anything yet. And who knows how long it will be before he even contacts me with an update.

I chew on my bottom lip while I war with myself over whether or not to wake her up. Would I want to know if I were in Cherry's place? Yes…I would. Despite not being able to do anything, I would still want to know if there was something going on with Dean.

I softly clear my throat, but it's enough to cause her to stir. "*Cherry,*" I whisper. She opens her eyes and carefully moves to look at me without waking Ace. I motion for her to come out into the hallway. She already looks concerned, but grabs the blanket at the foot of the bed to cover Ace with before she steps out of the room with me.

"What's going on?" she whispers as I quietly shut the door behind us.

"I don't want to wake him," I whisper back and start walking toward the kitchen to move away from the door.

"It's really quiet. Is the party over? How long was I asleep?" she asks, keeping pace beside me.

"Diesel and Maxie shut it down and sent everyone home."

"Why? What happened?"

"Dean got a call and had to leave. Viking, Chopper, and Viper went with him."

She looks perplexed. "From who?"

"Axel."

She gently grabs my arm, and we stop walking. "Did something happen to Axel?"

"Dean said he's okay, but they're on their way to him now."

"What happened to Axel?"

"He wouldn't say, but he did say Axel is okay. I know they were talking on the phone, and I asked if he crashed his bike, and Dean said no. They did send Chopper to get his flatbed, though."

"What?"

"Legion left earlier… It could have something to do with him."

"Oh, for fuck's sake. *Did Axel go after Legion?*"

I shake my head. "I honestly have no idea what is happening. Legion told me he was meeting someone tonight. All I know beyond that is Dean freaked out and took off, and it has something to do with Axel. I don't even know for sure if Legion is involved in any way."

"Would it surprise you?" For some reason, she doesn't seem as alarmed anymore.

"Are you mad at me for waking you up about this?"

"Of course not. This is the stupid shit we signed up for when we decided to hitch our lives to MC guys," Cherry says. "Let's go see what's left to clean up in the bar while we wait to hear something from them."

Sitting around really does just make waiting worse. I let out a sigh of relief. "I want to be like you when I grow up."

DEAN

"Bring Legion in the back door by the patio," I call up to Chopper behind the wheel of his flatbed truck, before turning to Viking. "Help carry him inside." I shift my angry gaze to Axel. "You go to the War Room. You sit your ass down at the table, and you wait there," I order him. Without any lip this time, Axel nods, dismounts his bike, and strides into the roadhouse.

"He's in bad shape," Viper says, once we've got Legion in a bed in one of the vacant bang-around rooms. "I don't know if he's gonna die or what, but he needs to be seen by a doctor. We should just dump him at the hospital."

"For all we know, whoever jumped him meant to kill him and left him for dead. We can't risk anyone coming to finish the job," I say.

"Then we need to get a doctor here," Chopper says. "Do any of us have a medical connection like that?"

"Maybe the Jokers' do?" Viper suggests.

"Hang on… I might know someone who can help." Viking pulls out his cell and makes a call to someone who answers pretty quickly. "Yeah, I know it's late, we've got a bit of a situation. We need a doctor, fast. It's an emergency… Yeah, I'm okay… He's okay, too… Do you know anyone who could help? Okay, let me put you on speaker. I'm with Dean, Viper, and Chopper."

"I think Jett dated someone who might help… But they're a vet," a woman's voice says through the speaker.

"A combat medic?" Viper asks.

"No, a *veterinarian*," the woman clarifies.

"Fuck…" Viking mutters, then turns to Viper. "Wait. Don't *you* know any combat medics?"

"None that could get here any time soon," Viper says.

"Alright, call Jett and meet us at our clubhouse as soon as you can," Viking says to the woman. "Thanks, Val."

"I thought I heard a commotion back here," Vanna says, stepping into the room and glancing around at us, before she lowers her gaze to the mangled mess that used to be Legion, lying unconscious on the bed. One hand flies to her mouth as she gasps in horror and clutches the door frame with the other. *"Oh god… What happened to him?"*

"Axel said he got jumped," Viking replies.

When she maneuvers herself into the small, already crowded room to be nearer to him…to sit down carefully on the edge of the bed beside him…and cautiously reaches as if she's going to touch his hand because she can't bear to see him like this… A surge of jealous rage courses through every fiber of my being, and I want to finish the motherfucker off myself. She doesn't touch him, though. That should be enough to settle me. She's not touching him, *yet*…but damn it, she *fucking wants to*. She wants to comfort him in that endless, bleeding-heart, compassionate way of hers. *Him.* The man I know is in love with my wife. The man who—*given half a fucking chance*—would take her from me in a heartbeat.

I exhale slowly through my nose, unclenching my jaw just enough to grit out, *"He'll fuckin' live."*

He'll fuckin' live just to fuckin' spite me!

She turns to me, her brows drawing together as if she doesn't understand my sudden hostility. "He needs help," she whimpers.

"We're working on it," I growl.

"I'll stay with him until then," she says, turning back to him as if he's the priority in her life now, and that's all I can fucking take. My heart aching, my stomach twisting, I storm out into the hall to head for the War Room with Viking, Viper, and Chopper right behind me.

"Dean...don't take this out on Axel," Viking says, keeping his concerned voice low. "I know you're fuckin' raging. And you know Vanna is just a kindhearted woman. That's all that was. She'd be that way about anyone, Dean. You know that."

I violently shove open the double doors of the War Room and step inside, causing Axel to startle and stare at me as I walk over to claim my seat at the head of the table. Viper, Viking, and Chopper take their seats as well.

"Dean... I...I was just trying to clean up my own mess," Axel leans forward, elbows on the table, and runs both hands through his disheveled hair, slicking it back. "Our club is at Legion's mercy because of me. I was just trying to get us free of him. I thought maybe he'd eventually lead me to wherever this *contingency plan* is. If I get the leverage, he's got nothing to hold over any of us anymore."

"That crew might have killed you had they caught you." It's impossible to keep the growl from my tone, and I slam my fist hard on the table. "Do you understand me? Do you have any fucking idea what that would do to us if something happened to you?" Axel is visibly shaken, sitting with his hands in his lap, eyes wide and glassy. My throat constricts around a painful knot as I stare back into his watery blue eyes.

"I'm sorry, Dean," he nearly whimpers. "I...I only did it because I love you guys."

"I would fucking kill Legion right now if it wasn't to the detriment of your freedom! This is why we tried to keep you out of it! To fucking protect you!"

Axel lets out a frustrated sigh. *"But that's why I—"*

"Talk to him." I turn to Viking. "Get through to him. Whatever I've said, whatever I've done clearly isn't working." I stand and head for the door. If I don't hit something soon, I'm going to fucking explode. *"I'm failing him... I'm fucking failing everyone around me!"*

"Dean, *breathe*, bro. Everyone is alright," Viking reminds me. "Everyone that matters, anyway. Go swing on something in the gym for a little while before you spiral out. I'll talk to him, okay?"

I'm just about to the door when Axel jumps up. Thankfully, Chopper prevents him from reaching me before I make it out of the room.

I don't bother wrapping my hands before I start throwing punches on the bag, each one landing with a thud that echoes through the empty gym. I keep punching until my knuckles ache, my muscles burn, but it's not enough.

I see her face in my mind. Her worry, her pain, *her compassion for him.*

I punch harder. The bag jerks back violently, swinging on its chain. My breaths are ragged, my chest tight with something I wish I could purge.

I shouldn't feel like this. I know what kind of person she is. That kindness of hers, that softness... It's why I fell in love with her. But right now, it's eating me alive.

I keep slugging the leather. Again and again. Until my fists feel as numb as I wish my heart would, until my arms are shaking. But it's still not enough.

I don't stop until a voice breaks through the haze of my thoughts.

"Hey," Viking says from the doorway. "Val's here, and the vet will be here any minute."

I drop my fists, catching my breath, only realizing now how much sweat I've got dripping down my face as my heart pounds in my ears.

"Great," I mutter. He'll be fine. But I still feel like I'm bleeding.

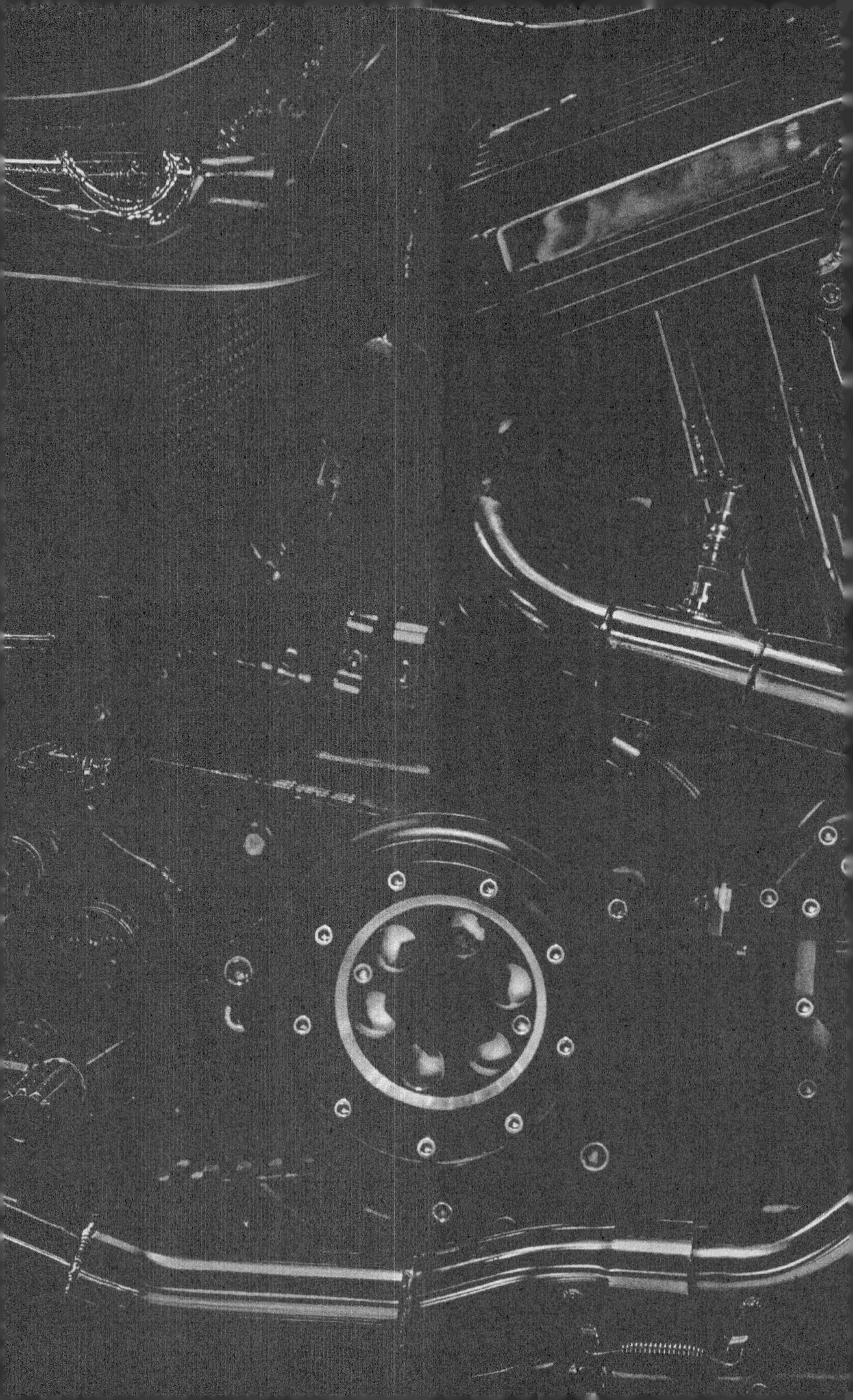

CHAPTER 29

DEAN

When I step back into Legion's room, Vanna is no longer with him, and a wave of relief rolls through me. She must have stepped out to get something he needs, and I know this reprieve will be short-lived. Viking and the woman he calls Val are standing at the foot of the bed.

"*Him?*" The blonde biker chick glares down at Legion's comatose form. "You should just let the son of a bitch die."

I already like her, but… "If he dies, we lose Axel," I say. "He's got leverage and a contingency plan that will put Axel away on a twenty-year federal stint."

The harshness in her eyes softens.

"Believe me," I sigh. "Nobody wants him gone more than I do."

The cellphone in her back pocket rings, and she grabs it to answer. "God damn it, Jett! Where are you?"

"Cool your pits! I'm in the parking lot, Val! I had to wake her up out of a dead sleep and take her by the clinic to pick up supplies she didn't have at the house," Jett snaps back. "We're walking through the corridor now," I can hear the clunk of boots approaching out in the hall. "Where the fuck are you? This place is deceptively huge."

Val hangs up and steps out into the hall to wave them inside. Another woman, who looks every bit a biker chick, too, with long black hair and a lot of ear piercings, stomps into the room with her veterinarian friend. The vet doesn't look like a biker, though. She's a timid brunette with a slight frame. Despite her obvious nervous demeanor, she rushes over to Legion.

Jett lets out a low whistle as she comes to stand beside her gal pal, Val. "Damn, this guy's really... *Wait a minute...*" She frowns before her eyes widen in shock. "Is that... *Oh, you gotta be shitting me!* You dragged our asses out of bed for this bastid?"

"They have their reasons," Val mutters.

Jett lets out an exasperated sigh. "Haven't you guys heard the expression, *only the good die young?* He might *look* like he's knockin' at death's door right now, but believe you me, this motherfucker is probably immortal!"

"Anything else you need, or can we get out of here?" Val asks.

Viking glances at her, and I note the suspicion in his narrowed eyes. "He was mumbling something about the name Jagger... *You know anything about that?*"

Val seems to tense at the question, but meets his glare straight on. "Why would I?"

"Maybe because you used to fuck him," Viking says flatly.

If looks could kill, we'd need more than this nervous vet to save Viking's life. "*Used to* being the key words here, *asshole*. I don't keep tabs on that prick," Val snaps at him.

"So, you don't know anything about him running drugs with a new crew?" Viking presses.

"Ask your trafficking friend when he wakes up. I don't know shit about shit!" Val shoves past Viking and storms out into the hall. Jett tells her vet friend they'll be waiting for her in the parking lot, and hurries after Val.

I turn to a disgruntled-looking Viking. "She seems nice."

"Shut up, Dean," he mutters.

Vanna

Ace is still sound asleep in the bed when I quietly step out of Dean's club room. When the vet showed up, I needed a moment alone to compose myself. Shutting the door carefully behind me so he doesn't wake up, I turn toward the sound of stomping heels quickly headed in my direction. I recognize the two angry biker chicks instantly and take a quivering breath, bracing myself for the encounter with Val and whatever her problem is with me.

"Should have told your vet friend to overdose him with Pentobarbital like the rabid, feral mutt he is," Val vehemently snaps at Jett before she notices me.

I can't help but narrow my glare at her hateful comment, causing a tear to roll down my cheek.

"He's not worth a single one of your tears," she hisses at me next as I brush the tear away. "Neither one of you! If you knew the truth about him, *it would make you sick!*"

"Alright, Val. Let's go," Jett insists, pulling her away from me. They continue down the hall to leave, I presume. I can't help but wonder who else is crying over Legion. Maybe the woman he was supposedly on that hot date with tonight?

When I step back inside the room, the vet has Legion hooked up to an IV and is injecting something into the line. "This should keep him asleep into tomorrow," she says, reaching into her medicine bag. "These I'll leave here," she places an unmarked bottle of pills on the nightstand. "It's a nonsteroidal anti-inflammatory to help with his pain when he wakes up. I'm not sure if any ribs are broken, but with all this bruising, I'm sure he's suffered a few fractures." She stands and inches toward the door, eager to leave.

"Thank you for coming so quickly and so late," Dean says, extending his hand to gently shake hers. "If there's ever anything we can do for you, please don't hesitate to ask."

She only offers him a little nod and smile before she scurries down the hall as well.

"Someone needs to stay with him," I say.

"*Not you,*" Dean growls.

"Who else?" I ask.

"I'm only a few doors away, so is Axel and Cherry," Viking says.

"What if you don't hear him?" I ask.

"Ace is coming home with us, so go take his baby monitors from our room," Dean says to Viking. "Problem solved."

I know if I press the issue, it's going to result in a fight with my husband. "Alright," I glance up at Viking. "Please check on him, even if you don't hear anything on the monitor. I'll be back first thing in the morning."

"And what about Ace?" Dean demands.

Legion: Book 3

"I'll bring him with me, *like I do ninety percent of the time I have to do anything.*" I frown at him for insinuating I'm putting Legion over my own son.

"What's that supposed to mean?" Dean asks.

"I should ask you the same question!"

Viking clears his throat and seems to cautiously interject, "Ace really shouldn't see Legion like this."

"Obviously, I wouldn't let him come in here." I sigh. On second thought, maybe Ace shouldn't be here at all with tensions running this high. "I'm sure Rosita and Mia wouldn't mind watching Ace for a few hours."

Dean brushes past Viking to exit the room, but Viking stops him. "Axel wants to talk to you."

"I've got nothing left to say," Dean mutters.

"So just listen," Viking presses.

"You should go to him, Dean," I say. "I'll try to clean out some of Legion's cuts while you do. Just come get me when you're ready to leave."

"Where's Ace? I'm ready now," he stubbornly declares.

"He's still in your old room. Sleeping," I say.

"Come on, bro," Viking urges. "It's Axel."

"Axel can fucking sleep on whatever he's got to say to me," Dean snaps.

"Well, now you're just being a grumpy dick," Viking huffs.

"You should go talk to him, Dean. I've never seen Axel so upset," I gently press.

His stubborn glare never falters, but Dean turns and storms out of the room.

"Why is Dean mad at Axel?" I ask before Viking can leave, too.

"I think Axel was just the straw that broke the camel's back. Dean made that comment again earlier about feeling like he's failing everyone around him." Viking lets out a heavy sigh. "Do what you can with Legion before Dean drags you out of here. I'll keep an eye on him tonight. You need to go home with him. I don't know what he'll do if you don't. He needs you to choose him, Vanna."

"I've already chosen him." I grab the first aid kit on the nightstand and sit down in the chair beside Legion. "It doesn't mean I can't care about anyone else."

When I find Axel, he's sitting with Cherry on one of the leather couches along the wall in the Twisted Throttle, looking more pitiful and depressed than I've ever seen him. They both peer up at me with slight worry in their expressions, and it tempers some of the rage storming within. I don't want either of them to dread my temper.

I let out a long sigh. "Cherry, doll… Would you give Axel and me a minute?"

"Sure," she says, rubbing his knee once more before getting up to grant us a little privacy. She stops when she reaches me to place her hand on my arm. "He loves you, you know. We all do. You're not failing anyone," she says. I only nod and wait until she's beyond the corridor before moving to grab a chair and taking a seat in front of Axel.

He glances up at me as if he expects me to wring his neck.

"I'm sorry I shouted at you. But I meant what I said."

"I know," Axel's weary gaze drops to stare down at his motorcycle boots. "I was just trying to take initiative… This is my mess…"

"It's *our* mess."

He scoffs. "You told me not to lash out at the Demons after what Legion did to you that night… I should have listened. We wouldn't be in this position if I had."

I place my hand on his shoulder, giving him a gentle squeeze. "I love that you care about this club so much, Axel."

"I care about *you* more."

"Same here, kid. Which is why I fly off the handle when you do stupid shit."

He chuckles, then sniffles, swiping at his nose with the back of his hand.

"It's great that you want to take initiative and pull your weight as a member of this club. But fill us in on what the fuck you plan to do *before* you do it. How can the rest of us return the favor and watch your back if you don't clue us in on what you're doing?"

"You're right. I'm sorry. From now on, if I get another bright idea, I'll bring it to the table first."

Legion: Book 3

"That's all I ask." I pat his arm and stand. Axel rises with me, and I pull him in for a hug. "I love you, kid. It would break me if anything ever happened to you."

"I love you too, Dean." Axel hugs me a little tighter before heading back to his room with Cherry. I realize Viking is standing by the bar. He pats Axel on the back as he passes, then steps behind the bar.

"You two kiss and make up?" Viking jokes, though I know he's always concerned where Axel is involved. "How about a beer after all this shit tonight? You look like you could use one." He grabs two Millers from the fridge and places one on the bar for me.

"Sure," I say, crossing the room to join him. I crack the top off and take a seat on one of the barstools. "So...that blonde chick... Is she the sweet-butt you've been hung up on? I thought there was something familiar about her. She was there that night, at the Knights Clubhouse, when we went to confront Legion."

"Yeah, that was Val. But she ain't a sweetbutt anymore, and if you value your fuckin' balls, don't let her hear you calling her one." Viking lets out a huff that tells me he's had reason for concern over his own balls regarding this chick.

"She seems to hate Legion as much as I do," I say, then take a swig before adding, "That already gives her a few brownie points in my book."

"He corrupted the Asphalt Knights while she was with them. She's the president of her own MC now."

"Nice. She's a real spitfire."

Viking scoffs. "You're telling me?" He takes a gulp of his beer. "Speaking of that night at the AK's clubhouse... Did you ever tell Vanna about Legion's *build-a-bitch*?"

"Didn't seem important after coming home to an eyeball in the sink," I say, though, there are other reasons I never mentioned it even after everything blew over, reasons I'd rather not think about in this current climate with her. I steer the topic back to his chick. "So, her name's *Val*?"

"Valerie. She prefers Val."

"Viking and Valkyrie. *Cute*." The small taunt earns me a slight scowl from him, and I realize how much fun revenge might be.

"*Valerie*."

"*If you say so*." I take another sip to prevent a chuckle. "She's got that Nordic, female warrior look about her. Attitude, too."

"She sure does."

"What exactly is a Valkyrie?" I ask, setting him up for my own amusement.

"In Nordic mythology, Valkyries choose which warriors are worthy of entering Valhalla."

"Yeah, *exactly*." It's damn near impossible to keep the smirk off my face when he shoots me another scalding glare.

"Is this what it was like when I was breaking your balls about Vanna keeping you in a cock cage?"

"Oh, I haven't even *begun* to give you your just deserts after all the shit you gave me about Vanna!"

He takes a swig of his beer, probably stewing in the realization that it's my turn to relentlessly break his balls.

"You've been the *real* mayor of the *friendzone* all along, haven't you? *Asshole*."

Viking places his beer on the bar and hard-eyes me. "*Shut up, Dean.*"

"Oh, this is far from being out of my system," I warn him. "But we've got bigger issues right now. You think her ex is the Jagger Legion was mumbling about?"

"I'm thinking there's a damn good chance. He was there that night, too." Viking takes another gulp of beer.

"The Sergeant at Arms. I remember now. You two looked like you wanted to kill each other before I got into it with Legion."

"Yup."

"We're going to have to talk to Valkyrie."

"*Valarie*."

"If Valkyrie was in a relationship with him, she knows everything we need to know in order to find him. He could lead us to the top of mount meth."

Viking lets out a gruff sigh. "We're gonna need to give her a minute to cool off before we pull her into this."

"Right… Wouldn't want her sending you to Valhalla early."

Viking shoots me a side-eyed glare. "Is this how it's going to be now?"

I smile at him. "You earned it."

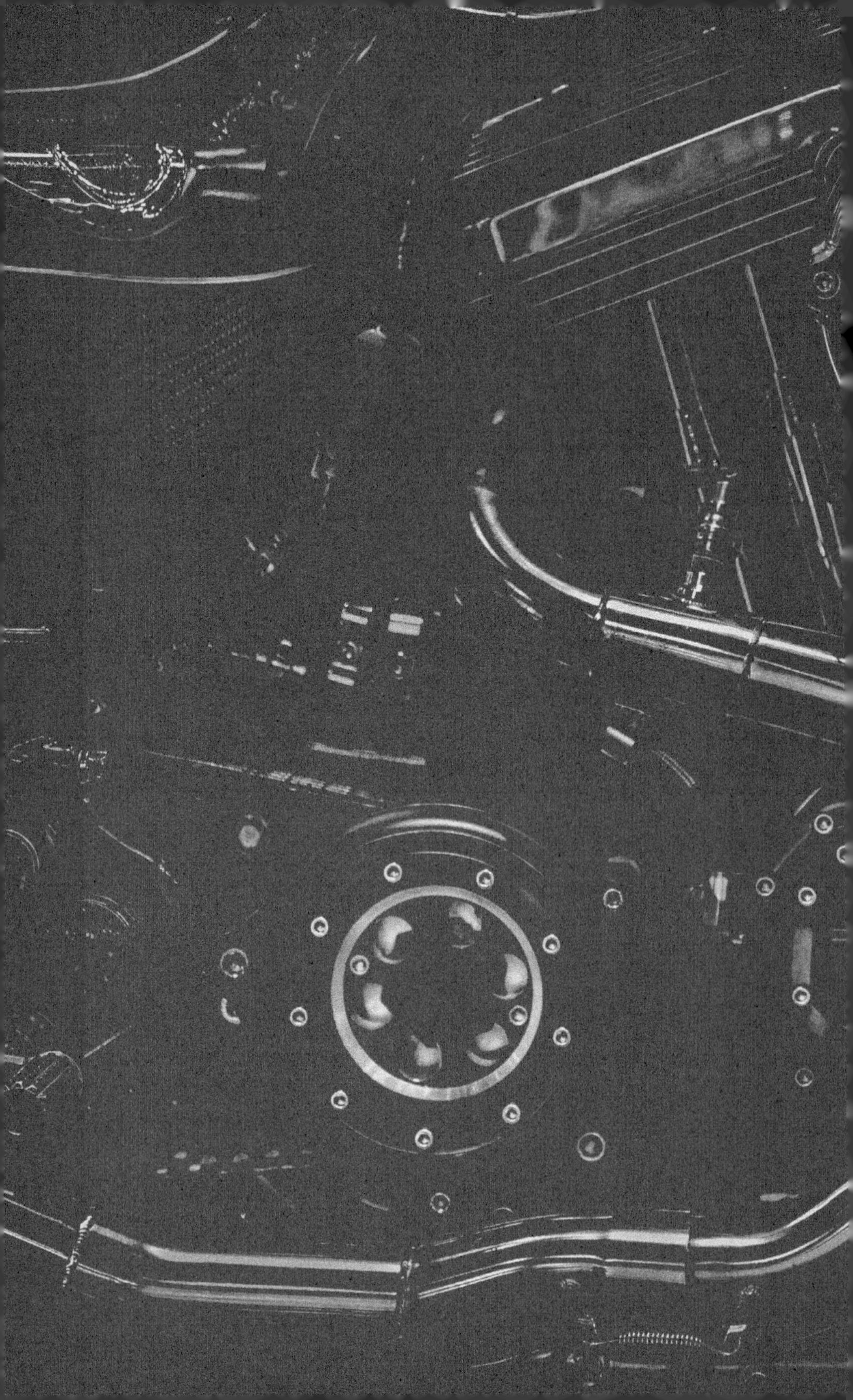

CHAPTER 30

DEAN

When I enter the War Room, my Brothers are already seated around the table waiting for me.

"Are you okay, bro?" Viking asks. "You don't look like you slept at all last night."

I didn't. In fact, I don't think I've had a worse night's rest since Jack Fuckin' Nero's release. "How'd our fucking guest fair last night?" I ask, avoiding the question while glancing at Viking and Axel as I claim my seat at the head of the table.

"I didn't hear anything," Axel says.

"I checked his pulse a few times to make sure he was still alive," Viking replies. "Whatever the vet gave him kept him pretty comatose, even into this morning."

"Those drugs should be wearing off soon," I say, eager to interrogate him.

"Val called me earlier this morning, too," Viking goes on. "Said if we need the vet to come back and check on him, she would after her practice closes, later. Mentioned a few of his cuts could probably use stitches."

Chopper lets out a gruff sigh. "I think this is a rude awakening that we need to keep Legion a little closer… I'm not saying *patch him in*… But fuck… He almost got killed. We either have to step up and take keeping him alive more seriously, or we have to dismantle his fucking contingency plan somehow."

The argument I got into with Vanna last night springs to the forefront of my mind. She had put Ace to bed and returned to the kitchen, where I was waiting in anticipation of round two with my double-shot of whiskey.

"Dean, Legion isn't the way he is because he just woke up one day and decided to be the villain in everyone's story," she'd said.

"Don't make excuses for him. We've all been through shit, Vanna," I argued back.

"And you told me yourself you weren't always a *good guy*."

"I was never the kind of dreg Legion is… *Do not compare me to that piece of shit.*"

"I'm not… I know… I'm just saying… He's trying to find the light, Dean… We should help him find it."

"*Help him*…after everything he's done to us… As soon as we manage to neutralize his contingency plan, *I'll help him find the fucking light all right.*"

"He killed his own brother to prove to you he was no longer your enemy… Give him a chance."

"*He's already forced that upon us!*"

Vanna nervously touched my hand, a gentle reminder to keep my voice down for Ace. I grabbed the shot glass and threw back the remainder of the whiskey in one hard swallow.

"Show him he doesn't need to," she said softly.

"Legion is as incapable of trusting me as I am of him… What you're asking is an *impossibility*, Vanna. The shit just runs too fucking deep."

"He'll trust me…"

"What does that mean?"

"You asked me for my help with Legion when he first came back to our town… I'll earn his trust and get the leverage from him."

"No… I don't want you forging anything with Legion."

"I'm the only one who can get it," she pushed.

"Vanna. *No.*"

"You don't think I'm capable?"

"I think you're very capable… I don't want you getting close to him." Why was this so difficult for her to comprehend?

"*Trust me…*"

"God-dammit! I forbid you to insert yourself in this! Do you hear me? *As your husband*, as the president of this fucking MC, I *fucking forbid it!* This is club business! Stay out of it!"

That defiant look settled over her expression after I'd yelled at her. She didn't say anything. She simply turned from me and stormed down the hallway to the bedroom. If Ace wasn't asleep in his room, I'm sure she would have slammed it.

I spent the night on the couch. Tried to talk to her, apologize to her for losing my temper when she got up this morning to make Ace breakfast.

"*You don't get to pull rank on me,*" she'd snapped at me while our son was occupied at the table with his meal. She'd kept her voice a low whisper so as not to alert him. "I'm not one of your MC Brothers, or one of your damn groupies. *I'm your wife.*"

I'd tried to tell her she was right, but she didn't want to hear it.

"I'm dropping Ace off with Rosita today, and I'm going to the clubhouse to make sure Legion is alive and looked after... I don't think Ace should be around us today, anyway."

As much as it hurt to hear, she was right about that, too. Ace would realize there is something off between his mother and me. I tried to touch her, but she brushed me away, busying herself with the dishes in the sink in an attempt to ignore me.

"I've got Church in a few hours with the guys, I'll drive you," I offered.

"I'd rather drive myself. I don't want to have to rely on a ride anywhere from anyone."

That might have been part of her refusal, but I knew she just wanted distance. "Fair enough," I'd reluctantly agreed and rode Serene here.

"Well, while we consider what all that looks like with Legion moving forward, we've got the next month's schedule with Medusa's gates to review," Viper announces, pulling my focus back to Church. "There are a few court appearances coming up that require our escort services. Oh, and we've got another bit of club business we need to discuss regarding our South Carolina chapter. They want to patch over a smaller crew from their region and expand. They've already conducted the background checks and interviews to ensure these new guys are a fit for our mission. They just need our Charter's nod of approval and blessing."

"As long as everyone is cleared, I have no objections," I say, but Viper winces. "What?" Like I need anything else piled onto this shit day.

"There may be a problem... I'm not sure whether you care or not, but...the VP of this patch-over crew...he's dating *Lucinda*," Viper explains.

"You think I care who she's fucking?" I sigh.

"No. But I think you might care when she starts showing up to Saviors' events, casting a dark cloud over everything we do."

Fuck. That's a valid point. "Fuck my life."

"This bitch is like a raging case of herpes," Viking scoffs. "Not that I've ever had herpes, but you know what I mean."

"Who am I to tell either of them they can't be together?" I sigh.

"As far as I'm concerned, as the original Charter's Sergeant at Arms, Lucinda is a security threat. Blame the call on me if you want to. I don't give a fuck," Viking offers. "Bitch is a loose cannon of toxic drama."

"The blame will still land on me. And despite all the vile shit she's done, I still feel like a dick agreeing to this stipulation before giving my approval for this patch-over," I admit.

"You could be saving this VP's life, bro," Viking says, and he isn't joking. "What did this sorry son of a bitch do to deserve being subjected to Lucinda? You know he hasn't seen her true colors yet."

"Still. Their relationship isn't my business."

"Alright. Then how's Vanna gonna feel about seeing her at our events? You gonna force that situation on the First Lady?" Viking presses.

"Maybe we should table this vote until I speak with our First Lady," I say, wondering when the fuck that will be. Vanna's still pissed at me, and I'm sure bringing this shit up to her is going to work fucking wonders on our present situation.

"Fair enough," Viking agrees. "Just keep in mind I'm happy to have this conversation with the VP before we vote."

"I appreciate it, bro," I say.

"Very well then, let's go over this next bit of business before we get into schedules with Medusa's Gates..." Viper says, gesturing to Diesel as he opens up his laptop. I let out another tense sigh in anticipation of more shit news.

"Our financials," Diesel announces.

Vanna

"I can't help but notice the way Dean's walking around like a lost puppy today, and you've barely said two words to anyone since you got in," Cherry says, leaning in the doorway of Legion's room. "Ace isn't here either… Are you guys fighting?"

I glance over my shoulder at her from my seat at Legion's bedside and offer her a little smile I hope is reassuring. "It was just a disagreement," I say. "How did Legion do last night?"

"I checked on him a few times. Viking and I got him out of his boots and jeans last night, so he'd be more comfortable. I'm not sure he can tell yet. But anyway, we should probably change a few of his bandages. I stopped by Walmart for some more supplies and to grab him some clean clothes." She nods to the chair against the wall, where there are a few plastic shopping bags. "Some sweatpants, t-shirts. A couple of boxers and socks. When he wakes up, if he can't change into them himself, one of the guys will help him. They'd rather do it than leave it to either of us."

"I'm sure he will appreciate this. Thank you, Cherry," I say, grateful that she seems to care to some small degree, too.

"The vet said she'd come by later today to remove the IV from his hand and reevaluate him."

"I hope she comes alone. That Val person is a real bitch." I frown at the memory of her callous comments last night, though I am curious where her hatred for Legion really stems from.

Cherry doesn't comment, asking instead, "Do you need me to get you anything?"

"How about some ice in a Ziploc and a towel? I'm sure the bruising on his torso is even worse today, and a cold compress of some sort will help. I'm going to start changing these bandages and cleaning him up a little while he's still out. One less unpleasant experience for him to go through when he wakes up."

"Okay. The nylon gloves are in the night table there," Cherry says with a nod. "I'll be right back."

Legion: Book 3

While Cherry goes to the kitchen, I slip on a pair of gloves and move the sheet covering Legion's battered body down to his waist, exposing his torso. As I anticipated, the bruising is worse. He looks like he was trampled, even with all of the tattoos covering a majority of his skin. My eyes land on one of the larger pieces that spans his chest. He didn't have this one that night at the wine cellar when he cut himself and swore his allegiance to me.

The greyscale tattoo depicts a demon and an angel embracing. The words *TRUE LOVE*, in bold lettering, are inked beneath them. Through the angel's feathered wings, I can still make out the Sigil of Asmodeus just below the left side of his clavicle. And despite his vast collection of tattoos, observing him this close up, they don't hide all the scars...some worse than others. My gaze traces the distinct V disguised within the large angel and demon piece. A cut he's made more than once, judging by the jaggedness of the raised scars left behind. As I scan his body, I can't help but wonder if he's done all of this to himself...

Before my mind is able to imagine what darkness lies behind these scars, Cherry returns with the ice-pack and towel, and we carefully place the makeshift compress on his chest, moving it around his torso every couple of minutes while we change his bandages. He barely stirs throughout the whole process, only slightly flinching when we move the ice towel.

"If these bruises are still bad in a few days, we can switch to a warm compress. The first few days, ice helps the swelling," I say, once we've finished. "But warmth will help him heal quicker once it subsides. I guess we'll see what the vet says about wrapping his ribs or not. We'll need the guys to help with that if Legion is still out by the time she gets here."

"He'll probably wake up soon," Cherry says, collecting the garbage where we discarded the used bandages, packaging, and our gloves.

"I'm going to sit with him for a little while," I say. I'm not eager to face off with my husband again, and he's dealing with whatever *MC business* he's got going on in the conference room down the hall, anyway. "He could use some more time with this ice, and it should be moved every couple of minutes." I remember Legion once expressed an interest in Reiki, back when we first met, and he showed up at the Ametrine Cauldron a short time after. Now seems like an appropriate time. There's not much else I can do to help him.

I wait for Cherry to leave the room before I try to focus on sending him healing energy and carefully place my hand on his bare shoulder, over the half-skull fortune-teller portrait tattoo there. His skin is alarmingly warm to the touch, now that I'm no longer wearing gloves, and I wonder if it's a side effect of the antibiotics he was given last night, or something more serious. Though I try not to think back on specific memories, I do recall running high fevers after Jack's beatings on a few of the more severe occasions. I hope Legion's fever is not indicative of something more serious.

As I hover beside him, my gaze wanders to his face. Even in a state of drugged sleep, the hint of a pained scowl strains his sharp features, and I can't help but wonder if it's because of his physical condition or if it's his tormented soul unable to find rest, even now. The thought distresses me, and I'm suddenly aware of the erratic beating of my heart as a swell of conflicting emotions begin to roil within.

Dean isn't wrong about anything he's said. Legion is the root cause of so much turmoil, and he would have killed the man I love had Dean not gotten through to him. I can't deny the fact that Legion is vicious, cunning, and dangerous… That he's been a lethal, strategic enemy in the past… But I've experienced his softer side… I know it exists, and I believe him when he says he is remorseful…that he wants redemption. I shouldn't trust him… Yet for some strange reason, I think I always have, to some degree, even before he shot his own brother… The fact that I do trust Legion feels like I'm betraying Dean.

The weight of this, *perhaps not-so-secret admission*, feels as though it might crush me, when something that hadn't occurred to me until this moment flitters into my thoughts… If I forgive Legion…if I say those words out loud…*would he leave*? Disappear from our lives? His self-inflicted mission…*accomplished?*

An odd, quiet dread seeps into my soul…followed by another crushing wave of guilt. Tears sting my eyes, and I force my mind to imagine what life with Dean and Ace will look like without the looming shadow of Legion's presence lingering on the perimeter of our lives… Dean would be elated…and it wouldn't take Ace long to move on… *But I…*

I choke back a quiet sob as the very thought of this scenario only elicits a heartbreaking emptiness that shouldn't exist within me at all... I wanted to share in the relief Dean would feel...but I do feel something for Legion...something I've tried to bury deep in a pit of denial and ignore all along.

Shame scorches my heart, pumping turmoil through my veins like a poison. I squeeze my eyes shut, forcing the tears to spill and run down my cheeks. I have to forgive Legion. I have to make him believe I do. And if he chooses to leave and disappear from my life, at least it will be his choice, and he will be free, too.

I remove my hand from his shoulder to wipe away the tears and move the cold compress from his chest to his lower abdomen. The adjustment causes him to jolt, but he doesn't awaken.

"I'm sorry," I shakily whisper, unsure if I startled him. "You're safe, Damien... I'm not going to let anybody hurt you ever again..."

His lips part, releasing a slight groan, then a whimper. He twists his face toward me, perspiration from the fever glistening on his tense brow and upper lip. I gently pat his face with a cool, damp rag, reassuring him once again that he's safe.

"Lies..." he whispers, before his jaw clenches and his eyes screw tighter, squeezing out a single tear. It slips down his chiseled face, and I carefully wipe it away. *"You knew..."* he whispers again...a voice riddled with such pain, I no longer believe it has anything to do with the current state of his physical injuries... *"You knew... You did this to us..."*

LEGION

Where the fuck am I...It's cold...Why can't I move...

A gritty cement floor scratches my bare knees while rough hands grip my face, squeezing painfully around my clenched jaw. Another rips my head back by my hair.

"Open up, you little bastard... You know this makes everything easier... Loosens you up..."

No... No... What is this? I've escaped this... Why am I back here? How?

Fingers continue to dig into my face, and the metallic tinge of blood seeps between my molars, coating the sides of my tongue. I attempt to thrash and jerk away, but my arms are bound tightly behind my back at the biceps and wrists.

I can't move... I can't escape... Have I died and gone to Hell?

I jerk my jaw free of the man's brutal grip and seize the opportunity to glance down at myself on my knees in the mostly dark.

This young, emaciated, un-inked body tressed up in bondage isn't mine... Not anymore, it isn't...

Wake up! Wake the fuck up!

Something is pulling me... Some dark force...dragging me deeper into my own tormented subconscious...

"I just need a few goddamned pictures of you in this gear! That's all!"

But that's never *all*...

This went on for years, but I never lost my will to fight back. Besides, *he likes me pretty*... He won't break my teeth or cause any physical damage. At least, nothing permanent.

A large, menacing hand pinches my nostrils closed and wrenches my head back again.

I'm in a losing battle. I'm barely fourteen again. Maybe one hundred pounds to his two hundred and fifty. He'll have his way with me again, but I won't go down on his terms... I won't go down without a fight...

Unscrewing my eyes, I glare up at him defiantly from behind the domino mask, clenching my jaw even tighter despite the pain. I'll hold my breath until I black out just to spite him!

Angered, he forces the rim of the glass between my lips, and it clanks grittily against my teeth.

"Come on! I don't want to hurt you!"

Lies.

"It's just a couple of pictures!"

More lies.

Burning pressure builds in my chest as I fight the increasing urge to exhale and gasp for breath.

It's always dark in this cement dungeon, but my vision is becoming spotty. I can hardly make out the cinderblock walls or the extra camera equipment set up in my peripheral vision anymore.

"Stubborn little asshole," he grunts, before the toe of his boot slams up into my groin.

Blinding pain causes my jaw to slacken involuntarily. Wind from my lungs rushes past my lips. Before I can suck in air, he forcibly pours the foul, bitter-tasting liquid into my mouth, then shoves my jaw shut again. Whatever it is, it burns the small cuts inside my cheeks, and I push as much of it as I can through my teeth with my tongue. Warm liquid dribbles out of the corners of my mouth, down my throat and the leather-studded collar secured tightly around it.

Angrily, he shoves away from me, storming back toward the cameras. I choke on what managed to trickle down my esophagus while attempting to catch my breath. Without him crowding me, I'm able to glance around the basement. There's a new piece of strange furniture he's dragging toward me. It screeches against the floor. Some kind of wooden bench with leather cuffs at the base of each leg.

He turns back to me, hooking his fingers into the metal ring of my choker, and violently hauls me to my feet, eye level with his sweaty chest. I stagger forward, my legs too weak from lack of circulation, and he shoves me face down onto the bench.

"Don't move." The threat of further violence in his tone is unmistakable. He loops another strap across my lower back, tightly securing me to it. "You earned this punishment tonight… And you're lucky there's a market for this, too."

He steps away from me briefly and repositions one of the tripods. The faint beep of the camera powering on is barely audible through his ragged breathing. When he flips the display screen open, the soft glow illuminates his angry, grimacing features. He makes a few height adjustments, and once satisfied with the angle of the shot, he twists the screen around to face me.

"*There.* Now we can *all* enjoy the show," he sneers, moving beyond my line of sight. I watch his shadowed form in the display screen as he pulls a leather mask from a trunk against the wall behind me and slips it over his head, completely obscuring his identity before returning to my side.

His fingers tug roughly at the strings of my mask, and a surge of panic floods my system…

No! No, please… I don't want anyone to see my face through this! The mask is all I have left!

The scrap of soft leather falls to the floor, and I stare at it as tears pool and sting my eyes.

Whatever he's about to do to me is not only going to be unpleasant. It's going to involve a level of humiliation and degradation I've yet to suffer through. He's always taken precautions to conceal our identities when he films or takes photos. Whenever my face is involved, he's permitted me the domino mask. Though it barely contributed anything in the way of maintaining anonymity, it was at least a psychological crutch I'd clung to in order to survive it all. A small shred of *something* that separates me from the depravity I suffered in these films and photos.

The stinging bite of his crop makes my body arch against the restraints of its own volition.

"You think covering yourself with little scars is going to turn me off? Think again! Now, let's see how many strikes it takes to make you bleed, and I'll add a few of my own to your collection!" He reaches forward, snaring my hair in his fist, and wrenches my head back. Dark laughter echoes off the cinderblock walls all around me. "Look up and cry for the camera, *pretty one!* Let them hear your lovely screams! Once I've beaten you back into submission, we'll have a little fun with the open-mouth gag I got especially for you!"

The whoosh of the crop cuts through the air before it bites me again…*and again…and again…*

"Damien…" a soft voice calls to me through the pain. I barely hear it over his maniacal laughter…through the cries I can no longer fight back… *"Damien… Damien, can you hear me?"*

Mom? Mom! Mom, I'm down here! Help me! Mom!

"Damien…"

Help me! Please! I'm going to break… Mom! Don't let me break!

"Damien… I need you to wake up, please, please wake up!"

Wake up? Wake…up…

It's bright… I'm no longer in a dungeon… Lukewarm water is crashing down against my chest… I'm sitting against the wall in a shower stall…watching bloody streams run like swirling rivers down the drain a few inches from my feet… There's blood all over my body…all over my legs, my torso…my arms and hands… There's blood smeared all over the fiberglass walls… Bloody handprints…streaks…

Someone is rubbing my arms with a rough cloth…

"Damien… I need you to listen to me, little bro… Can you hear me? Damien?"

Dom?

Legion: Book 3

I hear my brother's voice…but I can't seem to look away from the bloody rivulets winding down the drain…

"I did this, Damien… Do you hear me? If the cops ask you anything, you tell them I did this!"

He's so adamant…but, no… No, *he* didn't.

Mom did this… Mom knew… She let them, Dom… She let them hurt us… She didn't choose us…

"Promise me, Damien. *Promise me!* I love you so much, I'm so fucking sorry, Damien… You tell them I did it…please… I'm your big brother and you have to do what I tell you to do…"

Dominick is crying… I don't want him to cry…

"Promise me, little bro…"

Okay, Dom… Okay…

This ill-fitting uniform itches…

"You're going to live with the other boys at Saint Josephs," the foster care lady says…

Why? Where's my mother?

"Well, I'm sorry, dear, but…she just can't take care of you right now… The nice people at Saint Joseph's will, though…"

We're all orphans…but nobody likes me here…

"Your mother didn't want you!" they laugh and push me down…down in the dirt… *"Demon boy! Demon boy! The Devil owns your soul!"*

A sharp rock pierced a deep hole in my palm… More blood… What did I ever do to them?

I stand as they continue to sing-song and mock me…

"Demon boy! Demon boy! The Devil owns your soul!"

I raise my loosely closed fist to my mouth and blow hard through it, spraying the blood from my wound in one of their horrified faces. They scream and run away…

I'll be disciplined for defending myself…

Nothing is fair…

Mom… Why didn't you want me?

Where are you, Mom?

Mom?

"What do you even see in *The Omen* anyway?" he asks her…

The chains rattle and constrict around my throat…tighter and tighter…

They mean to kill me…
She didn't choose me either, Mom…

"Please, Damien… Wake up!"

My eyes snap open, and I'm greeted by screaming pain as I jackknife, simultaneously reaching for the gun that should have been at my side but isn't. *Fuck!*

"D-Damien?"

Vanna?

Her shaky voice pulls my attention to her seated form beside me. Even in the dimly lit room, I see her eyes are wide with concern. The events that led to this moment come rushing back to me. I am only able to recall bits and pieces, but I know I'm in the Saviors MC clubhouse, in a spare room, recuperating from getting my ass jumped.

"You…you were having a nightmare… I couldn't wake you up," she practically whispers, as if afraid I'd fault her for some inexplicable reason. "Are you alright? Do you want to…talk about it?"

"No…" I watch her delicate throat swallow as I lay my aching body back down against the bed. "No… I… I don't remember, anyway," I lie.

"Alright… Well…can I get you anything?" she offers, the slight wince in her expression a clear indication of how uncomfortable she feels in my presence now.

What the fuck did she witness? What the fuck did she hear? It must have been something for her to realize I was trapped in a nightmare. Fortunately, as the minutes tick by between us in silence, whatever I had dreamed really is rapidly fading into obscurity.

"I'm fine," I manage to croak out, though as I do so, I realize how dry and scratchy my throat feels. "On second thought, might I trouble you for a drink?"

She leans forward to grab something from the nightstand and produces a bottled water. "I didn't think the drugs would keep you under for so long." She twists the cap off, then hands it to me. I take a few eager swigs. When I pass it back to her, I realize there's an IV in my hand. "We're waiting for the vet to come remove that for you. The pain medicine has probably run its course, but there are painkillers in pill form if you need them, too."

"Vet?"

She practically winces again. "Yes… I'm afraid we don't have any *human doctor* connections."

"How long have I been out?"

"Since last night…and most of today… I've been looking after you." She swallows nervously again. "Well, Cherry and me, mostly …and Viking, overnight." She twists the cap back on. "Can you tell me what happened?"

"Axel didn't?"

A frustrated little sigh escapes her as she places the bottle back on the nightstand. "It's club business. I suppose I shouldn't be asking you about it at all. Never mind… I just remember the last thing you told me before you left the party was that you were going on a date."

Fuck… I left the Twisted Throttle, allowing her to believe her own assumption that there was another woman in my life. I try to shake my head, instantly regretting the painful motion. "No," I flinch from the acute ache in my neck and the way my head pounds harder. "I didn't leave to meet with a woman, Vanna… That was your assumption."

Her brows slightly furrow, but she doesn't seem annoyed, only curious. Perhaps invested… *One can hope…*

"I went to meet a man with information pertaining to the organization whose destruction I've been assisting your husband and the Jokers with," I reply, all too happy to undermine Keegan, especially to his wife. Sure, spousal testimonial privilege is a thing, but he still wouldn't break one of the club's golden rules. Not with any specific details anyway. She sits back in the chair, conflict further knitting her brows. I won't make her ask. "We were found out. They brought us to another location. He was killed. I got my ass beat."

"Nearly to death," she practically whispers, evidently distraught. Her concern eases something deep within me, but she's clearly distressed. "*Somebody got killed?*"

Should I tell her it was my doing?

Worry further eclipses her lovely features, and it suddenly occurs to me, Keegan's aversion to relaying pertinent details to her goes beyond abiding by one of the golden rules of MC life. *Keegan wouldn't burden her fragile soul…* But…is this how *she* wants it to be?

"Are we cohorts now?" I tease, attempting to alleviate the situation for her. "Shall I be your inside track to all things MC?"

It barely takes her a second to reply with a firm little, "No."

"Come now, you know you have but to ask anything of me, and all within my power to grant shall be yours."

She tilts her head. "Is that so?"

It hurts to smile, but I do so anyway.

"You're slick, but I saw that one coming a mile away." She smiles back at me, though something about her expression seems forced.

"One what?"

"*A deal with the devil,*" she teases, but still seems unsettled as she gets up from her chair and moves across the room to the dresser against the wall. She removes a blanket from the bottom drawer, then comes to stand at the foot of my borrowed bed. "I've been icing the bruises on your chest, and the temperature is supposed to drop some more with this second cold front coming in. You might need this tonight."

What I need is a hug...around my neck...with your thighs...heal me...

"*Will you tuck me in before you go?*" I mean it as a joke, but for some reason, the playful smile, though possibly forced, slides right off her face. She catches herself, glancing away from me to fuss with unfolding the blanket, then spreads it out over me.

"I'll be back to check on you, and again before I leave for the night," she says, picking up a small plastic shopping bag which appears to contain my clothes. I glance down and lift the sheet covering the lower half of my body to peek at the new sweatpants I've got on. "You can thank Cherry for the clothes...and Viking for getting you into them," she says. "I'll wash what you were wearing and bring it back... Try to get some rest." She grabs my filthy cut and leather moto-jacket from the back of a chair as well.

When the door shuts quietly behind her, I can't help but wonder if that peculiar reaction had something to do with my nightmares.

DEAN

"Is he awake?" I ask, meeting Vanna at the halfway point in the hall.

"I think you should let him rest and just talk to him in the morning," she practically insists, but it's without any of the anger she was harboring for me this morning. Still, she doesn't look up at me.

"Did he say something to you? What's wrong? I can clearly see something is bothering you... What did he do?"

"He was asleep when I went in," she says, barely sparing me a glance. "But he was having a nightmare while I was cleaning him up... I... I tried to wake him, but I couldn't at first. I almost left the room to come and get you... *It was bad*, Dean... Worse than the kind I used to have." Her eyes are glassy and pained when she finally peers up at me, and I'm not sure if it's over some sort of sympathetic emotional reaction to Legion, or if she's upset by the memories of her past triggered by witnessing whatever she did in that room with him.

I'm not happy about either scenario, but the thought of her having any more sympathy for the demonic prick sends another pang of jealousy ripping through my chest. It only gets worse when she speaks again.

"*He was calling out for his mother...*" Her voice nearly breaks, tears spilling over and down her cheeks. "H-he sounded like a little boy...a hurt, frightened little boy...and I couldn't help but think of Ace." She steps into me, needing to be held, and I'm grateful and eager to oblige, instantly wrapping my arms around her.

Maybe I'm a complete asshole, but I can't help but wonder if he knew damn well she was in the room with him, and this was all an act. Another fucking scheme to garner himself more of her sympathy, to wrap his fucking tentacles around her a little tighter. I keep this suspicion to myself for the time being. If I'm wrong, I'll definitely look like the asshole, and not only will she feel more sympathy for him, she'll be madder at me.

"Ace is safe, Vanna. No one will ever hurt him. I will always protect the both of you," I assure her. It's the truth, and I'd rather comfort her about our son, not my *wannabe rival*. I feel her head nod against my chest.

"I know." She sniffles, straightening to peer up at me again. "I should get these clothes in the laundry. I doubt he'll be up and about any time soon, but at least they'll be clean when he is."

Legion is sitting a little more propped up in the bed when I enter his room.

"*Ah*, you just missed your wife," the bastard grins despite a cracked lip.

"What's the intel?" I ask, shutting the door and ignoring his obvious attempt at baiting me.

"I'm feeling slightly better, thank you for inquiring."

"I'm gonna ask you one more time, before you're feeling a whole lot worse. What do you have for me?"

"*Scathing resentment.*" Legion scowls but rules in favor of self-preservation. "Blowing up that house in Jocsan really got their attention. And despite discovering Stanley, they're willing to cut a deal with you."

"What deal?"

"I need a smoke."

"Knock yourself out."

"I've had quite my fill of that, thank you." Legion slowly moves to grab his cigarettes and lighter from the nightstand and sits up on the side of the bed. I realize the IV is no longer embedded in his hand.

"Did the vet come and go already?" I ask, nodding at the discarded IV line.

"No. I removed it myself," he replies, placing a cigarette between his lips, about to light up.

"You might want to crack a window. Vanna's not a fan."

He attempts to stand, grimacing as he reaches for the blinds to slip his fingers through and unlatch the locking mechanism. Apparently, the reach is too much for his fractured ribs, and he sinks carefully back down to the mattress, defeated by the pain.

"This is a nonsmoking establishment anyway," I say.

"You're a real hard-ass," Legion mutters, plucking the cigarette from his lips and slipping it back in the pack. He places it, and the lighter, on the nightstand and grabs the bottle of painkillers.

"And you were just about to tell me what went down last night."

"Reaper's second in command is a prick who goes by the road name Jagger," Legion begins, twisting open the cap and popping two pills into his mouth. He swallows them dry before continuing. "*Jagger* informed me they were willing to pull out of Bermuda County completely if you agreed to back off. I pressed them for Jocsan County as well. They rejected it, but counter-offered a promise to stay out of the region where the Jokers' clubhouse is located. They won't give up the entirety of Jocsan because of the ports... *I tried...* I also warned you the strike in Jocsan would prompt a response." He lets out a heavy sigh as if frustrated. "*Apparently*, the house we hit with the Jokers was a setup, and they used us to take out one of their rivals."

"So, they knew about Stan."

He nods. "It was inevitable…but we squeezed him for what we could."

"What happened to Stan?"

"He wasn't aware they were on to him until just before he met me. I took him out."

"You killed him?"

"That was inevitable, too." Legion moves slowly and cautiously to lean back on the bed against the pillows, then studies me for a moment. "They offered me a spot in their crew. Thought you should know that."

I narrow my glare at him. "And why is that? Did you think I'd be inspired to offer you a place with us?"

"No. I know that will never happen. That you will never trust or forgive me. I accept it's a lost cause between us."

"Am I to assume they rocked your shit because you turned down the offer?"

Legion scoffs. "No. *My shit was destined to be rocked* regardless. They didn't ask me for a decision on the spot. I've been *granted time to consider their offer* while I heal from this *message*."

"Generous."

He glares at my sarcasm. "I haven't forgotten you're only tolerating my presence because of the fact I could have your little Road Captain locked up for felony arson."

"That's certainly not buying you any goodwill."

A sly grin twitches at the corner of his mouth. "Might the fact that your wife cares about me hold sway over your tolerance as well?"

"There you go, playing with fire again."

"*Indeed*."

"Get back to Jagger."

"*As I was saying*, he told me they'd be in touch in a few weeks." Legion smirks, adding, "I'm fairly certain I'll refuse the offer officially."

"Or so you would have me believe."

"The thought crossed my mind, I'll admit that. But then, *not only* would I be betraying you…"

"You'd be betraying *her*."

"*And I won't do that*," he sneers, mimicking the words of the song he danced with my wife to. I don't feel bad that he got jumped. But if I did, the sentiment would have evaporated into thin air at his antagonizing words.

"Did you recognize this Jagger?" I ask.

Legion tilts his head slightly. "He remained in the shadows, though his voice was familiar… Do *you* know him?"

"Not sure yet. This situation is beginning to require a level of trust I'm not sure either of us is capable of."

"*Beginning to?*" He chuckles.

"You could be lying to me right now. You could be playing me like you played Vanna before."

He cocks a cut brow. "Played Vanna?"

"Making her think you were trapped in some horrible nightmare, calling out for help… Way to garner a little extra sympathy from my wife, you manipulative asshole."

He seems to pale, swallowing hard before asking, "What did she say?"

Maybe he wasn't pulling any bullshit for once. Those cold grey eyes stare back at me with an unease I've rarely seen in Legion. I don't know the specific details of his childhood, but I know enough, having witnessed the exchange between Legion and his brother before he ended his brother's life… It isn't hard to guess what those nightmares may have been about.

I decide to spare him any further shame and embarrassment pertaining to the subject. "Nothing specific… Just that it was clear you were experiencing some kind of night terror."

Tension immediately leaves his body, and he grabs the bottle of water on the night table. After chugging a few gulps, he relaxes against the mattress once more. "I'm not playing anyone," he reiterates, "I would only consider the offer as an opportunity to maneuver myself into a position to better serve *you*. But they'd keep tabs on me…*test my loyalty*. I guarantee that would not only prove problematic for us both, but they would go for the jugular, and we both know what that would involve. It's a risky play, and the severity of this beating leads me to believe this is a *one-time offer*…Bear these facts in mind while you weigh all of your options. Hell, take it to the table and vote on it.

Legion: Book 3

I'll do what you decide. Just consider my cover blown if they require a move on Vanna."

The door creaks on its hinges, and his scowling eyes slide toward the sound, then widen instantly when Vanna steps into the room with us. She's holding a large, steaming mug with a stainless-steel utensil sticking out of it. I instantly recognize the savory aroma, and another wave of jealousy rolls through me.

"I heated you up some pastina soup from home," she says, quietly closing the door behind her. "It helps everything... I always keep some frozen in case of an emergency."

The way Legion's fucking mug morphs from concern over what she might have heard to elation at her thoughtful gesture makes me want to blacken his other fucking eye. I try not to grit my teeth as she steps further into the room to carefully hand him what I know tastes exactly like a bowl full of love.

"Italians jokingly call this *penicillin soup*," she says. "I figured you might be hungry and would have an easier time keeping this down with your pain pills."

"Your consideration is touching, sweet one," Legion says with a smile that might be the first genuine one I've ever seen stretch his demonic features. *I hope he burns his fucking mouth.*

I struggle to keep my expression neutral when Vanna turns to face me. "I didn't know if you had work to do at the shop after Church, but I made you lunch, too."

"Thank you," I say, trying to gauge whether or not she's still mad at me.

"Can we talk?" she asks, a slight level of timidness in her tone, as if concerned I might refuse her request.

"Of course." I gesture to the door and move to follow her the instant she takes a few steps toward it, but she stops to glance back at Legion.

"I hope it helps," she says, offering him a tight-lipped smile.

I spare him one last disdainful glare as I grab the doorknob and open it for her to proceed. He's still grinning like she handed him a pot of gold. Before he can swallow and reply with some irritating, exemplary compliment on her culinary skills or some other worshipful wordy praise of her kind nature, I herd her into the hall and shut the door behind us.

She glances up at me suspiciously but proceeds in the direction of the kitchen without commenting on our hasty departure. When we reach the kitchen, I take a seat at the table while she removes what looks like a wrapped hero from the fridge and brings it to me.

"Do you want a plate? It's a breaded cutlet from the other night when I made chicken parm. I put it on Italian bread with some lettuce, tomato, and vinaigrette."

My mouth is already watering. "No, I can use the wrapping," I say, eagerly separating the foil and grabbing the first half of the sandwich.

"Well, eat fast before Viking smells food." She isn't kidding, and I'm not about to share her cooking with anyone else right now.

"What did you want to talk about?" I ask around a big bite.

"Did you really think I would feed him and not bring you something too, you psycho?" she teases, grabbing a rag, a roll of paper towels from a cabinet, and a small plastic container with what appears to be soapy water from the counter beside the sink. She places them down on the table across from me, before grabbing the leather jacket I just noticed was draped over the back of the other kitchen chair. "Do you think I haven't picked up on a few of your…*quirks* after four years together?" She sits down with the jacket in her lap, and I catch a glimpse of the embroidered demon skull on the back of it.

That's Legion's fucking leather jacket she's about to hand-clean for him.

I finish chewing before attempting to speak again. "It's not a quirk. Any man who values his woman is territorial of her cooking, too. And don't think for a second Legion isn't aware of that fact. That's a majority of the reason he was so fuckin' pleased."

She presses her lips together, rolling them in for a moment to compose herself as she dips the rag into the container and begins to gently scrub his fucking jacket. "Dean…*maybe he was just hungry.*"

"When a woman makes food, it's an act of nurturing that the male species traditionally associates with *intimacy*. It's an *intimate*, personal gesture, and you're damn right I'm territorial and selective over who you cook for. Let this be the last time you cook anything for that prick."

"You never seem to mind when I cook for all of your friends for special occasions and holidays," she presses.

"That's completely different. That's a family setting. Not the same thing by a long shot. And I think you know that… Quit being a ball-buster."

She sighs and rolls her eyes at me while I take another large bite. "I really don't want to fight with you, Dean. But we need to be able to talk about Legion without you flying off the handle."

"Well, since we're on the topic, *my Old Lady* shouldn't be handling—*let alone cleaning*—another biker's fuckin' leather."

She stops scrubbing to sit up straight and stare back at me. "Is this a joke?"

"Do I look like I'm joking?"

She bites her bottom lip in another attempt to suppress a smile. "You're all insane. All of you."

"Yeah, well, can't say I didn't warn you."

She shakes her head at me, and I take another bite.

"Before I brought Legion his pastina—" she begins, but I interrupt to correct her.

"*My pastina.*"

"I heard you two talking," she continues, but her smile fades. "Should I be worried?"

In my rush to ask *what exactly she overheard*, I swallow too soon, and an unchewed piece of breaded chicken scrapes down my esophagus, delaying my ability to voice the question.

She must realize on her own and goes on to say, "What did Legion mean...'*make a move*' on me?"

"It was a hypothetical statement that will never come to pass. I don't want you worrying about it."

She nods, lowering her eyes from mine, but her brows pitch together as she leans back in the chair, pulling his jacket into her lap and picking at the white strings where his Chrome Demons' Vice President patch used to be.

"What else?" I ask. She peers up at me as if she expects to be on the receiving end of another outburst. "I'm sorry I raised my voice to you last night."

"You've been saying that a lot lately," she sighs, and I immediately lose my appetite as guilt wracks my system. "I know how stressed out you've been... But there's no reason to get yourself so worked up over Legion. He isn't a threat. Not to the club. Not to our relationship."

Now is not the time to incite round three. Instead, I tell her, "Christmas Eve is already next week. I still have to go up to the cabin and make sure it's winterized for the season. I should have already had that done. Why don't you and Ace come with me? It's not like we still have to decorate the house. And I'll help you wrap whatever gifts are left."

"Maybe a little getaway is a good idea," she says to my surprise and elation. "But don't you want to open presents with Ace at home under our tree? And you know Viking is looking forward to the meal on Christmas Eve."

"We could be back by then. I'll have us home the day before Christmas Eve. Plus, it will give Viking plenty of opportunity to sneak in Ace's big present."

"Which is?"

"You don't want to be surprised with him?"

"I don't know, I'll think about it. I know there's something *biker-business-wise* going on… Are you sure leaving town now is a good idea?"

"Legion's ass whooping bought us a couple of weeks' reprieve from all that," I say, reaching across the table for her hand. She places hers in mine, and I gently caress it with my thumb. "You and Ace are my priority, and I promised you only happy memories on Christmas Eve."

She playfully scowls at me. "But you just promised to have us home by Christmas Eve."

"Then I'll extend it to Eve's Eve." I sigh. "If I don't get a breather from Legion soon, doll, I might just kill him myself. Can we consider this mini getaway an early Christmas gift?"

"If you'll grant me one as well."

"You know I'll give you anything you want."

"We'll see," she says, placing the jacket back on the table and standing. She doesn't let go of my hand, and what levity I may have been feeling these last few moments with her, dissipates with every step we take in the direction of Legion's room.

Vanna

"What are you doing?" Dean asks as I lead him back down the hall.

"Ending this alpha-male-bullshit." I swing the door open and flick on the light to a grimacing Legion lying on the bed. He blinks from the sudden brightness, squinting up at me curiously.

Dean grips my hand tighter and tugs my arm as I move to take a step further into the room. "Vanna…." he growls in warning, but I'm determined.

"What's wrong?" Legion asks, his gaze never leaving me.

"Swear to me you will never hurt my husband."

"I have," Legion says.

"Swear to him, then," I insist.

He shifts his focus momentarily to Dean. "You both have my word. *Again.*"

I glance up at Dean. "Now promise me you won't do anything to hurt him."

Before Dean can say anything, Legion interrupts, "Your husband isn't the one responsible for what happ—"

"*Legion.*" I shoot him a look that shuts him right up. He lies back against his pillows, an amused smirk on his face now as he shifts his attention back to a fuming Dean, standing rigidly in the doorway.

"Promise." I glare up at him. "Promise me you're not going to do, *or let*, something like this or worse happen to him again, and especially not by the hand of a Savior. Including yours."

The scowl in Dean's eyes intensifies as he shifts his attention toward the bed. When I glance back at Legion, he's got his fingers threaded against his stomach, twiddling his thumbs, an antagonistic smile on his bruised face as he stares expectantly back at Dean.

"Dean…" I press, and my husband's gaze drops to stare into mine, lips pressing into a stubborn, hard line. "I'm pulling rank, honey."

"You're an Old Lady, Vanna… You have no official rank within this MC," Dean mutters.

"I do where it counts," I say, placing my hand over his heart.

Legion chuckles behind me. "She's got you by the balls there, too, *pres.*"

"*You* shut up." I glare over my shoulder at Legion once again. "I've never seen ice so thin as the spot you're standing on!"

"*Yes, ma'am.*" Legion grins as if he enjoyed being scolded.

Shifting so I'm able to look at them both, I let out an exasperated sigh. "I'm sick of this tension. I'm sick of dwelling on the past. None of us wants to keep reliving any of it. And I'm tired of the bloodshed. Make an effort to get along or at least *tolerate* each other. You don't have to be best friends, but this antagonistic bullshit," I glare at Legion pointedly, before turning back to Dean, "I'm tired of it all. I just want peace."

"*I promise I won't kill him,*" Dean grumbles.

I make my way over to the bedside table to retrieve Legion's soup mug and smile down at him. "How hard was that?" Neither of them comments. "Would you like some more pastina?"

"I would love some more of your pastina, sweet one." Legion cracks a suspicious smile.

I take Dean by the hand again and we exit Legion's room, heading back to the kitchen.

"What the fuck was that?" Dean asks.

"You're just going to have to trust me," I whisper, just in case. "He's not going to give up that leverage until he believes you're not going to kill him."

"Good luck with that."

I peer up at him as we continue to the kitchen. "If this doesn't work, I'll just bring in the big guns."

"*The big guns?*" Dean arches a curious brow.

"Yes. My feminine wiles."

The playful grin slides right off his face. "*Hold up…* There will be no slinging of *feminine wiles!*"

"Oh, stop," I laugh, stepping into the kitchen to prepare another serving of pastina soup. Dean practically hovers over me the entire time, internally panicking, I'm sure. "Don't you have repairs to wrap up in your shop and roadhouse arrangements to make before we head to the cabin tomorrow?"

"Vanna, Legion is already enamored with all your wiles… Don't encourage him."

I turn around to face him, leaning against the counter while I wait for the soup on the stove to heat up. He's got one fist balled against his hip, and the other gripping the back of his neck.

"You do realize feminine wiles encompass far more than seduction, don't you? At least in the sense you're clearly worried about," I say. He only continues to stare at me, eyes searching mine, warring with his own protective inclinations. "Just trust me, Dean. Legion isn't the only one who's learned to survive through psychological warfare."

"You care about him," he finally says.

I nod. "The way most women care for the lost and broken."

"You're not most women. *You're my woman.* And he wants what is mine."

I let out a sigh, and despite believing what I'm about to say, it feels wrong to do so out loud, as if I'm somehow betraying Legion. But Dean is my husband, *my true love*… And the only man who has earned my vow of loyalty. "Dean… I don't know if Legion has even realized this himself, but… I don't think it's a *woman's* love he craves so much…"

My throat tightens at the memory of his broken pleas. I swallow hard and force the revelation past my lips. "*It's a mother's.*"

CHAPTER 31

LEGION

"A man could definitely get used to this," I grin as Vanna places a breakfast tray across my lap. My mouth is already watering over the aroma and presentation of pancakes, maple syrup, scrambled eggs, and breakfast sausage.

"I wasn't sure what you like for breakfast, so it's a little bit of everything," she says.

"I'm surprised the *good warden* permitted this."

She gives me a slight frown, but then admits, "Well, Cherry and I made breakfast for Dean, Ace, Axel, and Viking, too. So technically, he can't complain." She lowers herself into the chair beside me. "I hope this is enough to hold you over until later. With Viking around, there will be no seconds."

"I'll eat whatever you place in front of me," I smile, unraveling the napkin she's rolled a knife and fork within. "Have you eaten?"

She waves her hand as if to brush the question away. "I'm rarely in the mood for breakfast. Please, eat before it gets cold."

"So, the young Keegan is here," I say, forking off a piece of pancake to shove into my mouth. The moment I do, I'm astonished. I've eaten a grand-slam-style breakfast before. They've all basically been the same. But I can taste the difference in this dish once again. That special ingredient she sprinkles into everything she prepares… *Love*.

"Yes, we just stopped by because we're taking Ace up to the cabin for two days."

"*Oh?*" Admittedly, I feel some type of indecipherable way about her departure… A vexatious emotion I do not wish to examine in her presence.

"There's a Christmas village up there we think he'll really enjoy," she goes on while I eat. "And Dean has to wrap up a few things with the cabin itself for the winter."

"I see."

She smiles warmly and leans forward to pick up the napkin on the tray, gently wiping my chin. "You're like Ace," she giggles. "We make him wear a designated shirt for meals involving syrup and sauce."

"My apologies,"

"Don't…he's three and you're injured," she says, sitting back in the chair. "I'm glad you seem to be doing a bit better."

"*It's the pastina,*" I wink, and her little laugh is a comfort in and of itself.

Once I've consumed every morsel, I thank her again for her efforts and compassion.

"I don't expect you to be up and about any time soon, but I hope you'll still be here when we get back," she says, standing to collect the tray. "There's no rush for you to leave. There's plenty of room here. I could always go get whatever you need, wherever you've been staying."

"That won't be necessary."

"It's really no trouble."

"I've spent the majority of my life as a nomad. There isn't much I own… Besides…our common enemies blew up my riverside retreat."

The plate and utensils clatter on the shaking tray before she clutches it against her abdomen to steady it. "*What?*"

"My *temporary dwelling* is no longer… It hasn't been for a few weeks now. I've been sampling all your county has to offer in the way of lodgings, becoming quite the *hotel connoisseur!*"

She isn't amused by my attempt at making light of the situation and spends a moment simply blinking back at me. Her mind is no doubt running through worst-case scenarios. I know precisely when she lands on one that strikes a nerve. Her brows shift from censurably knitted to pitched upward, and her knuckles turn white around the edge of the tray.

"I assure you, sweet one, my transitory stay here poses no threat. This beating I've endured bought us a little time... *An interim truce* while all parties ponder the offers and concessions exchanged."

We share in another bout of tense silence. She did not find any assurance in my words... *She is a good mother...*

"Vanna... If I believed my presence was in any way a threat to you or those you love, *I would crawl out of here...* Have I not proven all I'm willing to do for you?"

Besides... I'm not going anywhere, *including Hell*, until I've completed my mission. Earned my redemption... *God owes me that much!*

It isn't long after she departs when Keegan, *the bastard about to snatch her from my side*, graces me with his brooding presence next. That unremitting glare lands on the mostly empty glass of sweet tea perched on the bedside table, before it transfers to me. To rub salt in his wounds, I pick up the napkin she left behind and dab the corner of my pernicious grin.

Adept himself at reading others without the exchange of words, Keegan pulls in a long breath, attempting to quell the ever-roiling rage I incite within him.

"Relax, Keegan... I ate her pastina and pancakes...*not her pussy.*"

"I'll be doing that while we're up at the cabin," he gut-checks me with the statement...

Touché...asshole.

"And since we're on the subject, when were you going to mention yours was blown up? That was fucking weeks ago and might have been a pretty strong indication this shit was looming on the horizon." He gestures to my current state.

I attempt to shrug, but the stabbing sensation shooting through my ribcage convinces me to abandon the gesture. "It was a rental," I grunt through the pain.

"Well, you've managed to maneuver yourself into our clubhouse for the foreseeable future *after all.*" He crosses his arms contemptuously. "*Congratulations... Welcome home... Prick.*"

His disingenuous tone grates against my tempered patience. I've hurt men for far less. I haven't tolerated any measure of disrespect, belittlement, or condescension in close to two decades... Perhaps Keegan would benefit from a reminder of who he is talking to... *I don't require a knife to fucking cut him...*

Forcing a slight, insincere smile of my own, I tell him, "Once I am up and about, I am happy to help around the Twisted Throttle... I don't expect free room and board, and I do have more than a decade of bar experience, having owned one myself until recently."

"Did your enemies blow that up, too?" he mordaciously inquires.

"No. In fact, it fetched a fantastic price and more than bank-rolled my relocation to your precious Bermuda County...a gentleman's club I happened to remodel and name myself." Despite the discomfort from sneering, it's worth the paling expression on Keegan's face when I tell him, *"The Morning Star..."*

Let that eat at his sanity while he's away with her...

DEAN

The truck tires grind to a stop on the snow-dusted gravel of the driveway, and I grip the steering wheel a few seconds longer than I need to. My knuckles are stiff from death-gripping it for the majority of the way to our mountain cabin. Throwing the truck into park, I mentally remind myself to just *breathe. Smile. Keep my shit together for my family...*

"Hey..." Vanna's fingers touch my arm. "Everything okay?"

"Aces, baby." I force a smile for her and unbuckle my seatbelt. "Just a long drive in a cage is all." I pull the keys from the ignition and hand them to her. "Why don't you get Ace inside, and I'll bring in the bags and the groceries?"

She unbuckles her seatbelt and stretches before peering over her shoulder at our son soundly sleeping in his car seat. A loving smile stretches her lips, and she reaches back to gently rub his knee, stirring him awake. He blinks and glances around, craning his little neck to see out the window better.

"Are we there yet?" he asks, for probably the twentieth time, though with his nap, we got a brief reprieve.

"We made it," Vanna says, opening her door and getting out of the truck to unbuckle Ace and grab his backpack.

I exit the truck as well, pretending to need a moment to stretch myself, while they make their way inside the cabin. The cold mountain air has nothing on the block of ice in the pit of my stomach.

The Morning Star... The fucking way he said it with that demonic grin... *How could he know?* Vanna and I destroyed the spell together almost five years ago... Did she tell him about it? Is what he said about his former strip club even true? And if it is, did he reveal the connection to her? Why wouldn't she have told me if he did?

The fucking prick knows somehow. And he dropped that fucking brain-bomb on me to sabotage our getaway. Though there's a chance this is all a coincidence...a very slim fucking chance, and I need to know whether it is or not right now.

I slip my cellphone from my pocket and check to see if it has service. It's still hit or miss way up here, and I may just have to wait until we take a ride to that little Christmas town tomorrow.

Fuck my life... No signal.

I shove the useless thing back in my pocket and sling open the back passenger door. Grabbing the groceries to bring them inside first, I trudge up the wooden steps, determined to put this *Morning Star* situation out of my mind for now.

When I step inside, Vanna already has the lights on in the front of the cabin, the heat turned up, and is getting Ace situated in the living room near the stone fireplace. Once I get a fire going, we'll all be more comfortable. I put the groceries on the small kitchen island and turn to go back out for our suitcase, but she heads me off at the door.

"Are you sure everything is alright?" she quietly asks, placing her hand on my arm again.

"I told you, doll. I'm Aces, baby." I press a kiss to her forehead, but when I pull back to look at her, she folds her arms, clearly unconvinced. "I still have a bunch of shit to do before I can even think about relaxing, kitten. I'm just in *get-it-done mode*."

"Is there anything I can do to help?"

"You can put the groceries away. Unless you want to lug in firewood instead?"

She scrunches her nose, and I'm sure we're both thinking back to the last time she helped with the firewood and a spider crawled up her arm. I chuckle at the memory of the shriek she let out. It rivaled a hawk's.

"*Shut up*," she playfully warns, shoving me toward the door now. "*It was huge, and you know it!*"

Legion: Book 3

It isn't long before Vanna's got my mother's old records playing softly, the groceries put away, and our clothes unpacked and organized into the small dresser in the bedroom.

I wrap my arms around her waist as she attempts to walk by me, and pull her back against my chest, cherishing the way she relaxes in my hold. Pressing my lips against the back of her head, I breathe her in. God, how I've fought to get to this place with her. It's been over a year since I've felt her flinch or tense at an unexpected touch. The realization brings a smile to my face. I am her Knight, and she knows it. *Fuck Legion and his mind-fuckery.*

"Did you know your great-great-grandpa built this cabin, Ace?" Vanna asks. Our son is sitting in front of the stone hearth, unpacking the toys he brought from his backpack. "Daddy's family lived in these mountains when they came to America, isn't that cool? Do you remember the name of this mountain range?"

He pauses from his task, his little brows scrunching together as he considers the question. "Smoke?"

"That's right! The Great Smoky Mountains," Vanna says. I let her slip from my embrace as she walks over to him. "You're such a smart boy, Ace." She removes one of the iron candle holders from the mantle above the fireplace and crouches to show him. "Your Ancestors brought these all the way from Scotland when they immigrated. Guess how old they are?"

His little hand grips around the neck, and Vanna carefully allows him to test the weight of the object, letting him hold it but keeping her own hands near in case he does drop it. "A hundred!"

"Close," she replies, speaking as though it's an impressive span of time, "*Two hundred and fifty years!*"

"Wow!" Ace says, and I suppress a grin because I'm not sure if he is truly impressed, or if he just loves his mother enough to play into her enthusiasm for her sake.

"You're more than Scottish, though, kiddo," I add, "Your great-great-great...*maybe great*-grandmother married an Irishman, hence our last name, Keegan. But did you know you're also Italian on mommy's side?" Ace peers up at me, then looks at his mother. "Mommy's grandparents came to America from southern Italy. They settled in New York, where your Aunt Giuliana, grandma, and grandpa still live."

Vanna runs her fingers through the top of his dark hair, combing it back the way she does mine. "One day we'll go on another adventure, and we'll take you to the *Big Apple* to visit them and see where mommy used to live."

"Mommy lived in an apple?" Ace asks, making Vanna giggle. "*Like James and the Giant Peach?*"

Vanna places the candle holder down on the hearth and reaches into his backpack for his tablet. "I'll show you," she says, bringing up a map of the United States and zooming in on New York. "This area is nicknamed The Big Apple, but it's just a city." Ace seems mildly disappointed by this, and I have to suppress another laugh. "And this area here is Long Island, where your grandparents live now. You'll meet them someday."

Ace points at the map. "It looks like a fish!"

"It does!" Vanna laughs along with his gleeful observation. "What does Italy look like?" she asks, adjusting the map on the screen, then points to the country.

"A boot!" Ace smiles up at her.

"That's right! Your ancestors got on a ship and sailed all the way across the Atlantic Ocean, from here to here, to start a life for us in America."

"A big ship?"

"Mhmm."

"*Like Vikings did?*" Ace asks excitedly, pulling a chuckle from us both. "Am I a Viking, too?"

"Uncle Viking definitely makes you an honorary Viking, too!" Vanna's reply brings another proud smile to Ace's face.

"You're a pretty cool little dude," I tell him.

"Do you know where we are now on this map?" Vanna asks. Ace shakes his head, and she proceeds to show him where our cabin is nestled. Ace's eyes dance over the map for a moment.

"Everybody is so far," he says, thoughtfully.

"Do you want to know something really special about these mountains?" Vanna asks, and he nods. "The Great Smoky Mountains are part of the Appalachian Mountain range, and they are *over* one *billion* years old. Some of the oldest mountains on earth."

"*Wow...*"

Legion: Book 3

"One day we'll tell you about Pangea," I chuckle. Ace peers up at me quizzically. "These same mountains were once part of the Scottish Highlands, where our family came from. The world used to be one big piece of land."

He looks to his mother suspiciously, before glancing back up at me. "Is this a bedtime story?" he asks, making us both laugh again.

"No, but we have a lot to do while we're here, so you had better sleep tonight," Vanna says.

"Mountain things?" Ace asks.

"Mhmm. Did you know Daddy is Appalachian, too? You and your father have strong roots in these mountains."

Ace stares thoughtfully at the map again before asking, "Where is Legend from?"

I fight the knee-jerk reaction to reply *Hell*.

"Arizona," Vanna quickly shows him on the map.

"Is he a Viking, too?" Ace asks.

"I don't know where Legend's family comes from," Vanna says.

"*Maybe Hades*." I shrug, watching Vanna's reaction. She presses her lips together to suppress a smile.

"Where is Hades?" Ace asks, glancing back down at the map.

"I don't know, but this tablet needs to charge, and mommy has to get dinner going for us," Vanna quickly says, powering down the tablet. She holds it up for me to take, avoiding eye contact with me now. I know it's because she doesn't want to laugh and raise Ace's curiosity any further on the topic of Legion. I place it on the end table, and she grabs the candlestick, standing to place it back on the mantle. Ace resumes unpacking his toys.

Vanna peers up at me as she walks to the kitchen and whispers, "*You know he's going to repeat that.*"

I don't bother hiding my grin when I covertly grab her hand to stop her. "*I hope he does.*"

"You're a menace."

"I'm gonna wear him out before dinner, *so I can lay this strong root in you later.*" I wink at her.

"*And a rogue.*" She smirks.

While Vanna prepares dinner, Ace assists me with bringing in enough firewood to last us the two days we'll be staying. Half we stack neatly on the porch near the front door to be brought in later, and the rest we stack beside the stone hearth. Though the cabin has warmed up a little more from her cooking, I show Ace how to build a fire to keep the cabin warm through the night. Granted, he's three and will probably forget everything I've just shown him, but he still asks an abundance of questions, of which I'm happy to answer.

"Alright, my little lumber-snacks, come eat supper," Vanna announces, taking a seat at the already set table.

"Some of my favorites, but is he gonna eat steak?" I whisper to her as I sit.

"*I brought nuggets as backup,*" she conspiratorially whispers back, then smiles down at our son. "Besides, if Daddy eats it, you will too, right, Ace?"

Ace studies his plate and picks up his fork like he's got a job to do. "Yeah... Daddy is a fine male spess-man."

Vanna blinks, stunned, and I clear my throat to ask, *"A what now?"*

"Miss Dixie says Daddy is a fine spess...*spess-a-man.*"

"*My Gods,*" Vanna whispers under her breath while I try not to laugh. "I'm all for our son spending time with his biker uncles and you at the roadhouse a few nights a week, but maybe you should lay down the law with *certain talk* around him?"

"Are you mad, Momma?" Ace asks before I can reply.

"*No,* angel, eat your supper." Vanna pulls on a reassuring smile for him. "If you want to grow up to be big and strong like your Daddy, you have to eat your meat and veggies."

"Okay," he says, going straight for the mashed potatoes and gravy.

"Including those string beans, mister," Vanna says, nodding at his plate.

"*Lizard tails,*" Ace insists.

"Alright, eat your *lizard tails.*"

I love them myself, but they're not Ace's favorite, even though she prepares them with garlic and butter. But Ace makes an effort to please her, forgoing his mashed potatoes for a moment to pick up a string bean with his fingers and gnaw on it.

He peers up from his plate at us, as if seeking further encouragement. "These will make my root strong, too?"

Legion: Book 3

Vanna nearly chokes on her wine, a giggle escaping despite her effort to suppress it behind the hand she's got pressed to her mouth. He really does hear everything and repeat it.

"How are those mashed potatoes working out for you, buddy? Good?" I can't help chuckling at him as I cut into my steak. "Let's get some more of those in your mouth."

A little while after dinner, Vanna and I set Ace up on the new couch in the living room with his sleeping bag and extra blankets. I place a large piece of oak into the fire, which should burn for hours and keep the front of the cabin toasty until early morning. Ace is generally a pretty solid sleeper, and after lugging in firewood with me, I suspect he's down for the count like I was hoping for.

Vanna lightly kisses his cheek and carefully tucks him in a little tighter before she runs her fingers through my hair, flirtatiously gripping it and giving it a rough little tug that shoots right to my cock. She scampers off to the bedroom, smirking over her shoulder, and I'm eager to join her. Just in case Ace should toss in his sleep and roll off, I line the floor along the couch with a few extra pillows.

"Daddy?" Ace's sleepy voice draws me back to him before I can stand and make a break for the bedroom. His little fingers curl around the top of his sleeping bag. "I'm not tired," he mumbles, though his drooping eyelids beg to differ.

I gently stroke the top of his head. "We have lots to do tomorrow, buddy. You need to rest up."

"Can you tell me a story?" the little traitor bargains.

I let out a defeated sigh, repositioning myself to sit on the floor beside him. "Alright, buddy, but just one," I say, draping an arm gently across him in order to stroke his little forehead with my fingertips—a trick we discovered when he was a baby. Fortunately, it still works and never takes long for him to fall asleep.

"The Knight story," he insists, and although it's one of his favorites, the request only reminds me of Legion's *Morning Star* comment.

I keep my voice low, my words slow, watching his blinks as they stretch longer...and longer...until finally, his eyes remain closed and his breath evens out. I wait a few minutes more, just to be sure he's really down for the count, then inch by inch, I lift my arm from him and move away. Standing, slowly and cautiously, I walk around the couch and head for the bedroom.

"Took you long enough," Vanna teases, her voice warm and inviting. She's already discarded her pajama pants, wearing only her underwear and my faded Sturgis t-shirt, already in bed.

I grin, quietly closing the bedroom door and twisting the lock, just in case. "*Worth the wait?*"

She sits up and slowly slides her panties down her legs, then drops them over the side of the bed. "*Let's find out,*" she purrs.

I'm already hard in the seconds it takes to shed my clothes and jump into the bed with her. The springs creak beneath me when I land on my knees at the foot of the mattress, and she giggles as I cage her beneath me.

"*Shhh!*" she whisper-scolds, a finger pressed to her lips before she reaches up to stroke my jaw, coaxing me down to her. I slowly lower myself against her, studying her face in the dim glow of the tableside lamp, and gently smooth a whisp of hair from her forehead. "What is it?" she whispers. "Why are you staring like that?"

"Just committing this expression to memory," I murmur. "I don't want to forget it."

"Forget what?"

"The way you look at me when it's just us."

Her playful smile softens. "It is *just us.*"

"The way your hair spills down your shoulders," I go on before she feels the need to elaborate. "The way my shirt hangs off your body like it's always belonged there." I let my fingers trail up her side, brushing bare skin beneath the hem of the fabric. "The way you make me feel like I'm the luckiest man in the world, just by loving me."

She tips her face up to kiss me, soft and slow, her lips moving against mine. I settle between her parted legs and kiss her back deeper as her hands slide up my chest, into my hair, pulling me closer. The shirt slips higher as I move against her, baring more skin. She doesn't stop me when I grab the hem and pull it off of her, tossing it over the side of the bed, and she arches into the kisses I trail down her neck and to her breasts. A soft gasp escapes her when I take a pebbled peak into my mouth and suck. She writhes beneath me, attempting to rub herself against my hardened length.

She whispers my name, hot and needy. I claim her mouth once again as her legs slide up mine, heels anchoring against the back of my thighs. Her thighs part wider, inviting me in. She holds my face between her palms, eyes locked with mine, and I can see it. The fire. The trust. The history between us. Everything we don't need to say out loud.

Her breath catches when I push inside her, eyes fluttering closed, but only for a moment. She wants to watch me, too. I move slowly, giving her everything, and she meets me with every breath, every thrust, every whispered plea.

When we finish, I shift off of her and she curls into me, resting her head against my shoulder, palm pressed against my racing heart. I hold her tightly against me, skin warm against mine. Neither of us wants to part, but my gaze shifts to the door.

"I should check on Ace," I whisper, before pressing a kiss to the top of her head.

She lets out a sated little moan, reluctant to part. "Alright. I'll meet you back in here."

While I pull on my flannel pants, Vanna grabs a robe from the closet and quickly tiptoes to the bathroom. I pad quietly down the short hallway, barefoot against the cool boards.

I peek over the back of the couch. Ace is curled on his side, facing the fireplace, still tucked inside his sleeping bag. The soft, orange glow of the fire dimly illuminates his little face. He looks peaceful. Safe.

I return to Vanna, leaving the bedroom door slightly ajar this time, and slip beneath the covers, the mattress dipping as I pull her back into my arms. She melts into me instantly, her body warm against mine, and I breathe in the scent of her hair. Outside, the light breeze rustles the pine trees and swirls the thin layer of snow across the roof of the cabin, somehow making everything feel cozier, and I'm grateful she talked me out of selling this place.

"Is Ace okay out there?" she murmurs, tracing lazy patterns along my arm with her fingertips.

"Little bugger barely moved an inch." I tighten my arms around her, pressing a kiss to the side of her neck as she presses her sexy ass against my shaft. "*Round two?*" I growl.

She chuckles tiredly. "You seem to have shaken off whatever you brought up here with us," she says, hesitating for a moment at my silence before she continues. "I didn't want to bring it up earlier, but did Legion say something?"

"He's always saying something," I mutter.

"What was it this time?" When I don't answer, she wiggles her ass against me again. "*Dean?*"

I let out a sigh in an attempt to tame my rising anxiety. "Did you tell him?"

"Tell him what?"

"About the Knight spell."

"No. Why?"

"Are you sure?"

"Of course, I'm sure. The only people who knew about it besides us, are Laura, Ethan, and Marie Delai. Why are you asking? What did he say?"

"That he owned a strip joint called the *Morning Star.*"

"It's probably a coincidence."

"I don't know. Maybe." My gut is telling me otherwise. Especially the way he sneered when he said it.

"Legion isn't a threat, Dean," she says, as if she's reminding me for the thousandth time. Maybe she is.

"He makes my skin crawl," I mutter, "He's fuckin' weird, Vanna. He's too flamboyant and theatrical. His exaggerated gestures, like he's always playing to an audience that only exists in his twisted mind. The way he talks makes me want to choke him. Everything he says is always another elaborate performance. It's like he deliberately does it to piss me off."

Not to mention the way he looks at her. I see it every time…that glint in his eyes like a wolf circling its prey. The way his smile tightens when she mentions my name. And she doesn't even see the darkness beneath his already sinister exterior. What the fuck is it about him? How can she not? The way his eyes linger on her, the way he speaks to her as if they share some secret… The shit he's orchestrated. His every word, his every move, seems carefully designed to make himself indispensable in our lives. But I'll never trust him regardless. He's cunning, clever, and I know it's only a matter of time before his true nature shows.

"I don't think anyone's ever given Legion a real chance to heal…to be seen for who he really is beneath all of that," Vanna says, and I can feel her body tense in my arms as if she's worried how I'll react.

"I've seen plenty," I grumble, but still press a kiss against the top of her shoulder to show her she has nothing to fear from me.

"That wasn't him…and in the end, he chose us, Dean… Maybe he's never had anyone choose him… He's the way he is because he's been hurt, badly…repeatedly… When I look at him now, I can't help but see a scared little boy."

"Alright," I sigh. I suppose that's better than her seeing him as a hot-blooded man… A hot-blooded man who's desperately in love with her.

"Alright?"

"I'm choosing not to have this battle with you."

"I don't want to battle with you *at all.*"

Still, I can't resist scoffing, "If he's a little boy, he's the one that appears beside your bed in the middle of the night, watching you sleep with a giant kitchen knife clutched in his hands."

I have to press my lips together when I feel her body shaking with silent laughter before she expels a quivering breath in an attempt to compose herself.

"*Stop it,*" she whisper-laughs, "you're going to give me nightmares with that visual and make me want to lock the bedroom door every night."

"On Ace?" I chuckle. "He would never. He may have inherited my looks, but he has your pure, kind heart."

"No, it's just a creepy thing to think about right before we go to sleep. It's bad enough I've dreamed—"

She tenses, and I wait for her to continue, but she doesn't. "Dreamed what?"

"Dreams I can't remember, lately…" she clears her throat. "Watch this be the one that sticks, or I scream the next time Ace wakes me up in the middle of the night."

"Like you did when that spider ran up your arm from the firewood?" I tease her. "I swear, someone probably heard you in Tennessee."

After her next wave of giggles passes, it isn't long before her breath evens out, and her body relaxes, soft and trusting against mine. I let my own eyes drift shut to the sound of her sleeping and the wind brushing by our cabin. The mountains can howl all they want outside, cold and relentless. In here, I have everything I need. And as for Legion…he can plant all the psychological bombs he can manufacture. It won't change the fact that Vanna is mine, and together with Ace, we have something indestructible.

CHAPTER 32

Vanna

I'm not sure I'd consider last night's conversation about Legion progress, but at least it didn't spiral into another heated argument with my husband.

This morning, Dean is already outside working through a few chores on his *cabin winterization to-do-list*. We've already had breakfast, and Ace has just finished brushing his teeth with me in the nearly too-small-for-the-both-of-us bathroom.

"Okay, sweetie," I say, handing him a towel to wipe his mouth now that he's finished rinsing. "Go get your backpack and bring it into the bedroom so we can get you ready for today's adventures!"

"Yeah!" he says excitedly, throwing the hand-towel in the sink before bolting down the short hallway to the front of the cabin. I finish rinsing our toothbrushes and clipping them into their travel cases, then place them in the little mirrored cabinet above the sink. I grab my toiletry travel bag and unzip it, only to realize there's something I forgot to bring with me...

"*Shit...*"

I must have put the little blue disc of contraceptives back in the bathroom drawer at home after taking it yesterday morning. Nothing I can do about it now... What's one dose? We'll be home tomorrow, anyway.

Legion: Book 3

We spend the majority of the day exploring a little town not too far from the cabin, but it feels like we stepped into a giant Christmas snow globe or a Hallmark movie. The air is perfectly crisp with the scent of pine trees and cinnamon from the little shops. The freshness of the mountain air makes my lungs feel alive with every chilly breath, but there's a warmth radiating from my heart as I hold hands with both Ace and Dean, strolling along the snow-powdered sidewalks.

Ace is still practically bouncing with unbridled excitement, eyes wide, drinking in the sight of every twinkling light and frosted shop window. He points to every snowman, every Christmas tree, and every gingerbread house on display. His cheeks are flushed from the cold, but it doesn't deter the constant smile on his little face.

Whenever I glance up at Dean, he's smiling too, watching Ace with a gentle pride, knowing our son will remember this trip to the mountains and ask to return.

The irresistible aroma of freshly baked cinnamon rolls and hot cocoa draws us into a little cafe, and we sit down to enjoy a treat and a short reprieve from the cold.

"We needed this," Dean quietly says on our journey back to his truck. Ace is walking a few paces ahead of us. "To just slow down and appreciate what matters...realize how lucky we are to have this." He hugs me a little tighter against his side.

"Wow!" Ace shouts and darts off the sidewalk, onto the snow-covered lawn. He bends to pick up a pinecone in his mittened hands, holding it up for us to see. It's bigger than his entire face. "Can I keep it?"

"You sure can," Dean chuckles, then leans into me and whispers, "All these fancy decorations and he's most excited by a pinecone."

I frown up at him, ready to stick up for Ace. "So?"

"You think he takes after me...*but he's impressed by trees*, too." Dean smiles lovingly, and I can't help but smile back.

"*Funny*... But that pinecone just reminded me of something we can do with him back at the cabin after dinner."

"Oh?"

"You wanted more pagan traditions to do with Ace," I say, reaching up to pat his chest. "And you're going to participate, too."

"*Devil shit?*" He smirks.

I roll my eyes at him and slip out of his embrace. "Come on, Ace," I say, "We need to find another special pinecone for later."

He peers up at me curiously. "A special one?"

"That's right... We're going to do some pinecone magic!"

His eyes light up with renewed excitement, and he shoves the pinecone into Dean's hands, then scurries back into the snow to find another.

"We all get to make three wishes," Vanna explains, now that we've finished the baked ziti she made for dinner and washed and dried the dishes. She's got the materials needed for this *Yule pinecone wish spell*, which includes little slips of paper, Ace's colored pencils, and a white candle burning in the center of the table.

"Now, how this works is, we each write our wishes on the slips of paper first. And each color matches your wish. For example, *and to keep this as simple as possible*," Vanna says, holding up the green pencil. "Green is for health and abundance." She places that one down and picks up the others one at a time to explain. "Red is for love, black is for protection, and blue is for peace and trust."

"What's a bun dance?" Ace asks, watching me pick up the green pencil first.

"*Abundance,*" Vanna chuckles. "It means having lots and lots of something really good!"

"What is yellow for?" Ace asks.

"Yellow is for happiness," Vanna explains.

Ace stares at the pencils contemplatively. "I want to wish for a moto-cycle," he announces.

"That's my boy!" I say with pride.

Vanna shakes her head at me, but her smile doesn't falter. "What color motorcycle, Ace?"

"Black like S'reen!" he declares, and Vanna hands him the black pencil.

"I don't want to overcomplicate the whole color idea, but you can also match your colors to your wishes that way, too. Whatever color reminds you of your wish, that's the one you use."

Legion: Book 3

We both help Ace write his wishes down, which also include a Hot-Wheels spiral racetrack tower toy of some sort, and new books for bedtime stories, in the *bun-dance* category.

Vanna is quick to jot her three wishes down, and I'm content with my three wishes centering around the ability to keep my family happy, healthy, safe, and provided for.

"Now, we roll the wishes up, like this," Vanna instructs, using her fingers to roll one of her papers on the table into a cylinder. "We roll the paper toward us to represent bringing our wishes to us."

Ace is determined to do this part for himself, and he manages to, pretty well. At least well enough to move forward to the next step.

"And now we carefully dip the end into the candle wax, like this." Vanna slowly dips an end of one of her wishes into the pool of melted wax on the candle, then brings it to the pinecone, "And we tuck our wishes into the magic pinecone, so they stick inside between the crevices. See? Mommy will help you do yours, sweetie," she says, scooting closer to assist Ace.

"It sticks!" he smiles, grabbing for another one. They both seem to be enjoying this, and that's all I care about.

Once all of our wishes have been placed inside the pinecone, Ace spins it around to inspect our handiwork. "What happens now?" he asks.

"Well, now we put it in the fire so our wishes can float up into the universe and work on coming true," Vanna explains.

"Can I put it in?" Ace eagerly asks.

"Daddy can help you," she says.

Keeping him a safe distance from the fire, I help him with the iron tongs to place it on top of the logs, and we watch our magic pinecone burn together. Vanna slips her hand into mine, gently giving it a little squeeze as she peers up at me with a slight, hopeful smile.

I didn't get a chance to read her wishes, though I did notice she used a pink pencil. I have a sneaky suspicion she also used all three of her slips on the same wish.

A wish I'm still not sure I can grant.

The dull ache in my ribs stirs me from a restless sleep. But it isn't solely the physical pain disrupting my slumber. Sleep eludes me in her absence... Though it's just as well. When she isn't dominating my conscious thoughts, she's haunting my dreams. I suppose I've brought that upon myself as well… Working magic on her subconscious has backfired on my own… *Mr. Complicated*… A smile tugs at the corner of my mouth. Her friend, *Ethan,* called me that…whistled a song as if to playfully provoke her in my presence… So, she's dreamed of me, at least once…and his taunting words and telling smirk led me to believe it was a dream worth telling her friends about…

What I wouldn't do for a peep show in her cerebral cortex…

My own fantasies swirl to the forefront of my mind as I remember what it felt like to pin her against the stone wall of that wine cellar and kiss her…

What her hands felt like on my bare skin as she tended to my wounds…

Like the devious prick I am, I pretended to be asleep a bit longer the last time she came to tend to my injuries. I wanted her to feel at ease in my presence…to prolong the duration of her visit…to feel her cautious, nurturing touches, and savor them.

The fond memories turn bitter as self-loathing creeps back in…

I've brought every shred of misery upon myself. She is my one comfort…but she isn't mine…and Keegan dragged her away.

Though even as I wonder if she wanted to remain at my side, even by some minuscule, subconscious fraction, I also wonder if I'm being delusional. I thought I saw a hesitance in her eyes when he spoke of their cabin getaway… But like the cards laid out on her table depicted…*am I only seeing what I want to see?*

The moment plays over in my mind, analyzing her words and actions before she left me behind… I'm not sure if it's my cracked ribs or the weight of her departure, but it's hard to breathe… I feel like I'm suffocating under the weight of things I never asked for or ever wanted to feel. I tried not to love her… I tried so fucking hard… But I fell, and the torment of affection is more painful than any of the wounds canvasing my body.

Pain and I have always been intimately acquainted, often visiting uninvited, manifesting in cruel and twisted ways. Yet no form has quite compared to the bitter, tormenting sting of unrequited love.

The tremors are starting… Just breathe, you fucking fool! You're not hers to choose! These circumstances are not congruent!

Legion: Book 3

My heart hammers in my chest so hard it might fracture another fucking rib... I can hear it thudding... Can anyone else?

Sweat percolates on my skin, and I reach a shaking hand in the darkness to feel for my cigarettes and Zippo on the nightstand. Fuck opening the window...she's not here...

She's...not...here...

The door creeks on its hinges as I light up and take a cautious, shallow drag from the cigarette. I crack open an eye to see who is disrupting my internal meltdown.

"Oh, good, you're awake," Axel says, stepping all the way into the room. The now familiar aroma of Vanna's pastina soup permeates the air from the bowl he's holding. "I heated some soup up for you. Vanna left it. I've got a little more in the mini fridge in my room, so Viking can't get to it."

She thought to leave me food... The tightness in my chest eases, but I still don't feel much like conversing. Axel flicks on the dim lamp and places the bowl and spoon on the night table beside me.

"You might want to give this a minute to cool off," he rubs his hands on his jeans as he takes a step back. "How are you feeling today?"

I'm mildly surprised by the genuine tone in his words. My eyes are still fairly swollen. If I were to narrow my gaze at him, I might as well close them. I pull another leisurely drag and exhale. At least the young Road Captain is a distraction from my spiraling thoughts.

Axel reaches into the inner pocket of his cut and removes a joint. "I thought maybe you could use some, for the pain, you know," he says, placing it on the bedside table as well.

"Still alive," I reply, wondering if the joint is laced with something and young Axel is attempting to pull a *Stanley* on me. Though it is doubtful. Axel is acutely aware that if I go down, he goes with me.

He takes a seat in the chair against the wall near the foot of the bed, dragging a hand through his hair as he does so. "Yeah, good thing for the both of us," he scoffs, but it's without malice. "Would it change anything if I said I was sorry I burned down your old clubhouse?"

"I knew it was a matter of time before something happened to that shithole." I was banking on it being the Saviors, but any one of the crews we were stringing along could have lost sight of the bigger picture, faux as it had been, along with their already wavering patience. "There was only one thing I was invested in."

"Killing Dean."

"Initially."

"Do you have any regrets?"

"A few."

He hesitates for a moment, then asks, "Did your cabin really get blown up?"

I nod.

He tilts his head slightly as he appraises me. "You don't seem bothered by it."

"I'm a bit of a minimalist," I subtly joke, flicking my cigarette in the ashtray on the edge of the night table. "But I do miss the view."

A sly smirk pulls at the corner of his lips. "The hard copies of the leverage you're holding over me didn't happen to go up in flames, too, did it?"

I grin at the way Axel attempts to disguise his hope within the humor of his inquiry. Pulling another leisurely drag, I let him sweat it out before confessing on a cloud of smoke, "You know, for a brief moment that night...*you* were one of my prime suspects."

Axel manages to keep the smile stitched on, but his honest eyes betray his worry. I slowly shake my head as his shoulders sag ever so slightly. "It's nothing personal, kid… It never was with you."

"Not even when you had that junkie stab me at my first fight?"

"No. Just a means to an end. For whatever it's worth, what I have on you is just an insurance policy. As soon as I work out a better one, you'll be off the hook."

He arches a quizzical brow. "A better one?"

"I can assure you, I've been dedicating my full and unwavering attention to the matter."

He seems to stare more intently at me, his gaze unguarded, and I wonder if his innocence will hinder his ability to grasp my meaning. Keegan, in his paranoia—*granted, it is warranted*—would have already deciphered my meaning.

At Axel's age, I was already well on my way to becoming a hardened criminal. Axel still thinks the world operates on a clear right and wrong basis. He's been alive long enough to know better, though. I fault Keegan and the Saviors for the young man's naivety, how they've managed to safeguard him, keeping him practically unblemished by the wickedness of the world, despite his rough start in life.

"You mean Vanna," he finally says.

"Perhaps I owe you more credit."

He tenses, disturbed by the confirmation, I imagine. Despite his unease, he goes on to press, "I'll take an honest answer in exchange."

"Well…you did save my life, *I suppose…*" I reply, willing to entertain his emboldened request out of sheer curiosity. There's a bit more to the young Road Captain than I originally thought.

He straightens in his seat, squaring his shoulders. "What you said to Cherry… Was any of it true?" His vibrant blue eyes narrow, emphasizing the seriousness of his inquiry. "Did you really not know she was locked down in that basement?"

The cigarette between my fingers warms as I pull another long drag. The ember glows brighter in the dim light. The weight of his question renders us both silent enough to hear the crackling of the burning paper. I exhale the smoke on a sigh as Axel's unwavering blue stare bores into me with a skepticism I've admittedly earned. It's akin to the smoke drifting between us, thick and difficult to see through. I know my words alone may not ever convince him, but perhaps the steady calm behind them might.

"I never knew."

"But you always seem to know everything."

"Do I?" I chuckle, pulling one last drag as he slowly nods, studying me. I carefully move to extinguish the cigarette in the ashtray and exhale a smoky sigh. "Blind trust comes cloaked in the illusion of loyalty… A painful lesson I learned the hard way."

Chapter 33

LEGION

Bracing my hand against the bedside table, I carefully shift to place my feet on the ground. I haven't ventured outside of this room yet, only limped to the attached lavatory when necessary, but if I spend another moment tucked away in this closet, *out of sight, out of mind*, I'm going to *lose* my fucking mind.

My motorcycle boots are beside the bed, and my ribs protest every breath, as I stand and shove my feet into them. I don't risk further injury by bending to tie the laces. I'm not going far. I just need to get outside for a while. Before I do, I turn to the window behind the night table and carefully pull up the old blinds. The stale smell of cigarettes will surely be a deterrent to Vanna when she returns, and the last thing I want to do is repel her.

I unlatch the locking mechanism and shove the window up. Sharp pain tears through my sides as cool air hits me in the chest, nearly causing me to regret the effort. I gaze at the other window on the opposite side of the bed and rule against it. She's due back any time now, and I expect she will be along to check in on me, soon… *I hope…* When she does, I refuse to be the invalid she left behind.

As I stuff my smokes and lighter in the pocket of my sweatpants and step to the door, I spot my leather jacket draped across a chair, immediately noticing it's been cleaned. *Did she do this?* The thought of Vanna tending to my leather eases the slight resentment I've harbored since her departure. It is a line in this MC world…and she crossed it…*for me*. I carefully slip the leather jacket on over my sweatshirt. The welcome weight of it on my shoulders, congruent to the guilt over my bitterness at something she had little choice in. She belongs to Keegan. She did all she could for me...

I run my fingers over the smooth leather covering my arm. The blood, the dirt—all gone. Some harder clubs consider it bad luck. That you're removing the essence of all you've survived. All you've done to get where you are. But I allow what she's done to settle warmly in my chest, choosing to see this as a new beginning. My angel of light...my Goddess...wiping my slate clean.

The cool air hits me once again when I step out onto the back patio, crisp and refreshing against my bruised face. I drag in the breath of a new day, my ribs nearly making me regret it instantly, but I ease myself down into one of the chairs and light up a smoke.

What I can see of the parking lot is empty, aside from the section of lot by Keegan's repair shop. It appears *Mean Dean's Machine Shop* is open for business, and there are a few motorcycles and vehicles parked near the garage doors, my bike among them. The rest of the Saviors MC must have nine-to-fives, and the Twisted Throttle isn't open to the public until three this afternoon, which will be shortly.

So, this is what it's like in a club where everyone works for a living... *Poor bastards...* I wonder how many of them miss the days before redemption.

A little red mustang pulls into the lot near the roadhouse, and the vibrant Cherry scuttles inside with another club girl and a few grocery bags. The slamming of the steel door behind them echoes across the quiet lot.

When the steel door behind me creaks open a few minutes later, the sound of clicking heels on cement follows.

"I thought you might have ventured out here," Cherry says, stepping around the back of the chair to face me. "Are you hungry? I can fix you something."

"Might I trouble you for a ride? I'll make it worth your while if we stop by an ATM along the way."

"*Oh*, umm..." She pulls her own cell out to check the time. "The roadhouse opens in an hour..." The unease in her otherwise friendly tone is evident. I can't blame her.

"How do you feel about loaning me your ride, and I'll go myself?"

She purses her lips, green eyes scanning my visible injuries. "Do *you* think that's a good idea in your condition?"

"Alright... How about I give you my debit card, you run it as credit, and pick up a new cellphone *for* me?"

"They took your phone but didn't take your wallet? That's odd."

"Well, they took the cash I had in it. They took my weapons... They left me with my wallet and my smokes."

"That was an interesting choice," she says with a notable measure of suspicion.

"Actually, it was a message... But the next time I cross paths with them, they will be taking far more."

The apprehensive look on her face morphs to genuine concern, and I'm certain it has everything to do with Axel. "Then maybe you should just stay here. I'll go." She holds her hand out, and I remove my wallet from the inner pocket of my cut to retrieve the card and give it to her. "Any particular model?" she asks, gazing down at the card before her eyes dart back up to meet mine. "*Rusty Gunderson?*"

I simply sit back and watch the kaleidoscope of emotions dance behind her emerald eyes as her mind sorts through all of the theories as to why I have their former Tail Gunner's debit card. I witness the moment her racing thoughts land on hope...

"I'm afraid not," I say, "though it makes sense why you'd come to the conclusion."

She shifts in her boots and swallows before asking, "What conclusion?"

"That Rusty is the one I've entrusted my contingency plan to. He isn't. I have other uses for him."

"Clearly," she says, tapping the card in her hand before tucking it into the back pocket of her skinny jeans. "I should go if I'm going to be back here before Dean gets in."

"They're back?"

"Yes."

I fight the urge to smile. "Then you should hurry."

And I should shower.

*T*he Morning Star Gentlemen's Club... Sierra Vista... Arizona... I type the name of the strip joint Legion claims to have owned and

Legion: Book 3

sold into the web browser on my phone. I haven't had a private moment until now to check without risking Vanna asking any questions. The last thing I want to do is draw her attention to this unnerving connection. My heart sinks as results populate, confirming its existence. I scroll down to the business for sale link and click it. It's listed as off the market and last sold three months ago for...

"*Jesus fuck...*" I drag a hand down my face and pause to grip my ticking jaw as I stare at the seven-figure number on the listing... *The demonic bane of my existence is a fucking millionaire.*

"Dean?" Cherry's voice snaps me out of my trance, and I break my gaze away from the zeros on the screen to face her. She's carrying a plastic shopping bag and her keys in one hand, a debit card in the other. "Legion asked me to pick him up a new cellphone, and he gave me this to make the purchase with."

She strolls up to me and places the debit card down on the bar. I glance at the name, but before I can speak, she does.

"He said Rusty doesn't have the leverage... Do you think he could be lying?" She sounds both hopeful and worried.

"I wouldn't put anything past Legion," I say, picking up the card. She hands me the bag as well, but before I push away from the bar to go confront him about it, she places her hand on my arm to stop me.

"Dean, for whatever it's worth, I believe him about what happened the night he shot Asmodeus. He had no idea about his brother. In his own broken way, he did what he thought was best to keep us all alive. I know he drugged me to spare me the experience of being abducted and having to see that monster again. He did everything for reasons that made sense to him at the time... I'm sorry, but... I forgive him for it."

"But you don't believe him about this?" I ask, holding up the card between my fingers.

She lifts a dainty shoulder in a slight shrug. "Maybe Rusty doesn't have it... But maybe Rusty knows *who does?*"

"I'll find out." And if I can't, Vanna will.

When I shove the door to his room open and enter, Legion is stepping out of the bathroom, in the process of securing a towel around his waist.

"You never struck me as one to share in your Sergeant at Arms' rather odd fascination regarding the substantiality of my cock." He glares at me. "*Or are you simply above knocking before entering?*"

I'm already exhausted, and I haven't been in his presence longer than thirty seconds yet. I chuck the bag with the cellphone on the foot of the bed and hold up the debit card before tossing it onto the bed as well.

"Ah, yes…" Legion grins. "I had a feeling the little pixie may have still been clinging to hope, despite having informed her that *no*… Rusty *is not* the executor of my contingency plan." He pauses to tilt his head, his eyes narrowing as if insulted. "You don't actually believe I could possibly be this careless, do you?"

"You did suffer a concussion. Where is our old pal, Rusty?"

"I can tell you where he isn't. *Bermuda County*. Not after you unceremoniously gave him the boot and a threat never to return." Legion moves to grab the boxers from the folded pile of clothes on the corner of the bed, and I spot something else about him that unnerves me. A tattoo on his lower back… A demon with a tarot card clutched in its talons, depicting a knight in black armor upon a black horse…

I feel like I've just been slugged in the fucking gut… First, the Morning Star connection… *Now this.*

"Do you mind?" Legion growls, and I take the opportunity to turn away from him and gather my composure, playing it off as if I'm granting him privacy to dress. He pulls on the boxers beneath the towel before discarding it to maneuver himself into his jeans.

"Alright, I'm decent," he grunts, a little out of breath from the pain in his ribs, I'm sure. "At least, decent enough."

"That's still debatable," I mutter, shifting to face him once again. He's watching me closely, analyzing me with those piercing, pale eyes.

"How was your little getaway with the family?" he asks with an antagonistic, *knowing* sneer again.

"Just what we needed."

"And has your lovely bride accompanied you here?"

I take a bit of pleasure in telling him, "*No.* She hasn't."

Disappointment flickers behind his stare, but he recovers quickly. "Well, I imagine the young Keegan is tired after the journey home."

"Yeah. Anyway. Is Rusty's number still the same?"

"Why? Would you like to summon him here?"

When I hold his gaze without further comment, Legion lets out a resigned sigh. "Fine. I'll activate the phone and request a meet on your behalf."

"Why don't you activate it later," I say, pulling my phone from my pocket. I unlock the screen and toss it to him. Legion catches it awkwardly against his chest with a grimace. "Use mine. Then finish getting dressed and join me in the bar while we wait for him."

The corner of his mouth pulls into a half-grin. "Afraid I might warn him? *Coach him* before this meet, perhaps?"

"If you really have nothing to hide, it shouldn't be a problem."

Legion dials a number and puts the call on speaker. I watch him closely, but there doesn't seem to be any waver in his demeanor. He's either got one hell of a poker face and ice in his veins, or Rusty really isn't the one safekeeping Legion's leverage. The call picks up on the third ring, and a curious voice through the speakerphone answers, "Hello? *Dean?*"

"He's here as well," Legion replies. "We would like to cordially invite you to an evening at the Twisted Throttle. *Tonight.* ASAP, in fact."

Rusty is silent for a moment, then says, "But Dean said if I ever set foot in Bermuda County again..."

"I'm making an exception tonight," I interrupt. "You have my word, you will not be harmed. I just want a conversation."

"Why now?" Rusty asks, bitterness in his tone. "You wouldn't hear me out three years ago."

"You can come in, Rusty, and make this situation easier on everyone," I say, "*Or we can come find you,* and when we do, I can't guarantee you'll be on the receiving end of the civility I'm assuring you tonight."

"Legion?" Rusty seeks assurances from the demon.

"It's alright," Legion replies. "The bar's open tonight."

"It's a big place..." Rusty hesitates. "I haven't forgotten..."

"All I'm interested in is a conversation, Rusty. I'm ready to hear you out if you're willing to answer the questions I have," I say. "Final offer."

"Alright... I'll head there now. Give me an hour or so," Rusty agrees, and Legion ends the call.

"Satisfied?" Legion tosses the phone back to me.

"We'll see."

Jennifer Saviano

Vanna

The directions are clear: Take the missed dose as soon as you remember, even if it means taking two pills in one day. If it's been longer, consider an emergency contraceptive if you have had unprotected sex in the days prior to your missed dose... Well, it hasn't been that long, and a Plan B pill is out of the question.

I lift my eyes from the package of contraceptives in my hand and stare into the mirror. I didn't mean to forget. I took my dose the morning we left for the cabin. Out of habit, I simply placed them back in the bathroom drawer and forgot to pack them. It was an accident... But my fingers remain frozen on the plastic and foil-encased pill pinched between them. I just have to press it out...put it in my mouth...and swallow. Simple. Routine. I've been doing it for weeks... Nearly two months now... Since that day on the porch when Dean was so adamant about what he didn't want...

One missed dose—which was an accident—isn't a big deal. But skipping the backup...is a conscious choice...

Take it... Dean would tell me to take it.

My fingers tighten, and the foil splits, freeing the pill. I lift my hand to my mouth and just as I'm about to press the pill past my lips, it slips, landing with a soft *plink* in the sink.

I lower my gaze to the little white pill teetering on the edge of the drain.

I didn't mean to drop it... At least, I don't think I did...

The longer I stare at it, the more I feel the urge to turn on the faucet...just for a second...and walk away...

Ace and I have dinner together alone. Dean decided to go over to the clubhouse early to check in with Derek and the workload at his repair shop, before spending some time at the Twisted Throttle. I wouldn't go so far as to say he insisted Ace and I stay home tonight, but he made it a point to mention *it would be alright if we did.*

I expected Ace to be tired after dinner. Especially after the long ride home earlier today. He did nap for a majority of the journey, I suppose. Now, Ace is sprawled out on his belly beneath the Christmas tree, completely lost in his own little world as he lines up his toy cars and motorcycles along the edge of the tree skirt. Nico is curled up asleep beside him, unconcerned with anything beyond the warmth of the lights and the soft, murmuring engine sounds Ace is making while he plays.

I should feel settled in this peaceful, golden glow. Soak in the calm of our quiet moment at home. But my mind is elsewhere.

I didn't say anything for the sake of keeping the peace, especially in front of our son, but I know Dean doesn't want me to check in on Legion, to give Legion the impression I care. But I do care, and the thought of my absence convincing Legion I don't, bothers me more with every passing moment. He doesn't deserve to feel forgotten.

Dean won't like it, but he won't make an issue of it, not in front of his crew and especially not in front of Ace, who I'm sure would love to see a few of his biker Uncles.

I chew my bottom lip, staring at Ace for a moment before I cave and ask him, "Are you tired, sweetheart?"

"No," he says simply.

"Do you want to go see Uncle Viking at Daddy's bar?"

His big brown eyes light up, and he scrambles to his feet. "Yeah!"

I park my SUV beside Serene in her usual spot near Dean's repair shop, and glance in the rearview mirror. The neon sign of the Twisted Throttle casts a glow over the motorcycles and trucks parked closer to the roadhouse. Ace wiggles in his car seat, eager to get out.

"Hang on, sweetie, I'm coming," I chuckle, unbuckling my seatbelt to get him.

All of the ranking members of the Saviors MC's bikes are parked further down the lot, closest to the back entrance by the patio. Ace and I walk hand-in-hand to the steel door.

When we step inside the bar, we're met with the usual mix of laughter, boisterous conversation, clinking pool balls, and rock music coming from the jukebox. I'm happy to see the increase in patronage, but surprised we aren't greeted by Viking in his usual spot near the front entrance. Perched on his stool and taking up the position of bouncer tonight is the biker they've all come to call *Ford Focus*.

"Heyyyy, little man!" A big smile takes over his somewhat stern expression when he spots Ace and I walking in. Ford Focus leans down to offer Ace a low-five as we approach. Ace laughs and releases my hand to eagerly slap the biker's. Ford Focus chuckles and straightens to address me. "And our First Lady, always a pleasure to see you, Vanna."

"I didn't know the guys were meeting tonight," I say, speaking a little louder to be heard over the music.

"Weren't supposed to be, but that guy's to blame," Ford Focus replies, cocking his chin in the direction of the bar.

I turn to scan the row of patrons. Sitting at the bar, a few stools away from the regulars, is Legion. He's alone, swirling an amber liquid in a glass before he takes a sip, his shoulders hunched slightly under his leather jacket. The lights above the bar illuminate the demon skull rocker on his back, far more vibrant now that I cleaned the grit and grime out of the white embroidery.

"He's got some fuckin' balls wearing that shit in here," Ford Focus growls, then quickly apologizes for his choice of words in front of my son. Ace doesn't seem to be paying attention, though. He's preoccupied, searching the room for the familiar faces of his uncles. There are a few prospects dispersed throughout the room, helping Ford Focus keep an eye on things, but Ace doesn't know them well, and they know better than to approach us before the club deems them fully trustworthy.

Three of the patch-chasers running drinks for Cherry tonight come by to fuss over Ace and how he looks more and more like Dean every time they see him. The cooing and giggling of the women draws Legion's attention, and a slow, deliberate smile stretches his mouth when our eyes meet. He still looks a little rough, but I'm glad to see him up and about.

"Excuse us," I say to the women, picking up Ace and shifting him to my hip as I make my way across the room. I wave to Cherry, who is busy pouring shots for a few patrons at the end of the bar opposite Legion. Ace hasn't spotted Cherry or Legion yet, still busy scanning the crowded room, mostly likely for Viking. Legion repositions himself on his barstool to face me, just as Ace turns and realizes his *magic friend* is here.

"*Legend!*" he squeals with excitement. Before I can stop him, Ace lunges forward, nearly tumbling from my grasp.

Legion: Book 3

My heart seizes and I gasp aloud, "*Ace!*", but Legion moves fast, catching my son and clutching him protectively to his chest as Ace, oblivious to the fact he could have been seriously injured, wraps his little arms gleefully around Legion's neck. I grip the empty barstool beside me to catch my breath and attempt to recover from the near heart attack.

"It's alright, sweet one, I've got him," Legion says, though I notice he's wincing through his otherwise reassuring smile.

"Oh no, your ribs," I wince along with him, "I'm sorry, I had no idea he would do that. Here, let me take him," I say, stepping forward to lift Ace from his lap, who doesn't seem to want to leave Legion.

"Are you from Hades?" Ace asks him, refusing to let go. The question broadens Legion's smile, but I apologize anyway.

"Let go of the kid," Ford Focus growls, suddenly beside us, "Or I'll break those evil hands you've done God-knows-what with."

Legion loosens his hold on Ace but keeps his hands hovering close enough to Ace's back in case he should tumble again.

"Take him," Ford Focus orders me as if I'm one of the patch-chasers they boss around. I'm not impressed with his tone, but don't want this to escalate. I attempt to gently pull Ace from Legion's lap again.

"No!" Ace protests, his little fingers gripping onto Legion's jacket.

"You know," Legion says, his voice carrying a hint of resentment as he glares at Ford Focus. "kids are generally good judges of character."

"Sounds like something a groomer would say," Ford Focus mutters, and my heart rate skyrockets again. I can practically feel the murderous rage radiating off of Legion.

"*That's enough!*" I snap, glaring briefly at Ford Focus. I'm afraid to even look at Legion while I gently pry Ace's fingers from his jacket and pull him back into my arms.

"Is everything okay over here?" Cherry asks, stepping over to us on the other side of the bar. She smiles and waves at Ace, but I can tell in her eyes, she can feel the tension when she looks at me. "Do you want me to take him?" she asks. "The guys are in Church, I can bring Ace to the gym to play or just to Dean's room?"

"Sure," I say, "I'll handle the bar."

"No need," Cherry says, whistling at one of the patch-chasers. "I'm due for a break. Maxie can handle it until I come back." Her gaze shifts to Ford Focus as she walks around the bar to take Ace from me. "You should probably go back to your post," she says to him.

"I'm gonna have to tell Dean about this," Ford Focus says, more so to me, like I've done something wrong.

"I'll handle it." I frown at him. Ford Focus glares at Legion once more before he walks away.

"Should I even ask?" Cherry glances at Legion as he turns back to his drink and downs it.

"*Please don't,*" he growls.

Cherry takes Ace through the corridor beyond the bar. Once they're out of sight, I step closer to Legion and cautiously touch his arm. He's already tense and nearly flinches.

"*Probably shouldn't do that...* It is no doubt another *transgression* that will be promptly reported to the *good warden.*" He taps the bottom of his glass on the bar, grabbing Maxie's attention. She retrieves the bottle of whiskey from the shelf and saunters over to him.

"Another Whiskey, neat?" she bats her eyes, but her flirtatious efforts go unnoticed. His gaze is locked on the empty glass.

"Do you want to talk?" I ask, but he says nothing, so I nod for Maxie to pour him the drink. The moment she does, he lifts the glass and downs it, then slides it back to her.

"Put it on my tab. I'm going out for a smoke." Legion gets up from the bar, and I take a step back to give him some room.

"Let's go to the back patio," I suggest, not wanting to walk past Ford Focus by the front door.

"After you," Legion gestures toward the corridor.

Once we're clear of the bar and walking side by side down the hallway, I ask him how he's feeling.

"*How am I feeling...*" he mutters, tone dripping with resentment. I thought getting Legion away from Ford Focus would have helped ease the tension, but as I keep pace beside him, it only seems to intensify. I peer up at him. He's staring straight ahead, jaw locked, hands curled into fists at his sides.

I know that word cut him. Legion may be a killer. A man who has done unspeakable things. But harming a child is not something he is, or ever was, capable of.

I can practically feel the heat rolling off of him. The nearer we get to the back patio door, the slower his pace becomes, until we stop at the hall that leads to the gym and the War Room. He turns to glare down it. I don't hear Ace or Cherry in the gym playing on any of the equipment, so she must have taken him to Dean's or her and Axel's room.

"Legion?" I say his name questioningly.

"You'll have to excuse me, sweet one," he growls, then storms toward the War Room.

"*Wait!*" I hurry after him, unsure of what exactly he's going to do, but the anger in his expression is a clear indication it isn't anything good. He stands before the closed double doors. I can hear the men inside talking as Legion's shoulders tighten and he drags in a hissing breath. "*Don't!*" I warn, but he's beyond hearing me.

With one sharp kick, the doors burst open, slamming against the walls with a force that silences the entire room for a split second, before I hear the sound of chairs scraping against the floor as the men inside jump to their feet.

"What the fuck?" Viking's voice booms loudest, "You're gonna fucking pay for that!"

"I'm confident your president is well aware of the fact I can more than afford it!" Legion's voice dips dangerously low when he demands, "You want to tell me why your men think they can talk to me like I'm some *fucking chomo?*" Though he's clearly enraged, I can still hear the hurt in his words. "I've killed men for far less than the constant disrespect I've tolerated from you and your crew for the sake of our truce."

"Is that what we're calling *coercion*, now?" Dean sneers back at him.

"I murdered my own brother *for you!* I decimated my crew *for you!* I got my ass fucking pummeled *for you!*" Legion snaps.

"*For me?*" Dean scoffs. "*Really?* We both know that's a fucking lie."

"Damien…" I whisper, "Damien, come with me, please."

"Who's out there with you?" Dean demands, and I brace myself when I hear the heavy thud of his motorcycle boots round the table and approach the busted doorway.

"Vanna?" Dean's angry expression instantly transitions to surprised concern when he steps into the hall. "I thought you were staying home with Ace tonight?"

"He…he wanted to see his uncles… I didn't know there was a club meeting tonight," I stammer.

His gaze shifts between me and Legion. "What the fuck happened?" Dean asks, but Legion remains silent.

"Ace tried to jump out of my arms, but Legion caught him. Your bouncer for the night had a few choice words over it," I explain. "I wasn't thrilled with the way he spoke to me either."

Dean's stare narrows. "He disrespected you?"

"I don't know if I'd describe it that way, as far as what he said to me. But with Legion—" I begin to say when Dean interrupts.

"I don't give a fuck about Legion."

"Well, you should," I press, a bit aggravated. I square my shoulders and continue. "What I witnessed was wrong, and Legion should not be subjected to that type of disrespect, especially when you all know by now what was said couldn't be farther from who he is."

Dean glances at Legion, and when he does, I can't help but peer up at Legion, too. The hardness in his eyes has softened a bit, and he turns slightly to offer me a subtle nod in appreciation.

"Let's discuss this later," Dean says.

"With me? Fine. But while you already have everyone together, why don't you lay down that law now? Because if I ever hear an accusation like this again…" I shake my head, giving all within earshot a moment to let my request sink in. "*I just might forget my place.*"

"Alright," Dean nods, "Legion, why don't you give us a few minutes to wrap up and—"

Before Dean can finish, Legion turns and brushes past me to head for the hall, but I hear his barely audible whisper as he does. A strangled, simple, "*Thank you.*"

"Damien, wait," I begin to follow him, but Dean grabs my hand, and I turn to face him. "Stop. We'll have a conversation later. Can't you see he's hurt?"

Dean releases me, and I hurry after Legion. I didn't hear the back patio door open, so he must have gone back to the bar to wait like Dean asked.

As I round the corner of the corridor, expecting to find him on the barstool being attended to by his new admirer, Maxie, I realize there's a slight commotion in the bar. A couple of guys are laughing, pointing toward the steel door. I realize Ford Focus is holding his jaw, wearing a stunned, but also pained expression.

"What just happened?" I ask the blonde bartender.

Legion: Book 3

"Legion slugged Ford before he left like he was punching out on a Friday night headed for a hot date!" Maxie laughs. "I thought about callin' after him, *I'm right here, baby!* But he kind of scares me a little... I haven't decided yet if it's in a good way."

I didn't need to know all that. "Great," I sigh, hurrying to the door. Though I'm still annoyed with the way Ford Focus spoke to me earlier, I ask if he's alright. He nods, and I shove through the steel door. The cool night air slaps me in the face. Legion is already swinging his leg over his motorcycle across the lot, and he fires it up.

"Legion, wait!" I call out to him, but my voice is drowned out by the roar of his engine as he twists the throttle and takes off, barreling through the gates and into the city streets.

DEAN

Vanna's sitting alone on the leather couch, staring at the Christmas tree in our living room when I step through the front door. "Ace is sleeping," she tells me.

"Thought you were gonna stick around," I say, shrugging out of my leather and hanging it up on the rack. I remove my boots at the door as well, before joining her on the couch. "Are you pissed at me?"

"No," she says, leaning forward to place her phone on the slate coffee table. "Legion isn't answering calls or texts."

"They took his phone, doll," I remind her. "If he activated the new phone, I'm sure he's got a new number."

"Oh...right. I forgot." She sighs, then asks, "Did you talk to your MC?"

I nod. "Talked to Ford Focus too... He doesn't seem to think he was in the wrong about anything he said or did."

"Jerk," she mumbles.

"You wanna give me your version of events? I can't allow anyone to disrespect my woman. My queen. Our First Lady."

"Oh, you mean my voice counts for something?" she snarkily comments.

"Vanna, you know it does. And had you stuck around, I could have dealt with it then and there."

She lets out another frustrated sigh. "It was more so his tone. Like he was ordering me to do something like some of these guys talk to the patch-chasers."

"What did he tell you to do?"

Her pretty eyes narrow at me. *"It was his tone."* I wait patiently for her to elaborate, and she finally does. "After he called Legion *a groomer*, which by the way, is a terrible thing to say to someone *who actually is a victim!* He told me to take Ace from him, and then, like I was being written up or something for some kind of *bullshit misconduct*, he said he was going to *have to tell you about this."*

"Alright… I'm sorry you took offense. I'll speak with him the first chance I get."

"Good," she grumbles, shifting on the couch to place her feet in my lap. "I thought you were going to stay until closing tonight."

"You were upset. I wanted to come to you as soon as possible," I say, placing my hand on her shin to stroke her leg over her velour pajama pants.

"I really don't like the abuse Legion is subjected to," she says.

"Legion's done a lot to warrant it, baby."

She shakes her head. "Not when it comes to this kind of thing. Don't you remember how that particular *C-word* made you feel? And not to diminish what you went through, or excuse those who took part in it, but there's a difference between kink-shaming someone and accusing someone of a heinous crime involving children. Neither is okay, but one is clearly worse. If you truly believed Legion was capable of that, you would never have permitted him anywhere near us."

"I distinctly recall threatening his life if he did. That fucking leverage he's holding over us forced some leniency."

She gives me a wry look. "You don't believe he'd ever hurt a child."

"I don't know him, Vanna. And to be frank, neither do you."

"I know he's not one of those monsters."

"There's no way to *know* that."

"In my soul, I do. He'd kill himself before he'd ever do anything to harm a kid."

"You trust him enough to leave Ace alone with him?" I press her and silently pray for a little sanity here.

"No," she says, *thank the fucking Gods.* "But I wouldn't leave Ace with anyone besides Viking, Cherry, and Axel. Or Viper and Rosita. I don't think Diesel or Chopper or Dozer would ever harm Ace, either. It's just something I wouldn't do."

"Well, I'm glad we're on the same page."

Her head tilts slightly as she continues to stare at me. "Do you think I'm a bad mother?"

"Fuck no, Vanna. Where do you come up with this shit?"

"You don't want another kid with me," she starts, and I'm about to begin praying again. "I almost lost Ace at the Halloween shop. I almost dropped him, and he would have split his damn head open on the floor at the Twisted Throttle if Legion hadn't caught him."

"Vanna, kids pull stunts like this. It comes with the job. I think you're the best mother Ace could ever ask for." I sigh, then pull out my cellphone to check the tracking on a gift for him I'm hoping arrives by tomorrow. "Speaking of Ace splitting his head open, I ordered him a new helmet for Christmas to match his new bike."

"His new bike?"

"Viking put it up in the attic while we were at the cabin. He's gonna help me bring it down tomorrow night so you can wrap it in time for Christmas morning. We'll just hide it in our closet until then."

"*You two got him a motorcycle?*"

"A black one, looks like a miniature Serene, only Axel airbrushed the Saviors MC rocker on the tank. He's gonna lose his damn mind when he sees it. Viking's spending the night so he can see Ace's face when he opens it."

"I'm sure he's going to be thrilled, but... how fast does it go? He can't even ride a bicycle yet."

"Don't worry, I won't take off the governor until he can handle it, and it's got a set of detachable training wheels, too."

"How fast, Dean?"

"I can run faster, don't worry. It doesn't go over ten miles per hour, and he'll only be able to ride it when he's around me, okay?"

"Oh god, what if he falls?"

"He's probably gonna."

"*Dean!*"

"Kids fall, doll. You just have to gaslight them, dust off their asses, and put them back on the bike. He's gonna love it."

She shakes her head, but then finally admits, "He will love it. But you're all still insane." She shifts her position on the couch to sit beside me, and I drape an arm around her as she rests her head against me. "What was the meeting about tonight? Seemed important."

"Rusty. He came by to clear some things up about his dealings with Legion. Apparently, in exchange for some banking assistance, Legion is footing the expenses for Rusty's mother's medical bills. He still claims he never meant to hurt the MC. Wants us to reconsider letting him back in as a prospect again."

To my surprise, she doesn't comment or ask any questions. For a little while, we sit in silence, letting the quiet moment settle between us as we admire the golden-hued lights and ornaments on the Christmas tree. My gaze travels up to the star glowing at the top, and I feel the familiar block of ice forming in the pit of my stomach again as Legion's tattoo and taunting words play over in my mind.

"Dean?" Her voice breaks the stillness, soft but laced with a measure of anxiety as if she can sense my own.

"Yeah, doll?"

"What if Legion doesn't come back?"

If only...

"If it wasn't for the leverage situation, I'd say it would be fuckin' Aces, baby... We've got a standing truce with these drug runners to keep their shit out of our county and away from the Jokers' clubhouse. I can't save the world, doll. All I can do is keep you and Ace safe and our county clean to the best of our ability."

"You really don't trust him at all?"

"I trust that we share this common goal. Beyond that, baby...lies a really big leap of faith I'm not sure either of us is capable of making."

LEGION

The bass feels like it's vibrating my ribcage, still sore from the ride out to the Raunch Ranch. The lights paint the stage in pulsing red and blue like a crime scene, while I nurse another drink I really don't want. This joint reeks of whiskey and cheap perfume, mixed with sweat and desperation...and I wonder if the latter is me. I grip the glass, keeping my eyes locked on the stage as the music pounds, dulling the edges of my thoughts, but not enough. Not nearly enough.

Puppet moves like she was made for this. Every twist of her hips, every teasing slip of fabric designed to drag bills from wallets and make men forget themselves. But I don't forget. I remember everything in painful detail.

I should be concerned over who else might be watching her...*waiting for me*... Though I have been granted a stay of execution.

Legion: Book 3

Even if that weren't the case, I don't care. I feel too empty to care. I tell myself I'm only here to meet Rusty, to find out what little he told Keegan, to distract myself while I wait…that watching Puppet shed her clothes and her dignity, is some kind of twisted way to reclaim my pride…to remind myself I'm still the man I've always been, *un-fucking-touchable*.

Except that isn't true anymore…and there's another woman to blame… *Vanna…*

I hate that I give a fuck what she thinks of me, what anyone in that crew thinks of me. I let the shame crawl under my skin when she defended me in front of Keegan, like I needed saving, like I was fucking weak.

I take another drink, choking down the rage I still feel at what that little prick bouncer insinuated. I wanted to slash his throat and spray the bar with his blood. I know what I am. A bastard. A criminal. A killer. A man who never believed in redemption until I looked in *her* eyes…

Fuck… She knows I'm not that kind of monster… And maybe she doesn't think I'm beyond saving…

Perhaps this isn't reality, though. Perhaps this is simply the *Seven of Cups…*

Reality is Puppet on stage, peeling away the last scraps of lace…locking eyes with me as I lift my glass in salute of her degradation. She smirks at me like she knows why I'm here.

I force a smirk back because I know she doesn't. Not the entire scope of our demented dynamic, anyway. She slides down to her knees, hands trailing up her body, into her long, black hair, putting on a show…and I pretend I'm not drowning.

CHAPTER 34

Vanna

The snow is sticking. This is the first time, at least since I've been here, where the flakes are beginning to blanket the lawn, trees, and the swing-set Dean built for Ace last Christmas, in pure white. I smile at the thought of Ace's excitement, waking up to an actual white Christmas, along with the evidence of Santa's visit. Not only because there will be more presents under the tree, but Viking plans to stomp around in his big boots to leave imprints in the snow on our front porch for Ace to discover. Wrapping the Saviors MC Fleece around myself, I curl up in an Adirondack with my warm mug of chai tea and settle in to watch the snowflakes fall in the night.

I rest my head against the back of the chair and watch the fluffy snowflakes swirl beneath the glow of the floodlight in the backyard. The crisp silence is so peaceful, and such a contrast to only a few hours ago. Dean promised we would only have happy memories of Christmas Eve, and tonight was full of laughter, warmth, and the easy kind of chaos that comes with having a house full of bikers and their loved ones. Everyone had come and gone by now. Everyone, but Legion.

I let out another slow breath and watch the steam curl into the cold air. It's only been a day since he stormed out of the Twisted Throttle, but he's made no attempt to reach out to anyone, not even me. Every time I think about the exchange between him and Ford Focus, my stomach sinks. Legion didn't deserve such terrible treatment, especially not after preventing Ace from getting hurt. I hate the idea of him sitting alone somewhere, convinced no one is even thinking of him… That no one sees him trying… I see it.

I remove the little wrapped box from my pocket and place it on the side table to my left. Legion isn't coming. He may have even left for good… And the sorrow the thought stirs inside me mixes with the guilt nagging at my conscience.

As the temperature continues to drop, I wrap myself tighter in the blanket and close my eyes. What had started off as puffy snowflakes for the first while are becoming a bit icier, and now sound faintly like falling sand.

I don't hear the crunch of footsteps in the snow until they are a few yards before me. This time, I'm not startled by his abrupt presence when he approaches from the darkness. I'm relieved, and happier to see him than I should admit.

"I didn't think you were going to make it tonight," I say.

Legion stops walking when he reaches the foot of the porch steps in front of me, a light dusting of snow coating the shoulders of his leather jacket, and the hood pulled up over his head.

"Were you hoping I would?" he asks, though I'm not able to detect whether his words were spoken in sarcasm or sincerity.

"I didn't even hear your bike pull up out front… How come you didn't ring the front doorbell?"

"I ordered a ride. They dropped me at the end of your driveway… And, the *science of silence*, sweet one, dictates as a general rule that the atmospheric conditions of this cold night have increased the air density, which in turn makes it harder for soundwaves to travel…" I can almost make out the playfully sarcastic little sneer on his mouth as he explains the effect of snow and the absorption of sound.

"Thank you, *professor*. I think I understand," I smirk back at him. "Let's skip to the last question, please."

His cockiness seems to dissipate a bit. "I debated whether or not to disrupt your night." He removes something from beneath his leather jacket, holding it in front of himself awkwardly within his gloved hands. It's a flat box, packaged in what looks like shiny black wrapping paper with gold ribbon and a matching bow. "I was going to leave this for you to find…"

"You got me a Christmas gift?"

"Yule... Christmas... I have... And something for Ace, as well... You can tell him it's from *Old Saint Nick*, if you...do not wish for him to know I—"

"Damien..." I sigh. His sudden awkwardness is such a contrast from his usual demeanor, it tugs at my heart. His chin lifts from beneath the hood, and I know he's looking at me more intently now. I wonder if he's afraid I'm going to tell him to get lost and take his gifts with him. "Come up here, get out of the snow before I have to tell Ace you're *Frosty the Snowman.*"

Legion walks up the steps and comes to stand before me, pushing back his hood as he hands me the prettily wrapped gift. The weight of the box surprises me, and I rest it against my lap. It looks like a box that might contain a set of pretty gloves and a scarf, but whatever is inside is far heavier than any type of clothing accessory he might have purchased.

"Would you like to sit down?" I nod to the other Adirondack beside me.

Wordless, he takes a seat, spotting the little gift-wrapped box on the table between us. He clears his throat before saying, "I'm sure it will pale in comparison to whatever Keegan gifted you in that little jewelry box, but... I do hope you like it, just the same."

I suppress a smile at his assumption about the gift I actually got for him. "Are you sure you don't want me to wait until Christmas morning?"

He slowly shakes his head. "I think I would like to see you open it."

"I've always favored Christmas Eve, anyway." I smile at him, curious as to what he could have possibly gotten for me.

"The festive spirit... Time spent with the chosen... The heavy dose of anticipation?" he smiles back.

"There is an energy on Christmas Eve. It builds from the beginning of Yuletide. You don't feel it?"

"I do, this night... Open it." He cocks his chin at the gift in my lap.

I carefully untie the gold ribbon, peeling the thick cellophane wrapping back carefully. After lifting the top of the box off, I place it beside me on the table and unfold the tissue paper within to reveal a round, black disc.

"A scrying mirror?"

"Obsidian, yes," Legion replies. "We conversed about them once."

I glance up at him curiously. "We did?"

"That night…on the pier…" his tone seems a bit more deflated in a way.

I try to think back to what our conversation could have been three years ago.

"I'd asked if you'd ever used one."

"I haven't."

"I know. You said they were very expensive… Well, now you don't have to worry about it."

"Damien…" I don't know what else to say. Refusing his gift might hurt or offend him, but a real Obsidian scrying mirror, bigger than my face, certainly was expensive. I run my fingers across the smooth surface. "You didn't have to do this…"

"You have nothing to fear, you know."

When I peer up at him quizzically, he lets out another defeated sigh.

"You told me you were afraid of what you might see… There is no real darkness within you, sweet one."

"I don't know about that."

"You'd never harm anyone, unless it was in defense of a loved one… *That doesn't count.*"

"Well, thank you… This was very…thoughtful, Damien… And a little ironic."

"Ironic?"

After wrapping the Obsidian scrying mirror safely in its box for now, I lift the much smaller giftbox from the table between us and hold it out to him.

"This is actually for you." I smile.

His eyes widen in genuine surprise, but he doesn't move to take it.

"It's not a bomb…or a…*body part.*" I almost wince through my own halfhearted attempt at a dark joke.

Timorously, he finally takes the little box from me, resting it against his knee.

Jennifer Saviano

LEGION

I hadn't anticipated she would give me something. And although I am, for the most part, pleasantly surprised... A part of me...the broken, pessimistic part of me fixates on the fact that the only other women in my life to have ever gifted me anything eventually plunged a knife through my heart.

I force myself to chuckle at her pointed comment and proceed to open her gift. Lifting the necklace by its tightly braided leather cord, I inspect the dangling pendant in the light emanating through a window behind us.

A raw black tourmaline crystal set in silver with an accent stone which looks to be a polished quartz, or perhaps Selenite. It's difficult to identify in this low light. I rest the pendant in my hand, brushing a thumb over the small stone.

"Is this polished one quartz?"

"Rose quartz," she says, as if such a stone bears no significance at all.

I swallow before I speak, "Rose quartz... for?"

"Love." Again, she replies as if the word doesn't carry weight or worth.

"... Love?"

"I thought you could use some *fluffier energies* around you."

"Ah..." I nod, patting myself on the back for disallowing my emotions to get the better of me in her presence.

"You don't like it?" The hint of disappointment in her tone jabs at something inside of me, and my mind races to find the words to fix it while she goes on. "It's okay if you don't... I just thought that—"

"*I do like it...* I simply did not *expect* it."

"Oh... Well... I picked it up at that little shop in Southport," she chuckles, "Actually, we bumped into each other right outside it. Laura and Ethan were with me... I got you this as well." She produces a small glass bottle. "In case you ever want to try again."

"Try again?" I ask, twisting in my seat to get a better look at the label in the light through the window. Mullen, for detoxification of the lungs... I immediately recall her arms wrapped around me the night she insisted I mattered...

"So, you saw this and instantly thought of me, did you?" I attempt to pull the shielding cloak of arrogance around me once again. "And such a distance to travel. I am touched, Vanna."

Her gaze lowers from mine. "For a moment there, I thought you were serious. You don't have to be a dick about it."

Fuck... Too far.

"I'm not... I...I mean, I am...*serious*. Not a dick... Although I suppose that's highly subjective..." *Blundering idiot.* "My apologies, sweet one. I am simply not accustomed to receiving gifts. It's been quite a while... The better part of a decade, in fact..."

"Just say *thank you*."

"Thank you."

"You're welcome." She lifts her eyes, and another smile finally graces her lovely lips. I can breathe a little easier once more. "I hope you consider trying again."

"Why does that feel like a loaded request?"

She shrugs, "Probably because it is."

"Did you enjoy your excursion to Southport?" I ask, switching gears.

"It made me miss it." She sighs. "The Ametrine Cauldron... I know I didn't make a whole lot of money there with just Reiki appointments and the occasional card reading when Laura wasn't in. But I really loved it there. You know how people say, if you do what you love, it never feels like a job? I really had that there. Most days, anyway."

"I had to do what I did... You weren't safe there... And I had to make it look like retaliation."

She stares at me for a moment, then goes on as if I hadn't said anything at all. "For a while, Laura toyed with the idea of rebuilding and starting up again. She decided she was too close to retirement age. She sat on the property for a few months before deciding to sell it. It went pretty quick. She used the money to buy herself that dream cottage on the beach. Can't say I blame her. Sometimes I wonder what business is going to go up there. The lot is in the historical district, so whatever is built on the property has to come close to the original structure. Laura said it's just about finished, but I haven't driven by."

"Why not?"

She shrugs, pulling the blanket around herself, and I wonder if she's getting too cold. "It might make me sad. Like looking at the ghost of someone I used to know. It won't be the Ametrine Cauldron.

The property is commercial, so maybe it will be lawyers' offices, or a hair salon, or something, now that it has all new plumbing… I'll go back there…one day."

Her little sniffle solidifies my decision. The time has come for me to depart. "The temperature continues to drop. Get back inside, sweet one, before Santa brings you a cold for Christmas."

"Have you eaten tonight?" she asks, her hopeful tone taking me by surprise yet again. "We still have some food from tonight. And homemade eggnog… Not that eggnog is my forte. *Fair warning.*"

"I have not."

"Well, you must be hungry. It has to be after nine already," she says, situating herself to rise with her gift and blanket in hand before she stands and walks past me to the door.

I shove the giftbox into my pocket and quickly undo the clasp of the necklace. Standing as I secure her gift around my neck, I notice she's smiling at me again.

"It's backwards. The rose quartz is the accent piece. It's supposed to stand out," she explains.

"I think I like it better against my skin."

"*Or you don't like pink.*"

"Come now, Vanna… Wouldn't you guess pink is one of my favorite colors?" I tease.

She rolls her eyes at me, placing her hand on the doorknob before she twists it slowly. "*Ace is asleep.*"

I nod in acknowledgement of her maternal warning, quietly following her inside her warm abode and toward the spacious front rooms of their home. The kitchen island is lined with a few covered trays. The flat screen above the smoldering fireplace in the living room is playing some MMA fight.

Keegan and his Sergeant at Arms stand up from the couch as we enter, looking none too pleased to see me.

"I thought you went to bed," Keegan's gaze drifts to Vanna, and he steps around the couch to approach us. "I didn't know you went outside." He seems disturbed by the revelation.

"*Ace is sleeping,*" Vanna says again, placing her gift on the kitchen island.

"Speaking of Ace," I say, removing an enveloped card from my inner pocket. "This is for him."

Keegan snatches it from my hand, prompting a disapproving little glare from Vanna, which in turn brings his level of aggression to a low simmer. "Fine. You can go now."

"Come on, Dean. He just got here. Let him eat something," Vanna insists on my behalf. "Look at him, he's practically an icicle."

"*That's got little to do with the weather.*" Keegan glares at me, stepping closer to the kitchen island in order to inspect the gift I gave her. "What is this? *A black hole?*"

"From Legion, *that tracks*," Viking jokes, reclaiming his seat in the leather armchair.

"*Touché.*" I grin.

Vanna steps close to stand between us, arms crossed, gaze shifting back and forth like she's waiting for one of us to ruin something. "We need to put certain things behind us," she says, voice steady but laced with something softer... *A plea.* "We're all on the same side, whether you two like it or not."

I don't bother glancing at Keegan. I don't have to. I can feel his reluctance in the heavy silence. He exhales sharply, and I know he'll agree. He loves her.

"*For you,*" Keegan finally concedes. Though it's more so in surrender than agreement.

When I spare him a glance, there is no camaraderie, just the bitter acknowledgment of the one thing we do have in common...

Her.

"You have my sworn allegiance, sweet one... An allegiance which extends to your husband and his cause," I promise, reaching into my leather jacket once more. "And perhaps this gesture will solidify your trust in my commitment to this alliance."

Keegan cocks a skeptical brow at me as I hand him a small velvet box. "Is this going to blow up?" he sarcastically inquires, leaning past Vanna to place his half-empty beer on the marble island.

I patiently wait for him to open it.

When he does, his suspicious glare softens, and he glances back at me. "Your leverage, I presume?" he says, showing Vanna the SD card within. A little gasp brushes past her lips.

I nod once, but for all the relief in his eyes, there is something else, too. Something sharper. Something resentful. Not because I had held this over him and his MC, but because we both know why I am giving it up. I'm not doing this for him. I'm doing it for her. She is my shield, and this fact burns him more than anything else ever could. I see it in the way his stubbled jaw tightens, in the way his gaze shifts to her.

We both know she doesn't even realize it. She's too relieved by my *grand gesture* to sense the way the air has turned razor-sharp between he and I. He's well aware of the fact that it isn't respect or loyalty that keeps me in check. It's her. The one person in the world I will never betray. The one person I will burn for.

I meet his stare head-on, allowing him to see it in my eyes. Even without leverage, I will always be here.

Not as his enemy.

Not as his friend.

But as the man who will never stop loving his wife and doing whatever is necessary to prove it to her.

She smiles at me, eyes glassy with gratitude and completely unaware of the power she wields over us both. *"I'm so proud of you,"* she says on a trembling whisper, and I can tell it's with great effort she does not embrace me again in front of her husband. Perhaps on some subconscious level, she does recognize his renewed desire to blow my head off. "Please, come, sit down. Let me fix you a plate," she insists, rubbing her husband's arm for a brief moment to quell his murderous rage permeating the atmosphere. We both watch her scurry into the kitchen.

I slide my gaze back to Keegan and smile as I step around him to join his wife. *"Merry Christmas and Yuletide blessings, Dean…"*

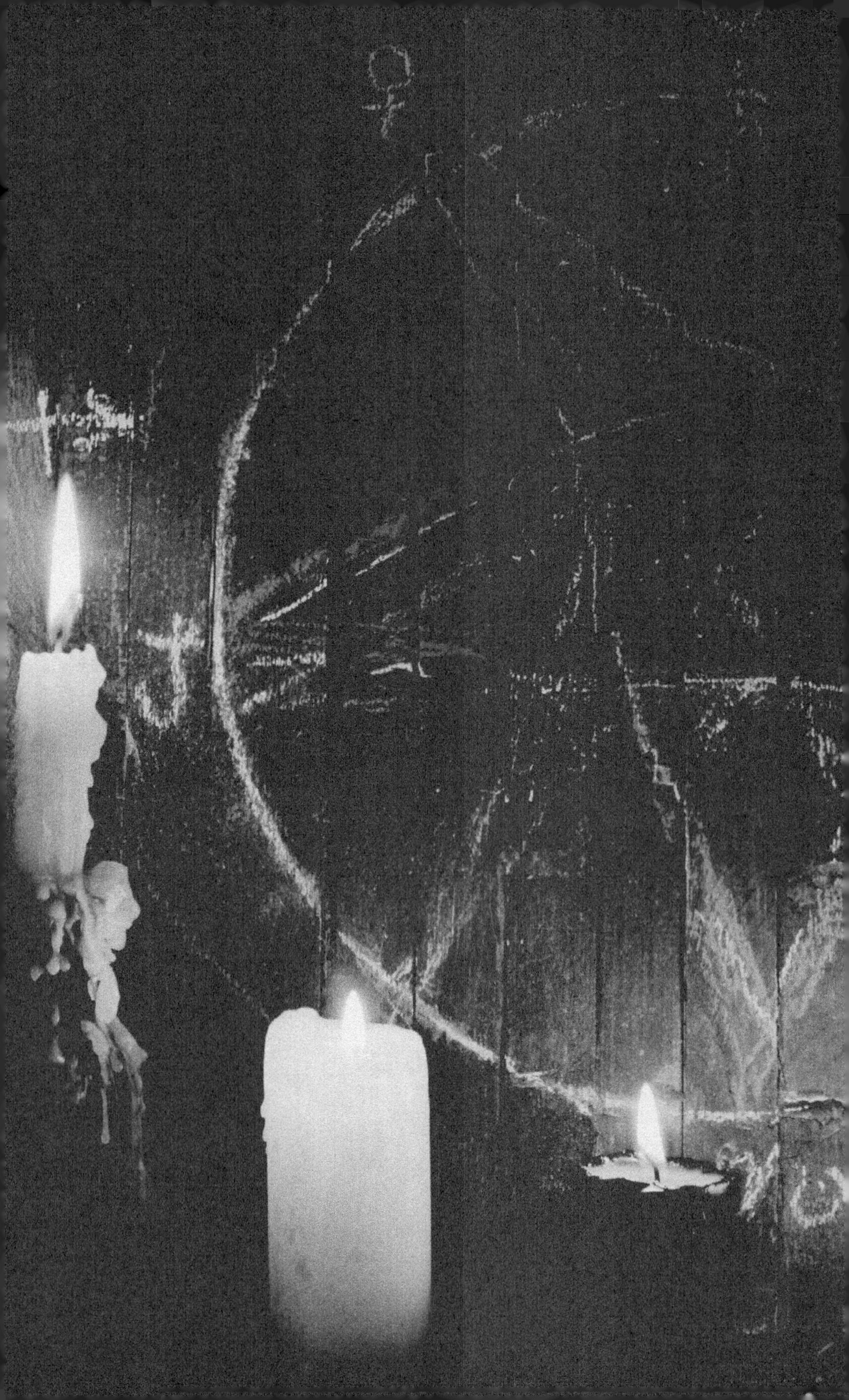

Chapter 35

EARLY SPRING
LEGION

W aiting is its own kind of hell, a purgatory I've subjected many to, myself. This type of mental warfare is a slow suffocation. A creeping silence under the weight of everything you can't control, trapped in the space between knowing and not knowing, between action and consequence, a gnawing thing that burrows under your skin and settles in your bones. It strips you down, minute by minute, until all that's left is raw nerves and the sound of your own thundering pulse, too damn loud in the silence.

The worst thing about waiting isn't the fear. I'm not afraid. I've been in precarious positions before—gun fights, ambushes, staring down men who were ready to put me in the dirt. That kind of danger is easy. It's sharp, immediate, *fucking preferable* to the way the passing of time hollows you out. Waiting makes your mind run through every possible scenario in an unremitting loop until they all blend together, and you *begin to feel your sanity slipping*…a dull blade at your patience… dragging across slowly…letting you wonder when it'll finally cut deep…

I light a cigarette just to keep my hands busy. The smoke tastes like nothing.

Ace's laughter echoes across the lot of the Twisted Throttle, loud and unrestrained, the kind of pure happiness only children have. I've been watching him and his mother play together on the small jungle gym behind the clubhouse. When I'm not preoccupied with covertly maneuvering human chess pieces, I'm watching them. She doesn't know how often. Or maybe she simply pretends not to notice the way my eyes eagerly find her, the way I steal these moments whenever I can, hoarding them like a man starved.

I think Keegan has reached the point of pretense as well… Though perhaps he tempers his territorial urges with the notion that if I'm watching her, too, it's one more pair of fiercely protective eyes surveilling his most prized possessions. I won't touch…but there is no line I wouldn't cross to keep them safe. I believe I've made that abundantly clear, and my devotion in this singular aspect has garnered his tolerance.

Ace climbs the ladder to go down the slide again while she regathers the top portion of her hair, clipping it back. The deep, natural undertones of red in her dark tresses are only evident in the sunlight. Suddenly, I'm craving a Cherry Coke.

An engine revs to life within Keegan's repair shop, where he's working, drawing her gaze in its direction. While scanning the lot, she spots me in what has become my usual haunt—the back patio, lounging alone with my smokes in a lawn chair. A smile pulls at her lips, but there is something off in her otherwise friendly expression. Something beneath the surface she's trying to hide. She turns away from me, abruptly, but not before I notice the way her smile falters and her shoulders tense, as if she's holding back something heavy.

I shouldn't care as much as I do. I shouldn't be getting up and striding over to her like some lovesick simp, hoping for scraps of her attention, hoping for her to make some trivial request of me so that I may *jump to it* in order to please her. But I do. Every fucking chance I get. Something is bothering her. *And I need to wipe whatever it is off the face of the earth…*so that her smile reaches her magnetic dark eyes once again.

I come to stand beside her, dropping my cigarette and snuffing it out beneath my boot. My stomach tightens when she peers up at me, softly smiling again as if summoning me to her side has somehow brought her a measure of comfort. Ace continues to play, oblivious to the way his mother makes my heart feel like it's caught in a vice.

"Hey," she says, a little breathless, as if the weight of whatever she's carrying is pressing harder on her now that I'm standing beside her.

"Hey," I reply, keeping my voice even and playing along for a moment.

She gestures to Ace. "We're just waiting for Rosita to drop Mia off. I'm watching her while Rosita goes to a doctor's appointment." She lowers her voice to further inform me, "Might take them to the library by the fairgrounds. You read a lot, so if there's anything I can pick up for you, please ask. I'd invite you to come along if it were just Ace and me, but…you know how Viper is."

Though deadly in his own right, Viper is the least of my concerns. "Why don't you tell me what's wrong?"

She stares at me as if surprised by the blunt inquiry, then glances back at her son, seeming to assure he's still distracted. Her hand trails up to gently stroke the smooth skin at the base of her throat, while the other rests against her hip. Ace waves at her from the top of the slide, and she chuckles and waves back to him. Her smile is practiced, though…her joy, a performance to shield him from whatever is bothering her.

"Vanna…" I press. She spares me a quick look, but otherwise keeps her attention fixed on Ace. "If *I* can see it, *he will*…"

"My sister sent an invitation in the mail a few days ago," she finally replies.

"And you have a scheduling conflict?" I sarcastically jest. When she peers up at me, there's a flicker of pain in her eyes. She forces a smile to disguise it, but I see her. I always see her. "What is it?"

"She sent a copy of her latest sonogram with it."

I shove my hands in my pockets, fists clenched, forcing myself not to reach for her. "I see…"

She only nods, then swallows.

I'm not supposed to be privy to this situation…this fault line in their relationship… One the darkness within is still tempted to exploit…if I allow it…if she ever gave me the slightest inkling of an opening. I want to say something else, something to let her know that I'd give her everything she wants in life if our circumstances were different…if she were mine… But she isn't. So, I remain silent, loving her the only way I can…from a distance…where it will never be enough…where I will slowly drive myself insane and…

Ace bounds over to us. She crouches to wrap him in a lingering embrace. He peers up at me over her shoulder, attempting to pull a few strands of her long hair from webbing over his little face in the slight spring breeze.

"Legend, what is 'Rizona like?" he asks.

"*Arizona*. It's hot," I reply, "generally speaking."

"Do you ever miss it?" Vanna inquires. She does so without looking at me, and the question rattles my system.

"No."

She stands, peering up at me again. "I've never been to the desert. It must be beautiful."

"Where I grew up, it was mostly barren and ugly."

Her brows bunch together. "*Ugly?* What about the Grand Canyon? Monument Valley? We've seen so many amazing pictures of Arizona, haven't we, Ace?" She glances down at him, stroking her fingers through the top of his hair before she looks back at me. "I've read that watching the sun rise over the Grand Canyon is like witnessing the first ever to exist. It's *that* breathtaking... You really haven't been there? No to any of the famous sites, ever?"

"We didn't have the means to venture anywhere when I was a kid... Then, I never had the time...or the desire."

She shakes her head. "It's so hard to imagine living a majority of your life in a state so rich with unique national parks, and never seeing any of it."

"I've ridden by sites." I shrug. "Never had a reason to stop."

"That's sad," she says quietly.

"Perhaps if I'd had someone worthwhile to point it out to me."

"You never had a girlfriend?"

I could use another cigarette. "For a short stint, once."

"I'm guessing that didn't..."

"*End well?*" I try not to scoff. "No. It didn't."

The sound of gravel crunching beneath tires diverts their attention from me.

"*Mia!*" Ace points enthusiastically to the sedan pulling into the lot.

Vanna glances back at me with a tight-lipped smile. "I guess we'll see you later," she says, allowing Ace to tug her in the direction of his playmate. I light up another cigarette and watch them stroll away.

Vanna

Ace and Mia make a dash for the pirate ship the moment our feet reach the perimeter of the playground. I settle onto the nearby bench and watch them scramble up the steps to get inside and up the ladder of the slide. Mia hesitates at the top, but Ace cheers her on. She finally pushes off, slides down, and lands in a giggling heap at the bottom before Ace joins her and they do it all over again.

Perfect. Let them wear themselves out a bit before I take them to the library. I stretch my legs out in front of me, rolling my shoulders back, willing myself to relax. The sun is warm on this spring noon, and the air is fresh with the scent of blooming flowers. I try to keep my mind from wandering back to that invitation sitting on my kitchen island…of the image she sent with it…a tiny, curled-up form with the first signs of a nose and little fingers. I left it where Dean would find it, and I wonder what he'll say when he does…or if he'll say anything at all…

I am happy for Giuliana. I really am. But I can't deny the ache deep inside, which only seems to grow more intense as the weeks pass. Will Dean ever come around? I press my palms against the denim over my thighs and exhale slowly, trying to push the thoughts from my mind for now.

"Vanna?" a familiar voice says from behind. I turn as she steps around the bench and takes a seat beside me.

"Meg," I say in surprise. "We haven't seen you in months. Did you move?"

"I have been so swamped with work, I've barely had the time to stop home," she says, adjusting the large, dark sunglasses she's wearing. "I've decided not to renew the lease with how seldom I'm there. I swear, you would think I'm running this company on my own."

"Are you still a pharmaceutical rep?" I ask.

A slight smile tugs at the corner of her mouth. "Drugs don't sell themselves," she chuckles. "At least, not at first." I can't see her green eyes behind her shades, but I follow the turn of her head as she glances toward the playground. "Ace has grown since I last saw him. Is that his cousin he's with?"

Ace is chasing Mia around the jungle gym, both of them laughing. He hasn't spotted Meg's vibrant red hair yet, and for some reason, I hope he remains distracted. "Yes, that's Mia. It's my turn to give her mother a break and watch them for a few hours."

"Oh, Rosita's daughter? Do you expect her along soon?" It's a simple question, but something about it feels…loaded.

"Yes, Viper and Rosita's daughter… Hey, did you ever get the cornucopia? Dean brought it over to your home before Thanksgiving, but you weren't there, so he left it on your porch."

"I did, it was fantastic, thank you," she replies quickly, but it only reinforces the odd feeling.

"Are you okay?"

Meg slowly shifts to face me. "I've been dealing with my father's estate. He passed away a few weeks ago."

"I'm so sorry, Meg," I say, feeling a bit guilty. No wonder she seems off. "Is there anything I can do?"

"Thanks, but no. I'm already back to work. Though, honestly, I'm exhausted. The men I work with have a difficult time following orders from a woman, especially when I have to travel out of town for conferences and trade shows."

"When is your lease up? I can help you pack if you'd like?"

"Oh, there's no rush to pack. I still have a few months, but I don't expect to be there much. I just wanted to let you know in case you and Ace start wondering."

"We'll miss you stopping by the farmstand. We open in a few weeks. Will you still be in the area?"

"Now and then." She smiles. "Would you mind if I say hello to Ace?"

"No, of course not," I say, standing to walk with her over to the playground. Ace finally spots her and dashes over to us.

"Hi Meg!" He smiles up at her. She bends to place a hand on his little shoulder and drags her sunglasses down the bridge of her nose to better look at him.

"Hello, sweetie, are you having fun?" Meg asks.

"Yeah!" Ace replies, winded from running around but otherwise happy. Mia comes to stand beside him, peering up at her curiously. "This is my cousin," Ace says.

"Hello, Mia," Meg smiles. "Aren't you a beautiful little girl."

"Hi," Mia replies, shyly tucking herself behind Ace.

"If I didn't know better, I'd think she was your daughter, Vanna," Meg peers over at me, "With this lovely, long, dark hair and pretty brown eyes."

I only force a smile.

"Well, I just wanted to come over and say hello to you, Ace," Meg goes on. "I've missed seeing you and mommy, and I hope one day I'll be able to visit you at the farmstand again, and you can help me pick out some fruits and veggies."

His little brows knit together in confusion. "You're going away?"

"I'm afraid so, big guy. But I will try very hard to visit whenever I can," Meg promises.

"Okay…" he lets out a little disheartened sigh.

"*Oh,*" Meg pouts, holding her arms out to him for a hug. "Don't look so sad, sweet one," she says as he steps into her embrace and hugs her back. "I promise to come see you again. Will you make me a promise, too?"

"Uh-huh," Ace says.

"Draw me a pretty picture so the next time I visit, I can take it with me."

"Okay," Ace agrees.

"Now, you go play and have fun with Mia," Meg says, releasing him and straightening. With one last glance, Ace takes Mia's hand, and they hurry back to the playground. "Well," she turns to me, "I should be on my way. We're hoping to land an important contract very soon, and I have a feeling the company is relying on me to close the deal on this one, too."

"Alright, well, best of luck with everything," I say.

"You, too, Vanna. Take care."

I watch Meg walk across the fairgrounds toward the parking lot before shifting my attention back to my kids. Ace is wearing a happy smile on his face again, and I'm glad Mia is here to distract him from Meg's departure. Something about her little *goodbye for now* felt rather final.

Sufficiently tuckered out, I have both tired toddlers safely strapped in their booster seats in the back seat of my SUV, ready to head to our next adventure.

"Everybody good?" I ask.

Mia smiles contentedly, sipping her juice box while Ace kicks his feet against his car seat, eager to get moving again.

"Where are we going now?" he asks.

Legion: Book 3

"*It's a surprise,*" I smile back at him before closing the car door. As I turn to open the driver's door, I'm met with a surprise myself. My front tire. Flat. Not just low, completely deflated, the rubber sagging against the pavement. I swear under my breath, about to reach into my back pocket to grab my cellphone, when I hear heavy footsteps on the other side of the car, too deliberate and swift to be someone simply passing by.

Viking's lessons on how to throw a real punch race through my mind as my fingers automatically press the lock button on the key fob. I clench my keys in my fist, allowing them to protrude between my fingers for maximum damage if I have to fight.

Two men approach me from either end of my car. They both look rough around the edges, one older with a scruffy beard, his hands shoved deep in his pockets. The other is younger, wiry, and his restless energy makes me instantly uneasy.

"Well, ain't this uncanny!" He grins, looking me up and down as if impressed by something.

"Afternoon," the older one says, voice too casual. "Car trouble?"

I swallow the spike of panic clawing up my throat. Did they do this? Are they going to rob me in broad daylight? I quickly glance around. We aren't alone. There are people enjoying the picnic tables beneath the trees in the park and playing catch, and there are others strolling along the sidewalk across the street by the ice cream parlor and other shops. All I have to do is scream…

Though my heart is hammering in my chest, I force myself to sound neutral when I reply, "Seems so."

"You're Dean Keegan's wife, yeah?" the younger one asks, stepping forward just enough to make me press my back up against Ace's door. I don't bother answering. They obviously know.

The older one sighs, like this is just another chore on his list. "You tell your Ol' Man, *time's up*. We've been more than patient. It's time to solidify the truce we've outlined, and given y'all such a generous taste of," he tilts his head, looking me over. "You want that to last, don't you? It's nice being able to trot that fine ass around a pristine little town like this, ain't it?"

The younger one chuckles, drawing my gaze to his sinister smirk. He cranes his neck to see inside the backseat window over my shoulder, at my kids, and my stomach knots before he even speaks.

"Be a shame if the club's decisions affected *more* than just the club, ya know?"

Jennifer Saviano

The fear wracking my system curdles into something sharper. Hotter. Before I can stop myself, I'm in his face, clenching both fists so tightly I can feel my fingernails digging into my palms.

"*I'll tell him,*" I snap, "Now get the fuck away from my kids!"

He licks his lips but slowly raises his hands and takes a step back. "*Easy, momma bear...*we're just delivering a message."

The older man turns and strolls off like they hadn't just threatened my entire world. With one last smirk, the young, wiry one jogs off after him.

My pulse pounds in my ears as I quickly unlock the car, jump into the driver's seat, and hit the lock button on the door after slamming it shut behind me. The keys rattle in my hand as I start the car and turn the AC on for the kids.

"What happened, Mommy?" Ace asks. "What did those men want?"

"They were just letting mommy know we have a flat tire," I say, pulling my cellphone from my back pocket. "Everything is okay. I'm just going to call daddy so he can come fix it."

I pause for a moment when I hear the low, slow growl of a motorcycle engine nearby. The black bike comes to a rolling stop in front of my car. The rider turns his head slowly to look at me through the windshield, and the afternoon sun bounces off his dark visor.

I had no idea Legion was watching us, or for how long, but relief floods my system.

He raises a gloved hand to his shielded face and taps the side of his index finger against the chin guard, a gesture to convey I should keep quiet about this. I don't know what else to do, so I simply nod in compliance. He seems to stare at me a moment longer before he shifts his focus to the corner of the block, where the two men disappeared moments ago. He waits, dangerous and calm all at once.

The loud rumbling of a pair of Harleys briefly pulls my attention to the end of the block. It's them. The two men barrel around the corner, fleeing our city now that they've delivered their message.

My heart beats faster again as Legion takes off after them...and I wonder if he's going to bring me back two more bloodstained patches.

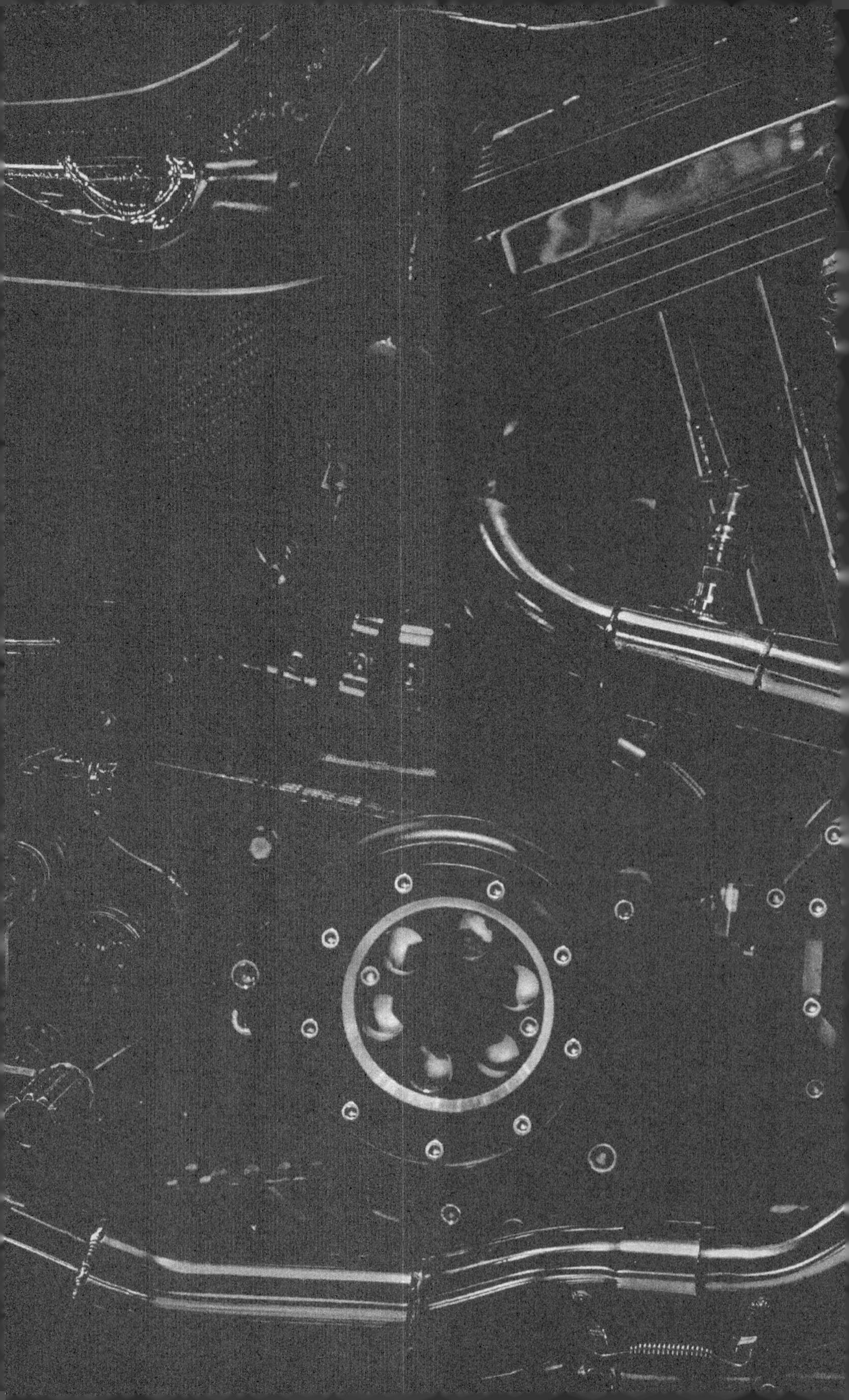

CHAPTER 36

DEAN

I don't know what pisses me off more...that he followed her...*or that he was there when I wasn't*... Like some guardian angel... *Like her dark knight*...

The water scalds, but it's got nothing on my heated temper. I press my palms against the stone shower wall as steam coils around me. I should be looking forward to tonight—the patch-over party, and what it means to this MC. But all I can see is the smug look on Legion's face two days ago, when he told me what he did to those thugs who approached Vanna... *What he arranged on behalf of my MC.*

I slam my fist against the wall, not hard enough to break the stone tiles or my knuckles, just enough to feel something sharper than these nagging thoughts. There's nothing to be done about it tonight. Tonight is about our MC. The future. Our growth. Proving to ourselves and the communities we serve that we are capable of rising above the chaos and building something worthwhile. Yet everything about keeping Legion around screams we're inviting chaos...

I kill the water and step out, dripping, still simmering, and grab a towel to secure it around my waist as I head toward the sink. The mirror is all fogged up, so I wipe it down with a washcloth before pulling open the drawer to rummage through what has become my wife's bathroom-bullshit collection in search of my comb. Once found among the clutter of makeup, lash curlers, and nail files she's acquired, I run the comb through my hair a few times, slicking it back. Before showering, I trimmed the sides low, as well as my facial scruff to little more than a five o'clock shadow, the way Vanna likes it. I'll add a little product after I get dressed and slick my hair back again before we head out. I chuck the comb onto the countertop, about to shut the disaster of a drawer, when I spot something that seems to spell disaster in a far more alarming way.

Half-hidden, shoved toward the back like it's trying to avoid me, lies her little disc of birth control. It's open and looking the worse for wear from being jostled among the rest of the shit in this drawer. I pull it out only to discover this pack is from *fucking December*...and there are still a week's worth of doses remaining...

Oh fuck, no...

I rummage through the drawer in search of another. Maybe she temporarily lost this one and got a replacement? Maybe she switched brands, and it's just someplace-the-fuck-else? Maybe she went back to the shot? *Fuck! Fuck! Fuck my life!*

Would she do this to me? To us?

It's possible I'm losing my shit over nothing. It's possible she just forgot to toss this old pack, and she really does have whatever she's taking currently somewhere else. She's switched contraceptives before. She could have switched again.

My guts continue to twist, and I just know she hasn't taken anything in weeks... *No, not weeks...months! Fucking months!*

I drop the disc in the drawer and shove it closed. Gripping the edge of the sink, I stare into the mirror at the wide-eyed asshole losing his shit right along with me.

Jesus fuck, we talked about this! Didn't we?

She knows how I feel... How reluctant I am. Not just because of money. *Because of her.* Because the last time nearly took her from me. Because I lay awake some nights still hearing the way she screamed... the machines beeping, and the hospital staff telling me they're doing all they can...

That's not all, though... Even if I could get past the fear, what if I simply *can't* do it? What if Ace really is our one miracle? *What if I fail her as a man and she...*

The bathroom door opens, but I keep my eyes fixed on the mirror. My heart is thudding in my chest like it wants to bust through my ribcage and run screaming down the hall.

"What?" Vanna asks, her bare feet padding up to me. "Did you find a grey or something?" she teases, wrapping her arms around me from behind. Her cheek presses against my back for a moment before I feel her lips graze my heated skin. "You know I love your salt and pepper," she murmurs, her hands skimming down my Adonis belt.

Jennifer Saviano

One of them drifts lower, over the towel, until it's resting against my cock. Her little groan causes the fucking traitor to stir beneath her gentle grip.

"My gorgeous husband… How lucky am I?" She peeks around my side with a sultry little smirk. *'Rosita has the kids for the night. Viper will meet us with the rest of the crew at the clubhouse… We have the house to ourselves for a while before we have to head out…"*

I force a smile at our reflection.

"Are you nervous about tonight?" she asks.

I can't form words.

A warm, loving smile spreads across her features, and she maneuvers herself to stand before me. I take a step back to give her more room. "You should be proud, Dean. All the club's hard work to expand the mission… You're succeeding. It's happening."

Her faith in me always feels like a gift I don't deserve. I should be willing to give her all within my power…or at the very least, *try*…

She turns around to grab her toothbrush and toothpaste, then proceeds to watch me through the mirror while she brushes her teeth, as if she's waiting for something. Her eyes flick to the drawer, then back to me, fast, but I saw it. She knows or suspects I saw.

Questions crowd at the back of my throat, but I choke them down. "I'm gonna get dressed," I say, leaning forward to press a kiss against the top of her head. She smells like warm vanilla with a hint of coconut and something else that feels like home.

"Did you see what came in the mail the other day?" she asks around a mouthful of foam. "I left it on the kitchen island." I can tell she's trying to sound offhand, like it's no big deal.

"I saw. Didn't bother opening it."

Her eyes drop for a second, and there it is again. That flicker of disappointment. She catches herself, playing it off with a small nod like *'it's fine'*. But I know her too well. That little pause speaks louder than anything else.

She spits, rinses, then cleans her toothbrush before telling me, "It's from my sister," even though we both already know.

"Yeah…" I nod, careful.

She doesn't say anything now, just begins to tidy the already organized counter, fidgeting, while I stand here attempting to decipher *why* she seems upset about it. Her family didn't show up for our wedding. No acknowledgment of the olive branch. No RSVP. Not even a damn text. Though that's all excusable compared to the fact that her family barely reached out when Ace—*their first grandchild*—was born. Why the fuck should we pretend like nothing ever happened?

I watch Vanna for another few seconds as the silence between us fills the room, thick and uncomfortable like the lingering steam, full of all the shit we should be able to just fucking say to each other.

"We're gonna be late." I sigh, eager to step away before it gets worse.

While she's in there doing herself up for this party, I slap on my usual biker attire, pull on my boots, and slip into my cut like it's all muscle memory. But everything I do now feels out of fucking sync, and denial rushes to the rescue…

Maybe it's nothing.

Maybe she forgot to toss the old pack.

Maybe her sister sent the invitation as a gesture of goodwill and not expectation.

I shove the thoughts aside. Denial's a hell of a drug, and I've been using it more than I'd like to admit. Because what if I'm wrong about the contraceptives? What if I'm the one holding the grudge against her family because it's easier than watching my wife make peace with people who hurt her?

I've been telling myself I'm only choosing my battles. That with everything going on with the MC, enemies circling, and *wanna-be-rivals playing politics,* I don't have the bandwidth for domestic landmines.

Denial is just a comforting delusion, and you're only lucky if it manages to buy you time. The truth is, it's a double-edged sword. It keeps the panic at bay, sure. Allows me to focus on the club, on earning a living to provide for my family… But the other edge is the one that cuts deep. Denial doesn't stop the truth from coming at you like a freight train. It just makes it hurt worse when it finally arrives. I learned that lesson the hard way in my first go-round with Legion. I saw the writing on the wall the night he showed up in my lot with the rest of his nomads…his taunting tagline on Lucinda's purple, jar of hearts stationery… Denial almost cost me everything.

Standing here now, cut on my back, keys in my hand, waiting for my wife to ride with me to the patch-over party, I feel both sides of the blade pressing in. Right now, we don't have the time the birth control conversation deserves, but I can at least open her sister's invitation and see what's got her out of sorts about it.

I walk over to the kitchen island, where the envelope has been sitting for the last few days. It's nothing too fancy. Cream colored, hand-addressed in a neat, practiced cursive. I pull out the invitation on thick card stock, foiled and elegant script informing us that *we are joyfully invited* to her baby shower.

Something slips out from within the card and lands on the marble island. Glossy…black and white…blurry but unmistakable.

I stare at the sonogram of Vanna's niece…*our niece,* I suppose, and all I can think about is the discarded birth control pack in the bathroom drawer. Was she hoping I'd see this and change my mind? Was she hoping I'd see this and imagine the little girl Vanna wants me to give her?

It's my fault. I've shut her down every time she's tried to talk to me about this.

I slide the sonogram back into the envelope with the invitation and place it down on the island as if I never touched it.

The rumbling engines of motorcycles shut down, one by one, as my crew parks their bikes around us in the section of the lot reserved for the original members of our founding charter. The Iron Saints' clubhouse is located near the halfway point between Bermuda County and our southern chapter, just outside Myrtle Beach.

I kick down the stand and twist Serene's key. She settles into silence beneath me, and I gaze up at the large Saviors MC banner draped across their old clubhouse sign. A warmth settles in my chest, temporarily quelling the turmoil wreaking quiet havoc inside of me. I am proud of this. We built this MC from the ground up and are making a difference with our mission, a mission others now want to join. We are growing. Tonight is proof.

I glance back at Vanna as she climbs off Serene and tucks her helmet into the saddlebag. She catches me watching her and smiles…at least on the surface. I have a feeling, despite the proud moment, we're both putting on a good face for the sake of not unraveling in front of people who look to us like we've got our shit together. I hang my helmet on Serene's handlebars and dismount, stepping up to Vanna, close enough she has to tilt her chin up to meet my eyes.

"You look good, baby." I let my gaze roam her pretty face and curvaceous figure clad in leather and denim. "My MC Queen. The finest First Lady a club could ask for."

"*Oh, stop it.*" She chuckles, playfully pushing away from me, but I grab her hand and pull her back. "Quit stalling and get in there. I'm sure they're all eager to get the party started."

Back when I was running with rougher MCs, patch-over parties were wild events fueled by booze, willing women, loud music, and raging bonfires. Usually, a fight or two as well, due to the combustible pairing of booze and women. But we aren't about that life anymore. Tonight, we celebrate a significant milestone.

When we step inside, we're welcomed with a mixture of applause and raised beers. My crew is standing on either side of the only remaining Iron Saints' banner on display, though the walls of the clubhouse are still lined with their history captured in framed photos, old patches, and the worn leather of the couches and stools lining the bar.

I'm forced to release Vanna's hand when the president and vice president step forward to shake ours and introduce us to the members about to be welcomed into our fold. Their First Lady escorts Vanna over to the bar, where Cherry is also waiting, and begins introducing her to the club's women. I make my way through the sea of new and familiar faces until I'm standing between my Sergeant at Arms and VP. Axel is standing with us, excitedly holding the banner we will be replacing the Iron Saints' one with momentarily.

A sharp whistle from their president quiets the room, and someone lowers the music playing through the sound system. He starts off by giving a brief speech about accepting our rules and bylaws, and their eagerness to join our mission, closing with, "Allow me to officially introduce the president of the founding charter… Dean Keegan."

I wait out the next brief eruption of applause while Viking slaps the back of my cut, jokingly taunting me, "*Don't fuck this up. I hope you prepared a speech. You better not bomb.*" And so on and so forth, in true to his nature, ball-busting fashion.

I don't know why it didn't occur to me to think of something to say prior to this occasion, but fuck it. Here goes…

I take another gander around the room at the men standing shoulder to shoulder, new cuts stitched fresh and proud. Brothers who have chosen to ride under the same banner, for the same cause. I step forward, trying to find my voice. When my gaze lands on Vanna, her pretty face staring back at me, full of pride and love, the words come easy.

"My uncle founded the Saviors MC, but he didn't do it to play badass or claim streets. This MC came together because the world is full of people who turn their backs on pain they don't have to feel. We decided not to be those people. We decided to fight for the afraid and the all-too-often forgotten. For the women and children locked behind closed doors with monsters who wear the masks of men."

When my wife's smile turns tearful, I swallow the knot that wants to form in my throat.

"We all know someone…unfortunately, and most likely, more than just someone… I've got a strong woman, one with more heart than most men I've ever met… Nobody saved her. No club came for her. No one stepped in to pull her out of the hell she escaped on her own before we met." I clear my throat in an effort to keep my voice from cracking. "She had to save herself, and that…that still fucks me up more than I can put into words… That's why this mission matters. That's why this patch *means* something. We show up when the system doesn't. We get them out. We protect. And we don't back down."

I close my eyes and let the silence stretch, mostly for a moment to pull my shit together before I go on. I take a breath, finding Vanna once again. Cherry has shifted closer to her among the group of women, and I smile at her as well.

"I know you hear this all the time. Hell, you may have even said it yourself… *'it's not all men'*… We know it isn't. This MC is proof it isn't. But too many self-proclaimed *'good men'* remain silent. If you are turning your head like it's not your business, then you're part of the problem. There aren't enough men willing to do something about it. Being a man isn't just about *not doing harm*. It's about *standing up to those who do*."

A few murmurs rise up around the room, agreeing, reflecting, maybe even hurting, and thinking back on pasts which have given them cause to seek redemption.

Legion: Book 3

"I'm not saying any of us are without our own faults. We all have a past. *We're Saviors, not saints*...but if we can be the hand that someone else never got...the protection they need, and the safe haven they deserve, then we're making a difference. So, here's to all of you joining us, to the road ahead, to the ones we protect. This isn't just a club. It's a calling. Welcome to the fight. Welcome to the Saviors MC."

Another roar of applause rises throughout the clubhouse as Axel and Viper remove their old banner, replacing it with the Saviors MC skull and wings. Their president hands me a beer and clanks his own against mine before we both raise them to the room in salute.

I keep tabs on Vanna from across the room as the patch-over party ensues, and I'm approached by multiple members of our new chapter. She's already knocked back a second drink since my little speech and is working on her third. We haven't been here long, so it's a red flag. The irony slices right through me, because the part of me that's bracing for the inevitable contraceptive conversation feels a cold kind of relief.

She's drinking. She wouldn't be if she were already pregnant.

The relief is hollow, though, because it also means something else.

I continue to shake every hand, clap every shoulder, and give each newly inducted member of the Saviors MC a nod and a few more words. They earned it and deserve my attention as well, but my gaze keeps gravitating to Vanna. At least she's with Cherry.

Just as I'm able to ease through the last couple of guys, I spot Viking coming at me with a determined stride, splitting the crowd.

"What's up?" I ask.

"*You know who* is outside," Viking says. "Figures he'd reappear tonight. Anyway, he wants a word with you."

"Alright. Let Vanna know I'll be right back."

I spot the glow of Legion's cigarette just beyond the club's floodlights in the parking lot. He's leaning against his bike in the shadows, the way he had been the night he first showed up in my lot. Though this time, he isn't surrounded by his Demons. He's alone.

The sounds of music, laughter, and conversations within the clubhouse fade behind me as I cross the lot. Legion stands to face me, wearing one of those sly grins that make me want to swing first and ask questions later. But his presence means something has either gone down or is about to.

"Congratulations." Legion cocks his chin toward the clubhouse. I can't tell if he's sincere or not, and I don't care either way. The way his gaze lingers on the door, hopeful for a glimpse of my wife, further grates my nerves.

"You've been MIA for a few days," I say, cutting right to the chase. "Have you decided what you're going to do about their offer?"

He shoots me a resentful glare. "*Declining it.* However, refusing them puts me in a precarious position, *as you well know*…and may even be counting on…"

I don't bother confirming or denying his assumption.

"The last thing anyone wants is a full-blown war. Killing a fully patched, ranking member of an MC is grounds for retaliation, which would spark a war. And since your club has made it abundantly clear that I will never receive the unanimous vote required to patch in as a Savior… *I've made other arrangements.*"

Motherfucker… "So, that's what you've been up to these last few weeks? Manipulating your way into a Jokers' cut?"

A sinister grin slowly stretches his mouth. "There's something else… Something you might equate to *stitching up a wound with barbed wire*, but it will solve all of our collective problems." Legion proceeds to relay the plan he's concocted while I finish off the half-empty beer sweating in my hand.

"You're a slippery son of a bitch."

Legion shrugs, pulling a long drag before expelling the smoke in my direction. "Considering where we are standing, I thought you'd be pleased. Besides, you still get to save face. How about a *thank you?*"

"How about a *fuck you*…You're still the cause."

He flicks his ash with his thumb, clearly agitated, and snaps, "*Are you going to veto the second phase of this plan?* Turn your back on your greatest allies, *simply to spite me?*"

"No."

He pulls a final drag. "Wise choice," he mutters on a breath of smoke, then chucks his cigarette on the ground between us and mounts his bike. "I'll see you at the meet."

I don't want to go back inside yet. Not with this storm of conflicting emotions about every-fucking-thing going on in my life converging all at once. After hearing the details of Legion's plan, the last thing I want to do is be around my crew. I turn away from the clubhouse, away from the music and laughter spilling out through the open front doors while my MC celebrates.

Legion: Book 3

I walk a distance away from the clubhouse, toward a picnic table out back, half-hidden in the shadows past the lot.

The wood creaks slightly under me as I sit on the table, rubbing a hand over my face. I close my eyes and let it drop into my lap.

Yeah, Legion's plan will most likely work, but my crew isn't going to like his *phase two* in order to secure all of Jocsan County. I know I have to give them a heads-up. They can't walk into this and be blindsided by the move... I should have fucking thought of this myself before Legion had a chance to sink his demonic claws into Slice's MC.

The motherfucker is always two steps ahead of me...

A subtle shift in the air penetrates my dark cloud of misery. A calm in the middle of everything. I always feel her before I see her, and when I lift my head, she's walking to me, boots soft against the grass. Vanna slides up beside me without a word and leans her shoulder against me.

"Why are you missing the party?" she asks.

"I've got a lot on my mind."

She reaches for my hand and laces her fingers through mine. "That was a touching speech."

"There isn't much I wouldn't give to rewrite that part of your past." I sigh, turning my hand over to grip hers tighter, grounding myself in the feel of her skin.

"The moment I saw you, Dean, I knew I was safe."

Those words always warm my heart, but... "You still think I'm your knight?"

She shifts to stand between my knees and places her hands on either side of my stubbled jaw, cradling my face. "Who else if not you, sweetheart?"

Her question only reminds me of Legion's connection to the Morning Star and the tattoo of the knight on his back. Regardless of what it all might mean, *he's too fucking late*... I married her. She's mine...*if I can manage to keep her.*

"Are you alright?" she asks. "You haven't been yourself since before we left the house."

"Big night... Things are happening."

"I'm proud of you." Her words hit harder than I expected, and I'm not sure why, but something in me cracks a little. "I know you don't always hear it. Not from the club. Not from the people who only see the cuts and the tattoos and the motorcycles and think they know who you are. But I do. And I need you to know it, too. I am proud of you, Dean. I couldn't ask for a better husband or father for Ace."

Her arms circle my neck, and I pull her closer, burying my face in her hair, breathing her in like she's the only thing keeping me from coming apart. Maybe we're gonna be okay.

"Do you remember that night on the picnic table?" She leans back to study me, resting her hands on my shoulders. She's wearing a little smirk, evident in the moonlight, our only source of illumination this distance from the clubhouse.

"Fondly," I reply.

She sinks her teeth into her bottom lip at my pun, then lets out a startled squeal as I grab her just below her ass, hoisting her up so she can straddle my lap. Her hips settle against mine, warm and inviting, and a wicked little grin quirks at the corners of her mouth.

She releases my shoulders to drag her fingers down my chest, leaning in close enough to brush her lips over mine. Not quite a kiss, but a temptation I succumb to.

I slip my hand to the nape of her neck and pull her to me. She lets out a quiet moan against my lips and rolls her body, grinding against me. She tastes like whiskey and fire and home. Her kiss is deep and slow, accompanied by a heat that promises to evaporate the pain.

"Love me," she whispers her command, and just like that, Legion's bullshit, the turmoil twisting my insides, and the patch-over party, couldn't be further away…

LEGION

Every fiber of my being is envious of him.

I have to adjust the steel rod growing in my pants as I watch her work his tongue…

Her pouty lips wrapped around it, their impassioned groans as she…*sucks* on it… *Making love* to it…

Of all the seasoned whores I've dealt with, I've never seen, nor have I experienced a kiss like *that*.

Pure witchcraft… What I would do to have that mouth again!

Staring in awe at her, wishing I were in his place, I attempt to console myself with the memory of our brief encounter in the wine cellar. I've thought of our stolen kiss quite often… Though what she's giving him of herself right now…she and I barely scratched the surface.

Resentment churns with desire, quickening my pulse as my jealous cock grows harder, still.

She seduces like an enchantress.
Loves like an angel.
Kisses like a demoness.
And fucks like a goddess.

She seems exceptionally eager for him tonight. The maddening sounds of her barely stifled gasps and moans drift from her parted lips into my ears…and I'm certain there isn't anything I wouldn't do to be the reason she cries out into the night…

Powerless against her pleas to be fucked, Keegan manhandles her into a position where she's bent over the table, and he's behind her, roughly yanking down her jeans. He fumbles with his own belt and fly, as if he can't get inside her fast enough.

The sound she makes when he finally does sends a rippling chill up my spine with another bolt of white-hot desire.

Unable to resist her siren's call any longer, I unzip, freeing my throbbing cock, already leaking with need, and spit in my hand before rubbing my fingers around the head, combining saliva with precum. I jerk myself in time with his quickening thrusts…her clipped little grunts and gasps… I close my eyes, zeroing in on only her. The wet sounds of her arousal…her heady words demanding to be filled…to be bred… It isn't long before the three of us are teetering on the edge of release…

"*Come in me!*" she demands of him again. And that's all I can fucking take. Gritting my teeth, cum shoots from my cock, spilling my seed in hot spurts somewhere on the dark ground as I pump every drop from myself, wishing I was emptying my balls into her womb.

"*No! What are you doing?*" Her voice, which was deep with heady lust mere seconds ago, suddenly sounds distraught.

I open my eyes to find them uncoupled. Keegan's hands are planted against the edge of the table, caging her between them. Hips that had been pounding into her now cocked back.

"Why didn't you—" she begins to ask when Keegan cuts her off.

"Because you haven't been taking your birth control, have you?" He's slightly out of breath as well. Seems neither of us shot our loads in Vanna tonight…

I quietly zip up and take a cautious step closer. Had my heart not already been racing from having just come so hard, it would be beating with excitement...

Vanna turns around and shoves at his shoulders. He takes a step back from her, tucking himself away as she hastily pulls up her pants. The defiant expression on her face loses its battle to the guilt she obviously feels. Her brows shift from furrowed to pitched. Her tightly pressed lips soften. It's evident she hasn't.

Trouble in paradise... Indeed.

My grin broadens, unseen in the darkness. My mind instinctively goes to work on all the possibilities of how this little rift in their relationship might work to my advantage. I listen to the rest of their exchange, eager for information to exploit...

"Jesus fuck, Vanna... We've talked about this," Keegan says.

"*Have we?*" she snaps back, a feistiness in her tone that nearly stirs my cock again. "Every time I try to talk to you about it, you dead the subject."

He runs a hand through his hair, stressed, and grips the back of his neck. "I'm not ready," he finally breaks the silence between them.

"I'm afraid you never will be," she says.

"Can you blame me?" he demands, and I find it impossible not to revel in his pain. She attempts to move past him, but he blocks her. "*Vanna...*" Keegan pleads.

"It's already a long shot regardless, isn't it?" she sighs, though her words are laced with frustration. "All things considered."

Fuck... That one had to hurt him... I sneer silently to myself.

"That was a low blow, Vanna... I gave you Ace."

"We were lucky."

"Yes, we are. *Lucky you're both still alive!*"

My excitement dwindles as memory pulls me back to that night in the warehouse...to what she told me when I delivered the evidence of my kept promises...

She had suffered complications...near fatal ones...

"The chances of that happening—" Vanna begins, but he cuts her off again.

"Are not something I'm willing to risk! You mean too much to me, Vanna... More than you seem to comprehend."

She softens under his discernible agony, releasing another sigh. "I don't want to have this fight here."

"*I don't want to have this fight at all...*" Remorse sinks Keegan's shoulders beneath the leather cut. Disappointing her truly does seem to devastate him. The way he reaches for her hand, not simply *taking it*, only waiting for her to accept him, speaks volumes without another word passing between them.

She truly would have been the death of him.

I find myself pitying him... Yet envying him even more deeply than before.

DEAN

The ride home felt longer than usual, even with the wind in my face and engine humming steady beneath me. The rides with Vanna's arms wrapped around me have always brought an additional layer of tranquility to my soul, reminding me why I'm willing to bleed for this life. But tonight, it feels like I'm riding towards a cliff I can't avoid.

The house is dark when we pull up, one porch light still burning. I kill the engine and wait for her to dismount before I do. She doesn't say anything to me as she trades her helmet with me for the house keys. I tuck Serene in for the night while Vanna lets herself inside our home.

When I finally enter, Vanna's reaching into a kitchen cabinet for Nico's snack before bed. He's rubbing against her legs, purring loud enough I can hear him across the room. I notice she's already discarded her boots, and her cut is draped across the back of a kitchen island stool.

"Vanna, we need to talk," I gently press, locking the front door behind me before hanging up my own cut. "I saw the contraceptives in the drawer. Have you come off them?"

She nods, a guarded expression in her eyes. "And I'm never taking it again."

"That's fine... I would never ask you to take something you don't want. There are procedures I could—"

With a tearful glare, she places Nico's dish on the kitchen floor before she turns and storms down the hall. I hurry after her before she gets the chance to slam and lock the bedroom door in my face.

"Vanna, we need to talk about this."

She doesn't bother turning around to face me, only continues her march into the bathroom, where I follow. "I tried talking to you about this. Multiple times. All you do is shut me down."

"That isn't true," I sigh, watching her yank open that cursed drawer and remove a hair clip. She hastily gathers her hair and clips it back. "I voiced my concerns the morning you first brought the idea up... There are a lot of things at play here...one of them being *I need to know that I can take care of what I have now.*"

She shoots daggers at me through the mirror. "*We. Us. Our...* I'm here, too."

"I know... I don't mean to come across like it's all about me or all about money, but...it is a factor we do need to consider."

She wrenches the faucet on, not even waiting for the water to warm before she begins scrubbing her face clean of the makeup. I wait patiently while she completes her task.

"I don't think this is about the money," she finally says, grabbing a hand towel to pat her face and hands dry.

"It's a factor. There are far more important ones." I take a step closer, gingerly placing a hand on her shoulder. "Like your health. Your safety. These are paramount concerns."

Her gaze lifts to meet mine, and she shifts to face me. "AFE is a rare occurrence, Dean. *One in forty thousand.*"

"But it happened, didn't it?"

She lets out a sigh laced with frustration, yanking the clip from her hair. It cascades around her shoulders, and she tosses the clip onto the counter. "You're just living in fear! I'm not willing to live like that anymore! Ever again!"

"Vanna..." I try to hold onto her, but she pushes away from me with a look that twists my guts and tightens my chest. I've never seen it in her eyes before. Not whenever she's looked at me... A flash of disappointment... there one second and gone the next... *But it was there...*

She shakes her head at me. "The chances of it happening again—"

"*I don't even want to fucking think about it!*"

"You can't keep shutting down on me! Dean...there are precautions the doctors can take."

"There are still other risks."

"I could argue your motorcycles are an even greater risk! And I've never asked you to give that up!"

Fuck. She has me there...

"Tell me the real reasons," she insists, crossing her arms.

"Vanna, you know all I want is to be able to give you everything..." She only stares at me. I can't fault her for wanting this. A sibling for Ace is the next natural step for our family, but I feel trapped in an impossible position... Torn between giving her what she wants, and protecting her...and that's *if* I'm even capable...

What if Ace really is our miracle, and I can't give her another baby? Will this be what destroys everything we *have* created together? Will I be less to her? Will that cause her love for me to fade and turn into a harbored resentment that erodes our perfect life together? An *irreconcilable difference?* Grounds for divorce?

"Dean..."

I can't lose her...

"Dean...honey..." She no longer seems cross with me, but the disappointment was there before...I saw it...

I can't fucking lose her... God damn it... Am I damned either way?

"*Breathe,* sweetheart..."

I glance down at her hand over mine as she attempts to pry my digging fingers from clawing at my own racing heart. Does she still know I would rip it out and give it to her?

Her hands move up to cradle my face as a pitying expression eclipses hers. "You really are terrified..."

"*Of losing you...yes, I am.*"

"You could never lose me, Dean."

"I almost did."

And still, the defeated look in her glassy eyes shatters my heart... If what we have now isn't enough...failing her as a man will surely be our undoing...

"I'm only asking for a chance..." she tearfully whispers. "I know what else you're afraid of... I'm not going to make you say it out loud... But Dean...can't we just see what's meant to be?"

Her hands lower to gently grip mine. "Do you really think I'd hold it against you if Ace is our only child?"

"*I don't think you'd intend to...*" I manage to choke out.

She offers a smile, but her eyes are full of sorrow. "I'm only asking you not to slam the door on hope… Don't let what happened with Lucinda dictate what happens with our family."

"Lucinda's got nothing to do with this. She's nothing to me. I wish you'd stop throwing it in my face."

"Throwing it in your face? I'm just trying to make you understand."

"*You don't understand!*"

"I want you to imagine holding our baby girl."

"Is that why you wanted me to see the invitation?"

"Do it!" she demands. "Picture her! Imagine her and tell me you don't want her!"

"Of course I would, Vanna… Don't be cruel…"

"I'm not being cruel. I'm trying to get through to you!"

I pull away from her and storm back to the kitchen. Back to that fucking invitation sitting on the kitchen island like it's waiting for a fucking verdict on my goddamned life.

I tear the damn thing open, whirling around on my wife to thrust the sonogram into her hands.

"I want you to imagine something, too, Vanna… *Imagine it never happening!* Imagine she never exists! *Now fucking look at me and tell me you won't resent me for it!*"

"I won't."

"I know you *want* to believe that… Fuck! *We both do.*"

She lowers her eyes from mine to gaze down at the sonogram. "If money wasn't an issue…if everything else was perfect…would you want another?"

"Everything *is* perfect."

She steps forward to place the sonogram on the kitchen island. "Then I guess there's nothing left to talk about."

"Is life with me and Ace *not* perfect, Vanna?"

"It is." She smiles at me, her eyes somehow tearful and hollow at the same time.

"Then why don't I believe you?"

"If we aren't meant to have another baby, so be it. I would never hold it against you. I would never resent you."

"You resent something."

Legion: Book 3

"Your opposition to possibility. Your stifling need to protect me, even if it means smothering my hopes."

"Fuck…twist the knife, why don't you… Is that really how you feel?"

"What would you do if I was pregnant? Would you want me to get rid of it?"

"Vanna, come on…"

"No. You're not the only one who gets to argue with hypotheticals. *I'm pregnant.*" She throws her arms up and lets them fall hopelessly to her sides. "What now? Are we keeping it?"

"Of course."

"Only because I want it? Or would you love this hypothetical baby like you love Ace?"

"Is this a serious question?"

"If you simply do not want another baby, *hypotheticals aside*, that changes things."

"*Irreconcilable things?*"

"It never crossed my mind after Ace that you would never want another baby with me."

"I'm not saying that either…"

A cautious hope flickers behind her eyes. "Do you just need more time?"

"Would you give it to me if I did?"

"Of course I would…within reason."

"Alright," I reach for her, immensely relieved when she steps into my arms without hesitation. I hold her in the silence between us now. A heavy silence that stretches on until I can no longer swallow back the words. *"I love you, you know that…don't you?"*

CHAPTER 37

DEAN

It's never just one thing. That's something else I've learned about life. It's never just the marriage hitting a tough patch, or the club getting backed into a corner under my leadership, or the town sitting on the edge of a fucking war our citizens are oblivious to. It's all of it. All at once. Like life's got a fucking vendetta against me or just a sick sense of timing, waiting until my arms are already full to drop another damn weight on my chest, just to see if I'll fold.

"When is all this going down?" Viper asks, dragging my attention back to the matter at hand. I turn to him from my place at the head of the table in the War Room, feeling more and more like the trust my men have in my judgment is being measured by the inch.

"Legion only informed me of the plan last night," I say. "*Phase one* is already in effect, and the meet is happening tomorrow night, in neutral territory outside of Jocsan. We'll be contacted with an exact time and location soon."

Viking lets out a gruff sigh. "I'm sorry I couldn't get anything with the Jagger connection… This is all happening fast."

"Gives them less time to come up with a plan to ambush or strong-arm us. *Like grabbing a loved one for leverage,*" I mutter. "The prospects will remain at the clubhouse to watch over any of those who feel safest here. The rest of us are riding out. We need the numbers to make an impression. Our South Carolina brothers from both chapters are riding with us. They'll be here tomorrow."

The room falls silent again. Not because my crew is on board with what is coming, but because we all know as much as we hate the *Ace up Legion's sleeve,* his plan puts our enemies in checkmate when it comes to our territory and Jocsan County.

"We don't have to like it...but we do have to vote on it, and it has to be unanimous to pass," I say. "We'll deal with Legion down the road. For now, the Demon is our best shot."

"It keeps our allies and our county safe." Viper sighs, glancing around the table at our ranking members. "All in favor?" He raises his hand, casting the first reluctant vote. The rest of us follow suit, one by one, until the unanimous decision is solidified.

"It's settled then." I hit the gavel against the sounding block.

"May our fallen brother forgive us," Viper quietly says, a level of remorse in his tone.

I lean forward to place my hand on his shoulder in an attempt to reassure him. "Snowy would have voted the same."

The rest of our brothers file out to inform their loved ones of the impending lockdown. Viper, Viking, and Axel remain behind with me.

"What's up?" Viking asks, a casual concern to his words.

I lean back, resting one hand on the arm of my chair, rubbing my stubbled jaw with the other. "I just need a goddamned minute to breathe."

"If you're stressed about this pact with Legion, I actually think he means well," Axel offers, sinking into his seat again.

"I'm not worried about Legion fucking us over," I say. Not if he's equating this negotiation with keeping Vanna safe.

Viper and Viking exchange a quick glance before Viking speaks up. "You cut out of the patch-over party early last night. Did you get into something with Vanna?"

I don't say anything. I don't need to. It's obvious. And although Vanna and I came to a pseudo-compromise, I know I've only managed to secure a short stay of execution.

"Club shit aside, we're still your brothers, Dean. You can talk to us, and it won't leave these four walls," Viking says.

Viper clears his throat, almost as if he's unsure of what he's about to say. "Rosita's been on me about it, too."

"And you're not on board?" I try not to sound relieved at the fact that he may be in a boat similar to mine.

Viper shrugs. "I'm perfectly content, but...two to four years seems to be the window when this conversation pops up."

"Pulling the blinds on the baby conversation pissed her off... Made me the enemy in her eyes," I explain.

Viking and Axel exchange glances next, obviously uncomfortable with the topic. "We're here for moral support, bro," Viking says, his large hand clapping the back of my shoulder before he chucks a thumb at Axel. "But our *areas of expertise* lie elsewhere. We should go make sure things are getting done for the lockdown. Vanna's already here with Ace. I'll make sure she understands what's going on. And we can't let Cherry or any of the girls go on a supply run without an escort."

"I can go pick up Rosita and Mia if you want?" Axel offers.

"I'll go get them in a minute," Viper says, cocking his chin at the door to dismiss them. "I got this."

Axel gives me a tight-lipped, sympathetic smile on his way out of the War Room with Viking. They shut the doors behind them, and I turn my attention back to Viper.

"She gave me time to think...but, what's fair?" I let out a sigh laced with frustration and building anxiety. "You know my... *situation*... She's been off the birth control for four months already... Started bringing up the *sibling talk* back in October of last year."

"She's clearly got an idea of a timeline in her head. This is all normal shit. I'd say a year is fair, but you're already seven months into it. I wouldn't take too long."

"Where are you on it with Rosita?"

"It feels right for us. Like we're building something together. But you gotta feel it. You already know what she wants... But nobody can do the soul searching for you."

"I just want to keep her happy... What if I can't?"

"You have Ace... Maybe things aren't as bleak as you fear?"

"Maybe."

"I can try putting it to you another way..." Viper leans back to fold his hands in his lap, surveying me the way he does. "Are you waiting for perfect? Because life doesn't give you perfect. There will always be shit to handle and time keeps marching forward, brother."

"That's the thing. Another kid is another worry," I sigh.

Viper lets out an empathetic huff. "Sure is... But it's something else, too."

I glance over at him curiously.

"*Purpose*, brother."

Vanna

The Twisted Throttle is closed tonight. The gates outside are locked and manned by a few prospects standing guard. The air inside feels heavier without the sound of laughter and music that usually fills the roadhouse on any given night. Instead of locals stopping in for a drink and conversation, or bikers shooting pool and blasting classic rock on the jukebox, the bar and a few of the guys' private rooms are occupied by their women and children. Their loved ones.

We're in lockdown.

I glance over at Ace, perfectly at ease on one of the leather couches Cherry and I thoroughly cleaned yesterday when we were informed the lockdown would be taking place. He's with Mia and a few of the other kids, watching *The Goonies* on a big screen Axel brought in.

"Has the MC ever had to do this before?" I quietly ask Cherry. She's standing beside me near the bar, surveying the room herself. The way she's got her arms folded, one hand tugging at her bottom lip, makes me wonder if this is a first time for her as well.

"I've only gone through it once," she says. "Shortly after I got here. This was more common when they were first carving out their territory. But that was decades ago. Axel said this is just a precaution. They don't expect anything to go wrong."

"Do you need us to do anything else right now?" Maxi asks, approaching us with three of the other patch-chasers who usually hang around the bar. As Dean's wife and the First Lady of this MC, it's on me to make sure everyone is as comfortable as we can make them. Most of the wives and girlfriends are sitting in small clusters at a few different bar tables, chatting quietly or scrolling their phones. Some are more at ease than others.

"I think everyone is alright for now," I say, glancing back at the clock behind the bar. "We should start making dinner soon. I hope everyone likes spaghetti and meatballs. I also grabbed a few loaves of Italian bread when we stopped at the store on the way here."

"If everything is in the kitchen, we can start prepping now," Maxie offers. I wonder if she's anxious and just wants something to do to keep busy. The Saviors haven't been one-percenters in a long time, and if they're all she's used to, this might be her first lockdown, too.

"Sure," I nod. "I brought fresh basil and garlic. There are a couple of onions in there, too. Maybe ask the kids if they want pasta or nuggets and fries."

"There's a head of lettuce and some cucumbers in the fridge. Tomatoes on the counter," Cherry adds. "Chop it up for a salad. We'll set up a buffet, and everyone can just take what they want. The guys will devour whatever's left when they get back. They aren't picky."

The patch-chasers head for the kitchen, just as I hear the distant growl of a motorcycle outside.

"All the guys are in the War Room, aren't they?" I ask.

Cherry clears her throat. "All but *one*."

When Legion steps through the steel door of the Twisted Throttle, heads turn and conversations stop. He walks in like he owns the place…or maybe he's just through taking any more shit. A few of the women tense under his searching gaze. I'm sure he's been the devil in whatever stories they've been told, not that I can't imagine why.

The moment he spots me, the air shifts again, and I don't know if I should find it more unsettling than being under lockdown.

"I'm going to see if they need help in the kitchen," Cherry says, as if she felt something too. She walks away when Legion crosses the room to me. The other wives and girlfriends pretend they aren't watching us, that they aren't aware of the strange kinetic energy building with every step he takes.

"Hey," I say, attempting to sound casual despite the cocktail of emotions making my pulse race. Instinctively, I cross my arms and bring my left hand to the base of my throat to toy with my wedding rings.

"Hey," he replies.

"I heard you joined the Jokers."

"A temporary arrangement." Legion studies me for a moment, and I can't help but feel like I'm missing something.

"Everyone keeps telling us not to worry. That this is all just a precaution."

"Both sides are eager for a truce," Legion attempts to assure me.

"So I've heard. But I'm still worried."

"Keegan will return to you unscathed and the hero of several counties," Legion sighs with a hint of resentment. "You have my word."

"I know. I trust you."

He seems surprised by the admission and remains silent.

"I know this meeting is necessary…but I need you to be careful, too."

His gaze narrows. "Why wouldn't I be?"

"I know you arranged this." I lower my voice, not wanting to cause him any sort of shame. I'm not sure how it would look to those pretending not to watch our exchange if I were to step away with him. But I want him to know someone, even if it's only me, wants him to come back alive, too. "I'm afraid this is you *tempting fate again*…throwing yourself between bullets and hoping one of them finally hits."

Legion's pale eyes flick past me for a brief moment, toward the corridor like he's checking for something, *or someone*, before he returns his stare to me. "I'm not trying to die…I'm trying to protect what's left."

"What's left?"

His hand twitches at his side, as if he wants to reach out to me, but he doesn't. He can't. Not here. Not now…not ever. Instead, his thumbs hook into his denim pockets, and he curls them into tight fists. "*What still matters to me…*"

A strange ache wraps around my heart, and I divert my eyes from his intense gaze to check on Ace. My son is still content with the other children watching their movie.

"*Him, too,*" Legion adds. When I peer back up at him, he's staring at me, jaw ticking, like he never looked away. As if he was memorizing my face. "You're still afraid."

I nod.

"There is nothing for you to fret over, sweet one. Your husband and I have everything well handled," Legion replies with an unwavering confidence I should find reassuring.

I offer him a timid smile, unable to confess that this arranged truce isn't the only thing about our situation I find increasingly concerning. He seems to sense it, tilting his head as he studies me more closely.

"Legion," an abrupt voice from the corridor startles me. "Come on, we've been waiting for you," Chopper gruffly informs him.

Legion lingers a moment longer, his stare hardening for some reason, as if a decision solidified in his complex mind. When he steps past me, his whispered words send a chill through my entire body... *"After tonight, you're my Queen, too."*

LEGION

Even as we pull into the large clearing around the abandoned cement factory, my thoughts aren't on the meeting about to commence, the guns and Kevlar we're wearing beneath our cuts, or the tension riding bitch with every man in this delicately brokered alliance. But it isn't tension *I* feel. It's exhilaration over everything I've managed to orchestrate, combined with the evident fraying of her illustrious restraint...

Sure, she hugged him and kissed him before we departed on this mission together. She pressed her body against his like she was trying to convey something only they shared. Sweet...loyal... The perfect Ol' Lady... I saw the way her hands trembled when she touched him... The flicker in her eyes when she spared me that parting glance...as if she needed to know I was still there...still watching... *Still hers...* Even if she'll never say it out loud.

My last words to her... She felt them. I *know* she did. The way her breath hitched under the slow, coiling tension whenever we're within proximity of one another... The way she stared at me... Her eyes always tell me the truth her lips refuse to.

Sure, she chose Keegan... She made sure that puny diamond and simple band on her finger glinted in my face as a reminder of the fact... As if it will keep me at a distance she deems safe...

She hasn't figured us out yet...but I warned her in the cellar before our stolen kiss... *I am a patient man.*

I don't bother fighting the grin stretching across my expression. Everyone will simply assume I'm smiling because everything is going according to plan.

There certainly is a war brewing... *Only it's within Keegan's wife.*

Legion: Book 3

The thunderous rumble of bikes echoes throughout the old cement factory as we roll to a stop on the far side of the clearing, leaving our guests room to join us. I made sure they wouldn't beat us here, and only gave them the exact location a short while ago, so there would be no chance of an ambush.

Neutral ground... I scoff to myself as I kill my engine and swing off my bike. It's all bullshit, really. There's no such thing. But it makes people feel safer, and the illusion is enough to get everyone here.

The cement factory, abandoned decades ago, looms around us—broken windows like hollow eyes, walls crumbling, exposing old wiring and rusted rebar. I light up a cigarette, my boots crunching against cracked concrete as I stroll a few feet further into the lot to survey the half perimeter of bikers with me. Both South Carolina chapters have joined Keegan's original crew, as well as their allies, the Jocsan County Jokers MC. It's enough of an impression of firepower to make anyone think twice, even if we end up slightly outnumbered.

Our engines now silenced, with only our headlights glowing in the dark to set the center stage, the low, warning rumble can be heard through the trees in the distance, rolling in as Reaper's crew approaches. I turn to face our mutual enemies, putting my back to Keegan and his crew.

"*How does it look?*" I jest, sneering over my shoulder at their president once more before it's show time.

Keegan's eyes narrow, but a half-grin twitches at the corner of his mouth, amused and probably appalled at what I've managed to accomplish.

No one saw this coming...and neither will Reaper, but it's my Ace in the hole...

DEAN

Silence falls sharp as Reaper's crew cuts off their bikes in near unison. Legion didn't flinch when they poured into the clearing. He simply stood there, smoking his damn cigarette in the center of it all like a stage illuminated by headlights, like he's the ringleader and we're all his circling ponies.

As the silence stretches on, it feels deliberate. Like Legion is pulling everyone's nerves taut. He's always had a way of letting an uncomfortable silence do the heavy lifting. I've been on the receiving end of this tactic before. He'll leave a sentence hanging in the air, like the smoke of his ever-present cigarettes, curling around your doubts and clouding your judgment.

I also know Legion never *just* talks. He performs. Sometimes in more theatrical ways than others, but always with an unnerving, charismatic charm that reads oddly threatening.

I shift my gaze to the biker I recognize from the Demons' Den the night I dragged Vanna out of that shit-hole clubhouse. He's still a big son of a bitch. A dark-haired, wiry-bearded version of Viking. He dismounts his bike and takes a few slow steps toward Legion.

"Oscar Wilde is famously quoted as saying, *Imitation is the sincerest form of flattery that mediocrity can pay to greatness*...Ballsy of you to step into my shoes...*assume my name and reputation* in order to take over what I had intended to collapse," Legion growls.

"Are you not impressed?" Reaper sneers.

Legion merely flicks his ash, ignoring the question. "And it was Benjamin Franklin who said, '*An ounce of prevention is worth a pound of cure.*'" He pulls a slow drag before going on. "War can easily become a consequence of unheeded words, so allow me to convey these terms *precisely*."

We all listen to Legion speak with that theatrical edge, accompanied by the odd flourish of a hand gesture timed just right. He isn't simply laying down the terms of the truce. He's selling a future.

"Territory claimed by the Saviors MC *is* and shall remain *completely off limits*. This includes any and all counties with a clubhouse under the banner of the Saviors MC. There will be no runs. No deals. No manufacturing. No muscle. No excuses. *No exceptions*... In return, we won't meddle in your organization. No sabotaging. No leaks. No shots fired. No more *explosions*... If you violate any of the terms, we'll prove Franklin right again...and you'll find that *pound of cure* far heavier than you can imagine."

"Fine," Reaper nods once, fighting to retain the poker face he rode in wearing.

"Then we have an agreement?" Legion presses, extending his open palm to seal the truce. A slow smile spreads across his face. "The *entirety* of the Saviors MC territory is off limits, henceforth?"

Reaper hesitates, glancing down at Legion's waiting hand, completely unaware of all the cunning demon has managed to pull off. I can't help but wonder if this was Legion's plan all along.

"Agreed," Reaper concedes, briefly clasping Legion's hand to shake it once. Cold and transactional. "All of the Saviors MC territory. We'll steer clear of Bermuda County, down through Horry."

"*And all of Jocsan*, as well," Legion adds with a sly grin.

Reaper's gaze narrows. "The Saviors have no claim on Jocsan. We generously agreed not to conduct business near the Jokers' clubhouse. Jocsan County as a whole isn't part of this truce."

"Oh, but it is, I'm afraid… You see, prior to this meeting, the Joco Jokers patched over to the Saviors MC, thereby making the *entirety* of Jocsan County…*off limits.*" Legion's grin turns dark, as if he's daring Reaper to challenge him. "Did you really think you'd outmaneuver me?" Legion tilts his head to the side, and I wonder if he's genuinely curious or just taunting him again.

But then he straightens, standing toe to toe with his former Sergeant at Arms. "Have you forgotten who it is you're dealing with? I've known it was you all along… And *as long* as you honor the truce, I won't come to claim your patch… *The devil you know, eh?*" Legion pulls another drag from his cigarette and lets his next words drift on the smoke. *"Ignore the warning, inherit the war."*

Reaper scoffs. "And who said that?"

"*Me,* motherfucker," Legion snaps. "You may have reconstructed something on the frayed threads of my coattails, but I'm back now."

"Yeah…you are," Reaper mutters, "And that leads us to our next order of business."

"I believe our business has concluded." Legion pulls a final drag from his cigarette and drops it between them. "I am *declining* your strong-armed offer to join your organization."

"You think that's wise? You may have weaseled Jocsan County away from us, but the Saviors MC will never *truly* have your back."

"You're right… Which is why I joined the Joco Jokers *prior* to the patch-over… *They have no choice…* I'm afraid you've just been bested by the Saviors MC's newest Enforcer." Legion grins deviously, taking a step closer to Reaper as if the King of Mount Meth isn't twice his size. "But don't look so put out, *old friend…* You aren't exactly leaving here *empty-handed*, now, *are you?*"

Jennifer Saviano

Vanna

Most of the women and all of the kids are tucked away in the back rooms, sleeping. It's a little after eleven pm. Cherry, Rosita, Diesel's wife Jaida, Maxie, and a few of the patch-chasers are waiting up with me in the bar. Having exhausted my capacity for small talk throughout the course of the day, we're sitting together quietly. Quiet enough to hear the sound of motorcycles approaching from down the street.

"It's them," Maxie says, anxiously standing up from one of the tables and smoothing down her denim skirt. "Should we turn the oven on and heat up the trays? Put on some coffee?"

"Might as well," Cherry says. "A few of them, in addition to Viking, are bound to be hungry."

"Be mindful of the sleeping kids nearby," I remind them.

While Maxie and the other patch-chasers head for the kitchen, I step outside with Cherry, Rosita, and Jaida. The prospects standing guard at the gates already have them open, and we watch our biker husbands pull into the lot.

Serene's tires are the first to hit the gravel, and relief floods my system at the sight of my husband returning, unscathed. While he parks Serene in her usual spot, I scan the rest of the crew to make sure they're all here, too, but I don't wait for Dean to dismount and come to me. I'm already halfway across the lot before he swings his leg off the bike and closes the distance between us. His eyes are softer than they were when he left earlier.

"Is everything alright?" he asks, just before I wrap my arms around him. He instantly holds me back in his warm, solid embrace. He presses a kiss to my temple, lingering to breathe me in as if he missed me, too, and I feel the tension leaving his shoulders the longer we hold onto each other.

"I was just worried," I whisper. He releases me only enough to study my expression. "We've never had to do this before. You've never gone off to meet a gang wearing bullet-proof vests beneath your cuts."

Dean lifts my chin with his finger before kissing my lips. He presses his forehead to mine for a moment, as if he's relieved by something more than this truce. "*It's all Aces, baby...* This was just a precaution. Everything went according to plan."

"Yeah... *You're welcome,* by the way," Legion's gravelly voice mutters behind Dean. I hear his Zippo ping open, and his thumb flick the striker.

Dean slips his arm around my waist, and we both turn to face him. "Let's not pretend you didn't end up exactly where you wanted all along."

Legion grins, pulling a drag on his cigarette while he plays with the brass Zippo in his other hand, but doesn't comment.

The rest of the crew follows Cherry, Rosita, and Jaida inside, but Viking stops to check on us.

"Everything good here?" he asks, glancing between Dean and Legion.

"*We'll see,*" Dean says, but his eyes narrow on Legion suspiciously. "Was it all you?"

"Define, *all...*" Legion smirks.

"*All.* Everything. Since the moment you rolled your sinister ass back into our town," Dean growls. "Did you know it would play out like this? *Did you orchestrate it?*"

"If I did, *you still benefited.*" Legion casually shrugs. "And I'm still waiting for that *thank you.*"

"Fuck you." Dean's sharp tone makes me anxiously shift in my boots beside him. "The last thing any of us wanted to see was our rocker on your fuckin' back after everything we *know you did* orchestrate."

Legion's wicked grin only broadens before he slides his gaze to me. With a slight bow, he winks at me. "*My Queen...*"

Dean's tightening, possessive grip on my hip almost hurts. "*My. Queen,*" he warns through gritted teeth.

As Legion steps past us to head for the steel door of the Twisted Throttle, he violently jerks the Zippo in his hand before a flame ignites his middle finger. He lifts it over his shoulder as he walks away, the flame illuminating the bright embroidered skull and angel wings on his back.

"Damn," Viking chuckles, clapping a hand on Dean's shoulder. "Legion didn't just flip you the bird, Dean. *He flipped you the fucking phoenix.*"

We watch Viking stroll into the roadhouse as well, and when Dean's grip loosens on me, his arm drops back to his side. I quickly

Jennifer Saviano

slip my hand into his. Not just to ground him, maybe to ground us both. Lacing my fingers between my husband's, I squeeze his hand a little tighter, trying to tell him without words that I'm here. *I'm his.* That I want this truce between him and Legion to hold.

Dean lets out a stress-ridden sigh as he gazes down at me, forcing a smile I know I'm meant to be reassured by. But a part of me still wonders if true peace between them is really possible… Or if I will always be the reason it never will be…

CHAPTER 38

1 MONTH LATER
Vanna

Ace situates himself on the seat of the mini-motorcycle in Dean's bike shop, completely dwarfed beside Serene, tongue poking out in fierce concentration as his little fingers clutch the handlebars. In his leather jacket and helmet, he looks just like his father—*Gods help me*—except for the knee and elbow pads I've insisted Ace wears. And since he is only allowed to ride under the supervision of Dean or Viking, the mini-bike stays at Dean's shop, at least until Ace really gets the hang of it. Keeping the bike at Dean's shop means Ace can't beg me to let him ride it around the yard at home, and I don't have to be the bad guy, which levels out my anxiety over the entire ordeal.

Still, my heart beats a little harder as I watch them. Dean crouches down beside Ace, patient and steady, while Ace, just a little too short to plant both boots firmly on the ground, wobbles to keep his balance, still wide-eyed and too fearless to know any better yet. Dean's laugh echoes across the lot as he catches Ace before he topples over. He catches me clutching the base of my throat, too.

"*Centrifugal force*, doll," Dean calls to me, "As soon as he gets rolling, he's good. Kid's a natural."

With a little boost from his proud father, Ace takes off on the mini-bike, buzzing around the wide-open parking lot at ten or so miles per hour. Dean jogs over to me, though he keeps an eye on our little bumblebee.

"You okay, baby?" he asks, all rough edges and soft eyes. I smile back at him briefly, before my attention drifts to our son, too wrapped up in his own little world to pay us any mind. "I meant to run something by you earlier, but time got away."

"What's going on?"

"Viking invited us all to his new place tonight. Kind of a housewarming thing for Beltane."

I turn to look at him curiously. "Viking bought a house?"

"Yeah, a real nice cabin on the river. Just closed on it a few weeks ago. Cash buy. Happened fast."

"Oh, wow. How wonderful for him. So, he's moving out of the clubhouse?"

"Apparently."

"How do you feel about that? I can't picture this place without him always around somewhere."

"I don't see that changing too much. He's still my bouncer. Still our Sergeant at Arms. Far as I know, he's keeping his room here. All his shit is still in there."

"Axel and Cherry are going to be next," I sigh. "Everybody is growing up."

Dean chuckles at my halfhearted joke. "They'll still be around. Just the other day, Axel was talking to me about going into business together. He wants to get into custom paint jobs for bikes and pinstriping and such. I'm not worried about anyone drifting away. This MC is family. It's been years since Viper has stayed at the clubhouse and we still see him often enough outside of church. Same for the others."

"The whole club is invited?" I ask, "*Even…*"

Dean lets out a gruff sigh as he watches Ace buzz by us again. "Legion *is* a fully-patched member."

"Well, I think this is wonderful for everyone. And what a perfect occasion for Beltane. Are we bringing the kids?"

"Rosita sends her love, but…this *Devil shit* isn't really her and Viper's scene," Dean jokes. "We can drop Ace off on our way over there, and just have our own little celebration with him tomorrow."

I glance up at him with a sly smirk. "Are we ditching Ace because you have other *Devil shit* in mind?"

Dean leans into me with a crooked grin. "Well, you did promise Beltane would be my favorite pagan celebration… It being a *sure thing* and all… *May's Eve is for adults only…*"

I giggle when he pulls me against him and ducks his head into the crook of my neck to tickle-kiss me. "Oh, please." I laugh, squirming within his strong hold at the sensation of his lips and rough stubble brushing against my sensitive skin. "Like you're at all deprived of carnal affections!"

"I want you to wear this tonight," he growls, fisting the fabric of my sundress and slowly curling it into his grip, pulling it higher up my leg. I swat at his hand and lean back enough to coax his lips to mine. Kissing him for a moment, I playfully nip his bottom lip and push my dress back down.

"Beltane is about more than sex, *you rogue*," I tease. "It's a celebration of life, new beginnings, and taking risks."

"*Like getting caught?*" Dean deviously growls, running the back of his knuckles down my cheek.

"*Aw fuck!*" We both hear from our three-and-a-half-year-old before he takes a tumble. Dean is beside him in a flash, helping Ace up from the ground. "*I'm okay, I'm okay!*" Ace insists, already eager to climb back onto the bike before Dean even has it straightened out for him. My heart is pounding again, but Dean is wearing the biggest grin as he readjusts Ace's helmet and pads.

"Good job, buddy," Dean says encouragingly, but then presses his lips together for a moment before adding, "Maybe a little less potty-mouth, though, for your momma."

"*I'm sorry, Momma!*" Ace calls to me before buzzing away again.

Dean returns to my side wearing another half-guilty grin. "See? He's fine. I didn't even have to gaslight him this time. He couldn't get back on the bike fast enough. *Now… Where were we?*"

I take a breath and let it out, attempting to settle my nerves as Dean leans into me suggestively again. "Beltane," I say, "I was about to tell you it's about surviving the winter…and what you fought like hell to keep burning."

His lust-drunk expression sobers a bit. "We've survived a lot."

I nod. "And when you survive a war, you don't just rebuild what you had. You build stronger. You build bigger. *You grow.* What's happening with the MC is an example of that. Expansion. Taking a risk on Legion."

"I wasn't talking about the MC."

I place my hand against his heart. "I know… But I agreed to give you time."

Legion: Book 3

Dean shifts his gaze to Ace, and although he's checking on our son, I know part of him doing so is avoidance.

"You bikers live life to the fullest. You know life isn't safe. Love isn't always safe... I know you've been betrayed, but I won't fail you. *Our love* is *safe*, Dean. No matter what. I will always love you."

"Yeah," he glances back at me with a rueful smile. "But a little magick doesn't hurt."

We reach the end of the dirt driveway at a clearing where Viking's cabin sits nestled a few yards from the riverbank, surrounded by woods. The sun just dipped below the tree line across the river, casting gold and orange light through the dark foliage that matches the glowing bonfire closer to the water. There are a few posts set up with string lights around the perimeter of the party area, which also leads to the back deck of the cabin.

The tires of Dean's truck crunch over the gravel as we pull into one of the remaining spots in the wide driveway, which is packed with a few other vehicles and motorcycles belonging to the MC. Dean kills the engine, and for a moment we linger, listening to the engine ticking as it cools.

Viking's cabin is lovely. Picture perfect, like a Kincaid painting. I turn to look at Dean. "Is this because of a woman?"

Dean chuckles. "Haven't you figured out that everything the male species does is because of women?"

"He's really serious about that Steel Vixen, isn't he?" I sigh, glancing past Dean to look through his window at the party raging on around the fire. "Is she going to be here tonight?"

He quirks a brow at me. "You don't like her?"

"I haven't decided," I say, unbuckling my seatbelt to grab the little good-luck witch jar I made for Viking's place-holder-house-warming-gift. With such short notice, it was the best I could do in a pinch. I'll get him something else in the near future.

The earthy smell of thick river mud, pine trees, and fire fills my lungs as we walk down the path along the side of the cabin, toward the gathering around the raging fire. Just as we reach the part of the path that merges with the one at the cabin's back deck, Viking steps out of the door carrying a big bag of ice for what I assume is meant for a cooler down near the riverbank.

"Hey! You made it!" he says, as if we would be anywhere else.

"You got room for these down there, or should I leave them here?" Dean asks, twisting to show him the two cases of beer tucked under his arm.

"Bring 'em," Viking says, descending the wooden steps.

"Congratulations, Viking," I smile up at him and hand him the jar. "You bury this outside your front porch for good luck and protection."

"Cool," he says, and I have to suppress a laugh as he looks at it and places it on the railing. "I'll get right on that in the morning."

"Perfect. This place is absolutely beautiful. I can't believe you kept this a secret. I hope this doesn't mean we're going to be seeing less of you at the clubhouse."

Viking scoffs, shrugging off my heartfelt words, as to be expected. "Place still needs work on the inside, but the view is bitchin'," he says, cocking his bearded chin toward the river. "And it wasn't a secret, it just happened fast. No way this place was gonna stay on the market long. I'm surprised Ace didn't say anything. He picked it out."

"Ace did?" I ask.

"Yeah, I brought him with me about a month ago when I was babysitting him. I asked if he liked it. He said *Yeah, it's a bitchin' place, bro.*"

"*He did not!*" I laugh.

Viking grins teasingly. "Anyway, he liked it, so I bought it. There's a pier to fish from, too, and it came with a boat slip, so that's next on the agenda."

"We're very happy for you. This place is just perfect."

"Well, you two know you're welcome here any time you want," Viking says, reaching into his pocket with his free hand. He tosses something small to Dean unexpectedly, who barely manages to catch it in the poor lighting, letting out a disgruntled sigh at his biker buddy. "Key to the place. Don't fuckin' lose it, asshole. *Mi casa es su casa.*" Viking gestures toward the gathering by the river. "Happy Beltane. Now, let's get this celebration started."

The men are mostly lounging around the fire with their beers, kicked back in lawn chairs or on the two picnic tables on either side of the clearing, talking, laughing, but mostly watching the women dance around the fire. They're all wearing flower crowns, and the moment Cherry spots us, she grabs one from a basket and brings it to me. Dean winks at Cherry in greeting, before I feel his hand brush the small of my back, moving over the curve of my waist. A slow, possessive touch that says without words, I belong to him. He must have already spotted Legion somewhere... I smile at Dean before he splits off to help Viking restock the coolers and greet his MC brothers.

Cherry places the flower crown made from daisies and other wildflowers on my head. "*She's here,*" she whispers.

"I figured... I guess this means they're serious."

"For the moment, anyway."

"Do we like her?"

Cherry shrugs. "She's a little standoffish. I'm still deciding."

I chuckle. "That's what I told Dean."

DEAN

I watch Vanna dancing just beyond the reach of the flames, that sexy sundress flaring up whenever she spins, allowing the glow of the fire to kiss those thick, smooth thighs... Her laughter rings out like a song as she adjusts the flower crown in her hair.

I'm standing a few paces back, beer nearly forgotten in my hand, just admiring the way she moves with the kind of ease that makes the world slow down.

Goddamn.

There's something ancient about her in the firelight. Something wild and pagan-esque, a Beltane goddess come to life. Everyone is watching the women dance, but my eyes are glued to the mystical creature I somehow managed to marry.

It isn't long before something dark beneath the awe twists in my gut...because I know he's watching, too, somewhere in the shadows that he always seems to gravitate into...always beyond the edge of light. *Fuckin' Legion...*the Demon who once wanted to burn the world down is probably staring at her the same way I am.

I hate that he gets to see her like this. Wild. Free. *Herself.*

She catches my eye and smiles, that little smirk that says she knows exactly what she's doing to me.

"You really have to admire it." Legion's rough voice materializes from the darkness, and although I knew the demonic fuck was lurking somewhere, every muscle in my body tenses.

"What?" I spare him a disdainful glance where he stands, half-lit by the fire, half-consumed by shadow, and *entirely* pushing every one of my buttons as he stares at her like he's got a right to. I grind my molars hard enough to feel it in my skull.

"The fire element... Purification. Transformation. The potential it holds for creation and destruction. The hypnotic effect fire holds over us... You know, fire gazing played a role in the evolution of the human mind's cognitive abilities."

"Yeah, I read that in National Geographic as a kid."

"Not all elements are a match for fire." He takes a slow swig of his beer, flicking the ash of his cigarette with his other hand. "And the more *air* it gets, the harder it is to control... *Air feeds fire.*"

I take a swig of my own beer, deciding whether or not to toss him in the river or the fire he fucking admires so much.

"Water, on the other hand..." *he goes on, naturally.* "Well...that combination is a far more precarious pairing, don't you think?" He pulls a slow drag and exhales the smoke in my direction, the way he used to when we hated each other openly. "Fire either evaporates water over time, or water drowns the fire out..."

I'm water.

He's air.

And she's the fire we're both orbiting.

The urge to grab him and shove him into the blaze is beginning to feel more and more like poetic justice... Then again, the fucker probably crawled out of hell... It might be satisfying to drown him in *my element.*

I swallow the urge with another gulp of beer, and with a parting glare to convey this *not too subtle* conversation is over, I turn from him to approach Vanna. I don't get far, though, when the woman Viking calls Val steps into my path.

"Dean... I need to speak with you," she says. Something in her eyes makes me bite back the frustration already rising.

I want nothing more than to reach Vanna in this moment, but out of respect for Viking, my best friend, my brother, and everything we've been through together, I force myself to pause and listen to what she has to say.

"I'm sorry I couldn't help with Jagger... I'm not proud of that time in my life... We were never anything real to each other. I only ever knew his road name," she says, before glancing somewhere

Legion: Book 3

behind me. Disdain eclipses her apologetic expression. "I can't imagine having to look at that monster every day."

"Did he do something to you?"

"No," she shakes her head slowly. "Not to me... For whatever it's worth, I'm sorry I couldn't help you avoid this."

"No worries, doll. What's done is done. We know you would have given us a name if you could have. If it makes you feel better, the former Knights we were able to track down and reach out to basically told us to go to hell." I wasn't surprised by the lack of cooperation. They not only blame me for Legion, but for the rift years ago with Shane. "If you'll excuse me," I say, nodding at my wife.

"Does she know?" Val asks, sparing Vanna a glance. I instinctively know what she's referring to.

"No. She doesn't. And I'd like to keep it that way," I say, firmly.

Her eyes lift to meet mine, a flicker of defiance in them. "You don't think she has a right to know?"

"It's not like that."

"What is it like, then?"

"Her knowing only benefits *him* in the end. Now, if you'll excuse me, I need to get to my wife."

Frustration renewed to near max capacity, I brush past her and continue toward Vanna.

She stops dancing when she sees me coming, her laughter fading like she can already feel the anger rolling off of me. I don't say anything. I just reach for her hand and tug her away with me, ignoring the way the other women raise their eyebrows and knowingly smirk. I lead my wife into the dark, away from him, toward the dock a few yards away.

"Dean?" she says softly as we walk out onto it. I turn to face her and back her up against one of the posts strung with mini lanterns, casting a barely-there glow.

I cage her with my body, hands sliding low around her hips, my forehead pressing to hers. I need her close. I need to feel her heartbeat hammering against my own. I need to remind myself, and her, exactly who we are.

"You're mine," I say, voice rough against her ear. "Don't ever forget it."

Her hands curl into my shirt, pulling me closer, and she kisses me as if she knows he said something...

I press her harder against the pole, parting her thighs with my leg as my hands slide back down to grip the curve of her hips, dragging her into me. Her heat against my denim-clad thigh stirs my cock, and a low growl rumbles up my throat. I kiss her harder, one hand slipping down to cup the back of her thigh, lifting her leg to hook it around my waist.

Without hesitation, she moves against me, grinding slow and needy. My other hand gathers the fabric of her sundress, bunching it up in my fist. If I lift it just a little bit higher, I can have her right here, right now, against this damn post, under the stars and his watchful, covetous gaze, I'm sure.

In this heated moment, I don't care if he's watching. I need to claim her. To remind her. To remind him. To remind myself, she's mine.

She whimpers into my mouth, hips tilting, eager, and I almost lose it, but her hands slide up my body to my face, cupping my stubbled jaw. "Dean," she whispers against my lips, breathless but steady. "Baby, not here."

I let her leg slide down, my hands falling away from her. But she keeps her hands on me as if she knows I need the anchor. As if she wants me to know she's not pulling away because she doesn't want me.

"We'll go home soon," she murmurs, brushing her nose playfully against mine. "We'll have the house to ourselves, and you can show me then."

I swallow hard and press my forehead to hers again, regaining my control. "Alright."

She smiles and kisses me, gentle this time. "We have one ritual to complete before we get to *this one*."

"A sacrifice?" I joke. "*I have someone in mind.*"

She giggles. "*No…* We have to jump over the fire."

I glance past her, back at the flames still roaring high, sending sparks into the dark sky like they'll reach the stars. "Ummm…well…"

"*When it dies down a bit,*" she adds with a hint of laughter.

I spot Legion's dark form lingering near the outer perimeter of the orange glow. Watching. Fuck him. Let him keep watching all the ways she belongs to me.

Legion: Book 3

LEGION

You know you're hurting when it doesn't get your dick hard anymore… It just churns a pain in your chest where once all you felt was a hollow chill… He knew I was watching them. Watching his hands roam her body, possessive and reverent… It's funny to think back on a time I would have gutted her like a doe, ripped her insides out right in front of his face, just to break him as thoroughly as possible. Now, I dream of experiencing her insides in a completely different way…

I wait patiently for her to return and dance around the fire once again, eager for another glimpse of her shapely legs whenever she lifts that skirt just a little higher than necessary to spin and twirl, flashing those glorious thighs in the glow of the flames. She knows I'm here watching. It's as much of a show for me as it is for him.

Fucking prick dragged her away, made out with her hot and heavy for all to see on the dock…*above the water*…daring the world to try and take her from him… Well, *perhaps not the world*…

The soft crack and brief hiss of a beer bottle being uncapped breaks the spiraling of my mind, and my gaze slides to the female form approaching me. I clock her from the corner of my eye. Blonde. Well-endowed. Tight little shorts, and a bottle in her hand like an invitation. She saunters up to me, all heat and easy promise.

"Thought you could use some company, all alone over here at a sex party." The hang-around the MC calls Maxi, slides her hand down my arm as if she already owns me. I permit her touch for a heartbeat, maybe two. I know I could fuck her, but I feel nothing. No rush. No fire. "Not much happening sex wise, but we could change that, baby. I've been thinking about your *May Pole* since before you patched in."

I catch her wrist, fingers closing tight enough to make her eyes widen. "*Beltane* isn't strictly a *sex party*." Despite the ever-present gravel in my voice, my tone is sharper than I intend. "I'll pass."

The blonde blinks, thrown, unaccustomed to being turned down. Or perhaps she's wondering what she might have read *beyond the first paragraph of her Beltane Google search*. "You sure?" she teases, tipping her chin in the direction of the dock. "*I don't mind sharing.*"

I scoff without humor. "You aren't even in the same league," I mutter, releasing her wrist and stepping back.

Her pretty little face twists with wounded pride.

"You're better off," another familiar blonde female says, approaching the disgruntled hang-around. "This prick will only hurt you. Go back to the party."

With a departing scowl, the patch whore turns and walks away with an exaggerated sway of her hips. I shift my gaze back to the fire and light up another cigarette.

"I don't know how you managed to pull this off, but it's just a matter of time before she learns the truth about you," the Vixen warns.

"It's in both our best interests for you to walk away, too," I say.

"Unfortunately for you, I'm not an emotionally unstable victim of your abuse. You don't intimidate me. I will stand up to you, Legion."

"I'm sure sinking your claws into Viking hasn't factored into your confidence," I sneer, sliding my gaze to her once more with an antagonistic grin. "But if it will ease the tension between us on this wonderful May's Eve... I haven't seen your friend in weeks... *How is she?*"

The blonde uncrosses her arms to ball her fists at her sides, and I laugh on a cloud of smoke.

"Val!" Viking calls from across the fire. "Get over here!"

Reluctant to obey, she glares harder at me. "*Stay away from her,*" she warns once again.

The old oak trees dripping in Spanish moss swallow the moonlight when I venture further into the woods to take a piss in private. When I return, so has Vanna. I spot her instantly, standing with Cherry and a few of the other club girls, laughing at something one of the Ol' ladies said. A breeze catches her hair, and as she brushes the strands from her face, unsnagging a few tendrils from her flower crown, her eyes lock with mine. She smiles, excusing herself from the group of women to approach me, only breaking her magnetic gaze from mine to glance briefly at the Steel Vixen standing beside Viking as she passes. The slight measure of hostility brewing just below the surface between them bodes well for me. The longer they avoid each other, the better, and they have done so all night.

Vanna makes one more pitstop at an ice cooler, bending to select two glass bottles.

"Another beer?" she offers when she reaches me. I could take it or leave it, I've had my fill, but she's the one offering, so I take it.

Legion: Book 3

"Would you mind?" she asks with a coy, little smile, holding out her hard lemonade to me. "The caps hurt my hands."

I remember, vividly, the feel of those petal-soft hands on my body... Without a word, I twist the cap off and tuck it into my cut pocket.

"Thanks." She smiles again, soft and easy. "Are you enjoying the party?"

"*I am now.*"

She takes a dainty sip from her bottle.

"Dance with me?"

She seems surprised by my sudden request, and although her friendly demeanor hasn't wavered, I can tell there is something delicate folding up inside her.

"I don't think that's a good idea..." she says, gentle, but firm, and low enough to spare me the embarrassment of rejection. There isn't any cruelty in her denial, though. Simply, walls. *Loyal fucking walls.*

I lean into her, though I'm cautious to maintain enough distance to seem respectful while still close enough for her to feel the weight of my attention. "Have you forgotten your promise to me, sweet one?" I allow a slight grin to tug at the corner of my mouth. "You still owe me a dance."

Her lips part in surprise, remembering, and a memory of my own forces its way to the forefront of my mind... What it felt like to slip my tongue between those luscious lips...

For a breathless moment, the air between us feels charged, so thick it hurts... *That pull.* That spark in the darkness she keeps pretending doesn't exist between us. It was a significant May's Eve that brought us together, years ago... The urge to divulge that secret churns within my tortured soul.

Not yet...

I stare at the way she chews her bottom lip, her nerves getting the better of her... Or perhaps, devil willing...*something more...*

"I haven't forgotten," she says, voice dipping soft. "I'll make it up to you. Two dances. You pick the songs."

Two dances...to spare Keegan the sight of her in my arms on this blessed Beltane...

Two dances... A collective seven minutes in Heaven where I can *pretend* she is mine.

I swallow back the things I can't say and give her a slow, easy grin instead. "As you wish, sweet one."

Her appreciative smile is both a balm and a blade.

When Keegan calls for her from across the yard, she spares me one last look, something almost apologetic, before she slips away from me like smoke through my fingers...

The old Beltane tradition hasn't been forgotten despite the thinning of the crowd. Only a few of the MC members with the closest bonds of brotherhood remain for the final ritual, though besides Vanna and Viking, the others participate for the sake of amusement.

One by one, and couple by couple, they leap over the flames of the low-burning fire, sealing vows, casting wishes...

I remain near enough in the shadows, arms crossed, cigarette dangling from my lips, waiting for it to happen... Wondering, though fairly certain, what she'll wish for when she leaps.

She laughs when Keegan catches her hand, pulling her toward the crackling fire, still burning just high enough to matter... The last leap before the flames burn themselves out.

She smiles that wild, unguarded smile at him that most men would kill to see aimed at them even once...

I would...

I have...

He pulls her closer, strong and sure, and lifts her hand to press a kiss against it. Fingers laced, they squeeze each other tighter, just before they run, vaulting the flames in one breathless leap.

Their friends cheer as they land on the other side, and she turns in his steady embrace, flushed and laughing, beautiful, like something worthy of worship. He spins her around in his arms like some fucking Hallmark movie.

I fight the urge to clench my fists, half-tempted to projectile vomit on the remaining flames like a scene from *The Exorcist!*

But I don't let the mask slip...

I can't...

And so, *I smile.*

I applaud.

I pretend the fire in my heart isn't mirroring the one dying at my feet ...

CHAPTER 39

Vanna

"You're really quiet tonight," Cherry says, nudging me with her elbow while I wipe down the bar counter more so out of habit than necessity. It's a Tuesday night, so it's not unusual for the Twisted Throttle to be a little slow.

I shrug, casting a quick glance at Legion across the room. He's nursing a beer in the corner of one of the leather couches, watching with borderline disinterest as a couple of the patch-chasers dance for him. He's been different since Beltane. Almost restless…

He wears our MC's colors now and shows up whenever asked. Although I'm happy he's making the effort, something just feels off, despite his admitted desire for redemption. I feel uneasy over the fact I might still be the only reason he's keeping himself tethered to this town.

Cherry follows my line of sight. "Axel says he's been good, and the sweetbutts seem to like him."

"He's trying…but something is different."

"He's an outlaw," Cherry says, pouring another shot for one of our regulars before she steps away to place it on the bar in front of the old biker. She offers him a friendly little wink and steps back to me. "It takes them time to adjust. Viking's been around since before I even got here, and he has only settled down in the last few years."

"Do you think he's going to stick around? For the long haul, I mean?"

Cherry studies me for a moment. "Are you hoping he doesn't?"

I let out a tense sigh. "I know how he feels… I'm not blind, and neither is Dean."

"Do you forgive him for everything?"

"I want to."

"Maybe he knows you're not quite there yet, and until you are…"

"Right…" I nod, glancing at the clock behind the bar. It's a little after 9 pm. Dean should be getting off his shift at the safehouse soon with Dozer, and Ace has been asleep in Dean's club room for about an hour. "I should go check on my son," I say.

"Okay." Cherry smiles. "Give the little munchkin a kiss for me. It's a slow night, I've got things up here, and Maxie should be back from her break any minute anyway."

Before I'm able to duck under the bar and head for the corridor, I notice a tension in Legion's expression. He's gone from looking nearly bored to death to glaring at a group of female patrons who just stepped through the steel door of the Twisted Throttle.

Four women, dressed in denim and leather. They're all wearing Steel Vixens MC cuts. I instantly recognize Jett and Val. They're all smiles for Viking at first, until Val scans the room and finds Legion. The moment their eyes lock, her expression turns cold, and Legion lifts his beer to her in what seems like a mock salute.

Viking is already rubbing his forehead and avoiding eye contact with her, like he already regrets something that hasn't even happened yet.

I duck under the counter and walk around the bar to see what the problem is, but I've already missed the beginning of their exchange.

"Doing you a favor," Val snaps.

"How is breaking my balls a favor?" Viking huffs.

"You said your boy was struggling," Val goes on, and Viking practically winces at her choice of words in front of me. "I thought we'd take our celebration to the Twisted Throttle. Make this place one of our hang-arounds. *But since we don't seem welcome here—*"

"You're welcome here," I interrupt, and she turns to look me over. I take the opportunity to do the same. She's a few inches taller than me in her leather boots. Her blonde, mid-length hair is pulled back in a high ponytail with a few thin braids at her temples. If her bitchy attitude wasn't an issue, I'd say her style at least pairs well with Viking's.

"Just because you avoided me at Beltane, and *I* apparently am not welcome in *your* establishment, doesn't mean I hold a grudge."

Val seems surprised, as if she didn't expect me to call her out on being blown off when I wanted to take those self-defense classes.

"Unless you really do have a problem with me?" I ask when she doesn't respond.

"Nothing I'm aware of," Viking says, shooting her a stern look. When I glance around at the other women, I notice they're all looking me over, too. Maybe it's because I'm not wearing bar or biker attire. I'm still wearing the button-down dress and ankle boots I put on this morning to spend time at the farm stand with Ace and Mia.

"We've been meaning to check out this place. And we've got no problems with *you*, gorgeous," Jett chimes in, throwing an arm around Val's shoulders before she lightly digs her stiletto-tipped nails into her friend's leather jacket like it's a warning.

"Yeah…you keep saying that… *Anyway*, would you ladies like a table? Feel free to sit wherever you like," I offer. "You're welcome to sit at the bar, too."

Val lifts her chin at the other women standing around me, and they all move to an empty table in the middle of the room, each claiming a seat. Jett grabs a chair and spins it around before straddling it. She glares over her shoulder at Legion while sweeping her long, black hair over the front of her shoulder, exposing the Steel Vixens MC rocker on her back. Then flips him off with both middle fingers.

I notice the taunting sneer on Legion's face as she does.

"We'll have a round of beers and shots while we wait for Ryder to get here," Val says, pulling my attention back to her.

"Start a tab for us on this," Jett says, plucking a credit card from her leather cut and handing it to me. "Ryder will be here soon," she adds when I glance at the name on the card.

"What kind?" I ask.

"Jameson and Budweiser," Val replies. "And thank you." She offers me a slight smile, making an effort. As long as she's willing to play nice, so am I, at least for Viking's sake. But I am curious what their deal really is with Legion, and if it has something more to do with his corruption and dismantling of the Asphalt Knights MC.

"I'll be right back with those." I return the smile.

Legion: Book 3

While I pour shots and load up their tray, I keep an eye on a still seemingly undeterred Legion.

"I can take it over to them if you want," Cherry offers, as if she's worried they're making me uncomfortable. "You can go check on Ace."

"I've got it. It won't take but a minute," I tell her, lifting the loaded tray. I make my way back to their table and place the beers and shots down in front of them.

"What's a club president's Ol' Lady doing handing out drinks? Aren't you supposed to be *above all that?*" one of the Steel Vixens I haven't officially met yet asks. The name displayed on the brunette's embroidered patch says her road name is *Boop*.

"I don't mind helping out on nights we're short-staffed or slow," I say, placing the last beer and shot down on the table before her.

"After everything that's gone down, are you really cool with *that* hanging around?" Boop angles her head in Legion's direction.

I tuck the tray under my arm, holding it against my side. "He's trying to right his wrongs..." My reply is met with more scoffing, and for some reason, it bothers me. Their disapproval spurs me to address Legion's presence further. "People change, you know... Learn from their mistakes."

Val practically scowls at me. "If you believe that, you should ask him about his *Puppet.*"

I glance at her curiously. "I'm sorry?"

"You will be if you actually think there's anything redeemable about Legion," she adds.

I'm not about to argue with a group of biker chicks in the middle of Dean's bar over Legion of all people. *Dean would love that.* It's best to simply diffuse the situation. "Can I get you all anything else?" I ask instead.

Jett glances at the clock on the wall. "Another round in about fifteen minutes... Ryder should be here soon."

I stop by the bar to drop off the tray with Cherry on my way to check on Ace.

"Is everything alright?" Cherry asks again. "I don't mind waiting on them tonight."

"Do you know anything about a *Puppet?*"

Cherry shakes her head, confused.

"I think they were referring to a *person.*"

"I've never met anyone by that road or pet name before," Cherry says.

"Alright." I suppose I'll just have to ask Legion myself.

LEGION

The blonde bitch of a pack leader stands up, blocking my path to the door, hostility etched across her expression as if I'd be intimidated.

I can't help but grin in her face. "If our girl services pussy as well as she does cock, I can understand why you're *so…enthralled* with her."

"Fuck you," she practically spits at me.

"How much?"

"You wish."

"*I meant me.* You're not my type. Everyone has a price, though. If your offer is generous enough, I might consider allowing you to ride my cock… You aren't wearing your man's patch… *fair game!*"

"Shall I run that offer by your club brother?" The Vixen crosses her arms and grins as if she managed to one-up me. I can feel Viking's watchful gaze boring into me, and I know he's moments from walking over. I haven't done anything wrong, though. Haven't broken any club rules. *She* stepped into *my* path.

"By all means," I call her bluff. "Nothing screams *girl power* like enlisting your man to fight your battles *for you.*"

She scowls before her eyes drift in Vanna's direction, scrutinizing my angel. "You're sick, you know that?" she mutters before her gaze cuts back to me. When I attempt to move past her, she slams her shoulder aggressively into my arm, and I can't help but chuckle as I resume course to the door for a smoke.

I've barely taken three drags off my cigarette before that steel door opens and shuts behind me again.

"Those girls inside don't seem to like you very much," Vanna says, walking up behind me. For once, I wish it wasn't her.

"I've got quite the fan club, as you can imagine, my sweet."

"They told me to ask you about *Puppet.*"

I'm not surprised Keegan has never mentioned my little fuck doll to her. I imagine he must often feel the pangs of temptation to weaponize this situation against me, to paint me as some obsessed freak in her mind. Not that I hadn't been... *Still am,* I suppose... Knowing he hasn't confirms what I've suspected all along...

Relishing in this small triumph, I fight the devious urge to grin.

"Well?" Vanna presses. "Are you going to answer me?" My lack of response seems to agitate her, and she lets out a sigh of frustration. "You promised me honesty. Do you remember that?"

"I do."

"I'm waiting."

"An ex." How else can I describe her?

Vanna blinks before her brows furrow. "You called her Puppet?"

"A term of endearment." *Technically...*

"Why would they want me to ask you about your ex? Did you do something to her?"

Fuck... "Rough breakup." I pull another drag, glancing at her briefly. She crosses her arms and shifts uneasily in her boots.

"When you say *rough*..." Vanna begins, and I turn to face her head-on. "You aren't implying you were violent with her...are you?"

"At the time of our breakup?"

Her eyes widen a bit at my inquiry, and her posture goes slightly rigid.

"Our breakup was not amicable... Nor is it anything I wish to rehash. I wanted out. She didn't. If you're worried as to whether or not *I beat her*, no. In my opinion, I did not."

"*In your opinion?*"

"During our times together...we...*dabbled* a bit."

"Dabbled in what?"

I search her expression more intently, wondering how vanilla her relationship with Keegan might be beyond what I've witnessed myself. He is a passionate, powerful lover... But I've never witnessed his hands around her throat...his belt secured around her wrists...

"Spanking. Asphyxiation. Restraints..."

"*Oh...*" Vanna's gaze immediately drops to the pavement.

"Shall I go on?"

"No... As long as you were both consenting adults," she shrugs awkwardly. "I mean, I don't need those details if..."

"Those women don't know me, Vanna. Their version of events is just that. *Their version.* Via the mouth of a disgruntled ex, no less. I deserve a fairer trial than this, no?"

"You're right... I'm sorry I asked."

"*Don't mention it,*" I wink at her as the sound of Keegan's approaching motorcycle echoes off the buildings down the street. "I'm sure the *good warden* would be less than thrilled to know *you've inquired about my sex life...* Fear not. *It's our little secret.*"

She lets out an uncomfortable little scoff, concurring without words.

We both watch Keegan dismount and cross the lot to her. He snakes an arm around her waist and plants a territorial kiss upon her lips, always eager to shove his claim on her in my face. Then he spares me a disdainful glance.

"Feel free to take off," he mutters.

"We have a few new patrons tonight," Vanna says in a chipper tone laced with mounting anxiety.

"Oh yeah?" he asks.

"Members of the Steel Vixens MC… I can't decide if they're here for a few drinks or to start trouble," she says, nodding at me. A slick smile etches across Keegan's face. "They don't seem to like Legion very much."

"In that case, their next round is on the house," Keegan jokes.

"Is that wise, oh fearless leader?" I needle him back. "I was under the impression *you were under* some financial hardship?"

"And I thought I told you to get the fuck out of here?"

"Oh, but I've come to collect."

"*Collect?*" Vanna asks.

"You still owe me a dance…*or two.*"

Keegan stiffens beside her while I pull the last drag from my cigarette. Did he honestly think I'd forgotten, or that I would willfully allow such an opportunity to slip through my grasp?

"Alright," Vanna sighs. "A deal is a deal. Why don't you pick a song to play before we dance? That way, you can give me a heads up when it comes on in case I'm busy with patrons."

Exhaling the smoke in Keegan's direction, I squeeze off the cherry and toss the butt into the receptacle behind him. "As you wish… How about Clapton's song, *Layla…*" I slide my eyes to Keegan in time to see him practically jolt and grip her tighter. I don't bother fighting my grin. He got the message. Our sweet Vanna remains unaware, and I wonder if he'll spoil my fun, or keep this little jab a secret as well…

Legion: Book 3

"Alright, that's a long one if I remember correctly," Vanna innocently replies.

I gesture toward the steel door of the Twisted Throttle, "*Beauty before evil*, sweet one."

Keegan grabs the handle, holding the door open for Vanna. She walks inside, and he shoots me another damning glare.

"*Husband* before *covetous fiend*," he growls, entering behind her and allowing the door to slam in my face. I half expect it to lock.

I'm familiar enough with their family routine to know she'll accompany him to check in on their son again. The roadhouse isn't crowded tonight, so there won't be a long wait for the songs of my choosing to play. Deciding to give her a little time, I light up again, just as another motorcycle pulls into the lot. A lady rider.

I've barely pulled a second drag before the steel door behind me bursts open and someone slams into my back, knocking the cigarette from my grasp.

"*Move, asshole!*" the brunette Brooklynite snaps as she storms past me, eager to greet her friend.

I stare at the dying glow of my cigarette against the gravel between my boots. It's astonishing, the things people forget about a person when they disappear for a while, or spend a few months playing by the rules of others... Perhaps a reminder is in order, a lesson in fear. I've always been such a good teacher.

DEAN

The noise from the bar fades with each step closer to my old club room, where Ace is sleeping. Vanna doesn't say a word, and I wonder if it's on purpose or if she's attempting to avoid another argument about Legion.

When we step into the room, the tension between us eases a bit at the sight of Ace fast asleep in the bed, his little chest rising and falling peacefully.

Vanna bends to adjust his blankets, then gently brushes his hair back from his face, the way she always does to both of us.

"He's exhausted," she whispers. "Rosita dropped Mia off with us at the farmstand today, and they both helped me tidy up and pick strawberries. Speaking of, we made mini strawberry shortcakes from scratch after lunch. There are some waiting for you at home in the fridge."

"Thanks," I say, keeping my voice low, despite her brief conversation with Legion still burning in my mind. "This better be the *last* dance, Vanna."

She hesitates, avoiding my gaze. "I promised him two."

My jaw tightens. "What inspired this generosity?"

She straightens slowly, finally turning to face me. "He tried to cash in his dance on Beltane... I didn't think you'd appreciate that...so I bargained my way out of it."

Another deal with the devil...

When I don't say anything, she continues with an almost pleading expression in her eyes. "He's trying to be part of something that doesn't come easy to him. This MC isn't what he's used to... He seems...restless."

I fold my arms and lean back against the dresser. "Maybe it's time he moved on."

She doesn't answer right away, but she absentmindedly lifts her hand to brush her fingertips across the base of her throat, as if the idea of him leaving distresses her.

The urge to break something begins to rise. "You don't want him to go," I say, studying her closely.

Her eyes lift to mine, but she doesn't deny it. "It's more complicated than that."

My guts twist, and I exit the room, taking a few strides down the hall, away from our sleeping son. Has she been so deprived of genuine affection prior to our life together that knowing Legion is in love with her is something she's come to find comfort in? *Validation*, even? *Jesus fuck...*

The door shuts quietly before she's by my side again. "I'm sorry," she says, stepping in front of me to halt my progression to the bar. "He's fragile, Dean... I don't know what he'll do if we tell him to go."

"Are you afraid of him?" I'm afraid to ask the questions I really want to know...

She seems to sense this and grips my hand in hers. "Not *of* him... For *him*."

Vanna always sees the good in people, even when they don't deserve it. Hell, especially when they don't fucking deserve it. It's one of the things I love most about her, *except* when I see it being used against her. Her soft heart and open soul...she doesn't realize how *evil* can fuckin' smell her kind of empathy, like blood in the water, or spot it like a crack in the foundation it can crawl through...

He noticed. He watches her with those pale eyes like he's starving, *hiding the pickaxe behind his back.* Playing the long game. The quiet one. The tragic past, the scars, the redemption arc he thinks we owe him. Fuck him and his evil plot to use the way she nurtures things that are broken to his advantage. I know she sees beauty in ruins... Potential in the fallen...and still believes people deserve to be whole. It's her gift. But it's also her goddamned blind spot, and he fucking knows it... *He uses it...*

But Vanna is mine to protect. I'm the fucking hero in her story. Her dark knight. Her Savior. And I always will be...*even if it means I have to become the villain temporarily in her eyes...*

I lift her hand and press a kiss against it. "I don't know how much patience I have left, Vanna."

We part ways upon reentering the Twisted Throttle. Vanna joins Cherry behind the bar, and I cross the room to sit with Viking in his usual spot near the door. Just before I make it to him, I cross paths with another Steel Vixen as she enters the bar.

"Welcome to the Twisted Throttle, doll." I force a smile, though, if she's *team Fuck Legion*, too, she's more than welcome. The brunette offers me a timid nod and eagerly veers off to join her friends waiting for her at the bar. I take a seat beside Viking and lean back against the bricks.

"You can go hang out with your chick for a while if you want. First time she's been here," I say, attempting to keep myself distracted with small talk. "Give her a quick tour if you want."

"Yeah, I told them they were welcome to come in. I figured it might help the bar," Viking replies.

"Huh?"

"You know, like that saying... *'If there's bitches, they will come.'*"

He actually manages to pull a chuckle out of me. "The logic is there, but that is absolutely not the quote you're thinking of." The humorous moment is short-lived when I scan the room and spot Legion, kicked back in a leather couch near the jukebox like he owns the place.

"He's gotta go," I mutter.

"What did he do now?"

"He's plotting something, I can feel it."

"Not to play devil's advocate, but he's been a team player since he got here, and he really came through for the Jokers."

"Look at him, sitting there all fuckin' smug with that fuckin' grin..." A grin that broadens the moment the opening riff of Layla begins to play. Legion raises his beer, just enough to make sure I know this is personal. A message. A taunt. Maybe even another promise...

"Son of a bitch."

"What?" Viking asks.

"Fuckin' Layla."

Viking quirks a brow at me. *"So?* It's a great Clapton hit."

"Legion selected it... Clapton wrote this song about Harrison's wife. He was in love with her. She wound up leaving him for Clapton."

"No shit?" Viking lets out an amused huff. "Gotta hand it to him, Dean...his mind-fuckery is on another level."

I waive a patch-chaser down to grab me a beer, though I probably should've asked for something stronger. Legion's had time to contemplate this dance. The song he's chosen will be presented to her as a confession of his love... Though there's no other way for me to take it than a quiet declaration of war.

LEGION

If Layla is a slap in the face, the song I chose for our dance will take the wind right out of him, like a kick in the balls... And I'm fairly certain, despite her promise, there will be no second dance tonight. At least not with her... *Keegan and I may end up in the parking lot,* however. Perhaps she'll grant me one last rain check...

The final few moments of Layla play through the speakers as Vanna steps out from behind the bar and crosses the room to me. I wonder how she will react to the song I've chosen for us... She'll know it's deliberate *because she knows me...*

Music has always lent a helping hand in the way of conveying the things we can't say out loud. Half the barflies in this joint have no doubt bared their souls through the jukebox, cuing up confessions one tune at a time. Love, regret, betrayal...there's a song for all of it.

Legion: Book 3

Layla ends as Vanna reaches me with a curious smile, just before our song begins to play. When it does, and its significance registers, her smile drops. Her lips part slightly, as if she isn't sure whether she wants to say my name or curse it.

I offer her my hand, but she hesitates, her gaze flicking to her husband. I know Keegan's leaning against the wall like a storm waiting to break. I can feel his stare burning through me. When she peers back up at me, her dark eyes reflect a war of emotions.

She's furious. Conflicted. *Afraid...* Though not of me...no, *never of me...*

The moment she places her hand in mine, I pull her into my arms, close...intimate...like I've got a right to. Her body tenses, but she doesn't deny me. She adjusts her hand in mine, cool but compliant. My other hand finds the curve of her waist as her palm rests against my chest, right over my racing heart. When she swallows, I know she can feel it, and when her wedding rings catch in the light above us, I ignore them.

"*You're playing with fire,*" she whispers, her sweet, warm breath against my throat.

I close my eyes for a moment and breathe her in, memorizing her scent and the feel of her in my embrace. "*Then burn with me...*"

The world falls away with each step, each sway, each lyric of Bryan Adams' *Please Forgive Me,* drifting through the speakers. I watch her eyes, waiting to see if she'll soften...

"*This song,* Legion..." She takes a quivering breath. "*He's watching us.*"

'It's not your wedding song."

"*It's close enough!*"

"I didn't choose it to hurt you," I murmur, "I chose it so you'd understand, so you'd know what I carry with me, so you'd know there isn't anything I wouldn't do for you."

Something flickers behind her gaze. Something deeper than guilt. Her hand trembles in mine, and I hold her closer still, allowing her to feel every beat of the song through me, every word I can't say out loud.

"*Damien... I can't give you what you want,*" she whispers, just before our song ends. The sadness in her tone, the bittersweet longing we both know she's too loyal to him to ever do anything about... They still soothe another broken part of my soul.

"You already did. You gave me this." I hold her a moment longer, and when she steps back, I let her go, despite feeling as though I'd rather peel off my own skin than let her slip away. We stare at each other, and I can still taste her perfume in the air, on my person. Some other song is playing now, but the echo of the one we claimed still vibrates in my chest...steady, punishing...

When I hear the heavy sound of his boots rapidly approaching, I know I'm in for more punishment.

The tsunami of his anger hits me, and I'm certain his fist is about to do the same. The room thins out around us, voices dip, conversations pause. Despite the skull and wings embroidered on my back, no club brother will be intervening on my behalf. Keegan's crew knows better than to get between him and the man who just slow-danced with his wife to a love song that cut too close to the bone.

To my surprise, the blow never arrives.

"You think you're slick?" Keegan growls, tone as sharp as the knives concealed on my body.

"No," I say, breaking my gaze from her to spare him a glance. "I think I'm in love with your wife... I daresay I will be until the day you put me in the ground for it."

The words hang between us, raw and unapologetic.

His jaw ticks, palpable rage a blazing fire held behind clenched teeth and muscle, but I don't flinch. I'm still wrapped up in the euphoria of what I'd just had in my arms for three and a half minutes of borrowed time.

"You and me. Outside. Now," my president commands.

"Dean, please..." Vanna nervously begs of him on my behalf, her hands slipping around his bicep.

"You stay here," he mutters, barely looking at her.

"Dean... *Please don't fight*," she anxiously presses.

"Enough!" Keegan steps away from her to get in my face. "Outside, of your own fucking accord, or I'll drag you the fuck out of here."

I could use a smoke, anyhow. I shift my gaze to Vanna. "There's nothing for you to fret over, sweet one. I will always keep my word to you."

"Should I come out there?" Viking asks as Keegan and I approach the steel door to the lot.

Legion: Book 3

"No," Keegan growls. "Don't let anyone out here."

"Got it," Viking shoots me a taunting sneer. *"No witnesses..."*

When we step outside, I light up a cigarette as Keegan comes to stand before me.

"What promise were you referring to?" he demands.

"The same one you made. That I wouldn't harm you."

Keegan leans into me, an intimidation tactic he means to emphasize his greater size. I'm well aware, with his honed skills, his brute strength, his ability to decipher body language to anticipate an opponent's next move in a battle. Dean Keegan could, *and eagerly would*, kick my ass in a *fair* fight. If he were anyone else, I'd slice him to bloody ribbons for the disrespect.

However, I expected this reaction, and this arrogant prick has a forcefield of impenetrable protection around him, rendering me unable to even lay a fucking finger upon him, *let alone a blade*, in wrath or even self-defense. A beautiful shield of blinding, white light. Protected by this promise I made to the love of both our lives...

I pull a long, leisurely drag, letting him know neither his posturing nor his proximity fazes me in the slightest. I meet his scowling gaze with a stoic expression of my own.

You don't scare me, Savior. I've had the fear fucked out of me long ago...

"I've never claimed to be a hero," he tells me. "You'd be wrong to think I'd ever put anything or anyone above Vanna and my son. You'd be *dead. Fucking. Wrong.*"

"Noted."

"*Note this, too,* asshole. When Vanna comes home with me tonight, I'll be making love to her. I'll be inside her. I'm the only man she wants. The only man she loves."

"Are you trying to convince me, or yourself?"

"I mean it when I tell you, I will do more than hurt you, Legion, if you fucking cross me again. Especially when it comes to *my wife.*"

He glares at me for a silent moment, as if deciding what to shove in my face next. "Maybe you should know exactly what I mean. Maybe a glimpse of what could be your final resting place will put things into perspective for you," he goes on, equally unreactive to the smoke I exhale in his glowering face.

"And where might that be, pray tell?" I sneer back at him.

"You might want to take this down." He eyes the cell in my pocket. "This is both a warning and a kindness that would be *detrimental to your existence*, should you mistake it for weakness."

Jennifer Saviano

"*A kindness?* I'm intrigued." I remove the cellphone from my cut pocket to punch in the coordinates he impressively rattles off from memory. "*Drear Swamp...*"

Keegan nods once. "Consider leaving the rest of your *black roses* at the end of the old pier you'll find there."

A slight chill forms in my solar plexus as I realize what he's just given me...

The kindness of closure, shrouded within the far more prominent threat of death...

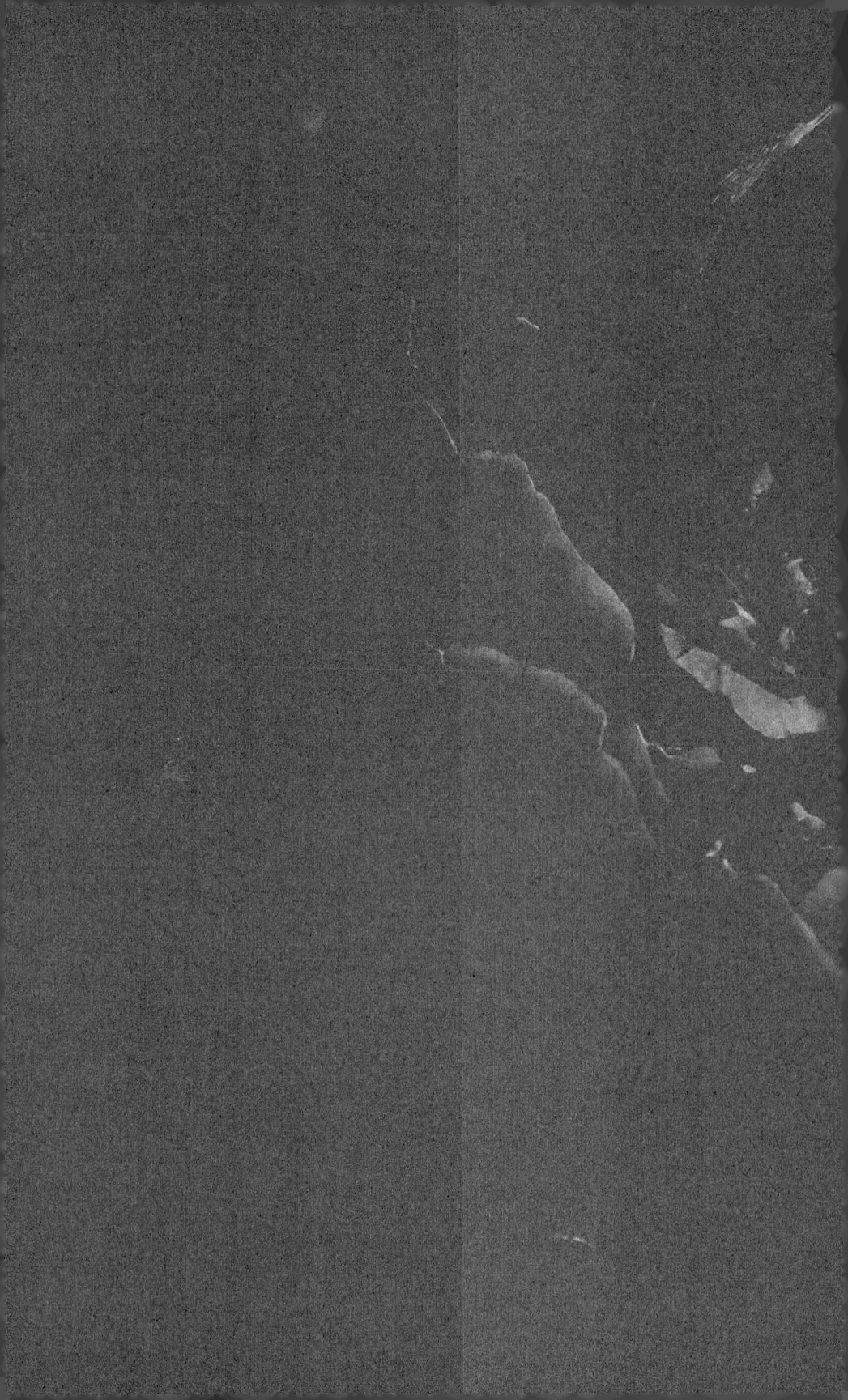

CHAPTER 40

Vanna

"Are you alright? You seem very angry tonight," I say softly to Dean as we enter our home. Ace is fast asleep in my arms, head resting against my shoulder, his little face pressed lightly against my neck.

"I'm not," Dean practically grumbles, shutting the door and locking it behind us. I let my purse slide down my arm and hand it over to him.

"I'm going to put Ace to bed."

He only nods.

Ace barely stirs while Nico watches me carefully finagle my son out of his clothes and into pajamas. Tucking him in, I brush a few strands of dark hair from his forehead and place a gentle kiss above his eyebrow. Nico curls up in his usual spot at Ace's feet. I stroke his fur as he settles himself in, buying a few moments to brace myself.

Dean can deny being pissed all he wants, but I know Legion got under his skin tonight. The murderous glare in my husband's eyes at Legion's song choice lingers in my memory, as well as the way he ordered me to remain inside the roadhouse. I'm sure he threatened Legion. He may have even tossed him a beating…but I'm afraid to ask if Legion left the lot in one piece.

I leave Ace's door cracked a few inches and make my way back to the kitchen, where Dean is still standing, leaning with his back against the front door. He's doing something on his phone and doesn't look up when I remove my jacket or when I hang it up on the rack next to his cut.

Soft music begins to play through the sound system of our home. It's low, not loud enough to wake Ace, but I instantly recognize the song, and the pain in Dean's eyes when he finally looks up at me. It's *Bryan Adams, Please Forgive Me.*

"Dean…" I sigh, unable to formulate a sentence beyond his name. I know part of the reason Legion chose the song tonight was to get at Dean. At least he didn't pick our actual wedding song. I would have turned him down. "It was just a dance he paid for…"

The sad look in Dean's eyes darkens, sending a shiver down my spine…and not entirely in a bad way. He places his phone on the edge of the bench below the coat rack, and I can see he has the song set to loop. As he begins to undo the buttons at the top of his shirt, enough to yank it off over his head, I know what is about to happen.

The shirt hits the floor, and I can't deny the devious part of me is smiling inside. Of course, his jealous, possessive side would kick into overdrive after Legion's little stunt. After ripping off the undershirt next, his hands drop to his belt, undoing it with an eager haste that has my face flushing with heat as I admire the rippling muscles of his sculpted body. So beautiful. So lethal. So mine.

I peer up into his lustful gaze. "Should I take off my—"

"Ain't gonna be a problem," he growls, stepping forward to roughly grab me around the waist, pulling me against his hot, hard body. In an instant, his mouth is on mine, kissing me roughly, and I submit to his need, parting my lips and allowing him to take possession of my mouth as I wrap my arms around his neck.

Strong hands move lower, gripping my ass, pressing me more firmly against him. I can feel his hard length undeniably now. He backs me up, maneuvering us toward the dining room table, until I'm pressed against the edge.

"Here?" I manage to gasp through the onslaught of his dominating kisses.

He doesn't respond with words. He simply hoists me up and drops me on it, barely breaking our kiss, and immediately shoves his hands up my skirt.

"Dean!" I whisper-shout at him, but he's on a mission. Grabbing behind my knees, he jerks me forward, forcing my legs around his waist. The old barnwood table groans in protest. Anxiety creeps in, shoving lust aside as worry over breaking the damn table is at the front of my mind now. *That would be so embarrassing!* I try to shove at his hands beneath the fabric of my skirt, then at his chest when I'm

unsuccessful. His fingers are already pulling at the waistband of my underwear.

"*Damnit, Dean! We're going to break the table!*" I harshly whisper, and though I'm not exactly cooperating, he is undeterred. "*It will wake up Ace!*"

"I haven't had you here yet," he says, just as I feel the knuckles of his fists ball up against my flesh. The muscles in his chest and arms flex, and the sound of fabric ripping cuts through the music.

His level of heady aggression doesn't at all match the lovingly mournful romantic song playing softly. After yanking the fabric from my body, he tosses the remnants of my now useless underwear onto the table beside us, then drops his hands to undo the rest of his fly, freeing himself between my parted thighs.

"Was that really necessary?"

He shrugs with complete indifference, grabbing the bunched-up hem of my skirt, hiked up and draped across my thighs in both fists. A devious smirk pulls at the corner of his mouth, just as his eyes flick up to meet mine again.

"*Wait!*" I barely get the word out before the fabric of my dress is ripping. Buttons fly away, clicking on the surface of the table and the hardwood floor around us. "*Damnit, Dean...*" I sigh, leaning back on my elbows defeatedly as he grabs and tears the rest of my dress open, all the way to the neckline. What used to be another one of my Practical Magic dresses now resembles a tattered, ankle-length cardigan. Maybe I should stop wearing anything I like around Legion. He seems to inadvertently ruin my favorite clothing.

With one hand, Dean grabs the base of his rigid cock and angles himself to press against my center. Hovering above me, he wraps his other hand around the nape of my neck, pulling me up to him until our mouths crash together again.

"*You're wet,*" he growls against my lips, almost accusatorily, as he slides his cock up and down my slit. I know the demons in his mind have him worried about my reaction to being in Legion's arms earlier.

"Well, *you're hot.* And mine. And I want you... *Only you.*" I nip his bottom lip before kissing him back. As his tongue thrusts against mine, he pushes inside of me, and I groan into his mouth at the sensation of him filling me. "I'm always ready for you, Dean," I whisper, tilting my head back to give him my throat. His rough stubble on my sensitive skin makes me quiver as he licks and kisses me there. "I belong to you, sweetheart. No one but you."

The table creaks with every pistoning slam of his body into mine. Clinging to each other, I allow him to work out his fears and frustrations until we're both on the verge of climax.

"Do you remember our first kiss? The first time we made love? *The fuckin' thousandth time?*" Dean pants as he fucks me.

"Of course, I do," I try to reassure him. "You love me exactly the way I need to be loved, Dean. You're the only man in the world for me..."

His fingers tangle in my hair, and he kisses me deeply again, before pressing his forehead to mine and confessing, as if I didn't already know, *"I need to erase it, Vanna... What he did to us tonight..."*

"He didn't do anything... I'm still yours... I'll always be yours..."

"I'm going to give you everything you want, baby... Everything."

"I know," I smile at his determined expression.

"*Everything,* Vanna..." he says, as if he's willing me to understand something unspoken.

He knows the instant I do, and claims my mouth once again with a deep, passionate kiss.

Nails digging into his back, holding onto him as if I might truly fall over a cliff, my body begins to convulse around his. He buries his face in the crook of my neck, holding me so tightly against him it's difficult to breathe.

"*Fuck,* Vanna! *Fuck...*" he grunts against my neck, one hand snaking down my back to grip my ass, anchoring me firmly against him as he thrusts as deep as he can get. Every muscle in his body tenses. A primal groan erupts from his throat, and I feel his powerful release.

Dean's hold on me relaxes just a bit as we both come back down in the aftermath, and he presses his forehead to mine once more. We listen to the music as our breaths slow to normal.

"I love you," he sighs. "*Insanely,* I love you."

I can't help but let out a sated, low laugh. "I know you do. That's why you married me, isn't it?"

"He can't have this song... He can't have any song. Not with you, Vanna... I don't care if he finds you in the lyrics. If he means every verse in this song... *I mean them more... I am your knight.*"

I reach up to hold his face in my hands and press a soft kiss against his lips. "I will never stop loving you, Dean. You're the only man I want to build a family with."

Another crooked ghost of a smile plays on his lips. "Well, the one thing I depend on...is for us to stay strong," he teases, stating the lyrics of the song in a matter-of-fact way that makes me giggle.

I drop my hand to take the one he has resting on my thigh. "Come on, goofball... *Now that I've got you on board*, round two is happening in the bedroom."

LEGION

*T*he one thing I'm sure of...is they're probably making love... Right now... I can't help the barrage of intrusive thoughts as the song we danced to plays over and over in my mind...

He couldn't let me fucking have it!

Rotting vegetation and thick humidity assault my senses the moment I pull down the raised dirt path, leading further into Drear Swamp. Black Gum and Cypress trees dripping in Spanish moss line both sides of the narrow trail through the scummy water. Downed trunks, now water-bogged logs among the Cypress Knees, serve as moss-covered stages for the millions of frogs and toads croaking in a constant crescendo, audible even over the exhaust pipes and engine of my motorcycle.

I make my way cautiously down the dark trail until I reach the end at a small embankment. The short, dilapidated wooden dock Keegan described sits crookedly in the dark, murky waters.

Killing the engine, I leave the headlights on and dismount, taking a few steps closer to the mold-encrusted, warped planks of the old pier. The air is heavy with a moisture I can almost taste. Precipitation causes the fabric of my shirt to cling uncomfortably to my skin. The lights from my Indian reflect in the glowing eyes of a few gators, moving stealthily through the black swamp.

I wonder if they are the very ones that may have devoured Asmodeus' remains...

I sigh his name into the darkness.

Legion: Book 3

The hiss of a gator near the muddy embankment pulls a half-grin from me, and my hand instinctively gravitates nearer to the gun holstered beneath my cut.

"Have you reincarnated already, brother?" I joke. "Or merely *possessed* the oversized reptile that consumed you?"

A whippoorwill's call for a mate clashes with the hoot of an owl as they both echo throughout the Tupelo and Cypress trees.

The gator hisses again, and I wonder if he's asking why I've come, after all this time...after what I did...

"I suppose...just to see...*to know*... *Closure*... Though I don't regret what transpired between us in our final moments... I already mourned the loss of my real brother...the night you unwittingly revealed the truth to me about what you had become... *Dominick* is the brother I miss... The brother I lost when we were parted as children... You, *Asmodeus*...are right where you belong... *Rest in pieces*. Though you're probably gator shit at this point...contributing to this rancid stench."

I light up a cigarette and pull a few long drags, listening to the constant serenade of nocturnal swamp creatures as my mind floods with memories stained with revenge.

Blind hatred.

Blind faith.

Denial...

Such a uniquely human defense mechanism, *denial*. No other species on this wretched earth matches our talent at disregarding reality for the sake of a little peace of mind.

Thinking back, I had often clung to denial throughout this entire revenge ride, as if I'd been dangling from a cliff. Fingers desperately digging into the jagged edge, knowing full well that if I slipped, complications would arise. Complications that even I might not have been able to manipulate the logistics of into a contented outcome. Yet all of the vacillating emotions warring within me, especially pertaining to one particular situation, disintegrated the moment I actually came face to face with the infamous *Jack Nero*.

What could have potentially been my greatest pawn in this twisted game of vengeance had become the epitome of said complication. A walking, talking complication that was of the utmost importance. One I not only kept to myself but kept under my complete control.

Seeing him in person for the first time solidified a fact I could no longer deny, or attempt to ignore. Not if harm would have befallen her for the sake of my own mission. There was no reconciling that fact.

The enemy of my enemy had become my enemy…

Though in order to gain any sort of influence over Jack Nero, I had to convince him otherwise. I knew there would be no deterring him from his own plans of retaliation against the woman who has haunted my thoughts since our eyes met. He was as determined to carry out his plans against her as I was mine against Keegan.

Jack Nero intended to do her great harm. I'd felt it through his handwritten letters. And it was clear to see in his tense, icy blue eyes. The mere thought of him carrying out those plans for her coiled my insides and spurred an entirely unfamiliar, soul-rattling, protective impulse that coursed through my entire being. Anger, fear, and a desire to cut his throat where he stood, crackled through my veins.

Denial about what I was beginning to feel for her died that day. Right there in that state prison visiting room.

Shackled at the wrists and ankles, wearing an orange uniform taut across his prison-sculpted torso, Jack Nero had been escorted into the visitation room by two large, military-esque correctional officers. They shoved him down onto the stool across the table from me. The indelible sound of his chains clanking against the metal seat bolted to the floor caused the muscles in my throat to involuntarily tense. Behind masks of impassivity, we studied each other in silence until the guards stepped away.

"Where is she?" Nero demanded, unable to keep the bloodthirst from his tone.

"We'll get to that," I bit out, already feigning hard for a cigarette.

Suspicion narrowed his eyes, persistent in his attempt to read me. "Are you the guy she's shacking up with now?" The corner of his mouth curved upward in a threatening, disingenuous grin. "Has she sent you here to warn me off?"

"No… *However*, I am very well versed in all things pertaining to *that* man."

The Adam's apple bobbed almost violently in his throat before he replied, "*So, she is with a man.*" Confirming this for him had significantly darkened his mood.

"She is. Shall I tell you about them?" I shifted in my seat to lean forward and threaded my fingers on top of the stainless-steel table. "He's madly in love with her. Willing to do anything for her."

"Is that so?"

"Very much so." I allowed an antagonistic smile to stretch my mouth. "I'd venture to say he worships her... *Every...inch...of her.*"

The muscles in his jaw ticked, and I could just about make out the pulse in his neck.

"Who the fuck are you?"

"The enemy of your enemy... In turn, one might deduce that makes me a *friend*... Perhaps, *your only friend*, now." I gestured to his restraints and prison garb.

"I'm listening..."

I knew I had to insert myself into this collision course with Jack Nero. Manipulate the situation to our benefit. I tried to convince myself it was more about my brother's revenge than it ever was about protecting Vanna. But that was denial speaking. Convincing everyone around us was done easily enough, at least for a while. I painted the entire situation in all shades of black, gave Asmodeus the updates he wanted to hear.

Yet even before I learned the truth about my brother, the thought of her actually being harmed ate away at me day and night. There was no quelling Jack Nero. The man's desire and determination to carry out his revenge were as steadfast as my brother's, and I had begun to regret pushing for the payback he became hell bent on claiming.

Had I only focused on hate, revenge would have been swift. I would have simply killed Keegan, perhaps in a similar fashion to how I dealt with my brother. But it would have been a pinpoint execution. This plan I'd concocted, this darkness I'd swept over his beloved county, which would have eventually corrupted and corroded everything he cared about... It had all been over the love I'd had for my brother. *Love* spawned this intricate, grandiose plan of complete annihilation.

Love is far deadlier an emotion than Hate.

I'd made that trip to the state penitentiary in the nick of time. The weeks before Jack Nero's early release, I'd been the one orchestrating everything for him. The mental warfare before his physical attacks had either been carried out by me or the man I had enlisted from my crew to keep close tabs on Nero. Vein had always been one to follow my exact orders to the letter.

However, convincing Asmodeus that the best course of action was allowing Jack Nero to carry out the actual murder of Dean Keegan had been no simple feat.

"Are you not exhausted, brother?" I'd asked. "We've opened the flood gates of Hell in Keegan's precious county. The moment we pull out, there will be gang wars for control of the territories. Further chaos will ensue. The town is doomed, regardless. Jack Nero is a man twisted by jealousy and a deep-rooted need for revenge as well. I assure you, whatever Nero does to Keegan, it will be an agonizing death, both mentally and physically. The years Nero has served in prison have warped him into something as ruthless as we... The blood of Dean Keegan on his hands keeps ours clean. Absolves us of this capital crime."

"I want the satisfaction! I want to *see* him suffer before we end him together!" Asmodeus shouted, a haunting look of both disappointment and betrayal in his eyes as he glared at me.

It tore at what remained of my heart. My brother...the only being I had ever truly loved in my life. After everything, I was letting him down. And the kicker... *I* had been the one from the beginning who pushed for this revenge. My brother was content to move on with whatever remained of a life. I had been the one who couldn't let it go... Who couldn't sleep or think of anything but Keegan's suffering, until now. I'd pushed for this. I'd pushed for him to *want* this...and when he finally did, *I did not*.

"My hand guides the hand that will end him, brother... Is that not close enough?"

"No! It isn't! You promised me vengeance! What's changed?"

"Nothing has changed... An opportunity to orchestrate his demise from a distance is at play. Be smart, Asmodeus...please!"

He slammed a deformed fist down on the arm of the leather chair he'd practically come to live in. Wordless...though his expression spoke volumes on its own.

I'd sighed, defeated, and cursed myself. What the fuck had I allowed to come over me? *A woman*...over my own flesh and blood.

Legion: Book 3

Over the only person who ever truly had my back… *Or so I had always believed.*

"If I were to arrange your attendance at his death…would that pacify you?" I'd asked, eager to appease him as I wracked my brain over the logistics of this promise. "Would that satisfy the debt owed to you?"

"Yes," he'd agreed.

"Then it shall be done."

What none of us had anticipated was Vanna jumping the gun on everyone's carefully laid plans… The rage and anxiety consuming me that wretched night were unlike anything I had ever experienced. The level of anger I felt toward her, and all the reasons *why*, both confused and enraged me further.

I had assigned Vein as Jack Nero's cohort. Maneuvered him like a chess piece into that cabin to assist Jack with Keegan, whilst simultaneously preventing him from actually killing Vanna. Something unbeknownst to me had spurred her into premature action. Foiling my plans and damn near getting herself killed in the process!

Too late had Vein informed me of the mad race to the cabin. There was no fulfilling my promise to my brother that he'd bear witness to Keegan's demise. I'd barely managed to derail Keegan's cavalry, dispatching a would-be prospect to stop Jason Caldwell and Viking by any means necessary. T-boning the Saviors' Sergeant at Arms' truck knocked them off the board only temporarily, but it was enough to prevent them from intervening at the cabin.

An involuntary shiver travels up my spine now, as Keegan's words in that rusty shed play over in my mind for the hundredth time. The thought of what transpired that night…what could have happened to her, jerks me violently back to the present.

I pull the last drag from my cigarette, sneering at the inky black waters speckled with green algae. Keegan's survival of the cabin only fueled Asmodeus's obsession with his demise and put Vanna directly in his crosshairs.

"I wish I could hate you for the monsters we've become," I mutter, tossing the butt into the muddy embankment a few feet from me.

The gator I've been conversing with crawls closer up the embankment, and I grip the handle of my gun.

Jennifer Saviano

"Don't make me kill you twice."

The prehistoric lizard tilts its head, snapping its deadly jaws sideways at something on the ground near the post of the saggy planked pier.

Hailing from the desert, swamps were never a familiar landscape to me. At first glance, I had thought the white balls along the water's edge were perhaps a species of mushroom.

Upon realization, a smile quirks up in the corner of my mouth. I recall reading about the affinity alligators have for a particular *sweet treat*.

"Marshmallows..." I grin with amusement as the beast gobbles up the last puffy white morsel left behind. It turns, thrashing a massive tail, and makes its way back into the dark waters. My eyes curiously scan Drear Swamp for any traces of what might be another, recently discarded corpse...

"Perhaps your soul isn't so *alone* out here after all, Asmodeus..."

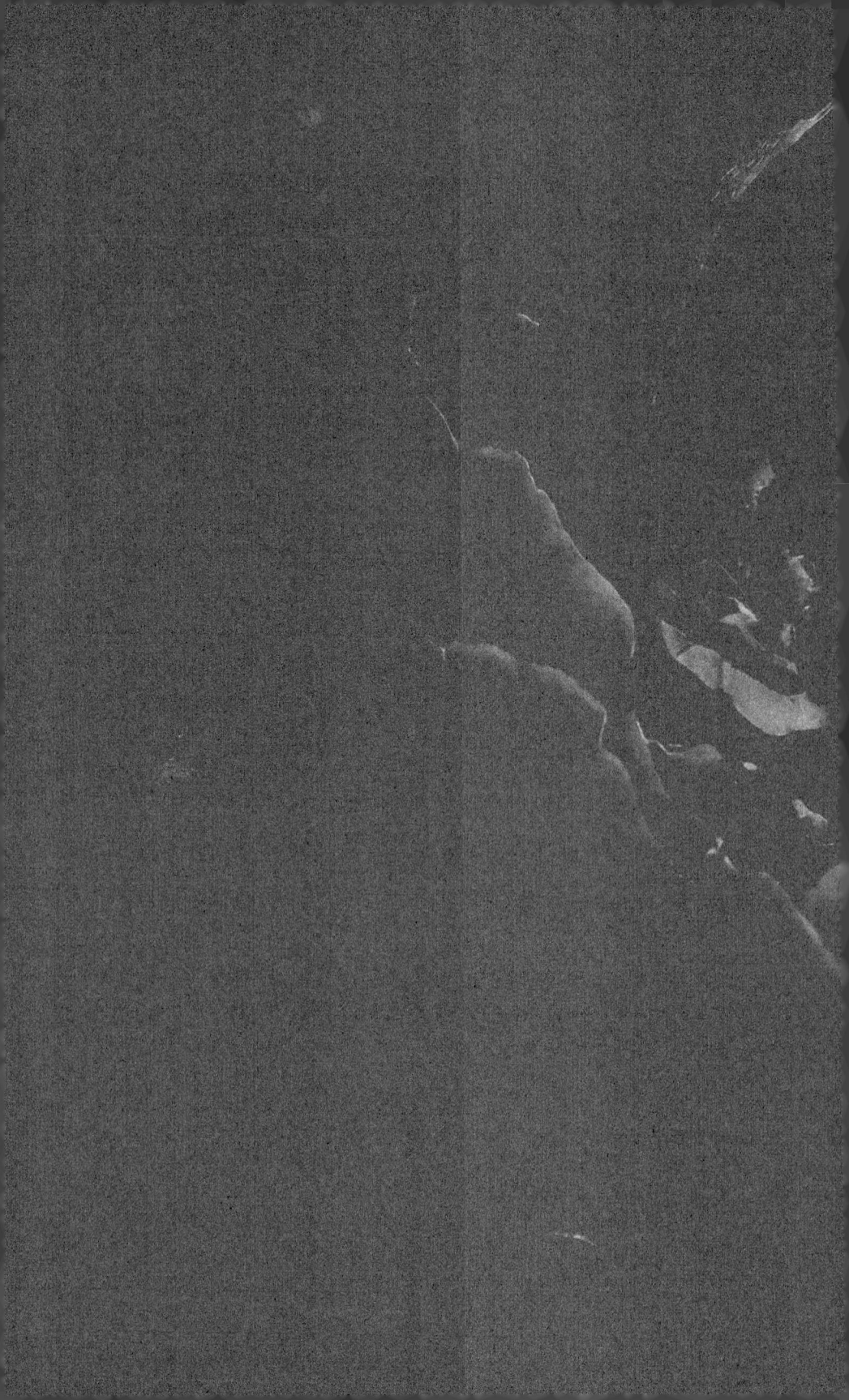

CHAPTER 41

Vanna

The warm spring breeze carries the sweet aroma of honeysuckle, which is growing all around the perimeter of the woods behind the farmstand and along the cornfield.

Ace helps me open up the farmstand, though customers usually don't begin showing up until after their church services. We have time to do a little foraging for ourselves.

"Do you want to pick some berries?" I ask Ace. "We might get lucky and find that raspberry patch again, too." I know exactly where the lone bush grows, down the trail that leads to the old farmhouse next door. When I lived there, I would stroll the little dirt path to Dean's blueberry and blackberry orchards and pick a few of those, too.

"We can make jam!" Ace smiles excitedly at first, but then his little brows scrunch, and he hurries to his art table. "Can I bring this for Miss Meg?" He holds up a slightly crinkled paper with both hands. He's been hanging onto this particular drawing for weeks, since the last time we ran into Meg. "This is me, and this is you, so she remembers us. And this is Daddy and S'reen," Ace says, pointing to each scribbled figure.

I crouch to his level and run my fingers through the top of his hair. "I don't think she's home anymore, sweetheart. Remember? Miss Meg said she was moving, and we haven't seen her car in the driveway in weeks."

"But... I *promised*," Ace says, lower lip about to wobble.

"*Okay*," I cave instantly. "How about this. We'll walk down the trail to her house and leave it on her front porch. She might be back, and if so, she'll find it and know you kept your promise."

"Yeah!" Ace enthusiastically agrees and bounds out the door. I follow after him, grabbing two baskets from the counter as I pass.

The trail behind the farmstand is shaded and cool, a blessing in what is shaping up to be a very warm, late spring morning. Birds rustle and chirp in the branches above us as we stroll along together, and Ace hums tunelessly beside me, drawing clutched in his little fist like a treasure map.

As we wander, so do my thoughts about everything that happened last night.

I know Legion thinks he's in love with me, and I don't know how to convince him he isn't. He can't be. And although I have come to care about Legion, I love my family. *I love my husband.* And after all the strain we've weathered, Dean is finally coming around. We aren't out of the woods yet, but for the first time in months, I feel like we're finally back in sync. Still, I can't help but wonder if Dean's change of mind has anything to do with Legion and his willingness to *be* or *give* anything I ask of him.

I push the thought aside as Ace darts ahead. "We're almost there!" he declares, rounding the curve where the lone raspberry bush sits beside the trail.

I can just make out the old farmhouse through the foliage, sitting tucked between two aging maples. The neglected yard beyond the back patio has been taken over by long grass and wildflowers, the old weeping willow's branches tangling within them.

Ace stops before the clearing and waits for me. "Can I take a dragon home?" he asks, peering up at me. I'm fairly certain the house is vacant, but I'm also sure Meg wouldn't mind. She never did in the past.

"Let's deliver Meg's picture and then we'll go pick some dragons," I smile at him.

The screen door creaks in the breeze as we venture around the side of the house to the front porch, its frame gently tapping against the wood trim. There's no car in the driveway. No flowerpots on the steps. No cushions left behind on the rocking chairs, but the porch swing still hangs crookedly from its chain, swaying like someone had just left.

"Where should we leave it, so it doesn't blow away?" Ace asks as we climb the steps.

"Is it okay if mommy folds it? We can probably tuck it into the knocker and shut the screen door all the way."

He nods and solemnly hands me the paper to do just that.

"There, now she will see it if she comes back," I say, pushing on the frame of the storm door once more for good measure. The light breeze doesn't affect it this time.

"I hope she likes it," Ace sighs.

"She'll love it," I smile at him. "Now, let's go get some dragons and berries!"

LEGION

She's usually here by now, especially with Keegan elbows deep in an engine in his shop, too busy to ride home for a lunch break...

Or is he?

Are they avoiding each other? Did our dance instigate a fight between them? It's well after noon... By this time, he's either already returned from home to finish the day, or Vanna's *been* here, checking in on things, dropping off lunch, playing with Ace on the little playground while they wait for Keegan to take a break. Just here, smiling at whomever is around like she isn't the only fucking reason this place ever feels remotely like a home.

My eyes drop to the empty cigarette pack sitting on the patio table before me. I pull a long drag off my last cigarette, inhaling the smoke like it might fill the emptiness I feel whenever she's not around. On a sigh, I watch the smoke dissipate into nothing.

A cigarette can convince your body you aren't starving, make you feel like you have control over the emptiness. What started out as survival turned into routine, then addiction, then comfort. In the beginning, each drag felt like a middle finger to everything that had its hands wrapped around my throat...every belt...every chain... I'm not sure at which point I began counting on it to kill me. Slowly, sure, but inevitably.

Vanna saw it...and it bothered her.

I reach into my pocket and retrieve the mullein tincture she gifted me, the cobalt-blue glass warm from my body. I stare at it, recalling

Legion: Book 3

the concern in her eyes when we spoke on her front porch, and the way she wrapped her arms around me.

She wants me to quit...*to be better*... Perhaps I'm capable of the change she believes in...

But there's an ever-present darkness in me that doesn't quit...

I shove the bottle back in my pocket and grab the empty cigarette pack as I stand. I crush it in my fist, the cardboard soft and useless, and toss it into the ashtray.

Maybe that's what love is for someone like me. Just another way to slowly die.

"Where is she?" I ask the moment I find myself standing in Keegan's shop.

He doesn't look up from the bike he's got on the lift. "You don't get to ask that."

"Is she alright?"

"Not your business, either."

I suck in a long breath through my nostrils, filling my lungs with the scent of oil, leather, and cold steel. "*I made it my business long before last night.*"

Keegan finally lifts his gaze to shoot me a glare and steps around the bike, grease on his hands, jaw tight. "*Maybe she needed a day without you in it.*"

To my surprise, that one lands.

"I want you out of the clubhouse," he adds. "I have to take this bike for a test ride. I want you gone by the time I get back."

"Very well." I'm surprised he's tolerated my presence here as long as he has, but my compliance without argument seems to anger him further.

Keegan moves to the workbench and grabs a rag to wipe off his hands while he studies me. "Were you hoping your stunt would cause us to fight?"

"Why? Did you witness something between us worth fighting about?"

Keegan's disdainful gaze narrows. "If she knew the depths of your depravity, she'd be disgusted by you."

"Are you referring to my little fuck doll?" I shrug. "If you truly believed that, you would have told her by now." He visibly tenses, and I can't help but grin and go on. "Astute of you to realize doing so would backfire on you. Perhaps initially she would be shocked and repulsed... But then she'd *think about it*... *Imagine it*... How deeply I crave her and all the things I'd do to her if given the chance… Disgust can easily warp into desire… She's a hot-blooded woman, Keegan…*and women love to be desired*…even the ones who don't suffer from a compromised self-esteem."

"*Watch it.*" Keegan growls, practically bristling like a wolf.

I raise my hand in a placating gesture. "I mean no offense to our sweet Vanna."

"You think you're so clever. Untouchable. You're so neck deep in your scheming, so caught up in finding the chink in everyone else's armor, you don't even realize how obvious yours are." Keegan scoffs and takes a step closer to me. "Allow me to enlighten you on a few things. When a person fixates all of their love on someone who doesn't reciprocate, it denotes a high probability you've had to imagine love where it didn't exist in order to survive."

I fight to keep the grin stitched on my face, but I don't think he missed the slight twitch in my left eye. He goes on, *emboldened*…

"I'm gonna bet that started for you in childhood. Whether you didn't get stable love or were straight-up neglected, you've survived by creating fantasies where a person actually has feelings for you. I see that you're hurting, that the origin of this pain inside you predates your fixation with my wife. And if you're not willing to acknowledge this, consider another angle… *You don't actually love her.* You don't actually want her. Not beyond a fleeting physical relationship, which, let's be honest, if that's all anyone has going, it's doomed to fail. You don't want a relationship. And I'll tell you why that is, too."

Keegan takes another step closer to me, lowering his voice so I'm forced to listen… "Deep down, you know you couldn't make it work with her. You couldn't keep her happy. You know you're beneath her. You're fixated on an *unavailable woman* because you don't truly want this." He raises his left hand in my face, and my gaze shifts to the wedding band on his finger. "You don't actually want to win her. You want to satiate a fantasy or two. *She's a conquest to you.* Not an end game."

My hands curl into fists at my side, and the muscle in my jaw ticks as my now seething glare slides back to his. I swallow down the Molotov cocktail of emotions erupting to the surface all at once.

The corner of Keegan's mouth tugs into a sly, crooked grin. "*How'd I do?*" Keegan taunts. "The chink in your armor is

Legion: Book 3

unworthiness... And if you actually ever did manage to steal her from me, admit this... *You'd think less of her.* She'd topple right off that pedestal in your fucked-up mind. You're pursuing an unavailable woman because you're broken. *And a piece of shit*, Legion. A shallow, *unworthy*, villainous piece of shit. *Analyze that*, prick."

"Well, you've certainly given me a lot of thought."

Keegan chuckles without humor. "Oh, you haven't had enough? Alright, try this on for size... *She doesn't even see you as a man*, Legion. Let that sink in. To her, you're just a broken child. A lost boy. She *pities* you. Now you tell me, *Legend... How does that make you feel?*"

Rage continues to boil my blood, and I can feel a vein throbbing in my corded neck. The constant, deafening *swoosh-swoosh-swoosh* in my ears drowns out even the roar of the motorcycle as he takes off, leaving me to stew over his hate-inducing words.

She doesn't even see you as a man...

Is that so, you self-righteous prick?

The heated blood in my veins turns cold as the thought of those words falling from *her* lips tears through my mind. I'd taken that as his personal assessment, but... *Has she actually voiced that to him?*

The darkness within tauntingly laughs... *'She pities you... You're unworthy of her love... Just a broken little boy... She thinks you're pathetic! You're her puppet!'*

Well, then... I'll simply have to rectify this unfortunate turn of events. I'm more than willing to facilitate the correction of her skewed assessment of me. Far more capable than *he is* of delivering everything her conflicted heart desires...

I scan his shop, and when my gaze lands on the calendar pinned to a corkboard above his workbench, a wicked grin returns to pull at the corners of my mouth. There are opportunities everywhere. One only has to be willing to reach out and grab them. To take advantage...

The darkness within wraps its claws around the throat of what remains of my conscience.

I will tear down that pedestal and fuck her in the ruins...

Snatching my phone from the inner pocket of my cut, I bring up a number I haven't called in years.

"Hello," a thick Irish accent answers.

"I assume you're stateside?"

"I am."

"I need you in Myrtle Beach in three days. I hope you haven't retired yet."

"Not yet, but I'm not keen on fighting Keegan again if that's what you're angling at."

"*Would twenty grand convince you otherwise?*"

"Dunno… *Thirty might.*"

I'd have paid fifty. "Done."

"Same place as the last time?"

"Yes."

"Am I taking a dive?"

"Of course not. Give it all you've got."

"Alright then. You know where to meet me with the cash."

"Indeed."

I hang up the phone and shove it back in my pocket, feigning hard for a fucking cigarette as I storm back to the clubhouse.

Villainous… I'll fucking show you villainous…

The motel stinks of mildew and dirty secrets. Once upon a time, I'd have felt right at home in a place that charges by the hour and gives you a discount for cash and keeping your complaints to yourself.

I kick the door shut behind me and toss my duffel bag on the foot of the bed before cracking a window, just enough to breathe. Then I remove my Sig Sauer and pack of smokes from my cut and place them on the nightstand. It looks familiar, and only takes me a second to remember.

I laugh once, dry and hollow, and strip out of my cut. After fishing my zippo and the joint I procured from another pocket, I toss the leather onto the bed as well. This is the same fucking room I came to the night she married him. The night I fucked a whore in a cheap wedding dress and imagined it was her.

I light up the joint and crash down on the bed. The old, worn mattress creaks beneath me as I reach over to the side table and switch on the radio to a local classic rock station. Leaning back against the headboard, I pull a long drag and listen to Steven Tyler taunt me with the lyrics of *Full Circle…*

My eyes snap open at the sound of a knock on my hotel room door. Grabbing my gun off the night table, I make my way silently to the peephole.

My heart beats faster as I tuck the gun into my waistband and immediately unlock the door to swing it open.

"*Vanna?* What are you doing here?"

She takes a determined step forward, and I back up, allowing her into the room with me. She shuts the door behind her. Her penetrating gaze never breaking from my own, though, her dark eyes seem a bit tearful.

"Did you fight with him?" I ask.

She doesn't answer, only takes another step closer to me, her hand reaching up to touch my face, and my heart races faster, still. I don't allow anyone to touch me. Ever. I've always recoiled on instinct. But *her* touch… I allow her to stroke my jaw. I'd allow her to do most anything to me. I lean my face into her palm, relishing the feel of her soft hand, the way her thumb strokes against the tense muscles of my jaw. Her hand slides down my neck until her fingers are suddenly working at the buttons of my shirt.

"Vanna?"

She shakes her head, her eyes dropping from mine to focus on the task of undoing my shirt.

I grab her hands, preventing her from going any further. "Did you fight with him?"

She wrenches her hands from my grasp to hastily remove her leather jacket, letting it drop to the floor beside her, before grabbing the hem of her shirt. She pulls it up over her head, and the garment lands atop her leather jacket on the floor, as well.

Vanna Keegan is standing before me…practically *topless*, in a lacy black bra…gazing up at me like I'm something to her…

She reaches up to cup my face in her hands, pulling me down to her, until our lips are almost touching. Like a damn fool, I hesitate, asking once more, "Vanna, did you fight with him?"

This time, she barely nods, pinning her bottom lip between her teeth.

"*Take it out on me…*" The whispered plea barely makes it past my lips before hers are crashing against mine. Her arms encircle my neck, locking me into this kiss as if I weren't desperate to partake in this fervent exchange myself. As if I'd ever pull away from her. I wrap my arms around her, crushing her voluptuous body against me, eager to take this as far as I possibly can.

All the nights I've dreamed of being with her over the last four years...the erotic fantasies that have played over and over in my mind... They're about to come true.

Keegan, you fucking fool! Whatever you did to drive her into my waiting arms, I thank you kindly, sir!

The need to feel her skin against mine is overwhelming, but I dare not break this kiss. This *willing* kiss! One I've craved since the first I stole from her in that wine cellar, nearly four long years ago.

Wrapped tightly in my embrace, I back her up toward the bed, silently praying she'll allow me to take her to it.

When I release her to undo the rest of the buttons of my shirt, she shoves me backwards and I land on the bed before her. She brings her foot up to the mattress and plants a heeled boot between my thighs. Unzipping the side before she slips it off her foot, she discards it with a thud on the carpet, then repeats the action with the other. I watch, enthralled, as she undoes the button of her jeans, then the fly, before slowly pushing them down over the sexy flare of her hips and supple thighs...her sensual body moving to work them down her shapely legs.

I rip off my shirt, then grab the gun tucked behind my back and toss it over the side of the bed without a care. It clunks heavily upon the carpet as I move to make quick work of discarding the rest of my clothing as well.

She steps out of her jeans as I kick mine off, shedding my boxers along with them. I watch with adrenaline pumping-anticipation as she reaches behind her back to unclasp her bra. The straps slide down her arms, and the bra falls to the floor between us. My mouth waters, and I swallow hard at the sight of her full, perfect breasts.

Reaching out, I grab her by the hips to pull her to me, burying my face in her soft, warm tits. Her fingers snake up the back of my skull, holding me to her bosom as my fingers dig into the firm flesh of her ass. These panties need to go, too. Taking a taught nipple into my mouth, I suck and flick her hardened bud with my tongue, while hooking my fingers into the waistband of her panties. As I rip them down, her fingers curl into my hair, forcing me to meet her heated gaze. I bite down on her nipple, and her head falls back, her other hand pushing down on my shoulder. My cock grows harder at her wordless demand to be worshipped.

Oh, how I've dreamed of this!

I kiss down her torso, licking and nipping her body until I'm on my knees at her feet, back against the foot of the mattress, mere inches from her pussy.

I've wanted this...prayed for this...worked dark magick to manifest this moment... I'm not stopping now!

Before she can come to her senses, I pull her hard against my face, burying my tongue between her hot, wet lips. Her fingernails dig into my shoulder as her other hand pulls at the back of my skull, forcing my face harder against her body, my tongue deeper inside her.

She doesn't make a sound, but she rocks and swerves her hips, riding my tongue. I grab her leg, hoisting her thigh over my shoulder with a desperate need to be as close to her as physically possible. She bends her knee, hooking her leg around me, forcing me closer still. The smooth skin of her calf and the heel of her foot anchor against my back. My cock is throbbing, desire already leaking from the swollen head.

I can do better than this... I want to ruin her for Keegan. If she's never thought of me while he was inside her before this night, *she will!*

I grip her ass, pulling her forward as I lean back on the bed, forcing her to kneel up onto the edge of the mattress so she can ride my face properly.

Wrapping my hands around her luscious thighs now, I pull her down onto my face and devour her like a death row inmate savoring his last meal. She grinds down on me greedily, and some warped part of me wouldn't mind dying by way of suffocation. I've nearly died a hundred times... If this is what finally takes me out, I'd die happy. It's more than I deserve or expect in this life, anyhow. Before I do expire by way of decadent flesh, she breaks away from my mouth, moving up the mattress.

I twist around immediately, following her up the bed as she lies down on her stomach against the comforter, looking back at me over her shoulder with a coy, little smile. I swipe her hair to the side, exposing her back to me as I lower myself to drag my tongue over her shoulder blades, making my way up to the shell of her ear. Nipping at her lobe, I feel her raise her lower body up to me, pressing her bare ass against my lower abdomen. She wiggles against me, maneuvering herself so that the heavy length of my engorged cock rests against her hot, slippery little slit. Sucking her lobe, I allow her to rub against me, slicking me with the combination of my saliva and her arousal.

I fight the urge to roll my hips into her, the head of my cock eagerly seeking her entrance. She tempts me further still, pushing back on me, beckoning to be penetrated.

"I'm not fucking you from behind, Vanna," I whisper against her ear. I've only fucked whores from behind, not wanting to see their faces. Not caring. Not wanting any form of connection. "You want me, baby? Turn over and look me in the eyes when I slide my cock inside you."

To my elation, she twists over onto her back between my caging limbs. That coy, little smile never falters, those dark, hooded eyes burning into me.

There's no way I'll be able to pull out of her.

Not a fucking chance in Hell.

As much as I despise the thought of anything between us, of not feeling the hot, bare, wet clench of her cunt around me, I force myself to reach for my cut and grab a condom.

Tearing it open between my teeth, I sit back on my heels, about to roll it down my shaft when she shakes her head at me, those pearly whites biting down on that plump lip once again.

I've never fucked a whore without a rubber…except Puppet that one time… I've only gone down on one other woman before in my life… I'm pretty sure I'm clean… And I'm sure she's clean… But…

"I'm going to come inside of you. I'm not pulling out. You don't want me to wear this?"

She shakes her head slowly, *no*.

No?

Bending her legs, she pulls them up from beneath my parted knees and opens her thighs, inviting me where I've longed to be since the night we met.

Fuck me…she mouths the words to me… *Fuck me now*…

Gripping my painfully erect cock, I slide my other hand up her body as I lean forward to mount and enter her. I wrap my hand around her throat, feeling her swallow. Her dark, half-lidded eyes plead for my cock. Her mouth opens to take a breath as I begin to push inside her. Her hands grip the wrist of my hand still wrapped around her throat. Her legs hook around me, heels digging into the back of my thighs as she attempts to force me deeper inside her.

Fuck! She's going to drive me to the edge too quickly!

I release her throat, slipping two fingers into her panting mouth as I begin to fuck her, attempting to distract from the glorious feeling of her cunt taking me in.

"How many times have you thought about this moment, Vanna?" I demand, fighting to cling to the threads of sanity remaining. "How long have you fantasized about giving yourself over to me?"

She doesn't answer, but she rocks her hips in time with my slow thrusts, gripping and fucking me back, all the while continuing to suck my fingers, swirling her tongue around and between them. Gritting my teeth, I grind into her, shoving myself as deeply inside of her as I can get, rubbing my body against her clit. My other hand curls into the bedding, gripping the fabric as I desperately battle the urge to coat her walls with my encroaching release.

She bites down on me, *hard*. Hard enough to cause quite a bit of burning pain. I slam into her, fucking her roughly. The headboard slams against the wall. When I try to remove my fingers, she bites down even harder, and I wince through the pain.

Devious little minx! Does she mean to mark me? Would she allow me to leave my mark on her, as well?

Bang! Bang! Bang!

The headboard slams against the wall. The springs of the shitty mattress creak beneath us.

I drive myself into her harder still. She doesn't let up, and I grin through the pain. Perhaps she wants to make me bleed? *Demoness...*

Bang! Bang! Bang!

Someone is yelling out in the hall... Probably bitching about the slamming headboard. I hear him more clearly when he shouts through the cracked window, "Put it out, asshole! And lower your fucking music!"

Vanna

*H*arder... *Faster...*

Sweat is dripping from my body as he works me over.

"Keep your guard up, Vanna!" Viking grunts at me from the weight bench where he's been curling dumbbells that weigh more than my entire child. "You're letting it drop whenever you throw that shin kick."

I pause to reset and wipe the sweat from stinging my eyes. "I know. I'm distracted."

"That's how you get punched in the face."

I can't help letting a small smile slip. Viking isn't the gentlest of trainers, but I appreciate his unfiltered pointers. His criticisms are easier to take now that I know they come from a place of love. Besides, I do want to learn effective techniques properly.

"What's got you so distracted?" he asks.

I give him a wry look. "After our last talk therapy session, I didn't think you'd want another one."

"Well, your strikes are half-assed. Spill it so we can stop wasting time and energy."

"It's difficult to be upset with my husband when he finally came around to trying for another baby."

"Oh shit, really?" Viking smiles genuinely. "That's great, Vanna."

"It is… But I'm still annoyed with him."

"Over the *recently evicted?*" Viking chuckles as if he approves. "Not gonna lie, Vanna. We've all barely managed to tolerate Legion's malicious alliance."

I sigh. "Legion is trying. We should help him as long as he is."

Viking lets out a scoff. "He was *trying* to get in your pants."

I roll my eyes. "No wonder you're best friends. You sound just like my husband."

"*Speaking of…*" Dean says, walking across the gym to us. His dark eyes scan me where I stand beside the punching bag, gloves up, face flushed, loose hair sticking uncomfortably to my neck. "What's this?" he asks. "I knew you were using the gym a few times a week, but I didn't know you were taking lessons from Viking."

"It's not a secret." I instantly go on the defensive. "He had time."

Dean looks at Viking, who just shrugs. "Hey, she came to me. It's not like I've shown her anything on the mat. Not that she didn't try to rope me into it."

"*You traitor!*" I laugh at how quickly he ratted me out.

"I didn't think you'd have a problem with me giving her some pointers," Viking adds.

"I don't," Dean says, stepping closer, not to confront but to close the distance between us. "I trust you both." He looks me up and down in my sweaty gym clothes, which consist of black leggings, sneakers, and a sports bra beneath a baggy, off-the-shoulder sweatshirt. Then his gaze slides to Viking.

"*Right,*" Viking chuckles in response to whatever *telepathic-man message* passed between them with just a look. "I'll make sure everyone knows the gym is off-limits for an hour or so." Viking grabs his gym bag before leaving us and closes the doors behind him.

When I look back at Dean, he's already shedding his cut, eyes still locked on me, a crooked grin playing at his mouth.

"I was gonna squeeze in a workout, but since we're both here, you might as well show me what you've learned," Dean says, voice nearly a growl.

"I think I'm done for the day."

He playfully scowls. "Stage fright?"

"*No,*" I mumble under my breath, bringing one of my wrists to my teeth in an attempt to undo the Velcro cuff of the boxing glove. Dean reaches out to assist me, and I let him.

"You should learn to throw bare-knuckle punches anyway," he says, tossing the gloves aside. "These should be worn when you're working out, but you won't have gloves on if you're ever in a situation where you have to hit someone." He gestures to the bag. "Throw a few. Not too hard. We can gradually increase the power. I just want to get a look at your form."

I playfully scowl back at him. "*I'm sure you do.*"

"Just imagine a particular *blonde bitch's* face right here," he jokes, patting an eye-level spot on the punching bag.

I arch a brow at him. "What makes you so sure I want to imagine a blonde?"

Dean chuckles. "Oh, you'll get your rematch with me, baby...*in the ring...* Right now, I want to see you make a tight, flat fist. Make sure your knuckles are the primary point of impact. Keep your wrists strong and aligned with your forearms. You want to avoid bending them on impact, which can lead to injury."

He moves so fast, I hear the thud of his fist against the leather before it even registers that he threw a punch. The bag sways from the powerful impact.

"I'm not as good as you," I say.

"You don't need to be. Now come on. Show me what you've got."

Dean spends the next few minutes coaching me, teaching me combination and elbow strikes.

"That's good, baby…" he circles me again to watch my form, and I feel his strong hands slide down my hips, digging into my thighs over my leggings, then back up again. The heat of his sigh brushes past my ear and sends a shiver through my body.

"You should have come to *me*, Vanna."

"You've got a lot on your plate."

"I'll always make time for you. Don't you know that?" He pulls my hips back and presses himself against my ass. "But now, since you didn't come to me, you'll come *for* me."

I spin around in his embrace to look him in the eyes. They're dark with lust, and he's wearing that trademark crooked grin of his.

"Not happening."

That grin broadens, and his eyes shift momentarily to the boxing ring. I know exactly what he's thinking as his hands travel down to squeeze my ass. "Spar with me."

I look at him wryly. "Like I'd stand a chance against you, *Mr. Underground Cage fighter*. And besides, I don't know how to grapple or wrestle or whatever those Jiu-Jitsu maneuvers are that you do on the ground. You'll have me pinned the moment we step in the ring."

"I'll go easy on you."

"No. I'm all sweaty and gross."

He curves his body into me, his pelvis grinding against me, and I can feel his hardness through his jeans. "You have no idea how many times I've jerked off about this… *Fucking you in the ring*… The way you've looked at me after I've won… *Come on, doll*. Let's have a little fun… Blow off some steam together. I'll teach you some moves first… Let you try them out on me."

"No. And besides, anybody could walk in at any moment."

"Viking has already spread the word that the gym is off limits for a while. He knows what's up."

"*Besides your dick,* nothing," I giggle.

He releases me to step back and strip off his shirt, revealing his muscular torso and vascular arms. I barely realize I'm biting my bottom lip as my gaze settles on his Adonis belt dipping into his jeans, before lingering a moment on the outline of his cock becoming more defined by the second.

I let out a nearly defeated sigh. "You're really pushing it."

"*I certainly intend to,*" Dean growls, unbuckling his belt as he teases me, "I won't *knock you out*, but I might *knock you up.*"

"Fine," I cave, pulling off my sweatshirt and tossing it at his feet.

Dean grins, salaciously and triumphantly, when he grabs my hips and pulls me against him. "*Fuckin' Aces, baby.*"

M y eyes snap open, and I immediately shake my hand in an attempt to stop the pain…

The fucking joint burned down to my fingers in my sleep…

My heart sinks as I glance around the empty hotel room, my vision blurring at the edges, warped by the remnants of the dream.

My gun is still on the nightstand…and I'm fully clothed, rocking a raging hard on.

Vanna isn't here… *She never was…* I'm alone… It was just a dream. *Just another…fucking…dream!*

I choke back a strangled sob, shoving myself out of bed to pick up the joint before it burns a hole in the rug. The asshole outside is still banging on my fucking door. I smash the roach into the top of the bedside table, extinguishing it before grabbing my gun and storming over to the door. When I wrench it open and stick the barrel in his face, he suddenly doesn't look so angry.

"I'm s-sorry…" he stammers.

"*You will be* if you ever touch this fucking door again!"

He nods, eyes wide with fear, frozen where he stands. I slam the door in his face, squeezing the handle of my gun at my side until my knuckles turn white and my arm is shaking.

Fuck! Fuck! Fuck!
That felt so fucking real!

I've cursed myself in my efforts to infiltrate her subconscious.

I place the gun on the bathroom counter and twist on the faucet, allowing the cool water to run over my burned fingers while I glare at myself in the cracked mirror.

The urge to slam my fist through it and finish the job surges through me, but I refrain.

Jennifer Saviano

I still have more moves to make…more cards to play.

Spells don't just vanish… What she ignited between us is real…raw… *ruinous!*

It's time she knows the truth of what she did.

And who she did it to…

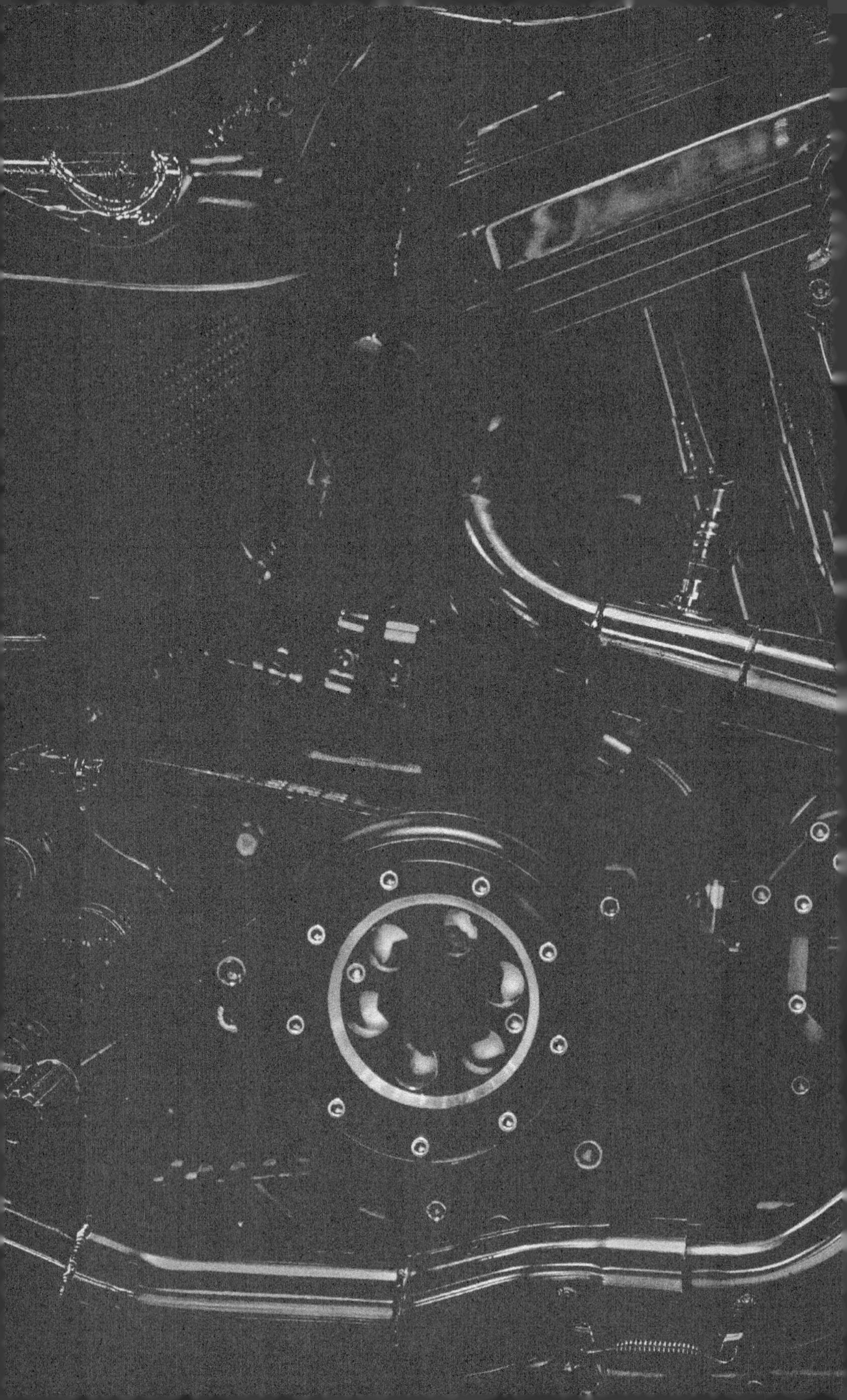

CHAPTER 42

DEAN

"Gonna need you to get a move on if you're coming with me," I say, grabbing a duffel bag from the bedroom closet to pack a few items of clothing into. I'm riding down for the bike rally in Myrtle Beach with my MC in an hour. We're meeting up with our southern chapter there, as well.

Vanna's leaning against the doorframe, arms crossed tight and stubbornly across her chest. "I already told you, if that Irish guy is going to be there, I'm not going. I know you're determined to fight him one more time, but I can't watch you go through that deathmatch insanity again."

I chuckle, tossing the bag at the foot of the bed before moving to the dresser to grab some clothes. "I don't have to go through all that again. You can wait for me in the hotel if you want."

"Is he going to be there? At the last three rallies, he was a no-show. He's probably avoiding you."

"He'll be there."

"How are you so sure?"

I shove the last pair of boxers into the bag and zip it shut before grabbing my phone off the night table. I bring up the latest text I received about an hour ago and present it to her. "Because Legion's already in Myrtle Beach, *having a drink with the motherfucker.*"

Conflicting emotions flicker behind her eyes as she studies the picture of them at the Lick Shoot Suck saloon. "I'm sure he sent this because he knows you've been waiting for the opportunity… He's just letting you know he's there… Legion means well…in his own way."

I try not to scoff and shove the phone in my back pocket. "Yeah, his middle finger front and center of the selfie really conveys *from Legion, with love.*"

"Don't be an asshole," she mumbles, wrapping her arms around her middle.

"How am *I* the asshole?"

"You're being snippy with me."

"I'm sorry." I place my hands on her arms. "I fucking hate it when you defend him, but I want you to come with me. Rosita is staying home with Mia. She's happy to take Ace for the two or three days we'll be down there. I promise to make alone time for us. We can have dinner at that Greek place you like and walk back to the hotel on the beach again."

She peers up at me, and her pleading expression pulls another resigned sigh from me.

"I'm not going to force you. You can say no, doll."

"I really don't want to… I'm perfectly fine staying home with Ace. We'll make a movie night out of it." She forces a smile in an attempt to convince me this is what she wants. "If you were riding down for a club thing, I'd go. But it's a fight thing. I meant it when I said I never wanted to see you fight like that again."

I press a kiss to her forehead. "It's not going to be like the last time. But, alright. Fair enough. One last fight, and I promise, unless someone needs me to toss them a beating, I'm hanging this part of my life up for good."

"Okay. Don't get arrested. *And don't kill him.*"

"Legion, or O'Keefe?" I joke.

She cracks a little smile. "*Neither of them.*"

It's the third day of the week-long event, and the bike rally is in full swing when we arrive. Roaring engines and glinting chrome as far as the eye can see. I dismount Serene and take a deep breath of sea air mixed with exhaust, sweat, and fried food.

I don't know if Legion is still at the L.S.S. Saloon, but that's the first place I'm checking. My boots feel heavy on the pavement as I determinedly move through the crowd, eyes scanning faces, ignoring the catcalls from bikini-clad women and throttle revs. I'm not here for the show this time. I'm here to find a little peace through violence.

"You got that picture text from him over four hours ago," Viking says, brushing shoulders through the crowd along with me. "You really think he's still at the bar?"

"Where else am I supposed to start looking? This rally stretches for miles. Even if he wandered off, he knows we're coming. He knows how long it takes to get here. He'll be back."

"Maybe *you* should have a drink while we wait. What if O'Keefe is with him?"

"It's on sight."

Viking's heavy hand lands firmly on my shoulder, halting me just as we reach the parking lot of the L.S.S.

"I know you've been looking forward to this reunion. The last three years we came down here, you were mostly searching for O'Keefe. But you can't just jump him in public. Wait for the fucking ring. At least we can make some money on it."

"I don't care about that."

"Then care about keeping your record clean for the sake of the club and the mission, Dean. For your family, too. You kick his ass out here in public, you're getting locked up. You might get a decent shot or two in before security tears you off him, but that's not going to satisfy you. If he's here with Legion, he already knows it's on. Save it for the ring."

Fuck. Viking is right. "Fine."

We make it to the packed bar, rowdy with bikers and babes looking to have a good time. I scan the bar and what I'm able to see beyond it, craning my neck around a bald biker with his face buried in the generous tits of a barmaid. She's perched on the edge of the bar, wearing a leather bikini and fishnets, serving thirty-dollar Motorboat and Hurricane shots.

Viking splits off to cover more ground, and we meet up again near the stairs to the upper deck.

When we reach the top, the air is thick with the smoke from the Burn-out box below, tires screaming over the sound of the crowd, before one of them blows out. Viking and I continue to weave our way through the sea of spectators, and just as the smoke clears, I spot

Legion leaning back on a bench, beer in one hand, arms stretched wide along the railing behind him.

He's got two women draped over him, dressed in leather and lace, more skin than clothing, laughing flirtatiously at something he said. When he spots me coming, his little grin turns sinister.

"*Beat it.*" He cocks his chin at one of the women, tapping the other's shoulder with his beer bottle.

They both pout, confused, until they notice me. I must not look too friendly at the moment, because they don't need further convincing. Grabbing their drinks, they quickly slip away in a swirl of perfume and tight leather, the braver—or perhaps the more intoxicated one—lingers for a second to run her hand down Viking's arm, before her giggling companion drags her away.

"Where is he?" I demand.

Legion glances behind us before his pale eyes meet mine again. "Just the two of you?"

"Not that it matters, but no. Everyone's here."

He seems pleased. *"Everyone?"*

"Not Vanna." For whatever reason, her absence doesn't seem to dampen his mild elation. "Where's O'Keefe? Did you warn him I was coming?"

"Of course not," Legion scoffs, standing up to toss his half-empty beer in the trash can a few feet away. "I paid him to be here. Everything is already arranged... *My gift to you.*"

"You what?"

"Consider it a peace offering," Legion says, though nothing about his antagonistic grin conveys peace.

Vanna

I can still feel Dean's parting kiss against my lips, and the rumble of Serene's engine in my bones, even though Dean left hours ago. I should be used to this by now. The long rides, the rallies, the occasional fight. But this fight is different. And although Dean is in the best physical shape I've ever seen him in, I still worry. How could I not? I love him, and part of loving him is accepting him for who he is. I know he needs this closure for his own inner peace.

Understanding him doesn't ease my anxiety, however. It doesn't stop my brain from looping the worst-case scenarios like a playlist I can't shut off. I go about my day, reminding myself that Dean is with his MC brothers, and they always have each other's backs. But it only takes the edge off so much. Despite that, I don't have the luxury of succumbing to the stress of *what-ifs*. Not with my little boy tugging at my shirt, asking for snacks and stories, and to go outside.

We play a few rounds of red-light-green-light and Simon Says on the front lawn before I bring Ace back inside for a fruit cup. My cellphone rings just as I set the snack down for him at the dining room table. The name on the caller ID brings a smile to my face, and I grab it with a still sticky hand.

"Hey stranger!"

"Girl, it's been too long!" The smile in Latisha's voice is evident. "Are you free tonight? We can grab a few drinks and catch up."

"Everyone is in Myrtle Beach for the rally. The Twisted Throttle is closed tonight, and I'm home with Ace. Let me give Rosita a call. She stayed behind, too."

"Why didn't you go?"

"Don't even get me started."

"Tell me over booze." Latisha laughs.

Once I confirm with Rosita that she's still happy to watch Ace tonight, I pack him an overnight bag while he chooses a couple of movies to bring. Just before we head out the door, I change into a pair of black jeans, boots, and one of Dean's old Guns N' Roses t-shirts, and grab my small makeup bag to shove in my purse. I'll have time to slap on some mascara and lip gloss and run a brush through my hair before I meet up with Latisha across town. She texted me that it's *90's Night* at the bar we're meeting at, so I quickly select one of Dean's flannel shirts as well and tie it around my waist. *Good enough.*

The moment Ace hugs me goodnight, and I kiss his little cheek, a flicker of guilt reignites the anxious feeling in my chest, and I hold onto him a little longer.

Rosita places her hand on my shoulder. "Go, have fun," she insists, as if she can read my mind. "The children are happy. Go be happy with your friend. It has been a while since you've seen her. We deserve a break now and again, no?"

Legion: Book 3

I kiss Ace one more time before he runs off to play with Mia, and I straighten to face Rosita. "Next time you do, let me know and we can have a sleepover at our house." I reach into my pocket and hand her some cash. "For dinner, in case you want to order a pizza or something. I'll come get him in the morning and bring them to the playground if you'd like."

"Sure," Rosita smiles. "Maybe I'll join you, and we can take them for a picnic. That would be nice."

"Let me know what you decide, and I'll pack a basket."

"*I'll bring the horchata,*" she teases.

Nirvana is blasting through the sound system when I enter the bar full of people wearing a mix of denim, flannel, and crop tops, all of them leaning hard into the theme. The bar tables around the perimeter of the room have lava lamps, and one of the lady bartenders is sporting crimped hair and butterfly clips.

I spot Latisha at the bar in a faded *Boyz II Men* tee and high-waisted jeans, already halfway through a cocktail with fruit skewered on the rim. Her face lights up the moment she sees me, and I weave my way through the crowd of strangers who are laughing and singing off-key to the music.

"Look at you, all snatched, nineties style!" Latisha laughs, tugging at the flannel shirt secured around my waist.

"Dean will be thrilled when I stretch the sleeves out beyond wear," I say, hugging her.

"You look great," she goes on.

"I don't have animal cracker crumbs in my bra, so that's a plus. But you look amazing, also. It's so good to see you. How are you?"

I take a seat at the bar beside her and order whatever she's having. The bartender is quick to bring me the '90s-themed cocktail, something sweet, spiked, and probably dangerous. While we catch up between sips and nostalgic music, some of the anxiety I've been carrying all day dissipates a bit. Latisha tells me about the new guy she's sort of seeing. I tell her about Ace morphing into Dean, including his obsession with motorcycles. Then we both crack up at how well we remember the lyrics to the string of *Salt N' Pepa* songs playing. By the time we finish our cocktails, we're both ready to hit the dance floor.

Jennifer Saviano

DEAN

We pull through the chain link fence and into the crowded lot of the old, familiar warehouse turned underground arena. As we kill the engines of our bikes, the muffled roar of the crowd inside spills through cracks in the steel.

Viking scans the lot, then checks his watch, then the street.

"What?" I ask as I remove my helmet and dismount Serene.

"You think he's gonna show?"

I hang my helmet on Serene's handlebars. "I hope so."

"I mean Legion. He said he'd be here, but I don't see his Indian anywhere."

I take a quick gander around the dark lot. "There's a lot of bikes here. And he said nine o'clock." I glance at my watch. "We still have forty minutes."

Viking slowly dismounts his bike with a heavy sigh. "Something doesn't feel right."

"Like there's gonna be a raid on this place, kind of *not right?*"

"No," he shakes his head. "I'm sure this circuit has all the right people on its payroll. I mean, we haven't seen Legion since he gave us the details. Are you so hell bent on beating the fuck out of O'Keefe, you haven't noticed?"

"This lot is full. His bike could be on the other side. It's possible he's already in there. And if he isn't, we're early. He's still got time."

"Alright," Viking shrugs out of his cut and folds it into the side bag of his bike. "Then let's go see what these *arrangements* are."

I tuck my cut away as well, and we cross the cracked lot to the main entrance. The night air is warm and slightly muggy, and it feels like being hit with an arctic breeze when we step inside. The industrial AC is blasting full force in an attempt to offset the heat from the hundreds of bodies packed into this place. Yelling, sweating, betting, and spilling over-priced beer on each other. The cold only half-masks the ripe odor of sweat and the faint, unmistakable metallic tang of blood.

We're greeted by a big guy in a suit, sporting a holstered semi-automatic under his open jacket. "Three hundred a head."

"He's fighting," Viking chucks a thumb at me. "We were told it's all been arranged."

"Name?" the suit gruffly demands.

"Keegan," Viking replies.

"This way." The suit leads us through the outer perimeter of the crowd, down a short hallway, and into a small locker room with a bench and a bathroom with a shower stall. "You can get ready in here. Pick a locker. There's a padlock and a key in each. Don't lose the key. When your fight's done, make sure you leave the key in the lock when you go. Your opponent hasn't checked in yet, but your fight isn't until nine. Center cage. Someone will let you know when he gets here, then you have the option of betting yourself to win." He shifts his attention momentarily to Viking. "You his coach or manager?"

Viking only stares silently back at the guy.

"Well, you came with him. You can bet your buddy here to win, or not bet at all."

"What's the buy-in to fight?" I ask. "It's been a few years."

"It's already been taken care of."

Viking waits until the suit shuts the door behind him and we're alone before he turns to me. "He even covered your fee to fight."

"Legion said everything was arranged."

"Yeah… Why does Legion seem as eager as you are for this fight, though?"

"Maybe he bet big money on me to win and wants to rake in another easy million," I mutter, though I'm only half serious. Before I shed my clothes down to my MMA shorts, I pull out the cash from my pocket and hand it to Viking. "When you get the chance, bet me to win."

Viking fingers through the cash. "Do you think O'Keefe really had any idea how bad he was fucking you over with Legion?"

"He knew he was selling me out for something. He might not have anticipated the amount of damage Legion caused, but he still fucked me over. I never thought we were friends, but his greed almost cost me everything."

"We should just go back to the rally and find our guys. Put this money in Ace's college fund," Viking says, attempting to hand it back to me.

I refuse to take it. "I'm gonna fuckin' triple it. No way I'm losing tonight. I'm in the best shape of my goddamned life. My only concern about tonight is not killing O'Keefe. I'm not losing this fight. I'm gonna paint the fuckin' ring with him."

"And imagine Legion while you're doing it." Viking reluctantly shoves the cash in his pocket.

I'm probably going to regret asking, but... "*What?*"

"Don't you think you might be a little unhinged when I'm the voice of reason?" Viking jokes, but the troubled expression on his face remains.

"Just say what you want to say, Viking."

"When has Legion ever done anything for anyone that wasn't in some way beneficial to him, too?"

"I'm aware the demonic prick hates me and wants everything I have. He knows he can't fight me. Maybe he wants to live vicariously through O'Keefe? Maybe he's hoping I end up one of the lucky clovers on the Irish prick's arm?"

"Or maybe there's another reason he wants you right here, right now. I just think it's a little suspicious we haven't seen Legion around, pretty much since we bumped into him earlier with those two chicks."

"I didn't expect him to hang out with us. And there are literally over three hundred *thousand* people who come to Bike Week every year. Easy for him to disappear for a while in a crowd that size."

"And he'd expect you to know that."

Fuck... Viking has a solid point. I wouldn't put it past Legion either. He would make a very brief appearance in order to convince me he's a couple hundred miles away from Vanna.

"For all we know, he's already high-tailed it back to Bermuda County. *Back to Vanna,*" Viking goes on, voicing my fears out loud.

Son of a bitch...that's exactly what he's done! He's probably been back in town for hours now!

If I didn't already have reason enough to beat O'Keefe to a bloody pulp, Legion's fucking antics have pushed me over the edge.

"Fuck... I know that look," Viking mutters.

Renewed rage courses through my veins. "*Bet me to win.*"

CHAPTER 43

Vanna

The music feels like it's thumping through the floor. An *Ace of Base* track vibrates in my chest as I laugh and dance with Latisha under the neon lights. A couple of guys in denim vests try to dance with us, but we turn them down and opt for a break.

Latisha leans in closer to my ear so I can hear her over the music. "Let's go get another drink!"

I've lost count of how many songs we've danced to. "Okay!" I say, a little breathless. My cheeks feel flushed, and I'm definitely already buzzed from the last cocktail.

Latisha grabs my hand and pulls me toward the bar as if she expects me to get lost otherwise. It's crowded, but it's not too bad. Being around bars and biker parties, I'm not as uncomfortable in these environments as I once was before Dean and the Saviors MC.

My laughter dies, though, when I spot Legion sitting with his back to the bar counter, staring at me. My stomach drops. Not because he's supposed to be in Myrtle Beach with my husband and the rest of the MC, but because of the way his intense stare makes me suddenly aware of the cling of my clothing and the spike in my heart rate. The way his gaze seems to stake a claim on my existence.

Of course, Latisha is pulling me toward the only vacant spot at the bar, right beside Legion. She flags down the bartender with the butterfly clips and orders us another one of the night's signature cocktails. "Heavy on the tequila!"

Without breaking his gaze from me, Legion leans back toward the bartender. "Allow me," he insists, reaching into his jacket for some cash.

"Thanks, buddy," Latisha begins to wave him off dismissively, without sparing him a glance. "But it's girls' night." She hands the bartender her debit card.

When Legion places his cash on the bar and slides it to her anyway, Latisha finally looks up at him. He grins at her, slow and dangerous, like he already knows exactly how to play her.

"*Oh,*" she blinks once, then sweeps her eyes along his razor-sharp jawline. She picks up his money and slips it into her bra. He pretends to appreciate the quick glimpse of her cleavage.

"Those drinks are gonna cost you a conversation." Legion's flirtatious words are laced with a level of command that seems to intrigue her further. I'm not surprised. Latisha has always had a thing for the cocky types. Specifically, the cocky *biker* types.

"I thought you were supposed to be at the rally," I say, and they both shift their attention to me.

"You know this guy?" Latisha asks.

"Latisha, this is Damien, aka Legion… Legion, Latisha."

Legion offers her his hand. "The pleasure is all mine."

She places her hand in his with a smirk as if to say she knows. "So, you're the new Enforcer for the club… Derek has mentioned you a time or two."

"Ah," Legion chuckles. "I see my reputation has preceded me."

"From what I've heard, it should," Latisha says, but I can tell she isn't joking.

"Where is Dean?" I ask, before things get any more awkward.

"Exactly where he has chosen to be." Legion gestures to the clock behind the bar. "His fight is at nine."

"It's nearly nine, now," I say, just as the bartender returns with our drinks and another beer and a shot of some dark liquid for Legion. I suddenly don't feel like drinking anymore.

"Then let's toast to victory," Legion grins, raising his beer bottle for us to clink our cocktails against. Latisha doesn't hesitate the way I do. She clinks her glass to mine next, watching me curiously. I don't want to make the situation uncomfortable for anyone else, so I clink my glass to Legion's beer and take a sip of the fruity cocktail, trying not to grimace at the noticeably stronger taste of tequila.

"Good girl," Legion winks.

I pretend not to notice. "Dean isn't alone, is he?"

"Of course not," he assures me. "And if it's of any consolation, I expect a rather large payoff."

"Huh?"

"*I bet your beloved to win*, my sweet. Would I have done so if I lacked faith in his ability?"

"How much?" Latisha bats her dark eyes at him while she sips her drink.

A sly grin teases the corners of Legion's mouth. "Oh, I'm winning big tonight."

"Do you dance, Damien?" she continues to flirt.

"On occasion," he replies.

She playfully rolls her eyes. *"Do you want to dance with me?"*

He takes his time considering her offer. "If you would be so kind as to grant me a private moment with our lovely Vanna."

She seems to force a little smile but gives in. "Alright, I'll just go request a few songs and give you two a minute." Drink in hand, she makes her way over to the DJ set up on the far side of the dance floor.

I turn back to Legion. "They don't know you're not in Myrtle Beach, do they?"

He shrugs and takes another swig. "They may suspect by now."

"*What did you do?*"

"I orchestrated a little time for us to talk, alone."

"That sounds serious." I sigh, feeling the buzz a little stronger. I place the remainder of the cocktail on the bar. "I should probably switch to water."

He studies me as I slide onto the barstool beside him, then abruptly asks, "Is it stifling?"

"What?"

"Your youth was stolen from you, sweet one. You never got the chance to live it up. You went from the innocent age of sixteen, straight to thirty… First a prisoner, then an *escapee*…only to find yourself betrothed after three measly years of freedom. A majority of those years lived in fear… *Was it really freedom?* And is it freedom even now, angel? Living under such restraint… *You are still young*, Vanna. *Live a little*… You *deserve* it."

He slides the cocktail closer to me, and I glance up at him wryly. "*The devil on my shoulder*, are you?"

Legion: Book 3

"Your humble Demon, Goddess… Who only wishes to be of service and to see you safe and *happy*."

My cellphone vibrates in my back pocket. I'm already certain who is calling.

"*The good warden*, I presume?" Legion mutters with a detectable level of disdain. He takes another gulp of beer while I take the call.

Between the static on Dean's end of the line and the loud music in this bar, I can't hear him at all. The call cuts out, so I type out a text instead.

I'm hanging out with Latisha. Ace is with Rosita. Everything is fine. Don't worry. Focus on your fight. Good luck. Be careful. I love you.

Dean: Thanks, I love you too. Have you seen Legion?

For a moment, I debate how to respond. Would it throw Dean off? Be a dangerous distraction while he's in the cage? It's not as if Dean has anything to worry about regarding Legion and I… I rule in favor of his peace of mind and focus and type out another text.

No. Don't worry about me. Focus on your fight. Get it out of your system. This is the last one!

Guilt instantly washes over me, and I take another sip of my drink as I watch the bouncing dots on my screen indicate he's typing…

Dean: <3 Promise. See you soon.

Me: 😘 For good luck, not that you need it.

Dean: Aces baby 😎

I tuck the cellphone into my back pocket and glance over at a smug-looking Legion. "I didn't tell him you're here… *for his sake*."

The Divinyls song, *I Touch Myself* begins to play. Legion finishes off his beer and slams the bottle down on the bar beside me.

"Well, this is my song," he growls against my ear, then walks off into the crowd on the dance floor behind me just as Latisha returns.

"What's this guy's deal?" Latisha asks, situating herself on a barstool to watch him. A moment later, she chuckles, "*Oh, wow…*"

"What?" I glance over at her to find an amused grin on her face.

"He's…"

"He's what?"

"Dancing…" She bites her bottom lip.

"Apparently, he enjoys that. It's probably his least destructive hobby."

"Now he's got two women dancing over to him… All he did was look at them from across the room."

I peek over my shoulder and immediately regret it. He's dancing with two drunk women. The moment we make eye contact, Legion grins, winking at me as he slips his hands to the napes of their necks and pulls them closer to his body. They're all too eager to touch on him and grind up against him.

"Is it wrong I want to go over there…" Latisha sighs.

"Didn't you just tell me you were sort of seeing someone?"

"Yeah, but it's not like we put an *official label* on it."

"Well, Legion should be required to wear a warning label."

I turn back around when—at his guided encouragement—the women dancing on him slowly begin to sink down the length of his body.

"Oh my god…" Latisha picks up a bar napkin and dramatically fans herself. "And they're just *going with it…*"

"I'm afraid to even ask."

Latisha only looks away from the spectacle on the dance floor long enough to grab her drink and take a quick sip before she goes on to describe what is happening. "He's got them crouched down on either side of him… One of them is holding onto his belt."

I know he wants me to watch *as if I'll get jealous* or something, which I am *not*. I finish the rest of my drink as the song comes to its close.

"Another round?" the bartender asks.

"Hell yes." Latisha hands over her glass.

"I'll have an ice water, please." I smile.

"And the gentleman?" The bartender nods somewhere in Legion's direction.

I don't want to be rude. "Sure," I say, digging in my jeans for my debit card.

"Should I start a tab?" she asks.

"Yes," Legion says, suddenly beside me, his hand jutting out to the bartender with a credit card between his fingers. "On this. And make mine a shot of Johnny Walker Black."

He's still got the two floosies hanging on him, laughing and touching him like they want to drag him off to the alley out back.

"You got it," the bartender says, taking his card.

Legion: Book 3

"You certainly have something." Latisha grins at Legion in that way she used to look at Viking. Legion scans her over slowly, head to toe and up again.

"You still want that dance?" he growls at her, and one of his groupies lets out a whimpering pout as if she thought she had staked her claim on him, at least, for the night.

Latisha slides off the barstool, lifting her arms to loosely circle them around his neck, effectively forcing the two women away from him. Legion slips a hand to the small of her back and pulls her to the dancefloor while Toni Braxton's song *You're Makin' Me High* blares from the speakers. His two shunned and disheartened groupies move on to other willing guys.

The bartender returns with our drinks and places them down before me. "Thanks," I say, before twisting on the stool to take another peek at what Legion and Latisha are doing on the dancefloor.

I don't know why I'm surprised to see them pressed against each other. He's got his hand jammed in her back pocket, grabbing her ass like she's already wearing his patch.

When the song ends, Latisha reclaims the barstool beside me, laughing like she just had the best time of her life. She grabs the cocktail I've been guarding for her and takes a gulp.

"*He's a wild one!*" She gasps like she has to catch her breath.

Within a second, Legion is on my other side. He shoots his Johnny Walker, then slides the shot glass across the bar top. It collides with a sharp clink against her cocktail. "You wanna go again?"

"Fuck yes." She grins back at him as if it's a challenge.

"You better finish that first." He cocks his chin at her drink, and when she chugs the rest of it, he rewards her with a growled, "*Good girl,*" before leaning into my ear. "You really should try to have a little fun, sweet one. Your friend is such a spitfire." Before I can say anything, they're back on the dancefloor, grinding to Rob Zombie's *Dragula*.

His insinuation that I'm not any fun plays over in my buzzed brain while I finish the rest of my cocktail, ignoring my water. I can be fun. *Asshole.* The next '90s hit begins to play, Meredith Brooks's *Bitch*. This could be my song. Fuck him. I can dance. And I can dance by myself, too.

I slide off the barstool and make my way to the edge of the dancefloor. When Latisha spots me, she ditches Legion and dances her way over to me. Immediately, I feel better, and the two of us are laughing together, having the time of our lives without him and his dark, manipulative energy tensing up the atmosphere. We dance to three more songs before Latisha says she needs to use the bathroom and will be back as soon as she can. There's always a significantly long line for the ladies' room, and tonight is no exception.

I'm fully buzzed and perfectly content to continue dancing on my own. I don't get to, though. The moment she leaves, a random guy moves in on me, zapping all the fun away with his bold, unsolicited advances. I turn away from him, bumping into someone else. Someone who smells like smoke and leather.

Why does it make me smile?

A finger lifts my chin up, forcing me to look him in the eyes. "Dance, sweet one." When I notice the shot in Legion's other hand, he offers it to me. "You're free tonight."

I don't feel like arguing with his choice of words. I take the shot and hand it back to him. A good song is playing. Another one I can really move to. Melissa Etheridge's *I'm The Only One*…

I think I'm getting drunk, though I'm not quite tipsy enough not to notice the way Legion has been using the proximity of his body to maneuver me away from the crowd. Over the duration of the next few songs, he's moved closer and closer, our bodies briefly touching, lightly bumping against each other, now and again. I'm sure I am meant to believe it's all been by accident.

Though now that he has me where he wants me…trapped between his hovering form and the brick wall, I lift my eyes to meet his intense stare.

"What?" I ask, still moving my body to an En Vogue song. He leans into me, planting one hand against the wall beside my head. "I just want to dance."

"Don't let me stop you."

"Are you sure? You're crowding me."

"I've seen what you can do in tighter corners than this." He grins. I scowl at him. "*Creeper.*"

His smile only broadens. However long his list of regrets might be, apparently *stalking me* is not on it. "The way you move…your body calls to mine…speaks to me."

"Oh? And what is my body saying to you, right now?"

Legion: Book 3

Smiling back at him, I thrust my middle finger into his smug expression. He startles me when he snatches my wrist and yanks my hand closer to his face. I watch in shock as he drags his tongue up my finger, then sucks it into his mouth. His teeth scrape gently against my skin as he slowly pulls my finger out and releases me before saying, "I believe that was the international sign for *fuck you*... Offer most eagerly accepted, sweet one. I would savor every moment between us."

I swallow hard, emotions I can't even begin to decipher in my inebriated mind riot throughout my body, and my heart pounds.

He wraps an arm around my waist, pulling me until his body presses against mine. Bowing his head, he brings his lips to my ear, and I can feel his warm, whispered breath through my hair. "Do you not realize the power you wield? The influence you have? That if you commanded it of me, even here...*right now*...with all of these cretins to bear witness... *I would drop to my fucking knees before you and...*"

"*Legion...stop.*" I can barely breathe. His words, his proximity, doing things to my body I should *not* be feeling.

"*I would worship you*... I would accept any terms you set forth... I would wait in the wings, in secret, for you... I would take our secret to the grave... *Keegan need never know.*"

"I would never betray him."

"Then I would go to him, and offer—"

"There is nothing you could offer him. Enough!"

"He's struggling...you know this..."

I attempt to push him away, but he cages me against the wall between his arms. It's his fault the patronage at the Twisted Throttle isn't what it once was. "My husband would never entertain what you're insinuating, no matter how bad the financial hardship *you caused!*"

"I was thinking more along the lines of a *timeshare*... Though I'm not *entirely* opposed to the idea of a threesome... *Are you?*"

"Just when I think it might be possible that you actually are, deep down, a decent human being, *you pull this!* Get off of me!" I shove at him.

"The only one playing games here is you. I've been straight with you about everything! You toy with me!"

"*Excuse me?*"

He grabs my hips, pulling the lower portion of my body flush against his. I push against his chest, leaning back as best I can.

"Deny the magnetism between us, Vanna." He growls, grinding himself against me. I gasp, and my awareness of his arousal seems to darken his lustful gaze. "Deny you feel anything for me. That you haven't thought about me these last long years I've been on a fucking quest for you and you alone!"

"Legion, you need to get off of me before someone sees us!"

"*Let them.* Tell me you haven't thought about me like this. That you haven't imagined us together."

"*Stop it.*"

"How many times have I fucked you?" he demands as I attempt to discreetly struggle out of his hold. "Tell me. How many times were you thinking of me when he was inside you?"

"You feel something for me?"

"I feel a lot of things for you."

"Then let go of me. Step away from me. Show me I can trust you. Show me you actually do have some level of respect for me. That you do see me differently than you have...*others* in your past."

"Whores?"

"If you see me differently, treat me as such... What you're doing now...this isn't respect. This isn't kindness, Damien... *please.*"

Legion steps back, his grim expression a mix between wounded and angered. I take the opportunity to storm back to the bar.

"Another water, please," I ask the bartender. I need to sober up and get out of here. I glance around for Latisha. Is she still waiting for the damn bathroom? I'm about to pull out my phone to text her when Legion brushes up against my side again.

"Hey, I'm sorry," he begins to say, when my night goes from bad to godawful. I've just locked eyes with a worst-case scenario, and my heart practically lurches up my throat along with that last shot I'm now regretting.

"Oh great." I'm buzzed, aggravated, and Lucinda is the last person on earth I want to see tonight. Or any night. *Ever again.* She lifts her drink from the other end of the bar and saunters toward me.

Wearing what would be considered an obscenely low-cut top on someone like me, and a pair of low-rise jeans to go with the sly little smirk on her face, she sneers, "What do we have here?"

Her gaze shifts momentarily from me to Legion, as he moves closer to my side. I can't help but wonder if he's being protective or just wants a front row seat. She looks him up and down with an air of dismissal before we lock eyes once again.

"Dean's so worried about who I'm fucking when he should be worried about you! I'm sure he will be *thrilled* to hear all about everything I just saw." Lucinda's red lips curve up in a grin that's just begging to be slapped off her face.

"Nothing you say to him will ever mean anything. Especially not about me. You're dead to him." I glare back at her. "Dean doesn't care who you're with. That ultimatum wasn't about who you're fucking. It was about keeping you away from the club. You're toxic."

Cold liquid splashes up into my face, and I gasp in surprise, tasting the cinnamon and whiskey flavor of her Fireball cocktail.

Before I even realize what I'm doing, her empty glass smashes on the floor, and her long blonde hair is ensnared in my fists. Shoving her backwards, I slam her up against a wall and jerk her head back, forcing her to meet my eyes again. Hers are wide with surprise.

"This has been a long time coming!" I snap, releasing her. Before she can do or say anything else, I ball my fist and throw a punch, nailing her in that devious mouth.

Her head snaps to the side, and I can't help but feel there isn't another person more deserving of my first *real* punch than Lucinda.

LEGION

Sometimes you get lucky. Sometimes, opportunity knocks harder than Vanna's fists currently slamming into Lucinda's not-so-pretty face. I know I have to break this catfight up, but Vanna needs the release, and Lucinda deserves whatever she dishes out. My blood runs hot as I take in the girl-on-girl action. Vanna looks alive, primal, hair falling wild around her shoulders, eyes lit with the kind of fire that always makes me wonder what else she'd do if I pushed her hard enough...

When Lucinda begins shrieking like a banshee, it's time to end this before cellphones start popping out. I swoop in and grab Vanna by her waist, possessive, firm, and yank her back against me. She struggles for a moment, wild-eyed and panting, but I hold her still. Her heat, her rage, seeps into my body, and it's a fucking rush.

"*You did good. Real good, baby,*" I whisper against her ear. "Let me take it from here. I need you to think about Ace now and calm down."

The fight instantly drains from her body, and she spins around in my embrace to face me, nearly panicked. "*Ace… What have I done?*"

"*Nothing.*" I cup her flushed cheek in my hand. "Do as I say. Go to your car and wait for me there. You can't drive, but you need to get out of here."

Vanna nods frantically, and I release her. She heads for the door, and I turn back to Lucinda. She's just gotten back to her feet and is pressing a napkin to her busted lip. I imagine her ego is just as bruised as her face. She looks mad enough to spit fire, but I beat her to the punch.

"You press charges, and I press *upload*."

Her bloodshot glare locks with mine. "*What?*"

Now that the brief excitement of the fight has passed, and the spectators have resumed minding their own fucking business, I lean in closer to Lucinda, lowering my voice when I tell her, "I wonder what the repercussions will be for Maddie when the town sees her mother sucking my dick in HD…Taking it on all fours in that hotel room we met in."

Her eyes widen in horrified realization. "You…*you recorded us?*"

"I took the liberty of cropping myself out, but what will this *proper little town* think of your…*degradation kink?* If you so much as *glare* in Vanna's direction, I'll send our sex tape to all of Maddie's teachers. Her principal. Her friends' parents. Hell, I'll have it playing at the local movie theater if you push me. Who knows where else the files will end up once I release them?" I sneer, making an evident display of raking my gaze up and down her disheveled form. "*You've got the body to go viral, babe.*"

Her eyes well up before she spins on her heels and storms off in the direction of the bathrooms, disappearing into the crowd. I immediately vacate the establishment in search of Vanna and spot her pacing down the street beside her car while on her phone.

As I reach her, I'm relieved she's speaking with Latisha, not Keegan. Not that there's much he can do about anything from Myrtle Beach.

"We need to go," I insist.

"But Latisha… And my car," Vanna gestures to the vehicle parked beside the curb.

Legion: Book 3

"I'll call a cab, just go!" Latisha pushes. "Lucinda's in here. She's pissed. I don't think she's called the cops, but that doesn't mean she or anyone else won't."

"I don't feel right leaving you here," Vanna hesitates.

"I'm fine, I'm calling a ride the second we hang up. Get out of here. I'll text you when I'm home."

"Alright," Vanna reluctantly agrees. "I'm sorry."

"Don't be." Latisha laughs. "I wish I got to see it!"

When they hang up, I pluck the phone from her trembling fingers. "Is there anything inside you need before we go?"

She blinks at me. "We're leaving my car?"

"You can't drive, so we're either leaving your car or my motorcycle."

She hesitates, conflicted for a moment. However, I know which she'll choose. Her people-pleasing conditioning will rule in my favor.

"Vanna, we don't have time," I urge.

"Shit. Let me grab my purse." She unlocks the passenger side door and crawls over the center console to retrieve the purse stashed somewhere inside. I take the opportunity to lower the volume of her phone and tap the power button to blacken the screen while she's preoccupied, then chuck it into the shadows beneath the glovebox.

"Okay," she says, straightening, and slips the purse strap over her shoulder. I shut the door before she can take a second glance and gently escort her by the arm in the direction of my bike.

"I'll have your car brought back to your home. Just let me get you out of here before she changes her mind and calls the cops." *I know she won't.*

"Do you think she will?" Vanna fretfully asks. "What was I thinking?"

"That she deserved it, and rightfully so." I don't release her until we reach my bike parked near the ally. "Get on."

"You were drinking, too."

"I had a beer and a shot. I'm fine. You started way before I did."

"Does the bartender still have your credit card?"

"It's not mine. I lifted it off one of the women earlier."

She blinks at me. "*Oh god!* We're both just out here committing drunken crimes!"

"Vanna, get on the fucking bike." I snatch my helmet off the handlebar and hand it to her before mounting up.

"Where are we going?" she asks, strapping it on.

"Wherever you want."

She simply stares at the seat behind me, clearly hesitant, and I know exactly why.

"It's a fucking ride, *not a goddamned affair*... Haven't you ever ridden with any of the others?"

She shakes her head as if it's some sort of sin. The good girl in her, *the faithful wife,* is still inside her mind, screaming through the haze of adrenaline and alcohol.

"Keeps you on a short leash, eh?"

"Dean's going to be so mad at me…"

"That would be rather hypocritical of him, considering where he's chosen to be tonight. Get on the bike, Vanna. Now. The wind in your face will do you good. Settle your nerves and cut through the heat still coursing through your veins."

She steps up to the bike to grip my shoulders and climbs on behind me. The instant I feel the warmth of her thick thighs pressed against me, my breath hitches. She wraps her arms around my body, and I grip the handlebars until my knuckles turn white. When she sighs, her warm breath against my neck sends a shiver down my spine. I twist the throttle, making the bike beneath us vibrate with a loud roar. If she felt my physical reaction to her touch, perhaps she'll attribute it to the rumbling bike.

I tear away from the curb and hit the road. The wind whips around us, but all I feel is her and the hunger twisting in my gut. I've wanted to experience this moment since I laid eyes on her at that bonfire. Countless times I've imagined her exactly like this. Wrapped around me, no one else in the world but us… A demon knight and his queen.

Every curve in the road, every shift of her weight, every time her grip tightens like I'm the only thing keeping her from crashing, my hands tremble with anticipation.

She's afraid I might let her fall. She's right to be afraid, but not of the road. She doesn't realize she fell a long time ago.

DEAN

The cage door slams shut behind me with a heavy clang, but we've been locked in on each other through the chain-link before I set foot on the mat. O'Keefe bounces in place across from me, chin down but I'm not fully convinced by his smug expression. He watches with his fists already raised as I roll my shoulders and jerk my head left to right, cracking the tension from my neck, attempting to shake off the nagging worry creeping to the forefront of my mind.

She said she hasn't seen him… Maybe Legion never left the rally…

My gut tells me otherwise. Legion wouldn't arrange this fight if it didn't benefit him in some way.

"For your sake, I hope the pot of gold the demon bought you with was worth it," I growl.

The Irishman grins. "What would you have me say, Keegan? Green's always been my color, mate. Thought you'd appreciate the Irish irony!"

"There's nothing you can say. But you can bleed."

The bell rings, and O'Keefe comes at me fast, throwing a jab-jab-cross combo. I manage to slip outside and pivot to deliver a brutal inside leg kick. The impact makes him grunt and shift his stance. When he lunges with a wild overhand right, I duck and wrap him up, underhooks in tight, my shoulder beneath his chin. I slam him back against the chain-link before lifting him and driving him down so hard, the mat shudders beneath us. I land in side-control, quickly maneuvering to pin his clover-tatted arm beneath my knee, the other across his torso.

"Where is he?" I demand while he struggles beneath me.

"Probably right where she wants him!"

I don't even feel the first few punches I rain down in his face, drawing first blood, and a lot of it at that.

The motherfucker played me. Used my desire for revenge against me to get me right where he wants me… But…*what has he done to manipulate Vanna?*

Where are they? Did she lie to me?

I imagine her on the back of his bike… Her arms around him… The way she'd look guilty…conflicted…scared…

What did he do to get her *where he wants her? And what is he planning to carry out?*

The crowd erupting around the cage cuts through my spiraling thoughts, the ringing in my ears dragging me back to the fight.

O'Keefe bucks and twists in an attempt to escape. I can feel his ribs heaving beneath me, but I can't hear his panicked breath over the roar of the spectators.

Only Viking's booming voice manages to reach me. A warning. *"Don't fucking kill him, Dean!"*

I allow the Irishman to shrimp out and stagger to his feet. He instantly throws a spinning backfist and misses.

I have no intention of granting him further mercy. I lunge, slamming him in the abdomen with another brutal kick that lands him against the cage, before locking him into a Muay Thai clinch.

O'Keefe attempts to grapple with me. The blood draining profusely from his nose and mouth, slickens his neck and shoulders, making it difficult to hold onto him.

I slam my knee up into his abdomen, again and again, while I've got him. Blood sputters from his busted face, spraying my chest and dripping onto the mat.

But I want to look him in the eyes when I end him, so I toss him like trash onto the mat. He lands heavy on his back. A bloody heap, desperately attempting to pull air into his lungs with a spasming diaphragm.

"Get up," I growl. "I want to watch your fucking lights go out."

O'Keefe slowly rises, positioning himself into another fighting stance. Fists raised, bouncing on the balls of his feet, but with far less ease than when we started.

"Come on, then!" he shouts. "We all have to sleep in the beds we make, don't we? I wonder if your wife hasn't already invited him into yours!"

I trust my wife, but this was a mistake. I'm four hundred miles away from where I should be.

And although I'm about to K.O. this Irish prick, Legion has already won this fight. He fucking won the moment I let vengeance blind me to what really matters.

I'd forfeit in this very moment, but that would be forfeiting money my family deserves. I promised Vanna this was the last fight. And when I return to her and apologize for allowing my foolish pride to chase retribution, I want to at least be able to do so with a stack of fucking cash to lay at her feet.

Legion: Book 3

When he charges me this time, I don't move. I don't flinch. I let him hit me. His shoulder slams into my abdomen, knocking me backward, but I'm already lining up my next move.

My back hits the mat as I hook my leg behind his and grip the back of his neck, using the momentum of his own weight to launch him. He flips clean over me, crashing down on his back with a thud that shakes the cage. Before he can even suck in a breath, I roll with him and mount him fast, pinning him beneath me.

My fist drips red with the vengeance I've waited for as I slam it into O'Keefe's mangled face until he's gurgling on the blood pouring profusely from his nose and mouth. Barely conscious now, the fight drains from his body, and his eyes roll back in his head. I release my grip on him and let the back of his skull thud against the mat.

The crowd roars like a hoard of bloodthirsty demons, feeding off the violence oozing from the center of the ring.

I leave him where he lies and exit the cage. Spectators scramble to move out of my way as I slice through the crowd toward Viking.

"You still got it, bro," Viking slaps the side of my arm.

"We need to get the fuck out of here," I say.

The shit I said to Legion before we left, I know it pissed him off. I can't shake the feeling now that my words may have unchained his vengeful tendencies. I don't think he'd hurt Vanna to hurt me, but he's up to something.

"Get cleaned up," Viking begins to say, when some drunk spectator stumbles out of the crowd and knocks into him. Without missing a beat, Viking shoves the guy away without a care, damn near launching him ten feet with ease. "I'll go collect our winnings and meet you by the bikes." He reaches into his pocket and hands me the key to the locker.

The walls in the locker room faintly echo with the distant roar of the crowd cheering on another set of fighters. I wrench on the sink and wet a towel to wipe the blood splatter from my chest. A few of my knuckles are split, but the slight pain takes a backseat to my worry as I scrub my hands clean, wishing I could wash away the stupid decision to come here, to leave her and Ace, to think for one fucking second that demonic prick didn't race back to her the moment I let him out of my goddamned sight.

"Hell of a fight," some guy mutters, poking his head into the room as I twist the key in the padlock and yank it free of the locker. I don't bother acknowledging his presence. I toss the lock inside and

Jennifer Saviano

grab my shit, quickly dressing while every fucking second wasted feels like another moment he could be manipulating her, working some fucking angle in an attempt to make her his.

It won't happen. Even if he tells her about the Morning Star. Even if he shows her that fucking tattoo.

He's too late… I'm her Knight. Her husband. Her choice.

I bring up her number on my cell and try to call again the moment my boots hit the pavement outside.

It rings a few times before going to voicemail, and I immediately check her location.

She's still at the bar. She probably can't hear over the music.

It's only a matter of time until she checks her phone, so I shoot her a text before mounting my bike.

I'm coming home. I'm sorry. I love you.

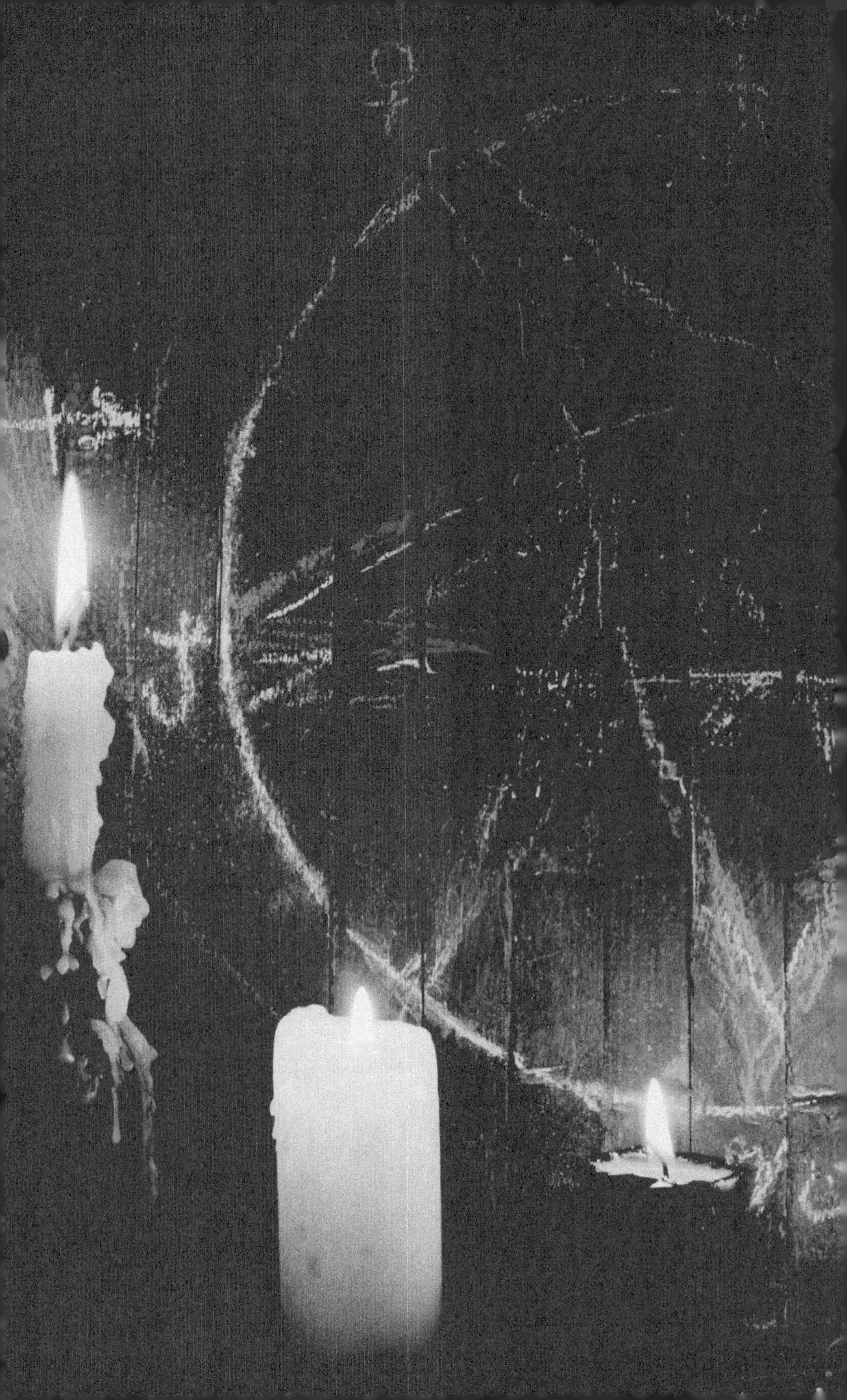

Chapter 44

LEGION

"I'll make us some coffee," Vanna says, flicking on the lights as we step inside her home. She moves quickly into the kitchen, heels clunking on the hardwood floor. I shut the door behind me, watching her busy herself with the task. "Afterward, you can bring me back to my car. I should be sober enough to drive by then."

That will monopolize too much of the time we have…

"Nonsense. I told you I'd arrange to have it brought here." I pull out my cellphone and delete the ten missed calls and several threatening texts from Keegan, before searching up a 24-hour tow service. "Just relax."

"I can't relax after what happened." She sighs, frustratedly pulling open a cabinet to retrieve two mugs.

"Then perhaps coffee isn't what you need right now."

She turns to face me as I lift the cell to my ear. "Legion, you don't have to—"

I silence her with a flippant gesture and proceed to make the arrangements. They invoice me the bill with assurances that her vehicle will be in transit within the next two hours.

I shove the cell in my pocket. "There, now. How hard was that?"

"How much is this going to be?"

"Five hundred." I don't tell her I've already paid it…*just in case.*

"That's ridiculously expensive for something we could have taken care of ourselves." She makes her way over to her purse sitting on the edge of the marble island and rummages inside it. "I don't even think I have half that much on me."

"I never asked to be reimbursed."

She tilts her head to the side, saying nothing, but looks at me wryly.

"I'll settle for a *thank you* and a drink." I smile.

"Coffee?" She forces a smile back and abandons her purse for the coffee pot again. "I think we've both had enough alcohol, and you still have to ride tonight."

"If you insist." *I'll take what I can get.* I slide onto one of the island barstools while she rinses out the pot.

A familiar feline hops up onto the island and saunters up to me.

"Hello, old friend." I stroke the sleek, black fur of his back while he greets me with a robust purr.

Vanna smiles as if her furry companion's acceptance of me puts her a little more at ease. "Nico remembers you."

"Indeed…"

She scoops him up and relocates him to a chair in the living room. "Sorry about that. Cat hair doesn't pair well with coffee." She chuckles and returns to the kitchen. "I'd feel better about this whole thing if you let me pay you back."

"It's nothing, sweet one. Let it go."

"You must still have quite a bit of that reward money left," she says, tapping some grinds into the filter.

"In addition to everything I've liquidated, yes. *I'm quite loaded.*"

She peeks over her shoulder at me curiously before cracking the tops off of two bottled waters and pouring them into the coffee-maker. After slapping the lid shut, she presses the brew button and turns to face me. "I should call Dean."

I keep my expression neutral while she pats down her pockets in search of her cellphone, to no avail of course, then moves to her purse once again. "Damn it! Don't tell me I dropped it on the sidewalk or something! I had it when I was talking to Latisha outside."

"It's not in your purse?" I feign concern. "I could have sworn I saw you tuck it inside after your call."

"Maybe I accidentally left it on the seat or something. I knew we shouldn't have gotten rid of the landline. We never used it, but it would come in handy now."

"Well, your vehicle will be here shortly, and you're welcome to use mine," I bluff with a grin. "I'm sure if he calls, he'll simply assume you didn't hear it over the ruckus in the bar."

She hesitates, considering my offer and weighing the consequences, then glances at the digital clock on the stove. It's only a quarter past eleven. There are still several hours before the bar closes. "If they don't get it here soon, I'll have to take you up on it."

Once the coffee is made, she joins me on the front porch while I smoke and wait for my next opportunity. When my cellphone chimes, she glances over at me.

"Is it Dean?" she asks.

I retrieve the phone from my pocket and glance at the notification with a smile. "Not exactly, though I am pleased to inform you he won the fight."

She lets out a heavy sigh of relief and finally relaxes into the Adirondack beside me. "I'm glad that's over."

"I told you there was nothing to worry about." I lean forward to flick my ash through the spindles of the porch railing.

"How much did you make?" She smiles at me with playful ease, now unburdened by the worry over Keegan's wellbeing.

"Well, your husband was the favored bet, so I had to put down a substantial amount in order to turn a decent profit." I pull another drag while she continues to study me curiously. "One hundred and fifty thousand was just deposited into my account."

Her eyes widen in shock. "*You just won one hundred and fifty grand?*"

"Well, no. I won fifty grand. One hundred thousand was the stake. I get that back."

I don't bring up the amusing fact that he won me that money thinking he was chasing justice. He won me that money while I'm here with his wife, about to show him the true meaning of *degradation... The formal term used in chivalric orders when a knight is stripped of his rank or title...*

"It's nice being able to talk to you without all of the cryptic head games." She scrunches her nose at me playfully.

"Ah? *Like friends do?*"

"Yes."

"Is that what we are to each other? *Friends,* Vanna?"

"I don't know... I suppose?"

"Between men and women, there is no friendship possible. There is passion, enmity, worship, love, but no friendship. Do you know who said that?"

"*Sounds like a man*... But I think friendship can be pure and simple."

I chuckle. "You're right. It was Oscar Wilde. Alas, you wish for me to speak plainly to you? Like friends?"

"Yes."

"Then let me plainly state...*loving you* is the only pure thing I've ever done in my entire life... You're both a blessing and a curse. An addiction I'll never purge from my system."

She winces and averts her gaze, seemingly afraid to even look at me now. "You can't say things like that." Her words are nearly a whisper, despite the ever-present tension radiating between us.

"Why not? Does it make you feel things for me you think you shouldn't?" I ask. She only fidgets with the flannel tied around her waist. "Do you not find it curious?" I press.

"What?"

"This...*comfortability* between us, this odd, familiar feeling we've shared since our first meeting... You've never truly feared me. *Why not,* Vanna?"

"I don't know..."

"I think you might."

The silence between us screams she does, though I know, she'll never admit it out loud. And where I do respect and admire her steadfast loyalty to him...knowing there is something there for me within her beautiful heart...that it will remain locked away and denied forever...churns an aching, longing pain within my chest.

"*I envy him.*" The words topple from my lips of their own volition. "I envy him to the marrow of my bones. I envy even the simplest of moments he has with you. That he can hold you in his arms and tell you exactly what you mean to him... *And it had better be the whole damn world,* Vanna."

"Damien... I don't think we should be talking like this."

"Intention empowers words. Without intention, they're nothing. I could spew played-out lines like *I'd burn the world for you!* Is that what you want to hear? Well, I have! I ended my brother's life for you. The only person who may have ever truly loved me... Vanna, I *have* burned the world for you... *My whole world...* And I did so without letting the lick of a single flame ever get near you… I've written you love letters in the blood of your enemies."

"Legion…"

My defeated sigh seems to concern her. As if fighting her better judgment, she reaches over to touch my hand. I relinquish my death grip upon the arm of the Adirondack, bending my wrist to lift my fingers and allow hers to gently slip between them. There is love in her touch. An undeniable apricity that has managed to seep into my frigid soul.

"Damien." She sighs my name in that godforsaken way that makes me want to cut out my heart and throw it into the deepest pits of flaming Hell.

I stare at our entwined fingers. "It's agony…being forced to love you from a distance… That a *friend* is all I'll ever be to you. I'm lost… *I'm fucking drowning*, Vanna. I ache in places I never knew existed, within depths of a soul I didn't know I had."

"You don't love me… You can't," she says the words almost fearfully, *pleadingly*.

"Because you believe I'm some loathsome monster? *Incapable*—"

"*No*. Because you don't actually know me. You're *infatuated* with some idea of me you've dreamed up over the last few years you were away. You don't know me. Whatever you think you feel, it isn't love. Maybe it's remorse, maybe it's *obligation* because of everything you regret. I don't know. But it isn't *love*… It can't be."

"When I'm with you… something inside of me…*hurts less*… Do you care about me, Vanna?"

"Yes."

My heart flutters with exhilaration, yet it is short-lived, for I know what is soon to follow her admission…

She slips her hand from mine and sits back in her chair. "But…my heart—"

"*Belongs to him*… I am painfully aware." I pull a long drag from my cigarette and let the smoky breath out slowly. *It's now or never*… "You know, it wasn't O'Keefe who led me to North Carolina." She peers at me over the rim of her coffee mug, brows furrowing inquisitively. "It wasn't until I was standing in your *former foyer* that the revelation struck me."

She sets the mug upon her knee, confusion further knitting her brows. I gesture to the old Victorian farmhouse down the street, barely visible in the darkness. "You summoned me."

Curiosity drains from her expression along with her blood as she seems to pale before my very eyes. *"What?"*

"I'm the knight. *Your* knight."

She tenses and quickly places the mug on the little table between us. "Legion…"

"Do you think I'd risk this revelation…*this confession*, if I lacked substantial proof?"

She nervously rubs her palms against the denim over her thighs, then stands. "Please, don't do this."

I rise with her. "It's always been me… Your spell worked exactly as you intended it… We worked our magick on the same night. *We called to each other on a significant May's Eve…* Your spell drew me to the Carolinas as much as Keegan had, if not more. You were the pull I felt all along. I couldn't harm you because I am your knight. I killed Jack by luring him to Keegan."

Unnerved, her hand moves to the base of her throat, and she takes a step back from me. I pull a final drag from my cigarette to settle my own nerves and toss the butt over the railing. *I'll need both hands if she tries to bolt from me…*

"Think about it," I gently push. "Hurting you would have destroyed Keegan… *But I couldn't do it.* From the moment I laid eyes on you, the very thought of causing you harm felt like an affront to my own soul. I'd sooner cut my own throat! Your spell rendered me incapable of hurting you. Incapable of allowing anything, *or anyone,* to harm you."

She's staring at me like a deer in headlights, like a frightened statue carved from white marble, except for her fingers digging at the base of her throat.

"I hated you for it… I hated you for making me love you so much! For ruining all of my plans to end Keegan! I tried to stop… I tried to cast it out of me… I beat myself bloody over it… *You saw the evidence…* But I fucking love you, Vanna… You are mine to protect."

My words seem to jolt life back into her, and she brushes past me. I follow her into the house while she goes on insisting, "This isn't love… Legion… You saw what you wanted to see…"

"No!" I grab her arm and spin her to face me.

"Legion, there were signs. It was Dean… It's always been Dean… *Don't do this…*"

"A black armored knight, upon a black steed, waving a red banner. I've had the tattoo depicting the same image on my body long before either of you was ever a thought. And the morning star…I fucking owned it!"

She shakes her head defiantly. "No."

"I'll show you." I release her and begin stripping off my jacket.

"No. Stop."

I toss the leather over the back of a barstool nearest us. "He doesn't even believe in witchcraft, in magick, not the way *we do.*"

She takes a few breaths, seemingly in an attempt to gather her composure, and walks further into the kitchen, positioning herself on the opposite side of the large marble island between us. "Let's pretend for a second, everything you're saying is true. You're the knight I summoned. If that's true, if you read my spell, then you read the part where love between us is an impossibility."

"Until you burned it."

She pales a little more, and I barely hear her whisper, "You've really been watching me…"

"I didn't love you at first. I just couldn't harm you. *But I loved you after.* I still do."

"Legion."

"You set our wills free… And my feelings for you haven't wavered. The more I watched you…the fonder I became. The way you cared so deeply for Ace from the moment you learned of his existence… You're everything a man could want. I love you. Accept it."

"I can't accept it. *I'm married.* I think you should leave."

I don't want to leave… "I've just given you my heart and—"

"Legion…" There's a tremble in her voice now… "Dean is coming back. You know he already suspects you're here. He's already on the road heading *directly here*… Do you realize what will happen if—"

"You think I fear your husband? *You think I fear anything?* After the shit I've survived… *I fear nothing.*"

Legion: Book 3

"*Alright.*" She raises her shaking hands. "Alright... I just... I need a little time to think on all of this... *Okay?*" Her nervous smile doesn't reach her pleading eyes.

I casually reclaim a barstool to ease her concern. "I understand. I was quite taken aback when I realized it myself... The raw magnetism between us from the start all makes perfect sense now...doesn't it?"

She only offers a tight-lipped smile.

"Why don't you make some more coffee while we wait for the tow truck?" I suggest. Perhaps giving her a chore with which to busy herself will alleviate some of her nervous energy... I have something else to aid in her ability to relax as well. "I still have to settle the bill."

"Oh, I'll just put it on my debit card... It's not a big deal."

"Now, now, I am a man of my word, and I said I'd pay it. It's the least I can do, considering how badly I've managed to rattle you."

"I'm fine," she lies through another strained and placating smile.

"No...*you're not*... I have a better idea. Why don't you go wash up? Put on something comfortable. You've had a rather eventful night, sweet one. Let me make the coffee."

"I'm comfortable," she claims, though she nearly flinches when I stand and step around the island to approach her. But she doesn't run.

"*I insist,*" I say, twirling a finger around the sleeve of the flannel shirt she has tied around her waist.

She peers timidly up at me. "There's um...more water in the fridge."

"Two sugars, was it?" I smile.

She nods.

I watch her walk down the hall before I set up a new pot and retrieve the mismatched mugs we left on the porch. Mine, a basic black glossy ceramic, and hers, purple with silver moons and stars, something that looks like she got it from a witchy pottery shop.

I take a quick gander down the hall to make sure she isn't near enough to witness the little gelatin capsule I crack open and sprinkle into her drink. I rinse the remnants down the drain before stirring in her two sugars. She rejoins me just as I place the mugs on the marble island near the barstools. She's wearing sweatpants that tie at the waist, and a faded Sturgis long-sleeved t-shirt.

I fight the urge to chuckle at her attempt to appear comfortable and casual, while covering up as much of her body as possible.

"Welcome back," I smile and gesture to the barstools.

She purses her lips, peering up at me guiltily. "I appreciate the effort, but I don't think I'll sleep at all tonight if I drink another coffee."

Oh, she'll sleep just fine... "It's decaf. I found it in the cabinet along with a bottle of Jameson. Would you like a shot?"

"Oh…No."

I grin as she joins me at the island, but she doesn't touch her mug. "Waste not want not." I lift mine, encouraging her to drink with me, but she still refuses. *Plan B…* "Let's toast to your charming Ace… It's *bad luck,* you know, *refusing a toast.*"

She picks up her coffee to humor me, superstitions working in my favor. I knew they would. "*Fine…* To Ace."

I clink my mug to hers. "May he grow up loving the ocean as much as you do…"

Her eyes dart up to meet mine, a flicker of recollection in them.

"May he look for shooting stars, but never have a reason to wish for happiness or safety…"

She sips hers slowly before stating, "I knew you were there that night…before I found the black rose at the beach… I had a feeling."

"You were right… We both wished upon that star that night… It may have been the very moment I fell in love with you."

She takes a hardy gulp then places the mug on the marble. I glance at the digital clock on the stove. The drug should take effect within fifteen minutes… Maybe faster since she's already had a few drinks tonight and nothing to eat.

"So…you broke into my rental home…."

"Yes. The night you went with Keegan down to Bike Week in Myrtle Beach."

"Wow…"

"I guess you could say, in a way…tonight is a strange anniversary for us."

She audibly swallows another gulp. "And you read Jack's letters?"

"Enough of them to know I had to insert myself into the situation."

"*That worked out really well for me.*" I barely hear the wry comment made under her breath.

"There was no way I could have anticipated your mad race to the cabin that night." Just thinking about it elevates my blood pressure.

"I don't want to talk about that night," she mutters, no longer meeting my gaze, but she lifts the mug to her lips once again.

A few quiet, contemplative moments pass between us. She's consumed more than half of her coffee and should be feeling the effects any moment now.

"Why?" she asks, leaning a little heavier on the back of her barstool.

"Why *what*, angel?"

"Why did you or-*orchestrate* this tonight?"

"*Love*, sweet one... Love, like power, corrupts absolutely. It may start out *wholesome* and *pure*...but the truth is... Love is deadlier than hate. There is no line between *good and evil* within the realms of *love*. People kill for love far more easily than they do for hate. Even your *white knight*. I may or may not have been able to drag his soul to Hell... But *you*, sweet one... You wield the power to *merely ask it of him*, and he would walk through the black gates of eternal damnation just to please you... We certainly have that in common."

"Then maybe it would be wise of you not to risk your life by an-*antagonizing* him over me." She lifts a hand to press the back of her fingers to her forehead.

"Are you alright?"

"I'm tired..."

"You've had an eventful night, sweet one."

She chuckles softly. "Yeah, don't tell anybody..."

"Your secrets are safe with me." I grin, moving from my seat to stand closer to her as she leans a little more. My body prevents her from toppling off the side of her barstool.

"Hitting Lucinda did feel good..." she giggles drowsily, nearly slumping against me. I tuck my chin in order to breathe in the barely-there, tropical fragrance of her hair.

"*Turned me the fuck on*." I growl the words against her ear, and she shudders against me...

Lying little minx... Her conscience disapproves, but her body welcomes my proximity.

I wrap an arm around her waist and pull her off the stool and against me fully. She grips my arms to steady herself.

"I think it's best you lie down for a while, sweet one. I'll come fetch you when your cage arrives."

"*Mmmhmm*." She sleepily complies, and I reposition her to my side, holding her upright as we proceed toward the hallway.

She's barely able to lift an arm when she points to the living room as we pass. "The couch is fine…"

"*Your bedroom is better.*"

By the time we reach the bedroom, she's leaning heavily against me, her face pressed sleepily into the base of my neck.

"*Damien…*" she says my name questioningly, but it's on a sultry, breathy whisper.

"You've got a cruel way of breathing my name," I growl, maneuvering her closer to the bed and allowing her body to slip away from me, limply falling upon the cobalt comforter.

I hastily strip off my shirt, catching sight of an apothecary-style bottle upon the dresser.

His cologne…

Inside, the Demon chuckles with a nasty sneer that I can feel slicing across my own features. I toss my shirt on the floor and snatch the bottle to spritz the air before me. Stepping closer to her through the mist of his signature scent, I feel the particles of moisture and deceit dance upon my heated skin.

There are consequences to playing with a Demon's fire, little witch! You don't get to toy with my emotions, my desire for you *like a common whore,* and then simply strut away, unbothered by my need for you! Not without repercussion! Not after *clawing open* this crack in my once impenetrable armor with *your wicked witchcraft!* You have seeped into my Vantablack soul… Turned me into this *pathetic, yearning simp for you!* It is only fair that I should make my way deep inside of you, as well… *Make you ache with consequence...*

Rage and lust lace the heated blood pumping through my veins as I stare down upon her unsuspecting form.

"Dean?" she groggily whispers. Another drowsy sigh escapes her luscious lips as the drug pulls her deeper into a dark oblivion.

'Do you really think it will be me?' She demanded of me once, the night I stole a kiss in the wine cellar. *'You will never have me present or willingly!'*

Oh, sweet one, I learned early on that sometimes we must settle for what we can get… I have also grown quite accustomed to simply *taking* that which I desire in this life.

I place the bottle on the dresser and move closer to the object of my burning obsession.

Legion: Book 3

She's barely conscious. I pluck at the ties of her sweatpants, undoing the knot before gripping the waistband on either side of her hips. She doesn't even stir as I roughly tug them down her legs. Her top, slightly pushed up past her naval, grants me a full, glorious view of her nearly naked lower body. My hungry gaze settles on the black lace, scantly shielding her pussy. The sweatpants slip from my grasp where I stand.

She's breathtaking.

A slumbering angel. Vulnerable and blissfully unaware of the lust-crazed Demon standing before her.

This may be the only chance I get... I have no intention of physically hurting her... She won't even remember this encounter. Only I will possess the memories of our night together.

Something to think back on...hold onto.

Screw it... Let's do it...

I kneel forward onto the bed, moving over her sleeping form. As if her subconscious senses a presence, her face twists forward. Her lips part and whisper *his name* once again...

I lower myself upon her, allowing the scent of his cologne to envelope her, lulling her into that feeling of safety and security she derives from his presence.

"Dean..."

That fucking name... *Sure, Angel... There isn't anything I wouldn't be for you... I'll be your Dean...*

I press my lips to hers, cautiously at first, watching her expression. Her eyes remain closed, dark lashes resting against porcelain skin, as she breathes in his scent. Her lips press forward, softly molding to mine in a returning kiss, and I am *instantly, painfully* throbbing for her.

Pushing my tongue inside the warm, sweet cavern of her mouth, I deepen this stolen kiss. She tastes of cream and sugar and pure, forbidden bliss.

A slight moan vibrates up her throat...and it is maddening.

On some level, she wants this. *She wants me.* The way she's looked at me since the first night we met. The way she allowed me to dance with her tonight. Our bodies moving closely together...touching, rubbing, bumping, and nearly grinding together... She's been putting out all the signals. *This can't be wrong if it feels so fucking right!*

I kiss her fully, sliding my tongue against hers, sucking, biting, licking her lips. My hands slide greedily up her body, shoving her top up over her breasts. Full, heavy, yet *so soft*. I grab them over her bra, and my cock pulses harder. I can't help but thrust my hips and grind myself against the warm apex of her thighs. Her decadent heat penetrates the denim prison of my rigid cock, and I grow feverishly more desperate for her.

Fuck! This is too much...

Breaking away from her lips, I trail kisses down her body until I'm on my knees, wedged between her sumptuous, thick thighs. I press my face against her soft stomach, kissing her flesh as my fingers slip inside the elastic waistband of her panties. My lips skim across her cesarean scar, and I kiss her lower still.

She doesn't even see you as a man... Keegan's words play over again in my mind, and I can't help the wicked sneer as I drag my tongue over her warm skin. *What will she think when I'm the one to give her everything she wants? How will you feel when the next kid she delivers looks up at you with pale eyes instead of dark?*

At least some part of me will know her love...

'Get on with it! She won't even remember tonight! Take what you want and slink back to the shadows where you belong!' The darkness within demands, its claws still in a stranglehold around my conscience. *Tear her down from her pedestal and fuck her in the ruins... She won't remember...*

She won't remember...

But I will...

Will I be able to keep this secret in the aftermath of this sinful act? Will I ever again be capable of meeting her soul-penetrating gaze?

A deep shame scorches me from the inside out.

No... No, I will not.

I remove my hands from her, though I take a final moment longer to cherish the feel of her warm thighs pressed against the sides of my body.

With a strangled groan, I force myself away from her.

Grabbing the edge of the comforter, I fling the blanket over her body as all-consuming, all-too-familiar feelings wash over me.

Self-loathing... Unworthiness...

Snatching my shirt off the floor, I quickly exit the room, slipping it back on as I storm down the hall to stage the kitchen in a desperate attempt to disguise what I can of my transgressions...or at the very least, stall my impending execution.

Legion: Book 3

She's going to hate me... She should hate me... What the fuck have I done?

Chapter 45

LEGION

If I possessed any semblance of decency, I would have kept riding. I would have cut myself from her life and put a bullet in the part of myself that still sees her face every time I close my eyes. But I don't. I'm not a decent man, and I've never been one. I'm hatred steeped in smoke, wrapped in leather and bad intentions. Regret seems to have become a common theme in my life, especially as of late. Against my better judgment, I find myself outside the apartment of a woman I should have left in my past a long time ago. Another regret.

The door swings open, and at first sight, she seems annoyed by my presence, yanking her black robes tightly around her body. Her brows pinch above false lashes and smoky, scowling eyes. She must have just come from the strip club. The silent seconds pass between us, but it isn't long before the anger radiating from her dissipates as she takes in my sorrowful state.

"Damien?" she sounds genuinely concerned, or at the very least, curious.

"*Puppet.*"

"What are you doing here?"

She hasn't moved from her doorframe. A subtle que she does not want to invite me in. We both know how this scene always plays out. I use her body like some sick combination of a confession booth and a whipping post, and we both pretend it fixes something…in us…between us… Fuck if I know anymore. What I do know is that I shouldn't be here, that the games between us have run their course. We're no good for each other. We never were.

Coming here was a mistake.

I turn to leave, but she grabs my hand. An alien wave of emotion tears through me at her touch, but is quickly consumed by the flames of rage and resentment roaring inside of me. Keegan's words continue to echo within my mind. An unrelenting torment of painful truth.

'You're pursuing an unavailable woman because you're broken, because you're a piece of shit… A shallow, unworthy, villainous piece of shit...'

I am the villain.

I am fucking pathetic, more so for seeking out another I find even more pathetic… A selfish attempt to ease my own pain.

Keegan is right, *and I hate us all for it!*

I sneer at the hand clutching mine, a war of choice raging within.

I don't owe this whore anything. I could simply walk away, spare her what remains of her sanity, and go drown my shame in more whiskey. I should slink off with my demons in tow and spark up a joint somewhere… somewhere I won't hurt anyone else tonight.

"Damien," she presses. "Look at me… What's wrong?"

"I just realized I'm out of cigarettes."

"I have some," she says, giving my hand a gentle tug.

"You don't smoke."

"Something happened to you tonight… I can see it all over your face. Just come inside."

The selfish desire to ease the ache in my chest allows her to pull me across the threshold.

"Would you like something to drink?" she offers. I don't respond, and she only hesitates for a moment before fixing a drink from the crystal decanter set on her dresser. She hands it to me and watches as I attempt to wash away the taste of shame still thick on my tongue with the whiskey.

I gesture to her closet with the empty tumbler in my hand. The wigs displayed on Styrofoam heads look like a collection of decapitated hookers. "Variety is the spice of life, huh?"

"You should try it sometime." She smirks. "Get off this *brunette* kick."

I scoff and hand the glassware back to her.

"There's something different about you…" She places the tumbler on the night table behind her. "She finally hurt you, didn't she?" The protective tone in her words surprises me.

"Of course not."

"*You're lying*," Puppet firmly insists. "She did, didn't she? What did she say to you?"

I scoff. "You're being ridiculous."

She shakes her head slowly. "No…you're Damien again… You're hurt, and I'm the only one who sees it. What did that bitch do?"

I pull in a breath to quell my rising temper. "You mentioned cigarettes."

Puppet turns and opens the drawer to remove a pack of my brand, then slowly approaches me. She opens the half-empty box and holds it out to me.

"You don't smoke," I say again, plucking one out. I light up and pull a much-needed drag. Maybe she keeps these on hand to offer her clients. *A fuck and a smoke* before she's on to the next trick. Or maybe… *"I didn't know Reaper took up smoking."*

The sly little smile ghosting across her lips confirms everything.

"I knew it."

She chuckles. "You *think* you know… Did you really tell him *at least you got the girl?*"

I shrug. "*Not verbatim*, though I was simply pointing out the silver lining after besting him."

"You're a dick. But I knew you'd be back." She smiles, then lets out a dreamy sigh as her eyes drop to linger on the brass zippo in my hand. "*The smell reminds me of you…*" Her words come slowly and longingly. "Sometimes, I just light one and let it burn, the way you used to burn incense. Sometimes I'll pull a drag, just to remember what you taste like."

I don't know whether to vomit or shed a tear—if I were even still capable. While staring at her blankly, memories of our twisted past play like a reel in my mind.

There was a brief moment in time when I entertained the idea of loving her… Where I thought perhaps it might be possible that she could love me, too, despite our pasts, despite what we've become. I was wrong about both of us. Love has never been in the cards for me…not with anyone.

"I shouldn't have come here," I say, resigned to our fate.

"Damien..." she whispers, reaching for me, but I take a step back, avoiding her touch. "Listen to me, Reaper is just—"

"You're not what I want." My words slap the lovesick expression off her face. "You never were, and you never will be... And I'm not, nor will I ever be, what *you* need... We're both losers, Puppet. I told you once to hate me. I mean it more now than I ever meant it before... You will always pale in comparison to her... I will never see you as anything worthy of my trust or respect. I apologize for intruding upon your evening, but now, do yourself a favor, Puppet. Hate me, as I have come to loathe the sight of you. Let this be the end of us. You will never hear from me again. I promise you that."

She's speechless this time. There's no flash of anger behind her dulling stare, no dramatics, no tears laced with pain and resentment streaming down her cheeks. Puppet simply stares at me as though my words have finally sunk in.

Vanna

The sun is too bright, burning my eyes like a punishment, even behind the aviator shades I took off of Dean this morning.

I'm sitting on a park bench beside Rosita, watching our kids play on the pirate ship playground they love so much.

"Coffee or horchata?" Rosita offers.

I've never been a big coffee drinker, but now...after last night...*the thought of coffee makes me sick.*

"Horchata, please." I force another smile and adjust the sunglasses on the bridge of my nose.

"I know how much you like it, but perhaps coffee will help your hangover better than horchata?" Rosita suggests.

I smile at her weakly. She seems to sense something is off and pours me a cup without further debate. "Did you mix liquors?"

I chuckle, soft and strained, and take a sip from the solo cup.

But inside, I'm breaking.

This isn't a hangover.

When I woke up this morning, everything felt wrong. I can't explain it. Just a weight in my limbs and a thick fog clinging to the edges of my mind like smoke that won't clear. I remember the fight with Lucinda. I remember speeding away on Legion's bike. I remember drinking coffee with him and the unsettling things he said...

I *don't* remember my car arriving. I don't remember texting Dean that I was home and all was well, or plugging my phone into the charger on my night table. I don't remember opening a bottle of Jameson and having more shots with Legion...and I don't remember getting into my bed...

I remember coffee and his confessions...

Dean came home last night to find me passed out in the bedroom after apparently drinking nearly all of his Jameson and leaving the evidence of such on the island.

I looked my husband in the eyes and acted like I remembered everything. Like I hadn't been violated in a way I can't even put into words yet. I don't know what happened... I don't know what to say that won't end in violence... Because what I do know is that Dean will kill him *if*...

I told him about the fight with Lucinda, about Legion showing up and getting me out of the bar before things with her could escalate. I didn't bring up the knight spell, even though he pressed me to know why Legion would make such an effort with O'Keefe. I told him about the money, what Legion won, perhaps that was it...but...I know he still suspects there's more...*I do too*...

Legion's been ignoring Dean's texts and calls since yesterday, and he hasn't responded to any of mine either. That only makes the strange heaviness settling in my bones *worse*. Panic rises in my chest whenever I try to remember what happened, *but can't*.

There are flashes. Sensations. Breath on my neck. Firm hands on my waist...

Shame and anxiety continue to ebb and flow like the tides of the ocean within my soul.

I let it happen... I went with him... I let him in... I trusted him... Despite my husband's warnings, *I trusted him*...

Rosita leans forward to get a better look at my face. "Vanna, are you alright?"

I nod. "Yes, I'll be fine."

And I will be. I don't have a choice. If I let myself fall apart over this now, in the middle of this sunny park, in front of our children, I might never pull myself back together.

I keep my focus on Ace and Mia.
I sip from my solo cup.
And I keep the scream buried behind my smile.

DEAN

It's way too fucking quiet, the kind of quiet before a storm, and I've felt this impending one brewing all morning.

The metallic click of the ratchet and the occasional hiss of a tentative sigh through my gritted teeth seem louder.

Vanna said nothing happened, other than busting Lucinda's lip and maybe blackening her eye. She said Legion showed up at the bar and got her home. They had a few more drinks to unwind from the fight. I'm not thrilled about any of it, but I trust my wife. Trusting her comes with knowing her.

And I know something isn't right.

I checked the time she texted me that she was home with the time logs on the tracking app on her phone. It all adds up. But I can't shake the feeling there's a major omission in the timeline of last night's events.

I tighten the bolt on the exhaust and wipe the grease off my fingers with a rag, more so to steady myself than anything else. The scent of oil and rubber usually grounds me, but not today.

She flinched when I touched her…tried to cover it with a smile too late. That simple split-second told me more than any of her words did. She was afraid, not just hungover from a rough night and an encounter with my ex.

The question tearing me apart…is she afraid of how I'm going to react to something she hasn't told me?

Did he do something to her?

I set the ratchet down, the heavy clink of it against the metal tray rings louder than it should. I run a hand through my hair, already feeling the cold pit forming in my solar plexus.

What did he do? And why aren't you telling me, baby?

"Hey, Dean?" Axel's voice calls from the lot just before he ducks under the open garage door.

The confused expression on Axel's face isn't what makes my stomach drop. It's what he's holding.

Black leather, worn at the seams, slung over his arm. The still crisp, white embroidered skull and angel wings patch stitched on the back of the cut.

Legion's cut.

Axel drops it onto the workbench beside me, and it lands with a dull slap. "Cherry just found it on the pool table, folded up like it was left there, waiting to be noticed."

"He quit?" I say quietly, mostly to myself.

Axel shrugs. "After everything he did to get in with us, why would he just up and leave?"

Did he leave? *Or did he fucking run?*

People don't run unless they've got a reason. He didn't just quit the MC...he abandoned the scene of a crime...

I snatch up the cut the motherfucker shed like snakeskin.

Whatever Vanna isn't telling me is something bad enough to make the demon run.

"Get Cherry. Have her drive the Mustang to my house. I need her to watch Ace for a bit."

Axel nods, concern in his searching eyes. "What happened, Dean?"

"I need you to contact the Jokers and let them know if they see Legion, strap him to that fucking chair in the basement until I can get there."

"What did he do?" Axel asks, practically leaping out of my way when I move past him to grab Serene's keys off my workbench.

"I'm going to find out."

T he sound of Ace's laughter rings out through the open windows in the front of our home as I walk up the porch steps, clutching Legion's cut in my fist like a piece of evidence drenched in betrayal. Cherry and Axel are right behind me. The crash of plastic toys hits me like a punch to the chest. This is the home I built with my family to protect them, and he slithered his way in and... I try not to let my thoughts spiral into worst-case scenarios.

Vanna opens the front door before I reach it. Her welcoming smile falters when she spots the cut in my hand.

Ace barrels over to me the moment I step inside, plastic truck still in hand. "Daddy!" he shouts, crashing into my leg the way he always does.

I drop to one knee and wrap him in my arms, kissing the top of his head. I try to keep my voice from cracking when I tell him, "Hey, buddy… Aunt Cherry and Uncle Axel are gonna take you to get some ice cream. Cool?"

He beams up at me, thankfully oblivious to the turmoil in my soul. I pick him up and hand him off to Axel.

Vanna steps closer, rubbing her hand against Ace's back. "What's going on?" she asks, making a valiant effort to keep smiling for Ace's sake, but I can hear the worry in her words.

I gently take her arm and pull her back from him, keeping my voice low when I tell her, "I don't want him to see either of us like this." Her eyes drop once more to the cut in my hands. "I don't know where this conversation's gonna go, and he doesn't need to see his mama cry, or his daddy lose it."

When she peers up at me, eyes already misted with tears, I can feel my heart breaking… *What did he do?*

"Mommy?" Ace frowns.

"We'll be right here when you get back, buddy." I force a smile in hopes of reassuring him. "You go have fun with Aunt Cherry and Uncle Axel." I nod at them, and they take Ace out to Cherry's car, distracting him with talk of sprinkles and whipped cream and maybe a trip to see his Uncle Viking.

I shut the door behind them and join Vanna where she's standing beside the kitchen island barstools, staring at the marble. I place Legion's cut down on it.

"He quit. Left it on one of the pool tables."

Her watery gaze shifts to stare at the leather, but she doesn't say anything.

"Why'd he run?" I press.

"I don't know…" she barely whispers.

"Vanna…this is one of those moments where I need you to tell me everything."

When she shakes her head, a tear rolls down her cheek, and she brushes it away.

"What did he do?"

"I…I don't know," she whimpers.

I try to keep my temper to an idle. "That was a sealed bottle of Jameson. Are you telling me you got so blackout drunk you don't remember what happened with him?"

"I didn't drink the Jameson... I was still a little tipsy from the bar. That's why I didn't drive home. I made us coffee while we waited for my car to get here."

"Wait... What?"

She lets out a quivering breath. "We left my car at the bar. I must have forgotten my phone inside it. We were in a rush to leave before Lucinda could call the cops. We left on Legion's motorcycle..."

That cunning motherfucker knew I'd be watching her location.

"I...I don't even remember when my car got here..." Vanna goes on, "Or texting you that I was home... Or plugging in my phone and getting in bed myself."

Jesus fuck... "Did he...?"

She shakes her head wildly. "No. No, I don't think so."

"But you aren't sure?"

She hesitates. "I think I'd know... I don't think he did."

"He just drugged you and tucked you in bed? Staged the fucking kitchen like you were both wasted? What else are you not telling me?"

"I swear that's all I remember."

"Vanna, if he took advantage of you... if he fucking raped you...it wasn't your fault."

"He didn't... I just know he didn't..."

"If you're fucking protecting him—"

"I'm not. Dean, I swear I'm not. I don't remember what happened after we talked, but... I think I'd know... *I know I'd know.*"

Did he stage this as well? Hope we'd fight about it? That I'd see her as damaged goods, tainted by him? Did he hope this would be what breaks us? Is he that fucking evil and vindictive? Or did he simply lose his nerve? Does he possess enough of an inkling of a conscience that he stopped himself?

"I'm sorry, Dean," she cries. "You were right, I never should have trusted him... This is all my fault."

I turn back to her and cup her face with hands that have broken bones and pulled triggers but never trembled like this.

"It's not your fault. I let this happen...and I'm so fucking sorry, Vanna." I kiss her forehead and wrap my arms around her as she sobs against my chest.

"I don't understand why he would do this now?" Vanna whimpers. "I know he was still adjusting to the club's ways, but..."

"I said some shit to him that probably set him off... Put him in his fucking place and that's all it took for his true colors to bleed through."

Bleed all over her...

She shifts in my arms to peer up at me. "What did you say?"

"I don't remember everything, but I ripped into him. Enough for him to snap..." I let out a tense sigh, partially regretting my words, but only because they led to this, not because they weren't true. "I told him you don't see him as a man. He's just a broken little boy in your eyes, incapable of loving you in all the ways you deserve. In all the ways *I do*. Something to that effect. I just wanted him to back off. I didn't think he'd..."

"*He didn't.*"

"Is that because he lost his nerve? Came to his senses? Or just wanted to put a crack in our foundation before he tucked-tail and ran?"

"He tried to convince me that he was the Knight I summoned. He broke into the old farmhouse when we went to Myrtle Beach. When I had the spell hidden in the closet under the stairs. That's how he found out about Jack, too...from the letters."

"And did he?" I have to swallow the knot forming in my throat. "Convince you?"

Her watery eyes soften, and she places a hand against my chest. "No, Dean. You are. You will *always* be. My rejection of his belief could have been what pushed him over the edge."

"It's no excuse," I growl. "And there will be a reckoning when I get my hands on him."

"Just let him go." She lets out another quivering sigh, wiping the remnants of tears from her cheeks as she takes a step back. "It was only a matter of time before he left anyway."

The fact that she seems saddened by this twists my guts, and I hold onto her arms a little tighter. She still cares about him. Even after this monumental betrayal of her trust.

"Jesus fuck, Vanna... Tell me you don't love him."

"What?"

"He did this to you…to us…and yet you're still concerned about him… You're upset he took off."

"I thought he wanted redemption. I wanted it for him. I thought he was trying… He *was* trying."

"Trying to pull us apart. You can't deny that now, doll. No matter how you slice it, that was his end goal in this final act. Cause as much damage as possible and vanish because he finally realized he'd never win you. That's what he does. He never changed. He's just patient."

"It didn't work, did it?"

I hold her tighter. "No. Never."

"Then just let him go. Let him disappear. Let us move on with our lives without him. Nothing happened, but if what he did was enough to make him realize there's nothing for him here, so be it. He made his choice." She touches my cheek. "And we made ours and sealed them with our wedding vows."

"He'll never touch you again. I promise."

"I know… Just let him go, Dean. Promise me you'll just let him go…"

CHAPTER 46

Vanna

What began as a cool, late-spring morning with a slow breeze rustling the leaves of the old oak towering over us is already heating up by midmorning. Humming gnats buzz in our faces while Ace and I collect fallen twigs around the farmstand. I toss another armful of brittle limbs into the burn barrel near the picnic tables between the farmstand and the strawberry patch, hoping the smoke will drive the annoying insects away. It's Sunday, so I don't expect any locals to show up for at least another hour or so.

I watch the smoke twist upward into the blue sky for a few moments. I've already swept the cement floor three times, reorganized the baskets, and even straightened every jam and honey jar label with Ace's assistance until they were all lined up perfectly. Busy work. Repetitive. But it's been keeping my hands full, keeping me from thinking too much about what happened the night before last.

Ace is sitting at his art table beside the register, a box of worn crayons dumped out in front of him. His adorable little tongue sticks out the corner of his mouth while he draws, laser-focused and unaware of my pacing and reorganizing.

Whenever I stop for too long, I begin to feel the shame of what happened like a stone in my chest.

I grab the rake from the garden toolshed and begin dragging dead leaves from where they've accumulated behind the thick row of

Madeline's rose bushes along the side of the farmstand. I rake until my arms ache and sweat prickles down my back.

The rake slips between my fingers and hits the ground with a dull thud when I hear it…low and familiar. A motorcycle growling down the road, and it isn't the louder, more throaty sound of a Harley… *It's his bike…*

Ace and I won't make it back to the house before he reaches us…

Dean might come home for a lunch break soon, but soon isn't now…

My heart is racing so fast it might come up my throat.

The motorcycle rips around the bend in the road and pulls into the gravel driveway leading directly to the small lot in front of the farmstand.

Ace is by my side, excitedly waving to *Legend.*

He kills the engine of his bike and quickly dismounts, boots crunching on the gravel with every step he takes toward us.

Instinctively, I push my son behind me. The tormented expression in Legion's eyes when he removes his black-shielded helmet nearly steals the breath from my lungs.

He looks haunted…

The helmet slips from his fingers and hits the gravel with a thud a moment before his knees do.

LEGION

Vanna takes a half step back, one arm protectively moving in front of her son, and my chest feels as though it's caving in on itself.

She's afraid of me.

After everything I've done…this is the first time she's looked at me like I'm dangerous…like I'm a threat to *her*…and it destroys me.

I drop to my knees before her, and the gravel bites through the denim straight through to my bones. But this is penance, and penance should hurt.

"Ace, sweetheart, go back to your table and finish your drawings," she says, her eyes never leaving mine. When he lingers, she nudges him gently. "*Go on now.*" He finally obeys. Tiny sneakers pad back through the entrance, leaving us with the weight of everything I've shattered.

Maybe it's because I know this is it...but she's never looked more heartbreakingly beautiful or more unreachable.

The words that have been burning a hole in my throat since I left her rasp out of me on a desperate breath. *"I didn't touch you... But I wanted to,"* I confess, hating the sound of my own voice. "I stopped myself before I went too far."

"Too far?" Her quiet voice sounds as strangled as my own. *"Everything you've done has been too far!"*

"I never wanted to hurt you...but I did... I broke something between us." My voice cracks, raw with a guilt I've never experienced. "You were the only person who ever saw me... You trusted me. And I spit on it. I let jealousy and obsession twist and mangle what we did have... What we could have had..."

The silence between us buzzes like static. I can barely look her in the eyes, but desperation drives me to search them for any minuscule sliver of understanding...or forgiveness.

"You were just going to run..." she whispers, distraught.

"I only made it seem that way, so I could return to you and—"

"And what?" Her voice quivers with hurt and rage. "You actually think there's anything left between us to salvage? That you haven't ruined everything? Every moment I thought was real...was just a manipulation..."

The weight of her words crushes me...

"I did wish you well the day of your wedding. I wished for your happiness and safety. I want you to have everything you desire in this life. When I left, I was glad to know I wouldn't be around to see *him* give it to you."

I swallow the painful lump in my throat.

"What I've done is unforgivable... But before I cut myself from your life, know this... From the moment we met, you stole the remnants of my heart. Not a day has passed that I haven't felt the pangs of regret. Everything I've ever had has always been ripped away from me... It's my own doing this time. You deserve peace and happiness... You'll never have either with me in your life. I'm here to say goodbye, my love. I'm sorry, and goodbye."

She takes a step forward like she wants to strike me, and I wish she would. When the question falls from her lips, it sounds like a plea, a wound still bleeding. *"Why wasn't my friendship enough?"*

Her question hits me like a punch to the gut. There's still fire behind her eyes, holding all the rage, betrayal, and loss of what we had.

"Why wasn't it enough?" she asks again, quieter, as if resolved not to receive an answer.

For once, I don't have one. The truth is crueler than anything else I can give her. It *was* enough...her friendship, her trust, her light. And I destroyed it anyway.

"Damien?"

"Because I wasn't."

She slowly shakes her head, tears welling behind her eyes until they spill, twisting the knife I plunged in my own heart, deeper.

"The second you looked at me like I was worth something, I needed all of you... I needed to possess it, to burn it into my skin, to fill some hole in my soul I can't even name. But I'm beyond redemption. I'm lost... sinking...drowning in darkness... There's so much in what I thought was just a hollow cavern in my chest... It was all stagnant for so long until you... Now there's only grief..."

She touches my shoulder and I recoil, unworthy of her touch, her sympathy, her kindness. But also because I know the innocent gesture won't curb the pain. It will only make me crave it more.

"I'm sorry," she says. "I should have forgiven you sooner. I was selfish, too. A part of me thought you would leave... I see now that it would have been best if you did. I don't want to keep hurting you."

Hurt is fleeting. Obliteration is more like it, but I've done that to myself...to her. She's shown me nothing but kindness. This is all on me. Grief and pain are simply consequences of love...unspent, unrequited love. I think all I've ever really wanted was love without having to beg for it...but I'm not a good person. I deserve to choke on these emotions, to swallow down these burning words whenever I'm around her. I should have... Yet I lack the will and decency even now to stop myself from telling her a selfish truth. *"I will always love you* more than what will ever be acceptable."

She brings her hands to her face to hide her own grief as silent sobs rack her body.

I hear it first. The rumble of an engine rolls in like a storm. And he is. We both know it.

She drops her hands to her chest, breath catching, eyes wide with sudden terror at the realization of what's about to happen next.

Keegan's close. Just past the bend beyond the pecan orchard down the road.

I don't move. I don't look away from her. I earned this. Every brutal second of it.

"*Legion…*" she gasps.

"I won't break this promise," I say quietly.

She blinks, confused, then horrified. *"No! Go!"*

"I mean it." My voice is low, steady, already bracing for what I've got coming to me. "We both know I deserve it, and your knight deserves to avenge you. I won't fight back."

"Please, just go!" she begs, voice breaking. When I don't move, she rushes to the farmstand, shutting the doors on Ace before Keegan arrives to deliver the justice I've earned.

Tires crunch on the gravel behind me. The engine winds down to an idle. She rushes past me to her husband, already pleading for my wretched life.

I reach for my smokes and light up.

Might as well enjoy one more…

The engine dies.

Boots hit gravel.

I pull a long drag and let it out slow…

Vanna

The roar of Serene's engine sends my heart into my throat. I turn fast, rushing back to the farmstand. Ace is still at his art table, little fists wrapped around crayons, working on something bright and messy. The moment he looks up at me, the sound of his father's bike registers, and he smiles.

"Ace, you keep working on your pictures. Mommy will be right outside," I say, breathless. His little smile falls, and he stares at me with curious worry. "I'm so sorry, baby. Stay here. I love you." Before he can ask any questions, I shut the barn-style doors, praying I'll be able to prevent what is about to happen.

I whirl back around. Legion is still on his knees in the gravel like some shattered offering. He isn't going to fight back. He isn't going

Legion: Book 3

to run. He's just going to take it because this is what he thinks redemption looks like...*ruin*.

"*He won't fight back!*" I shout before I even reach my husband. When I do, there's no stopping him. I'd have an easier time jumping in front of a train. "Dean! He's not going to fight you!"

"*I'll make him,*" Dean growls, rolling up his sleeves as he fast approaches Legion. I nearly slip on the gravel in an attempt to hold onto Dean's arm when his fist swings down on Legion.

The sickening crack of Dean's brutal right hook snaps Legion's head sideways.

"*Get up,*" Dean demands.

Legion pulls one more drag from his cigarette and gets to his feet before dropping it on the ground.

"Come on, asshole! Fight me!" Dean stands rigid and waiting as Legion straightens, saying nothing. He only stares back with determined defiance.

Dean throws another punch, a left hook this time, rocking Legion to the side once again. He didn't lift a hand to block it, or the next hit, or the one after that.

"*Stop it!*" I continue to shout at them.

Legion straightens once again, dabbing the corner of his mouth with his thumb where blood has begun to pool. Dropping both arms to his side, he stands and waits to be punched again.

"I'm gonna keep hitting you," Dean practically snarls. "You might as well swing back."

"*I won't,*" Legion mutters, sorrowful grey eyes shifting to me once more. "Your husband may break my bones, but he will never break my word to you. I am content to stand here and take whatever he—"

Dean grabs Legion by the collar of his leather jacket and slugs him hard in the stomach, keeling him over before uppercutting him in the face. This time, Legion staggers backward, landing on his back on the ground hard enough to hear the gravel crunch beneath his shoulders.

Dean mounts him, and still, he doesn't fight back.

"*I told you,*" Dean cocks his fist back again, breathing like an angry bull. "*I told you I'd fucking kill you!*"

"He didn't touch me!" I scream, but rage has Dean in a chokehold. There's only one thing that could possibly reach him, that would tear through his fury like a blade. "*Our son can hear you! He's in the farmstand! He's hearing all of this!*"

That does it.

Dean's fist lowers. Chest heaving, jaw locked, he shoves away from Legion and takes a step back. Then another. Then spits on the ground near Legion's boots before threatening him. "Crawl back to the desert where you belong, or I'll finish what I started."

I rush past them, back to the farmstand to pull open the doors. When I do, Ace isn't at his art table, and my heart sinks. *Is he hiding? My poor baby…*

"Ace?"

Silence.

I race inside to check behind the counter. He isn't there. He isn't hiding behind the shelves or the display cases.

A sliver of light cuts across the floor when a breeze catches the back door and creaks open on its hinges…

My breath escapes on another ragged scream. *"Ace!"*

Dean charges into the stand while Legion pushes himself to his feet, clutching his stomach and wiping at his bloody mouth as he hurriedly staggers toward us.

"He must have gotten scared and run out the back." I barely manage to get the words out. My chest feels as if it's splitting wide open with panic.

"He couldn't have gotten far," Dean says, but I can hear the worry in his words as he barrels out the back door, calling out to Ace.

I follow him, looking everywhere at once. I don't see Ace making his way up the hill toward our home. I don't think he'd have gotten that far that fast.

"The path in the woods!" I say. "He might have run to the neighbor's house! He knows the way!"

The three of us tear down the trail, calling out to him. When we reach the clearing, Dean splits off and rushes around the back of the house to cover more ground while I hurry to the front porch.

"Does he know the neighbor? Can you call them?" Legion asks, as out of breath as I am, one hand clutching the lower railing of the porch steps while he winces in pain.

"Meg doesn't live here anymore." I nearly rip the storm door off its flimsy hinges and grab the doorknob, trying it just in case. To my astonishment, it *isn't locked!* I shove the door open and stumble inside, shouting. *"Ace!* Where are you?"

Classical music is playing low from upstairs, the end of Vivaldi's Winter. As I approach the staircase, the song starts over again.

"There!" Legion rasps, pointing at the foyer table.

I recognize the scribbled paper sitting on the table instantly and snatch it up just as Dean reaches us. "He was just working on this one! He has to be here somewhere! *Ace! Ace!*"

"What the fuck?" Dean grabs the drawing from my hand, turning it over to reveal something that isn't our son's scribble, and my legs nearly give out.

There's a note on the back, scrawled across the paper in jagged, adult handwriting...

You created a monster.

K eegan's the first of us to bolt up the stairs, Vanna and I following on his heels. My guts twist with every lunge as I take the steps two at a time. The scrawled note...the music drifting from upstairs... *Vivaldi of all fucking things...* They might as well be warning bells...

I know what's coming. I should be running out the front door, not up the fucking steps!

The upstairs room is empty, except for a small stereo and another one of Ace's drawings, this time with the words *At least you got the girl,* scrawled across it. Keegan snatches something else off the floor. A messy flash of something orange.

"*Oh my god!*" Vanna screams upon the sight of it, her hand flying to her mouth.

"Jesus fuck," Keegan barely manages to mutter. "*Who the fuck is she?*"

When he turns, something white flutters from the long, fox-orange strands of the lace-front wig, landing softly on the carpet. A white, frayed ribbon I recognize instantly...

"What did you say your neighbor's name was?" I ask, picking up the worn sympathy ribbon. I turn it over, already expecting to find two significant words stamped into the white silk... *True Love...*

"*Meg. Meg Kaleb,*" Vanna hastily replies. "*Why?*"

But I'm not listening anymore.

Jennifer Saviano

I'm sliding down the banister before Keegan can grab me.

The moment my boots hit the hardwood, I dart out the front door, leap off the front porch, and sprint as fast as my legs and lungs will carry me through the trail...back to my bike.

Every inhale burns worse than the last, but not nearly as much as the inferno of rage building within me.

I grit my teeth and push harder. Keegan's hot on my trail, and if he catches me now, we may never see Ace again. Pain shoots up my side, hot and white, and I nearly drop to my knees again, but I can't stop, not with Ace in her hands, not with Vanna's eyes full of tears somewhere back there.

My bike comes into view through the foliage like fucking salvation, and I cut across the lot, nearly collapsing onto it, sucking in air like it might be my last breath. Every drag through my fucked-up windpipe is an act of punishment.

I fire up the engine, the vibration rattling through the ache in my spine and shoulder blades. Twisting the throttle just as Keegan clears the trail, I peel out, spitting gravel at him and barrel down the road.

When I spot Vanna stumbling from the forest, desperately waving both arms and begging me to stop, I almost do... I almost cut across the field to go to her and explain... But there's no time...

"I'll get him back!" I shout to her. And if I have to die to do so, I will. *"Vanna, I'll get him back, I swear to you! I'll get him back!"*

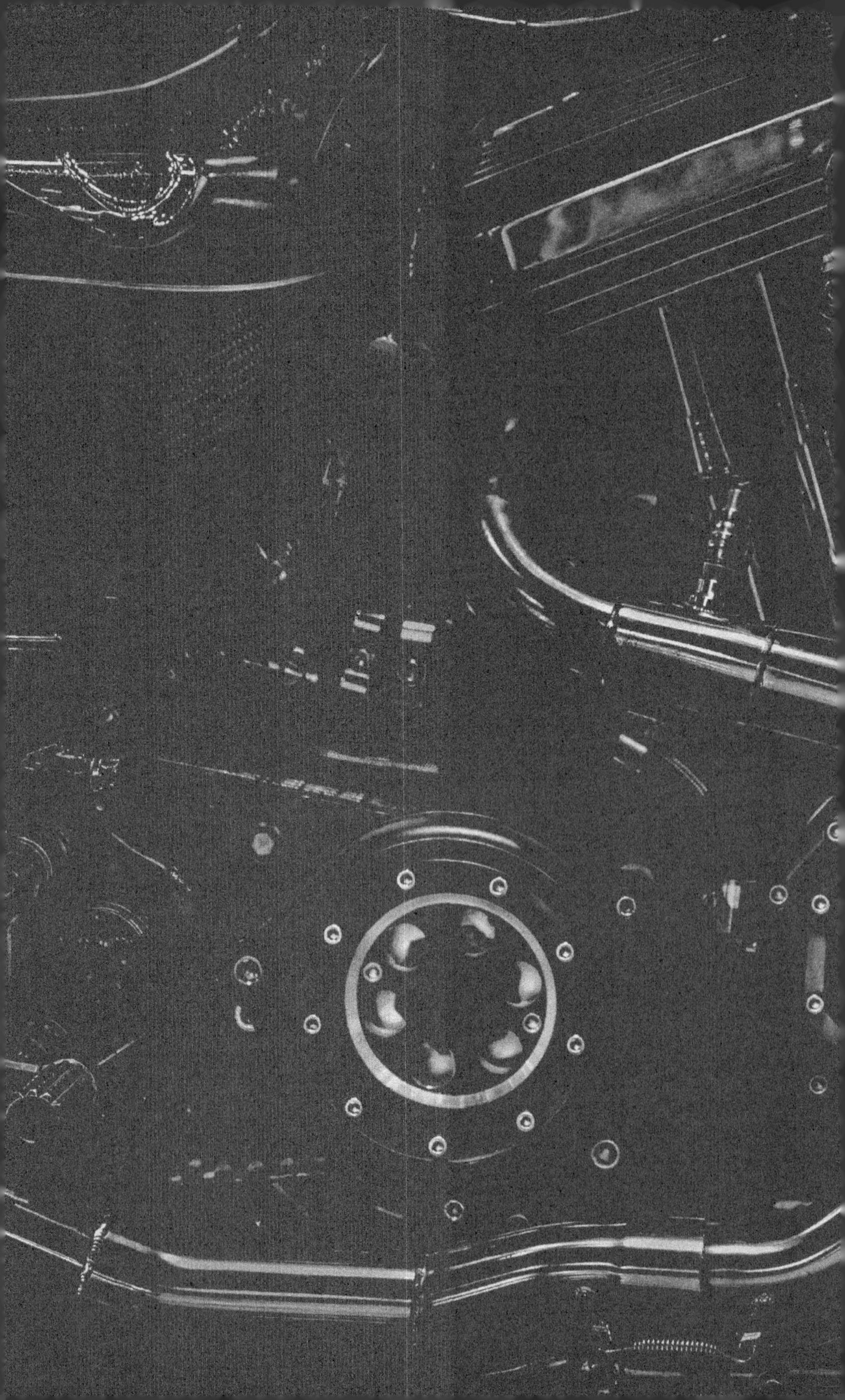

CHAPTER 47

DEAN

I've faced death. Stared it in the eye and smiled with blood in my teeth. But this… *Ace*…this is hell.

I had Jason Caldwell on the phone before Legion even made it around the bend in the road. I didn't hesitate. I don't care what stories the town will start whispering about us again…about my past…about my MC. *My son is missing.* That's all that fucking matters now.

I didn't wait for the cops to arrive before making my next call to my Sergeant at Arms. Viking rallied every brother in all charters. Word spread to the surrounding clubs and citizens. They came without question, without hesitation. Some brought their old ladies, their prospects, others brought drones and dogs. They spread out with the cops in a grid pattern, sweeping every inch of forest, ditch, and fence line. Those not involved with the search here are on the streets checking gas stations, truck stops, motels, anywhere within a hundred-mile radius that some sick fuck might duck into with a stolen kid…

My faith is in them. Ace isn't lost somewhere in the woods, and I can't help but feel this protocol the authorities insist upon is a waste of precious time. No, we didn't see someone take him. No, we didn't notice a car. No, we don't know what the letters left behind mean. No, we don't know why the former neighbor—*who apparently isn't a redhead*—would take our kid. We don't know anything!

But fuckin' Legion does…

My third call was worth the long shot, but as I feared, Axel regretfully informed me that Legion removed the tracking device on his bike weeks ago.

Now, I wait for the demon's call, clutching my cell in my fist so tightly I have to keep reminding myself to ease up, so I don't crack it. My lungs feel like they're collapsing, but not because of exertion from the search. It's from fear. A fear I can't let my wife see... Vanna's barely holding it together. She hasn't let herself fall apart, not yet. But every hour that ticks by, every time I check on her, I can see the crack in her composure widening. I feel it too, deep in my bones. We're both a breath away from breaking.

I circle back to the house to check on her again. The cops have insisted one of us remain at home *in case Ace wanders back*... We both feel fucking useless...powerless. It's beyond torment.

My frustration skyrockets the moment I spot the silver Lexus SUV in my driveway. Lucinda steps out of her cage, wearing hiking boots and a reflective vest.

"Dean!" she calls, rushing over to me. I'm surprised she isn't wearing makeup to cover the bruises from her fight with Vanna. Then again, she probably *wants* me to see them. *"Oh my god, I'm so sorry!* We came as soon as we heard!"

She slams into me, wrapping her arms around my neck. I'm about to pry her off me and cast her aside when I spot Maddie exiting the vehicle, dressed similarly to her mother.

"*Uncle Dean!*" She rushes to me as well.

"Please don't be here to make this about yourself." I defeatedly sigh. Lucinda releases me and has the nerve to look wounded. I crouch to catch Maddie in my arms. "Hey, Monkey." I hug her back tightly.

"We're here to help find Ace!" Maddie says.

"Thank you, *but you stay by your mother,* you hear me?" I say more firmly than I mean to. "*No more missing kids...*"

When the cell clutched in my hand rings, I stand and answer without looking at the caller ID. *"Yes, hello? Tell me something!"*

"Cops found a little sneaker and tire tracks in the back trail," Axel informs me. "Texting you a pic now, but I recognize Ace's kicks."

The text vibrates my phone just as another call beeps in.

"That's Jason, I'll call you back," I say before swiping to call-waiting. "Jason?"

"We've got tire tracks," he says. "Detectives are on it. Switching up protocol."

"*About fucking time.*" I barely hear my own voice as I stare at the little picture of Ace's sneaker on the dirt trail.

"The good news is we've already been looking into the details Vanna gave us earlier about the neighbor's car. We've got the composite sketch of the suspect on the news already airing with the pictures y'all gave us of Ace. *Things are happening,* Dean. I know it feels like we're all standing still. But I promise, we're gonna find your son."

LEGION

I got the fuck out of Dodge before Keegan could lock down the county. That's the thing about small towns and friendships with local police. Everyone knows each other, or at least *of* each other. When something tragic happens, especially involving a kid, they all band together. Unless, of course, the mother is a junkie whore, and the local judge is in on the pedo network...

I pull the last drag from my cigarette while staring through the broken blinds of this no-tell motel outside of Jocsan.

This shithole is starting to feel like a holding cell. I smash the butt out in the overflowing ashtray on the table beside me and light up another. The local news playing softly behind me has picked up Ace's story. They've been plastering his picture alongside the police sketch of Puppet for the last few hours. The emerald-green eyes are wrong, though...

Time is of the essence, and I need to decide how to proceed. I haven't been named as a person of interest yet. At least, it hasn't been broadcast. I can't help them if the man I've envied to the point of madness myself decides to hedge his bets and put my name on a statement. I doubt he will. Keegan might hate me, but he's a father first. And if there's a chance *I* can get Ace back, he'll buy me the time I need to take the shot. He knows I'm desperate enough...dangerous enough...*motivated.*

I fight the urge to call her. It's what she wants, and I'm already fairly certain where she is. It's all part of the game.

Legion: Book 3

Another torturous twenty minutes pass before my cellphone rings...

"Hello, Puppet."

"It's Reaper."

"Ah, I see she's roped you into this little game as well, *Legion*," I sneer. "You've always been a sucker for our little whore. Am I meant to assume we are to meet where I bested you last?"

"None of the cards, all of the arrogance," Reaper mutters. "You haven't changed much. But if you want to see this kid alive again, you'll do what she says."

"She went rogue on you, didn't she?"

His silence speaks volumes.

"Reaper...*give me the kid*, and you'll get to walk away from this mistake of epic proportions with your life."

"I'm choosing to take advantage of the leverage this unexpected turn of events has dropped in my lap."

"There are opportunities, Reaper, and then there are *massive fucking mistakes*. I'm afraid your choices thus far have landed you in the latter category. Allow me to help you out of this predicament. There's still time to diffuse the situation."

"It's nothing a little C-4 can't fix."

Fuck.

He chuckles, then there's a brief, muffled shuffling, before she picks up the line. "I thought you would have been here by now." I can hear the pout in her words.

"Come now, Puppet...you know there's only one woman I'd chase, and she isn't you."

"Keep pissing me off, Damien."

"I'd much rather come to some sort of agreement, *Gemma*." It's impossible to keep the growl from my tone.

She squeals excitedly, and I remove the cell from my ear until she's through. "You figured out my clues? They were a nod to you, of course."

"*Meg Kaleb*. An anagram for *Gem Blake*," I mutter. "How long has this been going on?"

"Feels like for-fucking-ever... It's been so long since you've called me by my real name. *Say it again?*"

"Where's the boy, Gemma?"

She laughs, an unhinged sound that might have made my hair stand on end if she hadn't sufficiently pissed me off already. "You told me to turn my unrequited love into hate," she says, ignoring my request for the only bit of information I give a damn about. "Well, I have, Legion. I hate you... I think a part of me has always hated you... And hate has a way of erasing whatever fear I had of you!"

"We can hash this out between us without the boy, Gem."

"He's the key to *her* heart... If I destroy him... *I destroy you all...*"

"Gemma... I need a definitive location."

"You hurt me..."

"Puppet."

"You hurt me...*and you killed them*... You turned me into something I don't even recognize. I told you this would happen... One day, I wouldn't want you anymore. You've destroyed me. It's *my* turn...to destroy *you*..."

"Give me the boy, and I'll agree to whatever terms you set forth. You have my word."

"I should have let you die... I wish I had just let you die... You're a monster... *You made me a monster...*"

"Give me the kid and I'll grant you your wish!"

"You will?"

"Show me proof of life and I'll come to you. This is what you want, isn't it? *I know you*... I know you'll be waiting for me at the old cement factory. Am I right? *Did I crack the code?*"

Another sinister little chuckle slithers through the line. A moment later, a photo text comes through. It's Ace, bound to a chair. Blindfolded, wearing a set of large headphones. I can practically see the trembling of his pouted lower lip. My chest tightens, old memories clawing up from places I keep locked down. He doesn't appear to have suffered any discernible injuries, but I note the chalk-like substance on his shirt and the knees of his pants, confirming my suspicions of their location.

Ace will never know what it's like to live every day praying someone will come, and no one ever does. I'll do whatever it takes to bring him back. He will never carry the scars I do. Not while I'm still breathing.

"Legion?"

"Yes, Puppet?"

"Come play with me..."

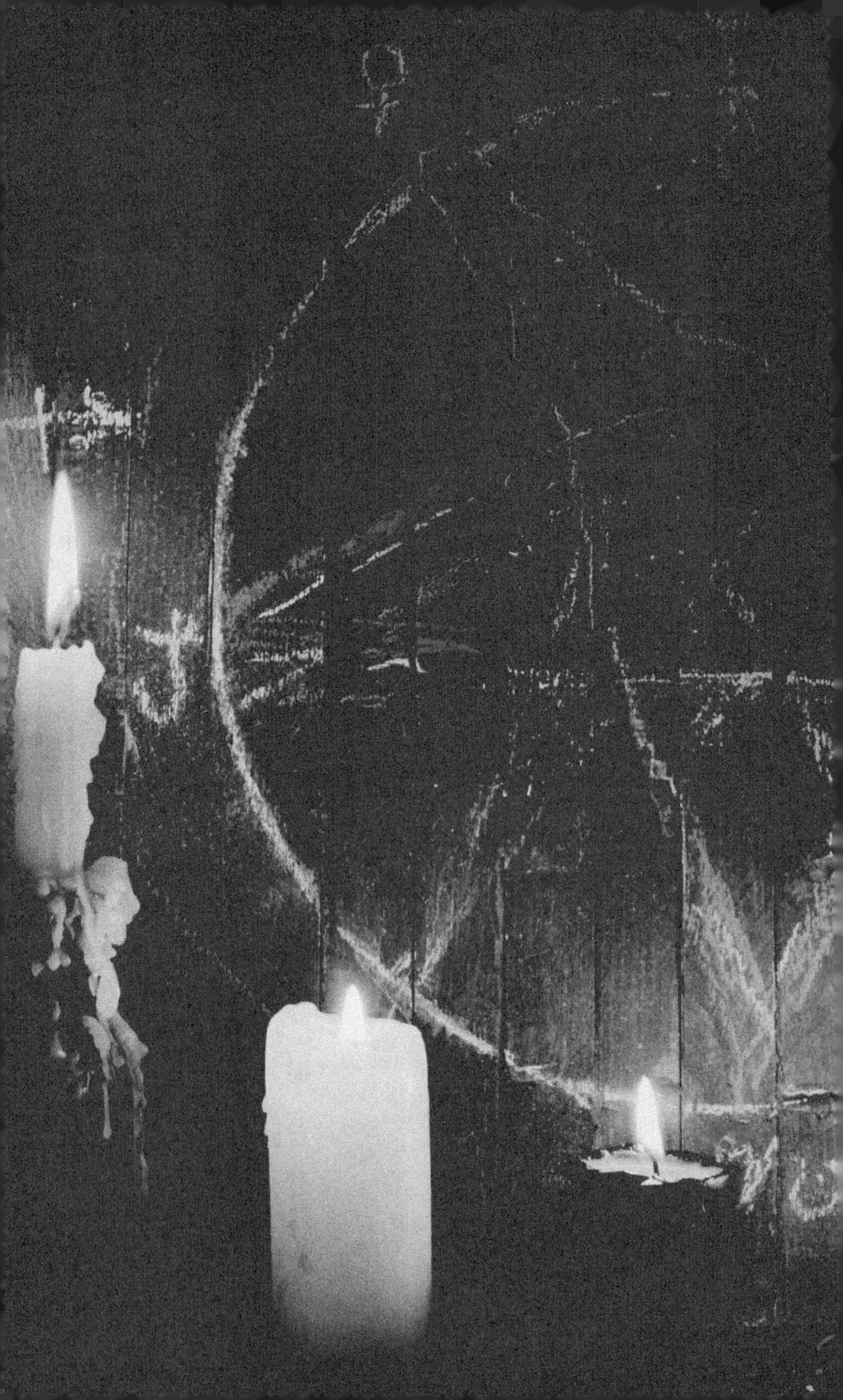

CHAPTER 48

LEGION

I drop the location pin to Keegan before I swing off my bike. Concrete dust kicks up around my boots, and I spot a chalked outline of hopscotch squares drawn on a mostly unblemished chunk of lot. The only other vehicle here matches the description Vanna gave on the news earlier.

Instinctively, my hand brushes the grip of the gun under my jacket, but I don't get far.

"Drop your weapons. All of them. Now." Reaper's voice echoes from within the old factory. "Or we drop you where you stand." The clicking, metallic sound of his revolver reinforces the command.

I slowly divest myself of weaponry, crouching to rest two Glocks and a few knives upon the cement lot. I raise my hands out to my sides, fingers spread, as I straighten and proceed toward the crumbling cathedral of ruin.

The two of them stand beside each other, illuminated by a couple of camping lanterns. I instantly notice the black det cord running along the base of the support beams...taped down with a care I could almost laugh at. Reaper always took pride in his work...

I'm unable to verify from this angle, but I am certain from experience that he has explosives strapped to the load-bearing beams, shaped charges designed to punch inward, not out. A classic implosion setup, meant to pull the whole structure down on itself. Nestled between the support beams, strung with wire and surgical care, are the real monsters... *Incendiary grenades*... military grade, unsurprisingly probably thermate or magnesium based. They'll burn hot enough to melt steel, hot enough to turn bone to dust.

"Nice party favors," I say, shifting my gaze back to them. Reaper still has his gun trained on me. Draped in tactical gear, his towering form makes the mad woman standing tensely beside him seem small and even more fragile than her broken mind. She appears harmless... at least physically... But I've been the victim of her puppeteering influences over men before...

Reaper smiles smugly. "Figured I'd give the Saviors a taste of Hell... *But I'll send you there first.*"

Puppet shifts in her boots beside him. Jittery.

I clear my throat. "An inward collapse...how *poetic*."

Puppet beams at me as if I just paid her a compliment. But then her empty hand darts inside Reaper's jacket, and before either of us can react...

BANG.

Point blank.

Blood sprays the already rust-stained support column beside him, and he crumples to the cement like a marionette slashed from its strings... One eye still open...mouth agape as if he died with a question on the tip of his tongue.

Puppet swings the gun back on me and smiles like a cracked doll, slowly crouching to pry the detonator from Reaper's dead hand. "You didn't think I'd let him hurt you, did you?" She cocks her head eerily to the side as she rises. "After all, I've done everything for you... He was just a placeholder... *My puppet*... Poor is the teacher whose student does not surpass him. *That's Da Vinci.*"

"*Delusions of grandeur*... Indicative of an inflated sense of one's own importance."

She scoffs. "I kept your kingdom from crumbling. Are you not impressed?"

"I'm tired."

She laughs, swaying oddly to a tune playing only in her mind while she sing-songs, *"There ain't no rest for the wicked!"*

"Where's Ace?" My question sobers her a bit, but she doesn't answer. "*Where's the boy*, Gem?"

She licks her lips, then cocks her chin toward a closed door a few yards across the wide space. "He's in there."

My vision tunnels, and I start moving in Ace's direction.

"Don't!" she warns, but I don't stop.

"*Fucking shoot me,*" I snarl through fury laced with guilt and desperation, "If that's what you need to do, do it. But I'm not leaving a three-year-old bound in a fucking closet!"

The gun rattles in her trembling hand, but she doesn't pull the trigger when I shove the door open.

The light from the dying lantern at his feet dimly illuminates the small room. His little wrists are bound with zip ties. Ankles too. His eyes are covered by a blindfold that shields a majority of his little face, and he's wearing a set of headphones.

I drop to my knees, throat catching, and immediately remove the headphones and blindfold. His eyes are wide and wet with tears, which have cut a trail down the dust canvasing his cheeks. He seems too traumatized to recognize me at first. I quickly undo the leather belt wrapped around his waist that's securing him to the chair.

"L-Legend?" his little voice cracks the heavy silence.

I have to swallow before I can respond. "Yeah, kid. I'm gonna get you to your momma." I grip the demon horns on my belt buckle and remove the small, concealed blade to cut his ties.

I can feel Puppet behind me, hovering near the doorway, still holding the gun on me.

"I didn't hurt him," she snaps defensively.

I slip the small push-blade back into my buckle and check Ace for injuries. He doesn't appear to have any scrapes or bruises, but the bottom of his sneaker-less foot is slightly damp. I remove the filth-covered sock.

"His foot is cut." I glare at her.

"We were playing hopscotch earlier. He was laughing!" Puppet guiltily insists. "It must have happened on a broken chunk of concrete… I needed him calm while they rigged the place… He was only tied up for a little while."

I try to wipe his foot clean as best I can with the bandana from my back pocket. "Don't," I snap at her without so much as a backward glance. "Don't try to justify it."

"I didn't *hurt* him! I like Ace!"

"*You locked a baby in a closet!*"

When I lift Ace from the chair, he clings to me like I'm the last solid thing left in the world. "It's okay, Ace…" I whisper, gently holding his head against my shoulder.

I brush past her, shielding him from Reaper's corpse.

"You want to compare sins?" she hisses, following closely behind.

"I want you to tell me about these fucking arrangements!" I snap. Ace's little body tenses in my arms. I hug him tighter and walk faster toward the lot.

"Reaper was going to kill you and then reach out to the Saviors to cut a deal in exchange for Ace. He was going to lure them here and blow them up," she explains, keeping pace, gun trained at my side.

"*The arrangements for Ace*," I press.

"Someone's coming to get him. They'll be here any minute. Damien... I would never hurt a kid."

I shoot her a damning glare. "There's a mountain of evidence that speaks to the contrary!"

The moment my boots hit the cracked concrete lot outside, I shift Ace slightly in my arms. "Look...look at the stars, Ace," I encourage him. The sun has set below the horizon, and the first twinkling stars of twilight shine in the darkening violet sky.

He twists his little face from where it's been tucked against my chest and peers up.

"You see that bright one there?" I point, and his curious gaze follows. "That's the North Star, *Polaris*. Do you know why it's special?"

He timidly shakes his head.

"It's always right there. All the other stars appear to move across the sky, but Polaris is unwavering in its position. People used to find their way home by looking up at the North Star. No matter how lost, they could figure out where they were supposed to go."

His small fingers clutch my jacket. "Is it magick?"

"Yes, buddy."

I stand in silence for a moment, cherishing the weight of him in my arms while we listen to the sounds of chirring insects in the overgrown weeds and the faint metallic ticking of my motorcycle cooling nearby. I hug him one last time, tighter than I remember ever being held myself, and the thought burns through me... If someone had come for me back then...if someone had cared enough to fight for me...maybe I wouldn't be the man I am now. Maybe the darkness wouldn't run so deep.

I peer down at him, his little face pressed against my shoulder. Ace deserves to grow up whole, unbroken. And if it's the last thing I ever do, I'll make damn sure he gets that chance.

The growl of an engine rumbles somewhere beyond the tree line. When a blue, older model mustang barrels into view, a slight wave of relief washes over me.

"Are we lost, Legend?" Ace whispers.

The ache in my chest intensifies, and I swallow the knot forming in my throat. "Not anymore, sweet one... Would you do something for me when you get back to your momma?"

"Yes."

"Tell her I love her…and that I'm sorry."

DEAN

The sun is already going down, and it feels like it'll never rise again. The authorities and volunteers have left, finally certain Ace isn't lost in the woods…*he was taken.*

Vanna is standing in the kitchen when I walk into our home, hands gripping the edge of the counter like it's the only thing keeping her from falling. Cherry steps away from her as I approach and wrap my arms around my wife from behind. She leans back into me, but the tension never leaves her, and I can feel her trembling with the weight of everything she's holding inside. For me. For us. For Ace.

The strength of this woman… I don't deserve her.

"The crew's still out," I murmur into her hair. "The cops are focusing on the car, and I've got eyes on every gas station in a fifty-mile radius. Every MC has his picture, baby. We're gonna find him."

"I'm sorry," she whispers.

"For what?" My voice nearly cracks.

"I never should have taken my eyes off him."

I turn her to face me, and her glassy eyes lift to meet mine. "This is not your fault."

"*But I'm his mother,*" she chokes out. "I'm supposed to keep him safe."

I cup her face in my hands. "*I'm supposed to keep you both safe.* We're going to find him. We're not giving up. Do you hear me? Do not give up."

Legion: Book 3

"I'm not…it's just getting harder to breathe… And I don't know how much longer I can stand here waiting as if he's actually going to wander back home."

I'm about to pull her into my arms again when my cell buzzes. I pull it from my pocket. It's a text. From Legion. No explanation, only a location.

"What is it?" she asks as if she can tell my blood just ran cold.

"Legion."

Her breath hitches. *"Did he find Ace?"*

"I don't know," I say, shoving the cell back in my pocket and grabbing my keys.

Her fingers cling to my leather jacket before I can turn. "I'm coming with you!"

"No," I say, too sharp. "You need to stay here, in case—"

"He's not walking through that door!" Her voice cracks, and the desperation in her eyes breaks my heart. She holds my arm tighter as if she can anchor me here. "Take me with you."

"I don't know what I'm walking into, Vanna."

"I don't care. He's my son."

"He's ours, and I'm not taking any chances," I say, gently prying her grip from my leather jacket. "Stay here. I will call you the moment I know anything."

"If you won't take me, take someone!"

I hold her arms firmly but gently at her sides and press a kiss to her forehead. "Call Viking and tell him I'm going to the spot we negotiated the truce with Reaper's crew. He'll know where."

I release her and dart out the door before she can grab me again. Heart pounding, I mount Serene and barrel out of the driveway.

If anything happens to Ace because of Legion, there won't be enough of him left to bury.

Vanna

"Let me call Viking. Sit down," Cherry gently insists at the sight of my trembling hands as I attempt to bring up Viking's number. When the phone buzzes and rings before I get the chance, I nearly jump out of my own skin.

I answer on a shaky breath. "I was just about to call you. Dean told me to—"

"*Ace is safe!*" Viking's voice is rough with urgency over the wind. "I'm riding to get him now!"

My knees almost give out. "*Oh my god! Are you sure? Where is he?*"

"With someone safe. I'm minutes away. They're racing to me as we speak. I tried to call Dean, but he's not answering his cell."

"Viking, *who has my son?*"

"Val and Jett. They just picked him up. He's alright."

I suddenly realize Cherry is squeezing my other hand. She leans in closer to the phone as I speak. "Dean said Legion sent him a location pin. He's going to where you met Reaper's crew."

"Legion traded himself for Ace there." I barely hear him over the roaring wind, but my heart stops for a beat.

"*What?*"

"He handed himself over. No backup. Just him. Whatever hell he's in now, he chose it to get Ace back."

Cherry and I stare at each other. Dean doesn't know what he's riding into or that Legion made a deal for Ace. What if whoever has Legion isn't satisfied with just him? What if they want Dean, too?

"Where is he? I'm going now," I say, rushing to my purse on the kitchen island to dig for my keys.

"I'll send some guys in that direction," Viking says. "Stay put."

"No!" I snap, already heading for the door. "Tell me where!"

"Ain't safe."

"Viking, *this is my family,* and if our friendship has ever meant anything to you, you'll tell me where my husband is going!"

He curses under his breath but finally gives me an address. "Don't go alone, you hear me?"

Cherry and I lock eyes as I pull open the front door. She nods, and we run to my car parked in the driveway. The moment we're both inside, I crank the ignition and slam my foot on the gas.

"Viking, promise me something," I say, whipping around the bend in the road so fast, Cherry grabs the handle above the passenger door to brace herself.

"What?" Viking reluctantly asks.

"You won't let Ace out of your arms until you're putting him in mine."

"Funny, isn't it? Love and hate. Hope and denial. Do you know what they have in common?" I let the question hang between us as I light up a cigarette. It might be my last.

I pull a long drag and allow the slight wave of calm I don't trust to settle over me. Releasing the words on a smokey sigh, I tell her, *"A very thin fucking line."*

Puppet doesn't say anything. She's still got the gun pointed at me. Her other hand is toying with the detonator at her side. Her smile is still stitched too tightly across her face, unhinged.

"So, what's the plan, Gem? Was all that talk earlier just a show for Reaper's sake?" I ask, smoke curling from my lips.

"Sometimes… Sometimes I hate you… Sometimes, I can't picture my life without you." She tilts her head. "That's always been our dance, hasn't it? Do you know why I tracked you down after Chad?"

I pull another drag and flick the ash with my thumb. "Revenge… *Despite the fact that you betrayed me first.*"

She smiles, soft, but *off*. "You could have killed me, too…the night of the graduation party… You spared me… You *love* me… I just needed to remind you."

I nearly choke on my smoke as I laugh. *"Is that what you've been telling yourself?"*

Her smile fades.

"My love for you died the night I nearly did at the end of that chain… You just got *lucky* and *happened* to survive. I didn't care whether you lived or died." I toss the cigarette on the ground and snuff out the ember beneath my boot. *"Until now…"*

Death has always been in my cards, but if I can make this my last act of *true love*…then maybe I can leave this wretched world with a shred of something that might look a little like redemption in Vanna's eyes. I was already leaving anyway. She can get on with her life, raise her son with Keegan, heal from the consequences and misfortunes of having drawn me—*a demon*—into her compassionate, magnanimous orbit…

My fingers slip around the horns of the demon belt buckle, and I slip the small push-blade free, turning to face the woman I've driven to madness head-on.

Jennifer Saviano

I can almost hear the haunting melody of Mozart's Lacrimosa in my mind as an insidious grin stretches my mouth.

"Did you know Wolfgang Amadeus Mozart died before completing the entire Requiem? His student, Franz Xaver Sussmayr, completed the work, including the rest of the Lacrimosa movement."

Puppet smiles. "I did, actually."

"It's such a shame you let your musical talents go to such tragic waste." I grip the horns tightly, the little blade—eager for her blood—protrudes between my fingers. "Let's dance, Gemma… *One last time…*"

I move fast, but her bullet is faster. The shot cracks through the air like a thunderclap and rips through my side, lightening hot. My body buckles, but I surge forward, and she stumbles back in fear, heel catching on the edge of broken concrete. The detonator slips from her hand and clatters to the ground, skidding beyond reach.

Panic flashes in her eyes, and she raises the gun to fire again, but I knock it wide and slam into her with everything I've got left.

Pain explodes through my side as we crash to the concrete. I barely hear her screams through the ringing in my ears. She kicks and claws beneath me, eyes going wide with terror when I slug her in the gut with the push-blade…once…twice…three times. The blade slips from my grip, the smooth metal horns of the handle too slick to hold onto. It clangs on the ground beside us, and I wrap my crimson-stained hands around her treacherous throat. It's fitting she should die this way…the way they killed whatever good remained in me years ago.

Her eyes bulge as I squeeze. She desperately bucks beneath me, kicking and clawing at my wrists, before abandoning the task in an attempt to grab for the gun just beyond reach.

"You always wanted to see the demon dwelling within me," I snarl. "Take a good look, Puppet! This is our blood sacrifice, and he's our escort to hell!"

I barely hear the metallic scrape of the push-blade against the concrete floor when her flailing hand finds purchase… She plunges it into my side, and hellfire erupts where the blade nicks my ribs through my leather jacket. She twists and pulls it out to stab me again, and I nearly lose my grip on her throat from the blinding pain and my draining strength.

"*Keep stabbing, you little bitch…*" I pant. "*I want your last breath soaked in failure…*"

Vanna

"Axel and the guys are ten minutes behind us," Cherry says, just as I cut down the old road leading up to the address I strongarmed out of Viking. It doesn't appear to have been maintained in years, but I don't ease up on the gas pedal.

The old factory comes into view when we reach the wide clearing, looking like something out of a nightmare—gray, cracked, rust stains from exposed rebar marring it as if the structure itself is bleeding.

Dean is already off of Serene, moving toward the looming structure with his gun drawn, muscles coiled tight like he's walking straight into hell. His head snaps in our direction the moment he hears my car, weapon still raised in the direction of the factory. I can read the muttering of *"Jesus Fuck, Vanna!"* on his lips.

The car skids to a halt, and I throw it in park, barely twisting the key from the ignition before flinging the door open as he hurriedly jogs toward us, gun still cautiously trained on the building.

"You shouldn't be here," he says, low but firm. He glances at Cherry when she steps from the passenger side door. "Either of you." His concerned gaze shifts back to me. "I told you to stay put for a reason."

"I had to come," I quickly say. "Ace is safe. Viking has him. He's at the clubhouse."

A mixture of relief and confusion eclipses Dean's stern expression. *"What?"*

"Ace is okay." I grip his tense shoulder and stare searchingly into his dark eyes. *"Legion might not be...* He traded himself for Ace. We can't just walk away."

Dean's eyes narrow, and he glances back at the condemnable structure. "It's dead quiet in there... If not for his bike and that *Meg* woman's car..." He cocks his chin in the direction of the parked vehicle and Legion's motorcycle. "I wouldn't think there's a living soul inside this place."

"We need to see if he's still here." I stare at the looming structure, looking more and more like a giant, decrepit mausoleum.

"Doll, I didn't come here to save Legion."

"I know there are things he's done that are unforgivable, but he saved our son. That counts for something, doesn't it?"

"I'll go. You stay here with the cage and Cherry," Dean insists. When I shake my head and he lets out a defeated sigh. "Fine. Just stay behind me, then. And Cherry—"

"I'll blow the horn if I see or hear anyone coming," Cherry says, moving around to the driver's side door. "Axel and a few of the guys should be here soon."

I brace myself for what we might find as I follow Dean into the old structure. Viking didn't give us many details, but if this had anything to do with the people who jumped Legion last time...

"Dean..." I whisper the moment we cautiously cross the threshold. The atmosphere is thick with tension and strange smells. Dust particles float through the air in the dim light cast by solar lanterns in the mostly dark. The moon above shines through the cracks in the roof, but it's still dark and unsettling.

Something becomes heavier the further inside we venture. I recognize a scent mingled within the air...something coppery that drags my memory back to the night Dean fought Jack in the cabin. I try to swallow down my rising anxiety and reach out to touch Dean's shoulder. He removes one hand from the raised gun to reach back and hold my hand.

"Do you smell that?" I shakily ask.

"Blood," he replies.

"Nobody ever made any ransom demands for Ace," I whisper. "This was about getting to Legion." I squeeze Dean's hand harder and pray silently to myself... *please don't let him be dead...*

Dean suddenly stops walking. "Oh shit..." he mutters under his breath.

I peek around his shoulder. There's a taped cord running across the concrete a few steps in front of us. Thin wires split off in different directions, disappearing into the darkness. "This fucking place is rigged to blow. We need to get out of here. *Now*." Dean instinctively shoves me behind his back, but then I hear it.

That familiar gravelly voice...

"You're late... *Too late...*"

I follow the sound of Legion's weary voice and spot him leaning against a support column on the ground, partially slumped with both arms wrapped around his stomach.

Legion: Book 3

Before Dean can stop me, I rush to Legion's side. He tilts his head back against the column, and when our eyes meet, he tiredly smiles. "I didn't think I'd get to see you again," he says on a pain-ridden sigh. My gaze drops to his hands clutching his stomach. I don't need the light of a lantern to tell they're soaked in blood.

I drop to my knees beside him, tears already stinging my eyes. I barely hear Dean's boots skidding on the gravel on Legion's other side.

"I'll call 911," Dean says, rummaging for his phone in his pocket.

"No," Legion firmly objects. "It's too late, and this place is rigged to implode… Get her out of here…"

"You're still breathing, it's not too late," I push.

His tired gaze slides back to me. "You asked me once…after I kissed you in the cellar…what a man like me could possibly know about True Love… Do you remember what I told you?"

I peer up at my husband for a brief moment, hesitating. If Legion is dying, he deserves to speak his piece.

Dean offers a single nod, and I know he's bracing for whatever Legion is about to say.

I settle my teary gaze back on Legion.

"I told you that, like smoking, it will eventually kill you…" Legion slips one bloody hand into his pocket and removes his brass Zippo. He flicks it open and runs his thumb through the flame. "I've never lied to you, sweet one… Despite my shortcomings, despite the evil I've committed… I've never lied to you." The hinges slowly creak, and the lid claps shut as he presses it closed. "I want you to keep this… I left it for you once…"

I nod, my throat tight, my eyes blurring as I gently take the Zippo from his bloody hand. I don't try to pull away when his fingers squeeze mine.

He swallows hard, and I'm not sure if it's from the pain he must be in, or the emotions swimming in his tearful gaze before he whispers, *"I love you… I always will."*

A whimper escapes me, and I have to choke back a sob. I can't even form the words. I want to say that I'm sorry… *I'm sorry I couldn't save you. I'm sorry I can't save you now… I'm sorry I can't tell you that I never expected you to be my deepest secret…*but I can't.

I squeeze his hand harder, and another weak grin pulls at the corner of his mouth as if he knows.

"I ain't gonna tell anybody…not where I'm going." He takes a shuddering breath and lifts his gaze to Dean. "Get her out of here, now…please… The bitch is still alive… There's a…*a detonator*…if she comes to…she's crazy enough to take us all out."

Dean grabs my arm, hard, and hauls me to my feet. My hand slips from Legion's, but I clutch his Zippo in my fist and hold it to my chest.

"*We can't just leave him!*" I scream as Dean drags me back the way we came. "*We can carry him out together!*"

"He's made his choice, doll," Dean urges, a level of desperation in his tone I cannot ignore either.

"*But he's not gone yet!*"

"*Go!*" Legion shouts, his words seeped in gut-wrenching torment as he looks past me to my husband. "*Get her out of here, Keegan! Before this fucking place comes down on us all!*"

"*No.*" I barely hear myself cry, but I'm no longer resisting my husband. "Damien, I'm sorry…"

"Go…sweet one…there isn't time…" Legion's voice cracks. He stares at me with a tearful finality that steals the breath from my lungs, and his final words shatter my heart. "In another life, baby…we don't end up this way… Somewhere…sometime…it's you and me…and we're sitting side by side…watching the sun go down across the desert… *You would have made it beautiful.*"

DEAN

The first pop behind us isn't loud. It's sharp. Precise. Then another and another and another rapidly follow. I grip Vanna's hand tighter and pull her to run faster as we bolt from the gaping mouth of the doomed structure already rumbling beneath our pounding feet.

"*Get down!*" I shout to Cherry, and she ducks behind Vanna's car door.

The roar of my crew's motorcycles approaching in the distance mingles with the concrete rumbling behind us, and I can feel the vibrations through the soles of my boots. Charges continue to detonate in a symphony of destruction designed to reduce the building to rubble. I pull Vanna into my arms before taking her to the ground and shielding her with my body as the final charges go off. *Boom. Boom. Boom*…like a heartbeat before it flatlines.

Legion: Book 3

The shockwave washes over us, and Vanna fearfully clings to me as the structure folds in on itself with cold, deliberate intent. Legion was right. It was rigged to implode. The walls sink into themselves, the roof buckles, and steel curls in on steel. We're hit with another wave of heat and the sharp stings of small debris pelting my back, but I don't move. I hold onto her like maybe if I grip her tight enough, I'll be able to keep the world from falling apart around us…

The second she bolted to the demon bleeding out against a cracked pillar, his expression riddled with pain and regret, I knew she forgave him for everything. She looked at him like he was still something to her… something I don't want to name. I hate that he managed to earn even a fraction of that look in her eyes…

I tried not to let his words seep into my soul…to taint the love between us. I wanted to rip her away from him the moment she dropped to her knees beside him.

"*She still has the detonator…*"

I didn't ask questions. I grabbed my wife by the arm and pulled her back toward the exit. She fought me. Of course she did. Fucking Vanna. She always does. But I didn't stop despite her cries to help him, despite the way she tried to twist free of my grip.

When Legion spoke again, soft, strained, and final, he'd convinced her this was the end. For half a heartbeat, I thought she might drop to the floor and shatter. But I held her upright, I kept her moving, I got her out, and I keep her shielded until the rumbling stops and the heavy silence is only broken by the random creak of metal.

When we sit up, everything is covered in grey. The structure is a pile of smoldering ruin, flames dancing in the ribs of broken beams, smoke rising like a funeral pyre… And I suppose it is… The final resting place of a demon.

"*He's gone,*" she whispers, staring heartbroken at the wreckage. It feels like my own heart is imploding as their final exchange plays over in my mind. She turns to peer up at me, eyes glassy. "Are you alright?"

"I'll survive."

Her brows knit with concern before her expression softens with understanding. She touches my stubbled jaw as if she needs to feel me, as if she knows I need her to need me. "I cared about Legion. I won't lie to you, Dean. But that doesn't change *this*." Her hand slides to my chest, over the heart she'll own forever. "You're still the one I wake up for, the one I've chosen to build my life with, the one I will *always* keep choosing. *You are the one I love.*"

Jennifer Saviano

The ache in my heart stills when she wraps her arms around my neck... But *I know myself*... His final words won't leave me...

Not the warning about the detonator, not the plea to get her out...those last ones and the way he looked at her like he still belonged somewhere inside her heart. His last, desperate swing at the foundation of our relationship. They were an implosive device. Measured, deliberate, personal, desperate... aimed straight at everything Vanna and I have built together.

"*I love you, Dean,*" she whispers against my ear, full of sorrow and relief.

"I love you, too." Enough to understand and pick up the pieces, enough to not hold her forgiving nature against her. She wouldn't be *my Vanna* without it.

My crew circles around us as I hold her tighter, asking if we're alright and what happened. I glance back at the ruins one last time. The flames are dying down. The steel beams groan as they cool.

Legion buried himself in the wreckage of his obsession. Whatever cracks he may have managed to leave in us, we'll fill them and rebuild stronger.

I press a kiss to her temple. "Let's go get Ace, doll, and bring our family home."

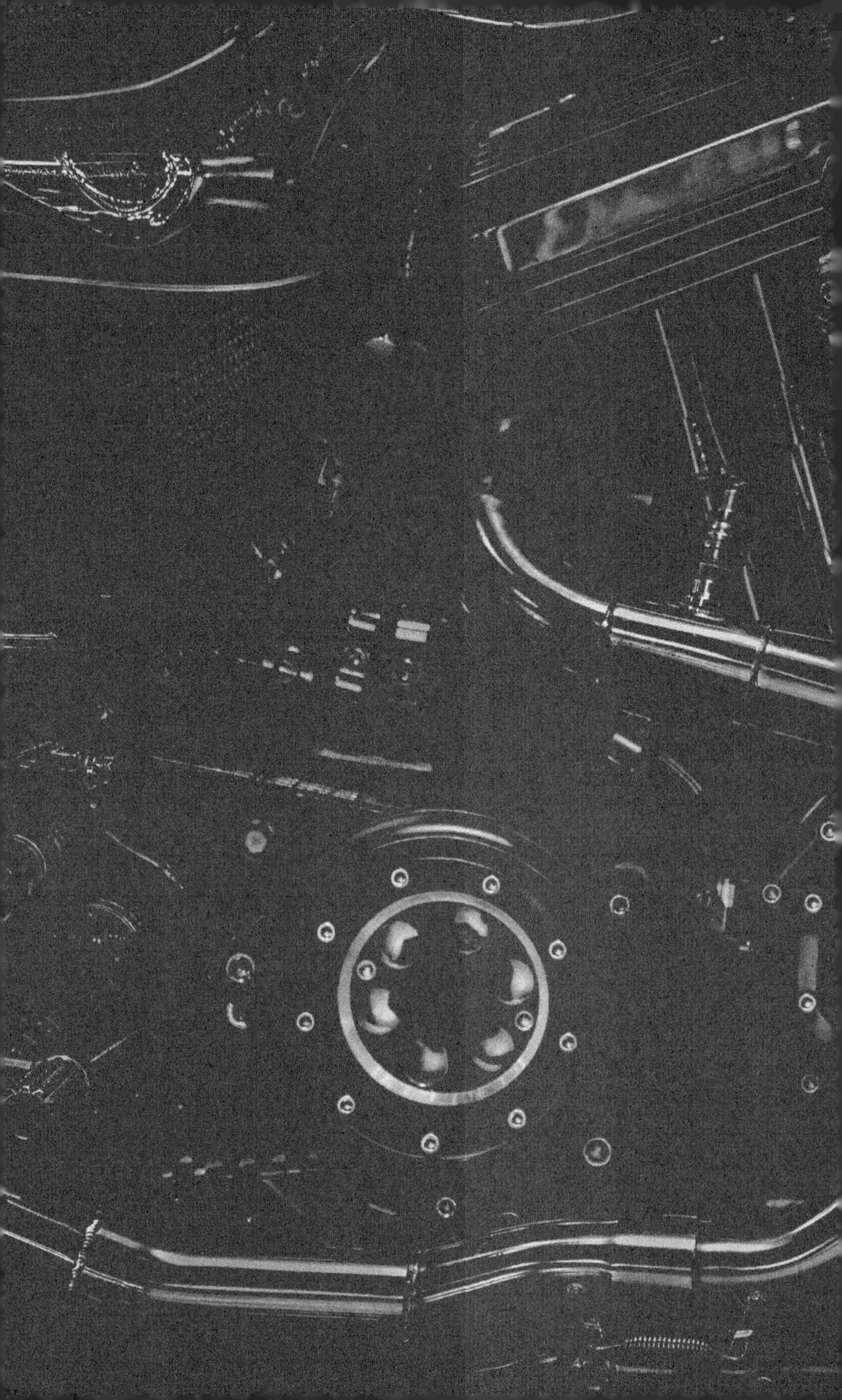

Chapter 49

DEAN

Laughter rings out across the backyard as the kids dart through the sprinklers, barefoot in bathing suits, wet hair plastered to their foreheads, red-white-and-blue popsicles dripping down their arms.

I wasn't sure we'd be here like this. At least, not so soon. I don't think Ace fully remembers what happened three weeks ago, judging by the big smile on his face as he jumps through the curtain of oscillating water for the hundredth time. He just knows he's safe now, surrounded by family who will do anything to keep him that way.

I'm tempted to join the kids in the sprinklers. It's the Fourth of July, and hot as hell in front of this grill. The scent of cooking meat, cut grass, and sunscreen fills the air and mingles with the soft classic rock music drifting from the outdoor speakers as I glance around the yard.

Axel, Chopper, Diesel, Dozer, Viper, and Derek are lounging in lawn chairs in the shade with beers, talking about motorcycles, MMA, and watching the kids play.

Vanna, Cherry, and Latisha just finished stringing the last few lanterns under the porch awning for later. Rosita emerges from the back door with a star-spangled tablecloth and a couple of food containers tucked under her arm. I hope one of them is that Mexican street corn salsa dish she made last year. The smiling group of women makes their way in their festive sundresses to the long picnic table beneath the canopy I set up earlier this morning.

Vanna smiles when she catches me admiring the cling of said sundress and blows me a little kiss.

Legion: Book 3

"*Less grinning, more grilling,*" Viking grunts, emerging from the side of the house with another hose, dish soap, and what looks like a tarp in his hands. "Old school slip-and-slide." He grins, and I chuckle, already imagining kids launching gleefully into the grass.

A few more beers in my crew, and the kids won't be the only ones fucking up my lawn. It'll turn into a competition to see who can fling themselves the furthest…*or who can bowl a toddler the best*. I glance at the packaged stack of red Solo cups on the table, already imagining the shenanigans.

"How are we doing over here, hot stuff?" Vanna teases, pushing the sunglasses up the bridge of her nose as she comes to stand beside me.

"Fuckin' Aces, baby." I grin, flipping and catching the stainless-steel spatula like a pro.

"Should I go grab the next batch of meat from the fridge?"

"Yeah, grab me a clean container for all this while you're at it and some foil to cover the top. Viking should be too preoccupied with setting up the slip-and-slide to notice just yet."

"Are the prospects and the patch chasers still coming? I texted Ford Focus to make sure he brings more buns with him. Maybe I should have delegated that to Trippy and Daniel. They should be here soon with Maddie, too."

"If he doesn't, Viking will waterboard him."

Vanna giggles as if I'm joking and tucks herself beneath my arm, wrapping hers around my waist. "He seems happy," she sighs, nodding toward Ace.

Our son has abandoned the sprinkler for the moment and has decided to assist Viking with his slip-and-slide project.

"What do we tell him when he asks?" She peers up at me, biting her bottom lip as if she expects some sort of outburst from me. "With everyone here, he's going to."

"I don't know… Maybe that he went back to Hades."

Her hold loosens, but she doesn't move away.

"I'm sorry, doll," I bite out. "I'm not as forgiving as you, Vanna."

"It's alright. I understand." She slips from beneath my arm and stands before me. Pushing the sunglasses up into her hair, she looks up at me as if she's got something important to say, when the back door swings open.

Maddie emerges and descends the steps, followed by Trippy and Daniel. She immediately runs up to us, carrying a bowl of fruit salad, which she hands to Vanna.

"Happy Independence Day!" She smiles before running off to join the other kids playing in the yard.

"Thanks for the invite," Daniel says, gingerly slapping my back while Trippy and Vanna exchange a greeting hug. I note the Saviors MC cut he's wearing, probably just to burn my ass.

"Everyone knows you got to weasel in with Maddie and Trippy." I force a smile.

"Yeah, well, be that as it may," Daniel goes on, seemingly unbothered by the dig. "There's a guy out on the front porch asking for you. Pulled up just as we did."

"A guy?" Vanna asks.

"Came in a cage. A Lincoln, I think. He's wearing a suit. Has a briefcase with him. Looks, I don't know, *official*," Daniel explains.

"Alright," I say, handing him the spatula. "Take over. There's a clean pan in the kitchen. This all needs to come off, and there's more meat inside."

"You got it, bro." Daniel smiles like this delegation was born from something other than necessity.

Trippy follows us inside as far as the kitchen to grab the pan, tin foil, and meat from the fridge, while Vanna and I join the suit on the front porch.

He's a man in his mid-thirties, already sweating through his collar and wearing a blazer too stiff for summer. He's clutching a briefcase like it's a lifeline. "Mr. and Mrs. Keegan?"

"That's us," I reply.

"My name is Kirk Creed. I'm sorry to interrupt the festivities, but do you have a moment to talk?" He lifts the briefcase and pats the leather. "This is all pretty straightforward. I just need a few signatures on a couple of documents to file."

"What for?" Vanna asks.

"I'm an attorney…the…executor of an estate."

My stomach sinks when I feel Vanna tense beside me. "W-whose estate?" she barely manages to whisper. We both already know.

Creed's voice softens when he tells her, "Damien Kane's, ma'am."

His name still hits like a punch, despite the fact that I've been expecting something. "I didn't realize the investigation turned up any

DNA. We were told the remains of the bodies recovered were burned beyond identification."

Legion's lawyer clears his throat. "My client had...*prior arrangements*. A conditional delivery, triggered either upon confirmation of death, or after twenty-one days of no contact."

A goddamn kill switch. Of course, Legion still had one. The demonic prick always played every angle.

"Do you have a few moments to go over the documents?" Creed asks, glancing nervously between us. "All I need you to sign today is a statement that you received them."

I step aside, reluctant and eager to be done with it at the same time. "Yeah. Come in."

We lead him over to the dining table before Vanna veers off to the kitchen cupboard. "Can I get you something to drink? Sweet tea?"

"Thank you, but no," Creed says politely and lowers himself into a chair at the table.

Vanna rejoins me, and we sit across from him. She slips her hand into mine. *"Don't hate me if I cry,"* she whispers shakily.

I squeeze her hand in silent reassurance that I won't. I could never hate her, not even the little sliver of her that loved Legion.

Kirk Creed sets the briefcase on the table and pops the latches, lifting the lid with a composed breath. He removes the files, eyes scanning the documents like he's double-checking every line before he speaks.

"To your son," he begins, "Erik Ace Keegan... Mr. Damien Kane left a trust in the amount of seventy-five thousand dollars."

Jesus fuck...

Vanna lets out a breath, sharp and fragile, and holds my hand a little tighter.

"Mr. Damien Kane's instructions were specific," Creed continues. "Educational or entrepreneurial purposes only. Not to be accessed until age twenty-one unless otherwise approved by both parents, or guardians in the case of an emergency." He sets those documents aside and picks up another file. "To the Saviors Motorcycle Club, he left three million dollars in unrestricted funds, though he expressed a desire that the money be used toward long-term mission goals, security, and legacy infrastructure."

I blink and run a hand over my stubbled jaw, unable to say a word. Vanna is just as stunned into silence.

"There's more," Creed says, flipping to another page. "He also left the deed to thirty acres of rural land off Highway 17 to the MC."

"*The Demons' Den*," Vanna whispers.

The realization makes my heart lurch as I recall a rare, civil conversation we had about my derailed plans for the MC.

Creed nods. "Mr. Damien Kane suggested in his accompanying documents that it be considered for a future compound or a safehouse site. It seems the original structure burned down a few years ago, but there are still water lines and a septic system where the former structure stood." He shifts in his seat and clears his throat.

"And to Mrs. Keegan…" he pauses to retrieve another document and places the folder on the table in front of her. "He left the deed to a property in Wilmington, a newly constructed Victorian-style house built to strict historical code, though it's zoned strictly for commercial use."

Her free hand quickly gravitates to her mouth, and the tears come, just like she warned me they would. "It was Legion…" she whispers. "He was the anonymous buyer Laura mentioned." She flips the file open to reveal the documents and photos of the resurrected Ametrine Cauldron.

"He wrote that it was a gift and an apology," Legion's lawyer adds, reaching into the briefcase once more. This time, he pulls out a sealed envelope and slides it toward us. "There's one more thing. He left this for your eyes only."

The envelope is black with a wax seal stamped with a pentacle.

Kirk Creed stands, slipping a business card from his jacket pocket and lays it beside the envelope. "I'll leave you with everything. Once you've had a chance to review, feel free to call me. I'll help facilitate the transfers, trust access, and all the necessary filings." He pulls one more piece of paper from inside his jacket and places it before me with a pen. "If you'll just sign on the tabbed lines that I've delivered these documents, I'll be on my way." After Vanna and I sign and date them, Creed offers a polite nod and lets himself out, quietly shutting the door behind him.

Vanna doesn't reach for the envelope, so I do. It smells like smoke and incense, like Legion is standing in the room with us. I turn it over in my hand, once…twice. It's somehow heavier than I expected it to be. As if it's actually filled with his regret. Inside are the last words he will ever say to us. The final card played by a man who tried to break us...

Vanna moves closer to me, her forehead resting against my shoulder, and I press a kiss to her hair.

"Are you ready for this?" I ask.

"No," she whispers. "But open it anyway."

I break the pentacle seal and slip the letter from within. It's wrapped around another stack of hundreds. At least a couple thousand, but I place the money aside to unfold the handwritten letter. He must have written it shortly before leaving his cut at the Twisted Throttle and showing up at the farmstand the day I nearly beat the life out of him.

"I can't read it," Vanna whimpers, wiping her eyes before leaning against me once again. "I can't see through the tears."

I curl my arm around her, holding her close, and clear my throat. As my eyes scan over his written words, I can hear them in his familiar, gravelly voice...

"To the two people I've wronged most, and the only woman I've ever truly loved... If I can't be the man you forgive, at least allow me to be the man who gives you back what I once tried to destroy.

If you're reading this, it means I'm gone. Doesn't matter how, only that I tried to go out doing one right thing. There's no redemption for what I've done. I betrayed trust. I crossed lines. I hurt people I claimed to care about, all because I couldn't let go of something that was never mine. I called it love, but it was need. Obsession under the guise of something purer. You were never mine to take. I see that now, and I'm sorry. But there are things I need you both to know. Things I wasn't able to admit even to myself, until now.

Dean Keegan, I hated how much I actually respected you. You were everything I wasn't. You built a life I didn't believe could exist—Solid, honest, a home full of love, and a crew you lead with integrity, who follow not because they fear you, but because they admire you. I envied you with everything in me. But I know you're the kind of man who'd ride into hell to bring a kid home. And given the chance, you would have saved me, too. For all I've done to you, I am truly sorry.

Vanna, your love changed the very composition of my soul. You saved me with your trust, and I shattered it. I'll regret that until my last breath, and probably after. I hope the Ametrine Cauldron brings you some of the happiness I stole from your life. I've left your son a trust, your husband's club a legacy I hope he can turn into something better than the ruins I created. You don't owe me forgiveness. You never did. But if there's anything left in your heart, remember me for this one last act. And as for Ace, the boy who looked up at me with your eyes, tell him to look to the stars. To wish upon them the way his mother does. Tell him the north star never moves, no matter how lost you get. And tell him Legends never die... Legion."

I place the letter on the table, and we sit in a moment of silence before her trembling hands reach for it. Without reading it again, she folds it up and slips it back inside the envelope, holding it in her lap.

Outside, the kids' laughter spills in from the backyard along with the distant snap and crackle of early fireworks somewhere up the street. But in here, it's still silent. Just her, me, and the echo of a man's last attempt to make something right.

Vanna gets up and slips the envelope into the kitchen drawer gently, like it's something sacred. She lifts the brass Zippo from within, smiling sadly at it before placing it on top of the envelope and shutting the drawer.

"I don't know what to do with this," she says softly, turning to look at me with tear-filled eyes. "The guilt. The grief. It's all tangled up in here," she whimpers, placing her hand over her heart. "I love you, Dean. I know you know that...but Legion...the way things ended with him... *I hate that it hurts so much."*

I get up and reach for her.

She clings to me.

"Then don't try to untangle it... Just let it be what it is. You're allowed to grieve, doll. It doesn't tarnish our love. Loving me doesn't mean you have to pretend he didn't matter to you. Grief is complicated. Love is, too."

And closure doesn't always come in words, I suppose. Sometimes it comes in silence, in sacrifice, in a last will and testament sitting on a table. Sometimes it looks like forgiveness, even when no one says the words out loud.

"I love you and Ace more than anything in this world." She wipes her eyes and peers up at me with a fragile smile. The kind that says she isn't okay yet, but will be, because she has us and she always will.

"Come on, doll," I say, taking her hand in mine once again.

When we step out onto the back porch, the warm breath of summer curls around us. Smoke from the grill drifts through the air in a mixture of charcoal and burgers. All of our people are here. *Our family.* The one we built out of broken parts and second chances. Leather cuts draped over lawn chairs. Boots in the grass. Kids squealing and dripping wet, being chased down by prospects with towels, attempting to wrangle them for dinner being set on the table.

"I'm glad Ace doesn't remember the worst of it," Vanna says, standing close enough I can feel the rise and fall of her breath. Her gaze follows Ace like she's memorizing every second.

"He doesn't. But he'll remember this," I assure her. "Family meals. Backyard fireworks. Games and laughter. All of us, together."

She leans closer against me, peering up at me with something softer in her eyes now. "Thank you," she whispers. "For not making me bury it all…"

"Legion might have crossed every line…but in the end, he gave everything to draw one that mattered," I admit.

"Legion mattered," she says. "But you're my home, Dean. Thank you for loving me in all the ways I've needed to be loved."

"My life's mission, doll." I lift her hand and press a kiss against her fingers, smiling at the way her wedding rings catch the light of the setting sun. "We've been to hell and back a few times. Love is what got us through the fire, loyalty keeps us standing strong, and together, we'll keep building something worth fighting for."

And for the first time in a long while, the silence between us feels like peace.

The Saviors MC Series continues with the next installment, Viking.

Until then, ride safe, love hard, leave nothing unsaid,
and never let the past keep you from fighting for something worth saving.

If you enjoyed Legion Book 3 in the Saviors MC Series, please consider taking the time to leave a review on Amazon. Reviews go a long way to help us Indie Authors connect with other readers who may enjoy our work.

AFTERWORD

This book took me a year longer than I ever intended it to. Not because I didn't love the story or the characters (even though they hijacked 90% of it and derailed my initial plans… I'm looking at you, Legion!) but because life hit harder than I expected.

There were days I couldn't write. Not because of laziness or lack of discipline, but because I was fighting to keep my love for writing alive in what can be an ugly industry at times. Because someone I once thought was a friend, betrayed me in ways that left me gutted. Picking up the pieces took time. Finding my voice again took even longer. But I have found it. And though I cannot speak for this person, I can state with pride and conviction that my work is my own, love it or hate it. IT'S MINE. And I've grown my readership without riding anyone else's coattails. Jealousy is an ugly thing, especially when it's hiding behind the smile of someone who claimed to be a friend. This experience hit me hard, but I came out of it wiser and bolder.

Authors don't often get to talk about the fact we're human, too. We grieve. We fight battles no one sees, and often, we write through those battles. Many of us pour our pain into the pages. We tuck fragments of ourselves into every chapter. Writing isn't just storytelling. It's survival. It's healing. It's how we try to make sense of the things that nearly broke us. So, if you're reading this series, just know it almost didn't happen. I'm in a place now where I'm glad it did. And I'm grateful you're here to read it.

To my Saviors MC fans, thank you for your patience. Thank you for understanding that creation takes the time it takes and doesn't always follow a schedule. And thank you for making space in your world for the parts of mine that needed to be told. Even the ones born from hurt. —*J Saviano*

About the Author

Jennifer Saviano

Jennifer Saviano is an award-winning author as well as an Amazon and Audible Best Seller in Vigilante Justice and Action-Adventure Romance. Saviano has a soft spot for damaged heroes and enjoys writing morally gray characters because heroes and villains are only a matter of perspective. She utilizes in-depth storytelling to bring her characters to life and make readers feel every emotion with them.

Her future writing endeavors include a Mafia Romance Series, delving into Paranormal Romance, as well as a few Psychological Thriller novellas.

When she isn't writing, you can find her with her own dark knight in the woods of the eastern Carolinas or beside the ocean at night. She enjoys crafting and spending time with their three rescue cats and crazy Belgian Malinois.

Saviano is also a tireless champion against human trafficking. She always strives to raise awareness and has coordinated multiple fundraisers to raise awareness.

To keep up with future projects and events,
check out the website at
www.JenniferSaviano.net

There you will find Detailed Content & Trigger Warnings, Autographed Books and Merch, Links to Social Media Accounts, The Saviors MC Spotify Playlist & Ways to join the Newsletter.